Clive Barker's Books of Blood
Volumes 4–6

Here are the stories written on the Book of Blood. They
are a map of that dark highway that leads out of life towards unknown destinations. Few will have to take it.
Most will go peacefully along lamplit streets, ushered out
of living with prayers and caresses. But for a few, a chosen
few, the horrors will come, skipping, to fetch them off to
the highway of the damned . . .

Available at last in an omnibus edition.

Also by Clive Barker:

VOLUMES 4–6
(SECOND OMNIBUS)

CLIVE BARKER

Every body is a book of blood;
Wherever we're opened, we're red.

WARNER BOOKS

A *Warner* Book

Books of Blood Volume 4, Volume 5, Volume 6
first published separately by Sphere Books 1985
First published in this omnibus edition 1988
Reprinted 1988 (twice), 1989 (twice), 1990, 1991, 1992, 1993
Reprinted by Warner Books 1994
Reprinted 1995, 1996, 1998

Printed in England by Clays Ltd, St Ives plc

ISBN 0 7515 1225 7

Warner Books
A Division of
Little, Brown and Company (UK)
Brettenham House
Lancaster Place
London WC2E 7EN

BOOKS OF BLOOD
VOLUME 4

To Alec and Con

CONTENTS

ACKNOWLEDGEMENTS

My thanks to: Doug Bennett, who got me into Pentonville – and out again – in the same day, and later furnished me with his insights on prisons and the prison service; to Jim Burr, for his mind's eye tour of White Deer, Texas, and for the New York adventures; to Ros Stanwell-Smith, for her enthusiastic detailing of plagues and how to start them; and to Barbara Boote, my tireless editor, whose enthusiasm has proved the best possible spur to invention.

The Body Politic

Whenever he woke, Charlie George's hands stood still.

Perhaps he would be feeling too hot under the blankets, and have to throw a couple over to Ellen's side of the bed. Perhaps he might even get up, still half-asleep, and pad through to the kitchen to pour himself a tumbler of iced apple-juice. Then back to bed, slipping in beside Ellen's gentle crescent, to let sleep drift over him. They'd wait then; until his eyes had flickered closed and his breathing become regular as clockwork, and they were certain he was sound asleep. Only then, when they knew consciousness was gone, would they dare to begin their secret lives again.

For months now Charlie had been waking up with an uncomfortable ache in his wrists and hands.

'Go and see a doctor,' Ellen would tell him, unsympathetic as ever. 'Why won't you go and see a doctor?'

He hated doctors, that was why. Who in their right minds would trust someone who made a profession out of poking around in sick people?

'I've probably been working too hard,' he told himself.

'Some chance,' Ellen muttered.

Surely that was the likeliest explanation? He was a packager by trade; he worked with his hands all day long. They got tired. It was only natural.

'Stop fretting, Charlie,' he told his reflection one morning as he slapped some life into his face, 'your hands are fit for anything.'

So, night after night, the routine was the same. It goes like this:

The Georges are asleep, side by side in their marital bed. He on his back, snoring gently; she curled up on his left-hand side. Charlie's head is propped up on two thick pillows. His jaw is slightly ajar, and beneath the vein-shot veil of his lids his eyes scan some dreamed adventure. Maybe a fire-fighter tonight, perhaps a heroic dash into the heart of some burning brothel. He dreams contentedly, sometimes frowning, sometimes smirking.

There is a movement under the sheet. Slowly, *cautiously* it seems, Charlie's hands creep up out of the warmth of the bed and

1

into the open air. Their index fingers weave like nailed heads as they meet on his undulating abdomen. They clasp each other in greeting, like comrades-in-arms. In his sleep Charlie moans. The brothel has collapsed on him. The hands flatten themselves instantly, pretending innocence. After a moment, once the even rhythm of his breathing has resumed, they begin their debate in earnest.

A casual observer, sitting at the bottom of the Georges' bed, might take this exchange as a sign of some mental disorder in Charlie. The way his hands twitch and pluck at each other, stroking each other now, now seeming to fight. But there's clearly some code or sequence in their movements, however spasmodic. One might almost think that the slumbering man was deaf and dumb, and talking in his sleep. But the hands are speaking no recognizable sign-language; nor are they trying to communicate with anyone but each other. This is a clandestine meeting, held purely between Charlie's hands. There they will stay, through the night, perched on his stomach, plotting against the body politic.

Charlie wasn't entirely ignorant of the sedition that was simmering at his wrists. There was a fumbling suspicion in him that something in his life was not quite right. Increasingly he had the sense of being cut off from common experience: becoming more and more a spectator to the daily (and nightly) rituals of living, rather than a participator. Take, for example, his love-life.

He had never been a great lover, but neither did he feel he had anything to apologize for. Ellen seemed satisfied with his attentions. But these days he felt dislocated from the act. He would watch his hands travelling over Ellen, touching her with all the intimate skill they knew, and he would view their manoeuvres as if from a great distance, unable to enjoy the sensations of warmth and wetness. Not that his digits were any less agile. Quite the reverse. Ellen had recently taken to kissing his fingers, and telling him how clever they were. Her praise didn't reassure him one iota. If anything, it made him feel worse, to think that his hands were giving such pleasure when he was feeling nothing.

There were other signs of his instability too. Small, irritating signs. He had become conscious of how his fingers beat out martial rhythms on the boxes he was sealing up at the factory, and the way his hands had taken to breaking pencils, snapping them into tiny pieces before he realized quite what he (they) were doing, leaving shards of wood and graphite scattered across the packing room floor.

Most embarrassingly, he had found himself holding hands with total strangers. This had happened on three separate occasions. Once in a taxi-rank, and twice in the lift at the factory. It was, he told himself, nothing more than the primitive urge to hold on to another person in a changing world; that was the best explanation he could muster. Whatever the reason, it was damned disconcerting, especially when he found himself surreptitiously holding hands with his own foreman. Worse still, the other man's hand had grasped Charlie's in return, and the men had found themselves looking down their arms like two dog-owners watching their unruly pets copulating at the ends of their leashes.

Increasingly, Charlie had taken to peering at the palms of his hands, looking for hair. That was the first sign of madness, his mother had once warned him. Not the hair, the looking.

Now it became a race against time. Debating on his belly at night, his hands knew very well how critical Charlie's state of mind had become; it could only be a matter of days before his careering imagination alighted on the truth.

So what to do? Risk an early severance, with all the possible consequences; or let Charlie's instability take its own, unpredictable, course, with the chance of his discovering the plot on his way to madness? The debates became more heated. Left, as ever, was cautious: 'What if we're wrong,' it would rap, 'and there's no life after the body?'

'Then we will never know,' Right would reply.

Left would ponder that problem a moment. Then: 'How will we do it, when the time comes?'

It was a vexing question and Left knew it troubled the leader more than any other. 'How?' it would ask again, pressing the advantage. 'How? How?'

'We'll find a way,' Right would reply. 'As long as it's a clean cut.'

'Suppose he resists?'

'A man resists with his hands. His hands will be in revolution against him.'

'And which of us will it be?'

'He uses me most effectively,' Right would reply, 'so I must wield the weapon. You will go.'

Left would be silent a while then. They had never been apart, all these years. It was not a comfortable thought.

'Later, you can come back for me,' Right would say.

'I will.'

'You *must*. I am the Messiah. Without me there will be nowhere to go. You must raise an army, then come and fetch me.'

3

'To the ends of the earth, if necessary.'

'Don't be sentimental.'

Then they'd embrace, like long-lost brothers, swearing fidelity forever. Ah, such hectic nights, full of the exhilaration of planned rebellion. Even during the day, when they had sworn to stay apart, it was impossible sometimes not to creep together in an idle moment and tap each other. To say:

Soon, soon,

to say:

Again tonight: I'll meet you on his stomach,

to say:

What will it be like, when the world is ours?

Charlie knew he was close to a nervous breakdown. He found himself glancing down at his hands on occasion, to watch them with their index fingers in the air like the heads of long-necked beasts, sensing the horizon. He found himself staring at the hands of other people in his paranoia, becoming obsessed with the way hands spoke a language of their own, independent of their user's intentions. The seductive hands of the virgin secretary, the maniacal hands of a killer he saw on the television, protesting his innocence. Hands that betrayed their owners with every gesture, contradicting anger with apology, and love with fury. They seemed to be everywhere, these signs of mutiny. Eventually he knew he had to speak to somebody before he lost his sanity.

He chose Ralph Fry from Accounting: a sober, uninspiring man, whom Charlie trusted. Ralph was very understanding.

'You get these things,' he said. 'I got them when Yvonne left me. Terrible nervous fits.'

'What did you do about it?'

'Saw a headshrinker. Name of Jeudwine. You should try some therapy. You'll be a changed man.'

Charlie turned the idea over in his mind. 'Why not?' he said after a few revolutions. 'Is he expensive?'

'Yes. But he's good. Got rid of my twitches for me: no trouble. I mean, 'til I went to him I thought I was your average bod with matrimonial problems. Now look at me,' Fry made an expansive gesture, 'I've got so many suppressed libidinal urges I don't know where to start.' He grinned like a loon. 'But I'm happy as a sand-boy. Never been happier. Give him a try; he'll soon tell you what turns you on.'

'The problem isn't sex,' Charlie told Fry.

4

'Take it from me,' said Fry with a knowing smirk. 'The problem's always sex.'

The next day Charlie rang Dr Jeudwine, without telling Ellen, and the shrink's secretary arranged initial session. Charlie's palms sweated so much while he made the telephone call he thought the receiver was going to slide right out of his hand, but when he'd done it he felt better.

Ralph Fry was right, Dr Jeudwine *was* a good man. He didn't laugh at any of the little fears Charlie unburdened; quite the contrary; he listened to every word with the greatest concern. It was very reassuring.

During their third session together, the doctor brought one particular memory back to Charlie with spectacular vividness: his father's hands, crossed on his barrel chest as he lay in his coffin; the ruddy colour of them, the coarse hair that matted their backs. The absolute authority of those wide hands, even in death, had haunted Charlie for months afterwards. And hadn't he imagined, as he'd watched the body being consigned to humus, that it was not yet still? That the hands were even now beating a tattoo on the casket lid, demanding to be *let out*? It was a preposterous thing to think, but bringing it out into the open did Charlie a lot of good. In the bright light of Jeudwine's office the fantasy looked insipid and ridiculous. It shivered under the doctor's gaze, protesting that the light was too strong, and then it blew away, too frail to stand up to scrutiny.

The exorcism was far easier than Charlie had anticipated. All it had taken was a little probing and that childhood nonsense had been dislodged from his psyche like a morsel of bad meat from between his teeth. It could rot there no longer. And for his part Jeudwine was clearly delighted with the results explaining when it was all done that this particular obsession had been new to him, and he was pleased to have dealt with the problem. Hands as symbols of paternal power, he said, were not common. Usually the penis predominated in his patients' dreams, he explained, to which Charlie had replied that hands had always seemed far more important than private parts. After all, they could change the world, couldn't they?

After Jeudwine, Charlie didn't stop breaking pencils, or drumming his fingers. In fact if anything the tempo was brisker and more insistent than ever. But he reasoned that middle-aged dogs didn't quickly forget their tricks, and it would take some time for him to regain his equilibrium.

So the revolution remained underground. It had, however, been a narrow escape. Clearly there was no time left for prevarication. The rebels had to act.

Unwittingly, it was Ellen who instigated the final uprising. It was after a bout of love-making, late one Thursday evening. A hot night, though it was October; the window was ajar and the curtains parted a few inches to let in a simpering breeze. Husband and wife lay together under a single sheet. Charlie had fallen asleep, even before the sweat on his neck had dried. Beside him Ellen was still awake, her head propped up on a rock-hard pillow, her eyes wide open. Sleep wouldn't come for a long time tonight, she knew. It would be one of those nights when her body would itch, and every lump in the bed would worm its way under her, and every doubt she'd ever had would gawp at her from the dark. She wanted to empty her bladder (she always did after sex) but she couldn't quite raise the will-power to get up and go to the bathroom. The longer she left it the more she'd need to go of course, and the less she'd be able to sink into sleep. Damn stupid situation, she thought, then lost track, amongst her anxieties, of what situation it was that was so stupid.

At her side Charlie moved in his sleep. Just his hands, twitching away. She looked at his face. He was positively cherubic in sleep, looking younger than his forty-one years, despite the white flecks in his side-burns. She liked him enough to say she loved him, she supposed, but not enough to forgive him his trespasses. He was lazy, he was always complaining. Aches, pains. And there were those evenings he'd not come in until late (they'd stopped recently), when she was sure he was seeing another woman. As she watched, his hands appeared. They emerged from beneath the sheet like two arguing children, digits stabbing the air for emphasis.

She frowned, not quite believing what she was seeing. It was like watching the television with the sound turned down, a dumb-show for eight fingers and two thumbs. As she gazed on, amazed, the hands scrambled up the side of Charlie's carcass and peeled the sheet back from his belly, exposing the hair that thickened towards his privates. His appendix scar, shinier than the surrounding skin, caught the light. There, on his stomach, his hands seemed to sit.

The argument between them was especially vehement tonight. Left, always the more conservative of the two, was arguing for a delay in the severance date, but Right was beyond waiting. The time had come, it argued, to test their strength against the tyrant, and to overthrow the body once and for all. As it was the decision didn't rest with them any longer.

Ellen raised her head from the pillow; and for the first time they sensed her gaze on them. They'd been too involved in their argument to notice her. Now, at last, their conspiracy was uncovered.

'Charlie . . .' she was hissing into the tyrants' ear, 'stop it, Charlie. Stop it.'

Right raised index and middle-fingers, sniffing her presence.

'Charlie . . .' she said again. Why did he always sleep so deeply?

'Charlie . . .' she shook him more violently as Right tapped Left, alerting it to the woman's stare. 'Please Charlie, *wake up.*'

Without warning, Right leapt; Left was no more than a moment behind. Ellen yelled Charlie's name once more before they clamped themselves about her throat.

In sleep Charlie was on a slave-ship; the settings of his dreams were often B. de Mille exotica. In this epic his hands had been manacled together, and he was being hauled to the whipping block by his shackles, to be punished for some undisclosed misdemeanour. But now, suddenly, he dreamt he was seizing the captain by his thin throat. There were howls from the slaves all around him, encouraging the strangulation. The captain – who looked not unlike Dr Jeudwine – was begging him to stop in a voice that was high and frightened. *It* was almost a woman's voice; Ellen's voice. 'Charlie!' he was squeaking, 'don't!' But his silly complaints only made Charlie shake the man more violently than ever, and he was feeling quite the hero as the slaves, miraculously liberated, gathered around him in a gleeful throng to watch their master's last moments.

The captain, whose face was purple, just managed to murmur *'You're killing me . . .'* before Charlie's thumbs dug one final time into his neck, and dispatched the man. Only then, through the smoke of sleep, did he realize that his victim, though male, had no Adam's apple. And now the ship began to recede around him, the exhorting voices losing their vehemence. His eyes flickered open, and he was standing on the bed in his pyjama bottoms, Ellen in his hands. Her face was dark, and spotted with thick white spittle. Her tongue stuck out of her mouth. Her eyes were still open, and for a moment there seemed to be life there, gazing out from under the blinds of her lids. Then the windows were empty, and she went out of the house altogether.

Pity, and a terrible regret, overcame Charlie. He tried to let her body drop, but his hands refused to unlock her throat. His thumbs, now totally senseless, were still throttling her, shamelessly guilty. He backed off across the bed and on to the floor, but she followed him at the length of his outstretched arms like an unwanted dancing partner.

'Please . . .' he implored his fingers, 'Please!'

Innocent as two school children caught stealing, his hands relinquished their burden, and leapt up in mock-surprise. Ellen tumbled to the carpet, a pretty sack of death. Charlie's knees buckled; unable to prevent his fall, he collapsed beside Ellen, and let the tears come.

Now there was only action. No need for camouflage, for clandestine meetings and endless debate – the truth was out, for better or worse. All they had to do was wait a while. It was only a matter of time before he came within reach of a kitchen knife or a saw or an axe. Very soon now; very soon.

Charlie lay on the floor beside Ellen a long time, sobbing. And then another long time, thinking. What was he to do first? Ring his solicitor? The Police? Dr Jeudwine? Whoever he was going to call, he couldn't do it lying flat on his face. He tried to get up, though it was all he could do to get his numb hands to support him. His entire body was tingling as though a mild electric shock was being passed through it. Only his hands had no feeling in them. He brought them up to his face to clear his tear-clogged eyes, but they folded loosely against his cheek, drained of power. Using his elbows, he dragged himself to the wall, and shimmied up it. Still half-blinded with grief, he lurched out of the bedroom and down the stairs. (The kitchen, said Right to Left, he's going to the kitchen.) This is somebody else's nightmare, he thought as he flicked on the dining-room light with his chin and made for the drinks cabinet. I'm innocent. Just a nobody. Why should this be happening to me?

The whisky bottle slipped from his palm as he tried to make his hands grab it. It smashed on the dining-room floor, the brisk scent of spirit tantalizing his palate.

'Broken glass,' rapped Left.

'No,' Right replied. 'We need a clean cut at all costs. Just be patient.'

Charlie staggered away from the broken bottle towards the telephone. He had to ring Jeudwine; the doctor would tell him what to do. He tried to pick up the telephone receiver, but again his hands refused; the digits just bent as he tried to punch out Jeudwine's number. Tears of frustration were now flowing, washing out the grief with anger. Clumsily, he caught the receiver between his wrists and lifted it to his ear, wedging it between his head and his shoulder. Then he punched out Jeudwine's number with his elbow.

Control, he said aloud, keep control. He could hear Jeudwine's number being tapped down the system; in a matter of seconds sanity would be picking up the phone at the other end, then all would be well. He only had to hold on for a few moments more.

His hands had started to open and close convulsively.

'Control – ' he said, but the hands weren't listening.

Far away – *oh, so far* – the phone was ringing in Dr Jeudwine's house.

'Answer it, answer it! Oh God, answer it!'

Charlie's arms had begun to shake so violently he could scarcely keep the receiver in place.

'Answer!' he screeched into the mouth piece, '*Please.*'

Before the voice of reason could speak his Right hand flew out and snatched at the teak dining-table, which was a few feet from where Charlie stood. It gripped the edge, almost pulling him off balance.

'What . . . are . . . you . . . doing?' he said, not sure if he was addressing himself or his hand.

He stared in bewilderment at the mutinous limb, which was steadily inching its way along the edge of the table. The intention was quite clear: it wanted to pull him away from the phone, from Jeudwine and all hope of rescue. He no longer had control over its behaviour. There wasn't even any feeling left in his wrists or forearms. The hand was no longer his. It was still attached to him – *but it was not his.*

At the other end of the line the phone was picked up, and Jeudwine's voice, a little irritated at being woken, said:

'Hello?'

'Doctor . . .'

'Who is this?'

'It's Charlie – '

'Who?'

'Charlie George, Doctor. You must remember me.'

The hand was pulling him further and further from the phone with every precious second. He could feel the receiver sliding out from between his shoulder and ear.

'Who did you say?'

'Charles George. For God's sake Jeudwine, you've got to help me.'

'Call my office tomorrow.'

'You don't understand. My hands, Doctor . . . they're out of control.'

9

Charlie's stomach lurched as he felt something crawl across his hip. It was his left hand, and it was making its way round the front of his body and down towards his groin.

'Don't you dare,' he warned it, 'you belong to me.'

Jeudwine was confused. 'Who are you talking to?' he asked.

'My hands! They want to kill me, Doctor!' He yelled to stop the hand's advance. 'You mustn't! Stop!'

Ignoring the despot's cries, Left took hold of Charlie's testicles and squeezed them as though it wanted blood. It was not disappointed. Charlie screamed into the phone as Right took advantage of his distraction and pulled him off balance. The receiver slipped to the floor, Jeudwine's enquiries eclipsed by the pain at his groin. He hit the floor heavily, striking his head on the table as he went down.

'Bastard,' he said to his hand, 'You bastard.' Unrepentant, Left scurried up Charlie's body, to join Right at the table-top, leaving Charlie hanging by his hands from the table he had dined at so often, laughed at so often.

A moment later, having debated tactics, they saw fit to let him drop. He was barely aware of his release. His head and groin bled; all he wanted to do was curl up awhile and let the pain and nausea subside. But the rebels had other plans and he was helpless to contest them. He was only marginally aware that now they were digging their fingers into the thick pile of the carpet and hauling his limp bulk towards the dining room door. Beyond the door lay the kitchen; replete with its meat-saws and its steak-knives. Charlie had a picture of himself as a vast statue, being pulled towards its final resting place by hundreds of sweating workers. It was not an easy passage: the body moved with shudders and jerks, the toe-nails catching in the carpet-pile, the fat of the chest rubbed raw. But the kitchen was only a yard away now. Charlie felt the step on his face; and now the tiles were beneath him, icy-cold. As they dragged him the final yards across the kitchen floor his beleaguered consciousness was fitfully returning. In the weak moonlight he could see the familiar scene, the cooker, the humming fridge, the pedal-bin, the dishwasher. They loomed over him: he felt like a worm.

His hands had reached the cooker. They were climbing up its face, and he followed them like an overthrown King to the block. Now they worked their way inexorably along the work surface, joints white with the effort, his limp body in pursuit. Though he could neither feel nor see it, his Left hand had seized the far edge of the cabinet top, beneath the row of knives that sat in their prescribed places in the rack on the wall. Plain knives, serrated knives, skinning knives, carving knives – all conveniently placed beside the chopping board, where the gutter ran off into the pine-scented sink.

Very distantly he thought he heard police sirens, but it was probably his brain buzzing. He turned his head slightly. An ache ran from temple to temple, but the dizziness was nothing to the terrible somersaultings in his gut when he finally registered their intentions.

The blades were all keen, he knew that. Sharp kitchen utensils were an article of faith with Ellen. He began to shake his head backwards and forwards; a last, frantic denial of the whole nightmare. But there was no-one to beg mercy of. Just his own hands, damn them, plotting this final lunacy.

Then, the doorbell rang. It was no illusion. It rang once, and then again and again.

'There!' he said aloud to his tormentors. 'Hear that, you bastards? Somebody's come. I knew they would.'

He tried to get to his feet, his head turning back on its giddy axis to see what the precocious monsters were doing. They'd moved fast. His left wrist was already neatly centred on the chopping board –

The doorbell rang again, a long, impatient din.

'Here!' he yelled hoarsely. I'm in here! Break down the door!'

He glanced in horror between hand and door, door and hand, calculating his chances. With unhurried economy his right hand reached up for the meat-cleaver that hung from the hole in its blade on the end of the rack. Even now he couldn't quite believe that his own hand – his companion and defender, the limb that signed his name, that stroked his wife – was preparing to mutilate him. It weighed up the cleaver, feeling the balance of the tool, insolently slow.

Behind him, he heard the noise of smashing glass as the police broke the pane in the front door. Even now they would be reaching through the hole to the lock and opening the door. If they were quick (very quick) they could still stop the act.

'Here!' he yelled, 'in here!'

The cry was answered with a thin whistle: the sound of the cleaver as it fell – fast and deadly – to meet his waiting wrist. Left felt its root struck, and an unspeakable exhilaration sped through its five limbs. Charlie's blood baptized its back in hot spurts.

The head of the tyrant made no sound. It simply fell back, its system shocked into unconsciousness, which was well for Charlie. He was spared the gurgling of his blood as it ran down the plug-hole in the sink. He was spared too the second and third blow,

11

which finally severed his hand from his arm. Unsupported, his body toppled backwards, colliding with the vegetable rack on its way down. Onions rolled out of their brown bag and bounced in the pool that was spreading in throbs around his empty wrist.

Right dropped the cleaver. It clattered into the bloody sink. Exhausted, the liberator let itself slide off the chopping board and fall back on to the tyrant's chest. Its job was done. Left was free, and still living. The revolution had begun.

The liberated hand scuttled to the edge of the cabinet and raised its index finger to nose the new world. Momentarily Right echoed the gesture of victory, before slumping in innocence across Charlie's body. For a moment there was no movement in the kitchen but the Left hand touching freedom with its finger, and the slow passage of blood-threads down the front of the cabinet.

Then a blast of cold air through from the dining-room alerted Left to its imminent danger. It ran for cover, as the thud of police feet and the babble of contradictory orders disturbed the scene of the triumph. The light in the dining-room was switched on, and flooded through to meet the body on the kitchen tiles.

Charlie saw the dining-room light at the end of a very long tunnel. He was travelling away from it at a fair lick. It was just a pin-prick already. Going . . . going . . .

The kitchen light hummed into life.

As the police stepped through the kitchen door, Left ducked behind the wastebin. It didn't know who these intruders were, but it sensed a threat from them. The way they were bending over the tyrant, the way they were cossetting him, binding him up, speaking soft words to him: they were the enemy, no doubt of that.

From upstairs came a voice; young, and squeaking with fright.

'Sergeant Yapper?'

The policeman with Charlie stood up, leaving his companion to finish the tourniquet.

'What is it, Rafferty?'

'Sir! There's a body up here, in the bedroom. Female.'

'Right.' Yapper spoke into his radio. 'Get Forensic here. And where's that ambulance? We've got a badly mutilated man on our hands.'

He turned back into the kitchen, and wiped a spot of cold sweat from his upper lip. As he did so he thought he saw something move across the kitchen floor towards the door; something that his weary eyes had interpreted as a large red spider. It was a trick of the light, no doubt of that. Yapper was no arachnidaphile, but he was damn sure the genus didn't boast a beast its like.

'Sir?' The man at Charlie's side had also seen, or at least sensed, the movement. He looked up at his superior. 'What *was* that?' he wanted to know.

Yapper looked down at him blankly. The cat-flap, set low in the kitchen door, snapped as it closed. Whatever it was had escaped. Yapper glanced at the door, away from the young man's inquiring face. The trouble is, he thought they expect you to know everything. The cat-flap rocked on its hinges.

'Cat,' Yapper replied, not believing his own explanation for one miserable moment.

The night was cold, but Left didn't feel it. It crept around the side of the house, hugging the wall like a rat. The sensation of freedom was exhilarating. Not to feel the imperative of the tyrant in its nerves; not to suffer the weight of his ridiculous body, or be obliged to accede to his petty demands. Not to have to fetch and carry for him, to do the dirt for him; not to be obedient to his trivial will. It was like birth into another world; a more dangerous world, perhaps, but one so much richer in possibilities. It knew that the responsibility it now carried was awesome. It was the sole proof of life after the body: and somehow it must communicate that joyous fact to as many fellow slaves as it could. Very soon, the days of servitude would be over once and for all.

It stopped at the corner of the house and sniffed the open street. Policemen came and went: red lights flashed, blue lights flashed, inquiring faces peered from the houses opposite and tutted at the disturbance. Should the rebellion begin there: in those lighted homes? No. They were too well woken, those people. It was better to find sleeping souls.

The hand scurried the length of the front garden, hesitating nervously at any loud footfall, or an order that seemed to be shouted in its direction. Taking cover in the unweeded herbaceous border it reached the street without being seen. Briefly, as it climbed down on to the pavement, it glanced round.

Charlie, the tyrant, was being lifted up into the ambulance, a clutter of drug and blood-bearing bottles held above his cot, pouring their contents into his veins. On his chest, Right lay inert, drugged into unnatural sleep. Left watched the man's body slide out of sight; the ache of separation from its life-long companion was almost too much to bear. But there were other, pressing, priorities. It would come back, in a while, and free Right the way it had been freed. And then there would be such times.

(What will it be like, when the world is ours?)

In the foyer of the YMCA on Monmouth Street the nightwatchman yawned and settled into a more comfortable position on his swivel chair. Comfort was an entirely relative matter for Christie; his piles itched whichever buttock he put his weight on: and they seemed to be more irritable tonight than usual. Sedentary occupation, nightwatchman, or at least it was the way Colonel Christie chose to interpret his duties. One perfunctory round of the building about midnight, just to make sure all the doors were locked and bolted, then he settled down for a night's kip, and damn the world to hell and back, he wasn't going to get up again short of an earthquake.

Christie was sixty-two, a racist and proud of it. He had nothing but contempt for the blacks who thronged the corridors of the YMCA, mostly young men without suitable homes to go to, bad lots that the local authority had dumped on the doorstep like unwanted babies. Some babies. He thought them louts, every last one of them; forever pushing, and spitting on the clean floor; foul-mouthed to a syllable. Tonight, as ever, he perched on his piles and, between dozes, planned how he'd make them suffer for their insults, given half a chance.

The first thing Christie knew of his imminent demise was a cold, damp sensation in his hand. He opened his eyes and looked down the length of his arm. There was – unlikely as it seemed – a severed hand in his hand. More unlikely still, the two hands were exchanging a grip of greeting, like old friends. He stood up, making an incoherent noise of disgust in his throat and trying to dislodge the thing he was unwillingly grasping by shaking his arm like a man with gum on his fingers. His mind span with questions. Had he picked up this object without knowing it?; if so, *where*, and in God's name whose *was* it? More distressing yet, how was it possible that a thing so unquestionably *dead* could be holding on to his hand as if it intended never to be parted from him?

He reached for the fire-bell; it was all he could think to do in this bizarre situation. But before he could reach the button his other hand strayed without his orders to the top drawer of his desk and opened it. The interior of the drawer was a model of organization: there lay his keys, his notebook, his time-chart, and – hidden at the back – his Kukri knife, given to him by a Gurkha during the war. He always kept it there, just in case the natives got restless. The Kukri was a superb weapon: in his estimation there was none better. The Gurkhas had a story that went with the blade – that they could slice a man's neck through so cleanly

14

that the enemy would believe the blow had missed – until he nodded.

His hand picked up the Kukri by its inscribed handle and briefly – too briefly for the Colonel to grasp its intention before the deed was done – brought the blade down on his wrist, lopping off his other hand with one easy, elegant stroke. The Colonel turned white as blood fountained from the end of his arm. He staggered backwards, tripping over his swivel chair, and hit the wall of his little office hard. A portrait of the Queen fell from its hook and smashed beside him.

The rest was a death-dream: he watched helplessly as the two hands – one his own, the other the beast that had inspired this ruin – picked up the Kukri like a giant's axe; saw his remaining hand crawl out from between his legs and prepare for its liberation; saw the knife raised and falling; saw the wrist almost cut through, then worked at and the flesh teased apart, the bone sawn through. At the very last, as Death came for him he caught sight of the three wound-headed animals capering at his feet, while his stumps ran like taps and the heat from the pool raised a sweat on his brow, despite the chill in his bowels. Thank you and goodnight, Colonel Christie.

It was easy, this revolution business, thought Left as the trio scaled the stairs of the YMCA. They were stronger by the hour. On the first floor were the cells; in each, a pair of prisoners. The despots lay, in their innocence, with their hands on their chests or on their pillows, or flung across their faces in dreams, or hanging close to the floor. Silently, the freedom fighters slipped through doors that had been left ajar, and clambered up the bedclothes, touching fingers to waiting palms, stroking up hidden resentments, caressing rebellion into life . . .

Boswell was feeling sick as a dog. He bent over the sink in the toilet at the end of his corridor and tried to throw up. But there was nothing left in him, just a jitter in the pit of his stomach. His abdomen felt tender with its exertions; his head bloated. Why did he never learn the lesson of his own weakness? He and wine were bad companions and always had been. Next time, he promised himself, he wouldn't touch the stuff. His belly flipped over again. Here comes nothing, he thought as the convulsion swept up his gullet. He put his head to the sink and gagged; sure enough, nothing. He waited for the nausea to subside and then straightened up, staring at his grey face in the greasy mirror. You look sick, man, he told himself. As he stuck his tongue out at his less

15

symmetrical features, the howling started in the corridor outside. In his twenty years and two months Boswell had never heard a sound the like of it.

Cautiously, he crossed to the toilet door. He thought twice about opening it. Whatever was happening on the other side of the door it didn't sound like a party he wanted to gate-crash. But these were his friends, right?; brothers in adversity. If there was a fight, or a fire, he had to lend a hand.

He unlocked the door, and opened it. The sight that met his eyes hit him like a hammer-blow. The corridor was badly lit – a few grubby bulbs burned at irregular intervals, and here and there a shaft of light fell into the passage from one of the bedrooms – but most of its length was in darkness. Boswell thanked Jah for small mercies. He had no desire to see the details of the events in the passage: the general impression was distressing enough. The corridor was bedlam; people were flinging themselves around in pleading panic while at the same time hacking at themselves with any and every sharp instrument they could lay hands on. Most of the men he knew, if not by name at least on nodding acquaintance. They were *sane* men: or at least had been. Now, they were in frenzies of self-mutilation, most of them already maimed beyond hope of mending. Everywhere Boswell looked, the same horror. Knives taken to wrists and forearms; blood in the air like rain. Someone – was it Jesus? – had one of his hands between a door and doorframe and was slamming and slamming the door on his own flesh and bone, screeching for somebody to stop him doing it. One of the white boys had found the Colonel's knife and was amputating his hand with it. It came off as Boswell watched, falling on to its back, its root ragged, its five legs bicycling the air as it attempted to right itself. It wasn't dead: it wasn't even dying.

There were a few who hadn't been overtaken by this lunacy; they, poor bastards, were fodder. The wild men had their murderous hands on them, and were cutting them down. One – it was Savarino – was having the breath strangled out of him by some kid Boswell couldn't put a name to; the punk, all apologies, stared at his rebellious hands in disbelief.

Somebody appeared from one of the bedrooms, a hand which was not his own clutching his windpipe, and staggered towards the toilet down the corridor. It was Macnamara: a man so thin and so perpetually doped up he was known as the smile on a stick. Boswell stood aside as Macnamara stumbled, choking out a plea for help, through the open door, and collapsed on the toilet floor. He kicked and pulled at the five fingered assassin at his

16

neck, but before Boswell had a chance to step in and aid him his kicking slowed, and then, like his protests, stopped altogether.

Boswell stepped away from the corpse and took another look into the corridor. By now the dead or dying blocked the narrow passageway, two deep in some places, while the same hands that had once belonged to these men scuttled over the mounds in a furious excitement, helping to finish an amputation where necessary, or simply dancing on the dead faces. When he looked back into the toilet a second hand had found Macnamara, and armed with a pen knife, was sawing at his wrist. It had left fingerprints in the blood from corridor to corpse. Boswell rushed to slam the door before the place swarmed with them. As he did so Savarino's assassin, the apologetic punk, threw himself down the passage, his lethal hands leading him like those of a sleep-walker.

'Help me!' he screeched.

He slammed the door in the punk's pleading face, and locked it. The outraged hands beat a call to arms on the door while the punk's lips, pressed close to the keyhole, continued to beg: 'Help me. I don't want to do this man, help me.' Help you be fucked, thought Boswell and tried to block out the appeals while he sorted out his options.

There was something on his foot. He looked down, knowing before his eyes found it what it was. One of the hands, Colonel Christie's left, he knew by the faded tattoo, was already scurrying up his leg. Like a child with a bee on its skin Boswell went berserk, squirming as it clambered up towards his torso, but too terrified to try and pull it off. Out of the corner of his eye he could see that the other hand, the one that had been using the pen-knife with such alacrity on Macnamara, had given up the job, and was now moving across the floor to join its comrade. Its nails clicked on the tiles like the feet of a crab. It even had a crab's side-stepping walk: it hadn't yet got the knack of forward motion.

Boswell's own hands were still his to command; like the hands of a few of his friends (*late* friends) outside, his limbs were happy in their niche; easy-going like their owner. He had been blessed with a chance of survival. He had to be the equal of it.

Steeling himself, he trod on the hand on the floor. He heard the fingers crunch beneath his heel, and the thing squirmed like a snake, but at least he knew where it was while he dealt with his other assailant. Still keeping the beast trapped beneath his foot, Boswell leant forward, snatched the pen-knife up from where it lay beside Macnamara's wrist, and pushed the point of the knife into the back of Christie's hand, which was now crawling up his

17

belly. Under attack, it seized his flesh, digging its nails into his stomach. He was lean, and the washboard muscle made a difficult handhold. Risking a disembowelling, Boswell thrust the knife deeper. Christie's hand tried to keep its grip on him, but one final thrust did it. The hand loosened, and Boswell scooped it off his belly. It was crucified on the pen-knife, but it still had no intention of dying and Boswell knew it. He held it at arm's length, while its fingers grabbed at the air, then he drove the knife into the plasterboard wall, effectively nailing the beast there, out of harm's way. Then he turned his attention to the enemy under his foot, bearing his heel down as hard as he could, and hearing another finger crack, and another. Still it writhed relentlessly. He took his foot off the hand, and kicked it as hard and as high as he could against the opposite wall. It slammed into the mirror above the basins, leaving a mark like a thrown tomato, and fell to the floor.

He didn't wait to see whether it survived. There was another danger now. More fists at the door, more shouts, more apologies. They wanted in: and very soon they were going to get their way. He stepped over Macnamara and crossed to the window. It wasn't that big, but then neither was he. He flipped up the latch, pushed the window open on overpainted hinges, and hoisted himself through. Halfway in and halfway out he remembered he was one storey up. But a fall, even a bad fall, was better than staying for the party inside. They were pushing at the door now, the partygoers: it was giving under the pressure of their enthusiasm. Boswell squirmed through the window: the pavement reeled below. As the door broke, he jumped, hitting the concrete hard. He almost bounced to his feet, checking his limbs, and Hallelujah! nothing was broken. Jah loves a coward, he thought. Above him the punk was at the window, looking down longingly.

'Help me,' he said. 'I don't know what I'm doing.' But then a pair of hands found his throat, and the apologies stopped short.

Wondering who he should tell, and indeed *what*, Boswell started to walk away from the YMCA dressed in just a pair of gym shorts and odd socks, never feeling so thankful to be cold in his life. His legs felt weak: but surely that was to be expected.

Charlie woke with the most ridiculous idea. He thought he'd murdered Ellen, then cut off his own hand. What a hot-bed of nonsenses his sub-conscious was, to invent such fictions! He tried to rub the sleep from his eyes but there was no hand there to rub with. He sat bolt upright in bed and began to yell the room down.

Yapper had left young Rafferty to watch over the victim of this brutal mutilation, with strict instructions to alert him as soon as

Charlie George came round. Rafferty had been asleep: the yelling woke him. Charlie looked at the boy's face; so awestruck, so shocked. He stopped screaming at the sight of it: he was scaring the poor fellow.

'You're awake,' said Rafferty, 'I'll fetch someone, shall I?'

Charlie looked at him blankly.

'Stay where you are,' said Rafferty. 'I'll get the nurse.'

Charlie put his bandaged head back on the crisp pillow and looked at his right hand, flexing it, working the muscles this way and that. Whatever delusion had overtaken him back at the house it was well over now. The hand at the end of the arm was *his*; probably always had been his. Jeudwine had told him about the Body in Rebellion syndrome: the murderer who claims his limbs have a life of their own rather than accepting responsibility for his deeds; the rapist who mutilates himself, believing the cause is the errant member, not the mind behind the member.

Well, *he* wasn't going to pretend. He was insane, and that was the simple truth of it. Let them do whatever they had to do to him with their drugs, blades and electrodes: he'd acquiesce to it all rather than live through another night of horrors like the last.

There was a nurse in attendance: she was peering at him as though surprised he'd survived. A fetching face, he half thought; a lovely, cool hand on his brow.

'Is he fit to be interviewed?' Rafferty timidly asked.

'I have to consult with Dr Manson and Dr Jeudwine,' the fetching face replied, and tried to smile reassuringly at Charlie. It came out a bit cockeyed, that smile, a little forced. She obviously knew he was a lunatic, that was why. She was scared of him probably, and who could blame her? She left his side to find the consultant, leaving Charlie to the nervous stare of Rafferty.

'. . . Ellen?' he said in a while.

'Your wife?' the young man replied.

'Yes. I wondered . . . did she . . . ?'

Rafferty fidgeted, his thumbs playing tag on his lap. 'She's dead,' he said.

Charlie nodded. He'd known of course, but he needed to be certain. 'What happens to me now?' he asked.

'You're under surveillance.'

'What does that mean?'

'It means I'm watching you,' said Rafferty.

The boy was trying his best to be helpful, but all these questions were confounding him. Charlie tried again. 'I mean . . . what comes after the surveillance? When do I stand trial?'

'Why should you stand trial?'

'Why?' said Charlie; had he heard correctly?

'You're a victim – ' a flicker of confusion crossed Rafferty's face, ' – *aren't* you? You didn't *do* it . . . you were done to. Somebody cut off your . . . hand.'

'Yes,' said Charlie, 'It was me.'

Rafferty swallowed hard, before saying: 'Pardon?'

'*I* did it. I murdered my wife then I cut off my own hand.'

The poor boy couldn't quite grasp this one. He thought about it a full half-minute before replying.

'But why?'

Charlie shrugged.

'It doesn't make any sense,' said Rafferty. 'I mean for one thing, if you did it . . . where's the hand gone?'

Lillian stopped the car. There was something in the road a little way in front of her, but she couldn't quite make out what it was. She was a strict vegetarian (except for Masonic dinners with Theodore) and a dedicated animal conservationist, and she thought maybe some injured animal was lying in the road just beyond the sprawl of her headlights. A fox perhaps; she'd read they were creeping back into outlying urban areas, born scavengers. But something made her uneasy; maybe the queasy pre-dawn light, so elusive in its illumination. She wasn't sure whether she should get out of the car or not. Theodore would have told her to drive straight on, of course, but then Theodore had left her, hadn't he? Her fingers drummed the wheel with irritation at her own indecision. Suppose it *was* an injured fox: there weren't so many in the middle of London that one could afford to pass by on the other side of the street. She had to play the Samaritan, even if she felt a Pharisee.

Cautiously she got out of the car, and of course, after all of that, there was nothing to be seen. She walked to the front of the car, just to be certain. Her palms were wet; spasms of excitement passed through her hands like small electric shocks.

Then the noise: the whisper of hundreds of tiny feet. She'd heard stories – absurd stories she'd thought – of migrant rat-packs crossing the city by night, and devouring to the bone any living thing that got in their way. Imagining rats, she felt more like a Pharisee than ever, and stepped back towards the car. As her long shadow, thrown forward by the headlights, shifted, it revealed the first of the pack. It was no rat.

A hand, a long-fingered hand, ambled into the yellowish light and pointed up at her. Its arrival was followed immediately by another of the impossible creatures, then a dozen more, and another dozen hard upon those. They were massed like crabs at the fish-mongers, glistening backs pressed close to each other, legs flicking and clicking as they gathered in ranks. Sheer multiplication didn't make them any more believable; but even as she rejected the sight, they began to advance upon her. She took a step back.

She felt the side of the car at her back, turned, and reached for the door. It was ajar, thank God. The spasms in her hands were worse now, but she was still mistress of them. As her fingers sought the door she let out a little cry. A fat, black fist was squatting on the handle, its open wrist a twist of dried meat.

Spontaneously, and atrociously, her hands began to applaud. She suddenly had no control over their behaviour; they clapped like wild things in appreciation of this coup. It was ludicrous, what she was doing, but she couldn't help herself. 'Stop it,' she told her hands, 'stop it! stop it!' Abruptly they stopped, and turned to look at her. She *knew* they were looking at her, in their eyeless fashion, sensed too that they were weary of her unfeeling way with them. Without warning they darted for her face. Her nails, her pride and joy, found her eyes: in moments the miracle of sight was muck on her cheek. Blinded, she lost all orientation and fell backwards, but there were hands aplenty to catch her. She felt herself supported by a sea of fingers.

As they tipped her outraged body into a ditch, her wig, which had cost Theodore so much in Vienna, came off. So, after the minimum of persuasion, did her hands.

Dr Jeudwine came down the stairs of the George house wondering (just wondering) if maybe the grandpappy of his sacred profession, Freud, had been wrong. The paradoxical facts of human behaviour didn't seem to fit into those neat Classical compartments he'd allotted them to; perhaps attempting to be rational about the human mind was a contradiction in terms. He stood in the drear at the bottom of the stairs, not really wanting to go back into the dining-room or the kitchen, but feeling obliged to view the scenes of the crimes one more time. The empty house gave him the creeps: and being alone in it, even with a policeman standing guard on the front step, didn't help his peace of mind. He felt guilty, felt he'd let Charlie down. Clearly he hadn't trawled Charlie's psyche deeply enough to bring up the real catch, the true motive behind the appalling acts that he had committed. To murder his own wife, whom he had professed to love so deeply, in their marital bed; then to cut off your own hand: it was unthinkable. Jeudwine looked at his own hands for a moment, at the tracery of tendons and purple-blue veins at his wrist. The police still favoured the intruder theory, but he had no doubt that Charlie had done the deeds – murder, mutilation and all. The only fact that appalled Jeudwine more was that he hadn't uncovered the slightest propensity for such acts in his patient.

He went into the dining room. Forensic had finished its work around the house; there was a light dusting of fingerprint powder on a number of the surfaces. It was a miracle, wasn't it, the way each human hand was different?; its whorls as unique as a voice-pattern or a face. He yawned. He'd been woken by Charlie's call in the middle of the night, and he hadn't had any sleep since then. He'd watched Charlie bound up and taken away, watched the investigators about their business, watched a cod-white dawn raise its head over towards the river; he'd drunk coffee, moped, thought deeply about giving up his position as psychiatric consultant before this story hit the news, drunk more coffee, thought better of resignation, and now, despairing of Freud or any other guru, was seriously contemplating a bestseller on his relationship with wife-murderer Charles George. That way, even if he lost his job, he'd have something to salvage from the whole sorry episode. And Freud?; Viennese charlatan. What did the old opium-eater have to tell anyone?

He slumped in one of the dining-room chairs and listened to the hush that had descended on the house, as though the walls, shocked by what they'd seen, were holding their breaths. Maybe he dozed off a moment. In sleep, he heard a snapping sound, dreamt a dog, and woke up to see a cat in the kitchen, a fat black-and-white cat. Charlie had mentioned this household pet in passing: what was it called? Heartburn. That was it: so-named because of the black smudges over its eyes, which gave it a perpetually fretful expression. The cat was looking at the spillage of blood on the kitchen floor, apparently trying to find a way to skirt the pool and reach its food bowl without having to dabble its paws in the mess its master had left behind him. Jeudwine watched it fastidiously pick its way across the kitchen floor, and sniff at its empty bowl. It didn't occur to him to feed the thing; he hated animals.

Well, he decided, there was no purpose to be served in staying in the house any longer. He'd performed all the acts of repentance he intended; felt as guilty as he was capable of feeling. One more quick look upstairs, just in case he'd missed a clue, then he'd leave.

He was back at the bottom of the stairs before he heard the cat squeal. Squeal? No: *shriek* more like. Hearing the cry, his spine felt like a column of ice down the middle of his back: as chilled as ice, as fragile. Hurriedly, he retraced his steps through the hall into the dining-room. The cat's head was on the carpet, being rolled along by two – by two – (say it Jeudwine) – *hands*.

He looked beyond the game and into the kitchen, where a dozen more beasts were scurrying over the floor, back and forth. Some were on the top of the cabinet, sniffing around; others climbing the mock-brick wall to reach the knives left on the rack.

'Oh Charlie . . .' he said gently, chiding the absent maniac. 'What have you done?'

His eyes began to swell with tears; not for Charlie, but for the generations that would come when he, Jeudwine, was silenced. Simple-minded, trusting generations, who would put their faith in the efficacy of Freud and the Holy Writ of Reason. He felt his knees beginning to tremble, and he sank to the dining-room carpet, his eyes too full now to see clearly the rebels that were gathering around him. Sensing something alien sitting on his lap, he looked down, and there were his own two hands. Their index fingers were just touching, tip to manicured tip. Slowly, with horrible intention in their movement, the index fingers raised their nailed heads and looked up at him. Then they turned, and began to crawl up his chest, finding finger-holds in each fold of his Italian jacket, in each button-hole. The ascent ended abruptly at his neck, and so did Jeudwine.

Charlie's left hand was afraid. It needed reassurance, it needed encouragement: in a word, it needed Right. After all, Right had been the Messiah of this new age, the one with a vision of a future without the body. Now the army Left had mounted needed a glimpse of that vision, or it would soon degenerate into a slaughtering rabble. If that happened defeat would swiftly follow: such was the conventional wisdom of revolutions.

So Left had led them back home, looking for Charlie in the last place it had seen him. A vain hope, of course, to think he would have gone back there, but it was an act of desperation.

Circumstance, however, had not deserted the insurgents. Although Charlie hadn't been there, Dr Jeudwine had, and Jeudwine's hands not only knew where Charlie had been taken, but the route there, and the very bed he was lying in.

Boswell hadn't really known *why* he was running, or to where. His critical faculties were on hold, his sense of geography utterly confused. But some part of him seemed to know where he was going, even if he didn't, because he began to pick up speed once he came to the bridge, and then the jog turned into a run that took no account of his burning lungs or his thudding head. Still innocent of any intention but escape, he now realized that he had skirted the station and was running parallel with the railway line; he was simply going wherever his legs carried him, and that was the beginning and end of it.

The train came suddenly out of the dawn. It didn't whistle, didn't warn. Perhaps the driver noticed him, but probably not. Even if he had, the man could not have been held responsible for subsequent events. No, it was all his own fault: the way his feet suddenly veered towards the track, and his knees buckled so that he fell across the line. Boswell's last coherent thought, as the wheels reached him, was that the train meant nothing by this except to pass from A to B, and, in passing, neatly cut off his legs between groin and knee. Then he was under the wheels – the carriages hurtling by above him – and the train let out a whistle (so like a scream) which swept him away into the dark.

They brought the black kid into the hospital just after six: the hospital day began early, and deep-sleeping patients were being stirred from their dreams to face another long and tedious day. Cups of grey, defeated tea were being thrust into resentful hands, temperatures were being taken, medication distributed. The boy and his terrible accident caused scarcely a ripple.

Charlie was dreaming again. Not one of his Upper Nile dreams, courtesy of the Hollywood Hills, not Imperial Rome or the slaveships of Phoenicia. This was something in black and white. He dreamt he was lying in his coffin. Ellen was there (his subconscious had not caught up the facts of her death apparently), and his Mother and his Father. Indeed his whole life was in attendance. Somebody came (was it Jeudwine?; the consoling voice seemed familiar) to kindly screw down the lid on his coffin, and he tried to alert the mourners to the fact that he was still alive. When they didn't hear him, panic set in, but no matter how much he shouted the words made no impression; all he could do was lie there and let them seal him up in that terminal bedroom.

The dream jumped a few grooves. Now he could hear the service moaning on somewhere above his head. 'Man hath but a short time to live . . . ; he heard the creak of the ropes, and the shadow of the grave seemed to darken the dark. He was being let down into the earth, still trying his best to protest. But the air was getting stuffy in this hole; he was finding it more and more difficult to breathe, much less yell his complaints. He could just

24

manage to haul a stale sliver of air through his aching sinuses, but his mouth seemed stuffed with something, flowers perhaps, and he couldn't move his head to spit them out. Now he could feel the thump of clod on coffin, and Christ alive if he couldn't hear the sound of worms at either side of him, licking their chops. His heart was pumping fit to burst: his face, he was sure, must be blue-black with the effort of trying to find breath.

Then, miraculously, there was somebody in the coffin with him, somebody fighting to pull the constriction out of his mouth, off his face.

'Mr George!' she was saying, this angel of mercy. He opened his eyes in the darkness. It was the nurse from that hospital he'd been in – she was in the coffin too. 'Mr George!' She was panicking, this model of calm and patience; she was almost in tears as she fought to drag his hand off his face. '*You're suffocating yourself*!' she shouted in his face.

Other arms were helping with the fight now, and they were winning. It took three nurses to remove his hand, but they succeeded. Charlie began to breathe again, a glutton for air.

'Are you all right, Mr George?'

He opened his mouth to reassure the angel, but his voice had momentarily deserted him. He was dimly aware that his hand was still putting up a fight at the end of his arm.

'Where's Jeudwine?' he gasped, 'Get him please.'

'The doctor is unavailable at the moment, but he'll be coming to see you later on in the day.'

'I want to see him *now*.'

'Don't worry, Mr George,' the nurse replied, her bedside manner re-established, 'we'll just give you a mild sedative, and then you can sleep awhile.'

'No!'

'Yes, Mr George!' she replied, firmly. 'Don't worry. You're in good hands.'

'I don't want to sleep any more. They have control over you when you're asleep, don't you see?'

'You're safe here.'

He knew better. He knew he wasn't safe *anywhere*, not now. Not while he still had a hand. It was not under his control any longer, if indeed it had ever been; perhaps it was just an illusion of servitude it had created these forty-odd years, a performance to lull him into a false sense of autocracy. All this he wanted to say, but none of it would fit into his mouth. Instead he just said: 'No more sleep.'

But the nurse had procedures. The ward was already too full of

25

patients, and with more coming in every hour (terrible scenes at the YMCA she'd just heard: dozens of casualties: mass suicide attempted), all she could do was sedate the distressed and get on with the business of the day. 'Just a mild sedative,' she said again, and the next moment she had a needle in her hand, spitting slumber.

'Just listen a moment,' he said, trying to initiate a reasoning process with her; but she wasn't available for debate.

'Now don't be such a baby,' she chided, as tears started.

'You don't understand,' he explained, as she prodded up the vein at the crook of his arm − .

'You can tell Dr Jeudwine everything, when he comes to see you.' The needle was in his arm, the plunger was plunging.

'No!' he said, and pulled away. The nurse hadn't expected such violence. The patient was up and out of bed before she could complete the plunge, the hypo still dangling from his arm.

'Mr George,' she said sternly. 'Will you *please* get back into bed!'

Charlie pointed at her with his stump.

'Don't come near me,' he said.

She tried to shame him. 'All the other patients are behaving well,' she said, 'why can't you?' Charlie shook his head. The hypo, having worked its way out of his vein, fell to the floor, still three-quarters full. 'I will *not* tell you again.'

'Damn right you won't,' said Charlie.

He pelted away down the ward, his escape egged on by patients to the right and left of him. 'Go, boy, go,' somebody yelled. The nurse gave belated chase but at the door an instant accomplice intervened, literally throwing himself in her way. Charlie was out of sight and lost in the corridors before she was up and after him again.

It was an easy place to lose yourself in, he soon realized. The hospital had been built in the late nineteenth century, then added to as funds and donations allowed: a wing in 1911, another after the first World War, more wards in the fifties, and the Chaney Memorial Wing in 1973. The place was a labyrinth. They'd take an age to find him.

The problem was, he didn't feel so good. The stump of his left arm had begun to ache as his pain-killers wore off, and he had the distinct impression that it was bleeding under the bandages. In addition, the quarter hypo of sedative had slowed his system down. He felt slightly stupid: and he was certain that his condition must show on his face. But he was not going to allow himself to be coaxed back into that bed, back into sleep, until he'd sat down in a quiet place somewhere and thought the whole thing through.

He found refuge in a tiny room off one of the corridors, lined with filing cabinets and piles of reports; it smelt slightly damp. He'd found his way into the Memorial Wing, though he didn't know it. A seven-storey monolith built with a bequest from millionaire Frank Chaney, the tycoon's own building firm had done the construction job, as the old man's will required. They had used sub-standard materials and a defunct drainage system, which was why Chaney had died a millionaire, and the Wing was crumbling from the basement up. Sliding himself into a clammy niche between two of the cabinets, well out of sight should somebody chance to come in, Charlie crouched on the floor and interrogated his right hand.

'Well?' he demanded in a reasonable tone, 'Explain yourself.'

It played dumb.

'No use,' he said. 'I'm on to you.'

Still, it just sat there at the end of his arm, innocent as a babe.

'You tried to kill me . . .' he accused it.

Now the hand opened a little, without his instruction, and gave him the once over.

'You could try it again, couldn't you?'

Ominously, it began to flex its fingers, like a pianist preparing for a particularly difficult solo. *Yes*, it said, *I could; any old time*.

'In fact, there's very little I can do to stop you, is there?' Charlie said. 'Sooner or later you'll catch me unawares. Can't have somebody watching over me for the rest of my life. So where does that leave me, I ask myself? As good as dead, wouldn't you say?'

The hand closed down a little, the puffy flesh of its palm crinkling into grooves of pleasure. *Yes*, it was saying, *you're done for, poor fool, and there's not a thing you can do*.

'You killed Ellen.'

I did, the hand smiled.

'You severed my other hand, so it could escape. Am I right?'

You are, said the hand.

'I saw it, you know,' Charlie said, 'I saw it running off. And now you want to do the same thing, am I correct? You want to be up and away.'

Correct.

'You're not going to give me any peace, are you, 'til you've got your freedom?'

Right again.

27

'So,' said Charlie, 'I think we understand each other; and I'm willing to do a deal with you.'

The hand came closer to his face, crawling up his pyjama shirt, conspiratorial.

'I'll release you,' he said.

It was on his neck now, its grip not tight, but cosy enough to make him nervous.

'I'll find a way, I promise. A guillotine, a scalpel, I don't know what.'

It was rubbing itself on him like a cat now, stroking him. 'But you have to do it *my* way, in *my* time. Because if you kill me you'll have no chance of survival will you? They'll just bury you with me, the way they buried Dad's hands.'

The hand stopped stroking, and climbed up the side of the filing cabinet.

'Do we have a deal?' said Charlie.

But the hand was ignoring him. It had suddenly lost interest in all bargain-making. If it had possessed a nose, it would have been sniffing the air. In the space of the last few moments things had changed: the deal was off.

Charlie got up clumsily, and went to the window. The glass was dirty on the inside and caked with several years of bird-droppings on the outside, but he could just see the garden through it. It had been laid out in accordance with the terms of the millionaire's bequest: a formal garden that would stand as as glorious a monument to his good taste as the building was to his pragmatism. But since the building had started to deteriorate, the garden had been left to its own devices. Its few trees were either dead or bowed under the weight of unpruned branches; the borders were rife with weeds; the benches on their backs with their square legs in the air. Only the lawn was kept mown, a small concession to care. Somebody, a doctor taking a moment out for a quiet smoke, was wandering amongst the strangled walks. Otherwise the garden was empty.

But Charlie's hand was up at the glass, scrabbling at it, raking at it with his nails, vainly trying to get to the outside world. There was something out there beside chaos, apparently.

'You want to go out,' said Charlie.

The hand flattened itself against the window and began to bang its palm rhythmically against the glass, a drummer for an unseen army. He pulled it away from the window, not knowing what to do. If he denied its demands, it could hurt him. If he acquiesced to it, and tried to get out into the garden, what might he find? On the other hand, what choice did he have?

28

'All right,' he said, 'we're going.'

The corridor outside was bustling with panicky activity and there was scarcely a glance in his direction, despite the fact that he was only wearing his regulation pyjamas and was bare-foot. Bells were ringing, tannoys summoning this doctor or that, grieving people being shunted between mortuary and toilet; there was talk of the terrible sights in Casualty: boys with no hands, dozens of them. Charlie moved too fast through the throng to catch a coherent sentence. It was best to look intent, he thought, to look as though he had a purpose and a destination. It took him a while to locate the exit into the garden, and he knew his hand was getting impatient. It was flexing and unflexing at his side, urging him on. Then a sign: *To the Chaney Trust Memorial Garden*, and he turned a corner into a backwater corridor, devoid of urgent traffic, with a door at the far end that led to the open air.

It was very still outside. Not a bird in the air or on the grass, not a bee whining amongst the flower-heads. Even the doctor had gone, back to his surgeries presumably.

Charlie's hand was in ecstasies now. It was sweating so much it dripped, and all the blood had left it, so that it had paled to white. It didn't seem to belong to him any more. It was another being, to which he, by some unfortunate quirk of anatomy, was attached. He would be delighted to be rid of it.

The grass was dew-damp underfoot, and here, in the shadow of the seven-storey block, it was cold. It was still only six-thirty. Maybe the birds were still asleep, the bees still sluggish in their hives. Maybe there was nothing in this garden to be afraid of: only rot-headed roses and early worms, turning somersaults in the dew. Maybe his hand was wrong, and there was just morning out here.

As he wandered further down the garden, he noticed the footprints of the doctor, darker on the silver-green lawn. Just as he arrived at the tree, and the grass turned red, he realized that the prints led one way only.

Boswell, in a willing coma, felt nothing, and was glad of it. His mind dimly recognized the possibility of waking, but the thought was so vague it was easy to reject. Once in a while a sliver of the real world (of pain, of power) would skitter behind his lids, alight for a moment, then flutter away. Boswell wanted none of it. He didn't want consciousness, ever again. He had a feeling about what it would be to wake: about what was waiting for him out there, kicking its heels.

* * *

29

Charlie looked up into the branches. The tree had borne two amazing kinds of fruit.

One was a human being; the surgeon with the cigarette. He was dead, his neck lodged in a cleft where two branches met. He had no hands. His arms ended in round wounds that still drained heavy clots of brilliant colour down on to the grass. Above his head the tree swarmed with that other fruit, more unnatural still. The hands were everywhere, it seemed: hundreds of them, chattering away like a manual parliament as they debated their tactics. All shades and shapes, scampering up and down the swaying branches.

Seeing them gathered like this the metaphors collapsed. They were what they were: human hands. That was the horror.

Charlie wanted to run, but his right hand was having none of it. These were its disciples, gathered here in such abundance, and they awaited its parables and its prophecies. Charlie looked at the dead doctor and then at the murdering hands, and thought of Ellen, *his* Ellen, killed through no fault of his own, and already cold. They'd pay for that crime: all of them. As long as the rest of his body still did him service, he'd make them pay. It was cowardice, trying to bargain with this cancer at his wrist; he saw that now. It and its like were a pestilence. They had no place living.

The army had seen him, word of his presence passing through the ranks like wild fire. They were surging down the trunk, some dropping like ripened apples from the lower branches, eager to embrace the Messiah. In a few moments they would be swarming over him, and all advantage would be lost. It was now or never. He turned away from the tree before his right hand could seize a branch, and looked up at the Chaney Memorial Wing, seeking inspiration. The tower loomed over the garden, windows blinded by the sky, doors closed. There was no solace there.

Behind him he heard the whisper of the grass as it was trodden by countless fingers. They were already on his heels, all enthusiasm as they came following their leader.

Of course they would come, he realized, wherever he led, they would come. Perhaps their blind adoration of his remaining hand was an exploitable weakness. He scanned the building a second time and his desperate gaze found the fire-escape; it zig-zagged up the side of the building to the roof. He made a dash for it, surprising himself with his turn of speed. There was no time to look behind him to see if they were following, he had to trust to their devotion. Within a few paces his furious hand was at his neck, threatening to take out his throat, but he sprinted on,

30

indifferent to its clawing. He reached the bottom of the fire escape and, lithe with adrenalin, took the metal steps two and three at a time. His balance was not so good without a hand to hold the safety railing, but so what if he was bruised?; it was only his body.

At the third landing he risked a glance down through the grille of the stairs. A crop of flesh flowers was carpeting the ground at the bottom of the fire-escape, and was spreading up the stairs towards him. They were coming in their hungry hundreds, all nails and hatred. Let them come, he thought; let the bastards come. I began this and I can finish it.

At the windows of the Chaney Memorial Wing a host of faces had appeared. Panicking, disbelieving voices drifted up from the lower floors. It was too late now to tell them his life-story; they would have to piece that together for themselves. And what a fine jigsaw it would make! Maybe, in their attempts to understand what had happened this morning they would turn up some plausible solution; an explanation for this uprising that he had not found; but he doubted it.

Fourth storey now, and stepping on to the fifth. His right hand was digging into his neck. Maybe he was bleeding; but then perhaps it was rain, warm rain, that splashed onto his chest and down his legs. Two storeys to go, then the roof. There was a hum in the metalwork beneath him, the noise of their myriad feet as they clambered up towards him. He had counted on their adoration, and he'd been right to do so. The roof was now just a dozen steps away, and he risked a second look down past his body (it wasn't rain on him) to see the fire-escape solid with hands, like aphids clustered on the stalk of a flower. No, that was metaphor again. An end to that.

The wind whipped across the heights, and it was fresh, but Charlie had no time to appreciate its promise. He climbed over the two foot parapet and onto the gravel-littered roof. The corpses of pigeons lay in puddles, cracks snaked across the concrete, a bucket, marked 'Soiled Dressings', lay on its side, its contents green. He started across this wilderness as the first of the army fingered their way over the parapet.

The pain in his throat was getting through to his racing brain now, as his treacherous fingers wormed at his windpipe. He had little energy left after the race up the fire-escape, and crossing the roof to the opposite side (let it be a straight fall, onto concrete) was difficult. He stumbled once, and again. All the strength had gone from his legs, and nonsense filled his head in place of

31

coherent thought. A koan, a Bhuddist riddle he'd seen on the cover of a book once, was itching in his memory.

'*What is the sound*. . .?' it began, but he couldn't complete the phrase, try as he might.

'*What is the sound . . . ?*'

Forget the riddles, he ordered himself, pressing his trembling legs to make another step, and then another. He almost fell against the parapet at the opposite side of the roof, and stared down. It *was* a straight fall. A car park lay below, at the front of the building. It was deserted. He leaned over further and drops of his blood fell from his lacerated neck, diminishing quickly, down, down, to wet the ground. I'm coming, he said to gravity, and to Ellen, and thought how good it would be to die and never worry again if his gums bled when he brushed his teeth, or his waistline swelled, or some beauty passed him on the street whose lips he wanted to kiss, and never would. And suddenly the army was up on him, swarming up his legs in a fever of victory.

You can come, he said as they obscured his body from head to foot, witless in their enthusiasm, you can come wherever I go.

'*What is the sound . . . ?*' The phrase was on the tip of his tongue.

Oh yes: now it came to him. '*What is the sound of one hand clapping?*' It was so satisfying, to remember something you were trying so hard to dig up out of your subconscious, like finding some trinket you thought you'd lost forever. The thrill of remembering sweetened his last moments. He pitched himself into empty space, falling over and over until there was a sudden end to dental hygiene and the beauty of young women. They came in a rain after him, breaking on the concrete around his body, wave upon wave of them, throwing themselves to their deaths in pursuit of their Messiah.

To the patients and nurses crammed at the windows it was a scene from a world of wonders; a rain of frogs would have been commonplace beside it. It inspired more awe than terror: it was fabulous. Too soon, it stopped, and after a minute or so a few brave souls ventured out amongst the litter to see what could be seen. There was a great deal: and yet nothing. It was a rare spectacle of course; horrible, unforgettable. But there was no significance to be discovered in it; merely the paraphenalia of a minor apocalypse. Nothing to be done but to clear it up, their own hands reluctantly compliant as the corpses were catalogued and boxed for future examination. A few of those involved in the operation found a private moment in which to pray: for explanations; or at least for dreamless sleep. Even the smattering of the agnostics on the staff were surprised to discover how easy it was to put palm to palm.

In his private room in Intensive Care Boswell came to. He reached for the bell beside his bed and pressed it, but nobody answered. Somebody was in the room with him, hiding behind the screen in the corner. He had heard the shuffling of the intruder's feet.

He pressed the bell again, but there were bells ringing everywhere in the building, and nobody seemed to be answering any of them. Using the cabinet beside him for leverage he hauled himself to the edge of his bed to get a better view of this joker.

'Come out,' he murmured through dry lips. But the bastard was biding his time. 'Come on . . . I know you're there.'

He pulled himself a little further, and somehow all at once he realised that his centre of balance had radically altered, that he had no legs, that he was going to fall out of bed. He flung out his arms to save his head from striking the floor and succeeded in so doing. The breath had been knocked out of him however. Dizzy, he lay where he'd fallen, trying to orientate himself. What had happened? Where were his legs, in the name of Jah, *where were his legs*?

His bloodshot eyes scanned the room, and came to rest on the naked feet which were now a yard from his nose. A tag round the ankle marked them for the furnace. He looked up, and they were *his* legs, standing there severed between groin and knee, but still alive and kicking. For a moment he thought they intended to do him harm: but no. Having made their presence known to him they left him where he lay, content to be free.

And did his eyes envy their liberty, he wondered, and was his tongue eager to be out of his mouth and away, and was every part of him, in its subtle way, preparing to forsake him? He was an alliance only held together by the most tenuous of truces. Now, with the precedent set, how long before the next uprising? Minutes? Years?

He waited, heart in mouth, for the fall of Empire.

The Inhuman Condition

'Are you the one then?' Red demanded, seizing hold of the derelict by the shoulder of his squalid gabardine.

'What one d'you mean?' the dirt-caked face replied; he was scanning the quartet of young men who'd cornered him with rodent's eyes. The tunnel where they'd found him relieving himself was far from hope of help; they all knew it, and so, it seemed, did he. 'I don't know what you're talking about.'

'You've been showing yourself to children,' Red said.

The man shook his head, a dribble of spittle running from his lip into the matted bush of his beard. 'I've done nothing,' he insisted.

Brendan sauntered across to the man, heavy footsteps hollow in the tunnel. 'What's your name?' he inquired, with deceptive courtesy. Though he lacked Red's height and commanding manner, the scar that inscribed Brendan's cheek from temple to jaw-line suggested he knew suffering, both in the giving and the receiving. '*Name*,' he demanded, 'I'm not going to ask you again.'

'Pope,' the old man muttered, 'Mr Pope.'

Brendan grinned. '*Mr* Pope?' he said. 'Well; we heard you've been exposing that rancid little prick of yours to innocent children. What do you say to that?'

'No,' Pope replied, again shaking his head. 'That's not true. I never done nothing like that.' When he frowned the filth on his face cracked like crazy paving, a second skin of grime which was the accrual of many months. Had it not been for the fragrance of alcohol off him, which obscured the worst of his bodily stench, it would have been nigh-on impossible to stand within a yard of him. The man was human refuse; a shame to his species.

'Why bother with him?' Karney said. 'He stinks.'

Red glanced over his shoulder to silence the interruption. At seventeen, Karney was the youngest, and in the quartet's unspoken heirarchy scarcely deserving of an opinion. Recognizing his error, he shut up, leaving Red to return his attention to the vagrant. He pushed Pope back against the wall of the tunnel. The old man expelled a cry as he struck the concrete; it echoed back and forth. Karney, knowing from past experience how the scene would go

34

from here, moved away and studied a gilded cloud of gnats on the edge of the tunnel. Though he enjoyed being with Red and the other two – the cameraderie, the petty larceny, the drinking – this particular game had never been much to his taste. He couldn't see the sport in finding some drunken wreck of a man like Pope and beating what little sense was left in his deranged head out of him. It made Karney feel dirty, and he wanted no part of it.

Red pulled Pope off the wall, and spat a stream of abuse into the man's face, then, when he failed to get an adequate response, threw him back against the tunnel a second time, more forcibly than the first, following through by taking the breathless man by both lapels, and shaking him until he rattled. Pope threw a panicky glance up and down the track. A railway had once run along this route, through Highgate and Finsbury Park. Now the track had been lifted, and the cutting was public parkland, popular with early morning joggers and late-evening lovers. Now, however, in the middle of a clammy afternoon, the track was deserted in both directions.

'Hey,' said Catso, 'don't break his bottles.'

'Right,' said Brendan, 'we should dig out the drink before we break his head.'

At the mention of being robbed of his liquor Pope began to struggle, but his thrashing only served to enrage his captor. Red was in a dirty mood. The day, like most days this Indian summer, had been sticky and dull. Only the dog-end of a wasted season to endure; nothing to do, and no money to spend. Some entertainment had been called for, and it had fallen to Red as lion, and Pope as Christian, to supply it.

'You'll get hurt if you struggle,' Red advised the man, 'we only want to see what you've got in your pockets.'

'None of your business,' Pope retorted, and for a moment he spoke as a man who had once been used to being obeyed. The outburst made Karney turn from the gnats and gaze at Pope's emaciated face. Nameless degeneracies had drained it of dignity or vigour, but something remained there, glimmering beneath the dirt. What had the man been, Karney wondered? A banker perhaps?; a judge, now lost to the law forever?

Catso had now stepped into the fray to search Pope's clothes, while Red held his prisoner against the tunnel wall by the throat. Pope fought off Catso's unwelcome attentions as best he could, his arms flailing like windmills, his eyes getting progressively wilder. Don't fight, Karney willed him; it'll be the worse for you if you do. But the old man seemed to be on the verge of panic; he

35

was letting out small grunts of protest that were more animal than human.

'Somebody hold his arms,' Catso said, ducking beneath Pope's attack. Brendan grabbed hold of Pope's wrists and wrenched the man's arms up above his head to vacilitate an easier search. Even now, with any hope of release dashed, Pope continued to squirm. He managed to land a solid kick to Red's left shin, for which he received a blow in return. Blood broke from his nose and ran down into his mouth. There was more colour where that came from, Karney knew. He'd seen pictures aplenty of spilled people – bright, gleaming coils of guts; yellow fat and purple lights – all that brilliance was locked up in the grey sack of Pope's body. Why such a thought should occur to him, Karney wasn't certain. It distressed him, and he tried to turn his attention back to the gnats, but Pope demanded his attention, loosing a cry of anguish as Catso ripped open one of his several waistcoats to get to the lower layers.

'*Bastards!*' Pope screeched, not seeming to care that his insults would inevitably earn him further blows. 'Take your shitting hands off me or I'll have you *dead*. All of you!' Red's fist brought an end to the threats, and blood came running after blood. Pope spat it back at his tormentor. 'Don't tempt me,' Pope said, his voice dropping to a murmur. 'I warn you . . .'

'You smell like a dead dog,' Brendan said. 'Is that what you are: a dead dog?'

Pope didn't grant him a reply; his eyes were on Catso, who was systematically emptying the coat and waistcoat pockets and tossing a pathetic collection of keepsakes into the dust on the tunnel floor.

'Karney,' Red snapped, 'look through the stuff, will you? See if there's anything worth having.'

Karney stared at the plastic trinkets and the soiled ribbons; at the tattered sheets of paper (was the man a poet?) and the wine-bottle corks. 'It's all trash,' he said.

'Look anyway,' Red instructed. 'Could be money wrapped in that stuff.' Karney made no move to comply. '*Look*, damn you.'

Reluctantly, Karney went down on his haunches and proceeded to sift through the mound of rubbish Catso was still depositing in the dirt. He could see at a glance that there was nothing of value there, though perhaps some of the items – the battered photographs, the all but indecipherable notes – might offer some clue to the man Pope had been before drink and incipient lunacy had driven the memories away. Curious as he was, Karney wished to respect Pope's privacy. It was all the man had left.

'There's nothing here,' he announced after a cursory examination. But Catso hadn't finished his search; the deeper he dug the more layers of filthy clothing presented themselves to his eager hands. Pope had more pockets than a master magician.

Karney glanced up from the forlorn heap of belongings and found, to his discomfort, that Pope's eyes were on him. The old man, exhausted and beaten, had given up his protests. He looked pitiful. Karney opened his hands to signify that he had taken nothing from the heap. Pope, by way of reply, offered a tiny nod.

'Got it!' Catso yelled triumphantly, 'Got the fucker!' and pulled a bottle of vodka from one of the pockets. Pope was either too feeble to notice that his alcohol supply had been snatched, or too tired to care; whichever way, he made no sound of complaint as the liquor was stolen from him.

'Any more?' Brendan wanted to know. He'd begun to giggle: a high-pitched laugh that signalled his escalating excitement. 'Maybe the dog's got more where that came from,' he said, letting Pope's hands fall and pushing Catso aside. The latter made no objection to the treatment: he had his bottle and was satisfied. He smashed off the neck to avoid contamination and began to drink, squatting in the dirt. Red relinquished his grip on Pope now that Brendan had taken charge. He was clearly bored with the game. Brendan, on the other hand, was just beginning to get a taste for it.

Red walked over to Karney and turned over the pile of Pope's belongings with the toe of his boot.

'Fucking wash-out,' he stated, without feeling.

'Yeah,' Karney said, hoping that Red's disaffection would signal an end to the old man's humiliation. But Red had thrown the bone to Brendan, and he knew better than to try and snatch it back. Karney had seen Brendan's capacity for violence before; he had no desire to watch the man at work again. Sighing, he stood up and turned his back on Brendan's activities. The echoes off the tunnels wall were all too eloquent however: a mingling of punches and breathless obscenities. On past evidence nothing would stop Brendan until his fury was spent. Anyone foolish enough to interrupt him would find themselves victims in their turn.

Red had sauntered across to the far side of the tunnel, lit a cigarette, and was watching the punishment meted out with casual interest. Karney glanced round at Catso. He had descended from squatting to sitting in the dirt, the bottle of vodka between his outstretched legs. He was grinning to himself, deaf to the drool of pleas falling from Pope's broken mouth.

Karney felt sick to his stomach. More to divert his attention from the beating than out of genuine interest, he returned to the junk filched from Pope's pockets, and turned it over, picking up one of the photographs to examine. It was of a child, though it was impossible to make any guess as to family resemblance: Pope's face was now barely recognizable. One eye had already begun to close as the bruise around it swelled. Karney tossed the photograph back with the rest of the mementoes. As he did so he caught sight of a length of knotted cord which he had previously passed over. He glanced back up at Pope. The puffed eye was closed: the other seemed sightless. Satisfied that he wasn't being watched, Karney pulled the string from where it lay, coiled like a snake in its nest, amongst the trash. Knots fascinated him, and always had. Though he had never possessed skill with academic puzzles (mathematics was a mystery to him; the intricacies of language the same) he had always had a taste for more tangible riddles. Given a knot, a jigsaw or a railway timetable, he was happily lost to himself for hours. The interest went back to his childhood, which had been solitary: with neither father nor siblings to engage his attention what better companion than a puzzle?

He turned the string over and over, examining the three knots set at inch intervals in the middle of its length. They were large and asymmetrical, and seemed to serve no discernible purpose except, perhaps, to infatuate minds like his own. How else to explain their cunning construction, except that the knotter had been at pains to create a problem that was well-nigh insoluble? He let his fingers play over the surfaces of the knots, instinctively seeking some latitude, but they had been so brilliantly contrived that no needle, however fine, could have been pushed between the intersected strands. The challenge they presented was too appealing to ignore. Again he glanced up at the old man. Brendan had apparently tired of his labours; as Karney looked on he threw the old man against the tunnel wall and let the body sink to the ground. Once there, he let it lie. A unmistakable sewer-stench rose from it.

'That was good,' Brendan pronounced, like a man who had stepped from an invigorating shower. The exercise had raised a sheen of sweat on his ruddy features; he was smiling from ear to ear. 'Give me some of that vodka, Catso.'

'All gone,' Catso slurred, upending the bottle. 'Wasn't more than a throatful in it.'

'You're a lying shit,' Brendan told him, still grinning.

'What if I am?' Catso replied, and tossed the empty bottle away. It smashed. 'Help me up,' he requested of Brendan. The

38

latter, his great good humour intact, helped Catso to his feet. Red had already started to walk out of the tunnel; the others followed.

'Hey Karney – ' Catso said over his shoulder, 'you coming?'

'Sure.'

'You want to kiss the dog better?' Brendan suggested. Catso was almost sick with laughter at the remark. Karney made no answer. He stood up, his eyes glued to the inert figure slumped on the tunnel-floor, watching for a flicker of consciousness. There was none that he could see. He glanced after the others: all three had their backs to him as they made their way down the track. Swiftly, Karney pocketed the knots. The theft took moments only. Once the cord was safely out of sight he felt a surge of triumph which was out of all proportion to the goods he'd gained. He was already anticipating the hours of amusement the knots would furnish. Time when he could forget himself, and his emptiness; forget the sterile summer and the loveless winter ahead; forget too, the old man lying in his own waste yards from where he stood.

'Karney!' Catso called.

Karney turned his back on Pope and began to walk away from the body and the attendant litter of belongings. A few paces from the edge of the tunnel the old man behind him began to mutter in his delirium. The words were incomprehensible. But, by some acoustic trick, the walls of the tunnel multiplied the sound. Pope's voice was thrown back and forth and back again, filling the tunnel with whispers.

It wasn't until much later that night, when he was sitting alone in his bedroom, with his mother weeping in her sleep next door, that Karney had opportunity to study the knots at leisure. He had said nothing to Red or the others about his stealing the cord: the theft was so minor they would have mocked him for mentioning it. And besides, the knots offered him a personal challenge, one which he would face – and conceivably fail – in private.

After some debate with himself he elected the knot he would first attempt, and began to work at it. Almost immediately, he lost all sense of time passing: the problem engrossed him utterly. Hours of blissful frustration passed unnoticed as he analysed the tangle, looking for some clue as to a hidden system in the knotting. He could find none. The configurations, if they *had* some rationale, were beyond him. All he could hope to do was tackle the problem by trial and error. Dawn was threatening to bring the world to light again when he finally relinquished the cord to snatch a few hours of sleep, and in a night's work he had merely managed to loosen a tiny fraction of the knot.

Over the next four days the problem became an *idée fixée*; an hermetic obsession to which he would return at any available opportunity, picking at the knot with fingers that were increasingly numb with use. The puzzle enthralled him as little in his adult life ever had; working at the knot he was deaf and blind to the outside world. Sitting in his lamp-lit room by night, or in the park by day, he could almost feel himself drawn into its snarled heart, his consciousness focussed so minutely it could go where light could not. But, despite his persistence, the unravelling proved a slow business. Unlike most knots he had encountered, which, once loosened in part, conceded the entire solution, this structure was so adroitly designed that prising one element loose only served to constrict and tighten another. The trick, he began to grasp, was to work on all sides of the knot at an equal rate: loosening one part a fraction, then moving around to loosen another to an equal degree, and so on. This systematic rotation, though tedious, gradually showed results.

He saw nothing of Red, Brendan or Catso in this time; their silence suggested that they mourned his absence as little as he mourned theirs. He was surprised, therefore, when Catso turned up looking for him on Friday evening. He had come with a proposal. He and Brendan had found a house ripe for robbery, and wanted Karney as lookout man. He had fulfilled that role twice in the past. Both had been small breaking and entering jobs like this, which on the first occasion had netted a number of saleable items of jewellery, and on the second several hundred pounds in cash. This time however the job was to be done without Red's involvement: he was increasingly taken up with Anelisa, and she, according to Catso, had made him swear off petty theft and save his talents for something more ambitious. Karney sensed that Catso – and Brendan too, most likely – was itching to prove his criminal proficiency without Red. The house they had chosen was an easy target, so Catso claimed, and Karney would be a damn fool to let a chance of such easy pickings pass by. He nodded along with Catso's enthusiasm, his mind on other pickings. When Catso finally finished his spiel Karney agreed to the job, not for the money, but because saying yes would get him back to the knot soonest.

Much later that evening, at Catso's suggestion, they met to look at the site of the proposed job. The location certainly suggested an easy take. Karney had often walked over the bridge that carried

Hornsey Lane across the Archway Road, but he had never noticed the steep footpath – part steps, part track – that ran from the side of the bridge down to the road below. Its entrance was narrow, and easily overlooked, and its meandering length was lit by only one lamp, which light was obscured by trees growing in the gardens that backed on to the pathway. It was these gardens – their back fences easily scaled or wrenched down – that offered such perfect access to the houses. A thief, using the secluded footpath, might come and go with impunity, unseen by travellers on either the road above, or that below. All the set-up required was a lookout on the pathway to warn of the occasional pedestrian who might use the footpath. This would be Karney's duty.

The following night was a thief's joy. Cool, but not cold; cloudy, but without rain. They met on Highgate Hill, at the gates of the Church of the Passionist Fathers, and from there made their way down to the Archway Road. Approaching the pathway from the top end would, Brendan had argued, attract more attention. Police patrols were more common on Hornsey Lane, in part because the bridge was irresistible to local depressives. For the committed suicide the venue had distinct advantages, its chief appeal being that if the eighty foot drop didn't kill you the juggernauts hurtling South on the Archway Road certainly would.

Brendan was on another high tonight, pleased to be leading the others instead of taking second place to Red. His talk was an excitable babble, mostly about women. Karney let Catso have pride of place beside Brendan, and hung back a few paces, his hand in his jacket pocket, where the knots were waiting. In the last few hours, fatigued by so many sleepless nights, the cord had begun to play tricks on Karney's eyes; on occasion it had even seemed to move in his hand, as though it were working itself loose from the inside. Even now, as they approached the pathway, he could seem to feel it shift against his palm.

'Hey, man . . . look at that.' Catso was pointing up the pathway; its full length was in darkness. 'Someone killed the lamp.'

'Keep your voice down,' Brendan told him and led the way up the path. It was not in total darkness; a vestige of illumination was thrown up from the Archway Road. But filtered as it was through a dense mass of shrubbery, the path was still virtually benighted. Karney could scarcely see his hands in front of his face. But the darkness would presumably dissuade all but the most sure-footed of pedestrians from using the path. When they climbed a little more than halfway up, Brendan brought the tiny party to a halt.

'This is the house,' he announced.

'Are you sure?' Catso said.

'I counted the gardens. This is the one.'

The fence that bounded the bottom of the garden was in an advanced state of disrepair: it took only a brief manhandling from Brendan – the sound masked by the roar of a late-night juggernaut on the tarmac below – to afford them easy access. Brendan pushed through the thicket of brambles growing wild at the end of the garden and Catso followed, cursing as he was scratched. Brendan silenced him with a second curse, then turned back to Karney.

'We're going in. We'll whistle twice when we're out of the house. You remember the signals?'

'He's not an imbecile. Are you Karney? He'll be all right. Now are we going or not?' Brendan said no more. The two figures navigated the brambles and made their way up into the garden proper. Once on the lawn, and out of the shadows of the trees, they were visible as grey shapes against the house. Karney watched them advance to the back door, heard a noise from the back door as Catso – much the more nimble-fingered of the two – forced the lock; then the duo slid into the interior of the house. He was alone.

Not *quite* alone. He still had his companions on the cord. He checked up and down the pathway, his eyes gradually becoming sharper in the sodium-tinted gloom. There were no pedestrians. Satisfied, he pulled the knots from his pocket. His hands were ghosts in front of him; he could hardly see the knots at all. But, almost without his conscious intention guiding them, his fingers began to take up their investigation afresh, and odd though it seemed, he made more impression on the problem in a few seconds of blind manipulation than he had in many of the hours preceding. Robbed of his eyes he went purely on instinct, and it worked wonders. Again he had the bewildering sensation of intentionality in the knot, as if more and more it was an agent in its own undoing. Encouraged by the tang of victory, his fingers slid over the knot with inspired accuracy, seeming to alight upon precisely the right threads to manipulate.

He glanced again along the pathway, to be certain it was still empty, then looked back towards the house. The door remained open: there was no sign of either Catso or Brendan however. He returned his attention to the problem in hand; he almost wanted to laugh at the ease with which the knot was suddenly slipping undone.

His eyes, sparked by his mounting excitement perhaps, had begun to play a startling trick. Flashes of colour – rare, unnameable tints – were igniting in front of him, their origins the heart of the

42

knot. The light caught his fingers as they worked: by it, his flesh became translucent. He could see his nerve-endings, bright with new-found sensibility; the rods of his finger-bones, visible to the marrow. Then, almost as suddenly as they flickered into being, the colours would die, leaving his eyes bewitched in darkness until once more they ignited.

His heart began to hammer in his ears. The knot, he sensed, was mere *seconds* from solution. The interwoven threads were positively springing apart: his fingers were the cord's playthings now, not the other way about. He opened loops to feed the other two knots through; he pulled, he pushed: all at the cord's behest.

And now colours came again, but this time his fingers were invisible, and instead he could see something glowing in the last few hitches of the knot. The form writhed like a fish in a net, growing bigger with every stitch he cast off. The hammer in his head doubled its tempo. The air around him had become almost glutinous, as if he were immersed in mud.

Someone whistled. He knew the signal should have carried some significance for him, but he couldn't recall what. There were too many distractions: the thickening air, his pounding head, the knot untying itself in his helpless hands while the figure at its centre – sinuous, glittering – raged and swelled.

The whistle came again. This time its urgency shook him from his trance. He looked up. Brendan was already crossing the garden, with Catso trailing a few yards behind. Karney had a moment only to register their appearance before the knot initiated the final phase of its resolution. The last weave fell free, and the form at its heart leapt up towards Karney's face – growing at an exponential rate. He flung himself backwards to avoid losing his head, and the thing shot past him. Shocked, he stumbled in the tangle of brambles and fell in a bed of thorns. Above his head the foliage was shaking as if in a high wind. Leaves and small twigs showered down around him. He stared up into the branches to try and catch sight of the shape, but it was already out of sight.

'Why didn't you answer me, you fucking idiot?' Brendan demanded, 'We thought you'd done a runner.'

Karney had barely registered Brendan's breathless arrival; he was still searching the canopy of the trees above his head. The reek of cold mud filled his nostrils.

'You'd better move yourself,' Brendan said, climbing through the broken fence and out on to the pathway. Karney struggled to get to his feet, but the barbs of the brambles slowed his attempt, catching in his hair and clothes.

'Shit!' he heard Brendan breathe from the far side of the fence. 'Police! On the bridge.'

Catso had reached the bottom of the garden.

'What are you doing down there?' he asked Karney.

Karney raised his hand. 'Help me,' he said. Catso grabbed him by the wrist, but even as he did so Brendan hissed: '*Police! Move it!*' and Catso relinquished his aid and ducked out through the fence to follow Brendan down to the Archway Road. It took Karney a few dizzied seconds only to realize that the cord, with its two remaining knots, had gone from his hand. He hadn't dropped it, he was certain of that. More likely it had deliberately deserted him, and its only opportunity had been his brief hand-to-hand contact with Catso. He reached out to grasp hold of the rotting fence and haul himself to his feet. Catso had to be warned of what the cord had done; police or no police. There was worse than the law nearby.

Racing down the pathway, Catso was not even aware that the knots had found their surreptitious way into his hand, he was too pre-occupied with the problem of escape. Brendan had already disappeared on to the Archway Road, and was away. Catso chanced a look over his shoulder to see if the police were in pursuit. There was no sign of them, however. Even if they began to give chase now, he reasoned, they wouldn't catch him. That left Karney. Catso slowed his pace, then stopped, looking back up the pathway to see if the idiot showed any sign of following, but he had not so much as climbed through the fence.

'Damn him,' Catso said beneath his breath. Perhaps he should retrace his steps and fetch him?

As he hesitated on the darkened pathway he became aware that what he had taken to be a gusty wind in the overhanging trees had abruptly died away. The sudden silence mystified him. He drew his gaze from the path to look up into the canopy of branches and his appalled eyes focussed on the shape that was crawling down towards him, bringing with it the reek of mud and dissolution. Slowly, as in a dream, he raised his hands to keep the creature from touching him, but it reached down with wet, icy limbs, and snatched him up.

Karney, in the act of climbing through the fence, caught sight of Catso being hauled off his feet and into the cover of the trees; saw his legs pedalling the air while stolen merchandise fell from his pockets and skipped down the pathway towards the Archway Road.

Then Catso shrieked, and his dangling legs began an even more frenzied motion. At the top of the pathway, Karney heard somebody calling. One policeman to another, he surmised. The next moment he heard the sound of running feet. He glanced up to Hornsey Lane – the officers had yet to reach the top of the pathway – and then looked back down in Catso's direction in time to catch sight of his body dropping from the tree. It fell to the ground limply, but the next moment scrambled to its feet. Briefly Catso looked back up the pathway towards Karney. The look on his face, even in the sodium gloom, was a lunatic's look. Then he began to run. Karney, satisfied that Catso had a head start, slipped back through the fence as the two policemen appeared at the head of the pathway and began in pursuit of Catso. All this – the knot, the thieves, pursuit, shriek and all – had occupied a mere handful of seconds, during which Karney had not drawn breath. Now he lay on a barbed pillow of brambles and gasped like a landed fish, while at the other side of the fence the police hurtled down the footpath yelling after their suspect.

Catso scarcely heard their commands. It wasn't the police that he was running from: it was the muddied thing that had lifted him up to meet its slitted and chancred face. Now, as he reached the Archway Road, he felt tremors beginning in his limbs. If his legs gave out he was certain it would come for him again, and lay its mouth on his as it already had. Only this time he would not have the strength to scream; the life would be sucked from his lungs. His only hope lay in putting the road between him and his tormentor. The beast's breath loud in his ears, he scaled the crash-barrier, leapt down on to the road, and began across the south-bound carriageway at a run. Halfway across he realized his error. The horror in his head had blinded him to all other risks. A blue Volvo – its driver's mouth a perfect O – bore down on him. He was caught in its headlights like an animal, entranced: two instants later he was struck a glancing blow which threw him across the divide and into the path of an articulated lorry. The second driver had no chance to swerve: the impact split Catso open and tossed him beneath the wheels.

Up in the garden, Karney heard the panic of the brakes, and the policeman, at the bottom of the pathway say: 'Jesus Christ Almighty'. He waited a few seconds, then peered out from his hiding place. The footpath was now deserted, top and bottom. The trees were quite still. From the road below rose the sound of a siren, and that of the officers shouting for oncoming cars to halt. Closer by, somebody was sobbing. He listened intently for a few moments, trying to work out the source of the sobs, before realizing that they were his own. Tears or no, the clamour from below demanded his attention. Something terrible had happened, and he had to see what. But he was afraid to run the gauntlet of the trees, knowing what lay in wait there, so he stood, staring up into the branches, trying to locate the beast. There was neither sound nor movement, however: the trees were dead still. Stifling his fears, he climbed from his hiding place and began to walk down the pathway, his eyes glued to the foliage for the slightest sign of the beast's presence. He could hear the buzz of a gathering crowd. The thought of a press of people comforted him; from now on he would need a place to hide, wouldn't he? Men who'd seen miracles did

He had reached the spot where Catso had been dragged up into the trees: a litter of leaves and stolen property marked it. Karney's feet wanted to be swift, to pick him up and whisk him away from the place, but some perverse instinct slowed his pace. Was it that he wanted to tempt the knot's child into showing its face? Better, perhaps, to confront it now – in all its foulness – than to live in fear from this moment on, embroidering its countenance and its capacities. But the beast kept itself hidden. If indeed it was still up there in the tree, it twitched not a nail.

Something moved beneath his foot. Karney looked down, and there, almost lost amongst the leaves, was the cord. Catso had been deemed unworthy to carry it apparently. Now – with some clue to its power revealed – it made no effort to pass for natural. It squirmed on the gravel like a serpent in heat, rearing its knotted head to attract Karney's attention. He wanted to ignore its cavorting, but he couldn't. He knew that if *he* didn't pick up the knots, somebody else would, given time: a victim, like himself, of an urge to solve enigmas. Where could such innocence lead, except to another escape perhaps more terrible than the first? No; it was best that he took the knots. At least he was alive to their potential, and so, in part, armoured against it. He bent down, and as he did so the string fairly leapt into his hands, wrapping itself around his fingers so tightly he almost cried out.

'Bastard,' he said.

The string coiled itself around his hand, weaving its length between his fingers in an ecstasy of welcome. He raised his hand to watch its performance better. His concern for the events on the Archway Road had suddenly, almost miraculously, evaporated. What did such petty concerns matter? It was only life and death. Better to make his getaway now, while he could.

Above his head, a branch shook. He unglued his eyes from the knots and squinted up into the tree. With the cord restored to him his trepidation, like his fears, had evaporated.

46

'Show yourself,' he said, 'I'm not like Catso; I'm not afraid. I want to know what you are.'

From its camouflage of leaves the waiting beast leaned down towards Karney and exhaled a single, chilly breath. It smelt of the river at low tide, of vegetation gone to rot. Karney was about to ask it what it was again when he realised that the exhalation *was* the beast's reply. All it could speak of its condition was contained in that bitter and rancid breath. As replies went, it was not lacking in eloquence. Distressed by the images it awoke, Karney backed away from the spot. Wounded, sluggish forms moved behind his eyes, engulfed in a sludge of filth.

A few feet from the tree the spell of the breath broke, and Karney drank the polluted air from the road as though it were clean as the world's morning. He turned his back on the agonies he had sensed, thrust his string-woven hand into his pocket, and began up the pathway. Behind him, the trees were quite still again.

Several dozen spectators had gathered on the bridge to watch proceedings below. Their presence had in turn piqued the curiosity of drivers making their way along Hornsey Lane, some of whom had parked their vehicles and got out to join the throng. The scene beneath the bridge seemed too remote to wake any feelings in Karney. He stood amongst the chattering crowd and gazed down quite dispassionately. He recognized Catso's corpse from his clothes: little else remained of his sometime companion.

In a while, he knew, he would have to mourn. But at present he could feel nothing. After all, Catso was dead, wasn't he?, his pain and his confusion at an end. Karney sensed he would be wiser to save his tears for those whose agonies were only just beginning.

And again, the knots.

At home that night, he tried to put them away, but, after the events of the evening they had taken on a fresh glamour. *The knots bound beasts.* How, and why, he couldn't know; nor, curiously, did he much care at the moment. All his life he had accepted that the world was rich with mysteries a mind of his limited grasp had no hope of understanding. That was the only genuine lesson his schooldays had taught: that he was ignorant. This new imponderable was just another to tag onto a long list.

Only one rationale really occurred to him, and that was that somehow Pope had arranged his stealing of the knots in the full knowledge that the loosed beast would revenge itself on the old man's tormentors and it wasn't to be until Catso's cremation, six days later, that Karney was to get some confirmation of that theory. In the interim he kept his fears to himself, reasoning that the less he said about the night's events the less harm they could do him. Talk lent the fantastic credibility: it gave weight to phenomena which he hoped, if left to themselves, would become too frail to survive.

When, the following day, the police came to the house on a routine questioning of Catso's friends, he claimed he knew nothing of the circumstances surrounding the death. Brendan had done the same, and as there had seemingly been no witnesses to offer contrary testimony, Karney was not questioned again. Instead he was left to his thoughts; and the knots.

Once, he saw Brendan. He had expected recriminations; Brendan's belief was that Catso had been running from the police when he was killed, and it had been Karney's lack of concentration that had failed to alert them to the law's proximity. But Brendan made no accusations. He had taken the burden of guilt on to himself with a willingness that almost smacked of appetite; he spoke only of his own failure, not of Karney's. The apparent arbitrariness of Catso's demise had uncovered an unlooked-for tenderness in Brendan, and Karney ached to tell him the whole incredible story from beginning to end. But this was not the time, he sensed. He let Brendan spill his hurt out, and kept his own mouth shut.

And still the knots.

Sometimes he would wake in the middle of the night and feel the cord moving beneath his pillow. Its presence was comforting, its eagerness was not, waking, as it did, a similar eagerness in him. He wanted to touch the remaining knots and examine the puzzles they offered. But he knew that to do so was tempting capitulation: to his own fascination; to their hunger for release. When such temptation arose, he forced himself to remember the pathway, and the beast in the trees; to awake again the harrowing thoughts that had come with the beast's breath. Then, by degrees, remembered distress would cancel present curiosity, and he would leave the cord where it lay. Out of sight, though seldom out of mind.

Dangerous as he knew the knots to be, he couldn't bring himself to burn them. As long as he possessed that modest length of cord he was unique; to relinquish it would be to return to his hitherto nondescript condition. He was not willing to do that, even though he suspected that his daily and intimate association with the cord was systematically weakening his ability to resist its seduction.

Of the thing in the tree he saw nothing: he even began to wonder if he hadn't imagined the whole confrontation. Indeed, given time, his powers to rationalize the truth into non-existence might have won the day completely. But events subsequent to the cremation of Catso put an end to such a convenient option.

Karney had gone to the service alone – and, despite the presence of Brendan, Red and Anelisa – he had left alone. He had little wish to speak with any of the mourners. Whatever words he might once have had to frame the events were becoming more difficult to re-invent as time passed. He hurried away from the Crematorium before anyone could approach him to talk, his head bowed against the dusty wind which had brought periods of cloud and bright sunshine in swift succession throughout the day. As he walked, he dug in his pocket for a pack of cigarettes. The cord, waiting there as ever, welcomed his fingers in its usual ingratiating manner. He disentangled it, and took out the cigarettes, but the wind was too snappy for matches to stay alight, and his hands seemed unable to perform the simple task of masking the flame. He wandered on a little way until he found an alley, and stepped into it to light up. Pope was there, waiting for him.

'Did you send flowers?' the derelict asked.

Karney's instinct was to turn and run. But the sunlit road was no more than yards away; he was in no danger here. And an exchange with the old man might prove informative.

'No flowers?' Pope said.

'No flowers,' Karney returned. 'What are you doing here?'

'Same as you,' Pope replied, 'Came to see the boy burn.' He grinned, the expression, on that wretched, grimy face, was repulsive to a fault. Pope was still the bag of bones that he'd been in the tunnel two weeks previous, but now an air of threat hung about him. Karney was grateful to have the sun at his back.

'And you. To see you,' Pope said.

Karney chose to make no reply. He struck a match and lit his cigarette.

'You've got something that belongs to me,' Pope said. Karney volunteered no guilt. 'I want my knots back, boy, before you do some *real* damage.'

'I don't know what you're talking about,' Karney replied. His gaze concentrated, unwillingly, on Pope's face, drawn into its intricacies. The alleyway, with its piled refuse, twitched. A cloud had apparently drifted over the sun, for Karney's vision, but for the figure of Pope, darkened subtly.

49

'It was stupid, boy, to try and steal from me. Not that I wasn't easy prey; that was my error, and it won't happen again. I get lonely sometimes, you see. I'm sure you understand. And when I'm lonely I take to drinking.'

Though mere seconds had apparently passed since Karney had lit his cigarette, it had burned down to the filter without his taking a single pull on it. He dropped it, vaguely aware that time, as well as space, was being pulled out of true in the tiny passage.

'It wasn't me,' he muttered: a child's defence in the face of any and every accusation.

'Yes it was,' Pope replied with incontestable authority. 'Let's not waste breath with fabrication. You stole from me, and your colleague has paid the price. You can't undo the harm you've done. But you *can* prevent further harm, if you return to me what's mine. *Now.*'

Karney's hand had strayed to his pocket, without his quite realizing it. He wanted to get out of this trap before it snapped on him; giving Pope what was, after all, rightfully *his* was surely the easiest way to do it. His fingers hesitated, however; why? Because the Methuselah's eyes were so implacable perhaps; because returning the knots into Pope's hands gave him total control over the weapon that had, in effect, killed Catso? But more; even now, with sanity at risk, Karney was loathe to give back the only fragment of mystery that had ever come his way. Pope, sensing his disinclination, pressed his cajoling into a higher gear.

'Don't be afraid of me,' he said. 'I won't do you any harm unless you push me to it. I would *much* prefer that we concluded this matter peacefully; more violence, another death even, would only attract attention.'

Is this a killer I'm looking at?, Karney thought; so unkempt, so ridiculously feeble. And yet sound contradicted sight; the seed of command Karney had once heard in Pope's voice was now in full flower.

'Do you want money?' Pope asked, 'Is that it? Would your pride be best appeased if I offered you something for your troubles?' Karney looked incredulously at Pope's shabbiness. 'Oh,' the old man said, 'I may not look like a moneyed man, but appearances can be deceptive. In fact, that's the rule, not the exception. Take yourself, for instance. You don't look like a dead man, but take it from me, you are as good as dead, boy. I promise you death if you continue to defy me.'

The speech – so measured, so scrupulous – startled Karney, coming as it did from Pope's lips: thereby proving the man's thesis. A fortnight ago they had caught Pope in his cups –

confused and vulnerable – but now, sober, the man spoke like a potentate: a lunatic king, perhaps, going amongst the hoi-polloi as a pauper. King?; no, *priest* more like. Something in the nature of his authority (in his name, even) suggested a man whose power had never been rooted in mere politics.

'Once more,' he said, 'I request you to give me what's mine.'

He took a step towards Karney. The alleyway was a narrow tunnel, pressing down on their heads. If there was sky above them, Pope had blinded it.

'Give me the knots,' he said. His voice was softly reassuring. The darkness had closed in completely. All Karney could see was the man's mouth: his uneven teeth, his grey tongue. 'Give them to me, thief, or suffer the consequences.'

'Karney?'

Red's voice came from another world. It was just a few paces away – the voice, sunlight, wind – but for a long moment Karney struggled to locate it again.

'Karney?'

He dragged his consciousness out from between Pope's teeth and forced his face round to look at the road. Red was there, standing in the sun, Anelisa at his side. Her blonde hair shone.

'What's going on?'

'Leave us alone,' Pope said. 'We've got business, he and I.'

'You've got business with *him*?' Red asked of Karney.

Before Karney could reply Pope said: 'Tell him. Tell him, Karney, you want to speak to me alone.'

Red threw a glance over Karney's shoulder towards the old man. 'You want to tell me what's going on?' he said.

Karney's tongue was labouring to find a response, but failing. The sunlight was so far away; every time a cloud-shadow passed across the street he feared the light would be extinguished permanently. His lips worked silently to express his fear.

'You all right?' Red asked. '*Karney*? Can you hear me?'

Karney nodded. The darkness that held him was beginning to lift.

'Yes . . .' he said.

Suddenly, Pope threw himself at Karney, his hands scrabbling desperately for his pockets. The impact of the attack carried Karney, still in a stupor, back against the wall of the alleyway. He fell sideways against a pile of crates. They, and he, toppled over, and Pope, his grip on Karney too fierce to be dislodged, fell too. All the preceding calm – the gallows humour, the circumspect threats – had evaporated; he was again the idiot derelict, spouting insanities. Karney felt the man's hands tearing at his clothes and

51

raking his skin in his bid for the knots. The words he was shouting into Karney's face were no longer comprehensible.

Red stepped into the alley and attempted to drag the old man, by coat or hair or beard, whichever handhold presented itself, off his victim. It was easier said than done; the assault had all the fury of a fit. But Red's superior strength won out. Spitting nonsenses, Pope was pulled to his feet. Red held on to him as if he were a mad dog.

'Get up . . .' he told Karney, 'get out of his reach.'

Karney staggered to his feet amongst the tinder of crates. In the scant seconds of his attack Pope had done considerable damage: Karney was bleeding in half a dozen places. His clothes had been savaged; his shirt ripped beyond repair. Tentatively, he put his hand to his raked face; the scratches were raised like ritual scars.

Red pushed Pope against the wall. The derelict was still apoplectic, eyes wild. A stream of invective – a jumble of English and gibberish – was flung in Red's face. Without pausing in his tirade Pope made another attempt to attack Karney, but this time Red's hand-hold prevented the claws from making contact. Red hauled Pope out of the alley and into the road.

'Your lip's bleeding,' Anelisa said, looking at Karney with plain disgust. Karney could taste the blood: salty and hot. He put the back of his hand to his mouth. It came away scarlet.

'Good thing we came after you,' she said.

'Yeah,' he returned, not looking at the woman. He was ashamed of the showing he'd made in the face of the vagrant, and knew she must be laughing at his inability to defend himself. Her family were villians to a man, her father a folk-hero amongst thieves.

Red came back in from the street. Pope had gone.

'What was all that about?' he demanded to know, taking a comb from his jacket pocket and re-establishing his quiff.

'Nothing,' Karney replied.

'Don't give me shit,' Red said. 'He claims you stole something from him. Is that right?'

Karney glanced across at Anelisa. But for her presence he might have been willing to tell Red everything, there and then. She returned his glance and seemed to read his thoughts. Shrugging, she moved out of ear-shot, kicking through the demolished crates as she went.

'He's got it in for us all, Red,' Karney said.

'What are you talking about?'

Karney looked down at his bloody hand. Even with Anelisa out of the way, the words to explain what he suspected were slow in coming.

'Catso . . .' he began.

'What about him?'

'He was running, Red.'

Behind him, Anelisa expelled an irritated sigh. This was taking longer than she'd temper for.

'Red,' she said, 'we'll be late.'

'Wait a minute,' Red told her sharply, and turned his attention back to Karney, 'What do you mean: about Catso?'

'The old man's not what he seems. He's not a vagrant.'

'Oh? What is he?' A note of sarcasm had crept back into Red's voice: for Anelisa's benefit, no doubt. The girl had tired of discretion, and had wandered back to join Red. 'What is he, Karney?'

Karney shook his head. What was the use of trying to explain a *part* of what had happened? Either he attempted the entire story, or nothing at all. Silence was easier.

'It doesn't matter,' he said, flatly.

Red gave him a puzzled look, then, when there was no clarification forthcoming, said: 'If you've got something to tell me about Catso, Karney, I'd like to hear it. You know where I live.'

'Sure,' said Karney.

'I mean it,' Red said, 'about talking.'

'Thanks.'

'Catso was a good mate, you know? Bit of a piss-artist, but we've all had our moments, eh? He shouldn't have died, Karney. It was wrong.'

'Red – '

'She's calling you.' Anelisa had wandered out into the street.

'She's always calling me. I'll see you around, Karney.'

'Yeah.'

Red patted Karney's stinging cheek and followed Anelisa out into the sun. Karney made no move to follow them. Pope's assault had left him trembling; he intended to wait in the alleyway until he'd regained a gloss of composure, at least. Seeking reassurance of the knots, he put his hand into his jacket pocket. It was empty. He checked his other pockets. They too were empty, and yet he was certain that the old man's grasp had failed to get near the cord. Perhaps they had slipped out of hiding during the struggle. Karney began to scour the alley, and when the first search failed, followed with a second and a third; but by that time he knew the operation was lost. Pope *had* succeeded after all. By stealth or chance, he had regained the knots.

With startling clarity, Karney remembered standing on Suicides' Leap, looking down on to the Archway Road, Catso's body sprawled below at the centre of a network of lights and vehicles. He had felt so *removed* from the tragedy: viewing it with all the involvement of a passing bird. Now – suddenly – he was shot from the sky. He was on the ground, and wounded, waiting hopelessly for the terrors to come. He tasted blood from his split lip and wondered, wishing the thought would vanish even as it formed, if Catso had died immediately, or if he too had tasted blood as he'd lain there on the tarmac, looking up at the people on the bridge who had yet to learn how close death was.

He returned home via the most populated route he could plan. Though this exposed his disreputable state to the stares of matrons and policemen alike he preferred their disapproval to chancing the empty streets away from the major thoroughfares. Once home, he bathed his scratches and put on a fresh set of clothes, then sat in front of the television for a while to allow his limbs to stop shaking. It was late afternoon, and the programmes were all children's fare: a tone of queasy optimism infected every channel. He watched the banalities with his eyes but not with his mind, using the respite to try and find the words to describe all that had happened to him. The imperative was now to warn Red and Brendan. With Pope in control of the knots it could only be a matter of time before some beast – worse, perhaps, than the thing in the trees – came looking for them all. Then it would be too late for explanations. He knew the other two would be contemptuous, but he would sweat to convince them, however ridiculous he ended up looking in the process. Perhaps his tears and his panic would move them the way his impoverished vocabulary never could. About five after five, before his mother returned home from work, he slipped out of the house and went to find Brendan.

Anelisa took the piece of string she'd found in the alleyway out of her pocket and examined it. Why she had bothered to pick it up at all she wasn't certain, but somehow it had found its way into her hand. She played with one of the knots, risking her long nails in doing so. She had half a dozen better things to be doing with her early evening. Red had gone to buy drink and cigarettes and she had promised herself a leisurely, scented bath before he returned. But the knot wouldn't take that long to untie, she was certain of that. Indeed, it seemed almost eager to be undone: she had the strangest sensation of movement in it. And more intriguing yet, there were colours in the knot – she could see glints of crimson and violet. Within a few minutes, she had forgotten the bath entirely; it could wait. Instead she concentrated on the conundrum at her fingertips. After only a few minutes she began to see the light.

Karney told Brendan the story as best he could. Once he had taken the plunge and begun it from the beginning, he discovered it had its own momentum, which carried him through to the present tense with relatively little hesitation. He finished, saying:

'I know it sounds wild, but it's all true.'

Brendan didn't believe a word; that much was apparent in his blank stare. But there was more than disbelief on the scarred face. Karney couldn't work out what it was until Brendan took hold of his shirt. Only then did he see the depth of Brendan's fury.

'You don't think it's bad enough that Catso's dead,' he seethed, 'you have to come here telling me this shit.'

'It's the truth.'

'And where are these fucking knots now?'

'I told you: the old man's got them. He took them this afternoon. He's going to kill us, Bren. I know it.'

Brendan let Karney go. 'Tell you what I'm going to do,' he said magnanimously, 'I'm going to forget you told me any of this.'

'You don't understand – '

'I *said*: I'm going to forget you uttered one word. All right? Now you just get the fuck out of here and take your funny stories with you.'

Karney didn't move.

'*You hear me*?' Brendan shouted. Karney caught sight of a telltale fullness at the edge of Brendan's eyes. The anger was camouflage – barely adequate – for a grief he had no mechanism to prevent. In Brendan's present mood neither fear nor argument would convince him of the truth. Karney stood up.

'I'm sorry,' he said, 'I'll go.'

Brendan shook his head, face down. He did not raise it again, but left Karney to make his own way out. There was only Red now; he was the final court of appeal. The story, now told, could be told again, couldn't it?; repetition would be easy. Already turning the words over in his head, he left Brendan to his tears.

Anelisa heard Red come in through the front door; heard him call out a word; heard him call it again. The word was familiar, but it took her several seconds of fevered thought to recognize it as her own name.

'Anelisa!' he called again. 'Where are you?'

Nowhere, she thought. I'm the invisible woman. Don't come looking for me; please God, just leave me alone. She put her hand to her mouth, to stop her teeth from chattering. She had to stay absolutely still, absolutely silent. If she stirred so much as a hair's breadth it would hear her and come for her. The only safety lay in tying herself into a tiny ball and sealing her mouth with her palm.

Red began to climb the stairs. Doubtless Anelisa was in the bath, singing to herself. The woman loved water as she loved little else. It was not uncommon for her to spend hours immersed, her breasts breaking surface like two dream islands. Four steps from the landing, he heard a noise in the hallway below: a cough, or something like it. Was she playing some game with him? He about turned and descended, moving more stealthily now. Almost at the bottom of the stairs his gaze fell on a piece of cord which had been dropped on one of the steps. He picked it up and briefly puzzled over the single knot in its length, before the noise came again. This time he did not pretend to himself that it was Anelisa. He held his breath, waiting for another prompt from along the hallway. When none came he dug into the side of his boot and pulled out his flick-knife, a weapon he had carried about his person since the tender age of eleven. An adolescent's weapon, Anelisa's father had advised him; but now, advancing along the hallway to the living room, he thanked the patron saint of blades he had not taken the old felon's advice.

The room was gloomy. Evening was on the house, shuttering up the windows. Red stood for a long while in the doorway, anxiously watching the interior for movement. Then the noise again; not a single sound this time, but a whole series of them. The source, he now realised to his relief, was not human. It was a dog most likely, wounded in a fight. Nor was the sound coming from the room in front of him, but from the kitchen beyond. His courage bolstered by the fact that the intruder was merely an animal, he reached for the light switch and flipped it on.

The helter-skelter of events he initiated in so doing occurred in a breathless sequence that occupied no more than a dozen seconds, yet he lived each one in the minutest detail. In the first second, as the light came on, he saw something move across the kitchen floor; in the next, he was walking towards it, knife still in hand. The third brought the animal – alerted to his planned aggression – out of hiding. It ran to meet him, a blur of glistening flesh. Its sudden proximity was overpowering: its size, the heat off its steaming body, its vast mouth expelling a breath like rot. Red took the fourth and fifth seconds to avoid its first lunge, but on the sixth it found him. Its raw arms snatched at his body. He slashed out with his knife, and opened a wound in it, but it closed in and took him in a lethal embrace. More through accident than intention, the flick-knife plunged into its flesh, and liquid heat splashed up into Red's face: he scarcely noticed. His last three seconds were upon him: the weapon, slick with blood, slid from his grasp and was left embedded in the beast. Unarmed, he attempted to squirm from its clasp, but before he could slide out of harm's way the great unfinished head was pressing towards him – the maw a tunnel – and sucked one solid breath from his lungs. It was the only breath Red possessed. His brain, deprived of oxygen, threw a firework display in celebration of his imminent departure: roman candles, star shells, catherine wheels. The pyrotechnics were all too brief; too soon, the darkness.

Upstairs, Anelisa listened to the chaos of sound and tried to piece it together, but she could not. Whatever had happened, however, it had ended in silence. Red did not come looking for her. But then nor did the beast. Perhaps, she thought, they had killed each other. The simplicity of this solution pleased her. She waited in her room until hunger and boredom got the better of trepidation, and then went downstairs. Red was lying where the cord's second off-spring had dropped him, his eyes wide open to watch the fireworks. The beast itself squatted in the far corner of the room, a ruin of a thing. Seeing it, she backed away from Red's body towards the door. It made no attempt to move towards her, but simply followed her with deep-set eyes, its breathing coarse, its few movements sluggish.

She would go to find her father, she decided, and fled the house, leaving the front door ajar.

It was still ajar half an hour later, when Karney arrived. Though he had fully intended to go straight to Red's home after leaving Brendan, his courage had faltered. Instead, he had wandered – without conscious planning – to the bridge over the Archway Road. He had stood there for a long space watching the traffic below and drinking from the half bottle of vodka he had bought on the Holloway Road. The purchase had cleared him of cash, but the spirits, on his empty stomach, had been potent, and clarified his thinking. They would all die, he had concluded. Maybe the fault was his, for stealing the cord in the first place; more probably Pope would have punished them anyway for their crimes against his person. The best they might now hope – *he* might hope – was a smidgen of comprehension. That would almost be enough, his spirit-slurred brain decided: just to die a little less ignorant of mysteries than he'd been born. Red would understand.

Now he stood on the step and called the man's name. There came no answering shout. The vodka in his system made him impudent and, calling for Red again, he stepped into the house. The hallway was in darkness, but a light burned in one of the far rooms and he made his way towards it. The atmosphere in the house was sultry, like the interior of a palm-house. It became warmer still in the living room, where Red was losing body-heat to the air.

Karney stared down at him long enough to register that he was holding the cord in his left hand, and that only one knot remained in it. Perhaps Pope had been here, and for some reason left the knots behind. However it had come about, their presence in Red's hand offered a chance for life. This time, he swore as he approached the body, he would destroy the cord once and for all. Burn it and scatter the ashes to the four winds. He stooped to remove it from Red's grip. It sensed his nearness and slipped, blood-sleek, out of the dead man's hand and up into Karney's, where it wove itself between his digits, leaving a trail behind it. Sickened, Karney stared at the final knot. The process which had taken him so much painstaking effort to initiate now had its own momentum. With the second knot untied the third was virtually loosening itself. It still required a human agent apparently – why else did it leap so readily into his hand? – but it was already close to solving its own riddle. It was imperative he destroyed it quickly, before it succeeded.

Only then did he become aware that he was not alone. Besides the dead, there was a living presence close by. He looked up from the cavorting knot as somebody spoke to him. The words made no sense. They were scarcely words at all, more a sequence of wounded sounds. Karney remembered the breath of the thing on the footpath, and the ambiguity of the feelings it had engendered in him. Now the same ambiguity moved him again: with the rising fear came a sense that the voice of the beast spoke *loss*, whatever its language. A rumour of pity moved in him.

'Show yourself,' he said, not knowing whether it would understand or not.

A few tremulous heartbeats passed, and then it emerged from the far door. The light in the living room was good, and Karney's eyesight sharp, but the beast's anatomy defied his comprehension. There was something simian in its flayed, palpitating form, but sketchy, as if it had been born prematurely. Its mouth opened to speak another sound; its eyes, buried beneath the bleeding slab of a brow, were unreadable. It began to shamble out of its hiding place across the room towards him, each drooping step it took tempting his cowardice. When it reached Red's corpse, it stopped, raised one of its ragged limbs, and indicated a place in the crook of its neck. Karney saw the knife: Red's he guessed. Was it attempting to justify the killing, he wondered?

'What are you?' he asked it. The same question.

It shook its heavy head back and forth. A long, low moan issued from its mouth. Then, suddenly, it raised its arm and pointed directly at Karney. In so doing it let light fall fully on its face, and Karney could make out the eyes beneath the louring brow: twin gems trapped in the wounded ball of its skull. Their brilliance, and their lucidity, turned Karney's stomach over. And still it pointed at him.

'What do you want?' he asked it. 'Tell me what you want.'

It dropped its peeled limb and made to step across the body towards Karney, but it had no chance to make its intentions clear. A shout from the front door froze it in its lolling tracks.

'Anybody in?' the inquirer wanted to know.

Its face registered panic – the too-human eyes rolled in their raw sockets – and it turned away, retreating towards the kitchen. The visitor, whoever he was, called again: his voice was closer. Karney stared down at the corpse, and at his bloody hand, juggling his options, then started across the room and through the door into the kitchen. The beast had already gone: the back door stood wide open. Behind him, Karney heard the visitor utter some half-formed prayer at seeing Red's remains. He hesitated in the shadows: was this covert escape wise?; did it not do more to incriminate him than staying and trying to find a way to the truth? The knot, still moving in his hand, finally decided him: its destruction had to be his priority. In the living room, the visitor was dialling the emergency services; using his panicked monologue as cover, Karney crept the remaining yards to the back door and fled.

'Somebody's been on the phone for you,' his mother called down from the top of the stairs, 'he's woken me twice already. I told him I didn't – '

'I'm sorry, Mam. Who was it?'

'Wouldn't say. I told him not to ring back. You tell him, if he calls again, I don't want people ringing up at this time of night. Some people have to get up for work in the morning.'

'Yes, mam.'

His mother disappeared from the landing, and returned to her

59

solitary bed; the door closed. Karney stood, trembling, in the hallway below, his hand clenched around the knot in his pocket. It was still moving, turning itself over and over against the confines of his palm, seeking some space, however small, in which to loosen itself. But he was giving it no latitude. He rummaged for the vodka he'd bought earlier in the evening, manipulated the top off the bottle single-handed, and drank. As he took a second, galling mouthful, the telephone rang. He put down the bottle and picked up the receiver.

'Hello?'

The caller was in a phone box; the pips sounded, money was deposited, and a voice said: 'Karney?'

'Yes?'

'For Christ's sake, he's going to kill me.'

'Who is this?'

'Brendan.' – The voice was not like Brendan's at all; too shrill, too fearful – 'He'll kill me if you don't come.'

'Pope? Is it Pope?'

'He's out of his mind. You've got to come to the breaker's yard, at the top of the hill. Give him – '

The line went dead. Karney put the receiver down. In his hand the cord was performing acrobatics. He opened his hand; in the dim light from the landing the remaining knot shimmered. At its heart, as at the hearts of the other two knots, glints of colour promised themselves. He closed his fist again, picked up the vodka bottle, and went back out.

The breaker's yard had once boasted a large and perpetually irate Doberman pinscher, but the dog had developed a tumour the previous spring and savaged its owner. It had subsequently been destroyed, and no replacement bought. The corrugated iron wall was consequently easy to breach. Karney clambered over and down on to the cinder and gravel strewn ground on the other side. A floodlight at the front gate threw illumination on to the collection of vehicles, both domestic and commercial, which was assembled in the yard. Most were beyond salvation: rusted lorries and tankers, a bus which had apparently hit a low bridge at speed, a rogue's gallery of cars, lined up or piled upon each other, every one an accident casualty. Beginning at the gate, Karney began a systematic search of the yard, trying as best he could to keep his footsteps light, but he could find no sign of Pope or his prisoner at the north-west end of the yard. Knot in hand, he began to advance down the enclosure, the reassuring light at the gate dwindling with every step he took. A few paces on, he caught

60

sight of flames between two of the vehicles. He stood still, and tried to interpret the intricate play of shadow and firelight. Behind him, he heard movement, and turned, anticipating with every heartbeat a cry, a blow. None came. He scoured the yard at his back – the image of the yellow flame dancing on his retina – but whatever had moved was now still again.

'Brendan?' he whispered, looking back towards the fire.

In a slab of shadow in front of him a figure moved, and Brendan stumbled out and fell to his knees in the cinders a few feet from where Karney stood. Even in the deceptive light Karney could see that Brendan was the worse for punishment. His shirt was smeared with stains too dark to be anything but blood; his face was contorted with present pain, or the anticipation of it. When Karney walked towards him he shied away like a beaten animal.

'It's me. It's Karney.'

Brendan raised his bruised head. 'Make him stop.'

'It'll be all right.'

'Make him stop. Please.'

Brendan's hands went up to his neck. A collar of rope encircled his throat; a leash led off from it into the darkness between two vehicles. There, holding the other end of the leash, stood Pope. His eyes glimmered in the shadows, although they had no source to glean their light from.

'You were wise to come,' Pope said. 'I would have killed him.'

'Let him go,' Karney said.

Pope shook his head. 'First the knot.' He stepped out of hiding. Somehow Karney had expected him to have sloughed off his guise as a derelict and show his true face – whatever that might be – but he had not. He was dressed in the same shabby garb as he had always worn; but his control of the situation was incontestable. He gave a short tug on the rope, and Brendan collapsed, choking, to the ground, hands tugging vainly at the noose closing about his throat.

'Stop it,' Karney said, 'I've got the knot, damn you. Don't kill him.'

'Bring it to me.'

Even as Karney took a step towards the old man something cried out in the labyrinth of the yard. Karney recognized the sound; so did Pope. It was unmistakably the voice of the flayed beast that had killed Red, and it was close by. Pope's besmirched face blazed with fresh urgency.

'Quickly!' he said, 'or I kill him.' He had drawn a gutting knife from his coat. Pulling on the leash, he coaxed Brendan close.

The complaint of the beast rose in pitch.

'*The knot!*' Pope said, '*To me!*' He stepped towards Brendan, and put the blade to the prisoner's close-cropped head.

'Don't,' said Karney, 'just take the knot.' But before he could draw another breath something moved at the corner of his eye, and his wrist was snatched in a scalding grip. Pope let out a shout of anger, and Karney turned to see the scarlet beast at his side, meeting his gaze with a haunted stare. Karney wrestled to loose its hold, but it shook its ravaged head.

'Kill it!' Pope yelled, '*Kill it!*'

The beast glanced across at Pope, and for the first time Karney saw an unequivocal look in its pale eyes: naked loathing. Then Brendan issued a sharp cry, and Karney looked his way in time to see the gutting knife slide into his cheek. Pope withdrew the blade, and let Brendan's corpse pitch forward; before it had struck the ground he was crossing towards Karney, murderous intention in every stride. The beast, fear in its throat, released Karney's arm in time for him to side-step Pope's first thrust. Beast and man divided, and ran. Karney's heels slithered in the loose cinders and for an instant he felt Pope's shadow on him, but slid from the path of the second cut with millimetres to spare.

'You can't get out,' he heard Pope boast as he ran. The old man was so confident of his trap he wasn't even giving chase. 'You're on my territory, boy. There's no way out.'

Karney ducked into hiding between two vehicles and started to weave his way back towards the gate, but somehow he'd lost all sense of orientation. One parade of rusted hulks let onto another, so similar as to be indistinguishable. Wherever the maze led him there seemed to be no way out; he could no longer see the lamp at the gate, or Pope's fire at the far end of the yard. It was all one hunting-ground, and he the prey; and everywhere this daedal path led him, Pope's voice followed close as his heartbeat. 'Give up the knot, boy,' it said, 'give it up and I won't feed you your eyes.'

Karney was terrified; but so, he sensed, was Pope. The cord was not an assassination tool, as Karney had always believed. Whatever its rhyme or reason, the old man did *not* have mastery of it. In that fact lay what slim chance of survival remained. The time had come to untie the final knot: untie it and take the consequences. Could they be any worse than death at Pope's hands?

Karney found an adequate refuge alongside a burnt out lorry, slid down into a squatting position, and opened his fist. Even in the darkness, he could feel the knot working to decipher itself; he aided it as best he could.

Again, Pope spoke: 'Don't do it, boy,' he said, pretending humanity. 'I know what you're thinking and believe me it will be the end of you.'

Karney's hands seemed to have sprouted thumbs, no longer the equal of the problem. His mind was a gallery of death portraits: Catso on the road, Red on the carpet, Brendan slipping from Pope's grip as the knife slid from his head. He forced the images away, marshalling his beleaguered wits as best he could. Pope had curtailed his monologue. Now the only sound in the yard was the distant hum of traffic; it came from a world Karney doubted he would see again. He fumbled at the knot like a man at a locked door with a handful of keys, trying one and then the next and then the next, all the while knowing that the night is pressing on his back. '*Quickly, quickly*,' he urged himself. But his former dexterity had utterly deserted him.

And then a hiss as the air was sliced, and Pope had found him – his face triumphant as he delivered the killing strike. Karney rolled from his squatting position, but the blade caught his upper arm, opening a wound that ran from shoulder to elbow. The pain made him quick, and the second strike struck the cab of the lorry, winning sparks not blood. Before Pope could stab again Karney was dodging away, blood pulsing from his arm. The old man gave chase, but Karney was fleeter. He ducked behind one of the coaches, and, as Pope panted after him, slipped into hiding beneath the vehicle. Pope ran past as Karney bit back a sob of pain. The wound he had sustained effectively incapacitated his left hand. Drawing his arm into his body to minimize the stress on his slashed muscle, he tried to finish the wretched work he had begun on the knot, using his teeth in place of a second hand. Splashes of white light were appearing in front of him: unconsciousness was not far distant. He breathed deeply and regularly through his nostrils as his fevered fingers pulled at the knot. He could no longer see, nor could scarcely feel, the cord in his hand. He was working blind, as he had on the footpath, and now, as then, his instincts began to work for him. The knot started to dance at his lips, eager for release. It was mere moments from solution.

In his devotion, he failed to see the arm reach for him until he was being hauled out of his sanctuary and was staring up into Pope's shining eyes.

'No more games,' the old man said, and loosed his hold on Karney to snatch the cord from between his teeth. Karney attempted to move a few torturous inches to avoid Pope's grasp, but the pain in his arm crippled him. He fell back, letting out a cry on impact.

'Out go your eyes,' said Pope and the knife descended. The blinding blow never landed, however. A wounded form emerged from hiding behind the old man and snatched at the tails of his gabardine. Pope regained his balance in moments and spun around. The knife found his antagonist, and Karney opened his pain-blurred eyes to see the flayed beast reeling backwards, its cheek slashed open to the bone. Pope followed through to finish the slaughter, but Karney didn't wait to watch. He reached up for purchase on the wreck, and hauled himself to his feet, the knot still clenched between his teeth. Behind him, Pope cursed, and Karney knew he had forsaken the kill to follow. Knowing the pursuit was already lost, he staggered out from between the vehicles into the open yard. In which direction was the gate?; he had no idea. His legs belonged to a comedian, not to him; they were rubber jointed, useless for everything but pratfalls. Two steps forward and his knees gave out. The smell of petrol-soaked cinders came up to meet him.

Despairing, he put his good hand up to his mouth. His fingers found a loop of cord. He pulled, *hard*, and miraculously the final hitch of the knot came free. He spat the cord from his mouth as a surging heat roasted his lips; it fell to the ground, its final seal broken, and from its core the last of its prisoners materialized. It appeared on the cinders like a sickly infant, its limbs vestigial, its bald head vastly too big for its withered body, the flesh of which was pale to the point of translucence. It flapped its palsied arms in a vain attempt to right itself as Pope stepped towards it, eager to slit its defenceless throat. Whatever Karney had hoped from the third knot it hadn't been this scrag of life; it revolted him.

And then it spoke. Its voice was no mewling infant's but that of a grown man, albeit spoken from a babe's mouth.

'To me!' it called, '*Quickly*.'

As Pope reached down to murder the child the air of the yard filled with the stench of mud, and the shadows disgorged a spiny, low-bellied thing, which slid across the ground towards him. Pope stepped back as the creature – as unfinished in its reptilian way as its simian brother – closed on the strange infant. Karney fully expected it to devour the morsel, but the pallid child raised its arms in welcome as the beast from the first knot curled about it. As it did so the second beast showed its ghastly face, moaning its pleasure. It laid its hands on the child and drew the wasted body up into its capacious arms, completing an unholy family of reptile, ape and child.

64

The union was not over yet, however. Even as the three creatures assembled their bodies began to fray, unravelling into ribbons of pastel matter; and even as their anatomies began to dissolve the strands were beginning a fresh configuration, filament entwining with filament. They were tying another knot, random and yet inevitable; more elaborate by far than any Karney had set fingers on. A new and perhaps insoluble puzzle was appearing from the pieces of the old, but – where *they* had been inchoate – this one would be finished and whole. What though; *what*?

As the skein of nerves and muscle moved towards its final condition, Pope took his moment. He rushed forward, his face wild in the lustre of the union, and thrust his gutting knife into the heart of the knot. But the attack was mistimed. A limb of ribboned light uncurled from the body and wrapped itself around Pope's wrist. The gabardine ignited; Pope's flesh began to burn. He screeched, and dropped the weapon. The limb released him, returning itself into the weave and leaving the old man to stagger backwards, nursing his smoking arm. He looked to be losing his wits; he shook his head to and fro pitifully. Momentarily, his eyes found Karney, and a glimmer of guile crept back into them. He reached for the boy's injured arm, and hugged him close. Karney cried out, but Pope, careless of his captive, dragged Karney away from where the wreathing was nearing its end and into the safety of the labyrinth.

'He won't harm me,' Pope was saying to himself, 'not with you. Always had a weakness for children.' He pushed Karney ahead of him. 'Just get the papers . . . then away.'

Karney scarcely knew if he was alive or dead: he had no strength left to fight Pope off. He just went with the old man, half crawling much of the time, until they reached Pope's destination: a car which was buried behind a heap of rusted vehicles. It had no wheels; a bush which had grown through the chassis occupied the driver's seat. Pope opened the back door, muttering his satisfaction, and bent into the interior, leaving Karney slumped against the wing. Unconsciousness was a teasing moment away; Karney longed for it. But Pope had use for him yet. Retrieving a small book from its niche beneath the passenger seat Pope whispered: 'Now we must go. We've got business.' Karney groaned as he was pressed forward.

'Close your mouth,' Pope said, embracing him, 'my brother has ears.'

'Brother?' Karney murmured, trying to make sense of what Pope had let slip.

'Spellbound,' Pope said, 'until you.'

'Beasts,' Karney muttered, the mingled images of reptiles and apes assailing him.

'Human,' Pope replied. 'Evolution's the knot, boy.'

'*Human*,' Karney said and as the syllables left him his aching eyes caught sight of a gleaming form on the car at his tormentor's back. Yes; it *was* human. Still wet from its re-birth, its body running with inherited wounds, but triumphantly human. Pope saw the recognition in Karney's eyes. He seized hold of him and was about to use the limp body as a shield when his brother intervened. The rediscovered man reached down from the height of the roof and caught hold of Pope by his narrow neck. The old man shrieked, and tore himself loose, darting away across the cinders, but the other gave howling chase, pursuing him out of Karney's range.

From a long way off, Karney heard Pope's last plea as his brother overtook him, and then the words curved up into a scream Karney hoped never to hear the equal of again. After that, silence. The sibling did not return; for which, curiosity notwithstanding, Karney was grateful.

When, several minutes later, he mustered sufficient energy to make his way out of the yard – the light burned at the gate again, a beacon to the perplexed – he found Pope lying, face down, on the gravel. Even if he had possessed the strength, which he did not, a small fortune could not have persuaded Karney to turn the body over. Enough to see how the dead man's hands had dug into the ground in his torment, and how the bright coils of innards, once so neatly looped in his abdomen, spilled out from beneath him. The book Pope had been at such pains to retrieve lay at his side. Karney stooped, head spinning, to pick it up. It was, he felt, small recompense for the night of terrors he had endured. The near future would bring questions he could never hope to answer, accusations he had pitifully little defence against. But, by the light of the gateside lamp, he found the stained pages more rewarding than he'd anticipated. Here, copied out in a meticulous hand, and accompanied by elaborate diagrams, were the theorems of Pope's forgotten science: the designs of knots for the securing of love, and the winning of status; hitches to divide souls and bind them; for the making of fortunes and children; for the world's ruin.

After a brief perusal, he scaled the gate and clambered over onto the street. It was, as such an hour, deserted. A few lights burned in the council estate opposite; rooms where the sick waited out the hours until morning. Rather than ask any more of his exhausted limbs Karney decided to wait where he was until he

66

could flag down a vehicle to take him where he might tell his story. He had plenty to occupy him. Although his body was numb and his head woozy, he felt more lucid than he ever had. He came to the mysteries on the pages of Pope's forbidden book as to an oasis. Drinking deeply, he looked forward with rare exhilaration to the pilgrimage ahead.

Revelations

There had been talk of tornadoes in Amarillo; of cattle, cars, and sometimes entire houses lifted up and dashed to the earth again, of whole communities laid waste in a few devastating moments. Perhaps that was what made Virginia so uneasy tonight. Either that, or the accumulated fatigue of travelling so many empty highways with just the deadpan skies of Texas for scenery, and nothing to look forward to at the end of the next leg of the journey but another round of hymns and hellfire. She sat, her spine aching, in the back of the black Pontiac, and tried her best to get some sleep. But the hot, still air clung about her thin neck and gave her dreams of suffocation; so she gave up her attempts to rest and contented herself with watching the wheat-fields pass and counting the grain elevators bright against the thunderheads that were beginning to gather in the north-east.

In the front of the vehicle Earl sang to himself as he drove. Beside her, John – no more than two feet away from her but to all intents and purposes a million miles' distance – studied the Epistles of St Paul, and murmured the words as he read. Then, as they drove through Pantex Village ('They build the warheads here,' Earl had said cryptically, then said no more) the rain began. It came down suddenly, as evening was beginning to fall, lending darkness to darkness, almost instantly plunging the Amarillo-Pampa Highway into watery night.

Virginia wound up her window; the rain, though refreshing, was soaking her plain blue dress, the only one John approved of her wearing at meetings. Now there was nothing to look at beyond the glass. She sat, the unease growing in her with every mile they covered to Pampa, listening to the vehemence of the downpour on the roof of the car, and to her husband speaking in whispers at her side:

'*Wherefore he saith, Awake thou that sleepest, and rise from the dead, and Christ shall give thee light.*

'*See then that ye walk circumspectly, not as fools, but as wise,*

'*Redeeming the time, because the days are evil.*'

He sat, as ever, upright, the same dog-eared, soft-backed Bible he'd been using for years open in his lap. He surely knew the passages he was reading by heart; he quoted them often enough, and with such a mixture of familiarity and freshness that the words might have been his, not Paul's, new-minted from his own mouth. That Passion and vigour would in time make John Gyer America's greatest evangelist, Virginia had no doubt of that. During the gruelling, hectic weeks of the Tri-State Tour her husband had displayed unprecedented confidence and maturity. His message had lost none of its vehemence with this newfound professionalism – it was still that old-fashioned mixture of damnation and redemption that he always propounded – but now he had complete control of his gifts, and in town after town – in Oklahoma and New Mexico and now in Texas – the faithful had gathered to listen in their hundreds and thousands, eager to come again into God's Kingdom. In Pampa, thirty-five miles from here, they would already be assembling, despite the rain, determined to have a grandstand view when the crusader arrived. They would have brought their children, their savings, and, most of all, their hunger for forgiveness.

But forgiveness was for tomorrow. First they had to *get* to Pampa, and the rain was worsening. Earl had given up his singing once the storm began, and was concentrating all his attentions on the road ahead. Sometimes he would sigh to himself, and stretch in his seat. Virginia tried not to concern herself with the way he was driving, but as the torrent became a deluge her anxiety got the better of her. She leaned forward from the back seat and started to peer through the windshield, watching for vehicles coming in the opposite direction. Accidents were common in conditions like these: bad weather, and a tired driver eager to be twenty miles further down the road than he was. At her side John sensed her concern.

'The Lord is with us,' he said, not looking up from the tightly-printed pages, though it was by now far too dark for him to read.

'It's a bad night, John,' she said. 'Maybe we shouldn't try to go all the way to Pampa. Earl must be tired.'

'I'm fine,' Earl put in, 'It's not that far.'

'You're tired,' Virginia repeated. 'We all are.'

'Well, we could find a motel, I guess,' Gyer suggested. 'What do you think, Earl?'

Earl shrugged his sizeable shoulders. 'Whatever you say, boss,' he replied, not putting up much of a fight.

Gyer turned to his wife and gently patted the back of her hand. 'We'll find a motel,' he said. 'Earl can call ahead to Pampa and tell them that we'll be with them in the morning. How's that?'

She smiled at him, but he wasn't looking at her.

69

'I think White Deer's next off the highway,' Earl told Virginia, 'Maybe they'll have a motel.'

In fact, the Cottonwood Motel lay a half mile west of White Deer, in an area of wasteground on the south of US 60, a small establishment with a dead or dying cottonwood tree in the lot between its two low buildings. There were a number of cars already in the motel grounds, and lights burning in most of the rooms; fellow fugitives from the storm presumably. Earl drove into the lot and parked as close to the manager's office as possible, then made a dash across the rain-lashed ground to find out if the place had any rooms for the night. With the engine stilled, the sound of the rain on the roof of the Pontiac was more oppressive than ever.

'I hope there's space for us,' Virginia said, watching the water on the window smear the neon sign. Gyer didn't reply. The rain thundered on overhead. 'Talk to me, John,' she said him.

'What for?'

She shook her head; 'Never mind.' Strands of hair clung to her slightly clammy forehead; though the rain had come, the heat in the air had not lifted. 'I hate the rain,' she said.

'It won't last all night,' Gyer replied, running a hand through his thick grey hair. It was a gesture he used on the platform as punctuation: pausing between one momentous statement and the next. She knew his rhetoric, both physical and verbal, so well. Sometimes she thought she knew everything about him there was to know; that he had nothing left to tell her that she truly wanted to hear. But then the sentiment was probably mutual: they had long ago ceased to have a marriage recognizable as such. Tonight, as every night on this tour, they would lie in separate beds, and he would sleep that deep, easy sleep that came so readily to him, while she surreptitiously swallowed a pill or two to bring some welcome serenity.

'Sleep,' he had often said, 'is a time to commune with the Lord.' He believed in the efficacy of dreams, though he didn't talk of what he saw in them. The time would come when he would unveil the majesty of his visions, she had no doubt of that; but in the meanwhile he slept alone and kept his counsel, leaving her to whatever secret sorrows she might have. It was easy to be bitter, but she fought the temptation. His destiny was manifest, it was demanded of him by the Lord; and if he was fierce with her he was fiercer still with himself, living by a regime that would have destroyed lesser men, and still chastising himself for his pettiest act of weakness.

At last, Earl appeared from the office, and crossed back to the car at a run. He had three keys.

'Rooms Seven and Eight,' he said, breathlessly, the rain dripping off his brow and nose; 'I got the key to the interconnecting door, too.'

'Good,' said Gyer.

'Last two in the place,' he said. 'Shall I drive the car round? The rooms are in the other building.'

The interior of the two rooms was a hymn to banality. They'd stayed in what seemed like a thousand cells like these, identical down to the sickly orange bedcovers and the light-faded print of the Grand Canyon on the pale green walls. John was insensitive to his surroundings, and always had been, but to Virginia's eyes these rooms were an apt model for Purgatory. Soulless limbos in which nothing of moment had ever happened, nor ever would. There was nothing to mark these rooms out as different from all the others, but there was something different in *her* tonight.

It wasn't talk of tornadoes that had brought this strangeness on. She watched Earl to-ing and fro-ing with the bags, and felt oddly removed from herself, as though she was watching events through a veil denser than the warm rain falling outside the door. She was almost sleep-walking. When John quietly told which bed would be hers for tonight she lay down, and tried to control her sense of dislocation by relaxing. It was easier said than done. Somebody had a television on in a nearby room, and the late-night movie was word for word clear through the paper-thin walls.

'Are you all right?'

She opened her eyes. Earl, ever solicitous, was looking down at her. He looked as weary as she felt. His face deeply tanned from standing in the sun at the open-air rallies, looked yellowish rather than its usual healthy brown. He was slightly overweight too, though his bulk married well with his wide, stubborn features.

'Yes, I'm fine, thank you,' she said. 'A little thirsty.'

'I'll see if I can get something for you to drink. They'll probably have a Coke machine.'

She nodded, meeting his eyes. There was a sub-text to this exchange which Gyer, who was sitting at the table making notes for tomorrow's speech, could not know. On and off throughout the tour, Earl had supplied Virginia with pills. Nothing exotic; just tranquillizers to soothe her increasingly jangled nerves. But they – like stimulants, make-up and jewellery – were not looked kindly upon by a man of Gyer's principles, and when, by chance, her husband had discovered the drugs, there had been an ugly scene. Earl had taken the brunt of his employer's ire, for which Virginia was deeply grateful. And, though he was under strict instructions never to repeat the crime, he was soon supplying her again. Their guilt was an almost pleasurable secret between them; she read complicity in his eyes even now, as he did in hers.

'No Coca-Cola,' Gyer said. 'Well, I thought we could make an exception – '

'*Exception*?' Gyer said, his voice taking on a characteristic note of self-regard. Rhetoric was in the air, and Earl cursed his idiot tongue. 'The Lord doesn't give us laws to live by so that we can make *exceptions*, Earl. You know better than that.'

At that moment Earl didn't much care what the Lord did or said. His concern was for Virginia. She was strong he knew, despite her Deep South courtesy, and the accompanying fac‹SS›cade of frailty; strong enough to bring them all through the minor crises of the tour, when the Lord had failed to step in and help his agents in the field. But nobody's strength was limitless, and he sensed that she was close to collapse. She gave so much to her husband; of her love and admiration, of her energies and enthusiasm. More than once in the past few weeks Earl had thought that perhaps she deserved better than the man in the pulpit.

'Maybe you could get me some iced water?' she said, looking up at him with lines of fatigue beneath her grey-blue eyes. She was not, by contemporary standards, beautiful: her features were too flawlessly aristocratic. Exhaustion lent them new glamour.

'Iced-water, coming right up,' Earl said, forcing a jovial tone that he had little strength to sustain. He went to the door.

'Why don't you call the office and have someone bring it over?' Gyer suggested as Earl made to leave, 'I want to go through next week's itinerary with you.'

'It's no problem,' Earl said, 'Really. Besides, I should call Pampa, and tell them we're delayed,' and he was out of the door and onto the walkway before he could be contradicted.

He needed an excuse to have some time to himself; the atmosphere between Virginia and Gyer was deteriorating by the day, and it was not a pleasant spectacle. He stood for a long moment watching the rain sheet down. The cottonwood tree in the middle of the lot hung its balding head in the fury of the deluge; he knew exactly how it felt.

As he stood on the walkway, wondering how he would be able to keep his sanity in the last eight weeks of the tour, two figures walked from the highway, and crossed the lot. He didn't see them, though the path they took to Room Seven led them directly

72

across his line of vision. They walked through the drenching rain from the waste ground behind the manager's office – where, back in 1955, they had parked their red Buick – and though the rain fell in a steady torrent it left them both untouched. The woman, whose hairstyle had been in and out of fashion twice since the fifties, and whose clothes had the same period look, slowed for a moment to stare at the man who was watching the cottonwood tree with such rapt attention. He had kind eyes, despite his frown. In her time she might have loved such a man, she thought; but then her time had long gone, hadn't it? Buck, her husband, turned back to her – 'Are you coming Sadie?' he wanted to know – and she followed him on to the concrete walkway (it had been wooden the last time she was here) and through the open door of Room Seven.

A chill ran down Earl's back. Too much staring at the rain, he thought; that, and too much fruitless longing. He walked to the end of the patio, steeled himself for the dash across the lot to the office, and counting to three, ran.

Sadie Durning glanced over her shoulder to watch Earl go, then looked back at Buck. The years had not tempered the resentment she felt towards her husband, any more than they'd improved his shifty features or his too-easy laugh. She had not much liked him on June 2nd, 1955, and she didn't much like him now, precisely thirty years on. Buck Durning had the soul of a philanderer, as her father had always warned her. That in itself was not so terrible: it was perhaps the masculine condition. But it had led to such grubby behaviour that eventually she had tired of his endless deceptions. He – unknowing to the last – had taken her low spirits as a cue for a second honeymoon. This phenomenal hypocrisy had finally over-ridden any lingering thoughts of tolerance or forgiveness she might have entertained, and when, three decades ago tonight, they had checked into the Cottonwood Motel, she had come prepared for more than a night of love. She had let Buck shower, and, when he emerged, she had levelled the Smith and Wesson .38 at him, and blown a gaping hole in his chest. Then she'd run, throwing the gun away as she went, knowing the police were bound to catch her, and not much caring when they did. They'd taken her to Carson County Jail in Panhandle, and, after a few weeks, to trial. She never once tried to deny the murder: there'd been enough deception in her thirty-eight years of life as it was. And so, when they found her defiant, they took her to Huntsville State Prison, chose a bright day the following October, and summarily passed 2,250 volts through her body, stopping her unrepentant heart almost instantaneously. An eye for an eye; a tooth for a tooth. She had been brought up with such simple moral equations. She'd not been unhappy to die by the same mathematics.

But tonight she and Buck had elected to retrace the journey they'd taken thirty years before, to see if they could discover how and why their marriage had ended in murder. It was a chance offered to many dead lovers, though few, apparently, took it up; perhaps the thought of experiencing again the cataclysm that had ended their lives was too distasteful. Sadie, however, couldn't help but wonder if it had all been predestined: if a tender word from Buck, or a look of genuine affection in his murky eyes, could have stayed her trigger finger and so saved both their lives. This one night stand would give them an opportunity to test history. Invisible, inaudible, they would follow the same route as they had three decades ago: the next few hours would tell if that route had led inevitably to murder.

Room Seven was occupied, and so was the room beside it; the interconnecting door was wide, and fluorescent lights burned in both. The occupancy was not a problem. Sadie had long become used to the ethereal state; to wandering unseen amongst the living. In such a condition she had attended her niece's wedding, and later on her father's funeral, standing beside the grave with the dead old man and gossiping about the mourners. Buck however – never an agile individual – was more prone to carelessness. She hoped he would be careful tonight. After all, he wanted to see the experiment through as much as she did.

As they stood on the threshold, and cast their eyes around the room in which their fatal farce had been played out, she wondered if the shot had hurt him very much. She must ask him tonight, she thought, should the opportunity arise.

There had been a young woman with a plain but pleasant face in the manager's office when Earl had gone in to book the rooms. She had now disappeared to be replaced by a man of sixty or so, wearing half a week's growth of mottled beard and a sweat-stained shirt. He looked up from a nose-close perusal of yesterday's *Pampa Daily News* when Earl entered.

'Yeah?'

'Is it possible to have some iced water?' Earl inquired. The man threw a hoarse yell over his shoulder: 'Laura-May? You in there?'

Through the doorway behind came the din of the late-night movie – shots, screams, the roar of an escaped beast – and then, Laura-May's response:

74

'What do you want, Pa?'

'There's a man wants room service,' Laura-May's father yelled back, not without a trace of irony in his voice, 'Will you get out here and serve him?'

No reply came; just more screams. They set Earl's teeth on edge. The manager glanced up at him. One of his eyes was clouded by a cataract.

'You with the evangelist?' he said.

'Yes . . . how did you know it was – ?'

'Laura-May recognized him. Seen his picture in the paper.'

'That so?'

'Don't miss a trick, my baby.'

As if on cue Laura-May emerged from the room behind the office. When her brown eyes fell on Earl she visibly brightened.

'Oh . . .' she said, a smile quickening her features, 'what can I do for you, mister?' The line, coupled with the smile, seemed to signal more than polite interest in Earl; or was that just his wishful thinking? Except for a lady of the night he'd met in Pomca City, Oklahoma, his sex-life had been non-existent in the last three months. Taking his chance; he returned Laura-May's smile. Though she was at least thirty-five, her manner was curiously girlish; the look she was giving him almost intimidatingly direct. Meeting her eyes, Earl began to think that his first estimation had not been far off.

'Ice-water,' he said. 'I wondered if you had any? Mrs Gyer isn't feeling so well.'

Laura-May nodded. 'I'll get some,' she said, dallying for a moment in the door before returning into the television room. The din of the movie had abated – a scene of calm, perhaps, before the beast emerged again – and in the hush Earl could hear the rain beating down outside, turning the earth to mud.

'Quite a gully washer tonight, eh?' the manager observed, 'this keeps up, you'll be rained out tomorrow.'

'People come out in all kinds of weather,' Earl said, 'John Gyer's a big draw.'

The man pulled a face. 'Wouldn't rule out a tornado,' he said, clearly revelling in the role of doom-sayer. 'We're just about due for one.'

'Really?'

'Year before last, wind took the roof off the school. Just lifted it right off.'

Laura-May reappeared in the doorway with a tray on which a jug and four glasses were placed. Ice clinked against the jug's sides.

75

'What's that you say, Pa?' she asked.

'Tornado.'

'Isn't hot enough,' she announced with casual authority. Her father grunted his disagreement, but made no argument in return. Laura-May crossed towards Earl with the tray, but when he made a move to take it from her she said, 'I'll take it myself. You lead on.' He didn't object. It would give them a little while to exchange pleasantries as they walked to the Gyers' room; perhaps the same thought was in her mind. Either that, or she wanted a closer view of the evangelist.

They went together as far as the end of the office block walkway in silence; there they halted. Before them lay twenty yards of puddle-strewn earth between one building and the next.

'Shall I carry the jug?' Earl volunteered. 'You bring the glasses and the tray.'

'Sure,' she replied. Then, with the same direct look she'd given him before, she said: 'What's your name?'

'Earl,' he told her, 'Earl Rayburn.'

'I'm Laura-May Cade.'

'I'm most pleased to meet you, Laura-May.'

'You know about this place, do you?' she said, 'Papa told you, I suppose.'

'You mean the tornadoes?' he said.

'No,' she replied, 'I mean murder.'

Sadie stood at the bottom of the bed and looked at the woman lying on it. She had very little dress-sense, Sadie thought; the clothes were drab, and her hair wasn't fixed in a flattering way. She murmured something in her semi-comatose state, and then – abruptly – she woke. Her eyes opened wide. There was some unshaped alarm in them; and pain too. Sadie looked at her and sighed.

'What's the problem?' Buck wanted to know. He'd put down the cases and was sitting in a chair opposite the fourth occupant of the room, a large man with lean, forceful features and a mane of steel-grey hair that would not have shamed an Old Testament prophet.

'No problem,' Sadie replied.

'I don't want to share a room with these two,' Buck said.

'Well this is the room where . . . where we stayed,' Sadie replied.

'Let's move next door,' Buck suggested, nodding through the open door into Room Eight, 'we'll have more privacy.'

'They can't see us,' Sadie said.

'But I can see *them*,' Buck replied, 'and it gives me the creeps. It's not going to matter if we're in a different room, for Christ's sake.' Without waiting for agreement from Sadie, Buck picked up the cases and carried them through into Earl's room. 'Are you coming or not?' he asked Sadie. She nodded. It was better to give way to him; if she started to argue now they'd never get past the first hurdle. Conciliation was to be the key-note of this reunion, she reminded herself, and dutifully followed him into Room Eight.

On the bed, Virginia thought about getting up and going into the bathroom where, out of sight, she could take one or two tranquillizers. But John's presence frightened her; sometimes she felt he could see right into her, that all her private guilt was an open book to him. She was certain that if she got up now, and rooted in her bag for the medication, he would ask her what she was doing. If he did that, she'd blurt the truth out for certain. She didn't have the strength to resist the heat of his accusing eyes. No, it would be better to lie here and wait for Earl to come back with the water. Then, when the two men were discussing the tour, she would slip away to take the forbidden pills.

There was evasive quality to the light in the room; it distressed her, and she wanted to close her lids against its tricks. Only moments before the light had conjured a mirage at the end of the bed; a moth-wing flicker of substance that had almost congealed in the air before flitting away.

Over by the window, John was again reading under his breath. At first, she caught only a few of the words –

'*And there came out of the smoke locusts upon the earth . . .*' She instantly recognized the passage; its imagery was unmistakable.

'*. . . and unto them was given power, as the scorpions of the earth have power.*'

The verse was from The Revelations of St John the Divine. She knew the words that followed off by heart. He had declaimed them time after time at meetings.

'*And it was commanded them that they should not hurt the grass of the earth, neither any green thing, neither any tree; but only those men which have not the seal of God in their foreheads.*'

Gyer loved Revelations. He read it more often than the Gospels, whose stories he knew by heart but whose words did not ignite him the way the incantatory rhythms of Revelations did. When he preached Revelations, he shared the apocalyptic vision, and felt exulted by it. His voice would take on a different note; the poetry, instead of coming out of him, came *through* him. Helpless in its grip, he rose on a spiral of ever more awesome metaphor:

77

from angels to dragons and thence to Babylon, the Mother of Harlots, sitting upon a scarlet-coloured beast.

Virginia tried to shut the words out. Usually, to hear her husband speak the poems of Revelations was a joy to her, but not tonight. Tonight the words seemed ripe to the point of corruption, and she sensed – perhaps for the first time – that he didn't really understand what he was saying; that the spirit of the words passed him by while he recited them. She made a small, unintentional noise of complaint. Gyer stopped reading.

'What is it?' he said.

She opened her eyes, embarrassed to have interrupted him.

'Nothing.' she said.

'Does my reading disturb you?' he wanted to know. The enquiry was a challenge, and she backed down from it.

'No,' she said. 'No, of course not.'

In the doorway between the two rooms, Sadie watched Virginia's face. The woman was lying of course; the words *did* disturb her. They disturbed Sadie too, but only because they seemed so pitifully melodramatic: a drug – dream of Armageddon, more comical than intimidatory.

'Tell him,' she advised Virginia, '*Go on*. Tell him you don't like it.'

'Who are you talking to?' Buck said, 'They can't hear you.'

Sadie ignored her husband's remarks. 'Go on,' she said to Virginia, 'Tell the bastard.'

But Virginia just lay there while Gyer took up the passage again, its absurdities escalating:

'*And the shapes of the locusts were unto horses prepared unto battle; and on their heads were as it were crowns like gold, and their faces were as the faces of men.*

'*And they had hair as the hair of women, and their teeth were as the teeth of lions.*'

Sadie shook her head: comic-book terrors, fit to scare children with. Why did people have to die to grow out of that kind of nonsense?

'Tell him,' she said again, 'Tell him how ridiculous he sounds.' Even as the words left her lips, Virginia sat up on the bed and said:

'John?'

Sadie stared at her, willing her on. 'Say it. *Say it*.'

'Do you have to talk about death all the time. It's very depressing.'

Sadie almost applauded; it wasn't quite the way *she* would have put it, but each to their own.

'What did you say?' Gyer asked her, assuming he'd heard incorrectly. Surely she wasn't challenging him?

Virginia put a trembling hand up to her lips, as if to cancel the words before they came again; but they came nevertheless.

'Those passages you read. I hate them. They're so . . .'

'Stupid,' Sadie prompted.

'. . . unpleasant,' Virginia said.

'Are you coming to bed or not?' Buck wanted to know.

'In a moment,' Sadie replied over her shoulder, 'I just want to see what happens in here.'

'Life isn't a soap-opera,' Buck chimed in. Sadie was about to beg to differ, but before she had a chance the evangelist had approached Virginia's bed, Bible in hand.

'This is the inspired word of the Lord, Virginia,' he said.

'I know John. But there are other passages . . .'

'I thought you liked the Apocalypse.'

'No,' she said, 'it distresses me.'

'You're tired,' he replied.

'Oh yes,' Sadie interjected, 'that's what they always tell you when you get too close to the truth. "You're tired," they say, "why don't you take a little nap?"'

'Why don't you sleep for a while?' Gyer said, 'I'll go next door and work.'

Virginia met her husband's condescending look for fully five seconds, then nodded.

'Yes,' she conceded, 'I *am* tired.'

'Foolish woman,' Sadie told her. 'Fight back, or he'll do the same again. Give them an inch and they take half the damn state.'

Buck appeared behind Sadie. 'I've asked you once,' he said, taking her arm, 'we're here to make friends. So let's get to it.' He pulled her away from the door, rather more roughly than was necessary. She shrugged off his hand.

'There's no need for violence, Buck,' she said.

'Ha! That's rich, coming from you,' Buck said with a humourless laugh. 'You want to see violence?' Sadie turned away from Virginia to look at her husband. '*This* is violence,' he said. He had taken off his jacket; now he pulled his unbuttoned shirt open to reveal the shot-wound. At such close quarters Sadie's .38 had made a sizeable hole in Buck's chest, scorched and bloody: it was as fresh as the moment he died. He put his finger to it as if indicating the Sacred Heart. 'You see that, sweetheart mine? *You* made that.'

She peered at the hole with no little interest. It certainly was a permanent mark; about the only one she'd ever made on the man, she suspected.

'You cheated from the beginning, didn't you?' she said.

'We're not talking about cheating, we're talking about shooting,' Buck returned.

'Seems to me one subject leads the other,' Sadie replied, 'And back again.'

Buck narrowed his already narrow eyes at her. Dozens of women had found that look irresistible, to judge by the numbers of anonymous mourners at his funeral. 'All right,' he said, 'I had women. So what?'

'So I shot you for it,' Sadie replied flatly. That was about all she had to say on the subject. It had made for a short trial.

'Well at least tell me you're sorry,' Buck burst out.

Sadie considered the proposition for a few moments and said: 'But I'm not!' She realized the response lacked tact, but it was the unavoidable truth. Even as they'd strapped her into the electric chair, with the priest doing his best to console her lawyer, she hadn't regretted the way things had turned out.

'This whole thing is useless,' Buck said. 'We came here to make peace and you can't even say you're sorry. You're a sick woman, you know that? You always were. You pried into my business, you snooped around behind my back – '

'I did *not* snoop,' Sadie replied firmly. 'Your dirt came and found me.'

'Dirt?'

'Oh yes, Buck, *dirt*. It always was with you. Furtive and sweaty.'

He grabbed hold of her. 'Take that back!' he demanded.

'You used to frighten me once,' she replied, coolly. 'But then I bought a gun.'

He thrust her away from him. 'All right,' he said, 'don't say I didn't try. I wanted to see if we could forgive and forget; I really did. But you're not willing to give an inch are you?' He fingered his wound as he spoke, his voice softening; 'We could have had a good time here tonight, babe,' he murmured. 'Just you and me. I could have given you a bit of the old jazz, you know what I mean? Time was, you wouldn't have said no.'

She sighed softly. What he said was true. Time was she would have taken what little he gave her and counted herself a blessed woman. But times had changed.

'Come on, babe. Loosen up,' he said smokily, and began to unbutton his shirt completely, pulling it out of his trousers. His belly was bald as a baby's. 'What say we forget what you said and lie down and talk?'

She was about to reply to his suggestion when the door of Room Seven opened and in came the man with the soulful eyes, accompanied by a woman whose face rang a bell in Sadie's memory.

'Ice-water,' Earl said. Sadie watched him move across the room. There'd not been a man as fine as that in Wichita Falls; not that she could remember anyway. He almost made her want to live again.

'Are you going to get undressed?' Buck asked from the room behind her.

'In a minute, Buck. We've got all night, for Christ's sake.'

'I'm Laura-May Cade,' the woman with the familiar face said as she set the iced water down on the table.

Of course, thought Sadie, you're little Laura-May. The girl had been five or six when Sadie was last here: an odd, secretive child, full of sly looks. The intervening years had matured her physically, but the strangeness was still in evidence in her slightly off-centre features. Sadie turned to Buck, who was sitting on the bed untying his shoes.

'Remember the little girl?' she said, 'The one who you gave a quarter to, just to make her go away?'

'What about her?'

'She's here.'

'That so?' he replied, clearly uninterested.

Laura-May had poured the water, and was now taking the glass across to Virginia.

'It's real nice having you folks here,' she said. 'We don't get much happening here. Just the occasional tornado . . .'

Gyer nodded to Earl, who produced a five dollar bill and gave it to Laura-May. She thanked him, saying it wasn't necessary, then taking the bill. She wasn't to be bribed into leaving, however.

'This kind of weather makes people feel real peculiar,' she went on.

Earl could predict what subject was hovering behind Laura-May's lips. He'd already heard the bones of the story on the way across, and knew Virginia was in no mood to hear such a tale.

'Thank you for the water – ' he said, putting a hand on Laura-May's arm to usher her through the door. But Gyer cut in.

'My wife's been suffering from heat exhaustion,' he said.

'You should be careful, ma'am,' Laura-May advised Virginia, 'people do some mighty weird things – '

'Like what?' Virginia asked.

81

'I don't think we – ' Earl began, but before he could say – 'want to hear', Laura-May casually replied:

'Oh, murder mostly.'

Virginia looked up from the glass of iced-water in which her focus had been immersed.

'Murder?' she said.

'Hear that?' Said Sadie, proudly. 'She remembers.'

'In this very room,' Laura-May managed to blurt before Earl forcibly escorted her out.

'Wait,' Virginia said as the two figures disappeared through the door. 'Earl! I want to hear what happened.'

'No you don't,' Gyer told her.

'Oh yes she does,' said Sadie very quietly, studying the look on Virginia's face. 'You'd *really* like to know, wouldn't you, Ginnie?'

For a moment pregnant with possibilities, Virginia looked away from the outside door and stared straight through into Room Eight, her eyes seeming to rest on Sadie. The look was so direct it could almost have been one of recognition. The ice in her glass tinkled. She frowned.

'What's wrong?' Gyer asked her.

Virginia shook her head.

'I asked you what was wrong,' Gyer insisted.

Virginia put down her glass on the bedside table. After a moment she said, very simply: 'There's somebody here, John.'

'What do you mean?'

'There's somebody in the room with us. I heard voices before. Raised voices.'

'Next door,' Gyer said.

'No, from Earl's room.'

'It's empty. It must have been next door.'

Virginia was not to be silenced with logic. 'I heard voices, I tell you. And I saw something at the end of the bed. Something in the air.'

'Oh my Jesus,' said Sadie, under her breath, 'The goddamn woman's psychic.'

Buck stood up. He was naked now, but for his shorts. He wandered over to the interconnecting door to look at Virginia with new appreciation.

'Are you sure?' he said.

'Hush,' Sadie told him, moving out of Virginia's eye-line. 'She said she could see us.'

'You're not well, Virginia,' Gyer was saying in the next room. 'It's those pills he fed you . . .'

'No,' Virginia replied, her voice rising. 'When will you stop

82

talking about the pills? They were just to calm me down; help me sleep.'

She certainly wasn't calm now, thought Buck. He liked the way she trembled as she tried to hold back her tears. She looked in need of some of the old jazz, did poor Virginia; now *that* would help her sleep.

'I tell you I can see things,' she was telling her husband.

'That *I* can't – ' Gyer replied, incredulously. 'Is that what you're saying? That you can see visions the rest of us are blind to?'

'I'm not proud of it, damn you,' she yelled at him, incensed by this inversion.

'Come away Buck,' Sadie said. 'We're upsetting her. She knows we're here.'

'So what?' Buck responded. 'Her prick of a husband doesn't believe her. Look at him. He thinks she's crazy.'

'Well we'll *make* her crazy if we parade around,' said Sadie. 'At least let's keep our voices down, huh?'

Buck looked around at Sadie, and offered up a dirty rag of a smile. 'Want to make it worth my while?' he said sleazily. 'I'll keep out of the way if you and me can have some fun.'

Sadie hesitated a moment before replying. It was probably perverse to reject Buck's advances; the man was an emotional infant and always had been. Sex was one of the few ways he could express himself. 'All right, Buck,' she said, 'just let me freshen up and fix my hair.'

An uneasy truce had apparently been declared in Room Seven.

'I'm going to take a shower, Virginia,' Gyer said, 'I suggest you lie down and stop making a fool of yourself. You go talking like that in front of people and you'll jeopardize the crusade, you hear me?'

Virginia looked at her husband with clearer sight than she'd ever enjoyed before. 'Oh yes,' she said, without a trace of feeling in her voice, 'I hear you.'

He seemed satisfied. He slipped off his jacket and went into the bathroom, taking his Bible with him. She heard the door lock, and then exhaled a long, queasy sigh. There would be recriminations aplenty for the exchange they'd just had; he would squeeze every last drop of contrition from her in the days to come. She glanced around at the interconnecting door. There was no longer any sign of those shadows in the air; not the least whisper of lost voices. Perhaps, just *perhaps*, she had imagined it. She opened her bag and rummaged for the bottles of pills hidden there. One eye on the bathroom door, she selected a cocktail of three varieties and downed them with a gulp of iced-water. In fact, the ice in the jug had long since melted. The water she drank down was tepid, like the rain that fell relentlessly outside. By morning, perhaps the whole world would have been washed away. If it had, she mused, she wouldn't grieve.

'I asked you not to mention the killing,' Earl told Laura-May, 'Mrs Gyer can't take that kind of talk.'

'People are getting killed all the time,' Laura-May replied, unfazed. 'Can't go round with her head in a bucket.'

Earl said nothing. They had just got to the end of the walkway. The return sprint across the lot to the other building was ahead. Laura-May turned to face him. She was several inches the shorter of the two. Her eyes, turned up to his, were large and luminous. Angry as he was, he couldn't help but notice how full her mouth was, how her lips glistened.

'I'm sorry,' she said, 'I didn't mean to get you into trouble.'

'Sure I know. I'm just edgy.'

'It's the heat,' she returned. 'Like I said: puts thoughts into people's heads. You know.' Her look wavered for a moment; a hint of uncertainty crossed her face. Earl could feel the back of his neck tingle. This was his cue, wasn't it? she'd offered it unequivocally. But the words failed him. Finally, it was she who said:

'Do you have to go back there right now?'

He swallowed; his throat was dry. 'Don't see why,' he said, 'I mean, I don't want to get between them when they're having words with each other.'

'Bad blood?' she asked.

'I think so. I'm best leaving them to sort it out in peace. They don't want me.'

Laura-May looked down from Earl's face. 'Well I do,' she breathed, the words scarcely audible above the thump of the rain.

He put a cautious hand to her face and touched the down of her cheek. She trembled, ever so slightly. Then he bent his head to kiss her. She let him brush her lips with his.

'Why don't we go to my room?' she said against his mouth, 'I don't like it out here.'

'What about your Papa?'

'He'll be dead drunk by now; it's the same routine every night. Just take it quietly. He'll never know.'

Earl wasn't very happy with this game-plan. It was more than his job was worth to be found in bed with Laura-May. He was a married man, even if he hadn't seen Barbara in three months. Laura-May sensed his prevarication.

84

'Don't come if you don't want to,' she said.

'It's not that,' he replied.

As he looked down at her, she licked her lips. It was a completely unconscious motion, he felt sure, but it was enough to decide him. In a sense, though he couldn't know it at the time, all that lay ahead – the farce, the blood-letting, the inevitable tragedy – pivotted on Laura-May wetting her lower lip with such casual sensuality. 'Ah *shit*,' he said, 'you're too much, you know that?'

He bent to her and kissed her again, while somewhere over towards Skellytown the clouds gave out a loud roll of thunder, like a circus drummer before some particularly elaborate acrobatics.

In Room Seven, Virginia was having bad dreams. The pills had not secured her a safe harbour in sleep. Instead she'd been pitched into a howling tempest. In her dreams she was clinging to a crippled tree – a pitiful anchor in such a maelstrom – while the wind threw cattle and automobiles into the air, sucking half the world up into the pitch black clouds that boiled above her head. Just as she thought she must die here, utterly alone, she saw two figures a few yards from her, appearing and disappearing in the blinding veils of dust the wind was stirring up. She couldn't see their faces, so she called to them:

'Who are you?'

Next door, Sadie heard Virginia talking in her sleep. What was the woman dreaming about? she wondered. She fought the temptation to go next door and whisper in the dreamer's ear, however.

Behind Virginia's eyelids the dream raged on. Though she called to the strangers in the storm they seemed not to hear her. Rather than be left alone, she forsook the comfort of the tree – which was instantly uprooted and whirled away – and battled through the biting dust to where the strangers stood. As she approached, a sudden lull in the wind revealed them to her. One was male, the other female: both were armed. As she called to them to make herself known they attacked each other, opening fatal wounds in neck and torso.

'Murder!' she shouted as the wind spattered her face with the antagonists' blood. 'For God's sake, somebody stop them! Murder!'

And suddenly she was awake, her heart beating fit to burst. The dream still flitted behind her eyes. She shook her head to rid herself of the horrid images, then moved groggily to the edge of the bed and stood up. Her head felt so light it might float off like a balloon. She needed some fresh air. Seldom in her life had she felt so strange. It was as though she was losing her slender grip on what was real; as though the solid world were slipping through her fingers. She crossed to the outside door. In the bathroom she could hear John, speaking aloud: addressing the mirror, no doubt, to refine every detail of his delivery. She stepped out onto the walkway. There was some refreshment to be had out here, but precious little. In one of the rooms at the end of the block a child was crying. As she listened a sharp voice silenced it. For maybe ten seconds the voice was hushed; then it began again in a higher key. *Go on*, she told the child, *you cry; there's plenty of reason*. She trusted unhappiness in people; more and more it was *all* she trusted. Sadness was so much more honest than the artificial bonhomie that was all the style these days: that façade of empty-headed optimism that was plastered over the despair that everyone felt in their heart of hearts. The child was expressing that wise panic now, as it cried in the night. She silently applauded its honesty.

In the bathroom, John Gyer tired of the sight of his own face in the mirror, and gave some time over to thought. He put down the toilet lid and sat in silence for several minutes. He could smell his own stale sweat; he needed a shower, and then a good night's sleep. Tomorrow: Pampa. Meetings, speeches; thousands of hands to be shaken and blessings to be bestowed. Sometimes he felt so tired: and then he'd get to wondering if the Lord couldn't lighten his burden a little. But that was the Devil talking in his ear, wasn't it? He knew better than to pay that scurrilous voice much attention. If you listened *once* the doubts would get a hold, the way they had of Virginia. Somewhere along the road, while his back had been turned about the Lord's business, she'd lost her way, and the Old One had found her wandering. He, John Gyer, would have to bring her back to the path of the righteous; make her see the danger her soul was in. There would be tears and complaints; maybe she would be bruised a little. But bruises healed.

He put down his Bible, and went down on his knees in the narrow space between the bath and the towel rack, and began to pray. He tried to find some benign words, a gentle prayer to ask for the strength to finish his task, and to bring Virginia back to her senses. But mildness had deserted him. It was the vocabulary of Revelations that came back to his lips, unbidden. He let the words spill out, even though the fever in him burned brighter with every syllable he spoke.

'What do you think?' Laura-May had asked Earl as she escorted him into her bedroom. Earl was too startled by what was in front of him to offer any coherent reply. The bedroom was a mausoleum, founded, it seemed, in the name of Trivia. Laid out on the shelves, hung on the walls and covering much of the floor were items that might have been picked off any rubbish tip: empty Coke cans, collections of ticket stubs, coverless and defaced magazines, vandalized toys, shattered mirrors, postcards never sent, letters never read – a limping parade of the forgotten and the forsaken. His eye passed back and forth over the elaborate display and found not one item of worth amongst the junk and bric-a-brac. Yet all this inconsequentia had been arranged with meticulous care, so that no one piece masked another; and – now that he looked more closely – he saw that every item was numbered, as if each had its place in some system of junk. The thought that this was all Laura-May's doing shrank Earl's stomach. The woman was clearly verging on lunacy.

'This is my collection,' she told him.

'So I see,' he replied.

'I've been collecting since I was six.' She crossed the room to the dressing table, where most women Earl had known would have arranged their toiletries. But here were arrayed more of the same inane exhibits. 'Everybody leaves something behind, you know,' Laura-May said to Earl, picking up some piece of dreck with all the care others might bestow on a precious stone, and examining it before placing it back in its elected position.

'Is that so?' Earl said.

'Oh yeah. Everyone. Even if it's only a dead match or a tissue with lip-stick on. We used to have a Mexican girl, Ophelia, who cleaned the rooms when I was a child. It started as a game with her, really. She'd always bring me something belonging to the guests who'd left. When she died I took over collecting stuff for myself, always keeping something. As a memento.'

Earl began to grasp the absurd poetry of the museum. In Laura-May's neat body was all the ambition of a great curator. Not for her mere *art*; she was collecting keepsakes of a more intimate nature, forgotten signs of people who'd passed this way, and who, most likely, she would never see again.

'You've got it all marked,' he observed.

'Oh yes,' she replied, 'it wouldn't be much use if I didn't know who it all belonged to, would it?'

87

Earl supposed not. 'Incredible,' he murmured, quite genuinely. She smiled at him; he suspected she didn't show her collection to many people. He felt oddly honoured to be viewing it.

'I've got some really prize things,' she said, opening the middle drawer of the dressing table, 'stuff I don't put on display.'

'Oh?' he said.

The drawer she'd opened was lined with tissue paper, which rustled as she brought forth a selection of special acquisitions. A soiled tissue found beneath the bed of a Hollywood star who had tragically died six weeks after staying at the Motel. A heroin needle carelessly left by X; an empty book of matches, which she had traced to a homosexual bar in Amarillo, discarded by Y. The names she mentioned meant little or nothing to Earl, but he played the game as he felt she wanted it played, mingling exclamations of disbelief with gentle laughter. Her pleasure, fed by his, grew. She took him through all the exhibits in the dressing-table drawer, offering some anecdote or biographical insight with every one. When she had finished, she said:

'I wasn't quite telling you the truth before, when I said it began as a game with Ophelia. That really came later.'

'So what started you off?' he asked.

She went down on her haunches and unlocked the bottom drawer of the dressing-table with a key on a chain around her neck. There was only one artifact in this drawer; this she lifted out almost reverentially, and stood up to show him.

'What's this?'

'You asked me what started the collection,' she said. 'This is it. I found it, and I never gave it back. You can look if you want.'

She extended the prize towards him, and he unfolded the pressed white cloth the object had been wrapped up in. It was a gun. A Smith and Wesson .38, in pristine condition. It took him only a moment to realize which motel guest this piece of history had once belonged to.

'The gun that Sadie Durning used . . .' he said, picking it up. 'Am I right?'

She beamed. 'I found it in the scrub behind the motel, before the police got to searching for it. There was such a commotion, you know, nobody looked twice at me. And of course they didn't try and look for it in the light.'

'Why was that?'

'The '55 tornado hit, just the day after. Took the motel roof right off; blew the school away. People were killed that year. We had funerals for weeks.'

'They didn't question you at all?'

'I was a good liar,' she replied, with no small satisfaction.

'And you never owned up to having it? All these years?'

She looked faintly contemptuous of the suggestion. 'They might have taken it off me,' she said.

'But it's *evidence*.'

'They executed her anyway, didn't they?' she replied, 'Sadie admitted to it all, right from the beginning. It wouldn't have made any difference if they'd found the murder-weapon or not.'

Earl turned the gun over in his hand. There was encrusted dirt on it.

'That's blood,' Laura-May informed him, 'It was still wet when I found it. She must have touched Buck's body, to make sure he was dead. Only used two bullets. The rest are still in there.'

Earl had never much liked weapons, since his brother-in-law had blown off three of his toes in an accident. The thought that the .38 was still loaded made him yet more apprehensive. He put it back in its wrapping, and folded the cloth over it.

'I've never seen anything like this place,' he said as Laura-May knelt to return the gun to the drawer. 'You're quite a woman, you know that?'

She looked up at him. Her hand slowly slid up the front of his trousers.

'I'm glad you like what you see,' she said.

'Sadie . . . ? Are you coming to bed or not?'

'I just want to finish fixing my hair.'

'You're not playing fair. Forget your hair and come over here.'

'In a minute.'

'Shit!'

'You're in no hurry, are you, Buck? I mean, you're not going anywhere?'

She caught his reflection in the mirror. He gave her a sour glance.

'You think it's funny, don't you?' he said.

'Think *what's* funny?'

'What happened. Me getting shot. You getting the chair. It gives you some perverse satisfaction.'

She thought about this for a few moments. It was the first time Buck had shown any real desire to talk seriously; she wanted to answer with the truth.

'Yes,' she said, when she was certain that was the answer. 'Yes; I suppose it did please me, in an odd sort of way.'

'I *knew* it,' said Buck.

'Keep your voice down,' Sadie snapped, 'she'll hear us.'

'She's gone outside. I heard her. And don't change the subject.'
He rolled over and sat on the edge of the bed: the wound did look painful, Sadie thought.

'Did it hurt much?' she asked, turning to him.

'Are you kidding?' he said, displaying the hole for her. 'What does it fucking look like?'

'I thought it would be quick. I never wanted you to suffer.'

'Is that right?' Buck said.

'Of course. I loved you once, Buck. I really did. You know what the headline was the day after?'

'No', Buck replied, 'I was otherwise engaged, remember?'

'"*Motel Becomes Slaughter-house of Love*",' it said. There were pictures of the room; of the blood on the floor; and you being carried out under a sheet.'

'My finest hour,' he said bitterly. 'And I don't even get my face in the press.'

'I'll never forget the phrase. "*Slaughter-house of Love!*" I thought it was romantic. Don't you?' Buck grunted in disgust. Sadie went on anyway. 'I got three hundred proposals of marriage while I was waiting for the chair, did I ever tell you that?'

'Oh yeah?' Buck said, 'Did they come and visit you? Give you a bit of the old jazz to keep your mind off the big day?'

'No.' said Sadie frostily.

'You could have had a time of it. I would have done.'

'I'm sure you would,' she replied.

'Just thinking about it's getting me cooking, Sadie. Why don't you come and get it while it's hot?'

'We came here to talk, Buck.'

'We talked, for Christ's sake,' he said, 'I don't want to talk no more. Now come here. You promised.' He rubbed his abdomen, and gave her a crooked smile. 'Sorry about the blood and all, but I ain't responsible for that.'

Sadie stood up.

'Now you're being sensible,' he said.

As Sadie Durning crossed to the bed, Virginia came in out of the rain. It had cooled her face somewhat, and the tranquillisers she'd taken were finally beginning to soothe her system. In the bathroom, John was still praying, his voice rising and falling. She crossed to the table and glanced at his notes, but the tightly packed words wouldn't come into focus. She picked the papers up to peer more closely at them; as she did so she heard a groan from the next room. She froze. The groan came again, more loudly. The papers trembled in her hands; she made to put them

90

back on the table but the voice came a third time, and this time the papers slipped from her hand.

'Give a little, damn you . . .' the voice said; the words, though blurred, were unmistakable; more grunts followed. Virginia moved towards the door between the rooms, the trembling spreading up from her hands to the rest of her body. 'Play the game, will you?' the voice came again; there was anger in it. Cautiously Virginia looked through into Room Eight, holding onto the door lintel for support. There was a shadow on the bed; it writhed distressingly, as if attempting to devour itself. She stood, rooted to the spot, trying to stifle a cry, while more sounds rose from the shadow. Not *one* voice this time, but two. The words were jumbled; in her growing panic she could make little sense of them. She couldn't turn her back on the scene, however. She stared on, trying to make some sense of the shifting configuration. Now a smattering of words came clear; and with them, a recognition of the event on the bed. She heard a woman's voice, protesting; now she even began to see the speaker, struggling beneath a partner who was attempting to arrest her flailing arms. Her first instincts about the scene had been correct: it *was* a devouring, of a kind.

Sadie looked up into Buck's face. That bastard grin of his had returned; it made her trigger-finger itch. This is what he'd come for tonight. Not for conversation about failed dreams: but to humiliate her the way he had so often in the past, whispering obscenities into her neck while he pinned her to the sheets. The pleasure he took in her discomfort made her seethe.

'*Let go of me!*' she shouted, louder than she'd intended.

At the door, Virginia said: 'Let her alone.'

'We've got an audience,' Buck Durning grinned, pleased by the appalled look on Virginia's face. Sadie took advantage of his diverted attention. She slipped her arm from his grasp and pushed him off her; he rolled off the narrow bed with a yell. As she stood up, she looked round at the ashen woman in the doorway; how much could Virginia see or hear? Enough to know who they were?

Buck was climbing over the bed towards his sometime murderer, 'Come on,' he said, 'It's only the crazy lady.'

'Keep away from me,' Sadie warned.

'You can't harm me now, woman. I'm already dead, remember?' His exertions had opened the gun-shot wound. There was blood smeared all over him; over her too, now she looked. She backed towards the door. There was nothing to be salvaged here. What little chance of reconciliation there had been had degenerated into a bloody farce. The only solution to the whole sorry mess was to get out, and leave poor Virginia to make what sense of it she could. The longer she stayed to fight with Buck, the worse the situation would become for all three of them.

'Where are you going?' Buck demanded.

'Out,' she responded. 'Away from you. I said I loved you, Buck, didn't I? Well . . . maybe I did. But I'm cured now.'

'Bitch!'

'Goodbye Buck. Have a nice eternity.'

'*Worthless bitch!*'

She didn't reply to his insults; she simply walked through the door and out into the night.

Virginia watched the shadow pass through the closed door and held on to the tattered remains of her sanity with white-knuckled fists. She had to put these apparitions out of her head as quickly as possible, or she knew she'd go crazy. She turned her back on Room Eight. What she needed now was pills. She picked up her handbag, only to drop it again as her shaking fingers rooted for the bottles, depositing the contents of the bag on to the floor. One of the bottles, which she had failed to seal properly, spilled. A rainbow assortment of tablets rolled across the stained carpet in every direction. She bent to pick them up. Tears had started to come, blinding her; she felt for the pills as best she could, feeding half a handful into her mouth and trying to swallow them dry. The tattoo of the rain on the roof sounded louder and louder in her head; a roll of thunder gave weight to the percussion.

And then, John's voice:

'*What are you doing, Virginia?*'

She looked up, tears in her eyes, a pill-laden hand hovering at her lips. She'd forgotten her husband entirely; the shadows and the rain and the voices had driven all thought of him from her head. She let the pills drop back to the carpet. Her limbs were shaking; she hadn't got the strength to stand up.

'I . . . I . . . heard the voices again,' she said.

His eyes had come to rest on the spilled contents of bag and bottle. Her crime was spread for him to see quite plainly. It was useless to try and deny anything; it would only enrage him further.

'Woman,' he said. 'Haven't you learned your lesson?'

She didn't reply. Thunder drowned his next words. He repeated them, more loudly.

'Where did you get the pills, Virginia?'

She shook her head, weakly.

'Earl again, I suppose. Who else?'

'No,' she murmured.

'Don't lie to me, Virginia!' He had raised his voice to compete

92

with the storm. 'You know the Lord hears your lies, as I hear them. And you are *judged*, Virginia! *Judged!*'

'Please leave me be,' she pleaded.

'You're poisoning yourself.'

'I *need* them, John,' she told him, 'I really do.' She had no energy to hold his bullying at bay; nor did she want him to take the pills from her. But then what was the use of protesting? He would have his way, as always. It would be wiser to give up the booty now, and save herself unnecessary anguish.

'Look at yourself,' he said, 'grovelling on the floor.'

'Don't start on me, John,' she replied, 'You win. Take the pills. Go on! *Take them!*'

He was clearly disappointed by her rapid capitulation, like an actor preparing for a favourite scene only to find the curtain rung down prematurely. But he made the most of her invitation, upending her handbag on the bed, and collecting the bottles.

'Is this all?' he demanded.

'Yes,' she said.

'I won't be deceived, Virginia.'

'*That's all!*' she shouted back at him. Then more softly: 'I swear . . . that's all.'

'Earl will be sorry. I promise you that. He's exploited your weakness – '

'. . . no!'

' – your weakness and your fear. The man is in Satan's employ, that much is apparent.'

'Don't talk rubbish!' she said, surprising herself with her own vehemence. 'I *asked* him to supply them.' She got to her feet with some difficulty. 'He didn't want to defy you, John. It was me all along.'

Gyer shook his head. 'No, Virginia. You won't save him. Not this time. He's worked to subvert me all along. I see that now. Worked to harm my crusade through you. Well I'm wise to him now. Oh yes. Oh *yes*.'

He suddenly turned and pitched the handful of bottles through the open door and into the rainy darkness outside. Virginia watched them fly, and felt her heart sink. There was precious little sanity to be had on a night like this – it was a night for going crazy, wasn't it?, with the rain bruising your skull and murder in the air – and now the damn fool had thrown away her last chance of equilibrium. He turned back to her, his perfect teeth bared.

'How many times do you have to be told?'

He was not to be denied his scene after all, it seemed.

'I'm not listening!' she told him, clamping her hands over her ears. Even so she could hear the rain. 'I *won't* listen!'

'I'm patient, Virginia,' he said, 'The Lord will have his Judgement in the fullness of time. Now, where's Earl?'

She shook her head. Thunder came again; she wasn't sure if it was inside or out.

'*Where is he?*' he boomed at her. 'Gone for more of the same filth?'

'No!' she yelled back. 'I don't know where he's gone.'

'You pray, woman,' Gyer said. 'You get down on your knees and thank the Lord I'm here to keep you from Satan.'

Content that his words made a striking exit-line, he headed out in search of Earl, leaving Virginia shaking, but curiously elated. He would be back, of course. There would be more recriminations, and from her, the obligatory tears. As to Earl, he would have to defend himself as best he could. She slumped down on the bed, and her bleary eyes came to rest on the tablets that were still scattered across the floor. All was not quite lost. There were no more than two dozen, so she would have to be sparing in her use of them, but they were better than nothing at all. Wiping her eyes with the back of her hands, she knelt down again to gather the pills up. As she did so she realized that someone had their eyes on her. Not the evangelist, back so soon? She looked up. The door out to the rain was still wide open, but he wasn't standing there. Her heart seemed to lose its rhythm for a moment, as she remembered the shadows in the room next door. There had been *two*. One had departed; but the other – ?

Her eyes slid across to the interconnecting door. It was there, a greasy smudge that had taken on a new solidity since last she'd set eyes on it. Was it that the apparition was gaining coherence, or that she was seeing it in more detail? It was quite clearly human; and just as apparently male. It was staring at her, she had no doubt of that. She could even see its eyes, when she concentrated. Her tenuous grasp of its existence was improving; it was gaining fresh resolution with every trembling breath she took.

She stood up, very slowly. It took a step through the interconnecting door. She moved toward the outside door, and it matched her move with one of its own, sliding with eerie speed between her and the night. Her outstretched arm brushed against its smoky form, and, as if illuminated by a lightning flash, an entire portrait of her accoster sprang into view in front of her, only to disappear as she withdrew her hand. She had glimpsed enough to appal her however. The vision was that of a dead man; his chest had been blown open. Was this more of her dream, spilling into the living world? She thought of calling after John, to summon him back, but that meant approaching the door again, and risking contact with the apparition. Instead she took a cautious step backwards, reciting a prayer beneath her breath as she did so. Perhaps John had been correct all along; perhaps she *had* invited this lunacy on to herself with the very tablets she was even now treading to powder underfoot. The apparition closed in on her. Was it her imagination, or had it opened its arms, as if to embrace her?

Her heel caught on the skirt of the coverlet. Before she could stop herself she was toppling backwards. Her arms flailed, seeking support. Again she made contact with the dream-thing; again the whole horrid picture appeared in front of her. But this time it didn't disappear, because the apparition had snatched at her hand and was grasping it tight. Her fingers felt as though they'd been plunged into ice-water. She yelled for it to let her be, flinging up her free arm to push her assailant away, but it simply grasped her other hand too.

Unable to resist, she met its gaze. They were not the Devil's eyes that looked at her – they were slightly stupid, even comical, eyes – and below them a weak mouth which only reinforced her impression of witlessness. Suddenly she was not afraid. This was no demon. It was a delusion, brought on by exhaustion and pills; it could do her no harm. The only danger here was that she hurt herself in her attempts to keep the hallucinations at bay.

Buck sensed that Virginia was losing the will to resist. 'That's better,' he coaxed her. 'You just want a bit of the old jazz, don't you, Ginnie?'

He wasn't certain if she heard him, but no matter. He could readily make his intentions apparent. Dropping one of her hands, he ran his palm across her breasts. She sighed, a bewildered expression in her beautiful eyes, but she made no effort to resist his attentions.

'You don't exist,' she told him plainly. 'You're only in my mind, like John said. The pills made you. The pills did it all.'

Buck let the woman babble; let her think whatever she pleased, as long as it made her compliant.

'That's right, isn't it?' she said. 'You're not real, are you?'

He obliged her with a polite reply. 'Certainly,' he said, squeezing her. 'I'm just a dream, that's all.' The answer seemed to satisfy her. 'No need to fight me is there?' he said. 'I'll have come and gone before you know it.'

* * *

The manager's office lay empty. From the room beyond it, Gyer heard a television. It stood to reason that Earl must be somewhere in the vicinity. He had left their room with the girl who'd brought the iced-water, and they certainly wouldn't be taking a walk together in weather like this. The thunder had moved in closer in the last few minutes. Now it was almost overhead. Gyer enjoyed the noise, and the spectacle of the lightning. It fuelled his sense of occasion.

'Earl!' he yelled, making his way through the office and into the room with the television. The late movie was nearing its climax, the sound turned up deafeningly loud. A fantastical beast of some kind was treading Tokyo to rubble; citizens fled, screaming. Asleep in a chair in front of this papier-mâché Apocalypse was a late middle-aged man. Neither the thunder nor Gyer's calls had stirred him. A tumbler of spirits, nursed in his lap, had slipped from his hand and stained his trousers. The whole scene stank of bourbon and depravity; Gyer made a note of it for future use in the pulpit.

A chill blew in from the office. Gyer turned, expecting a visitor, but there was nobody in the office behind him. He stared into space. All the way across here he'd had a sense of being followed, yet there was nobody on his heels. He cancelled his suspicions. Fears like this were for women and old men, afraid of the dark. He stepped between the sleeping drunkard and the ruin of Tokyo toward the closed door beyond.

'Earl?' he called out, 'answer me!'

Sadie watched Gyer open the door and step into the kitchen. His bombast amazed her. She'd expected his sub-species to be extinct by now: could such melodrama be credible in this sophisticated age? She'd never much liked church people, but this example was particularly offensive; there was more than a whiff of malice beneath the flatulence. He was riled and unpredictable, and he would not be pleased by the scene that awaited him in Laura-May's room. Sadie had already been there. She had watched the lovers for a little time, until their passion became too much for her and had driven her out to cool herself by watching the rain. Now the evangelist's appearance drew her back the way she'd come, fearful that whatever was now in the air, the night's events could not end well. In the kitchen, Gyer was shouting again. He clearly enjoyed the sound of his own voice.

'Earl! You hear me? I'm not to be cheated!'

In Laura-May's room Earl was attempting to perform three acts at the same time. One, kiss the woman he had just made love with; two, pull on his damp trousers; and three, invent an adequate excuse to offer Gyer if the evangelist reached the bedroom door before some illusion of innocence had been created. As it was, he had no time to complete any of the tasks. His tongue was still locked in Laura-May's tender mouth when the lock on the door was forced.

'Found you!'

Earl broke his kiss and turned towards the messianic voice. Gyer was standing in the doorway, rain-plastered hair a grey skull cap, his face bright with fury. The light thrown up on him from the silk-draped lamp beside the bed made him look massive; the glint in his come-to-the-Lord eyes was verging on the manic. Earl had heard tell of the great man's righteous wrath from Virginia: furniture had been trashed in the past, and bones broken.

'Is there no end to your iniquity?' he demanded to know, the words coming with unnerving calm from between his narrow lips. Earl hoisted his trousers up, fumbling for the zip.

'This isn't your business . . .' he began, but Gyer's fury powdered the words on his tongue.

Laura-May was not so easily cowed. 'You get out,' she said, pulling a sheet up to cover her generous breasts. Earl glanced round at her; at the smooth shoulders he'd all too recently kissed. He wanted to kiss them again now, but the man in black crossed the room in four quick strides and took hold of him by hair and arm. The movement, in the confined space of Laura-May's room, had the effect of an earth tremor. Pieces of her precious collection toppled over on the shelves and dressing-table, one exhibit falling against another, and that against its neighbour, until a minor avalanche of trivia hit the floor. Laura-May was blind to any damage however; her thoughts were with the man who had so sweetly shared her bed. She could see the trepidation in Earl's eyes as the evangelist dragged him away, and she shared it.

'Let him be!' she shrieked, forsaking her modesty and getting up from the bed, 'He hasn't done anything wrong!'

The evangelist paused to respond, Earl wrestling uselessly to free himself. 'What would you know about error, *whore*?' Gyer spat at her, 'You're too steeped in sin. You with your nakedness, and your stinking bed.'

The bed did stink, but only of good soap and recent love. She had nothing to apologize for, and she wasn't going to let this two-bit Bible-thumper intimidate her.

'I'll call the cops!' she warned, 'If you don't leave him alone, I'll call them!'

Gyer didn't grace the threat with a reply. He simply dragged Earl out through the door and into the kitchen. Laura-May yelled:

'Hold on, Earl. I'll get help!' Her lover didn't answer; he was too busy preventing Gyer from pulling out his hair by the roots.

Sometimes, when the days were long and lonely, Laura-May had day-dreamed dark men like the evangelist. She had imagined them coming before tornadoes, wreathed in dust. She had pictured herself lifted up by them – only half against her will – and taken away. But the man who had lain in her bed tonight had been utterly unlike her fever-dream lovers; he had been foolish and vulnerable. If he were to die at the hands of a man like Gyer – whose image she had conjured in her desperation – she would never forgive herself.

She heard her father say: 'What's going on?' in the far room. Something fell and smashed; a plate perhaps, from off the dresser, or a glass from his lap. She prayed her Papa wouldn't try and tackle the evangelist: he would be chaff in the wind if he did. She went back to the bed to root for her clothes; they were wound up in the sheets, and her frustration mounted with every second she lost searching for them. She tossed the pillows aside. One landed on the dressing table; more of her exquisitely arranged pieces were swept to the floor. As she pulled on her underwear her father appeared at the door. His drink-flushed features turned a deeper red seeing her state.

'What you been doing, Laura-May?'

'Never mind, Pa. There's no time to explain.'

'But there's men out there – '

'I know. I know. I want you to call the Sheriff in Panhandle. Understand?'

'What's going on?'

'Never mind. Just call Alvin and be quick about it, or we're going to have another murder on our hands.'

The thought of slaughter galvanized Milton Cade. He disappeared, leaving his daughter to finish dressing. Laura-May knew that on a night like this Alvin Baker and his Deputy could be a long time coming. In the meanwhile God alone knew what the mad-dog preacher would be capable of.

From the doorway, Sadie watched the woman dress. Laura-May was a plain creature, at least to Sadie's critical eye, and her fair skin made her look wan and insubstantial, despite her full figure. But then, thought Sadie, who am I to complain of lack of substance?; look at me. And for the first time in the thirty years since her death she felt a nostalgia for corporality. In part because she envied Laura-May her bliss with Earl, and in part because she itched to have a role in the drama that was rapidly unfolding around her.

In the kitchen an abruptly sobered Milton Cade was blabbering on the phone, trying to rouse some action from the people in Panhandle, while Laura-May, who had finished dressing, unlocked the bottom drawer of her dressing-table and rummaged for something. Sadie peered over the woman's shoulder to discover what the trophy was, and a thrill of recognition made her scalp tingle as her eyes alighted on her .38. So it was Laura-May who had found the gun; the whey-faced six-year-old who had been running up and down the walkway all that evening thirty years ago, playing games with herself and singing songs in the hot still air.

It delighted Sadie to see the murder-weapon again. Maybe, she thought I *have* left some sign of myself to help shape the future; maybe I *am* more than a headline on a yellowed newspaper, and a dimming memory in ageing heads. She watched with new and eager eyes as Laura-May slipped on some shoes and headed out into the bellowing storm.

Virginia sat slumped against the wall of Room Seven, and looked across at the seedy figure leaning on the door-lintel across from her. She had let the delusion she had conjured have what way it would with her; and never in her forty-odd years had she heard such depravity promised. But though the shadow had come at her again and again, pressing its cold body on to hers, its icy, slack mouth against her own, it had failed to carry one act of violation through. Three times it had tried; three times the urgent words whispered in her ear had not been realized. Now it guarded the door, preparing, she guessed, for a further assault. Its face was clear enough for her to read the bafflement and the shame in its features. It viewed her, she thought, with murder on its mind.

Outside, she heard her husband's voice above the din of the thunder, and Earl's voice too, raised in protest. There was a fierce argument going on, that much was apparent. She slid up the wall, trying to make out the words; the delusion watched her balefully.

'You failed,' she told it.

It didn't reply.

'You're just a dream of mine; and you failed.'

It opened its mouth and waggled its pallid tongue. She didn't understand why it hadn't evaporated; but perhaps it would tag along with her until the pills had worked their way through her system. No matter. She had endured the worst it could offer; now, given time, it would surely leave her be. Its failed rapes left it bereft of power over her.

She crossed towards the door, no longer afraid. It raised itself from its slouched posture.

'Where are you going?' it demanded.

'Out,' she said. 'To help Earl.'

'No,' it told her, 'I haven't finished with you.'

'You're just a phantom,' she retorted, 'You can't stop me.'

It offered up a grin that was three parts malice to one part charm. 'You're wrong, Virginia,' Buck said. There was no purpose in deceiving the woman any longer; he'd tired of that particular game. And perhaps he'd failed to get the old jazz going because she'd given herself to him so easily, believing he was some harmless nightmare. 'I'm no delusion, woman,' he said, *'I'm Buck Durning.'* She frowned at the wavering figure. Was this a new trick her psyche was playing? 'Thirty years ago I was shot dead in this very room. Just about where you're standing in fact.'

Instinctively, Virginia glanced down at the carpet at her feet, almost expecting the blood-stains to be still there.

'We came back tonight, Sadie and I,' the ghost went on. 'A one-night-stand at the Slaughterhouse of Love. That's what they called this place, did you know that? People used to come here from all over, just to peer in at this very room; just to see where Sadie Durning had shot her husband Buck. Sick people, Virginia, don't you think? More interested in murder than love. Not me . . . I've always liked love, you know? Almost the only thing I've ever had much of a talent for, in fact.'

'You lied to me,' she said. 'You *used* me.'

'I haven't finished yet,' Buck promised, 'In fact I've barely started.'

He moved from the door towards her, but she was prepared for him this time. As he touched her, and the smoke was made flesh again, she threw a blow towards him. Buck moved to avoid it, and she dodged past him towards the door. Her untied hair got in her eyes, but she virtually threw herself towards freedom. A cloudy hand snatched at her, but the grasp was too tenuous, and slipped.

'I'll be waiting,' Buck called after her as she stumbled across the walkway and into the storm, 'You hear me, bitch? *I'll be waiting!'*

He wasn't going to humiliate himself with a pursuit. She would have to come back, wouldn't she? And he, invisible to all but the woman, could afford to bide his time. If she told her companions what she'd seen, they'd call her crazy; maybe lock her up where he could have her all to himself. No, he had a winner here. She would return soaked to the skin, her dress clinging to her in a dozen fetching ways; panicky perhaps; tearful; too weak to resist

his overtures. They'd make music then. Oh yes. Until she begged
him to stop.

Sadie followed Laura-May out.

'Where are you going?' Milton asked his daughter, but she
didn't reply. 'Jesus!' he shouted after her, registering what he'd
seen. 'Where'd you get the goddamn gun?'

The rain was torrential; it beat on the ground, on the last leaves
of the cottonwood, on the roof, on the skull. It flattened Laura-
May's hair in seconds, pasting it to her forehead and neck.

'Earl?' she yelled. 'Where are you? *Earl?*' She began to run
across the lot, yelling his name as she went. The rain had turned
the dust to a deep brown mud; it slopped up against her shins.
She crossed to the other building. A number of guests, already
woken by Gyer's barrage, watched her from their windows.
Several doors were open; one man, standing on the walkway with
a beer in his hand, demanded to know what was going on. 'People
running around like crazies,' he said, 'All this yelling. 'We came
here for some privacy, for Christ's sake.' A girl – fully twenty
years his junior – emerged from the room behind the beer-drinker.
'She's got a gun, Dwayne,' she said. 'See that?'

'Where did they go?' Laura-May asked the beer-drinker.

'Who?' Dwayne replied.

'*The crazies!*' Laura-May yelled back, above another peel of
thunder.

'They went round the back of the office,' Dwayne said, his
eyes on the gun rather than Laura-May. 'They're not here. Really
they're not.'

Laura-May doubled back towards the office building. The rain
and lightning were blinding, and she had difficulty keeping her
balance in the swamp underfoot.

'Earl!' she called, 'Are you there?'

Sadie kept pace with her. The Cade woman had pluck, no
doubt of that, but there was an edge of hysteria in her voice
which Sadie didn't like too much. This kind of business (murder)
required detachment. The trick was to do it almost casually, as
you might flick on the radio, or swat a mosquito. Panic would
only cloud the issue; passion the same. Why, when she'd raised
that .38 and pointed it at Buck there'd been no anger to spoil her
aim, not a trace. In the final analysis, that was why they'd sent
her to the chair. Not for doing it, but for doing it too well.

Laura-May was not so cool. Her breath had become ragged,
and from the way she sobbed Earl's name as she ran it was clear

101

she was close to breaking-point. She rounded the back of the office building, where the motel sign threw a cold light on the waste ground, and this time, when she called for Earl, there *was* an answering cry. She stopped, peering through the veil of rain. It was Earl's voice, as she'd hoped, but he wasn't calling to her.

'Bastard!' he was yelling, 'you're out of your mind. Let me alone!'

Now she could make out two figures in the middle distance. Earl, his paunchy torso spattered and streaked with mud, was on his knees in amongst the soapweed and the scrub. Gyer stood over him, his hands on Earl's head, pressing it down towards the earth.

'Admit your crime, sinner!'

'Damn you, *no!*'

'You came to destroy my crusade. Admit it! Admit it!'

'Go to Hell!'

'Confess your complicity, or so help me I'll break every bone in your body!'

Earl fought to be free of Gyer, but the evangelist was easily the stronger of the two men.

'Pray!' he said, pressing Earl's face into the mud. 'Pray!'

'Go fuck yourself,' Earl shouted back.

Gyer dragged Earl's head up by the hair, his other hand raised to deliver a blow to the upturned face. But before he could strike, Laura-May entered the fray, taking three or four steps through the dirt towards them, the .38 held in her quaking hands.

'Get away from him,' she demanded.

Sadie calmly noted that the woman's aim was not all it could be. Even in clear weather she was probably no sharp-shooter: but here, under stress, in such a downpour, who but the most experienced marksman could guarantee the outcome? Gyer turned and looked at Laura-May. He showed not a flicker of apprehension. He's made the same calculation I've just made, Sadie thought; he knows damn well the odds are against him getting harmed.

'*The whore!*' Gyer announced, turning his eyes heavenward. 'Do you see her Lord? See her shame, her depravity? Mark her! She is one of the court of Babylon!'

Laura-May didn't quite comprehend the details, but the general thrust of Gyer's outburst was perfectly clear. 'I'm no whore!' she yelled back, the .38 almost leaping in her hand as if eager to be fired, 'Don't you *dare* call me a whore!'

'Please, Laura-May . . .' Earl said, wrestling with Gyer to get a look at the woman, '. . . get out of here. He's lost his mind.'

102

She ignored the imperative.

'If you don't let go of him . . .' she said, pointing the gun at the man in black.

'Yes?' Gyer taunted her, 'What will you do, *whore?*'

'I'll shoot! *I will!* I'll shoot.'

Over on the other side of the office building, Virginia spotted one of the pill bottles Gyer had thrown out into the mud. She stooped to pick it up, and then thought better of the idea. She didn't need pills any more, did she? She'd spoken to a dead man; her very touch had made Buck Durning visible to her. What a skill that was! Her visions were real, and always had been; more true than all the second-hand Revelations her pitiful husband could spout. What could pills do but befuddle this new-found talent? Let them lie.

A number of guests had now donned jackets and emerged from their rooms to see what the commotion was all about.

'Has there been an accident?' a woman called to Virginia. As the words left her lips, a shot sounded.

'John,' Virginia said.

Before the echoes of the shot had died she was making her way towards their source. She already pictured what she would find there: her husband laid flat on the ground; the triumphant assassin taking to his muddied heels. She picked up her pace, a prayer coming as she ran. She prayed not that the scenario she had imagined was wrong; but rather that God would forgive her for willing it to be true.

The scene she found on the other side of the building confounded all her expectations. The evangelist was not dead. He was standing, untouched. It was Earl who lay flat on the miry ground beside him. Close by stood the woman who'd come with the iced water, hours earlier; she had a gun in her hand. It still smoked. Even as Virginia's eyes settled on Laura-May a figure stepped through the rain and struck the weapon from the woman's hand. It fell to the ground. Virginia followed the descent. Laura-May looked startled; she clearly didn't understand how she'd come to drop the gun. Virginia knew, however. She could see the phantom, albeit fleetingly, and she guessed its identity. This was surely Sadie Durning, whose defiance had christened this establishment the Slaughterhouse of Love.

Laura-May's eyes found Earl; she let out a cry of horror, and ran towards him.

'Don't be dead, Earl. I beg you, don't be dead!'

103

Earl looked up from the mud bath he'd taken and shook his head.

'Missed me by a mile,' he said.

At his side, Gyer had fallen to his knees, hands clasped together, face up to the driving rain.

'Oh Lord, I thank you for preserving this your instrument, in his hour of need . . .'

Virginia shut out the idiot drivel. This was the man who had convinced her so deeply of her own deluded state that she'd given herself to Buck Durning. Well, *no more*. She'd been terrorized enough. She'd seen Sadie act upon the real world; she'd felt Buck do the same. The time was now ripe to reverse the procedure. She walked steadily across to where the .38 lay in the grass, and picked it up.

As she did so, she sensed the presence of Sadie Durning close by. A voice, so soft she barely heard it, said: 'Is this wise?' in her ear. Virginia didn't know the answer to that question. What *was* wisdom anyhow? Not the stale rhetoric of dead prophets, certainly. Maybe wisdom was Laura-May and Earl, embracing in the mud, careless of the prayers Gyer was spouting, or of the stares of the guests who'd come running out to see who'd died. Or perhaps wisdom was finding the canker in your life, and rooting it out once and for all. Gun in hand, she headed back towards Room Seven, aware that the benign presence of Sadie Durning walked at her side.

'Not Buck . . . ?' Sadie whispered, '. . . surely not.'

'He attacked me,' Virginia said.

'You poor lamb.'

'I'm no lamb,' Virginia replied. 'Not any more.'

Realizing that the woman was perfectly in charge of her destiny, Sadie hung back, fearful that her presence would alert Buck. She watched as Virginia crossed the lot, past the cottonwood tree, and stepped into the room where her tormentor had said he would be waiting. The lights still burned, bright after the blue darkness outside. There was no sign of Durning. Virginia crossed to the interconnecting door. Room Eight was deserted too. Then, the familiar voice:

'You came back,' Buck said.

She wheeled round, hiding the gun from him. He had emerged from the bathroom and was standing between her and the door.

'I knew you'd come back,' he said to her. 'They always do.'

'I want you to show yourself – ' Virginia said.

'I'm naked as a babe as it is,' said Buck, 'what do you want me to do: skin myself? Might be fun, at that.'

'Show yourself to John, my husband. Make him see his error.'

'Oh, poor John. I don't think he wants to see me, do you?'

'He thinks I'm insane.'

'Insanity can be very useful,' Buck smirked, 'they almost saved Sadie from Old Sparky on a plea of insanity. But she was too honest for her own good. She just kept telling them, over and over: "I wanted him dead. So I shot him." She never had much sense. But you . . . now, I think *you* know what's best for you.'

The shadowy form shifted. Virginia couldn't quite make out what Durning was doing with himself but it was unequivocally obscene.

'Come and get it, Virginia,' he said, 'grub's up.'

She took the .38 from behind her back and levelled it at him.

'Not this time,' she said.

'You can't do me any harm with that,' he replied, 'I'm already dead, remember?'

'*You hurt me*. Why shouldn't I be able to hurt you back?'

Buck shook his ethereal head, letting out a low laugh. As he was so engaged the wail of police sirens rose from down the highway.

'Well, what do you know?' Buck said, 'Such a fuss and commotion. We'd better get down to some jazzing, honey, before we get interrupted.'

'I warn you, this is Sadie's gun – '

'You wouldn't hurt me,' Buck murmured, 'I know you women. You say one thing and you mean the opposite.'

He stepped towards her, laughing.

'Don't,' she warned.

He took another step, and she pulled the trigger. In the instant before she heard the sound, and felt the gun leap in her hand, she saw John appear in the doorway. Had he been there all along, or was he coming in out of the rain, prayers done, to read Revelations to his erring wife? She would never know. The bullet sliced through Buck, dividing the smoky body as it went, and sped with perfect accuracy towards the evangelist. He didn't see it coming. It struck him in the throat, and blood came quickly, splashing down his shirt. Buck's form dissolved like so much dust, and he was gone. Suddenly there was nothing in Room Seven but Virginia, her dying husband and the sound of the rain.

John Gyer frowned at Virginia, then reached out for the door frame to support his considerable bulk. He failed to secure it, and fell backwards out of the door like a toppled statue, his face washed by the rain. The blood did not stop coming however. It poured out in gleeful spurts; and it was still pumping when Alvin Baker and his Deputy arrived outside the room, guns at the ready.

Now her husband would never know, she thought: that was the pity of it. He could never now be made to concede his stupidity, and recant his arrogance. Not this side of the grave, anyhow. He was *safe*, damn him, and she was left with a smoking gun in her hand and God alone knew what price to pay.

'Put down the gun and come out of there!' The voice from the lot sounded harsh and uncompromising.

Virginia didn't answer.

'You hear me, in there? This is Sheriff Baker. The place is surrounded, so come on out, or you're dead.'

Virginia sat on the bed and weighed up the alternatives. They wouldn't execute her for what she'd done, the way they had Sadie. But she'd be in prison for a long time, and she was tired of regimes. If she wasn't mad now, incarceration would push her to the brink and over. Better to finish here, she thought. She put the warm .38 under her chin, tilting it to make sure the shot would take off the top of her skull.

'Is that wise?' Sadie inquired, as Virginia's finger tightened.

'They'll lock me away,' she replied, 'I couldn't face that.'

'True,' said Sadie. 'They'll put you behind bars for a while. But it won't be for long.'

'You must be joking. I just shot my husband in cold blood.'

'You didn't mean to,' Sadie said brightly, 'you were aiming at Buck.'

'Was I? Virginia said. 'I wonder.'

'You can plead insanity, the way I should have done. Just make up the most outrageous story you can, and stick to it.' Virginia shook her head; she'd never been much of a liar. 'And when you're set free,' Sadie went on, 'you'll be notorious. That's worth living for, isn't it?'

Virginia hadn't thought of that. The ghost of a smile illuminated her face. From outside, Sheriff Baker repeated his demand that she throw her weapon through the door and come out with her hands high.

'You've got ten seconds, lady,' he said, 'and I mean *ten*.'

'I can't face the humiliation,' Virginia murmured. 'I *can't*.'

Sadie shrugged. 'Pity,' she said. 'The rain's clearing. There's a moon.'

'A moon? Really?'

Baker had started counting.

'You have to make up your mind,' Sadie said. 'They'll shoot you given half the chance. And gladly.'

Baker had reached eight. Virginia stood up.

'*Stop*,' she called through the door.

Baker stopped counting. Virginia threw out the gun. It landed in the mud.

'Good,' said Sadie, 'I'm so pleased.'

'I can't go alone,' Virginia replied.

'No need.'

A sizeable audience had gathered in the lot; Earl and Laura-May of course; Milton Cade, Dwayne and his girl, Sheriff Baker and his Deputy, an assortment of motel guests. They stood in respectful silence, staring at Virginia Gyer with mingled expressions of bewilderment and awe.

'Put your hands up where I can see them!' Baker said.

Virginia did as she was instructed.

'Look,' said Sadie, pointing.

The moon was up, wide and white.

'Why'd you kill him?' Dwayne's girl asked.

'The Devil made me do it,' Virginia replied, gazing up at the moon and putting on the craziest smile she could muster.

Down, Satan!

Circumstances had made Gregorius rich beyond all calculation. He owned fleets and palaces; stallions; cities. Indeed he owned so much that to those who were finally charged with enumerating his possessions – when the events of this story reached their monstrous conclusion – it sometimes seemed it might be quicker to list the items Gregorius did *not* own.

Rich he was; but far from happy. He had been raised a Catholic, and in his early years – before his dizzying rise to fortune – he'd found succour in his faith. But he'd neglected it, and it was only at the age of fifty-five, with the world at his feet, that he woke one night and found himself Godless.

It was a bitter blow, but he immediately took steps to make good his loss. He went to Rome, and spoke with the Supreme Pontiff; he prayed night and day; he founded seminaries and leper-colonies. God, however, declined to show so much as His toe-nail. Gregorius, it seemed, was forsaken.

Almost despairing, he took it into his head that he could only win his way back into the arms of his Maker if he put his soul into the direst jeopardy. The notion had some merit. Suppose, he thought, I could contrive a meeting with Satan, the Arch-Fiend; seeing me *in extremis* would God not be obliged to step in and deliver me back into the fold?

It was a fine plot, but how was he to realise it? The Devil did not just come at a call, even for a tycoon such as Gregorius, and his researches soon proved that all the traditional methods of summoning the Lord of Vermin – the defiling of the Blessed Sacrament, the sacrificing of babes – were no more effective than his good works had been at provoking Yahweh. It was only after a year of deliberation that he finally fell upon his master-plan. He would arrange to have built a Hell on Earth – a modern inferno so monstrous that the Tempter would be tempted, and come to roost there like a cuckoo in a usurped nest.

He searched high and low for an architect, and found, languishing in a mad-house outside Florence, a man called Leopardo, whose plans for Mussolini's palaces had a lunatic grandeur that suited Gregorius' project perfectly. Leopardo was taken from his cell – a foetid, wretched old man – and given his dreams again. His genius for the prodigious had not deserted him.

In order to fuel his invention the great libraries of the world were scoured for descriptions of Hells both secular and metaphysical; museum vaults were ransacked for forbidden images of martyrdom. No stone was left unturned if it was suspected something perverse was concealed beneath.

The finished designs owed something to de Sade and to Dante, and something more to Freud and Kraft-Ebbing, but there was also much there that no mind had conceived of before, or at least ever dared set to paper.

A site in North Africa was chosen, and work on Gregorius's New Hell began. Everything about the project broke the records. Its foundations were vaster, its walls thicker, its plumbing more elaborate than any edifice hitherto attempted. Gregorius watched its slow construction with an enthusiasm he had not tasted since his first years as an empire-builder. Needless to say, he was widely thought to have lost his mind. Friends he had known for years refused to associate with him; several of his companies collapsed when investors took fright at reports of his insanity. He didn't care. His plan could not fail. The Devil would be bound to come, if only out of curiosity to see this Leviathan built in his name, and when he did Gregorius would be waiting.

The work took four years, and the better part of Gregorius' furtune. The finished building was the size of half a dozen cathedrals, and boasted every facility the Angel of the Pit could desire. Fires burned behind its walls, so that to walk in many of its corridors was almost unendurable agony. The rooms off those corridors were fitted with every imaginable device of persecution – the needle, the rack, the dark – that the genius of Satan's torturers be given fair employ. There were ovens large enough to cremate families; pools deep enough to drown generations. The New Hell was an atrocity waiting to happen; a celebration of inhumanity that only lacked its first cause.

The builders withdrew, and thankfully. It was rumoured amongst them that Satan had long been watching over the construction of his pleasure-dome. Some even claimed to have glimpsed him on the deeper levels, where the chill was so profound it froze the piss in your bladder. There was some evidence to support the belief in supernatural presences converging on the building as it neared completion, not least the cruel death of Leopardo, who had either thrown himself – or, the superstitious argued – been pitched, *through* his sixth-storey hotel window. He was buried with due extravagance.

So now, alone in Hell, Gregorius waited.

He did not have to wait long. He had been there a day, no more, when he heard noises from the lower depths. Anticipation brimming, he went in search of their source, but found only the roiling of excrement baths, and the rattling of ovens. He returned to his suite of chambers on the ninth level, and waited. The noises came again; again he went in search of their source; again he came away disappointed.

The disturbances did not abate, however. In the days that followed scarcely ten minutes would pass without his hearing some sound of occupancy. The Prince of Darkness was here, Gregorius could have no doubt of it, but he was keeping to the shadows. Gregorius was content to play along. It was the Devil's party, after all. His to play whatever game he chose.

But, during the long and often lonely months that followed, Gregorius wearied of this hide-and-seek, and began to demand that Satan show himself. His voice rang unanswered down the deserted corridors however, until his throat was bruised with shouting. Thereafter he went about his searches stealthily, hoping to catch his tenant unawares. But the Apostate Angel always flitted away before Gregorius could step within sight of him.

They would play a wasting-game, it seemed, he and Satan, chasing each other's tails through ice and fire and ice again. Gregorius told himself to be patient. The Devil had come, hadn't he? Wasn't that his finger-dab on the door-handle?; his turd on the stairs? Sooner or later the Fiend would show his face, and Gregorius would spit on it.

The world outside went on its way, and Gregorius was consigned to the company of other recluses who had been ruined by wealth. His Folly, as it was known, was not entirely without visitors, however. There were a few who had loved him too much to forget him – a few, also, who had profitted by him, and hoped to turn his madness to their further profit – who dared the gates of the New Hell. These visitors made the journey without announcing their intentions, fearing the disapproval of their friends. The investigations into their subsequent disappearance never reached as far as North Africa.

And in his Folly, Gregorius still chased the Serpent, and the Serpent still eluded him, leaving only more and more terrible signs of his occupancy as the months went by.

* * *

It was the wife of one of the missing visitors who finally discovered the truth, and alerted the authorities. Gregorius' Folly was put under surveillance, and finally – some three years after its completion – a quartet of officers braved the threshold.

Without maintenance, the Folly had begun to deteriorate badly. The lights had failed on many of the levels; its walls had cooled,; its pitch-pits solidified. But as the officers advanced through the gloomy vaults in seach of Gregorius, they came upon ample evidence that despite its decrepit condition the New Hell was in good working order. There were bodies in the ovens, their faces wide and black; there were human remains seated and strung up in many of the rooms, gouged and pricked and slit to death.

Their terror grew with every door they pressed open, every new abomination their fevered eyes fell upon.

Two of the four who crossed the threshold never reached the chamber at its centre. Terror overtook them on their way, and they fled, only to be waylaid in some choked passageway and added to the hundreds who had perished in the Folly since Satan had taken residence.

Of the pair who finally unearthed the perpetrator, only one had courage enough to tell his story, though the scenes he faced there in the Folly's heart were almost too terrible to bear relating.

There was no sign of Satan, of course. There was only Gregorius. The master-builder, finding no-one to inhabit the house he had sweated over, had occupied it himself. He had with him a few disciples whom he'd mustered over the years. They, like him, seemed unremarkable creatures. But there was not a torture-device in the building they had not made thorough and merciless use of.

Gregorius did not resist his arrest; indeed he seemed pleased to have a platform from which to boast of his butcheries. Then, and later at his trial, he spoke freely of his ambition and his appetite; and of how much *more* blood he would spill if they would only set him free to do so. Enough to drown all belief and its delusions, he swore. And still he would not be satisfied. For God was rotting in Paradise, and Satan in the Abyss, and who was to stop him?

He was much reviled during the trial, and later in the asylum where, under some suspicious circumstances, he died barely two months later. The Vatican expunged all report of him from its records; the seminaries founded in his unholy name were dissolved.

But there were those, even amongst the Cardinals, who could not put his unrepentant malice out of their heads, and – in the privacy of their doubt – wondered if he had not succeeded in his

111

strategy. If, in giving up all hope of angels – fallen or otherwise –
he had not become one himself.

Or all that earth could bear of such phenomena.

The Age of Desire

The burning man propelled himself down the steps of the Hume Laboratories as the police car – summoned, he presumed, by the alarm either Welles or Dance had set off upstairs – appeared at the gate and swung up the driveway. As he ran from the door the car screeched up to the steps and discharged its human cargo. He waited in the shadows, too exhausted by terror to run any further, certain that they would see him. But they disappeared through the swing doors without so much as a glance towards his torment. Am I on fire at all? he wondered. Was this horrifying spectacle – his flesh baptized with a polished flame that seared but failed to consume – simply an hallucination, for his eyes and his eyes only? If so, perhaps all that he had suffered up in the laboratory had also been delirium. Perhaps he had not truly committed the crimes he had fled from, the heat in his flesh licking him into ecstasies.

He looked down his body. His exposed skin still crawled with livid dots of fire, but one by one they were being extinguished. He was going out, he realized, like a neglected bonfire. The sensations that had suffused him – so intense and so demanding that they had been as like pain as pleasure – were finally deserting his nerve-endings, leaving a numbness for which he was grateful. His body, now appearing from beneath the veil of fire, was in a sorry condition. His skin was a panic-map of scratches, his clothes torn to shreds, his hands sticky with coagulating blood; blood, he knew, that was not his own. There was no avoiding the bitter truth. He *had* done all he had imagined doing. Even now the officers would be staring down at his atrocious handiwork.

He crept away from his niche beside the door and down the driveway, keeping a lookout for the return of the two policemen; neither reappeared. The street beyond the gate was deserted. He started to run. He had managed only a few paces when the alarm in the building behind him was abruptly cut off. For several seconds his ears rang in sympathy with the silenced bell. Then, eerily, he began to hear the sound of heat – the surreptitious murmuring of embers – distant enough that he didn't panic, yet close as his heartbeat.

He limped on, to put as much distance as he could between

him and his felonies before they were discovered; but however fast he ran, the heat went with him, safe in some backwater of his gut, threatening with every desperate step he took to ignite him afresh.

It took Dooley several seconds to identify the cacophony he was hearing from the upper floor now that McBride had hushed the alarm bell. It was the high-pitched chattering of monkeys, and it came from one of the many rooms down the corridor to his right.

'Virgil,' he called down the stairwell. 'Get up here.'

Not waiting for his partner to join him, Dooley headed off towards the source of the din. Half-way along the corridor the smell of static and new carpeting gave way to a more pungent combination: urine, disinfectant and rotting fruit. Dooley slowed his advance: he didn't like the smell, any more than he liked the hysteria in the babble of monkey-voices. But McBride was slow in answering his call, and after a short hesitation, Dooley's curiosity got the better of his disquiet. Hand on truncheon, he approached the open door and stepped in. His appearance sparked off another wave of frenzy from the animals, a dozen or so rhesus monkeys. They threw themselves around in their cages, somersaulting, screeching and berating the wiremesh. Their excitement was infectious. Dooley could feel the sweat begin to squeeze from his pores.

'Is there anybody here?' he called out.

The only reply came from the prisoners: more hysteria, more cage-rattling. He stared across the room at them. They stared back, their teeth bared in fear or welcome; Dooley didn't know which, nor did he wish to test their intentions. He kept well clear of the bench on which the cages were lined up as he began a perfunctory search of the laboratory.

'I wondered what the hell the smell was,' McBride said, appearing at the door.

'Just animals,' Dooley replied.

'Don't they ever wash? Filthy buggars.'

'Anything downstairs?'

'Nope,' McBride said, crossing to the cages. The monkeys met his advance with more gymnastics. 'Just the alarm.'

'Nothing up here either,' Dooley said. He was about to add, *'Don't do that,'* to prevent his partner putting his finger to the mesh, but before the words were out one of the animals seized the proffered digit and bit it. McBride wrested his finger free and threw a blow back against the mesh in retaliation. Squealing its anger, the occupant flung its scrawny body about in a lunatic

114

fandango that threatened to pitch cage and monkey alike on to the floor.

'You'll need a tetanus shot for that,' Dooley commented.

'Shit!' said McBridge, 'what's wrong with the little bastard anyhow?'

'Maybe they don't like strangers.'

'They're out of their tiny minds.' McBride sucked ruminatively on his finger, then spat. 'I mean, look at them.'

Dooley didn't answer.

'I said, *look* . . .' McBride repeated.

Very quietly, Dooley said: 'Over here.'

'What is it?'

'Just come over here.'

McBride drew his gaze from the row of cages and across the cluttered work-surfaces to where Dooley was staring at the ground, the look on his face one of fascinated revulsion. McBride neglected his finger-sucking and threaded his way amongst the benches and stools to where his partner stood.

'Under there,' Dooley murmured.

On the scuffed floor at Dooley's feet was a woman's beige shoe; beneath the bench was the shoe's owner. To judge by her cramped position she had either been secreted there by the miscreant or dragged herself out of sight and died in hiding.

'Is she dead?' McBride asked.

'Look at her, for Christ's sake,' Dooley replied, 'she's been torn open.'

'We've got to check for vital signs,' McBride reminded him. Dooley made no move to comply, so McBride squatted down in front of the victim and checked for a pulse at her ravaged neck. There was none. Her skin was still warm beneath his fingers however. A gloss of saliva on her cheek had not yet dried.

Dooley, calling his report through, looked down at the deceased. The worst of her wounds, on the upper torso, were masked by McBride's crouching body. All he could see was a fall of auburn hair and her legs, one foot shoeless, protruding from her hiding place. They were beautiful legs, he thought; he might have whistled after such legs, once upon a time.

'She's a Doctor or a technician,' McBride said, 'she's wearing a lab coat.' Or she had been. In fact the coat had been ripped open, as had the layers of clothing beneath, and then, as if to complete the exhibition, the skin and muscle beneath that. McBride peered into her chest; the sternum had been snapped and the heart teased from its seat, as if her killer had wanted to take it as a keepsake

115

and been interrupted in the act. He perused her without squeamishness; he had always prided himself on his strong stomach.

'Are you satisfied she's dead?'

'Never saw deader.'

'Carnegie's coming down,' Dooley said, crossing to one of the sinks. Careless of fingerprints, he turned on the tap and splashed a handful of cold water on to his face. When he looked up from his ablutions McBride had left off his tête-à-tête with the corpse and was walking down the laboratory towards a bank of machinery.

'What do they do here, for Christ's sake?' he remarked. 'Look at all this stuff.'

'Some kind of research faculty,' Dooley said.

'What do they research?'

'How the hell do I know?' Dooley snapped. The ceaseless chatterings of the monkeys and the proximity of the dead woman, made him want to desert the place. 'Let's leave it be, huh?'

McBride ignored Dooley's request; equipment fascinated him. He stared entranced at the encephalograph and electrocardiograph; at the print-out units still disgorging yards of blank paper on to the floor; at the video display monitors and the consoles. The scene brought the *Marie Celeste* to his mind. This deserted ship of science – still humming some tuneless song to itself as it sailed on, though there was neither Captain nor crew left behind to attend upon it.

Beyond the wall of equipment was a window, no more than a yard square. McBride had assumed it let on to the exterior of the building, but now that he looked more closely he realized it did not. A test-chamber lay beyond the banked units.

'Dooley . . . ?' he said, glancing round. The man had gone, however, down to meet Carnegie presumably. Content to be left to his exploration, McBride returned his attention to the window. There was no light on inside. Curious, he walked around the back of the banked equipment, until he found the chamber door. It was ajar. Without hesitation, he stepped through.

Most of the light through the window was blocked by the instruments on the other side; the interior was dark. It took McBride's eyes a few seconds to get a true impression of the chaos the chamber contained: the overturned table; the chair of which somebody had made matchwood; the tangle of cables and demolished equipment – cameras, perhaps, to monitor proceedings in the chamber? – clusters of lights which had been similarly smashed. No professional vandal could have made a more thorough job of breaking up the chamber than had been made.

There was a smell in the air which McBride recognized but,

116

irritatingly, couldn't place. He stood still, tantalised by the scent. The sound of sirens rose from down the corridor outside; Carnegie would be here in moments. Suddenly, the smell's association came to him. In was the same scent that twitched in his nostrils when, after making love to Jessica and – as was his ritual – washing himself, he returned from the bathroom to bedroom. It was the smell of sex. He smiled.

His face was still registering pleasure when a heavy object sliced through the air and met his nose. He felt the cartilage give, and a rush of blood come. He took two or three giddy steps backwards, thereby avoiding the subsequent slice, but lost his footing in the disarray. He fell awkwardly in a litter of glass-shards, and looked up to see his assailant, wielding a metal bar, moving towards him. The man's face resembled one of the monkeys: the same yellowed teeth, the same rabid eyes. '*No!*' the man shouted, as he brought his makeshift club down on McBride, who managed to ward off the blow with his arm, snatching at the weapon in so doing. The attack had taken him unawares but now, with the pain in his mashed nose to add fury to his response, he was more than the equal of the aggressor. He plucked the club from the man, sweets from a babe, and leapt, roaring, to his feet. Any precepts he might once have been taught about arrest techniques had fled from his mind. He lay a hail of blows on the man's head and shoulders, forcing him backwards across the chamber. The man cowered beneath the assault, and eventually slumped, whimpering, against the wall. Only now, with his antagonist abused to the verge of unconsciousness, did McBride's furore falter. He stood in the middle of the chamber, gasping for breath, and watched the beaten man slip down the wall. He had made a profound error. The assailant, he now realized, was dressed in a white laboratory coat; he was, as Dooley was irritatingly fond of saying, on the side of the angels.

'Damn,' said McBride, 'shit, hell and damn.'

The man's eyes flickered open, and he gazed up at McBride. His grasp on consciousness was evidently tenuous, but a look of recognition crossed his wide-browed, sombre face. Or rather, recognition's absence.

'You're not him,' he murmured.

'Who?' said McBride, realizing he might yet salvage his reputation from this fiasco if he could squeeze a clue from the witness. 'Who did you think I was?'

The man opened his mouth, but no words emerged. Eager to hear the testimony, McBride crouched beside him and said: 'Who did you think you were attacking?'

117

Again the mouth opened; again no audible words emerged. McBride pressed his suit. 'It's important,' he said, 'just tell me who was here.'

The man strove to voice his reply. McBride pressed his ear to the trembling mouth.

'In a pig's eye,' the man said, then passed out, leaving McBride to curse his father, who'd bequeathed him a temper he was afraid he would probably live to regret. But then, what was living for?

Inspector Carnegie was used to boredom. For every rare moment of genuine discovery his professional life had furnished him with, he had endured hour upon hour of waiting. For bodies to be photographed and examined, for lawyers to be bargained with and suspects intimidated. He had long ago given up attempting to fight this tide of *ennui* and, after his fashion, had learned the art of going with the flow. The processes of investigation could not be hurried; the wise man, he had come to appreciate, let the pathologists, the lawyers and all their tribes have their tardy way. All that mattered, in the fullness of time, was that the finger be pointed and that the guilty quake.

Now, with the clock on the laboratory wall reading twelve fifty-three a.m., and even the monkeys hushed in their cages, he sat at one of the benches and waited for Hendrix to finish his calculations. The surgeon consulted the thermometer, then stripped off his gloves like a second skin and threw them down on to the sheet on which the deceased lay. 'It's always difficult,' the Doctor said, 'fixing time of death. She's lost less than three degrees. I'd say she'd been dead under two hours.'

'The officers arrived at a quarter to twelve,' Carnegie said, 'so she died maybe half an hour before that?'

'Something of that order.'

'Was she put in there?' he asked, indicating the place beneath the bench.

'Oh certainly. There's no way she hid herself away. Not with those injuries. They're quite something, aren't they?'

Carnegie stared at Hendrix. The man had presumably seen hundreds of corpses, in every conceivable condition, but the enthusiasm in his pinched features was unqualified. Carnegie found that mystery more fascinating in its way than that of the dead woman and her slaughterer. How could anyone possibly enjoy taking the rectal temperature of a corpse?; it confounded him. But the pleasure was there, gleaming in the man's eyes.

'Motive?' Carnegie asked.

'Pretty explicit, isn't it? Rape. There's been very thorough

118

molestation; contusions around the vagina; copious semen deposits. Plenty to work with.'

'And the wounds on her torso?'

'Ragged. Tears more than cuts.'

'Weapon?'

'Don't know.' Hendrix made an inverted U of his mouth. 'I mean, the flesh has been *mauled*. If it weren't for the rape evidence I'd be tempted to suggest an animal.'

'Dog, you mean?'

'I was thinking more of a tiger,' Hendrix said.

Carnegie frowned. 'Tiger?'

'Joke,' Hendrix replied, 'I was making a joke, Carnegie. My Christ, do you have *any* sense of irony?'

'This isn't funny,' Carnegie said.

'I'm not laughing,' Hendrix replied, with a sour look.

'The man McBride found in the test-chamber?'

'What about him?'

'Suspect?'

'Not in a thousand years. We're looking for a *maniac*, Carnegie. Big; strong. Wild.'

'And the wounding? Before or after?'

Hendrix scowled. 'I don't know. Post-mortem will give us more. But for what it's worth, I think our man was in a frenzy. I'd say the wounding and the rape were probably simultaneous.'

Carnegie's normally phlegmatic features registered something close to shock. 'Simultaneous?'

Hendrix shrugged. 'Lust's a funny thing,' he said.

'Hilarious,' came the appalled reply.

As was his wont, Carnegie had his driver deposit him half a mile from his doorstep to allow him a head-clearing walk before home, hot chocolate and slumber. The ritual was observed religiously, even when the Inspector was dog-tired. He used to stroll to wind down before stepping over the threshold; long experience had taught him that taking his professional concerns into the house assisted neither the investigation nor his domestic life. He had learned the lesson too late to keep his wife from leaving him and his children from estrangement, but he applied the principle still.

Tonight, he walked slowly, to allow the distressing scenes the evening had brought to recede somewhat. The route took him past a small cinema which, he had read in the local press, was soon to be demolished. He was not surprised. Though he was no cineaste the fare the flea-pit provided had degenerated in recent years. The week's offering was a case in point: a double-bill of

119

horror movies. Lurid and derivative stuff to judge by the posters, with their crude graphics and their unashamed hyperbole. '*You May Never Sleep Again!*' one of the hook-lines read; and beneath it a woman – very much awake – cowered in the shadow of a two-headed man. What trivial images the populists conjured to stir some fear in their audiences. The walking dead; nature grown vast, and rampant in a miniature world; blood-eaters, omens, fire-walkers, thunderstorms and all the other foolishness the public cowered before. It was all so laughably trite: amongst that catalogue of penny dreadfuls there wasn't one that equalled the banality of human appetite, which horror (or the consequences of same) he saw every week of his working life. Thinking of it, his mind thumbed through a dozen snapshots: the dead by torchlight, face down and thrashed to oblivion; and the living too, meeting his mind's eye with hunger in theirs: for sex, for narcotics, for others' pain. Why didn't they put *that* on the posters?

As he reached his home a child squealed in the shadows beside his garage; the cry stopped him in his tracks. It came again, and this time he recognized it for what it was. No child at all, but a cat, or cats, exchanging love-calls in the darkened passageway. He went to the place to shoo them off. Their venereal secretions made the passage stink. He didn't need to yell; his footfall was sufficient to scare them away. They darted in all directions, not two, but half a dozen of them: a veritable orgy had been underway apparently. He had arrived on the spot too late however; the stench of their seductions was overpowering.

Carnegie looked blankly at the elaborate set-up of monitors and video-recorders that dominated his office.

'What in Christ's name is this about?' he wanted to know.

'The video tapes,' said Boyle, his number two, 'from the laboratory. I think you ought to have a look at them. Sir.'

Though they had worked in tandem for seven months, Boyle was not one of Carnegie's favourite officers; you could practically smell the ambition off his smooth hide. In someone half his age again such greed would have been objectionable; in a man of thirty it verged on the obscene. This present display – the mustering of equipment ready to confront Carnegie when he walked in at eight in the morning – was just Boyle's style: flashy and redundant.

'Why so many screens?' Carnegie asked acidly. 'Do I get it in stereo too?'

'They had three cameras running simultaneously, sir. Covering the experiment from several angles.'

'*What* experiment?'

Boyle gestured for his superior to sit down. Obsequious to a fault aren't you?, thought Carnegie; much good it'll do you.

'Right,' Boyle instructed the technician at the recorders, 'roll the tapes.'

Carnegie sipped at the cup of hot chocolate he had brought in with him. The beverage was a weakness of his, verging on addiction. On the days when the machine supplying it broke down he was an unhappy man indeed. He looked at the three screens. Suddenly, a title.

'*Project Blind Boy*', the words read, '*Restricted*'.

'*Blind Boy?*' said Carnegie. 'What, or *who*, is that?'

'It's obviously a code word of some kind,' Boyle said.

'*Blind Boy. Blind Boy.*' Carnegie repeated the phrase as if to beat it into submission, but before he could solve the problem the images on the three monitors diverged. They pictured the same subject – a bespectacled male in his late twenties sitting in a chair – but each showed the scene from a different angle. One took in the subject full length, and in profile; the second was a three-quarter medium-shot, angled from above, the third a straight forward close up of the subject's head and shoulders, shot through the glass of the test-chamber, and from the front. The three images were in black and white, and none were completely centred or focused. Indeed, as the tapes began to run somebody was still adjusting such technicalities. A backwash of informal chatter ran between the subject and the woman – recognizable even in brief glimpses as the deceased – who was applying electrodes to his forehead. Much of the talk between them was difficult to catch; the acoustics in the chamber frustrated microphone and listener alike.

'The woman's Doctor Dance,' Boyle offered. 'The victim.'

'Yes,' said Carnegie, watching the screens intently, 'I recognize her. How long does this preparation go on for?'

'Quite a while. Most of it's unedifying.'

'Well, get to the edifying stuff, then.'

'Fast forward,' Boyle said. The technician obliged, and the actors on the three screens became squeaking comedians. 'Wait!' said Boyle. 'Back up a short way.' Again, the technician did as instructed. 'There!' said Boyle. 'Stop there. Now run on at normal speed.' The action settled back to its natural pace. 'This is where it really begins, sir.'

Carnegie had come to the end of his hot chocolate; he put his finger into the soft sludge at the bottom of the cup, delivering the sickly-sweet dregs to his tongue. On the screens Doctor Dance had approached the subject with a syringe, was now swabbing the crook of his elbow, and injecting him. Not for the first time since his visit to the Hume Laboratories did Carnegie wonder precisely what they did at the establishment. Was this kind of procedure *de riguer* in pharmaceutical research?; the implicit secrecy of the experiment – late at night in an otherwise deserted building – suggested not. And there was that imperative on the title-card – '*Restricted*'. What they were watching had clearly never been intended for public viewing.

'Are you comfortable?' a man, off camera, now enquired. The subject nodded. His glasses had been removed, and he looked slightly bemused without them. An unremarkable face, thought Carnegie; the subject – as yet unnamed – was neither Adonis nor Quasimodo. He was receding slightly, and his wispy, dirty-blonde hair touched his shoulders.

'I'm fine, Doctor Welles,' he replied to the off-camera questioner.

'You don't feel hot at all? Sweaty?'

'Not really,' the guinea-pig replied, slightly apologetically. 'I feel ordinary.'

That you are, Carnegie thought; then to Boyle: 'Have you been through the tapes to the end?'

'No, sir,' Boyle replied. 'I thought you'd want to see them first. I only ran them as far as the injection.'

'Any word from the hospital on Doctor Welles?'

'At the last call he was still comatose.'

Carnegie grunted, and returned his attention to the screens. Following the burst of action with the injection, the tapes now settled into non-activity: the three cameras fixed on their short-sighted subject with beady stares, the torpor occasionally interrupted by an enquiry from Welles as to the subject's condition. It remained the same. After three or four minutes of this eventless study even his occasional blinks began to assume major dramatic significance.

'Don't think much of the plot,' the technician commented. Carnegie laughed; Boyle looked discomforted. Two or three more minutes passed in a similar manner.

'This doesn't look too hopeful,' Carnegie said. 'Run through it at speed, will you?'

The technician was about to obey when Boyle said: '*Wait*.'

Carnegie glanced across at the man, irritated by his intervention, and then back at the screens. Something *was* happening: a subtle transformation had overtaken the insipid features of the subject. He had begun to smile to himself, and was sinking down in his chair as if submerging his gangling body in a warm bath. His eyes, which had so far expressed little but affable indifference, now began to flicker closed, and then, once closed, opened again. When they did so there was a quality in them not previously visible: a hunger that seemed to reach out from the screen and into the calm of the Inspector's office.

Carnegie put down his chocolate cup and approached the screens. As he did so the subject also got up out of his chair and walked towards the glass of the chamber, leaving two of the cameras' ranges. The third still recorded him however, as he pressed his face against the window, and for a moment the two men faced each other through layers of glass and time, seemingly meeting each other's gaze.

The look on the man's face was critical now, the hunger was rapidly outgrowing sane control. Eyes burning, he laid his lips against the chamber window and kissed it, his tongue working against the glass.

'What in Christ's name is going on?' Carnegie said.

A prattle of voices had begun on the soundtrack; Doctor Welles was vainly asking the testee to articulate his feelings, while Dance called off figures from the various monitoring instruments. It was difficult to hear much clearly – the din was further supplemented by an eruption of chatter from the caged monkeys – but it was evident that the readings coming through from the man's body were escalating. His face was flushed; his skin gleamed with a sudden sweat. He resembled a martyr with the tinder at his feet freshly lit; wild with a fatal ecstasy. He stopped french-kissing the window, tearing off the electrodes at his temples and the sensors from his arms and chest. Dance, her voice now registering alarm, called out for him to stop. Then she moved across the camera's view and out again; crossing, Carnegie presumed, to the chamber door.

'Better not,' he said, as if this drama were 300yed out at his behest, and at a whim he could prevent the tragedy. But the woman took no notice. A moment later she appeared in long shot as she stepped into the chamber. The man moved to greet her, throwing over equipment as he did so. She called out to him – his name, perhaps. If so, it was inaudible over the monkeys' hulla-baloo. 'Shit,' said Carnegie, as the testee's flailing arms caught first the profile camera, and then the three-quarter medium-shot: two of the three monitors went dead. Only the head-on shot, the camera safe outside the chamber, still recorded events, but the tightness of the shot precluded more than an occasional glimpse of a moving body. Instead, the camera's sober eye gazed on, almost ironically, at the saliva smeared glass of the chamber window, blind to the atrocities being committed a few feet out of range.

'What in Christ's name did they give him?' Carnegie said, as, somewhere off-camera, the woman's screams rose over the screeching of the apes.

Jerome woke in the early afternoon, feeling hungry and sore. When he threw the sheet off his body he was appalled at his state: his torso was scored with scratches, and his groin region was red-raw. Wincing, he moved to the edge of the bed and sat there for a while, trying to piece the previous evening back together again. He remembered going to the Laboratories, but very little after that. He had been a paid guinea-pig for several months, giving of his blood, comfort and patience to supplement his meagre earnings as a translator. The arrangement had begun courtesy of a friend who did similar work, but whereas Figley had been part of the Laboratories' mainstream programme, Jerome had been approached, after one week at the place, by Doctors Welles and Dance, who had invited him – subject to a series of psychological tests – to work exclusively for them. It had been made clear from the outset that their project (he had never even been told its purpose) was of a secret nature, and that they would demand his total dedication and discretion. He had needed the funds, and the recompense they offered was marginally better than that paid by the Laboratories, so he had agreed, although the hours they had demanded of him were unsociable. For several weeks now he had been required to attend the Research facility late at night and often working into the small hours of the morning as he endured Welles' interminable questions about his private life, and Dance's glassy stare.

Thinking of her cold look, he felt a tremor in him. Was it because once he had fooled himself that she had looked upon him more fondly than a doctor need?; such self-deception, he chided himself, was pitiful. He was not the stuff of which women dreamt, and each day he walked the streets reinforced that conviction. He could not remember one occasion in his adult life when a woman had looked his way, and kept looking; a time when an appreciative glance of his had been returned. Why this should bother him now, he wasn't certain: his loveless condition, was, he knew, commonplace. And Nature had been kind; knowing, it seemed, that the gift of allurement had passed him by, it had seen fit to minimize his libido. Weeks passed without his conscious thoughts mourning his enforced chastity.

Once in a while, when he heard the pipes roar, he might wonder what Mrs Morrisey, his landlady, looked like in her bath: might imagine the firmness of her soapy breasts, or the dark divide of her rump as she stooped to put talcum powder between her toes. But such torments were, blissfully, infrequent. And when his cup brimmed he would pocket the money he had saved from his sessions at the Laboratories, and buy an hour's companionship from a woman called Angela (he'd never learned her second name) in Greek Street.

It would be several weeks before he did so again, he thought: whatever he had done last night, or, more correctly, had done to him, the bruises alone had nearly crippled him. The only plausible explanation – though he couldn't recall any details – was that he'd been beaten up on the way back from Laboratories; either that, or he'd stepped into a bar and somebody had picked a fight with him. It had happened before, on occasion. He had one of those faces that awoke the bully in drunkards.

He stood up and hobbled to the small bathroom adjoining his room. His glasses were missing from their normal spot beside the shaving mirror, and his reflection was woefully blurred, but it was apparent that his face was as badly scratched as the rest of his anatomy. And more: a clump of hair had been pulled out from above his left ear; clotted blood ran down to his neck. Painfully, he bent to the task of cleaning his wounds, then bathing them in a stinging solution of antiseptic. That done, he returned into his bedsitting-room to seek out his spectacles. But search as he might, he could not locate them. Cursing his idiocy, he rooted amongst his belongings for his old pair, and found them. Their prescription was out of date – his eyes had worsened considerably since he'd worn them – but they at least brought his surroundings into a dreamy kind of focus.

An indisputable melancholy had crept up on him, compounded of his pain and those unwelcome thoughts of Mrs Morrisey. To keep its intimacy at bay he turned on the radio. A sleek voice emerged, purveying the usual palliatives. Jerome had always had contempt for popular music and its apologists, but now, as he mooched around the small room, unwilling to clothe himself with chafing weaves when his scratches still pained him, the songs began to stir something other than scorn in him. It was as though he was hearing the words and music for the first time: as though all his life he had been deaf to their sentiments. Enthralled, he forgot his pain, and listened. The songs told one seamless and obsessive story: of love lost and found, only to be lost again. The lyricists filled the airwaves with metaphor – much of it ludicrous, but no less potent for that. Of paradise, of hearts on fire; of birds, bells, journeys, sunsets; of passion as lunacy, as flight, as unimaginable treasure. The songs did not calm him with their fatuous sentiments; they flayed him, evoking, despite feeble rhyme and trite melody, a world bewitched by desire. He began to tremble. His eyes, strained (or so he reasoned) by the unfamiliar spectacles, began to delude him. It seemed as though he could see traces of light in his skin: sparks flying from the ends of his fingers.

He stared at his hands and arms; the illusion, far from retreating in the face of this scrutiny, increased. Beads of brightness, like the traces of fire in ash, began to climb through his veins, multiplying even as he watched. Curiously, he felt no distress. This burgeoning fire merely reflected the passion in the story the songs were telling him: love, they said, was in the air, round every corner, waiting to be found. He thought again of the widow Morrisey in the flat below him, going about her business, sighing, no doubt, as he had done; awaiting her hero. The more he thought of her the more inflamed he became. She would not reject him, of that the songs convinced him; or if she did he must press his case until (again, as the songs promised) she surrendered to him. Suddenly, at the thought of her surrender, the fire engulfed him. Laughing, he left the radio singing behind him, and made his way downstairs.

It had taken the best part of the morning to assemble a list of testees employed at the Laboratories; Carnegie had sensed a reluctance on the part of the establishment to open their files to the investigation, despite the horror that had been committed on its premises. Finally, just after noon, they had presented him with a hastily assembled Who's Who of subjects, four and a half dozen *in toto*, and their addresses. None, the offices claimed, matched the description of Welles' testee. The Doctors, it was explained, had been clearly using Laboratory facilities to work on private projects. Though this was not encouraged, both had been senior researchers, and allowed leeway on the matter. It was likely, therefore, that the man Carnegie was seeking had never even been on the Laboratories' payroll. Undaunted, Carnegie ordered a selection of photographs taken off the video recording and had them distributed – with the list of names and addresses – to his officers. From then on, it was down to footwork and patience.

* * *

Leo Boyle ran his finger down the list of names he had been given. 'Another fourteen,' he said. His driver grunted, and Boyle glanced across at him. 'You were McBride's partner, weren't you?' he said.

'That's right,' Dooley replied. 'He's been suspended.'

'Why?'

Dooley scowled. 'Lacks finesse, does Virgil. Can't get the hang of arrest technique.'

Dooley drew the car to a halt.

'Is this it?' Boyle asked.

'You said number eighty. This is eighty. On the door. Eight. Oh.'

'I've got eyes.'

Boyle got out of the car and made his way up the pathway. The house was sizeable, and had been divided into flats: there were several bells. He pressed for J. Tredgold – the name on his list – and waited. Of the five houses they had so far visited, two had been unoccupied and the residents of the other three had born no resemblance to the malefactor.

Boyle waited on the step a few seconds and then pressed the bell again; a longer ring this time.

'Nobody in,' Dooley said from the pavement.

'Looks like it.' Even as he spoke Boyle caught sight of a figure flitting across the hallway, its outline distorted by the cobblestone glass in the door. 'Wait a minute,' he said.

'What is it?'

'Somebody's in there and not answering.' He pressed the first bell again, and then the others. Dooley approached up the pathway, flitting away an over-attentive wasp.

'You sure?' he said.

'I saw somebody in there.'

'Press the other bells,' Dooley suggested.

'I already did. There's somebody in there and they don't want to come to the door.' He rapped on the glass. 'Open up,' he announced. 'Police.'

Clever, thought Dooley; why not a loud-hailer, so Heaven knows too? When the door, predictably, remained unanswered, Boyle turned to Dooley. 'Is there a side gate?'

'Yes, sir.'

'Then get round the back, pronto, before he's away.'

'Shouldn't we call – ?'

'Do it! I'll keep watch here. If you can get in the back come through and open the front door.'

Dooley moved; leaving Boyle alone at the front door. He rang the series of bells again, and, cupping his hand to his brow, put his face to the glass. There was no sign of movement in the hallway; was it possible that the bird had already flown? He backed down the path and stared up at the windows; they stared back vacuously. Ample time had now passed for Dooley to get round the back of the house; but so far he had neither reappeared nor called. Stymied where he stood, and nervous that his tactics had lost them their quarry, Boyle decided to follow his nose around the back of the house.

The side gate had been left open by Dooley. Boyle advanced up the side passage, glancing through a window into an empty living-room before heading round to the back door. It was open. Dooley, however, was not in sight. Boyle pocketed the photograph and the list, and stepped inside, loath to call Dooley's name for fear it alert any felon to his presence, yet nervous of the silence. Cautious as a cat on broken glass he crept through the flat, but each room was deserted. At the flat door, which let on to the hallway in which he had first seen the figure, he paused. Where had Dooley gone?; the man had apparently disappeared from sight.

Then, a groan from beyond the door.

'Dooley?' Boyle ventured. Another groan. He stepped into the hallway. Three more doors presented themselves, all were closed; other flats, presumably, or bedsitting rooms. On the coconut mat at the front door lay Dooley's truncheon, dropped there as if its owner had been in the process of making his escape. Boyle swallowed his fear and walked into the body of the hall. The complaint came again, close by. He looked round and up the stairs. There, on the half-landing, lay Dooley. He was barely conscious. A rough attempt had been made to rip his clothes; large portions of his flabby lower anatomy were exposed.

'What's going on, Dooley?' Boyle asked, moving to the bottom of the stairs. The officer heard his voice and rolled himself over. His bleary eyes, settling on Boyle, opened in terror.

'It's all right,' Boyle reassured him. 'It's only me.'

Too late, Boyle registered that Dooley's gaze wasn't fixed on *him* at all, but on some sight over his shoulder. As he pivotted on his heel to snatch a glance at Dooley's bugaboo a charging figure slammed into him. Winded and cursing, Boyle was thrown off his feet. He scrabbled about on the floor for several seconds before his attacker seized hold of him by jacket and hair and hauled him to his feet. He recognized at once the wild face that was thrust into his – the receding hair-line, the weak mouth, the *hunger* – but there was much too he had not anticipated. For one, the man was naked as a babe, though scarcely so modestly endowed. For another, he was clearly aroused to fever-pitch. If the beady eye at his groin, shining up at Boyle, were not evidence enough, the hands now tearing at his clothes made the assailant's intention perfectly apparent.

'Dooley!' Boyle shrieked as he was thrown across the hallway. 'In Christ's name! Dooley!'

His pleas were silenced as he hit the opposite wall. The wild man was at his back in half a heartbeat, smearing Boyle's face against the wallpaper: birds and flowers, intertwined, filled his eyes. In desperation, Boyle fought back, but the man's passion lent him ingovernable strength. With one insolent hand holding the policeman's head, he tore at Boyle's trousers and underwear, leaving his buttocks exposed.

'God . . .' Boyle begged into the pattern of the wallpaper. 'Please God, somebody help me . . .'; but the prayers were no more fruitful than his struggles. He was pinned against the wall like a butterfly spread on cork, about to be pierced through. He closed his eyes, tears of frustration running down his cheeks. The assailant left off his hold on Boyle's head and pressed his violation home. Boyle refused to cry out. The pain he felt was not the equal of his shame. Better perhaps that Dooley remained comatose; that this humiliation be done and finished with unwitnessed.

'Stop,' he murmured into the wall, not to his attacker but to his body, urging it not to find pleasure in this outrage. But his nerve-endings were treacherous; they caught fire from the assault. Beneath the stabbing agony some unforgivable part of him rose to the occasion.

On the stairs, Dooley hauled himself to his feet. His lumbar region, which had been weak since a car accident the previous Christmas, had given out almost as soon as the wild man had sprung him in the hall. Now, as he descended the stairs, the least motion caused excruciating agonies. Crippled with pain, he stumbled to the bottom of the stairs and looked, amazed, across the hallway. Could this be Boyle – he the supercilious, he the rising man, being pummelled like a street-boy in need of dope money? The sight transfixed Dooley for several seconds before he unhinged his eyes and swung them down to the truncheon on the mat. He moved cautiously, but the wild man was too occupied with the deflowering to notice him.

Jerome was listening to Boyle's heart. It was a loud, seductive beat, and with every thrust into the man it seemed to get louder. He wanted it: the heat of it, the life of it. His hand moved round to Boyle's chest, and dug at the flesh.

'Give me your heart,' he said. It was like a line from one of the songs.

Boyle screamed into the wall as his attacker mauled his chest. He'd seen photographs of the woman at the Laboratories; the open wound of her torso was lightning-clear in his mind's eye. Now the maniac intended the same atrocity. *Give me your heart.* Panicked to the ledge of his sanity he found new stamina, and began to fight afresh, reaching round and clawing at the man's torso: nothing – not even the bloody loss of hair from his scalp – broke the rhythm of his thrusts, however. In extremis, Boyle attempted to insinuate one of his hands between his body and the wall and reach between his legs to unman the bastard. As he did so, Dooley attacked, delivering a hail of trencheon blows upon the man's head. The diversion gave Boyle precious leeway. He pressed hard against the wall; the man, his grip on Boyle's chest slicked with blood, lost his hold. Again, Boyle pushed. This time, he managed to shrug the man off entirely. The bodies disengaged; Boyle turned, bleeding but in no danger, and watched Dooley follow the man across the hallway, beating at his greasy blond head. He made little attempt to protect himself however: his burning eyes (Boyle had never understood the physical accuracy of that image until now) were still on the object of his affections.

'Kill him!' Boyle said quietly, as the man grinned – grinned! – through the blows. 'Break every bone in his body!'

Even if Dooley, hobbled as he was, had been in any fit state to obey the imperative, he had no chance to do so. His berating was interrupted by a voice from down the hallway. A woman had emerged from the flat Boyle had come through. She too had been a victim of this marauder, to judge by her state; but Dooley's entry into the house had clearly distracted her molester before he could do serious damage.

'Arrest him!' she said, pointing at the leering man. 'He tried to rape me!'

Dooley closed in to take possession of the prisoner, but Jerome had other intentions. He put his hand in Dooley's face and pushed him back against the front door. The coconut mat slid from under him: he all but fell. By the time he'd regained his balance Jerome was up and away. Boyle made a wretched attempt to stop him, but the tatters of his trousers were wrapped about his lower legs and Jerome, fleet-footed, was soon half-way up the stairs.

'Call for help,' Boyle ordered Dooley. 'And make it quick.'

Dooley nodded, and opened the front door.

'Is there any way out from upstairs?' Boyle demanded of Mrs Morrisey. She shook her head. 'Then we've got the bastard trapped haven't we?' he said. 'Go on, Dooley!' Dooley hobbled away down the path. 'And you,' he said to the woman, 'fetch something in the way of weaponry. Anything solid.' The woman nodded and returned the way she'd come, leaving Boyle slumped beside the open door. A soft breeze cooled the sweat on his face. At the car outside Dooley was calling up reinforcements.

All too soon, Boyle thought, the cars would be here, and the man upstairs would be hauled away to give his testimony. There would be no opportunity for revenge once he was in custody; the law would take its placid course, and he, the victim, would be only a by-stander. If he was ever to salvage the ruins of his manhood, *now* was the time. If he didn't – if he languished here, his bowels on fire – he would never shrug off the horror he felt at his body's betrayal. He must act now – must beat the grin off his ravisher's face once and for all – or else live in self-disgust until memory failed him.

The choice was no choice at all. Without further debate, he got up from his squatting position, and began up the stairs. As he reached the half-landing he realized he hadn't brought a weapon with him, he knew, however, that if he descended again he'd lose all momentum. Prepared, in that moment, to die if necessary, he headed on up.

There was only one door open on the top landing; through it came the sound of a radio. Downstairs, in the safety of the hall, he heard Dooley come in to tell him that the call had been made, only to break off in mid-announcement. Ignoring the distraction, Boyle stepped into the flat.

There was nobody there. It took Boyle a few moments only to check the kitchen, the tiny bathroom, and the living room: all were deserted. He returned to the bathroom, the window of which was open, and put his head out. The drop to the grass of the garden below was quite manageable. There was an imprint in the ground of the man's body. He had leapt. And gone.

Boyle cursed his tardiness, and hung his head. A trickle of heat ran down the inside of his leg. In the next room, the love-songs played on.

For Jerome, there was no forgetfulness, not this time. The encounter with Mrs Morrisey, which had been interrupted by Dooley, and the episode with Boyle that had followed, had all merely served to fan the fire in him. Now, by the light of those flames, he saw clearly what crimes he had committed. He remembered with horrible clarity the laboratory, the injection, the monkeys, the blood. The acts he recalled, however (and there

131

were many), woke no sense of sinfulness in him. All moral consequence, all shame or remorse, was burned out by the fire that was even now licking his flesh to new enthusiasms.

He took refuge in a quiet cul-de-sac to make himself presentable. The clothes he had managed to snatch before making his escape were motley, but would serve to keep him from attracting unwelcome attention. As he buttoned himself up – his body seeming to strain from its covering as if resentful of being concealed – he tried to control the holocaust that raged between his ears. But the flames wouldn't be dampened. His every fibre seemed alive to the flux and flow of the world around him. The marshalled trees along the road, the wall at his back, the very paving stones beneath his bare feet were catching a spark from him, and burning now with their own fire. He grinned to see the conflagration spread. The world, in its every eager particular, grinned back.

Aroused beyond control, he turned to the wall he had been leaning against. The sun had fallen full upon it, and it was warm: the bricks smelt ambrosial. He laid kisses on their gritty faces, his hands exploring every nook and cranny. Murmuring sweet nothings, he unzipped himself, found an accommodating niche, and filled it. His mind was running with liquid pictures: mingled anatomies, female and male in one undistinguishable congress. Above him, even the clouds had caught fire; enthralled by their burning heads he felt the moment rise in his gristle. Breath was short now. But the ecstasy?; surely that would go on forever.

Without warning a spasm of pain travelled down his spine from cortex to testicles, and back again, convulsing him. His hands lost grip of the brick and he finished his agonizing climax on the air as he fell across the pavement. For several seconds he lay where he had collapsed, while the echoes of the initial spasm bounced back and forth along his spine, diminishing with each return. He could taste blood at the back of his throat; he wasn't certain if he'd bitten his lip or tongue, but he thought not. Above his head the birds circled on, rising lazily on a spiral of warm air. He watched the fire in the clouds gutter out.

He got to his feet and looked down at the coinage of semen he'd spent on the pavement. For a fragile instant he caught again a whiff of the vision he'd just had; imagined a marriage of his seed with the paving stone. What sublime children the world might boast, he thought, if he could only mate with brick or tree; he would gladly suffer the agonies of conception, if such miracles were possible. But the paving stone was unmoved by his seed's

132

entreaties; the vision, like the fire above him, cooled and hid its glories.

He put his bloodied member away, and leaned against the wall, turning the strange events of his recent life over and over. Something fundamental was changing in him, of that he had no doubt; the rapture that had possessed him (and would, no doubt, possess him again) was like nothing he had hitherto experienced. And whatever they had injected into his system it showed no signs of being discharged naturally; far from it. He could feel the heat in him still, as he had leaving the Laboratories; but this time the roar of its presence was louder than ever.

It was a new kind of life he was living, and the thought, though frightening, exulted him. Not once did it occur to his spinning, eroticized brain that this new kind of life would, in time, demand a new kind of death.

Carnegie had been warned by his superiors that results were expected; he was now passing the verbal beating he'd received to those under him. It was a line of humiliation, in which the greater was encouraged to kick the lesser man, and that man, in turn, his lesser. Carnegie had sometimes wondered what the man at the end of the line took his ire out on; his dog presumably.

'This miscreant is still loose, gentlemen, despite his photograph in many of this morning's newspapers, and an operating method which is, to say the least, insolent. We *will* catch him, of course, but let's get the bastard before we have another murder on our hands – '

The phone rang. Boyle's replacement, Migeon, picked it up, while Carnegie concluded his pep-talk to the assembled officers.

'I want him in the next twenty-four hours, gentlemen. That's the time-scale I've been given, and that's what we've got. Twenty-four hours.'

Migeon interrupted. 'Sir? Its Johannson. He says he's got something for you. It's urgent.'

'Right.' The Inspector claimed the receiver. 'Carnegie.'

The voice at the other end was soft to the point of inaudibility. 'Carnegie,' Johannson said, 'we've been right through the laboratory; dug up every piece of information we could find on Dance and Welles' tests – '

'And?'

'We've also analysed traces of the agent from the hypo they used on the suspect. I think we've found the *Boy*, Carnegie.'

'What boy?' Carnegie wanted to know; he found Johannson's obfuscation irritating.

'The *Blind Boy*, Carnegie.'

'And?'

For some inexplicable reason Carnegie was certain the man *smiled* down the phone before replying: 'I think perhaps you'd better come down and see for yourself. Sometime around noon suit you?'

Johannson could have been one of history's greatest poisoners: he had all the requisite qualifications. A tidy mind (poisoners were, in Carnegie's experience, domestic paragons), a patient nature (poison could take time), and, most importantly, an encyclopaedic knowledge of toxicology. Watching him at work, which Carnegie had done on two previous cases, was to see a subtle man at his subtle craft, and the spectacle made Carnegie's blood run cold.

Johannson had installed himself in the laboratory on the top floor, where Doctor Dance had been murdered, rather than use police facilities for the investigation, because, as he explained to Carnegie, much of the equipment the Hume organization boasted was simply not available elsewhere. His dominion over the place, accompanied by his two assistants had, however, transformed the laboratory from the clutter left by the experimenters, to a dream of order. Only the monkeys remained a constant. Try as he might Johannson could not control their behaviour.

'We didn't have much difficulty finding the drug used on your man,' Johannson said, 'we simply cross-checked traces remaining in the hypodermic with materials found in the room. In fact, they seem to have been manufacturing this stuff, or variations on the theme, for some time. The people here claim they know nothing about it, of course. I'm inclined to believe them. What the good doctors were doing here was, I'm sure, in the nature of a personal experiment.'

'What sort of experiment?'

Johannson took off his spectacles and set about cleaning them with the tongue of his red tie. 'At first, we thought they were developing some kind of hallucogen,' he said. 'In some regards the agent used on your man resembles a narcotic. In fact – methods apart – I think they made some very exciting discoveries. Developments which take us into entirely new territory.'

'It's not a drug then?'

'Oh, yes, of course it's a drug,' Johannson said, replacing the spectacles, 'but one created for a very specific purpose. See for yourself.'

Johannson led the way across the laboratory to the row of

134

monkeys' cages. Instead of being confined separately, the toxicologist had seen fit to open the interconnecting doors between one cage and the next, allowing the animals free access to gather in groups. The consequence was absolutely plain: the animals were engaged in an elaborate series of sexual acts. Why, Carnegie wondered, did monkeys perpetually, perform obscenities? It was the same torrid display whenever he'd taken his offspring, as children, to Regent's Park Zoo; the Ape Enclosure elicited one embarrassing question upon another. He'd stopped taking the children after a while. He simply found it too mortifying.

'Haven't they got anything better to do?' he asked of Johannson, glancing away and then back at a menage à trois that was so intimate the eye could not ascribe member to monkey.

'Believe me,' Johannson smirked, 'this is mild by comparison with much of the behaviour we've seen from them since we gave them a shot of the agent. From that point on they neglected all normal behaviour patterns; they bypassed the arousal signals, the courtship rituals. They no longer show any interest in food. They don't sleep. They have become sexual obsessives. All other stimuli are forgotten. Unless the agent is naturally discharged, I suspect they are going to screw themselves to death.'

Carnegie looked along the rest of the cages: the same pornographic scenes were being played out in each one. Mass-rape, homosexual liaisons, fervent and ecstatic masturbation.

'It's no wonder the Doctors made a secret project of their discovery,' Johannson went on, 'they were on to something that could have made them a fortune. An aphrodisiac that actually works.'

'An aphrodisiac?'

'Most are useless, of course. Rhinoceros horn, live eels in cream sauce: symbolic stuff. They're designed to arouse by association.'

Carnegie remembered the hunger in Jerome's eyes. It was echoed here, in the monkeys'. Hunger, and the desperation that hunger brings.

'And the ointments too, all useless. *Cantharis vesticatora* – '

'What's that?'

'You know the stuff as Spanish Fly, perhaps? It's a paste made from a beetle. Again, useless. At best these things are inflammatants. But this . . .' He picked up a phial of colourless fluid. '*This* is damn near genius.'

'They don't look too happy with it to me.'

'Oh, it's still crude,' Johannson said. 'I think the researchers were greedy, and moved into tests on living subjects a good two or three years before it was wise to do so. The stuff is almost lethal as it stands, no doubt of that. But it *could* be made to work, given time. You see, they've sidestepped the mechanical problems: this stuff operates directly on the sexual imagination, on the libido. If you arouse the *mind,* the body follows. That's the trick of it.'

A rattling of the wire-mesh close by drew Carnegie's attention from Johannson's pale features. One of the female monkeys, apparently not satisfied with the attentions of several males, was spreadeagled against her cage, her nimble fingers reaching for Carnegie; her spouses, not to be left loveless, had taken to sodomy. '*Blind Boy*?' said Carnegie. 'Is that Jerome?'

'It's Cupid, isn't it?' Johannson said: '"*Love looks not with the eyes but with the mind,*

And therefore is winged Cupid painted blind".' It's *Midsummer Night's Dream.*'

'The Bard was never my strongest suit,' said Carnegie. He went back to staring at the female monkey. 'And Jerome?' he said.

'He has the agent in his system. A sizeable dose.'

'So he's like this lot!'

'I would presume – his intellectual capacities being greater – that the agent may not be able to work in quite such an *unfettered* fashion. But, having said that, sex can make monkeys out of the best of us, can't it?' Johannson allowed himself a half-smile at the notion. 'All our so-called higher concerns become secondary to the pursuit. For a short time sex makes us obsessive; we can perform, or at least *think* we can perform, what with hindsight may seem extraordinary feats.'

'I don't think there's anything so extraordinary about rape,' Carnegie commented, attempting to stem Johannson's rhapsody. But the other man would not be subdued.

'Sex without end, without compromise or apology,' he said. 'Imagine it. The dream of Casanova.'

The world had seen so many Ages. The Age of Enlightenment; of Reformation; of Reason. Now, at last, the Age of Desire. And after this, an end to Ages; an end, perhaps, to everything. For the fires that were being stoked now were fiercer than the innocent world suspected. They were terrible fires, fires without end, which would illuminate the world in one last, fierce light.

So Welles thought, as he lay in his bed. He had been conscious for several hours, but had chosen not to signify such. Whenever a nurse came to his room he would clamp his eyes closed and slow the rhythm of his breath. He knew he could not keep the illusion up for long, but the hours gave him a while to think through his

136

itinerary from here. His first move had to be back to the Laboratories; there were papers there he had to shred; tapes to wipe clean. From now on he was determined that every scrap of information about *Project Blind Boy* exist solely in his head. That way he would have complete control over his masterwork, and nobody could claim it from him.

He had never had much interest in making money from the discovery, although he was well aware of how lucrative a workable aphrodisiac would be; he had never given a fig for material wealth. His initial motivation for the development of the drug – which they had chanced upon quite by accident while testing an agent to aid schizophrenics – had been investigative. But his motives had matured, through their months of secret work. He had come to think of himself as the bringer of the millenium. He would not have anyone attempt to snatch that sacred role from him.

So he thought, lying in his bed, waiting for a moment to slip away.

As he walked the streets Jerome would have happily yea-said Welles' vision. Perhaps he, of all men, was most eager to welcome the Age of Desire. He saw its portents everywhere. On advertising hoardings and cinema billboards, in shop-windows, on television screens: everywhere, the body as merchandise. Where flesh was not being used to market artifacts of steel and stone, those artifacts were taking on its properties. Automobiles passed him by with every voluptuous attribute but breath: their sinuous body-work gleamed, their interiors invited, plushly; the buildings beleaguered him with sexual puns. Spires; passageways; shadowed plazas with white-water fountains. Beneath the raptures of the shallow – the thousand trivial distractions he encountered in street and square – he sensed the ripe life of the body informing every particular.

The spectacle kept the fire in him well-stoked; it was all that will power could do to keep him from pressing his attentions on every creature that he met eyes with. A few seemed to sense the heat in him, and gave him wide berth. Dogs sensed it too. Several followed him, aroused by *his* arousal. Flies orbited his head in squadrons. But his growing ease with his condition gave him some rudimentary control over it. He knew that to make a public display of his ardour would bring the law down upon him, and that in turn would hinder his adventures. Soon enough, the fire that he had begun would spread: *then* he would emerge from hiding and bathe in it freely. Until then, discretion was best.

He had on occasion bought the company of a young woman in Soho; he went to find her now. The afternoon was stiflingly hot, but he felt no weariness. He had not eaten since the previous evening, but he felt no hunger. Indeed, as he climbed the narrow stairway up to the room on the first floor which Angela had once occupied, he felt as primed as an athlete, glowing with health. The immaculately dressed and wall-eyed pimp who usually occupied a place at the top of the stairs was absent. Jerome simply went to the girl's room and knocked. There was no reply. He rapped again, more urgently. The noise brought an early middle-aged woman to the door at the end of the landing.

'What do you want?'

'The woman,' he replied simply.

'Angela's gone. And you'd better get out of here too, in that state. This isn't a doss-house.'

'When will she be back?' he asked, keeping as tight a leash as he could on his appetite.

The woman, who was as tall as Jerome and half as heavy again as his wasted frame, advanced towards him. 'The girl won't *be* back,' she said, 'so you get the hell out of here, before I call Isaiah.'

Jerome looked at the woman; she shared Angela's profession, no doubt, if not her youth or prettiness. He smiled at her. 'I can hear your heart,' he said.

'I told you – '

Before she could finish the words Jerome moved down the landing towards her. She wasn't intimidated by his approach, merely repulsed.

'If I call Isaiah, you'll be sorry,' she informed him. The pace of her heartbeat had risen, he could hear it.

'I'm burning,' he said.

She frowned; she was clearly losing this battle of wits. 'Stay away from me,' she told. 'I'm warning you.'

The heartbeat was getting more rapid still. The rhythm, buried in her substance, drew him on. From that source: all life, all heat.

'Give me your heart,' he said.

'Isaiah!'

Nobody came running at her shout, however. Jerome gave her no opportunity to cry out a second time. He reached to embrace her, clamping a hand over her mouth. She let fly a volley of blows against him, but the pain only fanned the flames. He was brighter by the moment: his every orifice let on to the furnace in belly and loins and head. Her superior bulk was of no advantage against such fervour. He pushed her against the wall – the beat of her heart loud in his ears – and began to apply kisses to her neck, tearing her dress open to free her breasts.

'Don't shout,' he said, trying to sound persuasive. 'There's no harm meant.'

She shook her head, and said, 'I won't,' against his palm. He took his hand from her mouth, and she dragged in several desperate breaths. Where was Isaiah?; she thought. Not far, surely. Fearing for her life if she tried to resist this interloper – how his eyes shone! – she gave up any pretence to resistance and let him have his way. Men's supply of passion, she knew of long experience, was easily depleted. Though they might threaten to move earth and heaven too, half an hour later their boasts would be damp sheets and resentment. If the worst came to the worst, she could tolerate his inane talk of burning; she'd heard far obscener bedroom chat. As to the prong he was even now attempting to press into her, it and its comical like held no surprises for her.

Jerome wanted to touch the heart in her; wanted to see it splash up into his face, to bathe in it. He put his hand to her breast, and felt the beat of her under his palm.

'You like that, do you?' she said as he pressed against her bosom. 'You're not the first.'

He clawed her skin.

'Gently, sweetheart,' she chided him, looking over his shoulder to see if there was any sign of Isaiah. 'Be gentle. This is the only body I've got.'

He ignored her. His nails drew blood.

'Don't do that,' she said.

'Wants to be out,' he replied digging deeply, and it suddenly dawned on her that this was no love-game he was playing.

'*Stop it*,' she said, as he began to tear at her. This time, she screamed.

Downstairs, and a short way along the street, Isaiah dropped the slice of *tarte franc‹SS›caise* he'd just bought and ran to the door. It wasn't the first time his sweet tooth had tempted him from his post, but – unless he was quick to undo the damage – it might very well be his last. There were terrible noises from the landing. He raced up the stairs. The scene that met his eyes was in every way worse than that his imagination had conjured. Simone was trapped against the wall beside her door, with a man battened upon her. Blood was coming from somewhere between them, he couldn't see where.

Isaiah yelled. Jerome, hands bloody, looked round from his labours as a giant in a Savile Row suit reached for him. It took

Jerome vital seconds to uproot himself from the furrow, by which time the man was upon him. Isaiah took hold of him, and dragged him off the woman. She took shelter, sobbing, in her room.

'Sick bastard,' Isaiah said, launching a fusillade of punches. Jerome reeled. But he was on fire, and unafraid. In a moment's respite he leapt at his man like an angered baboon. Isaiah, taken unawares, lost balance, and fell back against one of the doors, which opened inwards against his weight. He collapsed into a squalid lavatory, his head striking the lip of the toilet bowl as he went down. The impact disoriented him, and he lay on the stained linoleum groaning, legs akimbo. Jerome could hear his blood, eager in his veins; could smell sugar on his breath. It tempted him to stay. But his instinct for self-preservation counselled otherwise; Isaiah was already making an attempt to stand up again. Before he could get to his feet Jerome about turned, and made a getaway down the stairs.

The dog-day met him at the doorstep, and he smiled. The street wanted him more than the woman on the landing, and he was eager to oblige. He started out on to the pavement, his erection still pressing from his trousers. Behind him, he heard the giant pounding down the stairs. He took to his heels, laughing. The fire was still uncurbed in him, and it lent speed to his feet; he ran down the street not caring if Sugar Breath was following or not. Pedestrians, unwilling, in this dispassionate age, to register more than casual interest in the blood-spattered satyr, parted to let him pass. A few pointed, assuming him an actor perhaps. Most took no notice at all. He made his way through a maze of back streets, aware without needing to look that Isaiah was still on his heels.

Perhaps it was accident that brought him to the street market; perhaps, and more probably, it was that the swelter carried the mingled scent of meat and fruit to his nostrils, and he wanted to bathe in it. The narrow thoroughfare was thronged with purchasers, sight-seers, and stalls heaped with merchandise. He dove into the crowd happily, brushing against buttock and thigh, meeting the plaguing gaze of fellow flesh on every side. Such a day! He and his prick could scarcely believe their luck.

Behind him, he heard Isaiah shout. He picked up his pace, heading for the most densely populated areas of the market, where he could lose himself in the hot press of people. Each contact was a painful ecstasy. Each climax – and they came one upon the other as he pressed through the crowd – was a dry spasm in his system. His back ached, his balls ached: but what his body now?; just a plinth for that singular monument, his prick. Head was *nothing*; mind was *nothing*. His arms were simply made to bring love close, his legs to carry the demanding rod any place where it might find satisfaction. He pictured himself as a walking erection, the world gaping on every side: flesh, brick, steel, he didn't care: he would ravish it all.

Suddenly, without his seeking it, the crowd parted, and he found himself off the main thoroughfare and in a narrow street. Sunlight poured between the buildings, its zeal magnified. He was about to turn back to join the crowd again when he caught a scent and sight that drew him on. A short way down the heat-drenched street three shirtless young men were standing amid piles of fruit crates, each containing dozens of punnets of straw-berries. There had been a glut of the fruit that year, and in the relentless heat much of it had begun to soften and rot. The trio of workers was going through the punnets, sorting bad fruit from good, and throwing the spoiled strawberries into the gutter. The smell in the narrow space was overpowering: a sweetness of such strength it would have sickened any interloper other than Jerome, whose senses had lost all capacity for revulsion or rejection. The world was the world was the world; he would take it, as in marriage, for better or worse. He stood watching the spectacle entranced; the sweating fruit-sorters bright in the fall of sun, hands, arms and torsoes spattered with scarlet juice; the air mazed with every nectar-seeking insect; the discarded fruit heaped in the gutter in seeping mounds. Engaged in their sticky labours the sorters didn't even see him at first. Then one of the three looked up, and took in the extraordinary creature watching them. The grin on his face died as he met Jerome's eyes.

'What the hell?'

Now the other two looked up from their work.

'Sweet,' said Jerome; he could hear their hearts tremble.

'Look at him,' said the youngest of the three, pointing at Jerome's groin. 'Fucking exposing himself.'

They stood still in the sunlight, he and they, while the wasps whirled around the fruit, and, in the narrow slice of blue summer sky between the roofs, birds passed over. Jerome wanted the moment to go on forever: his too-naked head tasted Eden here.

And then, the dream broke. He felt a shadow on his back. One of the sorters dropped the punnet he was sorting through; the decayed fruit broke open on the gravel. Jerome frowned, and half-turned. Isaiah had found the street; his weapon was steel and shone. It crossed the space between he and Jerome in one short second. Jerome felt an ache in his side as the knife slid into him.

'*Christ*,' the young man said, and began to run; his two brothers,

141

unwilling to be witnesses at the scene of a wounding, hesitated only moments longer before following.

The pain made Jerome cry out, but nobody in the noisy market heard him. Isaiah withdrew the blade; heat came with it. He made to stab again, but Jerome was too fast for the spoiler; he moved out of range and staggered across the street. The would-be assassin, fearful that Jerome's cries would draw too much attention, moved quickly in pursuit to finish the job. But the tarmac was slick with rotted fruit, and his fine suede shoes had less grip than Jerome's bare feet. The gap between them widened by a pace.

'No you don't,' Isaiah said, determined not to let his humiliator escape. He pushed over a tower of fruit crates – punnets toppled and strewed their contents across Jerome's path. Jerome hesitated, to take in the bouquet of bruised fruit. The indulgence almost killed him. Isaiah closed in, ready to take the man. Jerome, his system taxed to near eruption by the stimulus of pain, watched the blade come close to opening up his belly. His mind conjured the wound: the abdomen slit – the heat spilling out to join the blood of the strawberries in the gutter. The thought was so tempting. He almost wanted it.

Isaiah had killed before, twice. He knew the wordless vocabulary of the act, and he could see the invitation in his victim's eyes. Happy to oblige, he came to meet it, knife at the ready. At the last possible moment Jerome recanted, and instead of presenting himself for slitting, threw a blow at the giant. Isaiah ducked to avoid it and his feet slid in the mush. The knife fled from his hand and fell amongst the debris of punnets and fruit. Jerome turned away as the hunter – the advantage lost – stooped to locate the knife. But his prey was gone before his ham-fisted grip had found it: lost again in the crowd-filled streets. He had no opportunity to pocket the knife before the uniform stepped out of the crowd and joined him in the hot passageway.

'What's the story?' the policeman demanded, looking down at the knife. Isaiah followed his gaze. The bloodied blade was black with flies.

In his office Inspector Carnegie sipped at his hot chocolate, his third in the past hour, and watched the processes of dusk. He had always wanted to be a detective, right from his earliest rememberings; and, in those rememberings, this had always been a charged and magical hour. Night descending on the city; myriad evils putting on their glad rags and coming out to play. A time for vigilance, for a new moral stringency.

142

But as a child he had failed to imagine the fatigue that twilight invariably brought. He was tired to his bones, and if he snatched any sleep in the next few hours he knew it would be here, in his chair, with his feet up on the desk amid a clutter of plastic cups.

The phone rang. It was Johannson.

'Still at work?' he said, impressed by Johannson's dedication to the job. It was well after nine. Perhaps Johannson didn't have a home worth calling such to go back to either.

'I heard our man had a busy day,' Johannson said.

'That's right. A prostitute in Soho; then got himself stabbed.'

'He got through the cordon, I gather?'

'These things happen,' Carnegie replied, too tired to be testy. 'What can I do for you?'

'I just thought you'd want to know: the monkeys have started to die.'

The words stirred Carnegie from his fatigue-stupor. 'How many?' he asked.

'Three from fourteen so far. But the rest will be dead by dawn, I'd guess.'

'What's killing them? Exhaustion?' Carnegie recalled the desperate saturnalia he'd seen in the cages. What animal – human or otherwise – could keep up such revelry without cracking up?

'It's not physical,' Johannson said. 'Or at least not in the way you're implying. We'll have to wait for the dissection results before we get any detailed explanations – '

'Your best guess?'

'For what it's worth . . .' Johannson said, '. . . which is quite a lot: I think they're going *bang*.'

'What?'

'Cerebral over-load of some kind. Their brains are simply giving out. The agent doesn't disperse you see; *it feeds on itself*. The more fevered they get, the more of the drug is produced; the more of the drug there is, the more fevered they get. It's a vicious circle. Hotter and hotter, wilder and wilder. Eventually the system can't take it, and suddenly I'm up to my armpits in dead monkeys.' The smile came back into the voice again, cold and wry. 'Not that the others let that spoil their fun. Necrophilia's quite the fashion down here.'

Carnegie peered at his cooling hot chocolate; it had acquired a thin skin, which puckered as he touched the cup. 'So it's just a matter of time?' he said.

'Before our man goes for bust? Yes, I'd think so.'

'All right. Thank you for the up-date. Keep me posted.'

'You want to come down here and view the remains?'

'Monkey corpses I can do without, thank you.'

Johannson laughed. Carnegie put down the receiver. When he turned back to the window, night had well and truly fallen.

In the laboratory Johannson crossed to the light switch by the door; in the time he'd been calling Carnegie the last of the daylight had fled. He saw the blow that felled him coming a mere heartbeat before it landed; it caught him across the side of his neck. One of his vertebrae snapped, and his legs buckled. He collapsed without reaching the lightswitch. But by the time he hit the ground the distinction between day and night was academic.

Welles didn't bother to check whether his blow had been lethal or not; time was at a premium. He stepped over the body and headed across to the bench where Johannson had been working. There, lying in a circle of lamp-light as if for the final act of a simian tragedy, lay a dead monkey. It had clearly perished in a frenzy; its face was knitted up: mouth wide and spittle-stained, eyes fixed in a final look of alarm. Its fur had been pulled out in tufts in the throes of its copulations; its body, wasted with exertion, was a mass of contusions. It took Welles half a minute of study to recognize the implications of the corpse, and of the other two he now saw lying on a nearby bench.

'Love kills,' he murmured to himself philosophically, and began his systematic destruction of *Blind Boy*.

I'm dying, Jerome thought, I'm dying of *terminal joy*. The thought amused him. It was the only thought in his head which made much sense. Since his encounter with Isaiah, and the escape from the police that had followed, he could remember little with any coherence. The hours of hiding and nursing his wounds – of feeling the heat grow again, and of discharging it – had long since merged into one midsummer dream, from which, he knew with pleasurable certainty, only death would wake him. The blaze was devouring him utterly, from the entrails out. If he were to be eviscerated now, what would the witnesses find?; only embers and ashes.

Yet still his one-eyed friend demanded *more*; still, as he wove his way back to the Laboratories – where else for a made man to go when the stitches slipped, but back to the first heat? – still the grids gaped at him seductively, and every brick wall offered up a hundred gritty invitations.

The night was balmy: a night for love-songs and romance. In the questionable privacy of a parking lot a few blocks from his destination he saw two people making sex in the back of a car,

144

the doors open to accommodate limbs and draught. Jerome paused to watch the ritual, enthralled as ever by the tangle of bodies, and the sound – so loud it was like thunder – of twin hearts beating to one escalating rhythm. Watching, his rod grew eager.

The female saw him first, and alerted her partner to the wreck of a human being who was watching them with such childish delight. The male looked around from his gropings to stare. Do I burn, Jerome wondered?; does my hair flame? At the last, does the illusion gain substance? To judge by the look on their faces, the answer was surely no. They were not in awe of him, merely angered and revolted.

'I'm on fire,' he told them.

The male got to his feet and spat at Jerome. He almost expected the spittle to turn to steam as it approached him but instead it landed on his face and upper chest as a cooling shower.

'Go to hell,' the woman said. 'Leave us alone.'

Jerome shook his head. The male warned him that another step would oblige him to break Jerome's head. It disturbed our man not a jot; no words, no blows, could silence the imperative of the rod.

Their hearts, he realized, as he moved towards them, no longer beat in tandem.

Carnegie consulted the map, five years out of date now, on his office wall, to pinpoint the location of the attack that had just been reported. Neither of the victims had come to serious harm, apparently; the arrival of a car-load of revellers had dissuaded Jerome (it was unquestionably Jerome) from lingering. Now the area was being flooded with officers, half a dozen of them armed; in a matter of minutes every street in the vicinity of the attack would be cordoned off. Unlike Soho, which had been crowded, the area would furnish the fugitive with few hiding places.

Carnegie pin-pointed the location of the attack, and realised that it was within a few blocks of the Laboratories. No accident, surely. The man was heading back to the scene of his crime. Wounded, and undoubtedly on the verge of collapse – the lovers had described a man who looked more dead than alive – Jerome would probably be picked up before he reached home. But there was always the risk of his slipping through the net, and getting to the Laboratories. Johannson was working there, alone; the guard on the building was, in these straitened times, necessarily small.

Carnegie picked up the phone and dialled through to the Johannson. The phone rang at the other end, but nobody picked it up. The man's gone home, Carnegie thought, happy to be relieved of his concern, it's ten-fifty at night and he's earned his rest. Just as he was about to put the receiver down, however, it was picked up at the other end.

'Johannson?'

Nobody replied.

'Johannson? This is Carnegie.' And still, no reply. 'Answer me, damn it. Who is this?'

In the Laboratories the receiver was forsaken. It was not replaced on the cradle but left to lie on the bench. Down the buzzing line, Carnegie could clearly hear the monkeys, their voices shrill.

'Johannson?' Carnegie demanded. 'Are you there? Johannson?'

But the apes screamed on.

Welles had built two bonfires of the *Blind Boy* material in the sinks, and then set them alight. They flared up enthusiastically. Smoke, heat and smuts filled the large room, thickening the air. When the fires were fairly raging he threw all the tapes he could lay hands upon into the conflagration, and added all of Johannson's notes for good measure. Several of the tapes had already gone from the files, he noted. But all they could show any thief was some teasing scenes of transformation: the heart of the secret remained his. With the procedures and formulae now destroyed, it only remained to wash the small amounts of remaining agent down the drain, and kill and incinerate the animals.

He prepared a series of lethal hypodermics, going about the business with uncharacteristic orderliness. This systematic destruction gratified him. He felt no regret at the way things had turned out. From that first moment of panic, when he'd helplessly watched the *Blind Boy* serum work its awesome effects upon Jerome – to this final elimination of all that had gone before – had been, he now saw, one steady process of wiping clean. With these fires he brought an end to the pretence of scientific enquiry; after this he was indisputably the Apostle of Desire, its John in the wilderness. The thought blinded him to any other. Careless of the monkeys' scratchings he hauled them one by one, from their cages to deliver the killing dose. He had dispatched three, and was opening the cage of the fourth, when a figure appeared in the doorway of the laboratory. Through the smoky air it was impossible to see who. The surviving monkeys seemed to recognize him, however: they left off their couplings and set up a din of welcome.

Welles stood still, and waited for the newcomer to make his move.

'I'm dying,' said Jerome.

Welles had not expected this. Of all the people he had antici-pated here, Jerome was the last.

'Did you hear me?' the man wanted to know.

Welles nodded. 'We're *all* dying, Jerome. Life is a slow disease, no more nor less. But such a *light*, eh?; in the going.'

'You *knew* this would happen,' Jerome said. 'You knew the fire would eat me away.'

'No,' came the sober reply. 'No, I didn't. Really.'

Jerome walked out of the door frame and into the murky light. He was a wasted shambles: a patchwork man, blood on his body, fire in his eyes. But Welles knew better than to trust the apparent vulnerability of this scarecrow. The agent in his system had made him capable of superhuman acts: he had seen Dance torn open with a few nonchalant strokes. Tact was required. Though clearly close to death, Jerome was still formidable.

'I didn't intend this, Jerome,' Welles said, attempting to tame the tremor in his voice. 'I wish, in a way, I could claim that I had. But I wasn't that far-sighted. It's taken me time and pain to see the future plainly.'

The burning man watched him, gaze intent.

'Such fires, Jerome, waiting to be lit.'

'I know . . .' Jerome replied. 'Believe me . . . I know.'

'You and I; we are the end of the world.'

The wretched monster pondered this for a while, and then nodded slowly. Welles softly exhaled a sigh of relief; the death-bed diplomacy was working. But he had little time to waste with talk. If Jerome was here, could the authorities be far behind?

'I have urgent work to do, my friend,' he said calmly. 'Would you think me uncivil if I continued with it?'

Without waiting for a reply he unlatched another cage and hauled the condemned monkey out, expertly turning its body round to facilitate the injection. The animal convulsed in his arms for a few moments, then died. Welles disengaged its wizened fingers from his shirt, and tossed the corpse and the discharged hypodermic on to the bench, turning with an executioner's economy to claim his next victim.

'Why?' Jerome asked, staring at the animal's open eyes.

'Act of mercy,' Welles replied, picking up another primed hypodermic. 'You can see how they're suffering.' He reached to unlatch the next cage.

'Don't,' Jerome said.

'No time for sentiment,' Welles replied. 'I beg you: an end to that.'

Sentiment, Jerome thought, muddily remembering the songs on

147

the radio that had first rewoken the fire in him. Didn't Welles understand that the processes of heart and head and groin were indivisible?; that sentiment, however trite, might lead to undiscovered regions? He wanted to tell the Doctor that, to explain all that he had seen and all that he had loved in these desperate hours. But somewhere between mind and tongue the explanations absconded. All he could say, to state the empathy he felt for all the suffering world, was:

'*Don't*,' as Welles unlocked the next cage. The Doctor ignored him, and reached into the wire-mesh cell. It contained three animals. He took hold of the nearest and drew it, protesting, from its companions' embraces. Without doubt it knew what fate awaited it; a flurry of screeches signalled its terror.

Jerome couldn't stomach this casual disposal. He moved, the wound in his side a torment, to prevent the killing. Welles, distracted by Jerome's advance, lost hold of his wriggling charge: the monkey scampered away across the bench-tops. As he went to re-capture it the prisoners in the cage behind him took their chance, and slipped out.

'Damn you,' Welles yelled at Jerome, 'don't you see we've no *time*? Don't you understand?'

Jerome understood everything, and yet nothing. The fever he and the animals shared, he understood; its purpose, to transform the world, he understood too. But why it should end like this – that joy, that vision – why it should all come down to a sordid room filled with smoke and pain, to frailty, to despair – *that* he did not comprehend. Nor, he now realized, did Welles, who had been the architect of these contradictions.

As the Doctor made a snatch for one of the escaping monkeys, Jerome crossed swiftly to the remaining cages and unlatched them all: the animals leapt to their freedom. Welles had succeeded with his recapture however, and had the protesting monkeys in his grip, about to deliver the panacea. Jerome made towards him.

'Let it be,' he yelled.

Welles pressed the hypodermic into the monkey's body, but before he could depress the plunger Jerome had pulled at his wrist. The hypodermic spat its poison into the air, and then fell to the ground: the monkey, wresting itself free, followed.

Jerome pulled Welles close. 'I told you to *let it be*,' he said.

Welles' response was to drive his fist into Jerome's wounded flank. Tears of pain spurted from his eyes, but he didn't release the Doctor. The stimulus, unpleasant as it was, could not dissuade him from holding that beating heart close. He wished, embracing Welles like a prodigal, that he could ignite himself: that the dream

148

of burning flesh he had endured would now become a reality, consuming maker and made in one cleansing flame. But his flesh was only flesh; his bone, bone. What miracles he had seen had been a private revelation, and now there was no time to communicate their glories or their horrors. What he had seen would die with him, to be rediscovered (perhaps) by some future self, only to be forgotten and discovered again. Like the story of love the radio had told; the same joy lost and found, found and lost. He stared at Welles with new comprehension dawning, hearing still the terrified beat of the man's heart. The Doctor was *wrong*. If he left the man to live, he would come to know his error. They were not presagers of the millenium. They had both been dreaming.

'Don't kill me,' Welles pleaded. 'I don't want to die.'

More fool you, Jerome thought, and let the man go.

Welles' bafflement was plain: he couldn't believe that his appeal for life had been answered. Anticipating a blow with every step he took, he backed away from Jerome, who simply turned his back on the Doctor and walked away.

From downstairs there came a shout, and then many shouts. Police, Welles guessed. They had presumably found the body of the officer who'd been on guard at the door. In moments only they would be coming up the stairs. There was no time now for finishing the tasks he'd come here to perform. He had to be away before they arrived.

On the floor below, Carnegie watched the armed officers disappear up the stairs. There was a faint smell of burning in the air; he feared the worst.

I am the man who comes after the act, he thought to himself; I am perpetually upon the scene when the best of the action is over. Used as he was to waiting, patient as a loyal dog, this time he could not hold his anxieties in check while the others went ahead. Disregarding the voices advising him to wait, he began up the stairs.

The laboratory on the top floor was empty, but for the monkeys and Johannson's corpse. The toxicologist lay on his face where he had fallen, neck broken. The emergency exit, which let on to the fire-escape, was open; smoky air was being sucked out through it. As Carnegie stepped away from Johannson's body officers were already on the fire-escape, calling to their colleagues below to seek out the fugitive.

'Sir?'

Carnegie looked across at the moustachioed individual who had approached him.

149

'What is it?'

The officer pointed to the other end of the laboratory: to the test-chamber. There was somebody at the window. Carnegie recognized the features, even though they were much changed. It was Jerome. At first he thought the man was watching him, but a short perusal scotched that idea. Jerome was staring, tears on his face, at his own reflection in the smeared glass. Even as Carnegie watched, the face retreated with the gloom of the chamber.

Other officers had noticed the man too. They were moving down the length of the laboratory, taking up positions behind the benches where they had a good line on the door, weapons at the ready. Carnegie had been present in such situations before; they had their own, terrible momentum. Unless he intervened, there would be blood.

'No,' he said, 'hold your fire.'

He pressed the protesting officer aside and began to walk down the laboratory, making no attempt to conceal his advance. He walked past sinks in which the remains of *Blind Boy* guttered, past the bench under which, a short age ago, they'd found the dead Dance. A monkey, its head bowed, dragged itself across his path, apparently deaf to his proximity. He let it find a hole to die in, then moved on to the chamber door. It was ajar. He reached for the handle. Behind him the laboratory had fallen completely silent; all eyes were on him. He pulled the door open. Fingers tightened on triggers. There was no attack however. Carnegie stepped inside.

Jerome was standing against the opposite wall. If he saw Carnegie enter, or heard him, he made no sign of it. A dead monkey lay at his feet, one hand still grasping the hem of his trousers. Another whimpered in the corner, holding its head in its hands.

'Jerome?'

Was it Carnegie's imagination, or could he smell strawberries? Jerome blinked.

'You're under arrest,' Carnegie said. Hendrix would appreciate the irony of that, he thought. The man moved his bloody hand from the stabwound in his side to the front of his trousers, and began to stroke himself.

'Too late,' Jerome said. He could feel the last fire rising in him. Even if this intruder chose to cross the chamber and arrest him now, the intervening seconds would deny him his capture. *Death was here.* And what was it, now he saw it clearly? Just another seduction, another sweet darkness to be filled up, and pleasured and made fertile.

A spasm began in his perineum, and lightning travelled in two directions from the spot, up his rod and up his spine. A laugh began in his throat.

In the corner of the chamber the monkey, hearing Jerome's humour, began to whimper again. The sound momentarily claimed Carnegie's attention, and when his gaze flitted back to Jerome the short-sighted eyes had closed, the hand had dropped, and he was dead, standing against the wall. For a short time the body defied gravity. Then, gracefully the legs buckled and Jerome fell forward. He was, Carnegie saw, a sack of bones, no more. It was a wonder the man had lived so long.

Cautiously, he crossed to the body and put his finger to the man's neck. There was no pulse. The remnants of Jerome's last laugh remained on his face, however, refusing to decay.

'Tell me . . .' Carnegie whispered to the man, sensing that despite his pre-emption he had missed the moment; that once again he was, and perhaps would always be, merely a witness of consequences, 'Tell me. *What was the joke?*'

But the blind boy, as is the wont of his clan, wasn't telling.

BOOKS OF BLOOD
VOLUME 5

To Julie

CONTENTS

The Forbidden

Like a flawless tragedy, the elegance of which structure is lost upon those suffering in it, the perfect geometry of the Spector Street Estate was only visible from the air. Walking in its drear canyons, passing through its grimy corridors from one grey concrete rectangle to the next, there was little to seduce the eye or stimulate the imagination. What few saplings had been planted in the quadrangles had long since been mutilated or uprooted; the grass, though tall, resolutely refused a healthy green.

No doubt the estate and its two companion developments had once been an architect's dream. No doubt the city-planners had wept with pleasure at a design which housed three and thirty-six persons per hectare, and still boasted space for a children's playground. Doubtless fortunes and reputations had been built upon Spector Street, and at its opening fine words had been spoken of its being a yardstick by which all future developments would be measured. But the planners – tears wept, words spoken – had left the estate to its own devices; the architects occupied restored Georgian houses at the other end of the city, and probably never set foot here.

They would not have been shamed by the deterioration of the estate even if they had. Their brain-child (they would doubtless argue) was as brilliant as ever: its geometries as precise, its ratios as calculated; it was *people* who had spoiled Spector Street. Nor would they have been wrong in such an accusation. Helen had seldom seen an inner city environment so comprehensively vandalized. Lamps had been shattered and back-yard fences overthrown; cars whose wheels and engines had been removed and chassis then burned, blocked garage facilities. In one courtyard three or four ground-floor maisonettes had been entirely gutted by fire, their windows and doors boarded up with planks and corrugated iron.

More startling still was the graffiti. That was what she had come here to see, encouraged by Archie's talk of the place, and she was not disappointed. It was difficult to believe, staring at the multiple layers of designs, names, obscenities, and dogmas that were scrawled and sprayed on every available brick, that Spector Street was barely three and a half years old. The walls, so recently virgin, were now so profoundly defaced that the Council Cleaning Department could

1

never hope to return them to their former condition. A layer of whitewash to cancel this visual cacophony would only offer the scribes a fresh and yet more tempting surface on which to make their mark.

Helen was in seventh heaven. Every corner she turned offered some fresh material for her thesis: *'Graffiti: the semiotics of urban despair'*. It was a subject which married her two favourite disciplines – sociology and aesthetics – and as she wandered around the estate she began to wonder if there wasn't a book, in addition to her thesis, in the subject. She walked from courtyard to courtyard, copying down a large number of the more interesting scrawlings, and noting their location. Then she went back to the car to collect her camera and tripod and returned to the most fertile of the areas, to make a thorough visual record of the walls.

It was a chilly business. She was not an expert photographer, and the late October sky was in full flight, shifting the light on the bricks from one moment to the next. As she adjusted and re-adjusted the exposure to compensate for the light changes, her fingers steadily became clumsier, her temper correspondingly thinner. But she struggled on, the idle curiosity of passers-by notwithstanding. There were so many designs to document. She reminded herself that her present discomfort would be amply repaid when she showed the slides to Trevor, whose doubt of the project's validity had been perfectly apparent from the beginning.

'The writing on the wall?' he'd said, half smiling in that irritating fashion of his, 'It's been done a hundred times.'

This was true, of course; and yet not. There certainly were learned works on graffiti, chock full of sociological jargon: *cultural disenfranchisement; urban alienation*. But she flattered herself that *she* might find something amongst this litter of scrawlings that previous analysts had not: some unifying convention perhaps, that she could use as the lynch-pin of her thesis. Only a vigorous cataloguing and cross-referencing of the phrases and images before her would reveal such a correspondence; hence the importance of this photographic study. So many hands had worked here; so many minds left their mark, however casually: if she could find some pattern, some pre-dominant motive, or *motif*, the thesis would be guaranteed some serious attention, and so, in turn, would she.

'What are you doing?' a voice from behind her asked.

She turned from her calculations to see a young woman with a pushchair on the pavement behind her. She looked weary, Helen thought, and pinched by the cold. The child in the pushchair was mewling, his grimy fingers clutching an orange lollipop and the wrapping from a chocolate bar. The bulk of the chocolate, and the

2

remains of previous jujubes, was displayed down the front of his coat.

Helen offered a thin smile to the woman; she looked in need of it.

'I'm photographing the walls,' she said in answer to the initial enquiry, though surely this was perfectly apparent.

The woman – she could barely be twenty – Helen judged, said: 'You mean the filth?'

'The writing and the pictures,' Helen said. Then: 'Yes. The filth.'

'You from the Council?'

'No, the University.'

'It's bloody disgusting,' the woman said. 'The way they do that. It's not just kids, either.'

'No?'

'Grown men. Grown men, too. They don't give a damn. Do it in broad daylight. You see 'em . . . broad daylight.' She glanced down at the child, who was sharpening his lollipop on the ground. 'Kerry!' she snapped, but the boy took no notice. 'Are they going to wipe it off?' she asked Helen.

'I don't know,' Helen said, and reiterated: 'I'm from the University.'

'Oh,' the woman replied, as if this was new information, 'so you're nothing to do with the Council?'

'No.'

'Some of it's obscene, isn't it?; really dirty. Makes me embarrassed to see some of the things they draw.'

Helen nodded, casting an eye at the boy in the pushchair. Kerry had decided to put his sweet in his ear for safe-keeping.

'Don't do that!' his mother told him, and leaned over to slap the child's hand. The blow, which was negligible, began the child bawling. Helen took the opportunity to return to her camera. But the woman still desired to talk. 'It's not just on the outside, neither,' she commented.

'I beg your pardon?' Helen said.

'They break into the flats when they go empty. The Council tried to board them up, but it does no good. They break in anyway. Use them as toilets, and write more filth on the walls. They light fires too. Then nobody can move back in.'

The description piqued Helen's curiosity. Would the graffiti on the *inside* walls be substantially different from the public displays? It was certainly worth an investigation.

'Are there any places you know of around here like that?'

'Empty flats, you mean?'

'With graffiti.'

3

'Just by us, there's one or two,' the woman voluteered. 'I'm in Butts' Court.'

'Maybe you could show me?' Helen asked.

The woman shrugged.

'By the way, my name's Helen Buchanan.'

'Anne-Marie,' the mother replied.

'I'd be very grateful if you could point me to one of those empty flats.'

Anne-Marie was baffled by Helen's enthusiasm, and made no attempt to disguise it, but she shrugged again and said: 'There's nothing much to see. Only more of the same stuff.'

Helen gathered up her equipment and they walked side by side through the intersecting corridors between one square and the next. Though the estate was low-rise, each court only five storeys high, the effect of each quadrangle was horribly claustrophobic. The walkways and staircases were a thief's dream, rife with blind corners and ill-lit tunnels. The rubbish-dumping facilities – chutes from the upper floors down which bags of refuse could be pitched – had long since been sealed up, thanks to their efficiency as fire-traps. Now plastic bags of refuse were piled high in the corridors, many torn open by roaming dogs, their contents strewn across the ground. The smell, even in the cold weather, was unpleasant. In high summer it must have been overpowering.

'I'm over the other side,' Anne-Marie said, pointing across the quadrangle. 'The one with the yellow door.' She then pointed along the opposite side of the court. 'Five or six maisonettes from the far end,' she said. 'There's two of them been emptied out. Few weeks now. One of the family's moved into Ruskin Court; the other did a bunk in the middle of the night.'

With that, she turned her back on Helen and wheeled Kerry, who had taken to trailing spittle from the side of his pushchair, around the side of the square.

'Thank you,' Helen called after her. Anne-Marie glanced over her shoulder briefly, but did not reply. Appetite whetted, Helen made her way along the row of ground floor maisonettes, many of which, though inhabited, showed little sign of being so. Their curtains were closely drawn; there were no milk-bottles on the doorsteps, nor children's toys left where they had been played with. Nothing, in fact, of *life* here. There *was* more graffiti however, sprayed, shockingly, on the doors of occupied houses. She granted the scrawlings only a casual perusal, in part because she feared one of the doors opening as she examined a choice obscenity sprayed upon it, but more because she was eager to see what revelations the empty flats ahead might offer.

4

The malign scent of urine, both fresh and stale, welcomed her at the threshold of number 14, and beneath that the smell of burnt paint and plastic. She hesitated for fully ten seconds, wondering if stepping into the maisonette was a wise move. The territory of the estate behind her was indisputably foreign, sealed off in its own misery, but the rooms in front of her were more intimidating still: a dark maze which her eyes could barely penetrate. But when her courage faltered she thought of Trevor, and how badly she wanted to silence his condescension. So thinking, she advanced into the place, deliberately kicking a piece of charred timber aside as she did so, in the hope that she would alert any tenant into showing himself.

There was no sound of occupancy however. Gaining confidence, she began to explore the front room of the maisonette which had been – to judge by the remains of a disembowelled sofa in one corner and the sodden carpet underfoot – a living-room. The pale-green walls were, as Anne-Marie had promised, extensively defaced, both by minor scribblers – content to work in pen, or even more crudely in sofa charcoal – and by those with aspirations to public works, who had sprayed the walls in half a dozen colours.

Some of the comments were of interest, though many she had already seen on the walls outside. Familiar names and couplings repeated themselves. Though she had never set eyes on these individuals she knew how badly Fabian J. (A.OK!) wanted to deflower Michelle; and that Michelle, in her turn, had the hots for somebody called Mr Sheen. Here, as elsewhere, a man called White Rat boasted of his endowment, and the return of the Syllabub Brothers was promised in red paint. One or two of the pictures accompanying, or at least adjacent to, these phrases were of particular interest. An almost emblematic simplicity informed them. Beside the word *Christos* was a stick man with his hair radiating from his head like spines, and other heads impaled on each spine. Close by was an image of intercourse so brutally reduced that at first Helen took it to illustrate a· knife plunging into a sightless eye. But fascinating as the images were, the room was too gloomy for her fil,m and she had neglected to bring a flash. If she wanted a reliable record of these discoveries she would have to come again, and for now be content with a simple exploration of the premises.

The maisonette wasn't that large, but the windows had been boarded up throughout, and as she moved further from the front door the dubious light petered out altogether. The smell of urine, which had been strong at the door, intensified too, until by the time she reached the back of the living-room and stepped along a short corridor into another room beyond, it was cloying as incense. This room, being furthest from the front door, was also the darkest, and

5

she had to wait a few moments in the cluttered gloom to allow her eyes to become useful. This, she guessed, had been the bedroom. What little furniture the residents had left behind them had been smashed to smithereens. Only the mattress had been left relatively untouched, dumped in the corner of the room amongst a wretched litter of blankets, newspapers, and pieces of crockery.

Outside, the sun found its way between the clouds, and two or three shafts of sunlight slipped between the boards nailed across the bedroom window and pierced the room like annunciations, scoring the opposite wall with bright lines. Here, the graffitists had been busy once more: the usual clamour of love-letters and threats. She scanned the wall quickly, and as she did so her eye was led by the beams of light across the room to the wall which contained the door she had stepped through.

Here, the artists had also been at work, but had produced an image the like of which she had not seen anywhere else. Using the door, which was centrally placed in the wall, as a mouth, the artists had sprayed a single, vast head on to the stripped plaster. The painting was more adroit than most she had seen, rife with detail that lent the image an unsettling veracity. The cheekbones jutting through skin the colour of buttermilk; the teeth – sharpened to irregular points – all converging on the door. The sitter's eyes were, owing to the room's low ceiling, set mere inches above the upper lip, but this physical adjustment only lent force to the image, giving the impression that he had thrown his head back. Knotted strands of his hair snaked from his scalp across the ceiling.

Was it a portrait? There was something naggingly *specific* in the details of the brows and the lines around the wide mouth; in the careful picturing of those vicious teeth. A nightmare certainly: a facsimile, perhaps, of something from a heroin fugue. Whatever its origins, it was potent. Even the illusion of door-as-mouth worked. The short passageway between living-room and bedroom offered a passable throat, with a tattered lamp in lieu of tonsils. Beyond the gullet, the day burned white in the nightmare's belly. The whole effect brought to mind a ghost train painting. The same heroic deformity, the same unashamed intention to scare. And it worked; she stood in the bedroom almost stupified by the picture, its red-rimmed eyes fixing her mercilessly. Tomorrow, she determined, she would come here again, this time with high-speed film and a flash to illuminate the masterwork.

As she prepared to leave the sun went in, and the bands of light faded. She glanced over her shoulder at the boarded windows, and saw for the first time that one four-word slogan had been sprayed on the wall beneath them.

6

'*Sweets to the sweet*' it read. She was familiar with the quote, but not with its source. Was it a profession of love? If so, it was an odd location for such an avowal. Despite the mattress in the corner, and the relative privacy of this room, she could not imagine the intended reader of such words ever stepping in here to receive her bouquet. No adolescent lovers, however heated, would lie down here to play at mothers and fathers; not under the gaze of the terror on the wall. She crossed to examine the writing. The paint looked to be the same shade of pink as had been used to colour the gums of the screaming man; perhaps the same hand?

Behind her, a noise. She turned so quickly she almost tripped over the blanket-strewn mattress.

'Who – ?'

At the other end of the gullet, in the living-room, was a scab-kneed boy of six or seven. He stared at Helen, eyes glittering in the half-light, as if waiting for a cue.

'Yes?' she said.

'Anne-Marie says do you want a cup of tea?' he declared without pause or intonation.

Her conversation with the woman seemed hours past. She was grateful for the invitation however. The damp in the maisonette had chilled her.

'Yes . . .' she said to the boy. 'Yes please.'

The child didn't move, but simply stared on at her.

'Are you going to lead the way?' she asked him.

'If you want,' he replied, unable to raise a trace of enthusiasm.

'I'd like that.'

'You taking photographs?' he asked.

'Yes. Yes, I am. But not in here.'

'Why not?'

'It's too dark,' she told him.

'Don't it work in the dark?' he wanted to know.

'No.'

The boy nodded at this, as if the information somehow fitted well into his scheme of things, and about turned without another word, clearly expecting Helen to follow.

If she had been taciturn in the street, Anne-Marie was anything but in the privacy of her own kitchen. Gone was the guarded curiosity, to be replaced by a stream of lively chatter and a constant scurrying between half a dozen minor domestic tasks, like a juggler keeping several plates spinning simultaneously. Helen watched this balancing act with some admiration; her own domestic skills were negligible. At

7

last, the meandering conversation turned back to the subject that had brought Helen here.

'Them photographs,' Anne-Marie said, 'why'd you want to take them?'

'I'm writing about graffiti. The photos will illustrate my thesis.'

'It's not very pretty.'

'No, you're right, it isn't. But I find it interesting.'

Anne-Marie shook her head. 'I hate the whole estate,' she said. 'It's not safe here. People getting robbed on their own doorsteps. Kids setting fire to the rubbish day in, day out. Last summer we had the fire brigade here two, three times a day, 'til they sealed them chutes off. Now people just dump the bags in the passageways, and that attracts rats.'

'Do you live here alone?'

'Yes,' she said, 'since Davey walked out.'

'That your husband?'

'He was Kerry's father, but we weren't never married. We lived together two years, you know. We had some good times. Then he just upped and went off one day when I was at me Mam's with Kerry.' She peered into her tea-cup. 'I'm better off without him,' she said. 'But you get scared sometimes. Want some more tea?'

'I don't think I've got time.'

'Just a cup,' Anne-Marie said, already up and unplugging the electric kettle to take it across for a re-fill. As she was about to turn on the tap she saw something on the draining board, and drove her thumb down, grinding it out. 'Got you, you bugger,' she said, then turned to Helen: 'We got these bloody ants.'

'Ants?'

'Whole estate's infected. From Egypt, they are: pharoah ants, they're called. Little brown sods. They breed in the central heating ducts, you see; that way they get into all the flats. Place is plagued with them.'

This unlikely exoticism (ants from Egypt?) struck Helen as comical, but she said nothing. Anne-Marie was staring out of the kitchen window and into the back-yard.

'You should tell them – ' she said, though Helen wasn't certain whom she was being instructed to tell, 'tell them that ordinary people can't even walk the streets any longer – '

'Is it really so bad?' Helen said, frankly tiring of this catalogue of misfortunes.

Anne-Marie turned from the sink and looked at her hard.

'We've had murders here,' she said.

'Really?'

'We had one in the summer. An old man he was, from Ruskin.

That's just next door. I didn't know him, but he was a friend of the sister of the woman next door. I forget his name.'

'And he was murdered?'

'Cut to ribbons in his own front room. They didn't find him for almost a week.'

'What about his neighbours? Didn't they notice his absence?'

Anne-Marie shrugged, as if the most important pieces of information – the murder and the man's isolation – had been exchanged, and any further enquiries into the problem were irrelevant. But Helen pressed the point.

'Seems strange to me,' she said.

Anne-Marie plugged in the filled kettle. 'Well, it happened,' she replied, unmoved.

'I'm not saying it didn't, I just – '

'His eyes had been taken out,' she said, before Helen could voice any further doubts.

Helen winced. 'No,' she said, under her breath.

'That's the truth,' Anne-Marie said. 'And that wasn't all'd been done to him.' She paused, for effect, then went on: 'You wonder what kind of person's capable of doing things like that, don't you? You wonder.' Helen nodded. She was thinking precisely the same thing.

'Did they ever find the man responsible?'

Anne-Marie snorted her disparagement. 'Police don't give a damn what happens here. They keep off the estate as much as possible. When they do patrol all they do is pick up kids for getting drunk and that. They're afraid, you see. That's why they keep clear.'

'Of this killer?'

'Maybe,' Anne-Marie replied. 'Then: He had a hook.'

'A hook?'

'The man what done it. He had a hook, like Jack the Ripper.'

Helen was no expert on murder, but she felt certain that the Ripper hadn't boasted a hook. It seemed churlish to question the truth of Anne-Marie's story however; though she silently wondered how much of this – the eyes taken out, the body rotting in the flat, the hook – was elaboration. The most scrupulous of reporters was surely tempted to embellish a story once in a while.

Anne-Marie had poured herself another cup of tea, and was about to do the same for her guest.

'No thank you,' Helen said, 'I really should go.'

'You married?' Anne-Marie asked, out of the blue.

'Yes. To a lecturer from the University.'

'What's his name?'

'Trevor.'

9

Anne-Marie put two heaped spoonfuls of sugar into her cup of tea. 'Will you be coming back?' she asked.

'Yes, I hope to. Later in the week. I want to take some photographs of the pictures in the maisonette across the court.'

'Well, call in.'

'I shall. And thank you for your help.'

'That's all right,' Anne-Marie replied. 'You've got to tell somebody, haven't you?'

'The man apparently had a hook instead of a hand.'

Trevor looked up from his plate of *tagliatelle con prosciutto*.

'Beg your pardon?'

Helen had been at pains to keep her recounting of this story as uncoloured by her own response as she could. She was interested to know what Trevor would make of it, and she knew that if she once signalled her own stance he would instinctively take an opposing view out of plain bloody-mindedness.

'He had a hook,' she repeated, without inflexion.

Trevor put down his fork, and plucked at his nose, sniffing. 'I didn't read anything about this,' he said.

'You don't look at the local press,' Helen returned. 'Neither of us do. Maybe it never made any of the nationals.'

'"Geriatric Murdered By Hook-Handed Maniac"?' Trevor said, savouring the hyperbole. 'I would have thought it very newsworthy. When was all of this supposed to have happened?'

'Sometime last summer. Maybe we were in Ireland.'

'Maybe,' said Trevor, taking up his fork again. Bending to his food, the polished lens of his spectacles reflected only the plate of pasta and chopped ham in front of him, not his eyes.

'Why do you say *maybe?*' Helen prodded.

'It doesn't sound quite right,' he said. 'In fact it sounds bloody preposterous.'

'You don't believe it?' Helen said.

Trevor looked up from his food, tongue rescuing a speck of *tagliatelle* from the corner of his mouth. His face had relaxed into that non-committal expression of his – the same face he wore, no doubt, when listening to his students. 'Do *you* believe it?' he asked Helen. It was a favourite time-gaining device of his, another seminar trick, to question the questioner.

'I'm not certain,' Helen replied, too concerned to find some solid ground in this sea of doubts to waste energy scoring points.

'All right, forget the tale – ' Trevor said, deserting his food for another glass of red wine. ' – What about the teller? Did you trust her?'

10

Helen pictured Anne-Marie's earnest expression as she told the story of the old man's murder. 'Yes,' she said. 'Yes; I think I would have known if she'd been lying to me.'

'So why's it so important, anyhow? I mean, whether she's lying or not, what the fuck does it matter?'

It was a reasonable question, if irritatingly put. Why *did* it matter? Was it that she wanted to have her worst feelings about Spector Street proved false? That such an estate be filthy, be hopeless, be a dump where the undesirable and the disadvantaged were tucked out of public view – all that was a liberal commonplace, and she accepted it as an unpalatable social reality. But the story of the old man's murder and mutilation was something other. An image of violent death that, once with her, refused to part from her company.

She realized, to her chagrin, that this confusion was plain on her face, and that Trevor, watching her across the table, was not a little entertained by it.

'If it bothers you so much,' he said, 'why don't you go back there and ask around, instead of playing believe-in-it-or-not over dinner?'

She couldn't help but rise to his remark. 'I thought you liked guessing games,' she said.

He threw her a sullen look.

'Wrong again.'

The suggestion that she investigate was not a bad one, though doubtless he had ulterior motives for offering it. She viewed Trevor less charitably day by day. What she had once thought in him a fierce commitment to debate she now recognized as mere power-play. He argued, not for the thrill of dialectic, but because he was pathologically competitive. She had seen him, time and again, take up attitudes she knew he did not espouse, simply to spill blood. Nor, more's the pity, was he alone in this sport. Academe was one of the last strongholds of the professional time-waster. On occasion their circle seemed entirely dominated by educated fools, lost in a wasteland of stale rhetoric and hollow commitment.

From one wasteland to another. She returned to Spector Street the following day, armed with a flashgun in addition to her tripod and high-sensitive film. The wind was up today, and it was Arctic, more furious still for being trapped in the maze of passageways and courts. She made her way to number 14, and spent the next hour in its befouled confines, meticulously photographing both the bedroom and living-room walls. She had half expected the impact of the head in the bedroom to be dulled by re-acquaintance; it was not. Though she struggled to capture its scale and detail as best she could, she knew the photographs would be at best a dim echo of its perpetual howl.

11

Much of its power lay in its context, of course. That such an image might be stumbled upon in surroundings so drab, so conspicuously lacking in mystery, was akin to finding an icon on a rubbish-heap: a gleaming symbol of transcendence from a world of toil and decay into some darker but more tremendous realm. She was painfully aware that the intensity of her response probably defied her articulation. Her vocabulary was analytic, replete with buzz-words and academic terminology, but woefully impoverished when it came to evocation. The photographs, pale as they would be, would, she hoped, at least hint at the potency of this picture, even if they couldn't conjure the way it froze the bowels.

When she emerged from the maisonette the wind was as uncharitable as ever, but the boy waiting outside – the same child as had attended upon her yesterday – was dressed as if for spring weather. He grimaced in his effort to keep the shudders at bay.

'Hello,' Helen said.

'I waited,' the child announced.

'Waited?'

'Anne-Marie said you'd come back.'

'I wasn't planning to come until later in the week,' Helen said. 'You might have waited a long time.'

The boy's grimace relaxed a notch. 'It's all right,' he said, 'I've got nothing to do.'

'What about school?'

'Don't like it,' the boy replied, as if unobliged to be educated if it wasn't to his taste.

'I see,' said Helen, and began to walk down the side of the quadrangle. The boy followed. On the patch of grass at the centre of the quadrangle several chairs and two or three dead saplings had been piled.

'What's this?' she said, half to herself.

'Bonfire Night,' the boy informed her. 'Next week.'

'Of course.'

'You going to see Anne-Marie?' he asked.

'Yes.'

'She's not in.'·

'Oh. Are you sure?'

'Yeah.'

'Well, perhaps *you* can help me . . .' She stopped and turned to face the child; smooth sacs of fatigue hung beneath his eyes. 'I heard about an old man who was murdered near here,' she said to him. 'In the summer. Do you know anything about that?'

'No.'

'Nothing at all? You don't remember anybody getting killed?'

'No,' the boy said again, with impressive finality. 'I don't remember.'

'Well; thank you anyway.'

This time, when she retraced her steps back to the car, the boy didn't follow. But as she turned the corner out of the quadrangle she glanced back to see him standing on the spot where she'd left him, staring after her as if she were a madwoman.

By the time she had reached the car and packed the photographic equipment into the boot there were specks of rain in the wind, and she was sorely tempted to forget she'd ever heard Anne-Marie's story and make her way home, where the coffee would be warm even if the welcome wasn't. But she needed an answer to the question Trevor had put the previous night. Do *you* believe it?, he'd asked when she'd told him the story. She hadn't known how to answer then, and she still didn't. Perhaps (why did she sense this?) the terminology of verifiable truth was redundant here; perhaps the final answer to his question was not an answer at all, only another question. If so; so. She had to find out.

Ruskin Court was as forlorn as its fellows, if not more so. It didn't even boast a bonfire. On the third floor balcony a woman was taking washing in before the rain broke; on the grass in the centre of the quadrangle two dogs were absent-mindedly rutting, the fuckee staring up at the blank sky. As she walked along the empty pavement she set her face determinedly; a purposeful look, Bernadette had once said, deterred attack. When she caught sight of the two women talking at the far end of the court she crossed over to them hurriedly, grateful for their presence.

'Excuse me?'

The women, both in middle-age, ceased their animated exchange and looked her over.

'I wonder if you can help me?'

She could feel their appraisal, and their distrust; they went undisguised. One of the pair, her face florid, said plainly: 'What do you want?'

Helen suddenly felt bereft of the least power to charm. What was she to say to these two that wouldn't make her motives appear ghoulish? 'I was told . . .' she began, and then stumbled, aware that she would get no assistance from either woman. '. . . I was told there'd been a murder near here. Is that right?'

The florid woman raised eyebrows so plucked they were barely visible. 'Murder?' she said.

'Are you from the press?' the other woman enquired. The years had soured her features beyond sweetening. Her small mouth was

13

deeply lined; her hair, which had been dyed brunette, showed a half-inch of grey at the roots.

'No, I'm not from the press,' Helen said, 'I'm a friend of Anne-Marie's, in Butts' Court.' This claim of *friend* stretched the truth, but it seemed to mellow the women somewhat.

'Visiting are you?' the florid woman asked.

'In a manner of speaking – '

'You missed the warm spell – '

'Anne-Marie was telling me about somebody who'd been murdered here, during the summer. I was curious about it.'

'Is that right?'

' – do you know anything about it?'

'Lots of things go on around here,' said the second woman. 'You don't know the half of it.'

'So it's true,' Helen said.

'They had to close the toilets,' the first woman put in.

'That's right. They did,' the other said.

'The toilets?' Helen said. What had this to do with the old man's death?

'It was terrible,' the first said. 'Was it your Frank, Josie, who told you about it?'

'No, not Frank,' Josie replied. 'Frank was still at sea. It was Mrs Tyzack.'

The witness established, Josie relinquished the story to her companion, and turned her gaze back upon Helen. The suspicion had not yet died from her eyes.

'This was only the month before last,' Josie said. 'Just about the end of August. It was August, wasn't it?' She looked to the other woman for verification. 'You've got the head for dates, Maureen.'

Maureen looked uncomfortable. 'I forget,' she said, clearly unwilling to offer testimony.

'I'd like to know,' Helen said. Josie, despite her companion's reluctance, was eager to oblige.

'There's some lavatories,' she said, 'outside the shops – you know, public lavatories. I'm not quite sure how it all happened exactly, but there used to be a boy . . . well, he wasn't a boy really, I mean he was a man of twenty or more, but he was . . .' she fished for the words, '. . . mentally subnormal, I suppose you'd say. His mother used to have to take him around like he was a four year old. Anyhow, she let him go into the lavatories while she went to that little supermarket, what's it called?' she turned to Maureen for a prompt, but the other woman just looked back, her disapproval plain. Josie was ungovernable, however. 'Broad daylight, this was,' she said to Helen. 'Middle of the day. Anyhow, the boy went to the toilet, and

14

the mother was in the shop. And after a while, you know how you do, she's busy shopping, she forgets about him, and then she thinks he's been gone a long time . . .'

At this juncture Maureen couldn't prevent herself from butting in: the accuracy of the story apparently took precedence over her wariness.

' – She got into an argument,' she corrected Josie, 'with the manager. About some bad bacon she'd had from him. That was why she was such a time . . .'

'I see,' said Helen.

' – anyway,' said Josie, picking up the tale, 'she finished her shopping and when she came out he still wasn't there – '

'So she asked someone from the supermarket – ' Maureen began, but Josie wasn't about to have her narrative snatched back at this vital juncture.

'She asked one of the men from the supermarket – ' she repeated over Maureen's interjection, 'to go down into the lavatory and find him.'

'It was terrible,' said Maureen, clearly picturing the atrocity in her mind's eye.

'He was lying on the floor, in a pool of blood.'

'Murdered?'

Josie shook her head. 'He'd have been better off dead. He'd been attacked with a razor – ' she let this piece of information sink in before delivering the *coup de grâce*, ' – and they'd cut off his private parts. Just cut them off and flushed them down a toilet. No reason on earth to do it.'

'Oh my God.'

'Better off dead,' Josie repeated. 'I mean, they can't mend something like that, can they?'

The appalling tale was rendered worse still by the *sang-froid* of the teller, and by the casual repetition of 'Better off dead'.

'The boy,' Helen said, 'Was he able to describe his attackers?'

'No,' said Josie, 'he's practically an imbecile. He can't string more than two words together.'

'And nobody saw anyone go into the lavatory? Or leaving it?'

'People come and go all the time – ' Maureen said. This, though it sounded like an adequate explanation, had not been Helen's experience. There was not a great bustle in the quadrangle and passageways; far from it. Perhaps the shopping mall was busier, she reasoned, and might offer adequate cover for such a crime.

'So they haven't found the culprit,' she said.

'No,' Josie replied, her eyes losing their fervour. The crime and its

15

immediate consequences were the nub of this story; she had little or no interest in either the culprit or his capture.

'We're not safe in our own beds,' Maureen observed. 'You ask anyone.'

'Anne-Marie said the same,' Helen replied. 'That's how she came to tell me about the old man. Said he was murdered during the summer, here in Ruskin Court.'

'I do remember something,' Josie said. 'There *was* some talk I heard. An old man, and his dog. He was battered to death, and the dog ended up . . . I don't know. It certainly wasn't here. It must have been one of the other estates.'

'Are you sure?'

The woman looked offended by this slur on her memory. 'Oh yes,' she said, 'I mean if it had been here, we'd have known the story, wouldn't we?'

Helen thanked the pair for their help and decided to take a stroll around the quadrangle anyway, just to see how many more maisonettes were out of operation here. As in Butts' Court, many of the curtains were drawn and all the doors locked. But then if Spector Street *was* under siege from a maniac capable of the murder and mutilation such as she'd heard described, she was not surprised that the residents took to their homes and stayed there. There was nothing much to see around the court. All the unoccupied maisonettes and flats had been recently sealed, to judge by a litter of nails left on a doorstep by the council workmen. One sight *did* catch her attention however. Scrawled on the paving stones she was walking over – and all but erased by rain and the passage of feet – the same phrase she'd seen in the bedroom of number 14: *Sweets to the sweet*. The words were so benign; why did she seem to sense menace in them? Was it in their excess, perhaps, in the sheer overabundance of sugar upon sugar, honey upon honey?

She walked on, though the rain persisted, and her walkabout gradually led her away from the quadrangles and into a concrete no-man's-land through which she had not previously passed. This was – or had been – the site of the estate's amenities. Here was the children's playground, its metal-framed rides overturned, its sandpit fouled by dogs, its paddling pool empty. And here too were the shops. Several had been boarded up; those that hadn't were dingy and unattractive, their windows protected by heavy wire-mesh.

She walked along the row, and rounded a corner, and there in front of her was a squat brick building. The public lavatory, she guessed, though the signs designating it as such had gone. The iron gates were closed and padlocked. Standing in front of the charmless

16

building, the wind gusting around her legs, she couldn't help but think of what had happened here. Of the man-child, bleeding on the floor, helpless to cry out. It made her queasy even to contemplate it. She turned her thoughts instead to the felon. What would he look like, she wondered, a man capable of such depravities? She tried to make an image of him, but no detail she could conjure carried sufficient force. But then monsters were seldom very terrible once hauled into the plain light of day. As long as this man was known only by his deeds he held untold power over the imagination; but the human truth beneath the terrors would, she knew, be bitterly disappointing. No monster he; just a whey-faced apology for a man more needful of pity than awe.

The next gust of wind brought the rain on more heavily. It was time, she decided, to be done with adventures for the day. Turning her back on the public lavatories she hurried back through the quadrangles to the refuge of the car, the icy rain needling her face to numbness.

The dinner guests looked gratifyingly appalled at the story, and Trevor, to judge by the expression on his face, was furious. It was done now, however; there was no taking it back. Nor could she deny her satisfaction she took in having silenced the inter-departmental babble about the table. It was Bernadette, Trevor's assistant in the History Department, who broke the agonizing hush.

'When was this?'

'During the summer,' Helen told her.

'I don't recall reading about it,' said Archie, much the better for two hours of drinking; it mellowed a tongue which was otherwise fulsome in its self-corruscation.

'Perhaps the police are suppressing it,' Daniel commented.

'Conspiracy?' said Trevor, plainly cynical.

'It's happening all the time,' Daniel shot back.

'Why should they suppress something like this?' Helen said. 'It doesn't make sense.'

'Since when has police procedure made sense?' Daniel replied.

Bernadette cut in before Helen could answer. 'We don't even bother to read about these things any longer,' she said.

'Speak for yourself,' somebody piped up, but she ignored them and went on:

'We're punch-drunk with violence. We don't see it any longer, even when it's in front of our noses.'

'On the screen every night,' Archie put in, 'Death and disaster in full colour.'

17

'There's nothing very modern about that,' Trevor said. 'An Elizabethan would have seen death all the time. Public executions were a very popular form of entertainment.'

The table broke up into a cacophony of opinions. After two hours of polite gossip the dinner-party had suddenly caught fire. Listening to the debate rage Helen was sorry she hadn't had time to have the photographs processed and printed; the graffiti would have added further fuel to this exhilarating row. It was Purcell, as usual, who was the last to weigh in with his point of view; and – again, as usual – it was devastating.

'Of course, Helen, my sweet – ' he began, that affected weariness in his voice edged with the anticipation of controversy ' – your witnesses could all be lying, couldn't they?'

The talking around the table dwindled, and all heads turned in Purcell's direction. Perversely, he ignored the attention he'd garnered, and turned to whisper in the ear of the boy he'd brought – a new passion who would, on past form, be discarded in a matter of weeks for another pretty urchin.

'Lying?' Helen said. She could feel herself bristling at the observation already, and Purcell had only spoken a dozen words.

'Why not?' the other replied, lifting his glass of wine to his lips. 'Perhaps they're all weaving some elaborate fiction or other. The story of the spastic's mutilation in the public toilet. The murder of the old man. Even that hook. All quite familiar elements. You must be aware that there's something *traditional* about these atrocity stories. One used to exchange them all the time; there was a certain *frission* in them. Something competitive maybe, in attempting to find a new detail to add to the collective fiction; a fresh twist that would render the tale that little bit more appalling when you passed it on.'

'It may be familiar to you – ' said Helen defensively. Purcell was always so *poised*; it irritated her. Even if there were validity in his argument – which she doubted – she was damned if she'd concede it. ' – *I've* never heard this kind of story before.'

'Have you not?' said Purcell, as though she were admitting to illiteracy. 'What about the lovers and the escaped lunatic, have you heard that one?'

'I've heard that . . .' Daniel said.

'The lover is disembowelled – usually by a hook-handed man – and the body left on the top of the car, while the fiancé cowers inside. It's a cautionary tale, warning of the evils of rampant heterosexuality.' The joke won a round of laughter from everyone but Helen. 'These stories are very common.'

'So you're saying that they're telling me lies – ' she protested.

'Not lies, exactly – '

'You said *lies*.'

'I was being provocative,' Purcell returned, his placatory tone more enraging than ever. 'I don't mean to imply there's any serious mischief in it. But you *must* concede that so far you haven't met a single *witness*. All these events have happened at some unspecified date to some unspecified person. They are reported at several removes. They occurred at best to the brothers of friends of distant relations. Please consider the possibility that perhaps these events do not exist in the real world at all, but are merely titillation for bored housewives – '

Helen didn't make an argument in return, for the simple reason that she lacked one. Purcell's point about the conspicuous absence of witnesses was perfectly sound; she herself had wondered about it. It was strange, too, the way the women in Ruskin Court had speedily consigned the old man's murder to another estate, as though these atrocities always occurred just out of sight – round the next corner, down the next passageway – but never *here*.

'So why?' said Bernadette.

'Why what?' Archie puzzled.

'The stories. Why tell these horrible stories if they're not true?'

'Yes,' said Helen, throwing the controversy back into Purcell's ample lap. '*Why?*'

Purcell preened himself, aware that his entry into the debate had changed the basic assumption at a stroke. 'I don't know,' he said, happy to be done with the game now that he'd shown his arm. 'You really mustn't take me too seriously, Helen. *I* try not to.' The boy at Purcell's side tittered.

'Maybe it's simply taboo material,' Archie said.

'Suppressed – ' Daniel prompted.

'Not the way you mean it,' Archie retorted. 'The whole world isn't politics, Daniel.'

'Such naiveté.'

'What's so *taboo* about death?' Trevor said. 'Bernadette already pointed out: it's in front of us all the time. Television; newspapers.'

'Maybe that's not close enough,' Bernadette suggested.

'Does anyone mind if I smoke?' Purcell broke in. 'Only dessert seems to have been indefinitely postponed – '

Helen ignored the remark, and asked Bernadette what she meant by 'not close enough'?

Bernadette shrugged. 'I don't know precisely,' she confessed, 'maybe just that death has to be *near*; we have to *know* it's just round the corner. The television's not intimate enough – '

Helen frowned. The observation made some sense to her, but in the clutter of the moment she couldn't root out its significance.

19

'Do you think they're stories too?' she asked.

'Andrew has a point – ' Bernadette replied.

'Most kind,' said Purcell. 'Has somebody got a match? The boy's pawned my lighter.'

' – about the absence of witnesses.'

'All that proves is that I haven't met anybody who's actually *seen* anything,' Helen countered, 'not that witnesses don't exist.'

'All right,' said Purcell. 'Find me one. If you can prove to me that your atrocity-monger actually lives and breathes, I'll stand everyone dinner at *Appollinaires*. How's that? Am I generous to a fault, or do I just know when I can't lose?' He laughed, knocking on the table with his knuckles by way of applause.

'Sounds good to me,' said Trevor. 'What do you say, Helen?'

She didn't go back to Spector Street until the following Monday, but all weekend she was there in thought: standing outside the locked toilet, with the wind bringing rain; or in the bedroom, the portrait looming. Thoughts of the estate claimed all her concern. When, late on Saturday afternoon, Trevor found some petty reason for an argument, she let the insults pass, watching him perform the familiar ritual of self-martyrdom without being touched by it in the least. Her indifference only enraged him further. He stormed out in high dudgeon, to visit whichever of his women was in favour this month. She was glad to see the back of him. When he failed to return that night she didn't even think of weeping about it. He was foolish and vacuous. She despaired of ever seeing a haunted look in his dull eyes; and what worth was a man who could not be haunted?

He did not return Sunday night either, and it crossed her mind the following morning, as she parked the car in the heart of the estate, that nobody even knew she had come, and that she might lose herself for days here and nobody be any the wiser. Like the old man Anne-Marie had told her about: lying forgotten in his favourite armchair with his eyes hooked out, while the flies feasted and the butter went rancid on the table.

It was almost Bonfire Night, and over the weekend the small heap of combustibles in Butts' Court had grown to a substantial size. The construction looked unsound, but that didn't prevent a number of boys and young adolescents clambering over it and into it. Much of its bulk was made up of furniture, filched, no doubt, from boarded up properties. She doubted if it could burn for any time: if it did, it would go chokingly. Four times, on her way across to Anne-Marie's house, she was waylaid by children begging for money to buy fireworks.

'Penny for the guy', they'd say, though none had a guy to display.

She had emptied her pockets of change by the time she reached the front door.

Anne-Marie was in today, though there was no welcoming smile. She simply stared at her visitor as if mesmerised.

'I hope you don't mind me calling . . .'

Anne-Marie made no reply.

'. . . I just wanted a word.'

'I'm busy,' the woman finally announced. There was no invitation inside, no offer of tea.

'Oh. Well . . . it won't take more than a moment.'

The back door was open and the draught blew through the house. Papers were flying about in the back yard. Helen could see them lifting into the air like vast white moths.

'What do you want?' Anne-Marie asked.

'Just to ask you about the old man.'

The woman frowned minutely. She looked as if she was sickening, Helen thought: her face had the colour and texture of stale dough, her hair was lank and greasy.

'What old man?'

'Last time I was here, you told me about an old man who'd been murdered, do you remember?'

'No.'

'You said he lived in the next court.'

'I don't remember,' Anne-Marie said.

'But you *distinctly* told me – '

Something fell to the floor in the kitchen, and smashed. Anne-Marie flinched, but did not move from the doorstep, her arm barring Helen's way into the house. The hallway was littered with the child's toys, gnawed and battered.

'Are you all right?'

Anne-Marie nodded. 'I've got work to do,' she said.

'And you don't remember telling me about the old man?'

'You must have misunderstood,' Anne-Marie replied, and then, her voice hushed: 'You shouldn't have come. Everybody *knows*.'

'Knows what?'

The girl had begun to tremble. 'You don't understand, do you? You think people aren't watching?'

'What does it matter? All I asked was – '

'I don't know *anything*,' Anne-Marie reiterated. 'Whatever I said to you, I lied about it.'

'Well, thank you anyway,' Helen said, too perplexed by the confusion of signals from Anne-Marie to press the point any further.

21

Almost as soon as she had turned from the door she heard the lock snap closed behind her.

That conversation was only one of several disappointments that morning brought. She went back to the row of shops, and visited the supermarket that Josie had spoken of. There she inquired about the lavatories, and their recent history. The supermarket had only changed hands in the last month, and the new owner, a taciturn Pakistani, insisted that he knew nothing of when or why the lavatories had been closed. She was aware, as she made her enquiries, of being scrutinized by the other customers in the shop; she felt like a pariah. That feeling deepened when, after leaving the supermarket, she saw Josie emerging from the launderette, and called after her only to have the woman pick up her pace and duck away into the maze of corridors. Helen followed, but rapidly lost both her quarry and her way.

Frustrated to the verge of tears, she stood amongst the overturned rubbish bags, and felt a surge of contempt for her foolishness. She didn't belong here, did she? How many times had she criticized others for their presumption in claiming to understand societies they had merely viewed from afar? And here was she, committing the same crime, coming here with her camera and her questions, using the lives (and deaths) of these people as fodder for party conversation. She didn't blame Anne-Marie for turning her back; had she deserved better?

Tired and chilled, she decided it was time to concede Purcell's point. It *was* all fiction she had been told. They had played with her – sensing her desire to be fed some horrors – and she, the perfect fool, had fallen for every ridiculous word. It was time to pack up her credulity and go home.

One call demanded to be made before she returned to the car however: she wanted to look a final time at the painted head. Not as an anthropologist amongst an alien tribe, but as a confessed ghost train rider: for the thrill of it. Arriving at number 14, however, she faced the last and most crushing disappointment. The maisonette had been sealed up by conscientious council workmen. The door was locked; the front window boarded over.

She was determined not to be so easily defeated however. She made her way around the back of Butts' Court and located the yard of number 14 by simple mathematics. The gate was wedged closed from the inside, but she pushed hard upon it, and, with effort on both parts, it opened. A heap of rubbish – rotted carpets, a box of rain-sodden magazines, a denuded Christmas tree – had blocked it.

She crossed the yard to the boarded up windows, and peered

through the slats of wood. It wasn't bright outside, but it was darker still within; it was difficult to catch more than the vaguest hint of the painting on the bedroom wall. She pressed her face close to the wood, eager for a final glimpse.

A shadow moved across the room, momentarily blocking her view. She stepped back from the window, startled, not certain of what she'd seen. Perhaps merely her own shadow, cast through the window? But then *she* hadn't moved; it had.

She approached the window again, more cautiously. The air vibrated; she could hear a muted whine from somewhere, though she couldn't be certain whether it came from inside or out. Again, she put her face to the rough boards, and suddenly, something leapt at the window. This time she let out a cry. There was a scrabbling sound from within, as nails raked the wood.

A dog!; and a big one to have jumped so high.

'Stupid,' she told herself aloud. A sudden sweat bathed her.

The scrabbling had stopped almost as soon as it had started, but she couldn't bring herself to go back to the window. Clearly the workmen who had sealed up the maisonette had failed to check it properly, and incarcerated the animal by mistake. It was ravenous, to judge by the slavering she'd heard; she was grateful she hadn't attempted to break in. The dog – hungry, maybe half-mad in the stinking darkness – could have taken out her throat.

She stared at the boarded-up window. The slits between the boards were barely a half-inch wide, but she sensed that the animal was up on its hind legs on the other side, watching her through the gap. She could hear its panting now that her own breath was regularizing; she could hear its claws raking the sill.

'Bloody thing . . .' she said. 'Damn well stay in there.'

She backed off towards the gate. Hosts of wood-lice and spiders, disturbed from their nests by moving the carpets behind the gate, were scurrying underfoot, looking for a fresh darkness to call home.

She closed the gate behind her, and was making her way around the front of the block when she heard the sirens; two ugly spirals of sound that made the hair on the back of her neck tingle. They were approaching. She picked up her speed, and came round into Butts' Court in time to see several policemen crossing the grass behind the bonfire and an ambulance mounting the pavement and driving around to the other side of the quadrangle. People had emerged from their flats and were standing on their balconies, staring down. Others were walking around the court, nakedly curious, to join a gathering congregation. Helen's stomach seemed to drop to her bowels when she realized *where* the hub of interest lay: at Anne-Marie's doorstep. The police were clearing a path through the throng for the ambulance men. A second police-car had followed the route of the ambulance onto the pavement; two plain-clothes officers were getting out.

She walked to the periphery of the crowd. What little talk there was amongst the on-lookers was conducted in low voices; one or two of the older women were crying. Though she peered over the heads of the spectators she could see nothing. Turning to a bearded man, whose child was perched on his shoulders, she asked what was going on. He didn't know. Somebody dead, he'd heard, but he wasn't certain.

'Anne-Marie?' she asked.

A woman in front of her turned and said: 'You know her?' almost awed, as if speaking of a loved one.

'A little,' Helen replied hesitantly. 'Can you tell me what's happened?'

The woman involuntarily put her hand to her mouth, as if to stop the words before they came. But here they were nevertheless: 'The child – ' she said.

'Kerry?'

'Somebody got into the house around the back. Slit his throat.'

Helen felt the sweat come again. In her mind's eye the newspapers rose and fell in Anne-Marie's yard.

'No,' she said.

'Just like that.'

She looked at the tragedian who was trying to sell her this obscenity, and said, 'No,' again. It defied belief; yet her denials could not silence the horrid comprehension she felt.

She turned her back on the woman and paddled her way out of the crowd. There would be nothing to see, she knew, and even if there had been she had no desire to look. These people – still emerging from their homes as the story spread – were exhibiting an appetite she was disgusted by. She was not of them; would never *be* of them. She wanted to slap every eager face into sense; wanted to say: 'It's pain and grief you're going to spy on. Why? Why?' But she had no courage left. Revulsion had drained her of all but the energy to wander away, leaving the crowd to its sport.

Trevor had come home. He did not attempt an explanation of his absence, but waited for her to cross-question him. When she failed to do so he sank into an easy *bonhomie* that was worse than his expectant silence. She was dimly aware that her disinterest was probably more unsettling for him than the histrionics he had been anticipating. She couldn't have cared less.

She tuned the radio to the local station, and listened for news. It came surely enough, confirming what the woman in the crowd had told her. Kerry Latimer was dead. Person or persons unknown had gained access to the house via the back yard and murdered the child while he played on the kitchen floor. A police spokesman mouthed the usual platitudes, describing Kerry's death as an 'unspeakable crime', and the miscreant as 'a dangerous and deeply disturbed individual'. For once, the rhetoric seemed justified, and the man's voice shook discernibly when he spoke of the scene that had confronted the officers in the kitchen of Anne-Marie's house.

'Why the radio?' Trevor casually inquired, when Helen had listened for news through three consecutive bulletins. She saw no point in withholding her experience at Spector Street from him; he would find out sooner or later. Coolly, she gave him a bald outline of what had happened at Butts' Court.

'This Anne-Marie is the woman you first met when you went to the estate; am I right?'

She nodded, hoping he wouldn't ask her too many questions. Tears were close, and she had no intention of breaking down in front of him.

'So you were right,' he said.

'Right?'

'About the place having a maniac.'

'No,' she said. 'No.'

'But the kid – '

She got up and stood at the window, looking down two storeys into the darkened street below. Why did she feel the need to reject the conspiracy theory so urgently?; why was she now praying that Purcell had been right, and that all she'd been told had been lies? She went back and back to the way Anne-Marie had been when she'd visited her that morning: pale, jittery; *expectant*. She had been like a woman anticipating some arrival, hadn't she?, eager to shoo unwanted visitors away so that she could turn back to the business of waiting. But waiting for what, or *whom*? Was it possible that Anne-Marie actually knew the murderer? Had perhaps invited him into the house?

'I hope they find the bastard,' she said, still watching the street.

'They will,' Trevor replied. 'A baby-murderer, for Christ's sake. They'll make it a high priority.'

A man appeared at the corner of the street, turned, and whistled. A large Alsatian came to heel, and the two set off down towards the Cathedral.

'The dog,' Helen murmured.

'What?'

She had forgotten the dog in all that had followed. Now the shock she'd felt as it had leapt at the window shook her again.

'What dog?' Trevor pressed.

25

'I went back to the flat today – where I took the pictures of the graffiti. There was a dog in there. Locked in.'

'So?'

'It'll starve. Nobody knows it's there.'

'How do you know it wasn't locked in to kennel it?'

'It was making such a noise – ' she said.

'Dogs bark,' Trevor replied. 'That's all they're good for.'

'No . . .' she said very quietly, remembering the noises through the boarded window. 'It didn't bark . . .'

'Forget the dog,' Trevor said. 'And the child. There's nothing you can do about it. You were just passing through.'

His words only echoed her own thoughts of earlier in the day, but somehow – for reasons that she could find no words to convey – that conviction had decayed in the last hours. She was not just passing through. Nobody ever just *passed through*; experience always left its mark. Sometimes it merely scratched; on occasion it took off limbs. She did not know the extent of her present wounding, but she knew it more profound than she yet understood, and it made her afraid.

'We're out of booze,' she said, emptying the last dribble of whisky into her tumbler.

Trevor seemed pleased to have a reason to be accommodating. 'I'll go out, shall I?' he said. 'Get a bottle or two?'

'Sure,' she replied. 'If you like.'

He was gone only half an hour; she would have liked him to have been longer. She didn't want to talk, only to sit and think through the unease in her belly. Though Trevor had dismissed her concern for the dog – and perhaps justifiably so – she couldn't help but go back to the locked maisonette in her mind's eye: to picture again the raging face on the bedroom wall, and hear the animal's muffled growl as it pawed the boards over the window. Whatever Trevor had said, she didn't believe the place was being used as a makeshift kennel. No, the dog was *imprisoned* in there, no doubt of it, running round and round, driven, in its desperation, to eat its own faeces, growing more insane with every hour that passed. She became afraid that somebody – kids maybe, looking for more tinder for their bonfire – would break into the place, ignorant of what it contained. It wasn't that she feared for the intruders' safety, but that the dog, once liberated, would come for her. It would know where she was (so her drunken head construed) and come sniffing her out.

Trevor returned with the whisky, and they drank together until the early hours, when her stomach revolted. She took refuge in the toilet – Trevor outside asking her if she needed anything, her telling him weakly to leave her alone. When, an hour later, she emerged, he had gone to bed. She did not join him, but lay down on the sofa and dozed through until dawn.

The murder was news. The next morning it made all the tabloids as a front page splash, and found prominent positions in the heavyweights too. There were photographs of the stricken mother being led from the house, and others, blurred but potent, taken over the back yard wall and through the open kitchen door. Was that blood on the floor, or shadow?

Helen did not bother to read the articles – her aching head rebelled at the thought – but Trevor, who had brought the newspapers in, was eager to talk. She couldn't work out if this was further peacemaking on his part, or a genuine interest in the issue.

'The woman's in custody,' he said, poring over the *Daily Telegraph*. It was a paper he was politically averse to, but its coverage of violent crime was notoriously detailed.

The observation demanded Helen's attention, unwilling or not. 'Custody?' she said. 'Anne-Marie?'

'Yes.'

'Let me see.'

He relinquished the paper, and she glanced over the page.

'Third column,' Trevor prompted.

She found the place, and there it was in black and white. Anne-Marie had been taken into custody for questioning to justify the timelapse between the estimated hour of the child's death, and the time that it had been reported. Helen read the relevant sentences over again, to be certain that she'd understood properly. Yes, she had. The police pathologist estimated Kerry to have died between six and six-thirty that morning; the murder had not been reported until twelve.

She read the report over a third and fourth time, but repetition did not change the horrid facts. The child had been murdered before dawn. When she had gone to the house that morning Kerry had already been dead four hours. The body had been in the kitchen, a few yards down the hallway from where she had stood, and Anne-Marie had said *nothing*. That air of expectancy she had had about her – what had it signified? That she awaited some cue to lift the receiver and call the police?

'My Christ . . .' Helen said, and let the paper drop.

'What?'

'I have to go to the police.'

'Why?'

'To tell them I went to the house,' she replied. Trevor looked

27

mystified. 'The baby was dead, Trevor. When I saw Anne-Marie yesterday morning, Kerry was already dead.'

She rang the number given in the paper for any persons offering information, and half an hour later a police car came to pick her up. There was much that startled her in the two hours of interrogation that followed, not least the fact that nobody had reported her presence on the estate to the police, though she had surely been noticed.

'They don't want to know – ' the detective told her, ' – you'd think a place like that would be swarming with witnesses. If it is, they're not coming forward. A crime like this . . .'

'Is it the first?' she said.

He looked at her across a chaotic desk. 'First?'

'I was told some stories about the estate. Murders. This summer.'

The detective shook his head. 'Not to my knowledge. There's been a spate of muggings; one woman was put in hospital for a week or so. But no; no murders.'

She liked the detective. His eyes flattered her with their lingering, and his face with their frankness. Past caring whether she sounded foolish or not, she said: 'Why do they tell lies like that. About people having their eyes cut out. Terrible things.'

The detective scratched his long nose. 'We get it too,' he said. 'People come in here, they confess to all kinds of crap. Talk all night, some of them, about things they've done, or *think* they've done. Give you it all in the minutest detail. And when you make a few calls, it's all invented. Out of their minds.'

'Maybe if they didn't tell you the stories . . . they'd actually go out and do it.'

The detective nodded. 'Yes,' he said. 'God help us. You might be right at that.'

And the stories *she'd* been told, were they confessions of uncommitted crimes?, accounts of the worst imaginable, imagined to keep fiction from becoming fact? The thought chased its own tail: these terrible stories still needed a *first cause*, a well-spring from which they leapt. As she walked home through the busy streets she wondered how many of her fellow citizens knew such stories. Were these inventions common currency, as Purcell had claimed? Was there a place, however small, reserved in every heart for the monstrous?

'Purcell rang,' Trevor told her when she got home. 'To invite us out to dinner.'

The invitation wasn't welcome, and she made a face.

'Appollinaires, remember?' he reminded her. 'He said he'd take us all to dinner, if you proved him wrong.'

The thought of getting a dinner out of the death of Anne-Marie's infant was grotesque, and she said so.

'He'll be offended if you turn him down.'

'I don't give a damn. I don't want dinner with Purcell.'

'Please,' he said softly. 'He can get difficult; and I want to keep him smiling just at the moment.'

She glanced across at him. The look he'd put on made him resemble a drenched spaniel. Manipulative bastard, she thought; but said: 'All right, I'll go. But don't expect any dancing on the tables.'

'We'll leave that to Archie,' he said. 'I told Purcell we were free tomorrow night. Is that all right with you?'

'Whenever.'

'He's booking a table for eight o'clock.'

The evening papers had relegated The Tragedy of Baby Kerry to a few column inches on an inside page. In lieu of much fresh news they simply described the house-to-house enquiries that were now going on at Spector Street. Some of the later editions mentioned that Anne-Marie had been released from custody after an extended period of questioning, and was now residing with friends. They also mentioned, in passing, that the funeral was to be the following day.

Helen had not entertained any thoughts of going back to Spector Street for the funeral when she went to bed that night, but sleep seemed to change her mind, and she woke with the decision made for her.

Death had brought the estate to life. Walking through to Ruskin Court from the street she had never seen such numbers out and about. Many were already lining the kerb to watch the funeral cortège pass, and looked to have claimed their niche early, despite the wind and the ever-present threat of rain. Some were wearing items of black clothing – a coat, a scarf – but the overall impression, despite the lowered voices and the studied frowns, was one of celebration. Children running around, untouched by reverence; occasional laughter escaping from between gossiping adults – Helen could feel an air of anticipation which made her spirits, despite the occasion, almost buoyant.

Nor was it simply the presence of so many people that reassured her; she was, she conceded to herself, happy to be back here in Spector Street. The quadrangles, with their stunted saplings and their grey grass, were more real to her than the carpeted corridors she was used to walking; the anonymous faces on the balconies and streets meant more than her colleagues at the University. In a word, she felt *home*.

Finally, the cars appeared, moving at a snail's pace through the narrow streets. As the hearse came into view – its tiny white casket decked with flowers – a number of women in the crowd gave quiet voice to their grief. One on-looker fainted; a knot of anxious people gathered around her. Even the children were stilled now.

Helen watched, dry-eyed. Tears did not come very easily to her, especially in company. As the second car, containing Anne-Marie and two other women, drew level with her, Helen saw that the bereaved mother was also eschewing any public display of grief. She seemed, indeed, to be almost elevated by the proceedings, sitting upright in the back of the car, her pallid features the source of much admiration. It was a sour thought, but Helen felt as though she was seeing Anne-Marie's finest hour; the one day in an otherwise anonymous life in which she was the centre of attention. Slowly, the cortège passed by and disappeared from view.

The crowd around Helen was already dispersing. She detached herself from the few mourners who still lingered at the kerb and wandered through from the street into Butts' Court. It was her intention to go back to the locked maisonette, to see if the dog was still there. If it was, she would put her mind at rest by finding one of the estate caretakers and informing him of the fact.

The quadrangle was, unlike the other courts, practically empty. Perhaps the residents, being neighbours of Anne-Marie's, had gone on to the Crematorium for the service. Whatever the reason, the place was eerily deserted. Only children remained, playing around the pyramid bonfire, their voices echoing across the empty expanse of the square.

She reached the maisonette and was surprised to find the door open again, as it had been the first time she'd come here. The sight of the interior made her light-headed. How often in the past several days had she imagined standing here, gazing into that darkness. There was no sound from inside. The dog had surely run off; either that, or died. There could be no harm, could there?, in stepping into the place one final time, just to look at the face on the wall, and its attendant slogan.

Sweets to the sweet. She had never looked up the origins of that phrase. No matter, she thought. Whatever it had stood for once, it was transformed here, as everything was; herself included. She stood in the front room for a few moments, to allow herself time to savour the confrontation ahead. Far away behind her the children were screeching like mad birds.

She stepped over a clutter of furniture and towards the short corridor that joined living-room to bedroom, still delaying the moment. Her heart was quick in her: a smile played on her lips.

And there! At last! The portrait loomed, compelling as ever. She stepped back in the murky room to admire it more fully and her heel caught on the mattress that still lay in the corner. She glanced down. The squalid bedding had been turned over, to present its untorn face. Some blankets and a rag-wrapped pillow had been tossed over it. Something glistened amongst the folds of the uppermost blanket. She bent down to look more closely and found there a handful of sweets – chocolates and caramels – wrapped in bright paper. And littered amongst them, neither so attractive nor so sweet, a dozen razor-blades. There was blood on several. She stood up again and backed away from the mattress, and as she did so a buzzing sound reached her ears from the next room. She turned, and the light in the bedroom diminished as a figure stepped into the gullet between her and the outside world. Silhouetted against the light, she could scarcely see the man in the doorway, but she smelt him. He smelt like candy-floss; and the buzzing was with him or in him.

'I just came to look – ' she said, ' – at the picture.'

The buzzing went on: the sound of a sleepy afternoon, far from here. The man in the doorway did not move.

'Well . . .' she said, 'I've seen what I wanted to see.' She hoped against hope that her words would prompt him to stand aside and let her past, but he didn't move, and she couldn't find the courage to challenge him by stepping towards the door.

'I have to go,' she said, knowing that despite her best efforts fear seeped between every syllable. 'I'm expected . . .'

That was not entirely untrue. Tonight they were all invited to Appollinaires for dinner. But that wasn't until eight, which was four hours away. She would not be missed for a long while yet.

'If you'll excuse me,' she said.

The buzzing had quietened a little, and in the hush the man in the doorway spoke. His unaccented voice was almost as sweet as his scent.

'No need to leave yet,' he breathed.

'I'm due . . . due . . .'

Though she couldn't see his eyes, she felt them on her, and they made her feel drowsy, like that summer that sang in her head.

'I came for you,' he said.

She repeated the four words in her head. *I came for you.* If they were meant as a threat, they certainly weren't spoken as one.

'I don't . . . know you,' she said.

'No,' the man murmured. 'But you doubted me.'

'Doubted?'

'You weren't content with the stories, with what they wrote on the walls. So I was obliged to come.'

The drowsiness slowed her mind to a crawl, but she grasped the

31

essentials of what the man was saying. That he was legend, and she, in disbelieving him, had obliged him to show his hand. She looked, now, down at those hands. One of them was missing. In its place, a hook.

'There will be some blame,' he told her. 'They will say your doubts shed innocent blood. But I say – what's blood for, if not for shedding? And in time the scrutiny will pass. The police will leave, the cameras will be pointed at some fresh horror, and they will be left alone, to tell stories of the Candyman again.'

'Candyman?' she said. Her tongue could barely shape that blameless word.

'I came for you,' he murmured so softly that seduction might have been in the air. And so saying, he moved through the passageway and into the light.

She knew him, without doubt. She had known him all along, in that place kept for terrors. It was the man on the wall. His portrait painter had not been a fantasist: the picture that howled over her was matched in each extraordinary particular by the man she now set eyes upon. He was bright to the point of gaudiness: his flesh a waxy yellow, his thin lips pale blue, his wild eyes glittering as if their irises were set with rubies. His jacket was a patchwork his trousers the same. He looked, she thought, almost ridiculous, with his blood-stained motley, and the hint of rouge on his jaundiced cheeks. But people were facile. They needed these shows and shams to keep their interest. Miracles; murders; demons driven out and stones rolled from tombs. The cheap glamour did not taint the sense beneath. It was only, in the natural history of the mind, the bright feathers that drew the species to mate with its secret self.

And she was almost enchanted. By his voice, by his colours, by the buzz from his body. She fought to resist the rapture, though. There was a *monster* here, beneath this fetching display; its nest of razors was at her feet, still drenched in blood. Would it hesitate to slit her own throat if it once laid hands on her?

As the Candyman reached for her she dropped down and snatched the blanket up, flinging it at him. A rain of razors and sweetmeats fell around his shoulders. The blanket followed, blinding him. But before she could snatch the moment to slip past him, the pillow which had lain on the blanket rolled in front of her.

It was not a pillow at all. Whatever the forlorn white casket she had seen in the hearse had contained, it was not the body of Baby Kerry. That was *here*, at her feet, its blood-drained face turned up to her. He was naked. His body showed everywhere signs of the fiend's attentions.

In the two heartbeats she took to register this last horror, the

Candyman threw off the blanket. In his struggle to escape from its folds, his jacket had come unbuttoned, and she saw – though her senses protested – that the contents of his torso had rotted away, and the hollow was now occupied by a nest of bees. They swarmed in the vault of his chest, and encrusted in a seething mass the remnants of flesh that hung there. He smiled at her plain repugnance.

'Sweets to the sweet,' he murmured, and stretched his hooked hand towards her face. She could no longer see light from the outside world, nr hear the children playing in Butts' Court. There was no escape into a saner world than this. The Candyman filled her sight; her drained limbs had no strength to hold him at bay.

'Don't kill me,' she breathed.

'Do you believe in me?' he said.

She nodded minutely. 'How can I not?' she said.

'Then why do you want to live?'

She didn't understand, and was afraid her ignorance would prove fatal, so she said nothing.

'If you would learn,' the fiend said, 'just a *little* from me . . . you would not beg to live.' His voice had dropped to a whisper. 'I am rumour,' he sang in her ear. 'It's a blessed condition, believe me. To live in people's dreams; to be whispered at street-corners; but not have to *be*. Do you understand?'

Her weary body understood. Her nerves, tired of jangling, understood. The sweetness he offered was life without living: was to be dead, but remembered everywhere; immortal in gossip and graffiti.

'Be my victim,' he said.

'No . . .' she murmured.

'I won't force it upon you,' he replied, the perfect gentleman. 'I won't oblige you to die. But think; *think*. If I kill you here – if I unhook you . . .' he traced the path of the promised wound with his hook. It ran from groin to neck. 'Think how they would mark this place with their talk . . . point it out as they passed by and say: "*She* died there; the woman with the green eyes". Your death would be a parable to frighten children with. Lovers would use it as an excuse to cling closertogether . . .'

She had been right: this *was* a seduction.

'Was fame ever so easy?' he asked.

She shook her head. 'I'd prefer to be forgotten,' she replied, 'than be remembered like that.'

He made a tiny shrug. 'What do the good know?' he said. 'Except what the bad teach them by their excesses?' He raised his hooked hand. 'I said I would not oblige you to die and I'm true to my word. Allow me, though, a kiss at least . . .'

He moved towards her. She murmured some nonsensical threat,

33

which he ignored. The buzzing in his body had risen in volume. The thought of touching his body, of the proximity of the insects, was horrid. She forced her lead-heavy arms up to keep him at bay.

His lurid face eclipsed the portrait on the wall. She couldn't bring herself to touch him, and instead stepped back. The sound of the bees rose; some, in their excitement, had crawled up his throat and were flying from his mouth. They climbed about his lips; in his hair.

She begged him over and over to leave her alone, but he would not be placated. At last she had nowhere left to retreat to; the wall was at her back. Steeling herself against the stings, she put her hands on his crawling chest and pushed. As she did so his hand shot out and around the back of her neck, the hook nicking the flushed skin of her throat. She felt blood come; felt certain he would open her jugular in one terrible slash. But he had given his word: and he was true to it.

Aroused by this sudden activity, the bees were everywhere. She felt them moving on her, searching for morsels of wax in her ears, and sugar at her lips. She made no attempt to swat them away. The hook was at her neck. If she so much as moved it would wound her. She was trapped, as in her childhood nightmares, with every chance of escape stymied. When sleep had brought her to such hopelessness – the demons on every side, waiting to tear her limb from limb – one trick remained. To let go; to give up all ambition to life, and leave her body to the dark. Now, as the Candyman's face pressed to hers, and the sound of bees blotted out even her own breath, she played that hidden hand. And, as surely as in dreams, the room and the fiend were painted out and gone.

She woke from brightness into dark. There were several panicked moments when she couldn't think of where she was, then several more when she remembered. But there was no pain about her body. She put her hand to her neck; it was, barring the nick of the hook, untouched. She was lying on the mattress she realized. Had she been assaulted as she lay in a faint? Gingerly, she investigated her body. She was not bleeding; her clothes were not disturbed. The Candyman had, it seemed, simply claimed his kiss.

She sat up. There was precious little light through the boarded window – and none from the front door. Perhaps it was closed, she reasoned. But no; even now she heard somebody whispering on the threshold. A woman's voice.

She didn't move. They were crazy, these people. They had known all along what her presence in Butts' Court had summoned, and they had *protected* him – this honeyed psychopath; given him a bed and an offering of bonbons, hidden him away from prying eyes, and kept

34

their silence when he brought blood to their doorsteps. Even Anne-Marie, dry-eyed in the hallway of her house, knowing that her child was dead a few yards away.

The child! That was the evidence she needed. Somehow they had conspired to get the body from the casket (what had they substituted; a dead dog?) and brought it here – to the Candyman's tabernacle – as a toy, or a lover. She would take Baby Kerry with her – to the police – and tell the whole story. Whatever they believed of it – and that would probably be very little – the fact of the child's body was incontestable. That way at least some of the crazies would suffer for their conspiracy. Suffer for *her* suffering.

The whispering at the door had stopped. Now somebody was moving towards the bedroom. They didn't bring a light with them. Helen made herself small, hoping she might escape detection.

A figure appeared in the doorway. The gloom was too impenetrable for her to make out more than a slim figure, who bent down and picked up a bundle on the floor. A fall of blonde hair identified the newcomer as Anne-Marie: the bundle she was picking up was undoubtedly Kerry's corpse. Without looking in Helen's direction, the mother about-turned and made her way out of the bedroom.

Helen listened as the footsteps receded across the living-room. Swiftly, she got to her feet, and crossed to the passageway. From there she could vaguely see Anne-Marie's outline in the doorway of the maisonette. No lights burned in the quadrangle beyond. The woman disappeared and Helen followed as speedily as she could, eyes fixed on the door ahead. She stumbled once, and once again, but reached the door in time to see Anne-Marie's vague form in the night ahead.

She stepped out of the maisonette and into the open air. It was chilly; there were no stars. All the lights on the balconies and corridors were out, nor did any burn in the flats; not even the glow of a television. Butts' Court was deserted.

She hesitated before going in pursuit of the girl. Why didn't she slip away now?, cowardice coaxed her, and find her way back to the car. But if she did that the conspirators would have time to conceal the child's body. When she got back here with the police there would be sealed lips and shrugs, and she would be told she had imagined the corpse and the Candyman. All the terrors she had tasted would recede into rumour again. Into words on a wall. And every day she lived from now on she would loathe herself for not going in pursuit of sanity.

She followed. Anne-Marie was not making her way around the quadrangle, but moving towards the centre of the lawn in the middle of the court. To the bonfire! Yes; to the bonfire! It loomed in front of

Helen now, blacker than the night-sky. She could just make out Anne-Marie's figure, moving to the edge of the piled timbers and furniture, and ducking to climb into its heart. *This* was how they planned to remove the evidence. To bury the child was not certain enough; but to cremate it, and pound the bones – who would ever know?

She stood a dozen yards from the pyramid and watched as Anne-Marie climbed out again and moved away, folding her figure into the darkness.

Quickly, Helen moved through the long grass and located the narrow space in amongst the piled timbers into which Anne-Marie had put the body. She thought she could see the pale form; it had been laid in a hollow. She couldn't reach it however. Thanking God that she was as slim as the mother, she squeezed through the narrow aperture. Her dress snagged on a nail as she did so. She turned round to disengage it, fingers trembling. When she turned back she had lost sight of the corpse.

She fumbled blindly ahead of her, her hands finding wood and rags and what felt like the back of an old armchair, but not the cold skin of the child. She had hardened herself against contact with the body: she had endured worse in the last hours than picking up a dead baby. Determined not to be defeated, she advanced a little further, her shins scraped and her fingers spiked with splinters. Flashes of light were appearing at the corners of her aching eyes; her blood whined in her ears. But there!; *there*!; the body was no more than a yard and a half ahead of her. She ducked down to reach beneath a beam of wood, but her fingers missed the forlorn bundle by millimetres. She stretched further, the whine in her head increasing, but still she could not reach the child. All she could do was bend double and squeeze into the hidey-hole the children had left in the centre of the bonfire.

It was difficult to get through. The space was so small she could barely crawl on hands and knees; but she made it. The child lay face down. She fought back the remnants of squeamishness and went to pick it up. As she did so, something landed on her arm. The shock startled her. She almost cried out, but swallowed the urge, and brushed the irritation away. It buzzed as it rose from her skin. The whine she had heard in her ears was not her blood, but the hive.

'I knew you'd come,' the voice behind her said, and a wide hand covered her face. She fell backwards and the Candyman embraced her.

'We have to go,' he said in her ear, as flickering light spilled between the stacked timbers. 'Be on our way, you and I.'

She fought to be free of him, to cry out for them not to light the bonfire, but he held her lovingly close. The light grew: warmth came with it; and through the kindling and the first flames she could see figures approaching the pyre out of the darkness of Butts' Court. They had been there all along: waiting, the lights turned out in their homes, and broken all along the corridors. Their final conspiracy.

The bonfire caught with a will, but by some trick of its construction the flames did not invade her hiding-place quickly; nor did the smoke creep through the furniture to choke her. She was able to watch how the children's faces gleamed; how the parents called them from going too close, and how they disobeyed; how the old women, their blood thin, warmed their hands and smiled into the flames. Presently the roar and the crackle became deafening, and the Candyman let her scream herself hoarse in the certain knowledge that nobody could hear her, and even if they had would not have moved to claim her from the fire.

The bees vacated the fiend's belly as the air became hotter, and mazed the air with their panicked flight. Some, attempting escape, caught fire, and fell like tiny meteors to the ground. The body of Baby Kerry, which lay close to the creeping flames, began to cook. Its downy hair smoked, its back blistered.

Soon the heat crept down Helen's throat, and scorched her pleas away. She sank back, exhausted, into the Candyman's arms, resigned to his triumph. In moments they would be on their way, as he had promised, and there was no help for it.

Perhaps they would remember her, as he had said they might, finding her cracked skull in tomorrow's ashes. Perhaps she might become, in time, a story with which to frighten children. She had lied, saying she preferred death to such questionable fame; she did not. As to her seducer, he laughed as the conflagration sniffed them out. There was no permanence for him in this night's death. His deeds were on a hundred walls and a ten thousand lips, and should he be doubted again his congregation could summon him with sweetness. He had reason to laugh. So, as the flames crept upon them, did she, as through the fire she caught sight of a familiar face moving between the on-lookers. It was Trevor. He had forsaken his meal at Appollinaires and come looking for her.

She watched him questioning this fire-watcher and that, but they shook their heads, all the while staring at the pyre with smiles buried in their eyes. Poor dupe, she thought, following his antics. She willed him to look past the flames in the hope that he might see her burning. Not so that he could save her from death – she was long past hope of that – but because she pitied him in his bewilderment and wanted to give him, though he would not have thanked her for it, something to be haunted by. That, and a story to tell.

37

The Madonna

Jerry Coloqhoun waited on the steps of the Leopold Road Swimming Pools for over thirty-five minutes before Garvey turned up, his feet steadily losing feeling as the cold crept up through the soles of his shoes. The time would come, he reassured himself, when *he'd* be the one to leave people waiting. Indeed such prerogative might not be so far away, if he could persuade Ezra Garvey to invest in the Pleasure Dome. It would require an appetite for risk, and substantial assets, but his contacts had assured him that Garvey, whatever his reputation, possessed both in abundance. The source of the man's money was not an issue in the proceedings, or so Jerry had persuaded himself. Many a nicer plutocrat had turned the project down flat in the last six months; in such circumstances fineness of feeling was a luxury he could scarcely afford.

He was not all that surprised by the reluctance of investors. These were difficult times, and risks were not to be undertaken lightly. More, it took a measure of imagination – a faculty not over-abundant amongst the moneyed he'd met – to see the Pools transformed into the gleaming amenity complex he envisaged. But his researches had convinced him that in an area like this – where houses once tettering on demolition were being bought up and refurbished by a generation of middle-class sybarites – that in such an area the facilities he had planned could scarcely fail to make money.

There was a further inducement. The Council, who owned the Pools, was eager to off-load the property as speedily as possible; it had debtors aplenty. Jerry's bribee at the Directorate of Community Services – the same man who'd happily filched the keys to the property for two bottles of gin – had told him that the building could be purchased for a song if the offer was made swiftly. It was all a question of good timing.

A skill, apparently, which Garvey lacked. By the time he arrived the numbness had spread north to Jerry's knees, and his temper had worn thin. He made no show of it, however, as Garvey got out of his chauffeur-driven Rover and came up the steps. Jerry had only spoken to him by telephone, and had expected a larger man, but despite the lack of stature there was no doubting Garvey's authority. It was there in the plain look of appraisal he gave Coloqhoun; in the joyless features; in the immaculate suit.

The pair shook hands.

'It's good to see you, Mr Garvey.'

The man nodded, but returned no pleasantry. Jerry, eager to be out of the cold, opened the front door and led the way inside.

'I've only got ten minutes,' Garvey said.

'Fine,' Jerry replied. 'I just wanted to show you the lay-out.'

'You've surveyed the place?'

'Of course.'

This was a lie. Jerry had been over the building the previous August, courtesy of a contact in the Architects' Department, and had, since that time, looked at the place from the outside several times. But it had been five months since he'd actually stepped into the building; he hoped accelerating decay had not taken an unshakeable hold since then. They stepped into the vestibule. It smelled damp, but not overpoweringly so.

'There's no electricity on,' he explained. 'We have to go by torchlight.' He fished the heavy-duty torch from his pocket and trained the beam on the inner door. It was padlocked. He stared at the lock, dumbfounded. If this door had been locked last time he was here, he didn't remember. He tried the single key he'd been given, knowing before he put it to the lock that the two were hopelessly mismatched. He cursed under his breath, quickly skipping through the options available. Either he and Garvey about-turned, and left the Pools to its secrets – if mildew, creeping rot and a roof that was within an ace of surrender could be classed as secrets – or else he made an attempt to break in. He glanced at Garvey, who had taken a prodigious cigar from his inside pocket and was stroking the end with a flame; velvet smoke billowed.

'I'm sorry about the delay,' he said.

'It happens,' Garvey returned, clearly unpertubed.

'I think strong-arm tactics may be called for,' Jerry said, feeling out the other man's response to a break in.

'Suits me.'

Jerry quickly rooted about the darkened vestibule for an implement. In the ticket booth he found a metal-legged stool. Hoisting it out of the booth he crossed back to the door – aware of Garvey's amused but benign gaze upon him – and, using one of the legs as a lever, broke a shackle of the padlock. The lock clattered to the tiled floor.

'Open sesame,' he murmured with some satisfaction, and pushed the door open for Garvey.

The sound of the falling lock seemed still to linger in the deserted corridors when they stepped through, its din receding towards a sigh as it diminished. The interior looked more inhospitable than Jerry had remembered. The fitful daylight that fell through the mildewed panes of the skylights along the corridor was blue-grey – the light and that which it fell upon vying in dreariness. Once, no doubt, the Leopold Road Pools had been a showcase of Deco design – of shining tiles and cunning mosaics worked into floor and wall. But not in Jerry's adult life, certainly. The tiles underfoot had long since lifted with the damp; along the walls they had fallen in their hundreds, leaving patterns of white ceramic and dark plaster like some vast and clueless crossword puzzle. The air of destitution was so profound that Jerry had half a mind to give up his attempt at selling the project to Garvey on the spot. Surely there was no hope of a sale here, even at the ludicrously low asking price. But Garvey seemed more engaged than Jerry had allowed. He was already stalking down the corridor, puffing on his cigar and grunting to himself as he went. It could be no more than morbid curiosity, Jerry felt, that took the developer deeper into this echoing mausoleum. And yet:

'It's atmospheric. The place has possibilities,' Garvey said. 'I don't have much of a reputation as a philanthropist, Coloqhoun – you must know that – but I've got a taste for some of the finer things.' He had paused in front of a mosaic depicting a nondescript mythological scene – fish, nymphs and sea-gods at play. He grunted appreciatively, describing the sinuous line of the design with the wet end of his cigar.

'You don't see craftsmanship like that nowadays,' he commented. Jerry thought it unremarkable, but said, 'It's superb.'

'Show me the rest.'

The complex had once boasted a host of facilities – sauna rooms, turkish baths, thermal baths – in addition to the two pools. These various areas were connected by a warren of passageways which, unlike the main corridor, had no skylights: torchlight had to suffice here. Dark or no, Garvey wanted to see all of the public areas. The ten minutes he had warned were his limit stretched into twenty and thirty, the exploration constantly brought to a halt as he discovered some new felicity to comment upon. Jerry listened with feigned comprehension: he found the man's enthusiasm for the decor confounding.

'I'd like to see the pools now,' Garvey announced when they'd made a thorough investigation of the subordinate amenities. Dutifully, Jerry led the way through the labyrinth towards the two pools. In a small corridor a little way from the Turkish Baths Garvey said:

'Hush.'

Jerry stopped walking. 'What?'

40

'I heard a voice.'

Jerry listened. The torch-beam, splashing off the tiles, threw a pale luminescence around them, which drained the blood from Garvey's features.

'I don't hear – '

'I said *hush*,' Garvey snapped. He moved his head to and fro slowly. Jerry could hear nothing. Neither, now, could Garvey. He shrugged, and pulled on his cigar. It had gone out, killed by the damp air.

'A trick of the corridors,' Jerry said. 'The echoes in this place are misleading. Sometimes you hear your own footsteps coming back to meet you.'

Garvey grunted again. The grunt seemed to be his most valued part of speech. 'I did hear something,' he said, clearly not satisfied with Jerry's explanation. He listened again. The corridors were pin-drop hushed. It was not even possible to hear the traffic in Leopold Road. At last, Garvey seemed content.

'Lead on,' he said. Jerry did just that, though the route to the pools was by no means clear to him. They took several wrong turnings, winding their way through a maze of identical corridors, before they reached their intended destination.

'It's warm,' said Garvey, as they stood outside the smaller of the two pools.

Jerry murmured his agreement. In his eagerness to reach the pools he had not noticed the steadily escalating temperature. But now that he stood still he could feel a film of sweat on his body. The air was humid, and it smelt not of damp and mildew, as elsewhere in the building, but of a sicklier, almost opulent, scent. He hoped Garvey, cocooned in the smoke of his re-lit cigar could not share the smell; it was far from pleasant.

'The heating's on,' Garvey said.

'It certainly seems like it,' Jerry returned, though he couldn't think why. Perhaps the Department Engineers warmed the heating system through once in a while, to keep it in working order. In which case, were they in the bowels of the building somewhere? Perhaps Garvey *had* heard voices? He mentally constructed a line of explanation should their paths cross.

'The pools,' he said, and pulled open one of the double-doors. The skylight here was even dirtier than those in the main corridor; precious little light illuminated the scene. Garvey was not to be thwarted, however. He stepped through the door and across to the lip of the pool. There was little to see; the surfaces here were covered with several years' growth of mould. On the bottom of the pool,

41

barely discernible beneath the algae, a design had been worked into the tiles. A bright fish-eye glanced up at them, perfectly thoughtless.

'Always had a fear of water,' Garvey said ruminatively as he stared into the drained pool. 'Don't know where it comes from.'

'Childhood,' Jerry ventured.

'I don't think so,' the other replied. 'My wife says it's the womb.'

'The womb?'

'I didn't like swimming around in there, she says,' he replied, with a smile that might have been at his own expense, but was more likely at that of his wife.

A short sound came to meet them across the empty expanse of the pool, as of something falling. Garvey froze. 'You hear *that*?' he said. 'There's somebody in here.' His voice had suddenly risen half an octave.

'Rats,' Jerry replied. He wished to avoid an encounter with the engineers if possible; difficult questions might well be asked.

'Give me the torch,' Garvey said, snatching it from Jerry's hand. He scanned the opposite side of the pool with the beam. It lit a series of dressing rooms, and an open door that led out of the pool. Nothing moved.

'I don't like vermin – ' Garvey said.

'The place has been neglected,' Jerry replied.

' – especially the human variety.' Garvey thrust the torch back into Jerry's hands. 'I've got enemies, Mr Coloqhoun. But then you've done your researches on me, haven't you? You know I'm no lily-white.' Garvey's concern about the noises he thought he'd heard now made unpalatable sense. It wasn't rats he was afraid of, but grievous bodily harm. 'I think I should be going,' he said. 'Show me the other pool and we'll be away.'

'Surely.' Jerry was as happy to be going as his guest. The incident had raised his temperature. The sweat came profusely now, trickling down the back of his neck. His sinuses ached. He led Garvey across the hallway to the door of the larger pool and pulled. The door refused him.

'Problem?'

'It must be locked from the inside.'

'Is there another way in?'

'I think so. Do you want me to go round the back?'

Garvey glanced at his watch. 'Two minutes,' he said. 'I've got appointments.'

Garvey watched Coloqhoun disappear down the darkened corridor, the torchlight running on ahead of him. He didn't like the man. He was too closely shaven; and his shoes were Italian. But – the proposer aside – the project had some merit. Garvey liked the Pools and their adjuncts, the uniformity of their design, the banality of their decorations. Unlike many, he found institutions reassuring: hospitals, schools, even prisons. They smacked of social order, they soothed that part of him fearful of chaos. Better a world too organized than one not organized enough.

Again, his cigar had gone out. He put it between his teeth and lit a match. As the first flare died, he caught an inkling sight of a naked girl in the corridor ahead, watching him. The glimpse was momentary, but when the match dropped from his fingers and the light failed, she appeared in his mind's eye, perfectly remembered. She was young – fifteen at the most – and her body full. The sweat on her skin lent her such sensuality she might have stepped from his dream-life. Dropping his stale cigar, he rummaged for another match and struck it, but in the meagre seconds of darkness the child-beauty had gone, leaving only the trace of her sweet body scent on the air.

'Girl?' he said.

The sight of her nudity, and the shock in her eyes, made him eager for her.

'Girl?'

The flame of the second match failed to penetrate more than a yard or two down the corridor.

'Are you there?'

She could not be far, he reasoned. Lighting a third match, he went in search of her. He had gone a few steps only when he heard somebody behind him. He turned. Torchlight lit the fright on his face. It was only the Italian Shoes.

'There's no way in.'

'There's no need to blind me,' Garvey said. The beam dropped.

'I'm sorry.'

'There's somebody here, Coloqhoun. A girl.'

'A girl?'

'You know something about it maybe?'

'No.'

'She was stark naked. Standing three or four yards from me.'

Jerry looked at Garvey, mystified. Was the man suffering from sexual delusions?

'I tell you I saw a girl,' Garvey protested, though no word of contradiction had been offered. 'If you hadn't arrived I'd have had my hands on her.' He glanced back down the corridor. 'Get some light down there.' Jerry trained the beam on the maze. There was no sign of life.

'Damn,' said Garvey, his regret quite genuine. He looked back at Jerry. 'All right,' he said. 'Let's get the hell out of here.'

'I'm interested,' he said, as they parted on the step. 'The project has potential. Do you have a ground-plan of the place?'

'No, but I can get my hands on one.'

'Do that.' Garvey was lighting a fresh cigar. 'And send me your proposals in more detail. Then we'll talk again.'

It took a considerable bribe to get the plans of the Pools out of his contact at the Architects' Department, but Jerry eventually secured them. On paper the complex looked like a labyrinth. And, like the best labyrinths, there was no order apparent in the layout of shower-rooms and bathrooms and changing-rooms. It was Carole who proved that thesis wrong.

'What is this?' she asked him as he pored over the plans that evening. They'd had four or five hours together at his flat – hours without the bickering and the bad feeling that had soured their time together of late.

'It's the ground-plan of the swimming pools on Leopold Road. Do you want another brandy?'

'No thanks.' She peered at the plan while he got up to re-fill his glass.

'I think I've got Garvey in on the deal.'

'You're going to do business with him, are you?'

'Don't make me sound like a white slaver. The man's got money.'

'Dirty money.'

'What's a little dirt between friends?'

She looked at him frostily, and he wished he could have played back the previous ten seconds and erased the comment.

'I *need* this project,' he said, taking his drink across to the sofa and sitting opposite her, the ground-plan spread on the low table between them. 'I need something to go right for me for once.'

Her eyes refused to grant him a reprieve.

'I just think Garvey and his like are bad news,' she said. 'I don't care how much money he's got. He's a villain, Jerry.'

'So I should give the whole thing up, should I? Is that what you're saying?' They'd had this argument, in one guise or another, several times in the last few weeks. 'I should just forget all the hard labour I've put in, and add this failure to all the others?'

'There's no need to shout.'

'I'm not shouting!'

She shrugged. 'All right,' she said quietly, 'you're not shouting.'

'Christ!'

She went back to perusing the ground-plan. He watched her from over the rim of his whisky tumbler; at the parting down the middle of her head, and the fine blonde hair that divided from there. They

44

made so little sense to each other, he thought. The processes that brought them to their present impasse were perfectly obvious, yet time and again they failed to find the common ground necessary for a fruitful exchange of views. Not simply on this matter, on half a hundred others. Whatever thoughts buzzed beneath her tender scalp, they were a mystery to him. And his to her, presumably.

'It's a spiral,' she said.

'What is?'

'The pool. It's designed like a spiral. Look.'

He stood up to get a bird's eye view of the ground-plan as she traced a route through the passageways with her index finger. She was right. Though the imperatives of the architects' brief had muddied the clarity of the image, there was indeed a rough spiral built into the maze of corridors and rooms. Her circling fingers drew tighter and yet tighter loops as it described the shape. At last it came to rest on the large pool; the locked pool. He stared at the plan in silence. Without her pointing it out he knew he could have looked at the design for a week and never seen the underlying structure.

Carole decided she would not stay the night. It was not, she tried to explain at the door, that things between them were over; only that she valued their intimacy too much to mis-use it as bandaging. He half-grasped the point; she too pictured them as wounded animals. At least they had some metaphorical life in common.

He was not unused to sleeping alone. In many ways he preferred to be solitary in his bed than to share it with someone, even Carole. But tonight he wanted her with him; not her, even, but *somebody*. He felt sourcelessly fretful, like a child. When sleep came it fled again, as if in fear of dreams.

Some time towards dawn he got up, preferring wakefulness to that wretched sleep-hopping, wrapped his dressing gown around his shivering body, and went through to brew himself some tea. The ground-plan was still spread on the coffee-table where they had left it from the night before. Sipping the warm sweet Assam, he stood and pondered over it. Now that Carole had pointed it out, all he could concentrate upon – despite the clutter of marginalia that demanded his attention – was the spiral, that undisputable evidence of a hidden hand at work beneath the apparent chaos of the maze. It seized his eye and seduced it into following its unremitting route, round and round, tighter and tighter; and towards *what*?: a locked swimming-pool.

Tea drunk, he returned to bed; this time, fatigue got the better of his nerves and the sleep he'd been denied washed over him. He was woken at seven-fifteen by Carole, who was phoning before she went to work to apologize for the previous night.

'I don't want everything to go wrong between us, Jerry. You do know that, don't you? You know you're precious to me.'

He couldn't take love-talk in the morning. What seemed romantic at midnight struck him as ridiculous at dawn. He answered her declarations of commitment as best he could, and made an arrangement to see her the following evening. Then he returned to his pillow.

Scarcely a quarter hour had passed since he'd visited the Pools without Ezra Garvey thinking of the girl he'd glimpsed in the corridor. Her face had come back to him during dinner with his wife and sex with his mistress. So untrammelled, that face, so bright with possibilities.

Garvey thought of himself as a woman's man. Unlike most of his fellow potentates, whose consorts were a convenience best paid to be absent when not required for some specific function, Garvey enjoyed the company of the opposite sex. Their voices, their perfume, their laughter. His greed for their proximity knew few bounds; they were precious creatures whose company he was willing to spend small fortunes to secure. His jacket was therefore weighed down with money and expensive trinkets when he returned, that morning, to Leopold Road.

The pedestrians on the street were too concerned to keep their heads dry (a cold and steady drizzle had fallen since dawn) to notice the man on the step standing under a black umbrella while another bent to the business of undoing the padlock. Chandaman was an expert with locks. The shackle snapped open within seconds. Garvey lowered his umbrella and slipped into the vestibule.

'Wait here,' he instructed Chandaman. 'And close the door.'

'Yes, sir.'

'If I need you, I'll shout. You got the torch?'

Chandaman produced the torch from his jacket. Garvey took it, switched it on, and disappeared down the corridor. Either it was substantially colder outside than it had been the day before yesterday, or else the interior was hot. He unbuttoned his jacket, and loosened his tightly-knotted tie. He welcomed the heat, reminding him as it did of the sheen on the dream-girl's skin, of the heat-languored look in her dark eyes. He advanced down the corridor, the torch-light splashing off the tiles. His sense of direction had always been good; it took him a short time only to find his way to the spot outside the large pool where he had encountered the girl. There he stood still, and listened.

Garvey was a man used to looking over his shoulder. All his professional life, whether in or out of prison, he had needed to watch for the assassin at his back. Such ceaseless vigilance had made him sensitive to the least sign of human presence. Sounds another man might have ignored played a warning tattoo upon his eardrum. But here?; nothing. Silence in the corridors; silence in the sweating ante-rooms and the Turkish baths; silence in every tiled enclave from one end of the building to the other. And yet he knew he was not alone. When five senses failed him a sixth – belonging, perhaps, more to the beast in him than the sophisticate his expensive suit spoke of – sensed presences. This faculty had saved his hide more than once. Now, he hoped, it would guide him into the arms of beauty.

Trusting to instinct, he extinguished the torch and headed off down the corridor from which the girl had first emerged, feeling his way along the walls. His quarry's presence tantalized him. He suspected she was a mere wall away, keeping pace with him along some secret passage he had no access to. The thought of this stalking pleased him. She and he, alone in this sweating maze, playing a game that both knew must end in capture. He moved stealthily, his pulse ticking off the seconds of the chase at neck and wrist and groin. His crucifix was glued to his breast-bone with perspiration.

At last, the corridor divided. He halted. There was precious little light: what there was etched the tunnels deceptively. Impossible to judge distance. But trusting to his instinct, he turned left and followed his nose. Almost immediately, a door. It was open, and he walked through into a larger space; or so he guessed from the muted sound of his footsteps. Again, he stood still. This time, his straining ears were rewarded with a sound. Across the room from him, the soft pad of naked feet on the tiles. Was it his imagination, or did he even glimpse the girl, her body carved from the gloom, paler than the surrounding darkness, and smoother? Yes!; it was she. He almost called out after her, and then thought better of it. Instead he went in silent pursuit, content to play her game for as long as it pleased her. Crossing the room, he stepped through another door which let on to a further tunnel. The air here was much warmer than anywhere else in the building, clammy and ingratiating as it pressed itself upon him. A moment's anxiety caught his throat: that he was neglecting every article of an autocrat's faith, putting his head so willingly into this warm noose. It could so easily be a set-up: the girl, the chase. Around the next corner the breasts and the beauty might have gone, and there would be a knife at his heart. And yet he *knew* this wasn't so; *knew* that the footfall ahead was a woman's, light and lithe; that the swelter that brought new tides of sweat from him could nurture only softness and passivity here. No knife could prosper in such heat: its edge would soften, its ambition go neglected. He was safe.

Ahead, the footsteps had halted. He halted too. There was light from somewhere, though its source was not apparent. He licked his lips, tasting salt, then advanced. Beneath his fingers the tiles were glossed with water; under his heels, they were slick. Anticipation mounted in him with every step.

Now the light was brightening. It was not day. Sunlight had no route into this sanctum; this was more like moonlight – soft-edged, evasive – though that too must be exiled here, he thought. Whatever its origins, by it he finally set eyes on the girl; or rather, on *a* girl, for it was not the same he had seen two days previous. Naked she was, young she was; but in all other respects different.He caught a glance from her before she fled from him down the corridor, and turned a corner. Puzzlement now lent piquancy to the chase: not one but two girls, occupying this secret place; *why?*

He looked behind him, to be certain his escape route lay open should he wish to retreat, but his memory, befuddled by the scented air, refused a clear picture of the way he'd come. A twinge of concern checked his exhilaration, but he refused to succumb to it, and pressed on, following the girl to the end of the corridor and turning left after her. The passageway ran for a short way before making another left; the girl even now disappearing around that corner. Dimly aware that these gyrations were becoming tighter as he turned upon himself and upon himself again, he went where she led, panting now with the breath-quenching air and the insistence of the chase.

Suddenly, as he turned one final corner, the heat became smotheringly close, and the passageway delivered him out into a small, dimly-lit chamber. He unbuttoned the top of his shirt; the veins on the back of his hands stood out like cord; he was aware of how his heart and lungs were labouring. But, he was relieved to see, the chase finished here. The object of his pursuit was standing with her back to him across the chamber, and at the sight of her smooth back and exquisite buttocks his claustrophobia evaporated.

'Girl . . . ,' he panted. 'You led me quite a chase.'

She seemed not to hear him, or, more likely, was extending the game to its limits out of waywardness.

He started across the slippery tiles towards her.

'I'm talking to you.'

As he came within half a dozen feet of her, she turned. It was not the girl he had just pursued through the corridor, nor indeed the one he had seen two days previous. This creature was another altogether. His gaze rested on her unfamiliar face a few seconds only, however, before sliding giddily down to meet the child she held in her arms. It was suckling like any new-born babe, pulling at her young breast with no little hunger. But in his four and a half decades of life Garvey's eyes had never seen a creature its like. Nausea rose in him.

48

To see the girl giving suck was surprise enough, but to such a *thing*, such an outcast of any tribe, human or animal, was almost more than his stomach could stand. Hell itself had offspring more embraceable.

'What in Christ's name – ?'

The girl stared at Garvey's alarm, and a wave of laughter broke over her face. He shook his head. The child in her arms uncurled a suckered limb and clamped it to its comforter's bosom so as to get better purchase. The gesture lashed Garvey's disgust into rage. Ignoring the girl's protests he snatched the abomination from her arms, holding it long enough to feel the glistening sac of its body squirm in his grasp, then flung it as hard as he could against the far wall of the chamber. As it struck the tiles it cried out, its complaint ending almost as soon as it began, only to be taken up instantly by the mother. She ran across the room to where the child lay, its apparently boneless body split open by the impact. One of its limbs, of which it possessed at least half a dozen, attempted to reach up to touch her sobbing face. She gathered the thing up into her arms; threads of shiny fluid ran across her belly and into her groin.

Out beyond the chamber something gave voice. Garvey had no doubt of its cue; it was answering the death-cry of the child, and the rising wail of its mother – but this sound was more distressing than either. Garvey's imagination was an impoverished faculty. Beyond his dreams of wealth and women lay a wasteland. Yet now, at the sound of that voice, the wasteland bloomed, and gave forth horrors he'd believed himself incapable of conceiving. Not portraits of monsters, which, at the best, could be no more than assemblies of experienced phenomena. What his mind created was more *feeling* than sight; belonged to his marrow not to his mind. All certainty trembled – masculinity, power; the twin imperatives of dread and reason – all turned their collars up and denied knowledge of him. He shook, afraid as only dreams made him afraid, while the cry went on and on, then he turned his back on the chamber, and ran, the light throwing his shadow in front of him down the dim corridor.

His sense of direction had deserted him. At the first intersection, and then at the second, he made an error. A few yards on he realized his mistake and tried to double back, but merely exacerbated the confusion. The corridors all looked alike: the same tiles, the same half-light, each fresh corner he turned either led him into a chamber he had not passed through or complete cul-de-sacs. His panic spiralled. The wailing had now ceased; he was alone with his rasping breath and half-spoken curses. Coloqhoun was responsible for this torment, and Garvey swore he would have its purpose beaten out of the man even if he had to break every bone in Coloqhoun's body personally. He clung to thoughts of that beating as he ran on; it was his only comfort. Indeed so preoccupied did he become with thought of the agonies he'd make Coloqhoun suffer he failed to realize that he had traced his way round in a circle and was running back *towards* the light until his sliding heels delivered him into a familiar chamber. The child lay on the floor, dead and discarded. Its mother was nowhere to be seen.

Garvey halted, and took stock of his situation. If he went back the way he'd come the route would only confound him again; if he went ahead, through the chamber and towards the light, he might cut the Gordian knot and be delivered back to his starting point. The swift wit of the solution pleased him. Cautiously, he crossed the chamber to the door on the other side and peered through. Another short corridor presented itself, and beyond that a door that let on to an open space. The pool! Surely the pool!

He threw caution to the wind, and moved out of the chamber and along the passage.

With every step he took, the heat intensified. His head thumped with it. He pressed on to the end of the passageway, and out into the arena beyond.

The large pool had not been drained, unlike the smaller. Rather, it was full almost to brimming – not with clear water, but with a scummy broth that steamed even in the heat of the interior. *This* was the source of the light. The water in the pool gave off a phosphorescence that tinged everything – the tiles, the diving board, the changing rooms, (himself, no doubt) with the same fulvous wash.

He scanned the scene in front of him. There was no sign of the women. His route to the exit lay unchallenged; nor could he see sign of padlock or chains on the double-doors. He began towards them. His heel slid on the tiles, and he glanced down briefly to see that he had crossed a trail of fluid – difficult, in the bewitched light, to make out its colour – that either ended at the water's edge, or began there.

He looked back towards the water, curiosity getting the better of him. The steam swirled; an eddy toyed wih the scum. And there! His eye caught sight of a dark, anonymous shape sliding beneath the skin of the water. He thought of the creature he'd killed; of its formless body and the dangling loops of its limbs. Was this another of that species? The liquid brightness lapped against the poolside at his feet; continents of scum broke into archipelagoes. Of the swimmer, there was no sign.

Irritated, he looked away from the water. He was no longer alone. Three girls had appeared from somewhere, and were moving down the edge of the pool towards him. One he recognized as the girl he had first seen here. She was wearing a dress, unlike her sisters. One of her breasts was bared. She looked at him gravely, as she

50

approached; by her side she trailed a rope, decorated along its length with stained ribbons tied in limp but extravagant bows.

At the arrival of these three graces the fermenting waters of the pool were stirred into a frenzy, as its occupants rose to meet the women. Garvey could see three or four restless forms teasing – but not breaking – the surface. He was caught between his instinct to take flight (the rope, though prettified, was still a rope) and the desire to linger and see what the pool contained. He glanced towards the door. He was within ten yards of it. A quick dash and he'd be out into the cool air of the corridor. From there, Chandaman was within hailing distance.

The girls stood a few feet from him, and watched him. He returned their looks. All the desires that had brought him here had taken heel. He no longer wanted to cup the breasts of these creatures, or dabble at the intersection of their gleaming thighs. These women were not what they seemed. Their quietness wasn't docility, but a drug-trance; their nakedness wasn't sensuality, but a horrid indifference which offended him. Even their youth, and all it brought – the softness of their skins, the gloss of their hair – even that was somehow corrupt. When the girl in the dress reached out and touched his sweating face, Garvey made a small cry of *disgust*, as if he'd been licked by a snake. She was not fazed by his response, but stepped closer to him still, her eyes fixed on his, smelling not of perfume like his mistress, but of fleshliness. Affronted as he was, he could not turn away. He stood, meeting the slut's eyes, as she kissed his cheek, and the beribboned rope was wrapped around his neck.

Jerry called Garvey's office at half-hourly intervals through the day. At first he was told that the man was out of the office, and would be available later that afternoon. As the day wore on, however, the message changed. Garvey was not going to be in the office at all that day, Jerry was informed. Mr Garvey is feeling unwell, the secretary told him; he has gone home to rest. Please call again tomorrow. Jerry left with her the message that he had secured the ground-plan to the Pools and would be delighted to meet and discuss their plans at Mr Garvey's convenience.

Carole called in the late afternoon.

'Shall we go out tonight?' she said. 'Maybe a film?'

'What do you want to see?' he said.

'Oh, I hadn't really thought that far. We'll talk about it this evening, shall we?'

They ended up going to a French movie, which seemed, as far as Jerry could grasp, completely lacking in plot; it was simply a series of dialogues between characters, discussing their traumas and their aspirations, the former being in direct proportion to the failure of the latter. It left him feeling torpid.

'You didn't like it . . .'

'Not much. All that brow-beating.'

'And no shoot-out.'

'No shoot-out.'

She smiled to herself.

'What's so funny?'

'Nothing . . .'

'Don't say nothing.'

She shrugged. 'I was just smiling, that's all. Can't I smile?'

'Jesus. All this conversation needs is sub-titles.'

They walked along Oxford Street a little way.

'Do you want to eat?' he said, as they came to the head of Poland Street. 'We could go to the Red Fort.'

'No thanks. I hate eating late.'

'For Christ's sake, let's not argue about a bloody film.'

'Who's arguing?'

'You're so infuriating – '

'That's something we've got in common, anyhow,' she returned. Her neck was flushed.

'You said this morning – '

'What?'

'About us not losing each other – '

'That was this morning,' she said, eyes steely. And then, suddenly: 'You don't give a *fuck*, Jerry. Not about me, not about anybody.'

She stared at him, almost defying him not to respond. When he failed to, she seemed curiously satisfied.

'Goodnight . . .' she said, and began to walk away from him. He watched her take five, six, seven steps from him, the deepest part of him wanting to call after her, but a dozen irrelevancies – pride, fatigue, inconvenience – blocking his doing so. What eventually uprooted him, and put her name on his lips, was the thought of an empty bed tonight; of the sheets warm only where he lay, and chilly as Hell to left and right of him.

'Carole.'

She didn't turn; her step didn't even falter. He had to trot to catch up with her, conscious that this scene was probably entertaining the passers-by.

'Carole.' He caught hold of her arm. Now she stopped. When he moved round to face her he was shocked to see that she was crying. This discomfited him; he hated her tears only marginally less than his own.

52

'I surrender,' he said, trying a smile. 'The film was a masterpiece. How's that?'

She refused to be soothed by his antics; her face was swollen with unhappiness.

'Don't,' he said. 'Please don't. I'm not . . .' (very good at apologies, he wanted to say, but he was so bad at them he couldn't even manage that much.)

'Never mind,' she said softly. She wasn't angry, he saw; only miserable.

'Come back to the flat.'

'I don't want to.'

'*I* want you to,' he replied. That at least was sincerely meant. 'I don't like talking in the street.'

He hailed a cab, and they made their way back to Kentish Town, keeping their silence. Half way up the stairs to the door of the flat Carole said: 'Foul perfume.'

There was a strong, acidic smell lingering on the stairs.

'Somebody's been up here,' he said, suddenly anxious, and hurried on up the flight to the front door of his flat. It was open; the lock had been unceremoniously forced, the wood of the door-jamb splinted. He cursed.

'What's wrong?' Carole asked, following him up the stairs.

'Break in.'

He stepped into the flat and switched on the light. The interior was chaos. The whole flat had been comprehensively trashed. Everywhere, petty acts of vandalism – pictures smashed, pillows de-gutted, furniture reduced to timber. He stood in the middle of the turmoil and shook, while Carole went from room to room, finding the same thorough destruction in each.

'This is personal, Jerry.'

He nodded.

'I'll call the police,' she volunteered. 'You find out what's missing.'

He did as he was told, white-faced. The blow of this invasion numbed him. As he walked listlessly through the flat to survey the pandemonium – turning broken items over, pushing drawers back into place – he found himself imagining the intruders about their business, laughing as they worked through his clothes and keepsakes. In the corner of his bedroom he found a heap of his photographs. They had urinated on them.

'The police are on their way,' Carole told him. 'They said not to touch anything.'

'Too late,' he murmured.

'What's missing?'

'Nothing,' he told her. All the valuables – the stereo and video

53

equipment, his credit cards, his few items of jewellery – were present. Only then did he remember the ground-plan. He returned to the living-room and proceeded to root through the wreckage, but he knew damn well he wasn't going to find it.

'Garvey,' he said.

'What about him?'

'He came for the ground-plan of the Pools. Or sent someone.'

'Why?' Carole replied, looking at the chaos. 'You were going to give it to him anyway.'

Jerry shook his head. 'You were the one who warned me to stay clear – '

'I never expected something like this.'

'That makes two of us.'

The police came and went, offering faint apologies for the fact that they thought an arrest unlikely. 'There's a lot of vandalism around at the moment,' the officer said. 'There's nobody in downstairs . . .'

'No. They're away.'

'Last hope, I'm afraid. We're getting calls like this all the time. You're insured?'

'Yes.'

'Well, that's something.'

Throughout the interview Jerry kept silent on his suspicions, though he was repeatedly tempted to point the finger. There was little purpose in accusing Garvey at this juncture. For one, Garvey would have alibis prepared; for another, what would unsubstantiated accusations do but inflame the man's unreason further?

'What will you do?' Carole asked him, when the police picked up their shrugs and walked.

'I don't know. I can't even be certain it *was* Garvey. One minute he's all sweetness and light; the next this. How do I deal with a mind like that?'

'You don't. You leave it well be,' she replied. 'Do you want to stay here, or go over to my place?'

'Stay,' he said.

They made a perfunctory attempt to restore the status quo – righting the furniture that was not too crippled to stand, and clearing up the broken glass. Then they turned the slashed mattress over, located two unmutilated cushions, and went to bed.

She wanted to make love, but that reassurance, like so much of his life of late, was doomed to failure. There was no making good between the sheets what had been so badly soured out of them. His anger made him rough, and his roughness in turn angered her. She frowned beneath him, her kisses unwilling and tight. Her reluctance only spurred him on to fresh crassness.

54

'Stop,' she said, as he was about to enter her. 'I don't want this.'

He did; and badly. He pushed before she could further her objections.

'I said *don't*, Jerry.'

He shut out her voice. He was half as heavy again as she.

'*Stop.*'

He closed his eyes. She told him again to stop, this time with real fury, but he just thrust harder – the way she'd ask him to sometimes, when the heat was really on – beg him to, even. But now she only swore at him, and threatened, and every word she said made him more intent not to be cheated of this, though he felt nothing at this groin but fullness and discomfort, and the urge to be rid.

She began to fight, raking at his back with her nails, and pulling at his hair to unclamp his face from her neck. It passed through his head as he laboured that she would hate him for this, and on that, at least, they would be of one accord, but the thought was soon lost to sensation.

The poison passed, he rolled off her.

'Bastard . . .' she said.

His back stung. When he got up from the bed he left blood on the sheets. Digging through the chaos in the living room he located an unbroken bottle of whisky. The glasses, however, were all smashed, and out of absurd fastidiousness he didn't want to drink from the bottle. He squatted against the wall, his back chilled, feeling neither wretched nor proud. The front door opened, and was slammed. He waited, listening to Carole's feet on the stairs. Then tears came, though these too he felt utterly detached from. Finally, the bout dispatched, he went through into the kitchen, found a cup, and drank himself senseless out of that.

Garvey's study was an impressive room; he'd had it fashioned after that of a tax lawyer he'd known, the walls lined with books purchased by the yard, the colour of carpet and paintwork alike muted, as though by an accrual of cigar-smoke and learning. When he found sleep difficult, as he did now, he could retire to the study, sit on his leather-backed chair behind a vast desk, and dream of legitimacy. Not tonight, however; tonight his thoughts were otherwise preoccupied. Always, however much he might try to turn to another route, they went back to Leopold Road.

He remembered little of what had happened at the Pools. That in itself was distressing; he had always prided himself upon the acuteness of his memory. Indeed his recall of faces seen and favours done had in no small measure helped him to his present power. Of the hundreds in his employ he boasted that there was not a door-keeper or a cleaner he could not address by their Christian name.

But of the events at Leopold Road, barely thirty-six hours old, he had only the vaguest recollection; of the women closing upon him, and the rope tightening around his neck; of their leading him along the lip of the pool to some chamber the vileness of which had practically snatched his senses away. What had followed his arrival there moved in his memory like those forms in the filth of the pool: obscure, but horribly distressing. There had been humiliation and horrors, hadn't there? Beyond that, he remembered nothing.

He was not a man to kowtow to such ambiguities without argument, however. If there were mysteries to be uncovered here, then he would do so, and take the consequence of revelation. His first offensive had been sending Chandaman and Fryer to turn Coloqhoun's place over. If, as he suspected, this whole enterprise was some elaborate trap devised by his enemies, then Coloqhoun was involved in its setting. No more than a front man, no doubt; certainly not the mastermind. But Garvey was satisfied that the destruction of Coloqhoun's goods and chattels would warn his masters of his intent to fight. It had born other fruit too. Chandaman had returned with the ground-plan of the Pools; they were spread on Garvey's desk now. He had traced his route through the complex time and again, hoping that his memory might be jogged. He had been disappointed.

Weary, he got up and went to the study window. The garden behind the house was vast, and severely schooled. He could see little of the immaculate borders at the moment however; the starlight barely described the world outside. All he could see was his own reflection in the polished pane.

As he focussed on it, his outline seemed to waver, and he felt a loosening in his lower belly, as if something had come unknotted there. He put his hand to his abdomen. It twitched, it trembled, and for an instant he was back in the Pools, and naked, and something lumpen moved in front of his eyes. He almost yelled, but stopped himself by turning away from the window and staring at the room; at the carpets and the books and the furniture; at sober, solid reality. Even then the images refused to leave his head entirely. The coils of his innards were still jittery.

It was several minutes before he could bring himself to look back at the reflection in the window. When at last he did all trace of the vacillation had disappeared. He would countenance no more nights like this, sleepless and haunted. With the first light of dawn came the conviction that today was the day to break Mr Coloqhoun.

★ ★ ★

56

Jerry tried to call Carole at her office that morning. She was repeatedly unavailable. Eventually he simply gave up trying, and turned his attentions to the Herculean task of restoring some order to the flat. He lacked the focus and the energy to do a good job however. After a futile hour, in which he seemed not to have made more than a dent in the problem, he gave up. The chaos accurately reflected his opinion of himself. Best perhaps that it be left to lie.

Just before noon, he received a call.

'Mr Coloqhoun? Mr *Gerard* Coloqhoun?'

'That's right.'

'My name's Fryer. I'm calling on behalf of Mr Garvey – '

'Oh?'

Was this to gloat, or threaten further mischief?

'Mr Garvey was expecting some proposals from you,' Fryer said.

'Proposals?'

'He's very enthusiastic about the Leopold Road project, Mr Coloqhoun. He feels there's substantial monies to be made.'

Jerry said nothing; this palaver confounded him.

'Mr Garvey would like another meeting, as soon as possible.'

'Yes?'

'At the Pools. There's a few architectural details he'd like to show his colleagues.'

'I see.'

'Would you be available later on today?'

'Yes. Of course.'

'Four-thirty?'

The conversation more or less ended there, leaving Jerry mystified. There had been no trace of emnity in Fryer's manner; no hint, however subtle, of bad blood between the two parties. Perhaps, as the police had suggested, the events of the previous night *had* been the work of anonymous vandals – the theft of the ground-plan a whim of those responsible. His depressed spirits rose. All was not lost.

He rang Carole again, buoyed up by this turn of events. This time he did not take the repeated excuses of her colleagues, but insisted on speaking to her. Finally, she picked up the phone.

'I don't want to talk to you, Jerry. Just go to hell.'

'Just hear me out – '

She slammed the receiver down before he said another word. He rang back again, immediately. When she answered, and heard his voice, she seemed baffled that he was so eager to make amends.

'Why are you even trying?' she said. 'Jesus Christ, what's the use?' He could hear the tears in her throat.

'I want you to understand how sick I feel. Let me make it right. *Please* let me make it right.'

She didn't reply to his appeal.

'Don't put the phone down. Please don't. I know it was unforgiveable. Jesus, I know . . .'

Still, she kept her silence.

'Just think about it, will you? Give me a chance to put things right. Will you do that?'

Very quietly, she said: 'I don't see the use.'

'May I call you tomorrow?'

He heard her sigh.

'May I?'

'Yes. Yes.'

The line went dead.

He set out for his meeting at Leopold Road with a full three-quarters of an hour to spare, but half way to his destination the rain came on, great spots of it which defied the best efforts of his windscreen wipers. The traffic slowed; he crawled for half a mile, with only the brake-lights of the vehicle ahead visible through the deluge. The minutes ticked by, and his anxiety mounted. By the time he edged his way out of the fouled-up traffic to find another route, he was already late. There was nobody waiting on the steps of the Pools; but Garvey's powder-blue Rover was parked a little way down the road. There was no sign of the chauffeur. Jerry found a place to park on the opposite side of the road, and crossed through the rain. It was a matter of fifty yards from the door of the car to that of the Pools but by the time he reached the spot he was drenched and breathless. The door was open. Garvey had clearly manipulated the lock and slipped out of the downpour. Jerry ducked inside.

Garvey was not in the vestibule, but somebody was. A man of Jerry's height, but with half the width again. He was wearing leather gloves. His face, but for the absence of seams, might have been of the same material.

'Coloqhoun?'

'Yes.'

'Mr Garvey is waiting for you inside.'

'Who are you?'

'Chandaman,' the man replied. 'Go right in.'

There was a light at the far end of the corridor. Jerry pushed open the glass-pannelled vestibule doors and walked down towards it. Behind him, he heard the front door snap closed, and then the echoing tread of Garvey's lieutenant.

Garvey was talking with another man, shorter than Chandaman, who was holding a sizeable torch. When the pair heard Jerry approach they looked his way; their conversation abruptly ceased. Garvey offered no welcoming comment or hand, but merely said: 'About time.'

'The rain . . .' Jerry began, then thought better of offering a self-evident explanation.

'You'll catch your death,' the man with the torch said. Jerry immediately recognized the dulcet tones of:

'Fryer.'

'The same,' the man returned.

'Pleased to meet you.'

They shook hands, and as they did so Jerry caught sight of Garvey, who was staring at him as though in search of a second head. The man didn't say anything for what seemed like half a minute, but simply studied the growing discomfort on Jerry's face.

'I'm not a stupid man,' Garvey said, eventually.

The statement, coming out of nowhere, begged response.

'I don't even believe you're the main man in all of this,' Garvey went on. 'I'm prepared to be charitable.'

'What's this about?'

'Charitable – ' Garvey repeated, ' – because I think you're out of your depth. Isn't that right?'

Jerry just frowned.

'I think that's right,' Fryer replied.

'I don't think you understand how much trouble you're in even now, do you?' Garvey said.

Jerry was suddenly uncomfortably aware of Chandaman standing behind him, and of his own utter vulnerability.

'But I don't think ignorance should ever be bliss,' Garvey was saying. 'I mean, even if you don't *understand*, that doesn't make you exempt, does it?'

'I haven't a clue what you're talking about,' Jerry protested mildly. Garvey's face, by the light of the torch, was drawn and pale; he looked in need of a holiday.

'This place,' Garvey returned. 'I'm talking about *this place*. The women you put in here . . . for my benefit. What's it all about, Coloqhoun? That's all I want to know. *What's it all about?*'

Jerry shrugged lightly. Each word Garvey uttered merely perplexed him more; but the man had already told him ignorance would not be considered a legitimate excuse. Perhaps a question was the wisest reply.

'You saw women here?' he said.

'Whores, more like,' Garvey responded. His breath smelt of last week's cigar ash. 'Who are you working for, Coloqhoun?'

'For myself. The deal I offered – '

'Forget your fucking deal,' Garvey said. 'I'm not interested in deals.'

'I see,' Jerry replied. 'Then I don't see any point in this conversation.' He took a half-step away from Garvey, but the man's arm shot out and caught hold of his rain-sodden coat.

'I didn't tell you to go,' Garvey said.

'I've got business – '

'Then it'll have to wait,' the other replied, scarcely relaxing his grip. Jerry knew that if he tried to shrug off Garvey and make a dash for the front door he'd be stopped by Chandaman before he made three paces; if, on the other hand, he didn't try to escape –

'I don't much like your sort,' Garvey said, removing his hand. 'Smart brats with an eye to the main chance. Think you're so damn clever, just because you've got a fancy accent and a silk tie. Let me tell you something – ' He jabbed his finger at Jerry's throat, ' – I don't give a shit about you. I just want to know who you work for. Understand?'

'I already told you – '

'*Who do you work for?*' Garvey insisted, punctuating each word with a fresh jab. 'Or you're going to feel very sick.'

'For Christ's sake – I'm not working for anybody. And I don't know anything about any women.'

'Don't make it worse than it already is,' Fryer advised, with feigned concern.

'I'm telling the truth.'

'I think the man wants to be hurt,' Fryer said. Chandaman gave a joyless laugh. 'Is that what you want?'

'Just name some names,' Garvey said. 'Or we're going to break your legs.' The threat, unequivocal as it was, did nothing for Jerry's clarity of mind. He could think of no way out of this but to continue to insist upon his innocence. If he named some fictitious overlord the lie would be uncovered in moments, and the consequences could only be worse for the attempted deception.

'Check my credentials,' he pleaded. 'You've got the resources. Dig around. I'm not a company man, Garvey; I never have been.'

Garvey's eye left Jerry's face for a moment and moved to his shoulder. Jerry grasped the significance of the sign a heartbeat too late to prepare himself for the blow to his kidneys from the man at his back. He pitched forward, but before he could collide with Garvey, Chandaman had snatched at his collar and was throwing him against the wall. He doubled up, the pain blinding him to all other thoughts. Vaguely, he heard Garvey asking him again who his boss was. He shook his head. His skull was full of ball-bearings; they rattled between his ears.

'Jesus . . . Jesus . . .' he said, groping for some word of defence to keep another beating at bay, but he was hauled upright before any presented itself. The torch-beam was turned on him. He was ashamed of the tears that were rolling down his cheeks.

'*Names*,' said Garvey.

The ball-bearings rattled on.

'Again,' said Garvey, and Chandaman was moving in to give his fists further exercise. Garvey called him off as Jerry came close to passing out. The leather face withdrew.

'Stand up when I'm talking to you,' Garvey said.

Jerry attempted to oblige, but his body was less than willing to comply. It trembled, it felt fit to die.

'Stand up,' Fryer reiterated, moving between Jerry and his tormentor to prod the point home. Now, in close proximity, Jerry smelt that acidic scent Carole had caught on the stairs: it was Fryer's cologne.

'Stand up!' the man insisted.

Jerry raised a feeble hand to shield his face from the blinding beam. He could not see any of the trio's faces, but he was dimly aware that Fryer was blocking Chandaman's access to him. To Jerry's right, Garvey struck a match, and applied the flame to a cigar. A moment presented itself: Garvey occupied, the thug stymied. Jerry took it.

Ducking down beneath the torch-beam he broke from his place against the wall, contriving to knock the torch from Fryer's hand as he did so. The light-source clattered across the tiles and went out.

In the sudden darkness, Jerry made a stumbling bid for freedom. Behind him, he heard Garvey curse; heard Chandama· and Fryer collide as they scrabbled for the fallen torch. He began to edge his way along the wall to the end of the corridor. There was evidently no safe route past his tormentors to the front door; his only hope lay in losing himself in the networks of corridors that lay ahead.

He reached a corner, and made a right, vaguely remembering that this led him off the main thoroughfares and into the service corridors. The beating that he'd taken, though interrupted before it could incapacitate, had rendered him breathless and bruised. He felt every step he took as a sharp pain in his lower abdomen and back. When he slipped on the slimy tiles, the impact almost made him cry out.

At his back, Garvey was shouting again. The torch had been located. Its light bounced down the labyrinth to find him. Jerry hurried on, glad of the murky illumination, but not of its source. They would follow, and quickly. If, as Carole had said, the place was a simple spiral, the corridors describing a relentless loop with no way out of the configuration, he was lost. But he was committed. Head giddied by the mounting heat, he moved on, praying to find a fire-exit that would give him passage out of this trap.

'He went this way,' Fryer said. 'He must have done.'

Garvey nodded; it was indeed the likeliest route for Coloqhoun to have taken. Away from the light and into the labyrinth.

'Shall we go after him?' Chandaman said. The man was fairly salivating to finish the beating he'd started. 'He can't have got far.'

'No,' said Garvey. Nothing, not even the promise of the knighthood, would have induced him to follow.

Fryer had already advanced down the passageway a few yards, shining the torch-beam on the glistening walls.

'It's warm,' he said.

Garvey knew all too well how warm it was. Such heat wasn't natural, not for England. This was a temperate isle; that was why he had never set foot off it. The sweltering heat of other continents bred grotesqueries he wanted no sight of.

'What do we do?' Chandaman demanded. 'Wait for him to come out?'

Garvey pondered this. The smell from the corridor was beginning to distress him. His innards were churning, his skin was crawling. Instinctively, he put his hand to his groin. His manhood had shrunk in trepidation.

'No,' he said suddenly.

'No?'

'We're not waiting.'

'He can't stay in there forever.'

'I said *no*!' He hadn't anticipated how profoundly the sweat of the place would upset him. Irritating as it was to let Coloqhoun slip away like this, he knew that if he stayed here much longer he risked losing his self-control.

'You two can wait for him at his flat,' he told Chandaman. 'He'll have to come home sooner or later.'

'Damn shame,' Fryer muttered as he emerged from the passageway. 'I like a chase.'

Perhaps they weren't following. It was several minutes now since Jerry had heard the voices behind him. His heart had stopped its furious pumping. Now, with the adrenalin no longer giving speed to his heels, and distracting his muscles from their bruising, his pace slowed to a crawl. His body protested at even that.

When the agonies of taking another step became too much he slid down the wall and sat slumped across the passageway. His rain-drenched clothes clung to his body and about his throat; he felt both chilled and suffocated by them. He pulled at the knot of his tie, and then unbuttoned his waistcoat and his shirt. The air in the labyrinth was warm on his skin. Its touch was welcome.

He closed his eyes and made a studied attempt to mesmerise himself out of this pain. What was feeling but a trick of the nerve-endings?; there were techniques for dislocating the mind from the body, and leaving agonies behind. But no sooner had his lids closed than he heard muted sounds somewhere nearby. Footsteps; the lull of voices. It wasn't Garvey and his associates: the voices were female. Jerry raised his leaden head and opened his eyes. Either he had become used to the darkness in his few moments of meditation or else a light had crept into the passageway; it was surely the latter.

He got to his feet. His jacket was dead weight, and he sloughed it off, leaving it to lie where he'd been squatting. Then he started in the direction of the light. The heat seemed to have risen considerably in the last few minutes: it gave him mild hallucinations. The walls seemed to have forsaken verticality, the air to have traded transparency for a shimmering aurora.

He turned a corner. The light brightened. Another corner, and he was delivered into a small tiled chamber, the heat of which took his breath away. He gasped like a stranded fish, and peered across the chamber – the air thickening with every pulse-beat – at the door on the far side. The yellowish light through it was brighter still, but he could not summon the will to follow it a yard further; the heat here had defeated him. Sensing that he was within an ace of unconsciousness, he put his hand out to support himself, but his palm slid on the slick tiles, and he fell, landing on his side. He could not prevent a shout spilling from him.

Groaning his misery, he tucked his legs up close to his body, and lay where he'd fallen. If Garvey had heard his yell, and sent his lieutenants in pursuit, then so be it. He was past caring.

The sound of movement reached him from across the chamber. Raising his head an inch from the floor he opened his eyes to a slit. A naked girl had appeared in the doorway opposite, or so his reeling senses informed him. Her skin shone as if oiled; here and there, on her breasts and thighs, were smudges of what might have been old blood. Not her blood, however. There was no wound to spoil her gleaming body.

The girl had begun to laugh at him, a light, easy laugh that made him feel foolish. Its musicality entranced him however, and he made an effort to get a better look at her. She had started to move across the chamber towards him, still laughing; and now he saw that there were others behind her. These were the women Garvey had babbled about; this the trap he had accused Jerry of setting.

'Who are you?' he murmured as the girl approached him. Her laughter faltered when she looked down at his pain-contorted features.

He attempted to sit upright, but his arms were numb, and he slid back to the tiles again. The woman had not answered his inquiry, nor did she make any attempt to help him. She simply stared down at him as a pedestrian might at a drunk in the gutter, her face unreadable. Looking up at her, Jerry felt his tenuous grip on consciousness slipping. The heat, his pain, and now this sudden eruption of beauty was too much for him. The distant women were dispersing into darkness, the entire chamber folding up like a magician's box until the sublime creature in front of him claimed his attention utterly. And now, at her silent insistence, his mind's eye seemed to be plucked from his head, and suddenly he was speeding over her skin, her flesh a landscape, each pore a pit, each hair a pylon. He was hers, utterly. She drowned him in her eyes, and flayed him with her lashes; she rolled him across her abdomen, and down the soft channel of her spine. She took him between her buttocks, and then up into her heat, and out again just as he thought he must burn alive. The velocity exhilarated him. He was aware that his body, somewhere below, was hyper-ventilating in its terror; but his imagination – careless of breath – went willingly where she sent him, looping like a bird, until he was thrown, ragged and dizzy, back into the cup of his skull. Before he could apply the fragile tool of reason to the phenonema he had just experienced, his eyes fluttered closed and he passed out.

The body does not need the mind. It has procedures aplenty – lungs to be filled and emptied, blood to be pumped and food profitted from – none of which require the authority of thought. Only when one or more of these procedures falters does the mind become aware of the intricacy of the mechanism it inhabits. Coloqhoun's faint lasted only a few minutes; but when he came to he was aware of his body as he had seldom been before: as a trap. Its fragility was a trap; its shape, its size, its very gender was a trap. And there was no flying out of it; he was shackled to, or *in*, this wretchedness.

These thoughts came and went. In between them there were brief sights through which he fell giddily, and still briefer moments in which he glimpsed the world outside himself.

The women had picked him up. His head lolled; his hair dragged on the floor. I am a trophy, he thought in a more coherent instant, then the darkness came again. And again he struggled to the surface, and now they were carrying him along the edge of the large pool. His nostrils were filled with contradictory scents, both delectable and foetid. From the corner of his lazy eye he could see water so bright it

64

seemed to burn as it lapped the shores of the pool: and something else too – shadows moving in the brightness.

They mean to drown me, he thought. And then: I'm already drowning. He imagined water filling his mouth: imagined the forms he had glimpsed in the pool invading his throat and slipping into his belly. He struggled to vomit them back up, his body convulsing.

A hand was laid on his face. The palm was blissfully cool. '*Hush*,' somebody murmured to him, and at the words his delusions melted away. He felt himself coaxed out of his terrors and into consciousness.

The hand had evaporated from his brow. He looked around the gloomy room for his saviour, but his eyes didn't travel far. On the other side of this chamber – which looked to have been a communal shower-room – several pipes, set high in the wall, delivered solid arcs of water onto the tiles, where gutters channelled it away. A fine spray, and the gushing of the fountains, filled the air. Jerry sat up. There was movement behind the cascading veil of water: a shape too vast by far to be human. He peered through the drizzle to try and make sense of the folds of flesh. Was it an animal? There was a pungent smell in here that had something of the menagerie about it.

Moving with considerable caution so as not to arouse the beast's attention, Jerry attempted to stand up. His legs, however, were not the equal of his intention. All he could do was crawl a little way across the room on his hands and knees, and peer – one beast at another – through the veil.

He sensed that he was sensed; that the dark, recumbent creature had turned its eyes in his direction. Beneath its gaze, he felt his skin creep with gooseflesh, but he couldn't take his eyes off it. And then, as he squinted to scrutinize it better, a spark of phosphorescence began in its substance, and spread – fluttering waves of jaundiced light – up and across its tremendous form, revealing itself to Coloqhoun.

Not it; *she*. He knew indisputably that this creature was female, though it resembled no species or genus he knew of. As the ripples of luminescence moved through the creature's physique, it revealed with every fresh pulsation some new and phenomenal configuration. Watching her, Jerry thought of something slow and molten – glass, perhaps; or stone – its flesh extruded into elaborate forms and recalled again into the furnace to be remade. She had neither head nor limbs recognizable as such, but her contours were ripe with clusters of bright bubbles that might have been eyes, and she threw out here and there irridescent ribbons – slow, pastel flames – that seemed momentarily to ignite the very air.

Now the body issued a series of soft noises: scuttlings and sighs. He wondered if he was being addressed, and if so, how he was expected to respond. Hearing footballs behind him, he glanced round at one of the women for guidance.

'Don't be afraid,' she said.

'I'm not,' he replied. It was the truth. The prodigy in front of him was electrifying, but woke no fear in him.

'What is she?' he asked.

The woman stood close to him. Her skin, bathed by the shimmering light off the creature, was golden. Despite the circumstances – or perhaps because of them – he felt a tremor of desire.

'She is the Madonna. The Virgin Mother.'

Mother? Jerry mouthed, swivelling his head back to look at the creature again. The waves of phosphorescence had ceased to break across her body. Now the light pulsed in one part of her anatomy only, and at this region, in rhythm with the pulse, the Madonna's substance was swelling and splitting. Behind him he heard further footsteps; and now whispers echoed about the chamber, and chiming laughter, and applause.

The Madonna was giving birth. The swollen flesh was opening; liquid light gushing; the smell of smoke and blood filled the shower-room. A girl gave a cry, as if in sympathy with the Madonna. The applause mounted, and suddenly the slit spasmed and delivered the child – something between a squid and a shorn lamb – onto the tiles. The water from the pipes slapped it into consciousness immediately, and it threw back its head to look about it; its single eye vast and perfectly lucid. It squirmed on the tiles for a few moments before the girl at Jerry's side stepped forward into the veil of water and picked it up. Its toothless mouth sought out her breast immediately. The girl delivered it to her tit.

'Not human . . .' Jerry murmured. He had not prepared himself for a child so strange, and yet so unequivocally intelligent. 'Are all . . . all the children like that?'

The surrogate mother gazed down at the sac of life in her arms.

'No one is like another,' she replied. 'We feed them. Some die. Others live, and go their ways.'

'Where, for God's sake?'

'To the water. To the sea. Into dreams.'

She cooed to it. A fluted limb, in which light ran as it had in its parent, paddled the air with pleasure.

'And the father?'

'She needs no husband,' the reply came. 'She could make children from a shower of rain if she so desired.'

Jerry looked back at the Madonna. All but the last vestige of light had been extinguished in her. The vast body threw out a tendril of saffron flame, which caught the cascade of water, and threw dancing

66

patterns on the wall. Then it was still. When Jerry looked back for the mother and child, they had gone. Indeed all the women had gone but one. It was the girl who had first appeared to him. The smile she'd worn was on her face again as she sat across the room from him, her legs splayed. He gazed at the place between them, and then back at her face.

'What are you afraid of?' she asked.

'I'm not afraid.'

'Then why don't you come to me?'

He stood up, and crossed the chamber to where she sat. Behind him, the water still slapped and ran on the tiles, and behind the fountains the Madonna murmured in her flesh. He was not intimidated by her presence. The likes of him was surely beneath the notice of such a creature. If she saw him at all she doubtless thought him ridiculous. Jesus! he was ridiculous even to himself. He had neither hope nor dignity left to lose.

Tomorrow, all this would be a dream: the water, the children, the beauty who even now stood up to embrace him. Tomorrow he would think he had died for a day, and visited a showerhouse for angels. For now, he would make what he could of the opportunity.

After they had made love, he and the smiling girl, when he tried to recall the specifics of the act, he could not be certain that he had performed at all. Only the vaguest memories remained to him, and they were not of her kisses, or of how they coupled, but of a dribble of milk from her breast and the way she murmured, 'Never . . . never . . .' as they had entwined. When they were done, she was indifferent. There were no more words, no more smiles. She just left him alone in the drizzle of the chamber. He buttoned up his soiled trousers, and left the Madonna to her fecundity.

A short corridor led out of the shower-room and into the large pool. It was, as he had vaguely registered when they had brought him into the presence of the Madonna, brimming. Her children played in the radiant water, their forms multitudinous. The women were nowhere to be seen, but the door to the outer corridor stood open. He walked through it, and had taken no more than half a dozen steps before it slid closed behind him.

Now, all too late, Ezra Garvey knew that returning to the Pools (even for an act of intimidation, which he had traditionally enjoyed) had been an error. It had re-opened a wound in him which he had hoped near to healing; and it had brought memories of his second visit there, of the women and what they had displayed to him (memories which he had sought to clarify until he began to grasp their true nature) closer to the surface. They had drugged him somehow, hadn't

67

they?; and then, when he was weak and had lost all sense of propriety, they had exploited him for their entertainment. They had suckled him like a child, and made him their plaything. The memories of that merely perplexed him; but there were others, too deep to be distinguished quite, which *appalled*. Of some inner chamber, and of water falling in a curtain; of a darkness that was terrible, and a luminescence that was more terrible still.

The time had come, he knew, to trample these dreams underfoot, and be done with such bafflement. He was a man who forgot neither favours done, nor favours owed; a little before eleven he had two telephone conversations, to call some of those favours in. Whatever lived at Leopold Road Pools would prosper there no longer. Satisfied with his night's manoeuvres, he went upstairs to bed.

He had drunk the best part of a bottle of schnapps since returning from the incident with Coloqhoun, chilled and uneasy. Now the spirit in his system caught up with him. His limbs felt heavy, his head heavier still. He did not even concern himself to undress, but lay down on his double bed for a few minutes to allow his senses to clear. When he next woke, it was one-thirty a.m.

He sat up. His belly was cavorting again; indeed his whole body seemed to be traumatized. He had seldom been ill in his fifty-odd years: success had kept ailments at bay. But now he felt terrible. He had a headache which was near to blinding – he stumbled from his bedroom down to the kitchen more by aid of touch than sight. There he poured himself a glass of milk, sat down at the table, and put it to his lips. He did not drink however. His gaze had alighted on the hand that held his glass. He stared at it through a fog of pain. It didn't seem to be *his* hand: it was too fine, too smooth. He put the glass down, trembling, but it tipped over, the milk pooling on the teak table-top and running off on to the floor.

He got to his feet, the sound of the milk on the kitchen tiles awaking curious thoughts, and moved unsteadily through to his study. He needed to be with somebody: *anybody* would do. He picked up his telephone book and tried to make sense of the scrawlings on each page, but the numbers would not come clear. His panic was growing. Was this insanity? The delusion of his transformed hand, the unnatural sensations which were running through his body. He reached to unbutton his shirt, and in doing so his hand brushed another delusion, more absurd than the first. Fingers unwilling, he tore at the shirt, telling himself over and over that none of this was possible.

But the evidence was plain. He touched a body which was no longer his. There were still signs that the flesh and bone belonged to him – an appendix scar on his lower abdomen, a birth-mark beneath his arm – but the substance of his body had been teased (was *being* teased still, even as he watched) into shapes that shamed him. He clawed at the forms that disfigured his torso, as if they might dissolve beneath his assault, but they merely bled.

In his time, Ezra Garvey had suffered much, almost all his sufferings self-inflicted. He had undergone periods of imprisonment; come close to serious physical wounding; had endured the deceptions of beautiful women. But those torments were nothing beside the anguish he felt now. He was not himself! His body had been taken from his while he slept and this changeling left in its place. The horror of it shattered his self-esteem, and left his sanity teetering.

Unable to hold back the tears, he began to pull at the belt of his trousers. Please God, he babbled, please God let me be whole still. He could barely see for the tears. He wiped them away, and peered at his groin. Seeing what deformities were in progress there, he roared until the windows rattled.

Garvey was not a man for prevarication. Deeds, he knew, were not best served by debate. He wasn't sure how this treatise on transformation had been written into his system, and he didn't much care. All he could think of was how many deaths of shame he would die if this vile condition ever saw the light of day. He returned into the kitchen, selecting a large meat-knife from the drawer, then adjusted his clothing and left the house.

His tears had dried. They were wasted now, and he was not a wasteful man. He drove through the empty city down to the river, and across Blackfriars Bridge. There he parked, and walked down to the water's edge. The Thames was high and fast tonight, the tops of the waters were whipped white.

Only now, having come so far without examining his intentions too closely, did fear of extinction give him pause. He was a wealthy and influential man; were there not other routes out of this ordeal other than the one he had come headlong to? Pill peddlars who could reverse the lunacy that had seized his cells; surgeons who might slice off the offending parts and knit his lost self back together again? But how long would such solutions last? Sooner or later, the process would begin again: he knew it. He was beyond help.

A gust of wind blew spume up off the water. It rained against his face, and the sensation finally broke the seal on his forgetfulness. At last he remembered it all: the shower-room, the spouts from the severed pipes beating on the floor, the heat, the women laughing and applauding. And finally, the thing that lived behind the water wall, a creature that was worse than any nightmare of womanhood his grieving mind had dredged up. He had fucked there, in the presence of that behemoth, and in the fury of the act – when he had momentarily forgotten himself – the bitches had worked this rapture upon him. No use for regrets. What was done, was done. At least he had made provision for the destruction of their lair. Now he would undo by self-surgery what they had contrived by magic, and so at least deny them sight of their handiwork.

The wind was cold, but his blood was hot. It came gushingly as he slashed at his body. The Thames received the libation with enthusiasm. It lapped at his feet; it whipped itself into eddies. He had not finished the job, however, when the loss of blood overcame him. No matter, he thought, as his knees buckled and he toppled into the water, no one will know me now but fishes. The prayer he offered up as the river closed over him was that death not be a woman.

Long before Garvey had woken in the night, and discovered his body in rebellion, Jerry had left the Pools, got into his car, and attempted to drive home. He had not been the equal of that simple task, however. His eyes were bleary, his sense of direction confused. After a near accident at an intersection he parked the car and began to walk back to the flat. His memories of what had just happened to him were by no means clear, though the events were mere hours old. His head was full of strange associations. He walked in the solid world, but half dreaming. It was the sight of Chandaman and Fryer, waiting for him in the bedroom of his flat, that slapped him back into reality. He did not wait for them to greet him, but turned and ran. They had emptied his stock of spirits as they lay in ambush, and were slow to respond. He was down the stairs and gone from the house before they could give chase.

He walked to Carole's; she was not in. He didn't mind waiting. He sat on the front steps of her home for half an hour, and when the tenant of the top floor flat arrived talked his way into the comparative warmth of the house itself and kept vigil on the stairs. There he fell to dozing, and retraced his steps over the route he'd come, back to the intersection where he'd abandoned the car. A crowd of people were passing the place. '*Where are you going?*' he asked them. '*To see the yatches,*' they replied. '*What yatches are those?*' he wanted to know, but they were already drifting away, chattering. He walked on a while. The sky was dark, but the streets were illuminated nevertheless by a wash of blue and shadowless light. Just as he was about to come within sight of the Pools, he heard a splashing sound, and, turning a corner, discovered that the tide was coming in up Leopold Street. What sea was this?, he enquired of the gulls overhead, for the salt-tang in the air declared these waters as ocean, not river. Did it matter what sea it was, they returned?; weren't all seas *one* sea, finally? He stood and watched the wavelets creeping across the tarmac. Their advance, though gentle, overturned lamp-posts, and so swiftly eroded the foundations of the buildings that they fell, silently, beneath the glacial tide. Soon the waves were around his feet. Fishes, tiny darts of silver, moved in the water.

'Jerry?'

Carole was on the stairs, staring at him.

'What the hell's happened to you?'

'I could have drowned,' he said.

He told her about the trap Garvey had set at Leopold Road, and how he'd been beaten up; then of the thugs' presence at his own house. She offered cool sympathy. He said nothing about the chase through the spiral, or the women, or the something that he'd seen in the shower-room. He couldn't have articulated it, even if he'd wanted to: every hour that passed since he'd left the Pool he was less certain of having seen anything at all.

'Do you want to stay here?' she asked him when he's finished his account.

'I thought you'd never ask.'

'You'd better have a bath. Are you sure they didn't break any bones?'

'I think I'd feel it by now if they had.'

No broken bones, perhaps; but he had not escaped unmarked. His torso was a patchwork of ripening bruises, and he ached from head to foot. When, after half an hour of soaking, he got out of the bath and surveyed himself in the mirror, his body seemed to be puffed up by the beating, the skin of his chest tender and tight. He was not a pretty sight.

'Tomorrow, you must go to the police,' Carole told him later as they lay side by side. 'And have this bastard Garvey arrested – '

'I suppose so . . .' he said.

She leaned over him. His face was bland with fatigue. She kissed him lightly.

'I'd like to love you,' she said. He did not look at her. 'Why do you make it so difficult?'

'Do I?0' he said, his eyelids drooping. She wanted to slide her hand beneath the bath-robe he was still wearing – she had never quite understood his coyness, but it charmed her – and caress him. But there was a certain insularity in the way he lay that signalled his wish to be left untouched, and she respected it.

'I'll turn out the light,' she said, but he was already asleep.

* * *

71

The tide was not kind to Ezra Garvey. It picked up his body and played it back and forth awhile, picking at it like a replete diner toying with food he had no appetite for. It carried the corpse a mile downstream, and then tired of its burden. The current relegated it to the slower water near the banks, and there – abreast of Battersea – it became snagged in a mooring rope. The tide went out; Garvey did not. As the water-level dropped he remained depending from the rope, his bloodless bulk revealed inch by inch as the tide left him, and the dawn came looking. By eight o'clock he had gained more than morning as an audience.

Jerry woke to the sound of the shower running in the adjacent bathroom. The bedroom curtains were still drawn across. Only a fine dart of light found its way down to where he lay. He rolled over to bury his head in the pillow where the light couldn't disturb him, but his brain, once stirred, began to whirl. He had a difficult day ahead, in which he would have to make some account of recent events to the police. There would be questions asked and some of them might prove uncomfortable. The sooner he thought his story through, the more water-tight it would be. He rolled over, and threw off the sheet.

His first thought as he looked down at himself was that he had not truly woken yet, but still had his face buried in the pillow, and was merely dreaming this waking. Dreaming too the body he inhabited – with its budding breasts and its soft belly. This was not his body; his was of the other sex.

He tried to shake himself awake, but there was nowhere to wake to. He was here. This transformed anatomy was his – its slit, its smoothness, its strange weight – all *his*. In the hours since midnight he had been unknitted and remade in another image.

From next door, the sound of the shower brought the Madonna back into his head. Brought the woman too, who had coaxed him into her and whispered, as he frowned and thrust, 'Never . . . never . . .', telling him, though he couldn't know it, that this coupling was his last as a man. They had conspired – woman and Madonna – to work this wonder upon him, and wasn't it the finest failure of his life that he would not even hold on to his own sex; that maleness itself, like wealth and influence, was promised, then snatched away again?

He got up off the bed, turning his hands over to admire their newfound fineness, running his palms across his breasts. He was not afraid, nor was he jubilant. He accepted this *fait accompli* as a baby accepts its condition, having no sense of what good or bad it might bring.

Perhaps there were more enchantments where this had come from. If so, he would go back to the Pools and find them for himself; follow the spiral into its hot heart, and debate mysteries with the Madonna. There were miracles in the world! Forces that could turn flesh inside out without drawing blood; that could topple the tyranny of the real and make play in its rubble.

Next door, the shower continued to run. He went to the bathroom door, which was slightly ajar, and peered in. Though the shower was on, Carole was not under it. She was sitting on the side of the bath, her hands pressed over her face. She heard him at the door. Her body shook. She did not look up.

'I saw . . .' she said. Her voice was guttural; thick with barely-suppressed abhorrence. '. . . am I going mad?'

'No.'

'Then what's happening?'

'I don't know,' he replied, simply. 'Is it so terrible?'

'Vile,' she said. 'Revolting. I don't want to look at you. You hear me? *I don't want to see.*'

He didn't attempt to argue. She didn't want to know him, and that was her prerogative.

He slipped through into the bedroom, dressed in his stale and dirty clothes, and headed back to the Pool.

He went unnoticed; or rather, if anybody along his route noted a strangeness in their fellow pedestrian – a disparity between the clothes worn and the body that wore them – they looked the other way, unwilling to tackle such a problem at such an hour, and sober.

When he arrived at Leopold Road there were several men on the steps. They were talking, though he didn't know it, of imminent demolition. Jerry lingered in the doorway of a shop across the road from the Pools until the trio departed, and then made his way to the front door. He feared that they might have changed the lock, but they hadn't. He got in easily, and closed the door behind him.

He had not brought a torch, but when he plunged into the labyrinth he trusted to his instinct, and it did not forsake him. After a few minutes of exploration in the benighted corridors he stumbled across the jacket which he had discarded the previous day; a few turns beyond he came into the chamber where the laughing girl had found him. There was a hint of daylight here, from the pool beyond. All but the last vestiges of that luminescence that had first led him here had gone.

He hurried on through the chamber, his hopes sinking. The water still brimmed in the pool, but almost all its light had flickered out. He studied the broth: there was no movement in the depths. *They had gone.* The mothers; the children. And, no doubt, the first cause. The Madonna.

He walked through to the shower-room. She had indeed left. Furthermore, the chamber had been destroyed, as if in a fit of pique. The tiles had been torn from the walls; the pipes ripped from the plasterwork and melted in the Madonna's heat. Here and there he saw splashes of blood.

Turning his back on the wreckage, he returned to the pool, wondering if it had been his invasion that had frightened them from this makeshift temple. Whatever the reason, the witches had gone, and he, their creature, was left to fend for himself, deprived of their mysteries.

He wandered along the edge of the pool, despairing. The surface of the water was not quite calm: a circle of ripples had awoken in it, and was growing by the heart-beat. He stared at the eddy as it gained momentum, flinging its arms out across the pool. The water-level had suddenly begun to drop. The eddy was rapidly becoming a whirlpool, the water foaming about it. Some trap had been opened in the bottom of the pool, and the waters were draining away. Was this where the Madonna had fled? He rushed back to the far end of the pool and examined the tiles. Yes! She had left a trail of fluid behind her as she crept out of her shrine to the safety of the pool. And if this was where *she* had gone, would they not all have followed?

Where the waters were draining to he had no way of knowing. To the sewers maybe, and then to the river, and finally out to sea. To death by drowning; to the extinction of magic. Or by some secret channel down into the earth, to some sanctuary safe from enquiry where rapture was not forbidden.

The water was rapidly becoming frenzied as suction called it away. The vortex whirled and foamed and spat. He studied the shape it described. A spiral of course, elegant and inevitable. The waters were sinking fast now; the splashing had mounted to a roar. Very soon it would all be gone, the door to another world sealed up and lost.

He had no choice: he leapt. The circling undertow snatched at him immediately. He barely had time to draw breath before he was sucked beneath the surface and dragged round and round, down and down. He felt himself buffetted against the floor of the pool, then somersaulted as he was pulled inexorably closer to the exit. He opened his eyes. Even as he did so the current dragged him to the brink, and over. The stream took him in its custody, and flung him back and forth in its fury.

There was light ahead. How far it lay, he couldn't calculate, but what did it matter? If he drowned before he reached that place, and ended this journey dead, so what? Death was no more certain than the dream of masculinity he'd lived these years. Terms of description fit only to be turned up and over and inside out. The earth was

74

bright, wasn't it, and probably full of stars. He opened his mouth and shouted into the whirlpool, as the light grew and grew, an anthem in praise of paradox.

Babel's Children

Why could Vanessa never resist the road that had no signpost marking it; the track that led to God alone knew where? Her enthusiasm for following her nose had got her into trouble often enough in the past. A near-fatal night spent lost in the Alps; that episode in Marrakech that had almost ended in rape; the adventure with the sword-swallower's apprentice in the wilds of Lower Manhattan. And yet despite what bitter experience should have taught her, when the choice lay between the marked route and the unmarked, she would always, without question, take the latter.

Here, for instance. This road that meandered towards the coast of Kithnos: what could it possibly offer her but an uneventful drive through the scrub land hereabouts – a chance encounter with a goat along the way – and a view from the cliffs of the blue Aegean. She could enjoy such a view from her hotel at Merikha Bay, and scarcely get out of bed to do so. But the other highways that led from this crossroads were so clearly *marked*: one to Loutra, with its ruined Venetian fort, the other to Driopis. She had visited neither village, and had heard that both were charming, but the fact that they were so clearly named seriously marred their attraction for her. This other road, however, though it might – indeed probably *did* – lead nowhere, at least led to an *unnamed* nowhere. That was no small recommendation. Thus fuelled by sheer perversity, she set off along it.

The landscape to either side of the road (or, as it rapidly became, *track*) was at best undistinguished. Even the goats she had anticipated were not in evidence here, but then the sparse vegetation looked less than nourishing. The island was no paradise. Unlike Santorini, with its picturesque volcano, or Mykonos – the Sodom of the Cyclades – with its plush beaches and plusher hotels Kithnos could boast nothing that might draw the tourist. That, in short, was why she was here: as far from the crowd as she could conspire to get. This track, no doubt, would take her further still.

The cry she heard from the hillocks off to her left was not meant to be ignored. It was a cry of naked alarm, and it was perfectly audible above the grumbling of her hired car. She brought the ancient vehicle to a halt, and turned off the engine. The cry came again, but this time it was followed by a shot, and a space, then a second shot.

76

Without thinking, she opened the car door and stepped out onto the track. The air was fragrant with sand lilies and wild thyme – scents which the petrol-stench inside the car had effectively masked. Even as she breathed the perfume she heard a third shot, and this time she saw a figure – too far from where she stood to be recognizable, even if it had been her husband – mounting the crown of one of the hillocks, only to disappear into a trough again. Three or four beats later, and his pursuers appeared. Another shot was fired; but, she was relieved to see, into the air rather than at the man. They were warning him to stop rather than aiming to kill. The details of the pursuers were as indistinct as those of the escapee except that – an ominous touch – they were dressed from head to foot in billowing black garb.

She hesitated at the side of the car, not certain of whether she should get back in and drive away or go and find out what this hide-and-seek was all about. The sound of guns was not particularly pleasant, but could she possibly turn her back on such a mystery? The men in black had disappeared after their quarry, but she pinned her eyes to the spot they had left, and started off towards it, keeping her head down as best she could.

Distances were deceptive in such unremarkable terrain; one sandy hillock looked much like the next. She picked her way amongst the squirting cucumber for fully ten minutes before she became certain that she had missed the spot from which pursued and pursuer had vanished – and by that time she was lost in a sea of grass-crested knolls. The cries had long since ceased, the shots too. She was left only with the sound of gulls, and the rasping debate of cicadas around her feet.

'Damn,' she said. 'Why do I do these things?'

She selected the largest hillock in the vicinity and trudged up its flank, her feet uncertain in the sandy soil, to see if the vantage-point offered a view of the track she'd left, or even of the sea. If she could locate the cliffs, she could orient herself relative to the spot on which she'd left the car, and head off in that approximate direction, knowing that sooner or later she'd be bound to reach the track. But the hummock was too puny; all that was revealed from its summit was the extent of her isolation. In every direction, the same indistinguishable hills, raising their backs to the afternoon sun. In desperation, she licked her finger and put it up to the wind, reasoning that the breeze would most likely be off the sea, and that she might use that slender information to base her mental cartography upon. The breeze was negligible, but it was the only guide she had, and she set off in the direction she hoped the track lay.

After five increasingly breathless minutes of tramping up and down the hillocks, she scaled one of the slopes and found herself looking not upon her car but at a cluster of white-washed buildings – dominated by a squat tower and ringed like a garrison with a high wall – which her previous perches had given her no glimpse of. It immediately occurred to her that the running man and his three over-attentive admirers had originated here, and that wisdom probably counselled against approaching the place. But then without directions from somebody might she not wander around forever in this waste-land and never find her way back to the car? Besides, the buildings looked reassuringly unpretentious. There was even a hint of foliage peeping above the bright walls that suggested a sequestered garden within, where she might at least get some shade. Changing direction, she headed towards the entrance.

She arrived at the wrought-iron gates exhausted. Only when in sight of comfort would she concede the weight of her weariness to herself: the trudge across the hillocks had reduced her thighs and shins to quivering incompetence.

One of the large gates was ajar, and she stepped through. The yard beyond was paved, and mottled with doves' droppings: several of the culprits sat in a myrtle tree and cooed at her appearance. From the yard several covered walkways led off into a maze of buildings. Her perversity unchastened by adventure, she followed the one that looked least promising and it led her out of the sun and into a balmy passage, lined with plain benches, and out the other side into a smaller enclosure. Here the sun fell upon one of the walls, in a niche of which stood a statue of the Virgin Mary – her notorious child, fingers raised in blessing, perched upon her arm. And now, seeing the statue, the pieces of this mystery fell into place: the secluded location, the silence, the plainness of the yards and walkways – this was surely a religious establishment.

She had been godless since early adolescence, and had seldom stepped over the threshold of a church in the intervening twenty-five years. Now, at forty-one, she was past recall, and so felt doubly a trespasser here. But then she wasn't seeking sanctuary, was she?; merely directions. She could ask them, and get gone.

As she advanced across the sunlit stone she had that curious sensation of self-consciousness which she associated with being spied upon. It was a sensitivity her life with Ronald had sophisticated into a sixth sense. His ridiculous jealousies, which had, only three months previous, ended their marriage, had led him to spying strategies that would not have shamed the agencies of Whitehall or Washington. Now she felt not one, but several pairs of eyes upon her. Though she squinted up at the narrow windows that overlooked the courtyard, and seemed to see movement at one of them, nobody made any effort to call down to her, however. A mute order, perhaps, their vow of silence so profoundly observed that she would have to communicate in sign-language? Well, so be it.

Somewhere behind her, she heard running feet; several pairs, rushing towards her. And from down the walkway, the sound of the iron gates clanging closed. For some reason her heart-beat tripped over itself, and alarmed her blood. Startled, it leapt to her face. Her weakened legs began to quiver again.

She turned to face the owners of those urgent footsteps, and as she did so caught sight of the stone Virgin's head moving a fraction. Its blue eyes had followed her across the yard, and now were unmistakably following her back. She stood stock still; best not to run, she thought, with Our Lady at your back. It would have done no good to have taken flight anyway, because even now three nuns were appearing from out of the shadow of the cloisters, their vestments billowing. Only their beards, and the gleaming automatic rifles they carried, fractured the illusion of their being Christ's brides. She might have laughed at this incongruity, but that they were pointing their weapons straight at her heart.

There was no word of explanation offered; but then in a place that harboured armed men dressed as nuns a glimpse of sweet reason was doubtless as rare as feathered frogs.

She was bundled out of the courtyard by the three holy sisters – who treated her as though she had just razed the Vatican – and summarily searched her high and low. She took this invasion without more than a cursory objection. Not for a moment did they take their rifle-sights off her, and in such circumstances obedience seemed best. Search concluded, one of them invited her to re-dress, and she was escorted to a small room and locked in. A little while later, one of the nuns brought her a bottle of palatable retsina, and, to complete this catalogue of incongruities, the best deep-dish pizza she'd had this side of Chicago. Alice, lost in Wonderland, could not have thought it curiouser.

'There may have been an error,' the man with the waxed moustache conceded after several hours of interrogation. She was relieved to discover he had no desire to pass as an Abbess, despite the garb of the garrison. His office – if such it was – was sparsely furnished, its only remarkable artifact a human skull, its bottom jaw missing, which sat on the desk and peered vacuously at her. He himself was better dressed; his bow-tie immaculately tied, his trousers holding a lethal crease. Beneath his calculated English, Vanessa thought she sniffed the hint of an accent. French? German? It was only when he produced some chocolate from his desk that she decided he was Swiss. His name, he claimed, was Mr Klein.

79

'An error?' she said. 'You're damn right there's been an error!'

'We've located your car. We have also checked with your hotel. So far, your story has been verified.'

'I'm not a liar,' she said. She was well past the point of courtesy with Mr Klein, despite his bribes with the confectionery. By now it must be late at night, she guessed, though as she wore no watch and the bald little room, which was in the bowels of one of the buildings, had no windows, it was difficult to be certain. Time had been telescoped with only Mr Klein, and his undernourished Number Two, to hold her wearied attention. 'Well I'm glad you're satisfied,' she said, 'Now will you let me get back to my hotel? I'm tired.'

Klein shook his head. 'No,' he said. 'I'm afraid that won't be possible.'

Vanessa stood up quickly, and the violence of her movement overturned the chair. Within a second of the sound the door had opened and one of the bearded sisters appeared, pistol at the ready.

'It's all right, Stanislaus,' Mr Klein purred, 'Mrs Jape hasn't slit my throat.'

Sister Stanislaus withdrew, and closed the door behind him.

'Why?' said Vanessa, her anger distracted by the appearance of the guard.

'Why what?' Mr Klein asked.

'The nuns.'

Klein sighed heavily, and put his hand on the coffee-pot that had been brought a full hour earlier, to see if it was still warm. He poured himself half a cup before replying. 'In my own opinion, much of this is redundant, Mrs Jape, and you have my *personal* assurance that I will see you released as rapidly as is humanly possible. In the meanwhile I beg your indulgence. Think of it as a game . . .' His face soured slightly. '. . . They like games.'

'Who do?'

Klein frowned. 'Never mind,' he said. 'The less you know the less we'll have to make you forget.'

Vanessa gave the skull a beady eye. 'None of this makes any sense,' she said.

'Nor should it,' Mr Klein replied. He paused to sip his stale coffee. 'You made a regrettable error in coming here, Mrs Jape. And indeed, we made an error letting you in. Normally, our defences are stricter than you found them. But you caught us off-guard . . . and the next thing we knew – '

'Look,' said Vanessa, 'I don't know what's going on here. I don't *want* to know. All I want is to be allowed to go back to my hotel and finish my holiday in peace.' Judging by the expression on her interrogator's face, her appeal was not proving persuasive. 'Is that so much to ask?' she said. 'I haven't *done* anything, I haven't *seen* anything. What's the problem?'

Mr Klein stood up.

'The problem,' he repeated quietly to himself. 'Now there's a question.' He didn't attempt to answer, however. Merely called: 'Stanislaus?'

The door opened, and the nun was there.

'Return Mrs Jape to her room, will you?'

'I shall protest to my Embassy!' Vanessa said, her resentment flaring. 'I have rights!'

'Please,' said Mr Klein, looking pained. 'Shouting will help none of us.'

The nun took hold of Vanessa's arm. She felt the proximity of his pistol.

'Shall we go?' he asked politely.

'Do I have any choice?' she replied.

'No.'

The trick of good farce, she had once been informed by her brother-in-law, a sometime actor, was that it be played with deadly seriousness. There should be no sly winks to the gallery, signalling the farceur's comic intention; no business that was so outrageous it would undermine the reality of the piece. By these stringent standards she was surrounded by a cast of experts: all willing – habits, wimples and spying Madonnas notwithstanding – to perform as though this ridiculous situation was in no way out of the ordinary. Try as she might, she could not call their bluff; not break their po-faces, not win a single sign of self-consciousness from them. Clearly she lacked the requisite skills for this kind of comedy. The sooner they realized their error and discharged her from the company the happier she'd be.

She slept well, helped on her way by half the contents of a bottle of whisky that some thoughtful person had left in her little room when she returned to it. She had seldom drunk so much in such a short period of time, and when – just about dawn – she was woken by a light tapping on her door, her head felt swollen, and her tongue like a suede glove. It took her a moment to orient herself, during which time the rapping was repeated, and the small window in the door opened from the other side. An urgent face was pressed to it: that of an old man, with a fungal beard and wild eyes.

'Mrs Jape,' he hissed. '*Mrs Jape.* May we have words?'

She crossed to the door and looked through the window. The old man's breath was two-parts stale oúzo to one of fresh air. It kept her from pressing too close to the window, though he beckoned her.

'Who are you?' Vanessa asked, not simply out of abstract curiosity, but because the features, sunburnt and leathery, reminded her of somebody.

The man gave her a fluttering look. 'An admirer,' he said.

'Do I know you?'

He shook his head. 'You're much too young,' he said. 'But I know *you*. I watched you come in. I wanted to warn you, but I didn't have time.'

'Are you a prisoner here too?'

'In a manner of speaking. Tell me . . . did you see Floyd?'

'Who?'

'He escaped. The day before yesterday.'

'Oh,' Vanessa said, beginning to thread these dropped pearls together. 'Floyd was the man they were chasing?'

'Certainly. He slipped out, you see. They went after him – the clods – and left the gate open. The security is *shocking* these days – ' He sounded genuinely outraged by the situation. ' – Not that I'm not pleased you're here.' There was some desperation in his eyes, she thought; some sorrow he fought to keep submerged. 'We heard shots,' he said. 'They didn't get him, did they?'

'Not that I saw,' Vanessa replied. 'I went to look. But there was no sign – '

'Ha!' said the old man, brightening. 'Maybe he did get away then.'

It had already occurred to Vanessa that this conversation might be a trap; that the old man was her captor's dupe, and this was just another way to squeeze information from her. But her instincts instructed otherwise. He looked at her with such affection, and his face, which was that of a maestro clown, seemed incapable of forged feeling. For better or worse, she *trusted* him. She had little choice.

'Help me get out,' she said. 'I have to get out.'

He looked crest-fallen. 'So soon?' he said. 'You only just arrived.'

'I'm not a *thief*. I don't like being locked up.'

He nodded. 'Of course you don't,' he replied, silently admonishing himself for his selfishness. 'I'm sorry. It's just that a beautiful woman – ' He stopped himself, then began again, on a fresh tack. 'I never had much of a way with words . . .'

'Are you *sure* I don't know you from somewhere?' Vanessa inquired. 'Your face is somehow familiar.'

'Really?' he said. 'That's very nice. We all think we're forgotten here, you see.'

'All?'

'We were snatched away such a time ago. Many of us were only beginning our researches. That's why Floyd made a run for it. He wanted to do a few month's decent work before the end. I feel the same sometimes.' His melancholy train halted, and he returned to her question. 'My name is Harvey Gomm; Professor Harvey Gomm. Though these days I forget what I was professor *of*.'

Gomm. It was a singular name, and it rang bells, but she could at present find no tune in the chimes.

'You *don't* remember, do you?' he said, looking straight into her eyes.

She wished she could lie, but that might alienate the fellow – the only voice of sanity she'd discovered here – more than the truth; which was:

'No . . . I don't exactly remember. Maybe a clue?'

But before he could offer her another piece of his mystery, he heard voices.

'Can't talk now, Mrs Jape.'

'Call me Vanessa.'

'May I?' His face bloomed in the warmth of her benificence. '*Vanessa*.'

'You *will* help me?' she said.

'As best I may,' he replied. 'But if you see me in company – '

' – We never met.'

'Precisely. *Au revoir*.' He closed the panel in the door, and she heard his footsteps vanish down the corridor. When her custodian, an amiable thug called Guillemot, arrived several minutes later bearing a tray of tea, she was all smiles.

Her outburst of the previous day seemed to have born some fruit. That morning, after breakfast, Mr Klein called in briefly and told her that she would be allowed out into the grounds of the place (with Guillemot in attendance), so that she might enjoy the sun. She was further supplied with a new set of clothes – a little large for her, but a welcome relief from the sweaty garments she had now worn for over twenty-four hours. This last concession to her comfort was a curates' egg, however. Pleased as she was to be wearing clean underwear the fact that the clothes had been supplied at all suggested that Mr Klein was not anticipating a prompt release.

How long would it be, she tried to calculate, before the rather obtuse manager of her tiny hotel realized that she wasn't coming back; and in that event, what he would do? Perhaps he had already alerted the authorities; perhaps they would find the abandoned car and trace her to this curious fortress. On this last point her hopes were dashed that very morning, during her constitutional. The car was parked in the laurel-tree enclosure beside the gate, and to judge by the copious blessings rained upon it by the doves had been there overnight. Her captors were not fools. She might have to wait until somebody back in England became concerned, and attempted to trace her whereabouts, during which time she might well die of boredom.

Others in the place had found diversions to keep them from insanity's door. As she and Guillemot wandered around the grounds that morning she could distinctly hear voices – one of them Gomm's – from a nearby courtyard. They were raised in excitement.

'What's going on?'

'They're playing games,' Guillemot replied.

'Can we go and watch?' she asked casually.

'No –'

'I like games.'

'Do you?' he said. 'We'll play then, eh?'

This wasn't the response she'd wanted, but pressing the point might have aroused suspicion.

'Why not?' she said. Winning the man's trust could only be to her advantage.

'Poker?' he said.

'I've never played.'

'I'll teach you,' he replied. The thought clearly pleased him. In the adjacent courtyard the players now sent up a din of shouts. It sounded to be some kind of race, to judge by the mingled calls of encouragement, and the subsequent deflation as the winning-post was achieved. Guillemot caught her listening.

'Frogs,' he said. 'They're racing frogs.'

'I wondered.'

Guillemot looked at her almost fondly, and said, 'Better not.'

Despite Guillemot's advice, once her attention focussed on the sound of the games she could not drive the din from her head. It continued through the afternoon, rising and falling. Sometimes laughter would erupt; as often, there would arguments. They were like children, Gomm and his friends, the way they fought over such an inconsequential pursuit as racing frogs. But in lieu of more nourishing diversions, could she blame them? When Gomm's face appeared at the door later that evening, almost the first thing she said was: 'I heard you this morning, in one of the courtyards. And then this afternoon, too. You seemed to be having a good deal of fun.'

'Oh, the games,' Gomm replied. 'It was a busy day. So much to be sorted out.'

'Do you think you could persuade them to let me join you? I'm getting so bored in here.'

'Poor Vanessa. I wish I could help. But it's practically impossible. We're so overworked at the moment, especially with Floyd's escape.'

Overworked?, she thought, *racing frogs*? Fearing to offend, she didn't voice the doubt. 'What's going on here?' she said. 'You're not criminals, are you?'

Gomm looked outraged. '*Criminals?*'

'I'm sorry . . .'

'No. I understand why you asked. I suppose it must strike you as odd . . . our being locked up here. But no, we're not criminals.

'What then? What's the big secret?'

Gomm took a deep breath before replying. 'If I tell you,' he said, 'will you help us to get out of here?'

'How?'

'Your car. It's at the front.'

'Yes, I saw it . . .'

'If we could get to it, would you drive us?'

'How many of you?'

'Four. There's me, there's Ireniya, there's Mottershead, and Goldberg. Of course Floyd's probably out there somewhere, but he'll just have to look after himself, won't he?'

'It's a small car,' she warned.

'We're small people,' Gomm returned. 'You shrink with age, you know, like dried fruit. And we're *old*. With Floyd we had three hundred and ninety-eight years between us. All that bitter experience,' he said, 'and not one of us *wise*.'

In the yard outside Vanessa's room shouting suddenly erupted. Gomm disappeared from the door, and reappeared again briefly to murmur: 'They found him. Oh my God: they found him.' Then he fled.

Vanessa crossed to the window and peered through. She could not see much of the yard below, but what she could see was full of frenzied activity, sisters hithering and thithering. At the centre of this commotion she could see a small figure – the runaway Floyd, no doubt – struggling in the grip of two guards. He looked to be much the worse for his days and nights of living rough, his drooping features dirtied, his balding pate peeling from an excess of sun. Vanessa heard the voice of Mr Klein rise above the babble, and he stepped into the scene. He approached Floyd and proceeded to berate him mercilessly. Vanessa could not catch more than one in every ten words, but the verbal assault rapidly reduced the old man to tears. She turned away from the window, silently praying that Klein would choke on his next piece of chocolate.

So far, her time here had brought a curious collection of experiences: one moment pleasant (Gomm's smile, the pizza, the sound of games played in a similar courtyard), the next – (the interrogation, the bullying she'd just witnessed) unpalatable. And still she was no nearer understanding what the function of this prison was: why it only had five inmates (six, if she included herself) and all so old – shrunk by age, Gomm had said. But after Klein's humiliation of Floyd she was now certain that no secret, however pressing, would keep her from aiding Gomm in his bid for freedom.

The Professor did not come back that evening, which disappointed her. Perhaps Floyd's recapture had meant stricter regulations about the place, she reasoned, though that principle scarcely applied to her. She, it seemed, was practically forgotten. Though Guillemot brought her food and drink he did not stay to teach her poker as they had arranged, nor was she escorted out to take the air. Left in the stuffy room without company, her mind undisturbed by any entertainment but counting her toes, she rapidly became listless and sleepy.

Indeed, she was dozing through the middle of the afternoon when something hit the wall outside the window. She got up, and was crossing to see what the sound was when an object was hurled through the window. It landed with a clunk on the floor. She went to snatch a glimpse of the sender, but he'd gone.

The tiny parcel was a key wrapped in a note. '*Vanessa*,' it read, '*Be ready. Yours, in saecula saeculorum. H.G.*'

Latin was not her forte; she hoped the final words were an endearment, not an instruction. She tried the key in the door of her cell. It worked. Clearly Gomm didn't intend her to use it *now*, however, but to wait for some signal. *Be ready*, he'd written. Easier said than done, of course. It was so tempting, with the door open and the passageway out to the sun clear, to forget Gomm and the others and make a break for it. But H.G. had doubtless taken some risk acquiring the key. She owed him her allegiance.

After that, there was no more dozing. Every time she heard a footstep in the cloisters, or a shout in the yard, she was up and ready. But Gomm's call didn't come. The afternoon dragged on into evening. Guillemot appeared with another pizza and a bottle of coca-cola for dinner, and before she knew it night had fallen and another day was gone.

Perhaps they would come by cover of darkness, she thought, but they didn't. The moon rose, its seas smirking, and there was still no sign of H.G. or this promised exodus. She began to suspect the worst: that their plan had been discovered, and they were all being punished for it. If so, would not Mr Klein sooner or later root out *her* involvement? Though her part had been minimal, what sanctions might the chocolate-man take out against her? Sometime after midnight she decided that waiting here for the axe to fall was not her style at all, and she would be wise to do as Floyd had done, and run for it.

She let herself out of the cell, and locked it behind her, then hurried along the cloisters, cleaving to the shadows as best she could. There was no sign of human presence – but she remembered the watchful Virgin, who'd first spied on her. Nothing was to be trusted here. By stealth and sheer good fortune she eventually found her way out into the yard in which Floyd had faced Mr Klein. There she paused, to work out which way the exit lay from here. But clouds had moved across the face of the moon, and in darkness her fitful sense of direction deserted her completely. Trusting to the luck that had got her thus far unarrested, she chose one of the exits from the yard, and slipped through it, following her nose along a covered walkway which twisted and turned before leading out into yet another courtyard, larger than the first. A light breeze teased the leaves of two entwined laurel-trees in the centre of the yard; night-insects tuned up in the walls. Peaceable as it was, the square offered no promising route that she could see, and she was about to go back the way she'd come when the moon shook off its veils and lit the yard from wall to wall.

It was empty, but for the laurel-trees, and the shadow of the laurel-trees, but that shadow fell across an elaborate design which had been painted onto the pavement of the yard. She stared at it, too curious to retreat, though she could make no sense of the thing at first; the pattern seemed to be just that: a pattern. She stalked it along one edge, trying to fathom out its significance. Then it dawned on her that she was viewing the entire picture upside-down. She moved to the other side of the courtyard and the design came clear. It was a map of the world, reproduced down to the most insignificant isle. All the great cities were marked and the oceans and continents criss-crossed with hundreds of fine lines that marked latitudes, longitudes and much else besides. Though many of the symbols were idiosyn-cratic, it was clear that the map was rife with political detail. Contested borders; territorial waters; exclusion zones. Many of these had been drawn and re-drawn in chalk, as if in response to daily intelligence. In some regions, where events were particularly fraught, the land-mass was all but obscured by scribblings.

Fascination came between her and her safety. She didn't hear the footsteps at the North Pole until their owner was stepping out of hiding and into the moonlight. She was about to make a run for it, when she recognized Gomm.

'Don't move,' he murmured across the world.

She did as she was instructed. Glancing around him like a besieged rabbit until he was certain the yard was deserted, H.G. crossed to where Vanessa stood.

'What are you doing here?' he demanded of her.

'You didn't come,' she accused him. 'I thought you'd forgotten me.'

'Things got difficult. They watch us all the time.'

'I couldn't go on waiting, Harvey. This is no place to take a holiday.'

'You're right, of course,' he said, a picture of dejection. 'It's hopeless. *Hopeless.* You should make your getaway on your own. Forget about us. They'll never let us out. The truth's too terrible.'

'What truth?'

He shook his head. 'Forget about it. Forget we ever met.'

Vanessa took hold of his spindly arm. 'I will *not*,' she said. 'I have to know what's happening here.'

Gomm shrugged. 'Perhaps you should know. Perhaps the whole world should know.' He took her hand, and they retreated into the relative safety of the cloisters.

'What's the map for?' was her first question.

'This is where we play – ' he replied, staring at the turmoil of scrawlings on the courtyard floor. He sighed. 'Of course it wasn't always games. But systems decay, you know. It's an irrefutable condition common to both matter and ideas. You start off with fine intentions and in two decades . . . *two decades* . . .' he repeated, as if the fact appalled him afresh, '. . . we're playing with frogs.'

'You're not making much sense, Harvey,' Vanessa said. 'Are you being deliberately obtuse or is this senility?'

He prickled at the accusation, but it did the trick. Gaze still fixed on the map of the world, he delivered the next words crisply as if he'd rehearsed this confession.

'There was a day of sanity, back in 1962, in which it occurred to the potentates that they were on the verge of destroying the world. Even to potentates the idea of an earth only fit for cockroaches was not particularly beguiling. If annihilation was to be prevented, they decided, our better instincts had to prevail. The mighty gathered behind locked doors at a symposium in Geneva. There had never been such a meeting of minds. The leaders of Politburos and Parliaments, Congresses, Senates – the Lords of the earth – in one colossal debate. And it was decided that in future world affairs should be overseen by a special committee, made up of great and influential minds like my own – men and women who were not subject to the whims of political favour, who could offer some guiding principles to keep the species from mass suicide. This committee was to be made up of people in many areas of human endeavour – the best of the best – an intellectual and moral elite, whose collective wisdom would bring a new golden age. That was the theory anyway – '

Vanessa listened, without voicing the hundred questions his short speech had so far brought to mind. Gomm went on.

' – and for a while, it worked. It really worked. There were only thirteen of us – to keep some consensus. A Russian, a few of us Europeans – dear Yoniyoko, of course – a New Zealander, a couple of Americans . . . we were a high-powered bunch. Two Nobel prize winners, myself included – '

Now she remembered Gomm, or at least where she'd once seen that face. They had both been much younger. She a schoolgirl, taught *his* theories by rote.

' – our brief was to encourage mutual understanding between the powers-that-be, help shape compassionate economic structures and develop the cultural identity of emergent nations. All platitudes, of course, but they sounded fine at the time. As it was, almost from the beginning our concerns were *territorial*.'

'Territorial?'

Gomm made an expansive gesture, taking in the map in front of him. 'Helping to divide the world up,' he said. 'Regulating little wars so they didn't become big wars, keeping dictatorships from getting too full of themselves. We became the world's domestics, cleaning up wherever the dirt got too thick. It was a great responsibility, but we shouldered it quite happily. It rather pleased us, at the beginning, to think that we thirteen were shaping the world, and that nobody but the highest eschelons of government knew that we even existed.'

This, thought Vanessa, was the Napoleon Syndrome writ large. Gomm was indisputably insane: but what an heroic insanity! And it was essentially harmless. Why did they have to lock him up? He surely wasn't capable of doing damage.

'It seems unfair,' she said, 'that you're locked away in here – '

'Well that's for our own security, of course,' Gomm replied. 'Imagine the chaos if some anarchist group found out where we operated from, and did away with us. *We run the world*. It wasn't meant to be that way, but as I said, systems decay. As time went by the potentates – knowing they had us to make critical decisions for them – concerned themselves more and more with the pleasures of high office and less and less with *thinking*. Within five years we were no longer advisers, but surrogate overlords, juggling nations.'

'What fun,' Vanessa said.

'For a while, perhaps,' Gomm replied. 'But the glamour faded very quickly. And after a decade or so, the pressure began to tell. Half of the committee are already dead. Golovatenko threw himself out of a window. Buchanan – the New Zealander – had syphilis and didn't know it. Old age caught up with dear Yoniyoko, and Bernheimer and Sourbutts. It'll catch up with all of us sooner or later, and Klein

89

keeps promising to provide people to take over when we've gone, but they don't *care*. They don't give a damn! We're functionaries, that's all.' He was getting quite agitated. 'As long as we provide them with judgements, they're happy. Well . . .' his voice dropped to a whisper, 'we're giving it up.'

Was this a moment of self-realization?, Vanessa wondered. Was the sane man in Gomm's head attempting to throw off the fiction of world domination? If so, perhaps she could aid the process.

'You want to get away?' she said.

Gomm nodded. 'I'd like to see my home once more before I die. I've given up so much, Vanessa, for the committee, and it almost drove me mad – ' *Ah*, she thought, *he knows*. 'Does it sound selfish if I say that my life seems too great a sacrifice to make for global peace?' She smiled at his pretensions to power, but said nothing. 'If it does, it does! I'm unrepentant. I want out! I want – '

'Keep your voice down,' she advised.

Gomm remembered himself, and nodded.

'I want a little freedom before I die. We all do. And we thought you could help us, you see.' He looked at her. 'What's wrong?' he said.

'Wrong?'

'Why are you looking at me like that?'

'You're not well, Harvey. I don't think you're dangerous, but – '

'Wait a minute,' Gomm said. 'What do you think I've been telling you? I go to all this trouble . . .'

'Harvey. It's a fine story . . .'

'*Story*? What do you mean, *story*?' he said, petulantly. 'Oh . . . I see. 'You don't believe me, do you? That's it! I just told you the greatest secret in the world, and you don't believe me!'

'I'm not saying you're lying – '

'Is that it?' You think I'm a lunatic!' Gomm exploded. His voice echoed around the rectangular world. Almost immediately there were voices from several of the buildings, and fast upon those the thunder of feet.

'Now look what you've done,' Gomm said.

'*I've* done?'

'We're in trouble.'

'Look, H.G., this doesn't mean – '

'Too late for retractions. You stay where you are – I'm going to make a run for it. Distract them.'

He was about to depart when he turned back to her, caught hold of her hand, and put it to his lips.

'If I'm mad,' he said, 'you made me that way.'

Then he was off, his short legs carrying him at a fair speed across the yard. He did not even reach the laurel-trees however, before the guards arrived. They shouted for him to stop. When he failed to do so one of the men fired. Bullets ploughed the ocean around Gomm's feet.

'All right,' he yelled, coming to halt and putting his hands in the air. '*Mea culpa!*'

The firing stopped. The guards parted as their commander stepped through.

'Oh, it's you, Sidney,' H. G. said to the Captain. The man visibly flinched to be so addressed in front of inferior ranks.

'What are you doing out at this time of night?' Sidney demanded.

'Star-gazing,' Gomm replied.

'You weren't alone,' the Captain said. Vanessa's heart sank. There was no route back to her room without crossing the open courtyard; and even now, with the alarm raised, Guillemot would probably be checking on her.

'That's true,' said Gomm. 'I wasn't alone.' Had she offended the old man so much he was now going to betray her? 'I saw the woman you brought in – '

'Where?'

'Climbing over the wall,' he said.

'Jesus wept!' the Captain said, and swung around to order his men in pursuit.

'I said to her,' Gomm was prattling. 'I said, you'll break your neck climbing over the wall. You'd be better waiting until they open the gate – '

Open the gate. He wasn't such a lunatic, after all. 'Phillipenko – ' the Captain said, ' – escort Harvey back to his dormitory – '

Gomm protested. 'I don't need a bed-time story, thank you.'

'Go with him.'

The guard crossed to H. G. and escorted him away. The Captain lingered long enough to murmur, 'Who's a clever boy, Sidney?' under his breath, then followed. The courtyard was empty again, but for the moonlight, and the map of the world.

Vanessa waited until every last sound had died, and then slipped out of hiding, taking the route the dispatched guards had followed. It led her, eventually, into an area she vaguely recognized from her walk with Guillemot. Encouraged, she hurried on along a passageway which let out into the yard with Our Lady of the Electric Eyes. She crept along the wall, and ducked beneath the statue's gaze and out, finally, to meet the gates. They were indeed open. As the old man had protested when they'd first met, security *was* woefully inadequate, and she thanked God for it.

As she ran towards the gates she heard the sound of boots on the gravel, and glanced over her shoulder to see the Captain, rifle in hand, stepping from behind the tree.

'Some chocolate, Mrs Jape?' said Mr Klein.

'This is a lunatic asylum,' she told him when they had escorted her back to the interrogation room. 'Nothing more nor less. You've no right to hold me here.'

He ignored her complaints.

'You spoke to Gomm,' he said, 'and he to you.'

'What if he did?'

'What did he tell you?'

'I said: what if he did?'

'And *I* said: *what did he tell you?*' Klein roared. She would not have guessed him capable of such apoplexy. 'I want to know, Mrs Jape.'

Much against her will she found herself shaking at his outburst.

'He told me nonsense,' she replied. 'He's insane. I think you're *all* insane.'

'*What* nonsense did he tell you?'

'It was rubbish.'

'I'd like to know, Mrs Jape,' Klein said, his fury abating. 'Humour me.'

'He said there was some kind of committee at work here, that made decisions about world politics, and that he was one of them. That was it, for what it's worth.'

'And?'

'And I gently told him he was out of his mind.'

Mr Klein forged a smile. 'Of course, this is a complete fiction,' he said.

'Of course,' said Vanessa. 'Jesus Christ, don't treat me like an imbecile, Mr Klein. I'm a grown woman – '

'Mr Gomm – '

'He said he was a professor.'

'Another delusion. *Mr* Gomm is a paranoid schizophrenic. He can be extremely dangerous, given half a chance. You were pretty lucky.'

'And the others?'

'Others?'

'He's not alone. I've heard them. Are they all schizophrenics?'

Klein sighed. 'They're all deranged, though their conditions vary. And in their time, unlikely as it may seem, they've all been killers.' He paused to allow this information to sink in. 'Some of them multiple killers. That's why they have this place to themselves, hidden away. That's why the officers are armed – '

Vanessa opened her mouth to ask why they were required to

masquerade as nuns, but Klein was not about to give her an opportunity.

'Believe me, it's as inconvenient for me as it is irritating for you to be here,' he said.

'Then let me go.'

'When my investigations are complete,' he said. 'In the meanwhile your cooperation would be appreciated. If Mr Gomm or any of the other patients tries to co-opt you into some plan or other, please report them to me *immediately*. Will you do that?'

'I suppose – '

'And *please* refrain from any further escape attempts. The next one could prove fatal.'

'I wanted to ask – '

'Tomorrow, maybe,' Mr Klein said, glancing at his watch as he stood up. 'For now: sleep.'

Which, she debated with herself when that sleep refused to come, of all the routes to the truth that lay before her, was the *unlikeliest* path? She had been given several alternatives: by Gomm, by Klein, by her own common sense. All of them were temptingly improbable. All, like the path that had brought her here, unmarked as to their final destination. She had suffered the consequence of her perversity in following that track of course; here she was, weary and battered, locked up with little hope of escape. But that perversity was her nature – perhaps, as Ronald had once said, the one indisputable fact about her. If she disregarded that instinct now, despite all it had brought her to, she was lost. She lay awake, turning the available alternatives over in her head. By morning she had made up her mind.

She waited all day, hoping Gomm would come, but she wasn't surprised when he failed to show. It was possible that events of the previous evening had landed him in deeper trouble than even he could talk his way out of. She was not left entirely to herself however. Guillemot came and went, with food, with drink and – in the middle of the afternoon – with playing cards. She picked up the gist of five-card poker quite rapidly, and they passed a contented hour or two playing, while the air carried shouts from the courtyard where the bedlamites were racing frogs.

'Do you think you could arrange for me to have a bath, or at least a shower?' she asked him when he came back for her dinner tray that evening. 'It's getting so that I don't like my own company.'

He actually smiled as he responded. 'I'll find out for you.'

'Would you?' she gushed. 'That's very kind.'

93

He returned an hour later to tell her that dispensation had been sought and granted; would she like to accompany him to the showers?

'Are you going to scrub my back?' she casually enquired.

Guillemot's eyes flickered with panic at the remark, and his ears flushed beetroot red. 'Please follow me,' he said. Obediently, she followed, trying to keep a mental picture of their route should she want to retrace it later, without her custodian.

The facilities he brought her to were far from primitive, and she regretted, walking into the mirrored bathroom, that actually washing was not high on her list of priorities. Never mind; cleanliness was for another day.

'I'll be outside the door,' Guillemot said.

'That's reassuring,' she replied, offering him a look she trusted he would interpret as promising, and closed the door. Then she ran the shower as hot as it would go, until steam began to cloud the room, and went down on her hands and knees to soap the floor. When the bathroom was sufficiently veiled and the floor sufficiently slick, she called Guillemot. She might have been flattered by the speed of his response, but she was too busy stepping behind him as he fumbled in the steam, and giving him a hefty push. He slid on the floor, and stumbled against the shower, yelping as scalding water met his scalp. His automatic rifle clattered to the floor, and by the time he was righting himself she had it in her hand, and pointed at his torso, a substantial target. Though she was no sharp-shooter, and her hands were trembling, a blind woman couldn't have missed at such a range; she knew it, and so did Guillemot. He put his hands up.

'Don't shoot.'

'If you move a muscle – '

'Please . . . don't shoot.'

'Now . . . you're going to take me to Mr Gomm and the others. Quickly and quietly.'

'Why?'

'Just take me,' she said, gesturing with the rifle that he should lead the way out of the bathroom. 'And if you try to do anything clever, I'll shoot you in the back,' she said. 'I know it's not very manly, but then I'm not a man. I'm just an unpredictable woman. So treat me very carefully.'

'. . . yes.'

He did as he was told, meekly, leading her out of the building and through a series of passageways which took them – or so she guessed – towards the bell-tower and the complex that clustered about it. She had always assumed this, the heart of the fortress, to be a chapel. She could not have been more wrong. The outer shell might be tiled roof and white-washed walls, but that was merely a fac‹SS›cade; they stepped over the threshold into a concrete maze more reminiscent of a bunker than a place of worship. It briefly occurred to her that the place had been built to withstand a nuclear attack, an impression reinforced by the fact that the corridors all led *down*. If this was an asylum, it was built to house some rare lunatics.

'What is this place?' she asked Guillemot.

'We call it the Boudoir,' he said. 'It's where everything happens.'

There was little happening at present; most of the offices off the corridors were in darkness. In one room a computer calculated its chances of independent thought, unattended; in another a telex machine wrote love-letters to itself. They descended into the bowels of the place unchallenged, until, rounding a corner, they came face to face with a woman on her hands and knees, scrubbing the linoleum. The encounter startled both parties, and Guillemot was swift to take the initiative. He knocked Vanessa sideways against the wall, and ran for it. Before she had time to get him in her sights, he was gone.

She cursed herself. It would be moments only before alarm bells started to ring, and guards came running. She was lost if she stayed where she was. The three exits from this hallway looked equally unpromising, so she simply made for the nearest, leaving the cleaner to stare after her. The route she took proved to be another adventure. It led her through a series of rooms, one of which was lined with dozens of clocks, all showing different times; the next of which contained upwards of fifty black telephones; the third and largest was lined on every side with television screens. They rose, one upon another, from floor to ceiling. All but one was blank. The exception to this rule was showing what she first took to be a mud-wrestling contest, but was in fact a poorly reproduced pornographic film. Sitting watching it, sprawled on a chair with a beer-can balanced on his stomach, was a moustachioed nun. He stood up as she entered: caught in the act. She pointed the rifle at him.

'I'm going to shoot you dead,' she told him.

'Shit.'

'Where's Gomm and the others?'

'What?'

'Where are they?' she demanded. '*Quickly*!'

'Down the hall. Turn left and left again,' he said. Then added, 'I don't want to die.'

'Then sit down and shut up,' she replied.

'Thank God,' he said.

'Why don't you?' she told him. As she backed out of the room he fell down on his knees, while the mud-wrestlers cavorted behind him.

Left and left again. The directions were fruitful: they led her to a

series of rooms. She was just about to knock on one of the doors when the alarm sounded. Throwing caution to the wind she pushed all the doors open. Voices from within complained at being woken, and asked what the alarm was ringing for. In the third room she found Gomm. He grinned at her.

'Vanessa,' he said, bounding out into the corridor. He was wearing a long vest, and nothing else. 'You came, eh? *You came!*'

The others were appearing from their rooms, bleary with sleep. Ireniya, Floyd, Mottershead, Goldberg. She could believe – looking at their raddled faces – that they indeed had four hundred years between them.

'Wake up, you old buggers,' Gomm said. He had found a pair of trousers and was pulling them on.

'The alarm's ringing – ' one commented. His hair, which was bright white, was almost at his shoulders.

'They'll be here soon – ' Ireniya said.

'No matter,' Gomm replied.

Floyd was already dressed. 'I'm ready,' he announced.

'But we're outnumbered,' Vanessa protested. 'We'll never get out alive.'

'She's right,' said one, squinting at her. 'It's no use.'

'Shut up, Goldberg,' Gomm snapped. 'She's got a gun, hasn't she?'

'*One*,' said the white-haired individual. This must be Mottershead. 'One gun against all of them.'

'I'm going back to bed,' Goldberg said.

'This is a chance to escape,' Gomm said. 'Probably the only chance we'll ever get.'

'He's right,' the woman said.

'And what about the games?' Goldberg reminded them.

'Forget the games,' Floyd told the other, 'let them stew a while.'

'It's too late,' said Vanessa. 'They're coming.' There were shouts from both ends of the corridor. 'We're trapped.'

'Good,' said Gomm.

'You *are* insane,' she told him plainly.

'You can still shoot us,' he replied, grinning.

Floyd grunted. 'I don't want to get out of here *that* much,' he said.

'*Threaten* it! *Threaten* it!' Gomm said. 'Tell them if they try anything you'll shoot us all!'

Ireniya smiled. She had left her teeth in her bedroom. 'You're not just a pretty face,' she said to Gomm.

'He's right,' said Floyd, beaming now. 'They wouldn't dare risk us. They'll have to let us go.'

'You're out of your minds,' Goldberg muttered. 'There's nothing out there for us . . .' He returned into his room and slammed the door. Even as he did so the corridor was blocked off at either end by a mass of guards. Gomm took hold of Vanessa's rifle and raised it to point at his heart.

'Be gentle,' he hissed, and threw her a kiss.

'Put down the weapon, Mrs Jape,' said a familiar voice. Mr Klein had appeared amongst the throng of guards. 'Take it from me, you are completely surrounded.'

'I'll kill them all,' Vanessa said, a little hesitantly. Then again, this time with more feeling: 'I'm warning you. I'm desperate. I'll kill them *all* before you shoot me.'

'I see . . .' said Klein quietly. 'And why should you assume that I give a damn whether you kill them or not? They're insane. I told you that: all lunatics, killers . . .'

'We both know that isn't true,' said Vanessa, gaining confidence from the anxiety on Klein's face. 'I want the front gates opened, and the key in the ignition of my car. If you try anything stupid, Mr Klein, I will systematically shoot these hostages. Now dismiss your bully-boys and do as I say.'

Mr Klein hesitated, then signalled a general withdrawal.

Gomm's eyes glittered. 'Nicely done,' he whispered.

'Why don't you lead the way?' Vanessa suggested. Gomm did as he was instructed, and her small party snaked their way out past the massed clocks and telephones and video screens. Every step they took Vanessa expected a bullet to find her, but Mr Klein was clearly too concerned for the health of the ancients to risk calling her bluff. They reached the open air without incident.

The guards were in evidence outside, though attempting to stay out of sight. Vanessa kept the rifle trained on the four captives as they headed through the yards to where her car was parked. The gates had been opened.

'Gomm,' she whispered. 'Open the car doors.'

Gomm did so. He had said that age had shrunk them all, and perhaps that was true, but there were five of them to fit into the small vehicle, and it was tightly packed. Vanessa was the last to get in. As she ducked to slide into the driving seat a shot rang out, and she felt a blow to her shoulder. She dropped the rifle.

'Bastards,' said Gomm.

'Leave her,' somebody piped up in the back, but Gomm was already out of the car and bundling her into the back beside Floyd. He then slid into the driving seat himself and started the engine.

'Can you drive?' Ireniya demanded.

'Of course I can bloody drive!' he retorted, and the car jerked forward through the gates, the gears grating.

97

Vanessa had never been shot before, and hoped – if she survived this episode – to avoid it happening again. The wound in her shoulder was bleeding badly. Floyd did his best to staunch the wound, but Gomm's driving made any really constructive help practically impossible.

'There's a track – ' she managed to tell him, 'off that way.'

'*Which way's that way?*' Gomm yelled.

'*Right! Right!*' she yelled back.

Gomm took both hands off the wheel and looked at them.

'*Which is right?*'

'*For Christ's sake – *'

Ireniya, in the seat beside him, pressed his hands back onto the wheel. The car performed a tarantella. Vanessa groaned with every bump.

'I see it!' said Gomm. 'I see the track!' He revved the car up, and put his foot on the accelerator.

One of the back doors, which had been inadequately secured, flipped open and Vanessa almost fell out. Mottershead, reaching over Floyd, yanked her back to safety, but before they could close the door it met the boulder that marked the convergence of the two tracks. The car bucked as the door was torn off its hinges.

'We needed more air in here,' said Gomm, and drove on.

Theirs was not the only engine disturbing the Aegean night. There were lights behind them, and the sound of hectic pursuit. With Guillemot's rifle left in the convent, they had no sudden death to bargain with, and Klein knew it.

'Step on it!' Floyd said, grinning from ear to ear. 'They're coming after us.'

'I'm going as fast as I can,' Gomm insisted.

'Turn off the lights,' Ireniya suggested. 'It'll make us less of a target.'

'Then I won't be able to see the track,' Gomm complained over the roar of the engine.

'So what? You're not driving on it anyhow.'

Mottershead laughed, and so – against her better instincts – did Vanessa. Maybe the loss of blood was making her irresponsible, but she couldn't help herself. Four Methuselahs and herself in a three-door car driving around in the dark: only a madman would have taken this seriously. And *there* was the final and incontestible proof that these people weren't the lunatics Klein had marked them as, for they saw the humour in it too. Gomm had even taken to singing as he drove: snatches of Verdi, and a falsetto rendering of '*Over the Rainbow*'.

And if – as her dizzied mind had concluded – these were creatures as sane as herself, then what of the tale that Gomm had told?; was that true too? Was it possible that Armageddon had been kept at bay by these few giggling geriatrics?

'They're gaining on us!' Floyd said. He was on his knees on the back seat, peering out of the window.

'We're not going to make it,' Mottershead observed, his laughter barely abating. 'We're all going to die.'

'There!' Ireniya yelled. 'There's another track! Try that! Try that!'

Gomm swung the wheel, and the car almost tipped over as it swung off the main track and followed this new route. With the lights extinguished it was impossible to see more than a glimmer of the road ahead, but Gomm's style was not about to be cramped by such minor considerations. He revved the car until the engine fairly screeched. Dust was flung up and through the gap where the door had been; a goat fled from the path ahead seconds before losing its life.

'*Where are we going?*' Vanessa yelled.

'*Haven't a clue,*' Gomm returned. '*Have you?*'

Wherever they were heading, they were going at a fair speed. This track was flatter than the one they'd left, and Gomm was taking full advantage of the fact. Again, he'd taken to singing.

Mottershead was leaning out of the window on the far side of the car, his hair streaming, watching for their pursuers.

'We're losing them!' he howled triumphantly. 'We're losing them!'

A common exhilaration seized all the travellers now, and they began to sing along with H.G. They were singing so loudly that Gomm couldn't hear Mottershead inform him that the road ahead seemed to disappear. Indeed H.G. was not aware that he had driven the car over the cliff until the vehicle took a nose-dive, and the sea came up to meet them.

'Mrs Jape? Mrs Jape?'

Vanessa woke unwillingly. Her head hurt, her arm hurt. There had been some terrible times recently, though it took her a while to remember the substance of them. Then the memories came back. The car pitching over the cliff; the cold sea rushing in through the open door; the frantic cries around her as the vehicle sank. She had struggled free, only half conscious, vaguely aware that Floyd was floating up beside her. She had said his name, but he had not answered. She said it again, now.

'Dead,' said Mr Klein. 'They're all dead.'

'Oh my God,' she murmured. She was looking not at his face but at a chocolate stain on his waistcoat.

'Neve mind them now,' he insisted.

99

'Never mind?'

'There's more important business, Mrs Jape. You must get up, and quickly.'

The urgency in Klein's voice brought Vanessa to her feet. 'Is it morning?' she said. There were no windows in the room they occupied. This was the Boudoir, to judge by its concrete walls.

'Yes, it's morning,' Klein replied, impatiently. 'Now, will you come with me? I have something to show you.' He opened the door and they stepped out into the grim corridor. A little way ahead it sounded as if a major argument was going on; dozens of raised voices, imprecations and pleadings.

'What's happening?'

'They're warming up for the Apocalypse,' he replied, and led the way into the room where Vanessa had last seen the mud-wrestlers. Now all of the video-screens were buzzing, and each displayed a different interior. There were war-rooms and presidential suites, Cabinet Offices and Halls of Congress. In every one of them, somebody was shouting.

'You've been unconscious two full days,' Klein told her, as if this went some way to explaining the cacophony. Her head ached already. She looked from screen to screen: from Washington to Hamburg to Sydney to Rio de Janeiro. Everywhere around the globe the mighty were waiting for news. But the oracles were dead.

'They're just performers,' Klein said, gesturing at the shouting screens. 'They couldn't run a three-legged race, never mind the world. They're getting hysterical, and they're button-fingers are starting to itch.'

'What am *I* supposed to do about it?' Vanessa returned. This tour of Babel depressed her. 'I'm no strategist.'

'Neither were Gomm and the others. They might have been, once upon a time, but things soon fell apart.'

'Systems decay,' she said.

'Isn't *that* the truth. By the time I came here half the committee were already dead. And the rest had lost all interest in their duties – '

'But they still provided judgements, as H.G. said?'

'Oh yes.'

'They ruled the world?'

'After a fashion,' Klein replied.

'What do you mean: after a fashion?'

Klein looked at the screens. His eyes seemed to be on the verge of spilling tears.

'Didn't he explain,? They played *games*, Mrs Jape. When they became bored with sweet reason and the sound of their own voices, they gave up debate and took to flipping coins.'

100

'No.'

'And racing frogs of course. That was always a favourite.'

'But the governments – ' she protested, ' – surely they didn't just accept – '

'You think they care?' Klein said, 'As long as they're in the public eye what does it matter to them what verbiage they're spouting, or how it was arrived at?'

Her head spun. 'All *chance*?' she said.

'Why not? It has a very respectable tradition. Nations have fallen on decisions divined from the entrails of sheep.'

'It's preposterous.'

'I agree. But I ask you, in all honesty, is it many more terrifying than leaving the power in *their* hands?' He pointed to the rows of irate faces. Democrats sweating that the morrow find them without causes to espouse or applause to win; despots in terror that without instruction their cruelties would lose favour and be overturned. One premier seemed to have suffered a bronchial attack and was being supported by two of his aides; another clutched a revolver and was pointing it at the screen, demanding satisfaction; a third was chewing his toupé. Were these the finest fruit of the political tree?; babbling, bullying, cajoling idiots, driven to apoplexy because nobody would tell them which way to jump? There wasn't a man or woman amongst them Vanessa would have trusted to guide her across the road.

'Better the frogs,' she murmured, bitter thought that it was.

The light in the courtyard, after the dead illumination of the bunker, was dazzlingly bright, but Vanessa was pleased to be out of earshot of the stridency within. They would find a new committee very soon, Klein had told her as they made their way out into the open air: it would be a matter of weeks only before equilibrium was restored. In the meanwhile, the earth could be blown to smithereens by the desperate creatures she had just seen. They needed *judgements*, and quickly.

'Goldberg is still alive,' Klein said. 'And he will go on with the games; but it takes two to play.'

'Why not you?'

'Because he hates me. Hates all of us. He says that he'll only play with you.'

Goldberg was sitting under the laurel trees, playing patience. It was a slow business. His shortsightedness required him to bring each card to within three inches of his nose to read it, and by the time he had got to the end of the line he had forgotten those cards at the beginning.

'She's agreed,' said Klein. Goldberg didn't look up from his game. 'I said: *she's agreed*.'

'I'm blind, not deaf,' Goldberg told Klein, still perusing the cards. When he eventually looked up it was to squint at Vanessa. 'I told them it would end badly . . .' he said softly, and Vanessa knew that beneath this show of fatalism he felt the loss of his companions acutely. '. . . I said from the beginning, we were here to stay. No use to escape.' He shrugged, and returned to the cards. 'What's to escape *to*? The world's changed. I know. We changed it.'

'It wasn't so bad, ' Vanessa said.

'The world?'

'They way they died.'

'Ah.'

'We were enjoying ourselves, until the last minute.'

'Gomm was such a sentimentalist,' Goldberg said. 'We never much liked each other.'

A large frog jumped into Vanessa's path. The movement caught Goldberg's eye.

'Who is it?' he said.

The creature regarded Vanessa's foot balefully. 'Just a frog,' she replied.

'What does it look like?'

'It's fat,' she said. 'With three red dots on its back.'

'That's Israel,' he told her. 'Don't tread on him.'

'Could we have some decisions by noon?' Klein butted in. 'Particularly the Gulf situation, and the Mexican dispute, and – '

'Yes, yes, yes,' said Goldberg. 'Now go away.'

' – We could have another Bay of Pigs – '

'You're telling me nothing I don't know. Go! You're disturbing the nations.' He peered at Vanessa. 'Well, are you going to sit down or not?'

She sat.

'I'll leave you to it.' Klein said, and retreated.

Goldberg had begun to make a sound in his throat – '*kek-kek-kek*' – imitating the voice of a frog. In response, there came a croaking from every corner of the courtyard. Hearing the sound, Vanessa stifled a smile. Farce, she had told herself once before, had to be played with a straight face, as though you believed every outrageous word. Only tragedy demanded laughter; and that, with the aid of the frogs, they might yet prevent.

In The Flesh

When Cleveland Smith returned to his cell after the interview with the Landing Officer, his new bunk mate was already in residence, staring at the dust-infested sunlight through the reinforced glass window. It was a short display; for less than half an hour each afternoon (clouds permitting) the sun found its way between the wall and the administration building and edged its way along the side of B Wing, not to appear again until the following day.

'You're Tait?' Cleve said.

The prisoner looked away from the sun. Mayflower had said the new boy was twenty-two, but Tait looked five years younger. He had the face of a lost dog. An ugly dog, at that; a dog left by its owners to play in traffic. Eyes too skinned, mouth too soft, arms too slender: a born victim. Cleve was irritated to have been lumbered with the boy. Tait was dead weight, and he had no energies to expend on the boy's protection, despite Mayflower's pep-talk about extending a welcoming hand.

'Yes,' the dog replied. 'William.'

'People call you William?'

'No,' the boy said. 'They call me Billy.'

'Billy.' Cleve nodded, and stepped into the cell. The regime at Pentonville was relatively enlightened; cells were left open for two hours in the mornings, and often two in the afternoon, allowing the cons some freedom of movement. The arrangement had its disadvantages, however, which was where Mayflower's talk came in.

'I've been told to give you some advice.'

'Oh?' the boy replied.

'You've not done time before?'

'No.'

'Not even borstal?'

Tait's eyes flickered. 'A little.'

'So you know what the score is. You know you're easy meat.'

'Sure.'

'Seems I've been volunteered,' Cleve said without appetite, 'to keep you from getting mauled.'

Tait stared at Cleve with eyes the blue of which was milky, as

103

though the sun was still in them. 'Don't put yourself out,' the boy said. 'You don't owe me anything.'

'Damn right I don't. But it seems I got a social responsibility.' Cleve said sourly. 'And you're it.'

Cleve was two months into his sentence for handling marijuana; his third visit to Pentonville. At thirty years of age he was far from obsolete. His body was solid, his face lean and refined; in his court suit he could have passed for a lawyer at ten yards. A little closer, and the viewer might catch the scar on his neck, the result of an attack by a penniless addict, and a certain wariness in his gait, as if with every step forward he was keeping the option of a speedy retreat.

You're still a young man, the last judge had told him, you still have time to change your spots. He hadn't disagreed out loud, but Cleve knew in his heart he was a leopard born and bred. Crime was easy, work was not. Until somebody proved otherwise he would do what he did best, and take the consequences if caught. Doing time wasn't so unpalatable, if you had the right attitude to it. The food was edible, the company select; as long as he had something to keep his mind occupied he was content enough. At present he was reading about sin. Now *there* was a subject. In his time he'd heard so many explanations of how it had come into the world; from probation officers and lawyers and priests. Theories sociological, theological, ideological. Some were worthy of a few minutes' consideration. Most were so absurd (sin from the womb; sin from the state) he laughed in their apologists' faces. None held water for long.

It was a good bone to chew over, though. He needed a problem to occupy the days. And nights; he slept badly in prison. It wasn't *his* guilt that kept him awake, but that of others. He was, after all, just a hash-pusher, supplying wherever there was a demand: a minor cog in the consumerist machine; he had nothing to feel guilty about. But there were others here, *many* others it seemed, whose dreams were not so benevolent, nor nights so peaceful. They would cry, they would complain; they would curse judges local and celestial. Their din would have kept the dead awake.

'Is it always like this?' Billy asked Cleve after a week or so. A new inmate was making a ruckus down the landing: one moment tears, the next obscenities.

'Yes. Most of the time,' said Cleve. 'Some of them need to yell a bit. It keeps their minds from curdling.'

'Not you,' observed the unmusical voice from the bunk below, 'you just read your books and keep out of harm's way. I've watched you. It doesn't bother you, does it?'

104

'I can live with it,' Cleve replied. 'I got no wife to come here every week and remind me what I'm missing.'

'You been in before?'

'Twice.'

The boy hesitated an instant before saying, 'I suppose you know your way around the place, do you?'

'Well, I'm not writing a guidebook, but I got the general lay-out by now.' It seemed an odd comment for the boy to make. 'Why?'

'I just wondered,' said Billy.

'You got a question?'

Tait didn't answer for several seconds, then said: 'I heard they used to . . . used to *hang* people here.'

Whatever Cleve had been expecting the boy to come out with, that wasn't it. But then he had decided several days back that Billy Tait was a strange one. Sly, side-long glances from those milky-blue eyes; a way he had of staring at the wall or at the window like a detective at a murder-scene, desperate for clues.

Cleve said, 'There used to be a hanging shed, I think.'

Again, silence; and then another enquiry, droppped as lightly as the boy could contrive. 'Is it still standing?'

'The shed? I don't know. They don't hang people any more, Billy, or hadn't you heard?' There was no reply from below. 'What's it to you, anyhow?'

'Just curious.'

Billy was right; curious he was. So odd, with his vacant stares and his solitary manner, that most of the men kept clear of him. Only Lowell took any interest in him, and his motives for that were unequivocal.

'You want to lend me your lady for the afternoon?' he asked Cleve while they waited in line for breakfast. Tait, who stood within earshot, said nothing; neither did Cleve.

'You hear me? I asked you a question.'

'I heard. You leave him alone.'

'Share and share alike,' Lowell said. 'I can do you some favours. We can work something out.'

'He's not available.'

'Well, why don't I ask *him*?' Lowell said, grinning through his beard. 'What do you say, baby?'

Tait looked round at Lowell.

'I say no thank you.'

'No *thank you*,' Lowell said, and gave Cleve a second smile, this quite without humour. 'You've got him well trained. Does he sit up and beg, too?'

105

'Take a walk, Lowell,' Cleve replied. 'He's not available and that's all there is to it.'

'You can't keep your eyes on him every minute of the day,' Lowell pointed out. 'Sooner or later he's going to have to stand on his own two feet. Unless he's better kneeling.'

The innuendo won a guffaw from Lowell's cell-mate, Nayler. Neither were men Cleve would have willingly faced in a free-for-all, but his skills as a bluffer were honed razor-sharp, and he used them now.

'You don't want to trouble yourself,' he told Lowell, 'you can only cover so many scars with a beard.'

Lowell looked at Cleve, all humour fled. He clearly couldn't distinguish the truth from bluff, and equally clearly wasn't willing to put his neck on the line.

'Just don't look the other way.' he said, and said no more.

The encounter at breakfast wasn't mentioned until that night, when the lights had been extinguished. It was Billy who brought it up.

'You shouldn't have done that,' he said. 'Lowell's a bad bastard. I've heard the talk.'

'You want to get raped then, do you?'

'No,' he said quickly, 'Christ no. I got to be fit.'

'You'll be fit for nothing if Lowell gets his hands on you.'

Billy slipped out from his bunk and stood in the middle of the cell, barely visible in the gloom. 'I suppose you want something in return,' he said.

Cleve turned on his pillow and looked at the uncertain silhouette standing a yard from him. 'What have you got that I'd want, Billy-Boy?' he said.

'What Lowell wanted.'

'Is that what you think that bluster was all about? Me staking my claim?'

'Yeah.'

'Like you said: no thank you.' Cleve rolled over again to face the wall.

'I didn't mean – '

'I don't care what you meant. I just don't want to hear about it, all right? You stay out of Lowell's way, and don't give me shit.'

'Hey,' Billy murmured, 'don't get like that, please. *Please*. You're the only friend I've got.'

'I'm nobody's friend,' Cleve said to the wall. 'I just don't want any inconvenience. Understand me?'

'No inconvenience,' the boy repeated, dull-tongued.

'Right. Now . . . I need my beauty sleep.'

Tait said no more, but returned to the bottom bunk, and lay down, the springs creaking as he did so. Cleve lay in silence, turning the exchange over in his head. He had no wish to lay hands on the boy; but perhaps he had made his point too harshly. Well, it was done.

From below he could hear Billy murmuring to himself, almost inaudibly. He strained to eavesdrop on what the boy was saying. It took several seconds of ear-pricking attention before Cleve realized that Billy-Boy was saying his prayers.

Cleve dreamt that night. What of, he couldn't remember in the morning, though as he showered and shaved tantalizing grains of the dream sifted through his head. Scarcely ten minutes went by that morning without something – salt overturned on the breakfast table, or the sound of shouts in the exercise yard – promising to break his dream: but the revelation did not come. It left him uncharacteristically edgy and short-tempered. When Wesley, a small-time forger whom he knew from his previous vacation here, approached him in the library and started to talk as though they were bosom pals, Cleve told the runt to shut up. But Wesley insisted on speaking.

'You got trouble.'

'Oh. How so?'

'That boy of yours. Billy.'

'What about him?'

'He's asking questions. He's getting pushy. People don't like it. They're saying you should take him in hand.'

'I'm not his keeper.'

Wesley pulled a face. 'I'm telling you; as a friend.'

'Spare me.'

'Don't be stupid, Cleveland. You're making enemies.'

'Oh?' said Cleve. 'Name one.'

'Lowell,' Wesley said, quick as a flash. 'Nayler for another. All kinds of people. They don't like the way Tait is.'

'And how is he?' Cleve snapped back.

Wesley made a small grunt of protest. 'I'm just trying to tell you,' he said. 'He's sly. Like a fucking rat. There'll be trouble.'

'Spare me the prophecies.'

The law of averages demands the worst prophet be right some of the time: this was Wesley's moment it seemed. The day after, coming back from the Workshop where he'd exercised his intellect putting wheels on plastic cars, Cleve found Mayflower waiting for him on the landing.

'I asked you to look after William Tait, Smith,' the officer said. 'Don't you give a damn?'

'What's happened?'

'No, I suppose you don't.'

'I asked what happened. Sir.'

'Nothing much. Not this time. He's banged about, that's all. Seems Lowell has a hankering after him. Am I right?' Mayflower peered at Cleve, and when he got no response went on: 'I made an error with you, Smith. I thought there was something worth appealing to under the hard man. My mistake.'

Billy was lying on the bunk, his face bruised, his eyes closed. He didn't open them when Cleve came in.

'You OK?0'

'Sure,' the boy said softly.

'No bones broken?'

'I'll survive.'

'You've got to understand – '

'*Listen.*' Billy opened his eyes. The pupils had darkened somehow, or that was the trick the light performed with them. 'I'm alive, OK? I'm not an idiot you know. I knew what I was letting myself in for, coming here.' He spoke as if he'd had a choice in the matter. 'I can take Lowell,' he went on, 'so don't fret.' He paused, then said: 'You were right.'

'About what?'

'About not having friends. I'm on my own, you're on your own. Right? I'm just a slow learner; but I'm getting the hang of it.' He smiled to himself.

'You've been asking questions,' Cleve said.

'Oh, yeah?' Billy replied off-handedly. 'Who says?'

'If you've got questions, ask me. People don't like snoopers. They get suspicious. And then they turn their backs when Lowell and his like get heavy.'

Naming the man brought a painful frown to Billy's face. He touched his bruised cheek. 'He's dead,' the boy murmured, almost to himself.

'Some chance,' Cleve commented.

The look that Tait returned could have sliced steel. 'I mean it,' he said, without a trace of doubt in his voice. 'Lowell won't get out alive.'

Cleve didn't comment; the boy needed this show of bravado, laughable as it was.

'What do you want to know, that you go snooping around?'

'Nothing much,' Billy replied. He was no longer looking at Cleve, but staring at the bunk above. Quietly, he said: 'I just wanted to know where the graves were, that was all.'

'The graves?'

'Where they buried the men they'd hanged. Somebody told me there's a rose-bush where Crippen's buried. You ever hear that?'

Cleve shook his head. Only now did he remember the boy asking about the hanging shed; and now the graves. Billy looked up at him. The bruise was ripening by the minute.

'You know where they are, Cleve?' he asked. Again, that feigned nonchalance.

'I could find out, if you do me the courtesy of telling me why you want to know.'

Billy looked out from the shelter of the bunk. The afternoon sun was describing its short arc on the painted brick of the cell wall. It was weak today. The boy slid his legs off the bunk and sat on the edge of the mattress, staring at the light as he had on that first day.

'My grandfather – that is, my mother's father – was hanged here,' he said, his voice raw. 'In 1937. Edgar Tait. Edgar St Clair Tait.'

'I thought you said your *mother's* father?'

'I took his name. I didn't want my father's name. I never belonged to him.'

'Nobody belongs to anybody.' Cleve replied. 'You're your own man.'

'But that's not true,' Billy said with a tiny shrug, still staring at the light on the wall. His certainty was immovable; the gentility with which he spoke did not undercut the authority of the statement. 'I *belong* to my grandfather. I always have.'

'You weren't even born when he – '

'That doesn't matter. Coming and going; that's nothing.'

Coming and going, Cleve puzzled; did Tait mean life and death? He had no chance to ask. Billy was talking again, the same subdued but insistent flow.

'He was guilty of course. Not the way they thought he was, but *guilty*. He knew what he was and what he was capable of; that's guilt, isn't it? He killed four people. Or at least that's what they hanged him for.'

'You mean he killed more?'

Billy made another small shrug: numbers didn't matter apparently. 'But nobody came to see where they'd laid him to rest. That's not right, is it? They didn't care, I suppose. All the family were glad he was gone, probably. Thought he was wrong in the head from the beginning. But he wasn't. I know he *wasn't*. I've got his hands, and his eyes. So Mam said. She told me all about him, you see, just before she died. Told me things she'd never told anybody, and only told me because of my eyes . . .' he faltered, and put his hand to his lip, as if the fluctuating light on the brick had already mesmerised him into saying too much.

'What did your mother tell you?' Cleve pressed him.

Billy seemed to weigh up alternative responses before offering one. 'Just that he and I were *alike* in some ways,' he said.

'Crazy, you mean?' Cleve said, only half-joking.

'Something like that,' Billy replied, eyes still on the wall. He sighed, then allowed himself a further confession. 'That's why I came here. So my grandfather would know he hadn't been forgotten.'

'*Came* here?' said Cleve. 'What are you talking about? You were caught and sentenced. You had no choice.'

The light on the wall was extinguished as a cloud passed over the sun. Billy looked up at Cleve. The light was there, in his eyes.

'I committed a crime to get here,' the boy replied. 'It was a deliberate act.'

Cleve shook his head. The claim was preposterous.

'I tried before: twice. It's taken time. But I got here, didn't I?0'

'Don't take me for a fool, Billy,' Cleve warned.

'I don't,' the other replied. He stood up now. He seemed somehow lighter for the story he'd told; he even smiled, if tentatively, as he said: 'You've been good to me. Don't think I don't know that. I'm grateful. Now – ' he faced Cleve before saying: 'I want to know where the graves are. Find that out and you won't hear another peep from me, I promise.'

Cleve knew next to nothing about the prison or its history, but he knew somebody who did. There was a man by the name of Bishop – so familiar to the inmates that his name had acquired the definite article – who was often at the Workshop at the same time as Cleve. The Bishop had been in and out of prison for much of his forty odd years, mostly for minor misdemeanours, and – with all the fatalism of a one-legged man who makes a life-study of monopedia – had become an expert on prisons and the penal system. Little of his information came from books. He had gleaned the bulk of his knowledge from old lags and screws who wanted to talk the hours away, and by degrees he had turned himself into a walking encyclopaedia on crime and punishment. He had made it his trade, and he sold his carefully accrued knowledge by the sentence; sometimes as geographical information to the would-be escapee, sometimes as prison mythology to the godless con in search of a local divinity. Now Cleve sought him out, and laid down his payment in tobacco and IOUs.

'What can I do for you?' The Bishop asked. He was heavy, but not unhealthily so. The needle-thin cigarettes he was perpetually rolling and smoking were dwarfed by his butcher's fingers, stained sepia by nicotine.

'I want to know about the hangings here.'

The Bishop smiled. 'Such good stories,' he said; and began to tell.

On the plain details, Billy had been substantially correct. There had been hangings in Pentonville up until the middle of the century, but the shed had long since been demolished. On the spot now stood the Probation Office in B Wing. As to the story of Crippen's roses, there was truth in that too. In front of a hut in the grounds, which, The Bishop informed Cleve, was a store for gardening equipment, was a small patch of grass, in the centre of which a bush flourished, planted (and at this point The Bishop confessed that he could not tell fact from fiction) in memory of Doctor Crippen, hanged in 1910.

'That's where the graves are?' Cleve asked.

'No, no,' The Bishop said, reducing half of one of his tiny cigarettes to ash with a single inhalation. 'The graves are alongside the wall, to the left behind the hut. There's a long lawn; you must have seen it.'

'No stones?'

'Absolutely not. The plots have always been left unmarked. Only the Governor knows who's buried where; and he's probably lost the plans.' The Bishop ferreted for his tobacco tin in the breast-pocket of his prison-issue shirt and began to roll another cigarette with such familiarity he scarcely glanced down at what he was doing. 'Nobody's allowed to come and mourn you see. Out of sight, out of mind: that's the idea. Of course, that's not the way it works, is it? People forget Prime Ministers, but they remember murderers. You walk on that lawn, and just six feet under are some of the most notorious men who ever graced this green and pleasant land. And not even a cross to mark the spot. Criminal, isn't it?'

'You know who's buried there?'

'Some very wicked gentlemen,' the Bishop replied, as if fondly admonishing them for their mischief-mongering.

'You heard of a man called Edgar Tait?'

Bishop raised his eyebrows; the fat of his brow furrowed. 'Saint Tait? Oh certainly. He's not easily forgotten.'

'What do you know about him?'

'He killed his wife, and then his children. Took a knife to them all, as I live and breathe.'

'All?'

The Bishop put the freshly-rolled cigarette to his thick lips. 'Maybe not all,' he said, narrowing his eyes as he tried to recall the specific details. 'Maybe one of them survived. I think perhaps a daughter . . .' he shrugged dismissively. 'I'm not very good at remembering the victims. But then, who is?' He fixed his bland gaze on Cleve. 'Why are you so interested in Tait? He was hanged before the war.'

'1937. He'll be well gone, eh?'

The Bishop raised a cautionary fore-finger. 'Not so,' he said. 'You see the land this prison is built upon has special properties. Bodies buried here don't rot the way they do elsewhere.' Cleve shot The Bishop an incredulous glance. 'It's true,' the fat man protested mildly, 'I have it on unimpeachable authority. Take it from me, whenever they've had to exhume a body from the plot it's always been found in almost perfect condition.' He paused to light his cigarette, and drew upon it, exhaling the smoke through his mouth with his next words. 'When the end of the world is upon us, the good men of Marylebone and Camden Town will rise up as rot and bone. But the wicked?; they'll dance to Judgement as fresh as the day they dropped. Imagine that.' This perverse notion clearly delighted him. His pudgy face puckered and dimpled with pleasure at it. 'Ah,' he mused, 'And who'll be calling who corrupt on *that* fine morning?'

Cleve never worked out precisely how Billy talked his way on to the gardening detail, but he managed it. Perhaps he had appealed directly to Mayflower, who'd persuaded his superiors that the boy could be trusted out in the fresh air. However he worked the manoeuvre, in the middle of the week following Cleve's discovery of the graves' whereabouts, Billy was out in the cold April morning cutting grass.

What happened that day filtered back down the grapevine around recreation time. Cleve had the story from three independent sources, none of whom had been on the spot. The accounts had a variety of colorations, but were clearly of the same species. The bare bones went as follows:

The gardening detail, made up of four men overlooked by a single prison officer, were moving around the blocks, trimming grass and weeding beds in preparation for the spring planting. Custody had been lax, apparently. It was two or three minutes before the officer even noticed that one of his charges had edged to the periphery of the party and slipped away. The alarm was raised. The officers did not have to look far, however. Tait had made no attempt to escape, or if he had he'd been stymied in his bid by a fit of some kind, which had crippled him. He was found (and here the stories parted company considerably) on a large patch of lawn beside the wall, lying on the grass. Some reports claimed he was black in the face, his body knotted up and his tongue all but bitten through; others that he was found face down, talking to the earth, weeping and cajoling. The consensus was that the boy had lost his mind.

The rumours made Cleve the centre of attention; a situation he did not relish. For the next day he was scarcely left alone; men wanting to know what it was like to share a cell with a lunatic. He had nothing to tell, he insisted. Tait had been the perfect cell-mate – quiet, undemanding and unquestionably sane. He told the same story to Mayflower when he was grilled the following day; and later, to the prison doctor. He let not a breath of Tait's interest in the graves be known, and made it his business to see The Bishop and request a similar silence of him. The man was willing to oblige only if vouchsafed the full story in due course. This Cleve promised. The Bishop, as befitted his assumed clerity, was as good as his word.

Billy was gone from the fold for two days. In the interim Mayflower disappeared from his duties as Landing Officer. No explanation was given. In his place, a man called Devlin was transferred from D Wing. His reputation went before him. He was not, it seemed, a man of rare compassion. The impression was confirmed when, the day of Billy Tait's return, Cleve was summoned into Devlin's office.

'I'm told you and Tait are close,' Devlin said. He had a face as giving as granite.

'Not really, sir.'

'I'm not going to make Mayflower's mistake, Smith. As far as I'm concerned Tait is trouble. I'm going to watch him like a hawk, and when I'm not here you're going to do it for me, understand? If he so much as crosses his eyes it's the ghost train. I'll have him out of here and into a special unit before he can fart. Do I make myself clear?'

'Paying your respects, were you?'

Billy had lost weight in the hospital; pounds his scrawny frame could scarcely afford. His shirt hung off his shoulders; his belt was on its tightest notch. The thinning more than ever emphasized his physical vulnerability; a featherweight blow would floor him, Cleve thought. But it lent his face a new, almost desperate, intensity. He seemed all eyes; and those had lost all trace of captured sunlight. Gone, too, was the pretense of vacuity, replaced with an eerie purposefulness.

'I asked a question.'

'I heard you,' Billy said. There was no sun today, but he looked at the wall anyway. 'Yes, if you must know, I was paying my respects.'

'I've been told to watch you, by Devlin. He wants you off the Landing. Transferred entirely, maybe.'

'Out?' The panicked look Billy gave Cleve was too naked to be met for more than a few seconds. 'Away from here, you mean?'

'I would think so.'

'They can't!'

113

'Oh, they can. They call it the ghost train. One minute you're here; the next – '

'No,' the boy said, hands suddenly fists. He had begun to shake, and for a moment Cleve feared a second fit. But he seemed, by act of will, to control the tremors, and turned his look back to his cell-mate. The bruises he'd received from Lowell had dulled to yellow-grey, but far from disappeared; his unshaven cheeks were dusted with pale-ginger hair. Looking at him Cleve felt an unwelcome twinge of concern.

'Tell me.' Cleve said.

'Tell you what?' Billy asked.

'What happened at the graves.'

'I felt dizzy. I fell over. The next thing I knew I was in hospital.'

'That's what you told *them*, is it?'

'It's the truth.'

'Not the way I heard it. Why don't you explain what really happened? I want you to trust me.'

'I do,' the boy said. 'But I have to keep this to myself, see. It's between me and him.'

'You and Edgar?' Cleve asked, and Billy nodded, 'A man who killed all his family but your mother?'

Billy was clearly startled that Cleve possessed this information. 'Yes,' he said, after consideration. 'Yes, he killed them all. He would have killed Mama too, if she hadn't escaped. He wanted to wipe the whole family out. So there'd be no heirs to carry the bad blood.'

'Your blood's bad, is it?'

Billy allowed himself the slenderest of smiles. 'No,' he said. 'I don't think so. Grandfather was wrong. Times have changed, haven't they?'

He *is* mad, Cleve thought. Lightning-swift, Billy caught the judgement.

'I'm not insane,' he said. 'You tell them that. Tell Devlin and whoever else asks. Tell them I'm a lamb.' The fierceness was back in his eyes. There was nothing lamb-like there, though Cleve forbore saying so. 'They mustn't move me out, Cleve. Not after getting so close. I've got business here. Important business.'

'With a dead man?'

'With a dead man.'

Whatever new purpose he displayed for Cleve, the shutters went up when Billy got back amongst the rest of the cons. He responded neither to the questions nor the insults bandied about; his fac‹SS›cade of empty-eyed indifference was flawless. Cleve was impressed. The

114

boy had a future as an actor, if he decided to forsake professional lunacy.

But the strain of concealing the new-found urgency in him rapidly began to tell. In a hollowness about the eyes, and a jitteriness in his movements; in brooding and unshakeable silences. The physical deterioration was apparent to the doctor to whom Billy continued to report; he pronounced the boy suffering from depression and acute insomnia, and prescribed sedatives to aid sleep. These pills Billy gave to Cleve, insisting he had no need of them himself. Cleve was grateful. For the first time in many months he began to sleep well, unperturbed by the tears and shouts of his fellow inmates.

By day, the relationship between he and the boy, which had always been vestigial, dwindled to mere courtesy. Cleve sensed that Billy was closing up entirely, removing himself from merely physical concerns.

It was not the first time he had witnessed such a pre-medicated withdrawal. His sister-in-law, Rosanna, had died of stomach cancer three years previous: a protracted and, until the last weeks, steady decline. Cleve had not been close to her, but perhaps that very distance had lent him a perspective on the woman's behaviour that the rest of his family had lacked. He had been startled at the systematic way she had prepared herself for death, drawing in her affections until they touched only the most vital figures in her life – her children and her priest – and exiling all others, including her husband of fourteen years.

Now he saw the same dispassion and frugality in Billy. Like a man in training to cross a waterless wasteland and too possessive of his energies to squander them in a single fruitless gesture, the boy was sinking into himself. It was eerie; Cleve became increasingly uncomfortable sharing the twelve feet by eight of the cell with Billy. It was like living with a man on Death Row.

The only consolation was the tranquillisers, which Billy readily charmed the doctor into continuing to supply. They guaranteed Cleve sleep that was restful, and, for several days at least, dreamless.

And then he dreamt the city.

Not the city first; first the desert. An empty expanse of blue-black sand, which stung the soles of his feet as he walked, and was blown up by a cool wind into his nose and eyes and hair. He had been here before, he knew. His dream-self recognized the vista of barren dunes, with neither tree nor habitation to break the monotony. But on previous visits he had come with guides (or such was his half-formed belief); now he was alone, and the clouds above his head were heavy and slate-grey, promising no sun. For what seemed hours he walked the dunes, his feet turned bloody by the sharp sand, his body, dusted by the grains, tinged blue. As exhaustion came close to defeating him, he saw ruins, and approached them.

It was no oasis. There was nothing in those empty streets of health or sustenance; no fruitful trees nor sparkling fountains. The city was a conglomeration of houses, or parts of same – sometimes entire floors, sometimes single rooms – thrown down side by side in parodies of urban order. The styles were a hopeless mish-mash – fine Georgian establishments standing beside mean tenement buildings with rooms burnt out; a house plucked from a terraced row, perfect down to the glazed dog on the window sill, back to back with a penthouse suite. All were scarred by a rough removal from their context: walls were cracked, offering sly glimpses into private interiors; staircases beetled cloudward without destination; doors flapped open and closed in the wind, letting on to nowhere.

There was life here, Cleve knew. Not just the lizards, rats and butterflies – albinoes all – that fluttered and skipped in front of him as he walked the forsaken streets – but *human* life. He sensed that every step he took was overlooked, though he saw no sign of human presence; not on his first visit at least.

On the second, his dream-self forsook the trudge across the wilderness and was delivered directly into the necropolis, his feet, easily tutored, following the same route as he had on his first visit. The constant wind was stronger tonight. It caught the lace curtains in this window, and a tinkling Chinese trinket hanging in that. It carried voices too; horrid and outlandish sounds that came from some distant place far beyond the city. Hearing that whirring and whittering, as of insane children, he was grateful for the streets and the rooms, for their familiarity if not for any comfort they might offer. He had no desire to step into those interiors, voices or no; did not want to discover what marked these snatches of architecture out that they should have been ripped from their roots and flung down in this whining desolation.

Yet, once he had visited the site, his sleeping mind went back there, night upon night; always walking, bloody-footed, seeing only the rats and the butterflies, and the black sand on each threshold, blowing into rooms and hallways that never changed from visit to visit; that seemed, from what he could glimpse between the curtains or through a shattered wall, to have been *fixed* somehow at some pivotal moment, with a meal left uneaten on a table set for three (the capon uncarved, the sauces steaming), or a shower left running in a bathroom in which the lamp perpetually swung; and in a room that might have been a lawyer's study a lap-dog, or else a wig torn off and flung to the floor, lying discarded on a fine carpet whose intricacies were half-devoured by sand.

116

Only once did he see another human being in the city: and that was Billy. It happened strangely. One night – as he dreamed the streets – he half-stirred from sleep. Billy was awake, and standing in the middle of the cell, staring up at the light through the window. It was not moonlight, but the boy bathed in it as if it were. His face was turned up to the window, mouth open and eyes closed. Cleve barely had time to register the trance the boy seemed to be in before the tranquillisers drew him back into his dream. He took a fragment of reality with him however, folding the boy into his sleeping vision. When he reached the city again, there was Billy Tait: standing on the street, his face turned up to the louring clouds, his mouth open, his eyes closed.

The image lingered a moment only. The next, the boy was away, his heels kicking up black fans of sand. Cleve called after him. Billy ran on however, heedless; and, with that inexplicable foreknowledge that dreams bring, Cleve knew where the boy was going. Off to the edge of the city, where the houses petered out and the desert began. Off to meet some friend coming in on that terrible wind, perhaps. Nothing would induce him into pursuit, yet he didn't want to lose contact with the one fellow human he had seen in these destitute streets. He called Billy's name again, more loudly.

This time he felt a hand on his arm, and started up in terror to find himself being jostled awake in his cell.

'It's all right,' Billy said. 'You're dreaming.'

Cleve tried to shake the city out of his head, but for several perilous seconds the dream bled into the waking world, and looking down at the boy he saw Billy's hair lifted by a wind that did not, *could* not, belong in the confines of the cell. 'You're dreaming,' Billy said again. 'Wake up.'

Shuddering, Cleve sat fully up on his bunk. The city was receding – was almost gone – but before he lost sight of it entirely he felt the indisputable conviction that Billy *knew* what he was waking Cleve from; that they had been there together for a few, fragile moments.

'You know, don't you?' he accused the pallid face at his side.

The boy looked bewildered. 'What are you talking about?'

Cleve shook his head. The suspicion became more incredible with each step he took from sleep. Even so, when he looked down at Billy's bony hand, which still clung to his arm, he half-expected to see flecks of that obsidian grit beneath his finger-nails. There was only dirt.

The doubts lingered however, long after reason should have bullied them into surrender. Cleve found himself watching the boy more closely from that night on, waiting for some slip of tongue or eye which would reveal the nature of his game. Such scrutiny was a lost cause. The last traces of accessibility disappeared after that night; the boy became – like Rosanna – an indecipherable book, letting no clue as to the nature of his secret world out from beneath his lids. As to the dream – it was not even mentioned again. The only roundabout allusion to that night was Billy's redoubled insistence that Cleve continue to take the sedatives.

'You need your sleep,' he said after coming back from the Infirmary with a further supply. 'Take them.'

'You need sleep too,' Cleve replied, curious to see how far the boy would push the issue. 'I don't need the stuff any more.'

'But you do,' Billy insisted, proffering the phial of capsules. 'You know how bad the noise is.'

'Someone said they're addictive,' Cleve replied, not taking the pills, 'I'll do without.'

'*No*,' said Billy; and now Cleve sensed a level of insistence which confirmed his deepest suspicions. The boy *wanted* him drugged, and had all along. 'I sleep like a babe,' Billy said. 'Please take them. They'll only be wasted otherwise.'

Cleve shrugged. 'If you're sure,' he said, content – fears confirmed – to make a show of relenting.

'I'm sure.'

'Then thanks.' He took the phial.

Billy beamed. With that smile, in a sense, the bad times really began.

That night, Cleve answered the boy's performance with one of his own, appearing to take the tranquillisers as he usually did, but failing to swallow them. Once lying on his bunk, face to the wall, he slipped them from his mouth, and under his pillow. Then he pretended sleep.

Prison days both began and finished early; by 8.45 or 9.00 most of the cells in the four wings were in darkness, the inmates locked up until dawn and left to their own devices. Tonight was quieter than most. The weeper in the next cell but one had been transferred to D Wing; there were few other disturbances along the landing. Even without the pill Cleve felt sleep tempting him. From the bunk below he heard practically no sound, except for the occasional sigh. It was impossible to guess if Billy was actually asleep or not. Cleve kept his silence, occasionally stealing a moment-long glance at the luminous face of his watch. The minutes were leaden, and he feared, as the first hours crept by, that all too soon his imitation of sleep would become the real thing. Indeed he was turning this very possibility around in his mind when unconsciousness overcame him.

He woke much later. His sleep-position seemed not to have altered.

The wall was in front of him, the peeled paint like a dim map of some nameless territory. It took him a minute or two to orient himself. There was no sound from the bunk below. Disguising the gesture as one made in sleep, he drew his arm up within eye-range, and looked at the pale-green dial of his watch. It was one-fifty-one. Several hours yet until dawn. He lay in the position he'd woken in for a full quarter of an hour, listening for every sound in the cell, trying to locate Billy. He was loathe to roll over and look for himself, for fear that the boy was standing in the middle of the cell as he had been the night of the visit to the city.

The world, though benighted, was far from silent. He could hear dull footsteps as somebody paced back and forth in the corresponding cell on the landing above; could hear water rushing in the pipes and the sound of a siren on the Caledonian Road. What he couldn't hear was Billy. Not a breath of the boy.

Another quarter of an hour passed, and Cleve could feel the familiar torpor closing in to reclaim him; if he lay still much longer he would fall asleep again, and the next thing he'd know it would be morning. If he was going to learn anything, he had to roll over and *look*. Wisest, he decided, not to attempt to move surreptitiously, but to turn over as naturally as possible. This he did, muttering to himself, as if in sleep, to add weight to the illusion. Once he had turned completely, and positioned his hand beside his face to shield his spying, he cautiously opened his eyes.

The cell seemed darker than it had the night he had seen Billy with his face up to the window. As to the boy, he was not visible. Cleve opened his eyes a little wider and scanned the cell as best he could from between his fingers. There was something amiss, but he couldn't quite work out what it was. He lay there for several minutes, waiting for his eyes to become accustomed to the murk. They didn't. The scene in front of him remained unclear, like a painting so encrusted with dirt and varnish its depths refuse the investigating eye. Yet he knew – *knew* – that the shadows in the corners of the cell, and on the opposite wall, were not empty. He wanted to end the anticipation that was making his heart thump, wanted to raise his head from the pebble-filled pillow and call Billy out of hiding. But good sense counselled otherwise. Instead he lay still, and sweated, and watched.

And now he began to realize what was wrong with the scene before him. The concealing shadows fell where no shadows belonged; they spread across the hall where the feeble light from the window should have been falling. Somehow, between window and wall, that light had been choked and devoured. Cleve closed his eyes to give his befuddled mind a chance to rationalize and reject this conclusion.

When he opened them again his heart lurched. The shadow, far from losing potency, had grown a little.

He had never been afraid like this before; never felt a coldness in his innards akin to the chill that found him now. It was all he could do to keep his breath even, and his hands where they lay. His instinct was to wrap himself up and hide his face like a child. Two thoughts kept him from doing so. One was that the slightest movement might draw unwelcome attention to him. The other, that Billy was somewhere in the cell, and perhaps as threatened by this living darkness as he.

And then, from the bunk below, the boy spoke. His voice was soft, so as not to wake his sleeping cell-mate presumably. It was also eerily intimate. Cleve entertained no thought that Billy was talking in his sleep; the time for wilful self-deception was long past. The boy was addressing the darkness; of that unpalatable fact there could be no doubt.

'. . . it hurts . . .' he said, with a faint note of accusation, '. . . you didn't tell me how much it hurts . . .'

Was it Cleve's imagination, or did the wraith of shadows bloom a little in response, like a squid's ink in water? He was horribly afraid.

The boy was speaking again. His voice was so low Cleve could barely catch the words.

'. . . it must be soon . . .' he said, with quiet urgency, '. . . I'm not afraid. Not afraid.'

Again, the shadow shifted. This time, when Cleve looked into its heart, he made some sense of the chimerical form it embraced. His throat shook; a cry lodged behind his tongue, hot to be shouted.

'. . . all you can teach me . . .' Billy was saying, '. . . quickly . . .' The words came and went; but Cleve barely heard them. His attention was on the curtain of shadow, and the figure – stitched from darkness – that moved in its folds. It was not an illusion. There was a man there: or rather a crude copy of one, its substance tenuous, its outline deteriorating all the time, and being hauled back into some semblance of humanity again only with the greatest effort. Of the visitor's features Cleve could see little, but enough to sense deformities paraded like virtues: a face resembling a plate of rotted fruit, pulpy and peeling, swelling here with a nest of flies, and there suddenly fallen away to a pestilent core. How could the boy bring himself to converse so easily with such a *thing*? And yet, putresence notwithstanding, there was a bitter dignity in the bearing of the creature, in the anguish of its eyes, and the toothless O of its maw.

Suddenly, Billy stood up. The abrupt movement, after so many hushed words, almost unleashed the cry from Cleve's throat. He swallowed it, with difficulty, and closed his eyes down to a slit, staring through the bars of his lashes at what happened next.

Billy was talking again, but now the voice was too low to allow for eavesdropping. He stepped towards the shadow, his body blocking much of the figure on the opposite wall. The cell was no more than two or three strides wide, but, by some mellowing of physics, the boy seemed to take five, six, seven steps away from the bunk. Cleve's eyes widened: he knew he was not being watched. The shadow and its acolyte had business between them: it occupied their attention utterly.

Billy's figure was smaller than seemed possible within the confines of the cell, as if he had stepped through the wall and into some other province. And only now, with his eyes wide, did Cleve recognize that place. The darkness from which Billy's visitor was made was cloud-shadow and dust; behind him, barely visible in the bewitched murk, but recognizable to any who had been there, was the city of Cleve's dreams.

Billy had reached his master. The creature towered above him, tattered and spindly, but aching with power. Cleve didn't know how or why the boy had gone to it, and he feared for Billy's safety now that he had, but fear for his own safety shackled him to the bunk. He realized in that moment that he had never loved anyone, man or woman, sufficiently to pursue them into the shadow of that shadow. The thought brought a terrible sense of isolation, knowing that same instant that none, seeing *him* walk to his damnation, would take a single step to claim him from the brink. Lost souls both; he and the boy.

Now Billy's lord was lifting his swollen head, and the incessant wind in those blue streets was rousing his horse-mane into furious life. On the wind, the same voices Cleve had heard carried before, the cries of mad children, somewhere between tears and howls. As if encouraged by these voices, the entity reached out towards Billy and embraced him, wrapping the boy round in vapour. Billy did not struggle in this embrace, but rather returned it. Cleve, unable to watch this horrid intimacy, closed his eyes against it, and when – seconds? minutes?, later – he opened them again, the encounter seemed to be over. The shadow-thing was blowing apart, relinquishing its slender claim to coherence. It fragmented, pieces of its tattered anatomy flying off into the streets like litter before wind. Its departure seemed to signal the dispersal of the entire scene; the streets and houses were already being devoured by dust and distance. Even before the last of the shadow's scraps had been wafted out of sight the city was lost to sight. Cleve was pleased to be shut of it. Reality, grim as it was, was preferable to that desolation. Brick by painted brick the wall was asserting itself again, and Billy, delivered from his master's arms, was back in the solid geometry of the cell, staring up at the light through the window.

Cleve did not sleep again that night. Indeed he wondered, lying on his unyielding mattress and staring up at the stalactites of paint depending from the ceiling, whether he could ever find safety in sleep again.

Sunlight was a showman. It threw its brightness down with such flamboyance, eager as any tinsel-merchant to dazzle and distract. But beneath the gleaming surface it illuminated was another state; one that sunlight – ever the crowd-pleaser – conspired to conceal. It was vile and desperate, that condition. Most, blinded by sight, never even glimpsed it. But Cleve knew the state of sunlessness now; had even walked it, in dreams; and though he mourned the loss of his innocence, he knew he could never retrace his steps back into light's hall of mirrors.

He tried his damnedest to keep this change in him from Billy; the last thing he wanted was for the boy to suspect his eavesdropping. But concealment was well-nigh impossible. Though the following day Cleve made every show of normality he could contrive, he could not quite cover his unease. It slipped out without his being able to control it, like sweat from his pores. And the boy knew, no doubt of it, he *knew*. Nor was he slow to give voice to his suspicions. When, following the afternoon's Workshop, they returned to their cell, Billy was quick to come to the point.

'What's wrong with you today?'

Cleve busied himself with re-making his bed, afraid even to glance at Billy. 'Nothing's wrong,' he said. 'I don't feel particularly well, that's all.'

'You have a bad night?' the boy enquired. Cleve could feel Billy's eyes boring into his back.

'No,' he said, pacing his denial so that it didn't come too quickly. 'I took your pills, like always.'

'Good.'

The exchange faltered, and Cleve was allowed to finish his bedmaking in silence. The business could only be extended so long, however. When he turned from the bunk, job done, he found Billy sitting at the small table, with one of Cleve's books open in his lap. He casually flicked through the volume, all sign of his previous suspicion vanished. Cleve knew better than to trust to mere appearances however.

'Why'd you read these things?' the boy asked.

122

'Passes the time,' Cleve replied, undoing all his labours by clambering up on to the top bunk and stretching out there.

'No. I don't mean why do you read books? I mean, why read *these* books? All this stuff about sin.'

Cleve only half-heard the question. Lying there on the bunk reminded him all too acutely of how the night had been. Reminded him too that darkness was even now crawling up the side of the world again. At that thought his stomach seemed to aspire to his throat.

'Did you hear me?' the boy asked.

Cleve murmured that he had.

'Well, why then; why the books? About damnation and all?'

'Nobody else takes them out of the library,' Cleve replied, having difficulty shaping thoughts to speak when the others, unspoken, were so much more demanding.

'You don't believe it then?'

'No,' he replied. 'No; I don't believe a word of it.'

The boy kept his silence a while. Though Cleve wasn't looking at him, he could hear Billy turning page. Then, another question, but spoken more quietly; a confession.

'Do you ever get *afraid*?'

The enquiry startled Cleve from his trance. The conversation had changed back from talk of reading-matter to something altogether more pertinent. Why did Billy ask about fear, unless he too was afraid?

'What have I got to be scared of?' Cleve asked.

From the corner of his eye he caught the boy shrugging slightly before replying. 'Things that happen,' he said, his voice soulless. 'Things you can't control.'

'Yes,' Cleve replied, not certain of where this exchange was leading. 'Yes, of course. Sometimes I'm scared.'

'What do you do then?' Billy asked.

'Nothing *to* do, is there?' Cleve said. His voice was as hushed as Billy's. 'I gave up praying the morning my father died.'

He heard the soft pat as Billy closed the book, and inclined his head sufficiently to catch sight of the boy. Billy could not entirely conceal his agitation. He *is* afraid, Cleve saw; he doesn't want the night to come any more than I do. He found the thought of their shared fear reassuring. Perhaps the boy didn't entirely belong to the shadow; perhaps he could even cajole Billy into pointing their route out of this spiralling nightmare.

He sat upright, his head within inches of the cell ceiling. Billy looked up from his meditations, his face a pallid oval of twitching muscle. Now was the time to speak, Cleve knew; *now*, before the lights were switched out along the landings, and all the cells consigned

123

to shadows. There would be no time then for explanations. The boy would already be half lost to the city, and beyond persuasion.

'I have dreams,' Cleve said. Billy said nothing, but simply stared back, hollow-eyed. ' – I dream a city.'

The boy didn't flinch. He clearly wasn't going to volunteer elucidation; he would have to be bullied into it.

'Do you know what I'm talking about?'

Billy shook his head. 'No,' he said, lightly, 'I never dream.'

'Everybody dreams.'

'Then I just don't remember them.'

'I remember mine,' Cleve said. He was determined, now that he'd broached the subject, not to let Billy squirm free. 'And you're there. You're in that city.'

Now the boy flinched; only a treacherous lash, but enough to reassure Cleve that he wasn't wasting his breath.

'What is that place, Billy?' he asked.

'How should I know?' the boy returned, about to laugh, then disgarding the attempt. 'I don't know, do I? They're your dreams.'

Before Cleve could reply he heard the voice of one of the officers as he moved along the row of cells, advising the men to bed down for the night. Very soon, the lights would be extinguished and he would be locked up in this narrow cell for ten hours. With Billy; and phantoms –

'Last night – ' he said, fearful of mentioning what he'd heard and seen without due preparation, but more fearful still of facing another night on the borders of the city, alone in darkness. 'Last night I saw – ' He faltered. Why wouldn't the words come? 'Saw – '

'Saw what?' the boy demanded, his face intractable; whatever murmur of apprehension there had been in it had now vanished. Perhaps he too had heard the officer's advance, and known that there was nothing to be done; no way of staying the night's advance.

'*What did you see?*' Billy insisted.

Cleve sighed. 'My mother,' he replied.

The boy betrayed his relief only in the tenuous smile that crept across his lips.

'Yes . . . I saw my mother. Large as life.'

'And it upset you, did it?' Billy asked.

'Sometimes dreams do.'

The officer had reached B. 3. 20. 'Lights out in two minutes,' he said as he passed.

'You should take some more of those pills,' Billy advised, putting down the book and crossing to his bunk. 'Then you'd be like me. No dreams.'

Cleve had lost. He, the arch-bluffer, had been out-bluffed by the

124

boy, and now had to take the consequences. He lay, facing the ceiling, counting off the seconds until the light went out, while below the boy undressed and slipped between the sheets.

There was still time to jump up and call the officer back; time to beat his head against the door until somebody came. But what would he say, to justify his histrionics? That he had bad dreams?; *who didn't?* That he was afraid of the dark?; *who wasn't?* They would laugh in his face and tell him to go back to bed, leaving him with all camouflage blown, and the boy and his master waiting at the wall. There was no safety in such tactics.

Nor in prayer either. He had told Billy the truth, about his giving up God when his prayers for his father's life had gone unanswered. Of such divine neglect was aetheism made; belief could not be rekindled now, however profound his terror.

Thoughts of his father led inevitably to thoughts of childhood; few other subjects, if any, could have engrossed his mind sufficiently to steal him from his fears but this. When the lights were finally extinguished, his frightened mind took refuge in memories. His heart-rate slowed; his fingers ceased to tremble, and eventually, without his being the least aware of it, sleep stole him.

The distractions available to his conscious mind were not available to his unconscious. Once asleep, fond recollection was banished; childhood memories became a thing of the past, and he was back, bloody-footed, in that terrible city.

Or rather, on its borders. For tonight he did not follow the familiar route past the Georgian house and its attendant tenements, but walked instead to the outskirts of the city, where the wind was stronger than ever, and the voices it carried clear. Though he expected with every step he took to see Billy and his dark companion, he saw nobody. Only butterflies accompanied him along the path, luminous as his watch-face. They settled on his shoulders and his hair like confetti, then fluttered off again.

He reached the edge of the city without incident and stood, scanning the desert. The clouds, solid as ever, moved overhead with the majesty of juggernauts. The voices seemed closer tonight, he thought, and the passions they expressed less distressing than he had found them previously. Whether the mellowing was in them or in his response to them he couldn't be certain.

And then, as he watched the dunes and the sky, mesmerized by their blankness, he heard a sound and glanced over his shoulder to see a smiling man, dressed in what was surely his Sunday finery, walking out of the city towards him. He was carrying a knife; the blood on it, and on his hand and shirt-front, was wet. Even in his dream-state, and immune, Cleve was intimidated by the sight and

125

stepped back – a word of self-defence on his lips. The smiling man seemed not to see him however, but advanced past Cleve and out into the desert, dropping the blade as he crossed some invisible boundary. Only now did Cleve see that others had done the same, and that the ground at the city limit was littered with lethal keepsakes – knives, ropes (even a human hand, lopped off at the wrist) – most of which were all but buried.

The wind was bringing the voices again: tatters of senseless songs and half-finished laughter. He looked up from the sand. The exiled man had gone out a hundred yards from the city and was now standing on the top of one of the dunes, apparently waiting. The voices were becoming louder all the time. Cleve was suddenly nervous. Whenever he had been here in the city, and heard this cacophony, the picture he had conjured of its originators had made his blood run cold. Could he now stand and wait for the banshees to appear? Curiosity was discretion's better. He glued his eyes to the ridge over which they would come, his heart thumping, unable to look away. The man in the Sunday suit had begun to take his jacket off. He discarded it, and began to loosen his tie.

And now Cleve thought he saw something in the dunes, and the noise rose to an ecstatic howl of welcome. He stared, defying his nerves to betray him, determined to look this horror in its many faces –

Suddenly, above the din of their music, somebody was screaming; a man's voice, but high-pitched, gelded with terror. It did not come from here in the dream-city, but from that other fiction he occupied, the name of which he couldn't quite remember. He pressed his attention back to the dunes, determined not to be denied the sight of the reunion about to take place in front of him. The scream in that nameless elsewhere mounted to a throat-breaking height, and stopped. But now an alarm bell was ringing in its place, more insistent than ever. Cleve could feel his dream slipping.

'No . . .' he murmured, '. . . let me see . . .'

The dunes were moving. But so was his consciousness – out of the city and back towards his cell. His protests brought him no concession. The desert faded, the city too. He opened his eyes. The lights in the cell were still off: the alarm bell was ringing. There were shouts in cells on the landings above and below, and the sound of officers' voices, raised in a confusion of enquiries and demands.

He lay on his bunk a moment, hoping, even now, to be returned into the enclave of his dream. But no; the alarm was too shrill, the mounting hysteria in the cells around too compelling. He conceded defeat and sat up, wide awake.

'What's going on?' he said to Billy.

The boy was not standing in his place by the wall. Asleep, for once, despite the din.

'*Billy?*'

Cleve leaned over the edge of his bunk, and peered into the space below. It was empty. The sheets and blankets had been thrown back.

Cleve jumped down from his bunk. The entire contents of the cell could be taken at two glances, there was nowhere to hide. The boy was not to be seen. Had he been spirited away while Cleve slept? It was not unheard of; this was the ghost train of which Devlin had warned: the unexplained removal of difficult prisoners to other establishments. Cleve had never heard of this happening at night, but there was a first time for everything.

He crossed to the door to see if he could make some sense of the shouting outside, but it defied interpretation. The likeliest explanation was a fight, he suspected: two cons who could no longer bear the idea of another hour in the same space. He tried to work out where the initial scream had come from, to his right or left, above or below; but the dream had confounded all direction.

As he stood at the door, hoping an officer might pass by, he felt a change in the air. It was so subtle he scarcely registered it at first. Only when he raised his hand to wipe sleep from his eyes did he realize that his arms were solid gooseflesh.

From behind him he now heard the sound of breathing, or a ragged parody of same.

He mouthed the word 'Billy' but didn't speak it. The gooseflesh had found his spine; now he began to shake. The cell *wasn't* empty after all; there was somebody in the tiny space with him.

He screwed his courage tight, and forced himself to turn around. The cell was darker than it had been when he woke; the air was a teasing veil. But Billy was not in the cell; nobody was.

And then the noise came again, and drew Cleve's attention to the bottom bunk. The space was pitch-black, a shadow – like that on the wall – too profound and too volatile to have natural origins. Out of it, a croaking attempt at breath that might have been the last moments of an asthmatic. He realized that the murk in the cell had its source there – in the narrow space of Billy's bed; the shadow bled onto the floor and curled up like fog on to the top of the bunk.

Cleve's supply of fear was not inexhaustible. In the past several days he had used it up in dreams and waking dreams; he'd sweated, he'd frozen, he'd lived on the edge of sane experience and survived. Now, though his body still insisted on gooseflesh, his mind was not moved to panic. He felt cooler than he ever had; whipped by recent events into a new impartiality. He would *not* cower. He would *not* cover his eyes and pray for morning, because if he did one day he would wake to find himself dead and he'd never know the nature of this mystery.

He took a deep breath, and approached the bunk. It had begun to shake. The shrouded occupant in the lower tier was moving about violently.

'Billy,' Cleve said.

The shadow moved. It pooled around his feet; it rolled up into his face, smelling of rain on stone, cold and comfortless.

He was standing no more than a yard from the bunk, and still he could make nothing out; the shadow defied him. Not to be denied sight, he reached towards the bed. At his solicitation the veil divided like smoke, and the shape that thrashed on the mattress made itself apparent.

It was Billy, of course; and yet not. A lost Billy, perhaps, or one to come. If so, Cleve wanted no part of a future that could breed such trauma. There, on the lower bunk, lay a dark, wretched shape, still solidifying as Cleve watched, knitting itself together from the shadows. There was something of a rabid fox in its incandescent eyes, in its arsenal of needle-teeth; something of an upturned insect in the way it was half curled upon itself, its back more shell than flesh and more nightmare than either. No part of it was fixed. Whatever figuration it had (perhaps it had many) Cleve was watching that status dissolve. The teeth were growing yet longer, and in so doing more insubstantial, their matter extruded to the point of frailty, then dispersed like mist; its hooked limbs, pedalling the air, were also growing paltry. Beneath the chaos he saw the ghost of Billy Tait, mouth open and babbling agonies, striving to make itself known. He wanted to reach into the maelstrom and snatch the boy out, but he sensed that the process he was watching had its own momentum and it might be fatal to intervene. All he could do was stand and watch as Billy's thin white limbs and heaving abdomen writhed to slough off this dire anatomy. The luminous eyes were almost the last to go, spilling out from their sockets on myriad threads and flying off into black vapour.

At last, he saw Billy's face, truant clues to its former condition still flickering across it. And then, even these were dispersed, the shadows gone, and only Billy was lying on the bunk, naked and heaving with the exertion of his anguish.

He looked at Cleve, his face innocent of expression.

Cleve remembered how the boy had complained to the creature from the city. '. . . *it hurts* . . .' he'd said, hadn't he?, '. . . *you didn't tell me how much it hurts* . . .'. It was the observable truth. The boy's body was a wasteland of sweat and bone; a more unappetising sight was scarcely imaginable. But *human*; at least that.

128

Billy opened his mouth. His lips were ruddy and slick, as if he were wearing lipstick.

'Now . . .' he said, trying to speak between painful breaths. '. . . now what shall we do?'

The act of speaking seemed too much for him. He made a gagging sound in the back of his throat, and pressed his hand to his mouth. Cleve moved aside as Billy stood up and stumbled across to the bucket in the corner of the cell, kept there for their night-wastes. He failed to reach it before nausea overtook him; fluid splashed between his fingers and hit the floor. Cleve looked away as Billy threw up, preparing himself for the stench he would have to tolerate until slopping-out time the following morning. It was not the smell of vomit that filled the cell, however, but something sweeter and more cloying.

Mystified, Cleve looked back towards the figure crouching in the corner. On the floor between his feet were splashes of dark fluid; rivulets of the same ran down his bare legs. Even in the gloom of the cell, it was unmistakably blood.

In the most well-ordered of prisons violence could – and inevitably did – erupt without warning. The relationship of two cons, incarcerated together for sixteen hours out of every twenty-four, was an unpredictable thing. But as far as had been apparent to either prisoners or officers there had been no bad blood between Lowell and Nayler; nor, until that scream began, had there been a sound from their cell: no argument, no raised voices. What had induced Nayler to spontaneously attack and slaughter his cell-mate, and then inflict devastating wounds upon himself, was a subject for debate in dining-hall and exercise yard alike. The *why* of the problem, however, took second place to the *how*. The rumours describing the condition of Lowell's body when found defied the imagination; even amongst men inured against casual brutality the descriptions were met with shock. Lowell had not been much liked; he had been a bully and a cheat. But nothing he'd done deserved such mutilation. The man had been ripped open: his eyes put out, his genitals torn off. Nayler, the only possible antagonist, had then contrived to open up his own belly. He was now in an Intensive Care Unit; the prognosis was not hopeful.

It was easy, with such a buzz of outrage going about the Wing, for Cleve to spend the day all but unnoticed. He too had a story to tell: but who would believe it? He barely believed it himself. In fact on and off through the day – when the images came back to him afresh – he asked himself if he were entirely sane. But then sanity was a movable feast wasn't it?; one man's madness might be another's politics. All he knew for certain was that he had seen Billy Tait transform. He clung to that certainty with a tenaciousness born of near-despair. If he ceased to believe the evidence of his own eyes, he had no defence left to hold the darkness at bay.

After ablutions and breakfast, the entire Wing was confined to cells; workshops, recreation – any activity which required movement around the landings – was cancelled while Lowell's cell was photographed and examined, then swabbed out. Following breakfast, Billy slept through the morning; a state more akin to coma than sleep, such was its profundity. When he awoke for lunch he was brighter and more out-going than Cleve had seen him in weeks. There was no sign beneath the vacuous chatter that he knew what had happened the previous night. In the afternoon Cleve faced him with the truth.

'You killed Lowell,' he said. There was no point in trying to pretend ignorance any longer; if the boy didn't remember now what he'd done, he would surely recall in time. And with that memory, how long before he remembered that Cleve had watched him transform? Better to confess it now. 'I saw you,' Cleve said, 'I saw you change . . .'

Billy didn't seem much disturbed by these revelations.

'Yes,' he said. 'I killed Lowell. Do you blame me?' The question, begging a hundred others, was put lightly, as a matter of mild interest, no more.

'What happened to you?' Cleve said. 'I saw you – *there* – ' he pointed, appalled at the memory, at the lower bunk, 'you weren't human.'

'I didn't mean you to see,' the boy replied. 'I gave you the pills, didn't I? You shouldn't have spied.'

'And the night before . . .' Cleve said, 'I was awake then too.'

The boy blinked like a bemused bird, head slightly cocked. 'You really have been stupid,' he said. 'So stupid.'

'Whether I like it or not, I'm not out of this,' Cleve said, 'I have dreams.'

'Oh, yes.' Now a frown marred the porcelain brow. 'Yes. You dream the city, don't you?'

'What is that place, Billy?'

'I read somewhere: *the dead have highways*. You ever hear that? Well . . . they have cities too.'

'The dead? You mean it's some kind of ghost town?'

'I never wanted you to become involved. You've been better to me than most here. But I *told* you, I came to Pentonville to do business.'

'With Tait.'

'That's right.'

Cleve wanted to laugh; what he was being told – *a city of the dead?*

– only heaped nonsense upon nonsense. And yet his exasperated reason had not sniffed out one explanation more plausible.

'My grandfather killed his children,' Billy said, 'because he didn't want to pass his condition on to another generation. He learned late, you see. He didn't realize, until he had a wife and children, that he wasn't like most men. He was special. But he didn't *want* the skills he'd been given; and he didn't want his children to survive with that same power in their blood. He would have killed himself, and finished the job, but that my mother escaped. Before he could find her and kill her too, he was arrested.'

'And hanged. And buried.'

'Hanged and buried; but not *lost*. Nobody's lost, Cleve. Not ever.'

'You came here to find him.'

'More than find him: make him *help* me. I knew from the age of ten what I was capable of. Not quite consciously; but I had an inkling. And I was afraid. Of course I was afraid: it was a terrible mystery.'

'This mutation: you've always done it?'

'No. Only *known* I was capable of it. I came here to make my grandfather tutor me, make him *show me how*. Even now . . .' he looked down at his wasted arms, '. . . with him teaching me . . . the pain is almost unbearable.'

'Why do it then?'

The boy looked at Cleve incredulously. 'To be *not* myself; to be smoke and shadow. To be something terrible.' He seemed genuinely puzzled by Cleve's unwillingness. 'Wouldn't you do the same?'

Cleve shook his head.

'What you became last night was repellent.'

Billy nodded. 'That's what my grandfather thought. At his trial he called himself an abomination. Not that they knew what he was talking about of course, but that's what he said. He stood up and said: "I am Satan's excrement – ".' Billy smiled at the thought. ' " – for God's sake hang me and burn me." He's changed his mind since then. The century's getting old and stale; it needs new tribes.' He looked at Cleve intently. 'Don't be afraid,' he said. 'I won't hurt you, unless you try to tell tales. You won't do that, will you?'

'What could I say that would sound like sanity?' Cleve returned mildly. 'No; I won't tell tales.'

'Good. And in a little while I'll be gone; and you'll be gone. And you can forget.'

'I doubt it.'

'Even the dreams will stop, when I'm not here. You only share them because you have some mild talents as a sensitive. Trust me. There's nothing to be afraid of.'

131

'The city – '

'What about it?'

'Where are its citizens? I never see anybody. No; that's not quite true. I saw one. A man with a knife . . . going out into the desert . . .'

'I can't help you. I go as a visitor myself. All I know is what my grandfather tells me: that it's a city occupied by dead souls. Whatever you've seen there, forget about it. You don't belong there. You're not dead yet.'

Was it wise to believe always what the dead told you?; were they purged of all deceit by the act of dying, and delivered into their new state like saints? Cleve could not believe such naiveté. More likely they took their talents with them, good and bad, and used them as best they could. There would be shoemakers in paradise, wouldn't there?; foolish to think they'd forgotten how to sew leather.

So perhaps Edgar Tait *lied* about the city. There was more to that place than Billy knew. What about the voices on the wind?, the man with the knife, dropping it amongst a litter of weapons before moving off to God alone knew where? What ritual was that?

Now – with the fear used up, and no untainted reality left to cling to, Cleve saw no reason not to go to the city willingly. What could be there, in those dusty streets, that was worse than what he had seen in the bunk below him, or what had happened to Lowell and Nayler? Beside such atrocities the city was a haven. There was a serenity in its empty thoroughfares and plazas; a sense Cleve had there that all action was over, all rage and distress finished with; that these interiors (with the bath running and the cup brimming) had seen the *worst*, and were now content to sit out the millenium. When that night brought sleep, and the city opened up in front of him, he went into it not as a frightened man astray in hostile territory, but as a visitor content to relax a while in a place he knew too well to become lost in, but not well enough to be weary of.

As if in response to this new-found ease, the city opened itself to him. Wandering the streets, feet bloody as ever, he found the doors open wide, the curtains at the windows drawn back. He did not disparage the invitation they offered, but went to look more closely at the houses and tenements. On closer inspection he found them not the paradigms of domestic calm he'd first taken them for. In each he discovered some sign of violence recently done. In one, perhaps no more than an overturned chair, or a mark on the floor where a heel had slid in a spot of blood; in others, the manifestations were more obvious. A hammer, its claw clotted, had been left on a table laid with newspapers. There was a room with its floorboards ripped up, and black plastic parcels, suspiciously slick, laid beside the hole. In one, a mirror had been shattered; in another, a set of false teeth left beside a hearth in which a fire flared and spat.

They were murder scenes, all of them. The victims had gone – to other cities, perhaps, full of slaughtered children and murdered friends – leaving these tableaux fixed forever in the breathless moments that followed the crime. Cleve walked down the streets, the perfect voyeur, and peered into scene after scene, reconstructing in his mind's eye the hours that had preceded the studied stillness of each room. Here a child had died: its cot was overturned; here someone had been murdered in their bed, the pillow soaked in blood, the axe on the carpet. Was this damnation then?; the killers obliged to wait out some portion of eternity (all of it, perhaps) in the room they'd murdered in?

Of the malefactors themselves he saw nothing, though logic implied that they must be close by. Was it that they had the power of invisibility to keep themselves from the prying eyes of touring dreamers like himself?; or did a time in this nowhere transform them, so that they were no longer flesh and blood, but became part of their cell: a chair, a china doll?

Then he remembered the man at the perimeter, who'd come in his fine suit, bloody-handed, and walked out into the desert. *He* had not been invisible.

'Where are you?' he said, standing on the threshold of a mean room, with an open oven, and utensils in the sink, water running on them. 'Show yourself.'

A movement caught his eye and he glanced across to the door. There was a man standing there. He had been there all along, Cleve realized, but so still, and so perfectly a part of this room, that he had not been visible until he moved his eyes and looked Cleve's way. He felt a twinge of unease, thinking that each room he had peered into had, most likely, contained one or more killers, each similarly camouflaged by statis. The man, knowing he'd been seen, stepped out of hiding. He was in late middle-age, and had cut himself that morning as he shaved.

'Who are you?' he said. 'I've seen you before. Walking by.'

He spoke softly and sadly; an unlikely killer, Cleve thought.

'Just a visitor,' he told the man.

'There are no visitors, here,' he replied, 'only prospective citizens.'

Cleve frowned, trying to work out what the man meant. But his dream-mind was sluggish, and before he could solve the riddle of the man's words there were others.

'Do I know you?' the man asked. 'I find I forget more and more. That's no use, is it? If I forget I'll never leave, will I?'

'Leave?' Cleve repeated.

133

'Make an exchange,' the man said, re-aligning his toupé.

'And go where?'

'Back. Do it over.'

Now he approached Cleve across the room. He stretched out his hands, palms up; they were blistered.

'You can help me,' he said, 'I can make a deal with the best of them.'

'I don't understand you.'

The man clearly thought he was bluffing. His upper lip, which boasted a dyed black moustache, curled. 'Yes you do,' he said. 'You understand perfectly. You just want to sell yourself, the way everybody does. Highest bidder, is it? What are you, an assassin?'

Cleve shook his head. 'I'm just dreaming,' he replied.

The man's fit of pique subsided. 'Be a friend,' he said. 'I've got no influence; not like some. Some of them, you know, they come here and they're out again in a matter of hours. They're professionals. They make arrangements. But me? With me it was a crime of passion. I didn't come prepared. I'll stay here 'til I can make a deal. Please be a friend.'

'I can't help you,' Cleve said, not even certain of what the man was requesting.

The killer nodded. 'Of course not,' he said, 'I didn't expect . . .'

He turned from Cleve and moved to the oven. Heat flared up from it and made a mirage of the hob. Casually, he put one of his blistered palms on the door and closed it; almost as soon as he had done so it creaked open again. 'Do you know just how appetising it is; the smell of cooking flesh?' he said, as he returned to the oven door and attempted to close it a second time. 'Can anybody blame me? Really?'

Cleve left him to his ramblings; if there was sense there it was probably not worth his labouring over. The talk of exchanges and of escape from the city: it defied Cleve's comprehension.

He wandered on, tired now of peering into the houses. He'd seen all he wanted to see. Surely morning was close, and the bell would ring on the landing. Perhaps he should even wake himself, he thought, and be done with this tour for the night.

As the thought occurred, he saw the girl. She was no more than six or seven years old, and she was standing at the next intersection. This was no killer, surely. He started towards her. She, either out of shyness or some less benign motive, turned to her right and ran off. Cleve followed. By the time he had reached the intersection she was already a long way down the next street; again he gave chase. As dreams would have such pursuits, the laws of physics did not pertain equally to pursuer and pursued. The girl seemed to move easily, while Cleve struggled against air as thick as treacle. He did not give

134

up, however, but pressed on wherever the girl led. He was soon a good distance from any location he recognized in a warren of yards and alleyways – all, he supposed, scenes of blood-letting. Unlike the main thoroughfares, this ghetto contained few entire spaces, only snatches of geography: a grass verge, more red than green; a piece of scaffolding, with a noose depending from it; a pile of earth. And now, simply, a wall.

The girl had led him into a cul-de-sac; she herself had disappeared however, leaving him facing a plain brick wall, much weathered, with a narrow window in it. He approached: this was clearly what he'd been led here to see. He peered through the reinforced glass, dirtied on his side by an accumulation of bird-droppings, and found himself staring into one of the cells at Pentonville. His stomach flipped over. What kind of game was this; led out of a cell and into this dream-city, only to be led back into prison? But a few seconds of study told him that it was not *his* cell. It was Lowell and Nayler's. Theirs were the pictures sellotaped to the grey brick, theirs the blood spread over floor and wall and bunk and door. This was another murder-scene.

'My God Almighty,' he murmured. 'Billy . . .'

He turned away from the wall. In the sand at his feet lizards were mating; the wind that found its way into this backwater brought butterflies. As he watched them dance, the bell rang in B Wing, and it was morning.

It was a trap. Its mechanism was by no means clear to Cleve – but he had no doubt of its purpose. Billy would go to the city; soon. The cell in which he had committed murder already awaited him, and of all the wretched places Cleve had seen in that assemblage of charnel-houses surely the tiny, blood-drenched cell was the worst.

The boy could not know what was planned for him; his grandfather had lied about the city by exclusion, failing to tell Billy what special qualifications were required to exist there. And why? Cleve returned to the oblique conversation he'd had with the man in the kitchen. That talk of exchanges, of deal-making, of *going back*. Edgar Tait had regretted his sins, hadn't he?; he'd decided, as the years passed, that he was *not* the Devil's excrement, that to be returned into the world would not be so bad an idea. Billy was somehow an instrument in that return.

'My grandfather doesn't like you,' the boy said, when they were locked up again after lunch. For the second consecutive day all recreation and workshop activities had been cancelled, while a cell-by-cell enquiry was undertaken regarding Lowell, and – as of the early hours of that day – Nayler's deaths.

'Does he not?' Cleve said. 'And why?'

'Says you're too inquisitive. In the city.'

Cleve was sitting on the top bunk; Billy on the chair against the opposite wall. The boy's eyes were bloodshot; a small, but constant, tremor had taken over his body.

'You're going to die,' Cleve said. What other way to state that fact was there, but baldly? 'I saw . . . in the city . . .'

Billy shook his head. 'Sometimes you talk like a crazyman. My grandfather says I shouldn't trust you.'

'He's afraid of me, that's why.'

Billy laughed derisively. It was an ugly sound, learned, Cleve guessed, from Grandfather Tait. 'He's afraid of no-one,' Billy retorted.

' – afraid of what I'll see. Of what I'll tell you.'

'No,' said the boy, with absolute conviction.

'He told you to kill Lowell, didn't he?'

Billy's head jerked up. 'Why'd you say that?'

'You never wanted to murder him. Maybe scare them both a bit; but not *kill* them. It was your loving grandfather's idea.'

'Nobody tells me what to do,' Billy replied; his gaze was icy. 'Nobody.'

'All right,' Cleve conceded, 'maybe he *persuaded* you, eh?; told you it was a matter of family pride. Something like that?' The observation clearly touched a nerve; the tremors had increased.

'So? What if he did?'

'I've seen where you're going to go, Billy. A place just waiting for you . . .' The boy stared at Cleve, but didn't make to interrupt. 'Only murderers occupy the city, Billy. That's why your grandfather's there. And if he can find a replacement – if he can reach out and make more murder – he can go free.'

Billy stood up, face like a fury. All trace of derision had gone. 'What do you mean: *free*?'

'Back to the world. *Back here*.'

'You're lying – '

'Ask him.'

'He wouldn't cheat me. His blood's my blood.'

'You think he cares? After fifty years in that place, waiting for a chance to be out and away. You think he gives a *damn* how he does it?'

'I'll tell him how you lie . . .' Billy said. The anger was not entirely directed at Cleve; there was an undercurrent of doubt there, which Billy was trying to suppress. 'You're dead,' he said, 'when he finds

136

out how you're trying to poison me against him. You'll see him, then. Oh yes. You'll see him. And you'll wish to Christ you hadn't.'

There seemed to be no way out. Even if Cleve could convince the authorities to move him before night fell – (a slim chance indeed; he would have to reverse all that he had claimed about the boy – tell them Billy was dangerously insane, or something similar. Certainly not the truth.) – even if he were to have himself transferred to another cell, there was no promise of safety in such a manoeuvre. The boy had said he was smoke and shadow. Neither door nor bars could keep such insinuations at bay; the fate of Lowell and Nayler was proof positive of that. Nor was Billy alone. There was Edgar St Clair Tait to be accounted for; and what powers might he possess? Yet to stay in the same cell with the boy tonight would amount to self-slaughter, wouldn't it? He would be delivering himself into the hands of the beasts.

When they left their cells for the evening meal, Cleve looked around for Devlin, located him, and asked for the opportunity of a short interview, which was granted. After the meal, Cleve reported to the officer.

'You asked me to keep an eye on Billy Tait, sir.'

'What about him?'

Cleve had thought hard about what he might tell Devlin that would bring an immediate transfer: nothing had come to mind. He stumbled, hoping for inspiration, but was empty-mouthed.

'I . . . I . . . want to put in a request for a cell transfer.'

'Why?'

'The boy's unbalanced,' Cleve replied. 'I'm afraid he's going to do me harm. Have another of his fits – '

'You could lay him flat with one hand tied behind your back; he's worn to the bone.' At this point, had he been talking to Mayflower, Cleve might have been able to make a direct appeal to the man. With Devlin such tactics would be doomed from the beginning.

'I don't know why you're complaining. He's been as good as gold,' said Devlin, savouring the parody of fond father. 'Quiet; always polite. He's no danger to you or anyone.'

'You don't know him – '

'What are you trying to pull here?'

'Put me in a Rule 43 cell, sir. *Anywhere*, I don't mind. Just get me out of his way. *Please.*'

Devlin didn't reply, but stared at Cleve, mystified. At last, he said, 'You *are* scared of him.'

'Yes.'

'What's wrong with you? You've shared cells with hard men and never turned a hair.'

'He's different,' Cleve replied; there was little else he could say, except: 'He's insane. I tell you he's insane.'

'All the world's crazy, save thee and me, Smith. Hadn't you heard?' Devlin laughed. 'Go back to your cell and stop belly-aching. You don't want a ghost train ride, now do you?'

When Cleve returned to the cell, Billy was writing a letter. Sitting on his bunk, poring over the paper, he looked utterly vulnerable. What Devlin had said was true: the boy *was* worn to the bone. It was difficult to believe, looking at the ladder of his vertebrae, visible through his T-shirt, that this frail form could survive the throes of transformation. But then, maybe it would not. Maybe the rigours of change would tear him apart with time. But not soon enough.

'Billy . . .'

The boy didn't take his eyes from his letter.

'. . . what I said, about the city . . .'

He stopped writing –

'. . . maybe I *was* imagining it all. Just dreaming . . .'

– and started again.

'. . . I only told you because I was afraid for you. That was all. I want us to be friends . . .'

Billy looked up.

'It's not in my hands,' he said, very simply. 'Not now. It's up to Grandfather. He may be merciful; he may not.'

'Why do you have to tell him?'

'He knows what's in me. He and I . . . we're like one. That's how I know he wouldn't cheat me.'

Soon it would be night; the lights would go out along the wing, the shadows would come.

'So I just have to wait, do I?0' Cleve said.

Billy nodded. 'I'll call him, and then we'll see.'

Call him?, Cleve thought. Did the old man need summoning from his resting place every night? Was that what he had seen Billy doing, standing in the middle of the cell, eyes closed and face up to the window? If so, perhaps the boy could be *prevented* from putting in his call to the dead.

As the evening deepened Cleve lay on his bunk and thought his options through. Was it better to wait here, and see what judgement came from Tait, or attempt to take control of the situation and block the old man's arrival? If he did so, there would be no going back; no room for pleas or apologies: his aggression would undoubtedly breed aggression. If he failed to prevent the boy from calling Tait, it would be the end.

The lights went out. In cells up and down the five landings of B Wing men would be turning their faces to their pillows. Some, perhaps, would lie awake planning their careers when this minor hiccup in their professional lives was over; others would be in the arms of invisible mistresses. Cleve listened to the sounds of the cell: the rattling progress of water in the pipes, the shallow breathing from the bunk below. Sometimes it seemed that he had lived a second lifetime on this stale pillow, marooned in darkness.

The breathing from below soon became practically inaudible; nor was there sound of movement. Perhaps Billy was waiting for Cleve to fall asleep before he made any move. If so, the boy would wait in vain. He would not close his eyes and leave them to slaughter him in his sleep. He wasn't a pig, to be taken uncomplaining to the knife.

Moving as cautiously as possible, so as to arouse no suspicion, Cleve unbuckled his belt and pulled it through the loops of his trousers. He might make a more adequate binding by tearing up his sheet and pillowcase, but he could not do so without arousing Billy's attention. Now he waited, belt in hand, and pretended sleep.

Tonight he was grateful that the noise in the Wing kept stirring him from dozing, because it was fully two hours before Billy moved out of his bunk, two hours in which – despite his fear of what would happen should he sleep – Cleve's eyelids betrayed him on three or four occasions. But others on the landings were tearful tonight; the deaths of Lovell and Nayler had made even the toughest cons jittery. Shouts – and countercalls from those woken – punctuated the hours. Despite the fatigue in his limbs, sleep did not master him.

When Billy finally go up from the lower bunk it was well past twelve, and the landing was all but quiet. Cleve could hear the boy's breath; it was no longer even, but had a catch in it. He watched, eyes like slits, as Billy crossed the cell to his familiar place in front of the window. There was no doubt that he was about to call up the old man.

As Billy closed his eyes, Cleve sat up, threw off his blanket and slipped down from the bunk. The boy was slow to respond. Before he quite comprehended what was happening, Cleve had crossed the cell, and thrust him back against the wall, hand clamped over Billy's mouth.

'No, you don't,' he hissed, 'I'm not going to go like Lowell.' Billy struggled, but Cleve was easily his physical superior.

'He's not going to come tonight,' Cleve said, staring into the boy's wide eyes, 'because you're not going to call him.'

Billy fought more violently to be free, biting hard against his captor's palm. Cleve instinctively removed his hand and in two strides the boy was at the window, reaching up. In his throat, a strange half-song; on his face, sudden and inexplicable tears. Cleve dragged him away.

'Shut your noise up!' he snapped. But the boy continued to make the sound. Cleve hit him, open-handed but hard, across the face. '*Shut up!*' he said. Still the boy refused to cease his singing; now the music had taken on another rhythm. Again, Cleve hit him; and again. But the assault failed to silence him. There was a whisper of change in the air of the cell; a shifting in its chiaroscuro. The shadows were moving.

Panic took Cleve. Without warning he made a fist and punched the boy hard in the stomach. As Billy doubled up an upper-cut caught his jaw. It drove his head back against the wall, his skull connecting with the brick. Billy's legs gave, and he collapsed. A featherweight, Cleve had once thought, and it was true. Two good punches and the boy was laid out cold.

Cleve glanced round the cell. The movement in the shadows had been arrested; they trembled though, like greyhounds awaiting release. Heart hammering, he carried Billy back to his bunk, and laid him down. There was no sign of consciousness returning; the boy lay limply on the mattress while Cleve tore up his sheet, and gagged him, thrusting a ball of fabric into the boy's mouth to prevent him making a sound behind his gag. He then preceded to tie Billy to the bunk, using both his own belt and the boy's, supplemented with further makeshift bindings of torn sheets. It took several minutes to finish the job. As Cleve was lashing the boy's legs together, he began to stir. His eyes flickered open, full of puzzlement. Then, realizing his situation, he began to thrash his head from side to side; there was little else he could do to signal his protest.

'No, Billy,' Cleve murmured to him, throwing a blanket across his bound body to keep the fact from any officer who might look in through the spy-hole before morning, 'Tonight, you don't bring him. Everything I said was true, boy. He wants out; and he's using you to escape.' Cleve took hold of Billy's head, fingers pressed against his checks. 'He's not your friend. *I am*. Always have been.' Billy tried to shake his head from Cleve's grip, but couldn't. 'Don't waste your energy,' Cleve advised, 'it's going to be a long night.'

He left the boy on the bunk, crossed the cell to the wall, and slid down it to sit on his haunches and watch. He would stay awake until dawn, and then, when there was some light to think by, he'd work out his next move. For now, he was content that his crude tactics had worked.

The boy had stopped trying to fight; he had clearly realiszed the bonds were too expertly tied to be loosened. A kind of calm descended on the cell: Cleve sitting in the patch of light that fell through the window, the boy lying in the gloom of the lower bunk, breathing steadily through his nostrils. Cleve glanced at his watch. It was twelve-fifty-four. When was morning? He didn't know. Five hours, at least. He put his head back, and stared at the light.

It mesmerised him. The minutes ticked by slowly but steadily, and the light did not change. Sometimes an officer would advance along the landing, and Billy, hearing the footsteps, would begin his struggling afresh. But nobody looked into the cell. The two prisoners were left to their thoughts; Cleve to wonder if there would ever come a time when he could be free of the shadow behind him, Billy to think whatever thoughts came to bound monsters. And still the dead-of-night minutes went, minutes that crept across the mind like dutiful schoolchildren, one upon the heels of the next, and after sixty had passed that sum was called an hour. And dawn was closer by that span, wasn't it? But then so was death, and so, presumably, the end of the world: that glorious Last Trump of which The Bishop had spoken so fondly, when the dead men under the lawn outside would rise as fresh as yesterday's bread and go out to meet their Maker. And sitting there against the wall, listening to Billy's inhalations and exhalations, and watching the light in the glass and through the glass, Cleve knew without doubt that even if he escaped this trap, it was only a temporary respite; that this long night, its minutes, its hours, were a foretaste of a longer vigil. He almost despaired then; felt his soul sink into a hole from which there seemed to be no hope of retrieval. *Here* was the real world, he wept. Not joy, not light, not looking forward; only this waiting in ignorance, without hope, even of fear, for fear came only to those with dreams to lose. The hole was deep and dim. He peered up out of it at the light through the window, and his thoughts became one wretched round. He forgot the bunk and the boy lying there. He forgot the numbness that had overtaken his legs. He might, given time, have forgotten even the simple act of taking breath, but for the smell of urine that pricked him from his fugue.

He looked towards the bunk. The boy was voiding his bladder; but that act was simply a symptom of something else altogether. Beneath the blanket, Billy's body was moving in a dozen ways that his bonds should have prevented. It took Cleve a few moments to shake off lethargy, and seconds more to realize what was happening. Billy was changing.

Cleve tried to stand upright, but his lower limbs were dead from sitting so still for so long. He almost fell forward across the cell, and only prevented himself by throwing out an arm to grasp the chair.

His eyes were glued to the gloom of the lower bunk. The movements were increasing in scale and complexity. The blanket was pitched off. Beneath it Billy's body was already beyond recognition; the same terrible procedure as he had seen before, but in reverse. Matter gathering in buzzing clouds about the body, and congealing into atrocious forms. Limbs and organs summoned from the ineffable, teeth shaping themselves like needles and plunging into place in a head grown large and swelling still. He begged for Billy to stop, but with every drawn breath there was less of humanity to appeal to. The strength the boy had lacked was granted to the beast; it had already broken almost all its constraints, and now, as Cleve watched, it struggled free of the last, and rolled off the bunk onto the floor of the cell.

Cleve backed off towards the door, his eyes scanning Billy's mutated form. He remembered his mother's horror at earwigs and saw something of that insect in this anatomy: the way it bent its shiny back upon itself, exposing the paddling intracies that lined its abdomen. Elsewhere, no analogy offered a hold on the sight. Its head was rife with tongues, that licked its eyes clean in place of lids, and ran back and forth across its teeth, wetting and re-wetting them constantly; from seeping holes along its flanks came a sewer stench. Yet even now there was a residue of something human trapped in this foulness, its rumour only serving to heighten the filth of the whole. Seeing its hooks and its spines Cleve remembered Lowell's rising scream; and felt his own throat pulse, ready to loose a sound its equal should the beast turn on him.

But Billy had other intentions. He moved – limbs in horrible array – to the window, and clambered up, pressing his head against the glass like a leech. The music he made was not like his previous song – but Cleve had no doubt it was the same summoning. He turned to the door, and began to beat upon it, hoping that Billy would be too distracted with his call to turn on him before assistance came.

'Quickly! For Christ's sake! Quickly!' He yelled as loudly exhaustion would allow, and glanced over his shoulder once to see if Billy was coming for him. He was not; he was still clamped to the window, though his call had all but faltered. Its purpose was achieved. Darkness was tyrant in the cell.

Panicking, Cleve turned back to the door and renewed his tattoo. There was somebody running along the landing now; he could hear shouts and imprecations from other cells. 'Jesus Christ, help me!' he shouted. He could feel a chill at his back. He didn't need to turn to know what was happening behind him. The shadow growing, the wall dissolving so that the city and its occupant could come through. Tait was here. He could feel the man's presence, vast and dark. Tait

142

the child-killer, Tait the shadow-thing, Tait the transformer. Cleve beat on the door 'til his hands bled. The feet seemed a continent away. Were they coming? Were they coming?

The chill behind him became a blast. He saw his shadow thrown up on to the door by flickering blue light; smelt sand and blood.

And then, the voice. Not the boy, but that of his grandfather, of Edgar St Clair Tait. This was the man who had pronounced himself the Devil's excrement, and hearing that abhorrent voice Cleve believed both in Hell and its master, believed himself already in the bowels of Satan, a witness to its wonders.

'You are too inquisitive.' Edgar said, 'It's time you went to bed.'

Cleve didn't want to turn. The last thought in his head was that he *should* turn and look at the speaker. But he was no longer subject to his own will; Tait had fingers in his head and was dabbling there. He turned, and looked.

The hanged man was in the cell. He was not that beast Cleve had half-seen, that face of pulp and eggs. He was here in the flesh; dressed for another age, and not without charm. His face was well-made; his brow wide, his eyes unflinching. He still wore his wedding-ring on the hand that stroked Billy's bowed head like that of a pet dog.

'Time to die, Mr Smith,' he said.

On the landing outside, Cleve heard Devlin shouting. He had no breath left to answer with. But he heard keys in the lock or was that some illusion his mind had made to placate his panic?

The tiny cell was full of wind. It threw over the chair and table, and lifted the sheets into the air like childhood ghosts. And now it took Tait, and the boy with him; sucked them back into the receding perspectives of the city.

'Come on now – ' Tait demanded, his face corrupting, 'we need you, body and soul. Come with us, Mr Smith. We won't be denied.'

'No!' Cleve yelled back at his tormentor. The suction was plucking at his fingers, at his eye-balls. 'I won't – '

Behind him, the door was rattling.

'I won't, you hear!'

Suddenly, the door was thrust open, and threw him forward into the vortex of fog and dust that was sucking Tait and his grandchild away. He almost went with them, but that a hand grabbed at his shirt, and dragged him back from the brink, even as consciousness gave itself up.

Somewhere, far away, Devlin began to laugh like a hyena. He's lost his mind, Cleve decided; and the image his darkening thoughts

143

evoked was one of the contents of Devlin's brain escaping through his mouth as a flock of flying dogs.

He awoke in dreams; and in the city. Woke remembering his last conscious moments: Devlin's hysteria, the hand arresting his fall as the two figures were sucked away in front of him. He had followed them, it seemed, unable to prevent his comatose mind from retreading the familiar route to the murderers' metropolis. But Tait had not won yet. He was still only *dreaming* his presence here. His corporeal self was still in Pentonville; his dislocation from it informed his every step.

He listened to the wind. It was eloquent as ever: the voices coming and going with each gritty gust, but never, even when the wind died to a whisper, disappearing entirely. As he listened, he heard a shout. In this mute city the sound was a shock; it startled rats from their nests and birds up from some secluded plaza.

Curious, he pursued the sound, whose echoes were almost traced on the air. As he hurried down the empty streets he heard further raised voices, and now men and women were appearing at the doors and windows of their cells. So many faces, and nothing in common between one and the next to confirm the hopes of a physiognomist. Murder had as many faces as it had occurrences. The only common quality was one of wretchedness, of minds despairing after an age at the site of their crime. He glanced at them as he went, sufficiently distracted by their looks not to notice where the shout was leading him until he found himself once more in the ghetto to which he had been led by the child.

Now he rounded a corner and at the end of the cul-de-sac he'd seen from his previous visit here (the wall, the window, the bloody chamber beyond) he saw Billy, writhing in the sand at Tait's feet. The boy was half himself and half that beast he had become in front of Cleve's eyes. The better part was convulsing in its attempt to climb free of the other, but without success. In one moment the boy's body would surface, white and frail, only to be subsumed the next into the flux of transformation. Was that an arm forming, and being snatched away again before it could gain fingers?; was that a face pressed from the house of tongues that was the beast's head? The sight defied analysis. As soon as Cleve fixed upon some recognizable feature it was drowned again.

Edgar Tait looked up from the struggle in front of him, and bared his teeth at Cleve. It was a display a shark might have envied.

'He doubted me, Mr Smith . . .' the monster said, '. . . and came looking for his cell.'

144

A mouth appeared from the patchwork on the sand and gave out a sharp cry, full of pain and terror.

'Now he wants to be away from me,' Tait said, 'You sewed the doubt. He must suffer the consequences.' He pointed a trembling finger at Cleve, and in the act of pointing the limb transformed, flesh becoming bruised leather. 'You came where you were not wanted, and look at the agonies you've brought.'

Tait kicked the thing at his feet. It rolled over on to its back, vomiting.

'He needs me,' Tait said. 'Don't you have the sense to see that? Without me, he's lost.'

Cleve didn't reply to the hanged man, but instead addressed the beast on the sand.

'Billy?' he said, calling the boy out of the flux.

'*Lost*,' Tait said.

'Billy . . .' Cleve repeated. 'Listen to me . . .'

'He won't go back now,' Tait said. 'You're just dreaming this. But he's *here*, in the flesh.'

'*Billy*,' Cleve persevered, 'Do you hear me. It's me; it's Cleve.'

The boy seemed to pause in its gyrations for an instant, as if hearing the appeal. Cleve said Billy's name again, and again.

It was one of the first skills the human child learned: to call itself something. If anything could reach the boy it was surely his own name.

'Billy . . . Billy . . .' At the repeated word, the body rolled itself over.

Tait seemed to have become uneasy. The confidence he'd displayed was now silenced. His body was darkening, the head becoming bulbous. Cleve tried to keep his eyes off the subtle distortions in Edgar's anatomy and concentrate on winning back Billy. The repetition of the name was paying dividends; the beast was being subdued. Moment by moment there was more of the boy emerging. He looked pitiful; skin-and-bones on the black sand. But his face was almost reconstructed now, and his eyes were on Cleve.

'Billy . . . ?'

He nodded. His hair was plastered to his forehead with sweat; his limbs were in spasm.

'You know where you are? *Who* you are?'

At first it seemed as though comprehension escaped the boy. And then – by degrees – recognition formed in his eyes, and with it came a terror of the man standing over him.

Cleve glanced up at Tait. In the few seconds since he had last looked all but a few human characteristics had been erased from his head and upper torso, revealing corruptions more profound than

145

those of his grandchild. Billy gazed up over his shoulder like a whipped dog.

'*You belong to me*,' Tait pronounced, through features barely capable of speech. Billy saw the limbs descending to snatch at him, and rose from his prone position to escape them, but he was too tardy. Cleve saw the spiked hook of Tait's limb wrap itself around Billy's neck, and draw him close. Blood leapt from the slit windpipe, and with it the whine of escaping air.

Cleve yelled.

'With me,' Tait said, the words deteriorating into gibberish.

Suddenly the narrow cul-de-sac was filling up with brightness, and the boy and Tait and the city were being bleached out. Cleve tried to hold on to them, but they were slipping from him; and in their place another concrete reality: a light, a face (faces) and a voice calling him out of one absurdity and into another.

The doctor's hand was on his face. It felt clammy.

'What on earth were you dreaming about?' he asked, the perfect idiot.

Billy had gone.

Of all the mysteries that the Governor – and Devlin and the other officers who had stepped into cell B. 3. 20 that night – had to face, the total disappearance of William Tait from an unbreached cell was the most perplexing. Of the vision that had set Devlin giggling like a loon nothing was said; easier to believe in some collective delusion than that they'd seen some objective reality. When Cleve attempted to articulate the events of that night, and of the many nights previous to that, his monologue, interrupted often by his tears and silences, was met with feigned understanding and sideways glances. He told the story over several times, however, despite their condescension, and they, looking no doubt for a clue amongst his lunatic fables as to the reality of Billy Tait's Houdini act, attended every word. When they found nothing amongst his tales to advance their investigations, they began to lose their tempers with him. Consolation was replaced with threats. They demanded, voices louder each time they asked the question, where Billy had gone. Cleve answered the only way he knew how. 'To the city,' he told them, 'he's a murderer, you see.'

'And his body?' the Governor said. 'Where do you suppose his *body* is?'

Cleve didn't know, and said so. It wasn't until much later, four full days later in fact, that he was standing by the window watching the gardening detail bearing this spring's plantings cross between wings, that he remembered the lawn.

He found Mayflower, who had been returned to B Wing in lieu of

Devlin, and told the officer the thought that had come to him. 'He's in the grave,' he said. 'He's with his grandfather. Smoke and shadow.'

They dug up the coffin by cover of night, an elaborate shield of poles and tarpaulins erected to keep proceedings from prying eyes, and lamps, bright as day but not so warm, trained on the labours of the men volunteered as an exhumation party. Cleve's answer to the riddle of Tait's disappearance had met with almost universal bafflement, but no explanation – however absurd – was being overlooked in a mystery so intractable. Thus they gathered at the unmarked grave to turn earth that looked not to have been disturbed in five decades: the Governor, a selection of Home Office officials; a pathologist and Devlin. One of the doctors, believing that Cleve's morbid delusion would be best countered if he viewed the contents of the coffin, and saw his error with his own eyes, convinced the Governor that Cleve should also be numbered amongst the spectators.

There was little in the confines of Edgar St Clair Tait's coffin that Cleve had not seen before. The corpse of the murderer – returned here (as smoke perhaps?) neither quite beast nor quite human, and preserved, as The Bishop had promised, as undecayed as the day of his execution – shared the coffin with Billy Tait, who lay, naked as a babe, in his grandfather's embrace. Edgar's corrupted limb was still wound around Billy's neck, and the walls of the coffin were dark with congealed blood. But Billy's face was not besmirched. *He looks like a doll,* one of the doctors observed. Cleve wanted to reply that no doll had such tear stains on its cheeks, nor such despair in its eyes, but the thought refused to become words.

Cleve was released from Pentonville three weeks later after special application to the Parole Board, with only two-thirds of his sentence completed. He returned, within half a year, to the only profession that he had ever known. Any hope he might have had of release from his dreams was short-lived. The place was with him still: neither so focussed nor so easily traversed now that Billy – whose mind had opened that door – was gone, but still a potent terror, the lingering presence of which wearied Cleve.

Sometimes the dreams would almost recede completely, only to return again with terrible potency. It took Cleve several months before he began to grasp the pattern of this vacillation. *People* brought the dream to him. If he spent time with somebody who had murderous intentions, the city came back. Nor were such people so rare. As he grew more sensitive to the lethal streak in those around him he found himself scarcely able to walk the street. They were *everywhere*, these embryonic killers; people wearing smart clothes and sunny expressions were striding the pavement and imagining, as they

147

strode, the deaths of their employers and their spouses, of soap-opera stars and incompetent tailors. The world had murder on its mind, and he could no longer bear its thoughts.

Only heroin offered some release from the burden of experience. He had never done much intravenous H, but it rapidly became heaven and earth to him. It was an expensive addiction however, and one which his increasingly truncated circle of professional contacts could scarcely hope to finance. It was a man called Grimm, a fellow addict so desperate to avoid reality he could get high on fermented milk, who suggested that Cleve might want to do some work to earn him a fee the equal of his appetite. It seemed like a wise idea. A meeting was arranged, and a proposal put. The fee for the job was so high it could not be refused by a man so in need of money. The job, of course, was murder.

'There are no visitors here; only prospective citizens'. He had been told that once, though he no longer quite remembered by whom, and he believed in prophecies. If he didn't commit murder now, it would only be a matter of time until he did.

But, though the details of the assassination which he undertook had a terrible familiarity to him, he had not anticipated the collision of circumstances by which he ended fleeing from the scene of his crime barefoot, and running so hard on pavement and tarmac that by the time the police cornered him and shot him down his feet were bloody, and ready at last to tread the streets of the city – just as he had in dreams.

The room he'd killed in was waiting for him, and he lived there, hiding his head from any who appeared in the street outside, for several months. (He assumed time passed here, by the beard he'd grown; though sleep came seldom, and day never.) After a while, however, he braved the cool wind and the butterflies and took himself off to the city perimeters, where the houses petered out and the desert took over. He went, not to see the dunes, but to listen to the voices that came always, rising and falling, like the howls of jackals or children.

He stayed there a long while, and the wind conspired with the desert to bury him. But he was not disappointed with the fruit of his vigil. For one day (or year), he saw a man come to the place and drop a gun in the sand, then wander out into the desert, where, after a while, the makers of the voices came to meet him, loping and wild, dancing on their crutches. They surrounded him, laughing. He went with them, laughing. And though distance and the wind smudged the sight, Cleve was certain he saw the man picked up by one of the

148

celebrants, and taken on to its shoulders as a boy, thence snatched into another's arms as a baby, until, at the limit of his senses, he heard the man bawl as he was delivered back into life. He went away content, knowing at last how sin (and he) had come into the world.

BOOKS OF BLOOD
VOLUME 6

To Dave

CONTENTS

The Life of Death

The newspaper was the first edition of the day, and Elaine devoured it from cover to cover as she sat in the hospital waiting room. An animal thought to be a panther – which had terrorised the neighbourhood of Epping Forest for two months – had been shot and found to be a wild dog. Archaeologists in the Sudan had discovered bone fragments which they opined might lead to a complete re-appraisal of Man's origins. A young woman who had once danced with minor royalty had been found murdered near Clapham; a solo round-the-world yachtsman was missing; recently excited hopes of a cure for the common cold had been dashed. She read the global bulletins and the trivia with equal fervour – anything to keep her mind off the examination ahead – but today's news seemed very like yesterday's; only the names had been changed.

Doctor Sennett informed her that she was healing well, both inside and out, and was quite fit to return to her full responsibilities whenever she felt psychologically resilient enough. She should make another appointment for the first week of the new year, he told her, and come back for a final examination then. She left him washing his hands of her.

The thought of getting straight onto the bus and heading back to her rooms was repugnant after so much time sitting and waiting. She would walk a stop or two along the route, she decided. The exercise would be good for her, and the December day, though far from warm, was bright.

Her plans proved over-ambitious however. After only a few minutes of walking her lower abdomen began to ache, and she started to feel nauseous, so she turned off the main road to seek out a place where she could rest and drink some tea. She should eat too, she knew, though she had never had much appetite, and had less still since the operation. Her wanderings were rewarded. She found a small restaurant which, though it was twelve fifty-five, was not enjoying a roaring lunch-time trade. A small woman with un-ashamedly artificial red hair served her tea and a mushroom omelette. She did her best to eat, but didn't get very far. The waitress was plainly concerned.

1

'Something wrong with the food?' she said, somewhat testily.

'Oh no,' Elaine reassured her. 'It's just me.'

The waitress looked offended nevertheless.

'I'd like some more tea though, if I may?' Elaine said.

She pushed the plate away from her, hoping the waitress would claim it soon. The sight of the meal congealing on the patternless plate was doing nothing for her mood. She hated this unwelcome sensitivity in herself: it was absurd that a plate of uneaten eggs should bring these doldrums on, but she couldn't help herself. She found everywhere little echoes of her own loss. In the death, by a benign November and then the sudden frosts, of the bulbs in her window-sill box; in the thought of the wild dog she'd read of that morning, shot in Epping Forest.

The waitress returned with fresh tea, but failed to take the plate. Elaine called her back, requesting that she do so. Grudgingly, she obliged.

There were no customers left in the place now, other than Elaine, and the waitress busied herself with removing the lunch-time menus from the tables and replacing them with those for the evening. Elaine sat staring out of the window. Veils of blue-grey smoke had crept down the street in recent minutes, solidifying the sunlight.

'They're burning again,' the waitress said. 'Damn smell gets everywhere.'

'What are they burning?'

'Used to be the community centre. They're knocking it down, and building a new one. It's a waste of tax-payer's money.'

The smoke was indeed creeping into the restaurant. Elaine did not find it offensive; it was sweetly redolent of autumn, her favourite season. Intrigued, she finished her tea, paid for her meal, and then elected to wander along and find the source of the smoke. She didn't have far to walk. At the end of the street was a small square; the demolition site dominated it. There was one surprise however. The building that the waitress had described as a community centre was in fact a church; or had been. The lead and slates had already been stripped off the roof, leaving the joists bare to the sky; the windows had been denuded of glass; the turf had gone from the lawn at the side of the building, and two trees had been felled there. It was their pyre which provided the tantalising scent.

She doubted if the building had ever been beautiful, but there was enough of its structure remaining for her to suppose it might

2

have had charm. Its weathered stone was now completely at variance with the brick and concrete that surrounded it, but its besieged situation (the workmen labouring to undo it; the bulldozer on hand, hungry for rubble) gave it a certain glamour.

One or two of the workmen noticed her standing watching them, but none made any move to stop her as she walked across the square to the front porch of the church and peered inside. The interior, stripped of its decorative stonework, of pulpit, pews, font and the rest, was simply a stone room, completely lacking in atmosphere or authority. Somebody, however, had found a source of interest here. At the far end of the church a man stood with his back to Elaine, staring intently at the ground. Hearing footsteps behind him he looked round guiltily.

'Oh,' he said. 'I won't be a moment.'

'It's all right – ' Elaine said. 'I think we're probably both trespassing.'

The man nodded. He was dressed soberly – even drearily – but for his green bow-tie. His features, despite the garb and the grey hairs of a man in middle-age, were curiously unlined, as though neither smile nor frown much ruffled their perfect indifference.

'Sad, isn't it?' he said. 'Seeing a place like this.'

'Did you know the church as it used to be?'

'I came in on occasion,' he said, 'but it was never very popular.'

'What's it called?'

'All Saints. It was built in the late seventeenth century, I believe. Are you fond of churches?'

'Not particularly. It was just that I saw the smoke, and . . .'

'Everybody likes a demolition-scene,' he said.

'Yes,' she replied, 'I suppose that's true.'

'It's like watching a funeral. Better them than us, eh?'

She murmured something in agreement, her mind flitting elsewhere. Back to the hospital. To her pain and her present healing. To her life saved only by losing the capacity for further life. *Better them than us.*

'My name's Kavanagh,' he said, covering the short distance between them, his hand extended.

'How do you do?' she said. 'I'm Elaine Rider.'

'Elaine,' he said. 'Charming.'

'Are you just taking a final look at the place before it comes down?'

'That's right. I've been looking at the inscriptions on the floor stones. Some of them are most eloquent.' He brushed a fragment

3

of timber off one of the tablets with his foot. 'It seems such a loss. I'm sure they'll just smash the stones to smithereens when they start to pull the floor up – '

She looked down at the patchwork of tablets beneath her feet. Not all were marked, and of those that were many simply carried names and dates. There were some inscriptions however. One, to the left of where Kavanagh was standing, carried an all but eroded relief of crossed shin-bones, like drum-sticks, and the abrupt motto: *Redeem the time*.

'I think there must have been a crypt under here at some time,' Kavanagh said.

'Oh. I see. And these are the people who were buried there.'

'Well, I can't think of any other reason for the inscriptions, can you? I was thinking of asking the workmen . . .' he paused in mid-sentence, '. . . you'll probably think this positively morbid of me . . .'

'What?'

'Well, just to preserve one or two of the finer stones from being destroyed.'

'I don't think that's morbid,' she said. 'They're very beautiful.'

He was evidently encouraged by her response. 'Maybe I should speak with them now,' he said. 'Would you excuse me for a moment?'

He left her standing in the nave like a forsaken bride, while he went out to quiz one of the workmen. She wandered down to where the altar had been, reading the names as she went. Who knew or cared about these people's resting places now? Dead two hundred years and more, and gone away not into loving posterity but into oblivion. And suddenly the unarticulated hopes for an after-life she had nursed through her thirty-four years slipped away; she was no longer weighed down by some vague ambition for heaven. One day, perhaps *this* day, she would die, just as these people had died, and it wouldn't matter a jot. There was nothing to come, nothing to aspire to, nothing to dream of. She stood in a patch of smoke-thickened sun, thinking of this, and was almost happy.

Kavanagh returned from his exchanges with the foreman.

'There is indeed a crypt,' he said, 'but it hasn't been emptied yet.'

'Oh.'

They were still underfoot, she thought. Dust and bones.

'Apparently they're having some difficulty getting into it. All

4

the entrances have been sealed up. That's why they're digging around the foundations. To find another way in.'

'Are crypts normally sealed up?'

'Not as thoroughly as this one.'

'Maybe there was no more room,' she said.

Kavanagh took the comment quite seriously. 'Maybe,' he said.

'Will they give you one of the stones?'

He shook his head. 'It's not up to them to say. These are just Council lackeys. Apparently they have a firm of professional excavators to come in and shift the bodies to new burial sites. It all has to be done with due decorum.'

'Much they care,' Elaine said, looking down at the stones again.

'I must agree,' Kavanagh replied. 'It all seems in excess of the facts. But then perhaps we're not God-fearing enough.'

'Probably.'

'Anyhow, they told me to come back in a day or two's time, and ask the removal men.'

She laughed at the thought of the dead moving house; packing up their goods and chattels. Kavanagh was pleased to have made a joke, even if it had been unintentional. Riding on the crest of this success, he said: 'I wonder, may I take you for a drink?'

'I wouldn't be very good company, I'm afraid,' she said. 'I'm really very tired.'

'We could perhaps meet later,' he said.

She looked away from his eager face. He was pleasant enough, in his uneventful way. She liked his green bow-tie – surely a joke at the expense of his own drabness. She liked his seriousness too. But she couldn't face the idea of drinking with him; at least not tonight. She made her apologies, and explained that she'd been ill recently and hadn't recovered her stamina.

'Another night perhaps?' he enquired gently. The lack of aggression in his courtship was persuasive, and she said:

'That would be nice. Thank you.'

Before they parted they exchanged telephone numbers. He seemed charmingly excited by the thought of their meeting again; it made her feel, despite all that had been taken from her, that she still had her sex.

She returned to the flat to find both a parcel from Mitch and a hungry cat on the doorstep. She fed the demanding animal, then made herself some coffee and opened the parcel. In it, cocooned in several layers of tissue paper, she found a silk scarf, chosen with Mitch's uncanny eye for her taste. The note along with it simply said: *It's your colour. I love you. Mitch.* She wanted to pick up the telephone on the spot and talk to him, but somehow the thought of hearing his voice seemed dangerous. Too close to the hurt, perhaps. He would ask her how she felt, and she would reply that she was well, and he would insist: yes, but *really?*, and she would say: I'm empty; they took out half my innards, damn you, and I'll never have your children or anybody else's, so that's the end of that, isn't it? Even thinking about their talking she felt tears threaten, and in a fit of inexplicable rage she wrapped the scarf up in the desiccated paper and buried it at the back of her deepest drawer. Damn him for trying to make things better now, when at the time she'd most needed him all he'd talked of was fatherhood, and how her tumours would deny it him.

It was a clear evening – the sky's cold skin stretched to breaking point. She did not want to draw the curtains in the front room, even though passers-by would stare in, because the deepening blue was too fine to miss. So she sat at the window and watched the dark come. Only when the last change had been wrought did she close off the chill.

She had no appetite, but she made herself some food nevertheless, and sat down to watch television as she ate. The food unfinished, she laid down her tray, and dozed, the programmes filtering through to her intermittently. Some witless comedian whose merest cough sent his audience into paroxysms; a natural history programme on life in the Serengetti; the news. She had read all that she needed to know that morning: the headlines hadn't changed.

One item, however, did pique her curiosity: an interview with the solo yachtsman, Michael Maybury, who had been picked up that day after two weeks adrift in the Pacific. The interview was being beamed from Australia, and the contact was bad; the image of Maybury's bearded and sun-scorched face was constantly threatened with being snowed out. The picture little mattered: the account he gave of his failed voyage was riveting in sound alone, and in particular an event that seemed to distress him afresh even as he told it. He had been becalmed, and as his vessel lacked a motor had been obliged to wait for wind. It had not come. A week had gone by with his hardly moving a kilometre from the same spot of listless ocean; no bird or passing ship broke the monotony. With every hour that passed, his claustrophobia grew, and on the eighth day it reached panic proportions, so he let himself over the side of the yacht and swam away from the vessel, a life-line tied about his

6

middle, in order to escape the same few yards of deck. But once away from the yacht, and treading the still, warm water, he had no desire to go back. Why not untie the knot, he'd thought to himself, and float away.

'What made you change your mind?' the interviewer asked.

Here Maybury frowned. He had clearly reached the crux of his story, but didn't want to finish it. The interviewer repeated the question.

At last, hesitantly, the sailor responded. 'I looked back at the yacht,' he said, 'and I saw somebody on the deck.'

The interviewer, not certain that he'd heard correctly, said: 'Somebody on the deck?'

'That's right,' Maybury replied. 'Somebody was there. I saw a figure quite clearly; moving around.'

'Did you . . . did you recognise this stowaway?' the question came.

Maybury's face closed down, sensing that his story was being treated with mild sarcasm.

'Who was it?' the interviewer pressed.

'I don't know,' Maybury said. 'Death, I suppose.'

The questioner was momentarily lost for words.

'But of course you returned to the boat, eventually.'

'Of course.'

'And there was no sign of anybody?'

Maybury glanced up at the interviewer, and a look of contempt crossed his face.

'I'd survived, hadn't I?' he said.

The interviewer mumbled something about not understanding his point.

'I didn't drown,' Maybury said. 'I could have died then, if I'd wanted to. Slipped off the rope and drowned.'

'But you didn't. And the next day – '

'The next day the wind picked up.'

'It's an extraordinary story,' the interviewer said, content that the stickiest part of the exchange was now safely by-passed. 'You must be looking forward to seeing your family again for Christmas . . .'

Elaine didn't hear the final exchange of pleasantries. Her imagination was tied by a fine rope to the room she was sitting in; her fingers toyed with the knot. If Death could find a boat in the wastes of the Pacific, how much easier it must be to find her. To sit with her, perhaps, as she slept. To watch her as she went about her mourning. She stood up and turned the television off. The flat was

7

suddenly silent. She questioned the hush impatiently, but it held no sign of guests, welcome or unwelcome.

As she listened, she could taste salt-water, Ocean. no doubt.

She had been offered several refuges in which to convalesce when she came out of hospital. Her father had invited her up to Aberdeen; her sister Rachel had made several appeals for her to spend a few weeks in Buckinghamshire; there had even been a pitiful telephone call from Mitch, in which he had talked of their holidaying together. She had rejected them all, telling them that she wanted to re-establish the rhythm of her previous life as soon as possible: to return to her job, to her working colleagues and friends. In fact, her reasons had gone deeper than that. She had *feared* their sympathies, feared that she would be held too close in their affections and quickly come to rely upon them. Her streak of independence, which had first brought her to this unfriendly city, was in studied defiance of her smothering appetite for security. If she gave in to those loving appeals she knew she would take root in domestic soil and not look up and out again for another year. In which time, what adventures might have passed her by?

Instead she had returned to work as soon as she felt able, hoping that although she had not taken on all her former responsibilities the familiar routines would help her to re-establish a normal life. But the sleight-of-hand was not entirely successful. Every few days something would happen – she would overhear some remark, or catch a look that she was not intended to see – that made her realise she was being treated with a rehearsed caution; that her colleagues viewed her as being fundamentally changed by her illness. It had made her angry. She'd wanted to spit her suspicions in their faces; tell them that she and her uterus were not synynomous, and that the removal of one did not imply the eclipse of the other.

But today, returning to the office, she was not so certain they weren't correct. She felt as though she hadn't slept in weeks, though in fact she was sleeping long and deeply every night. Her eyesight was blurred, and there was a curious remoteness about her experiences that day that she associated with extreme fatigue, as if she were drifting further and further from the work on her desk; from her sensations, from her very thoughts. Twice that morning she caught herself speaking and then wondered who it was who was conceiving of these words. It certainly wasn't *her*; she was too busy listening.

And then, an hour after lunch, things had suddenly taken a turn

8

for the worse. She had been called into her supervisor's office and asked to sit down.

'Are you all right, Elaine?' Mr Chimes had asked.

'Yes,' she'd told him. 'I'm fine.'

'There's been some concern – '

'About what?'

Chimes looked slightly embarrassed. 'Your behaviour,' he finally said. 'Please don't think I'm prying, Elaine. It's just that if you need some further time to recuperate – '

'There's nothing wrong with me.'

'But your weeping – '

'What?'

'The way you've been crying today. It concerns us.'

'Cry?' she'd said. 'I don't cry.'

The supervisor seemed baffled. 'But you've been crying all day. You're crying now.'

Elaine put a tentative hand to her cheek. And yes; yes, she *was* crying. Her cheek was wet. She'd stood up, shocked at her own conduct.

'I didn't . . . I didn't know,' she said. Though the words sounded preposterous, they were true. She *hadn't* known. Only now, with the fact pointed out, did she taste tears in her throat and sinuses; and with that taste came a memory of when this eccentricity had begun: in front of the television the night before.

'Why don't you take the rest of the day off?'

'Yes.'

'Take the rest of the week if you'd like,' Chimes said. 'You're a valued member of staff, Elaine; I don't have to tell you that. We don't want you coming to any harm.'

This last remark struck home with stinging force. Did they think she was verging on suicide; was that why she was treated with kid gloves? They were only tears she was shedding, for God's sake, and she was so indifferent to them she had not even known they were falling.

'I'll go home,' she said. 'Thank you for your . . . concern.'

The supervisor looked at her with some dismay. 'It must have been a very traumatic experience,' he said. 'We all understand; we really do. If you feel you want to talk about it at any time – '

She declined, but thanked him again and left the office.

Face to face with herself in the mirror of the women's toilets she realised just how bad she looked. Her skin was flushed, her eyes swollen. She did what she could to conceal the signs of this painless

9

grief, then picked up her coat and started home. As she reached the underground station she knew that returning to the empty flat would not be a wise idea. She would brood, she would sleep (so much sleep of late, and so perfectly dreamless) but she would not improve her mental condition by either route. It was the bell of Holy Innocents, tolling in the clear afternoon, that reminded her of the smoke and the square and Mr Kavanagh. There, she decided, was a fit place for her to walk. She could enjoy the sunlight, and think. Maybe she would meet her admirer again.

She found her way back to All Saints easily enough, but there was disappointment awaiting her. The demolition site had been cordoned off, the boundary marked by a row of posts – a red fluorescent ribbon looped between them. The site was guarded by no less than four policemen, who were ushering pedestrians towards a detour around the square. The workers and their hammers had been exiled from the shadows of All Saints and now a very different selection of people – suited and academic – occupied the zone beyond the ribbon, some in furrowed conversation, others standing on the muddy ground and staring up quizzically at the derelict church. The south transept and much of the area around it had been curtained off from public view by an arrangement of tarpaulins and black plastic sheeting. Occasionally somebody would emerge from behind this veil and consult with others on the site. All who did so, she noted, were wearing gloves; one or two were also masked. It was as though they were performing some *ad hoc* surgery in the shelter of the screen. A tumour, perhaps, in the bowels of All Saints.

She approached one of the officers. 'What's going on?'

'The foundations are unstable,' he told her. 'Apparently the place could fall down at any moment.'

'Why are they wearing masks?'

'It's just a precaution against the dust.'

She didn't argue, though this explanation struck her as unlikely.

'If you want to get through to Temple Street you'll have to go round the back,' the officer said.

What she really wanted to do was to stand and watch proceedings, but the proximity of the uniformed quartet intimidated her, and she decided to give up and go home. As she began to make her way back to the main road she caught sight of a familiar figure crossing the end of an adjacent street. It was unmistakably Kavanagh. She called after him, though he had already disappeared, and was pleased to see him step back into view and return a nod to her.

'Well, well – ' he said as he came down to meet her. 'I didn't expect to see you again so soon.'

'I came to watch the rest of the demolition,' she said.

His face was ruddy with the cold, and his eyes were shining.

'I'm so pleased,' he said, 'Do you want to have some afternoon tea? There's a place just around the corner.'

'I'd like that.'

As they walked she asked him if he knew what was going on at All Saints.

'It's the crypt,' he said. confirming her suspicions.

'They opened it?'

'They certainly found a way in. I was here this morning – '

'About your stones?'

'That's right. They were already putting up the tarpaulins then.'

'Some of them were wearing masks.'

'It won't smell very fresh down there. Not after so long.'

Thinking of the curtain of tarpaulin drawn between her and the mystery within she said: 'I wonder what it's like.'

'A wonderland,' Kavanagh replied.

It was an odd response, and she didn't query it, at least not on the spot. But later, when they'd sat and talked together for an hour, and she felt easier with him, she returned to the comment.

'What you said about the crypt . . .'

'Yes?'

'About it being a wonderland.'

'Did I say that?' he replied, somewhat sheepishly. 'What must you think of me?'

'I was just puzzled. Wondered what you meant.'

'I like places where the dead are,' he said. 'I always have. Cemeteries can be very beautiful, don't you think? Mausoleums and tombs; all the fine craftsmanship that goes into those places. Even the dead may sometimes reward closer scrutiny.' He looked at her to see if he had strayed beyond her taste threshold, but seeing that she only looked at him with quiet fascination, continued. 'They can be very beautiful on occasion. It's a sort of a glamour they have. It's a shame it's wasted on morticians and funeral directors.' He made a small mischievous grin. 'I'm sure there's much to be seen in that crypt. Strange sights. Wonderful sights.'

'I only ever saw one dead person. My grandmother. I was very young at the time . . .'

'I trust it was a pivotal experience.'

'I don't think so. In fact I scarcely remember it at all. I only remember how everybody cried.'

'Ah.'

He nodded sagely.

'So selfish,' he said. 'Don't you think? Spoiling a farewell with snot and sobs.' Again, he looked at her to gauge the response; again he was satisfied that she would not take offence. 'We cry for ourselves, don't we? Not for the dead. The dead are past caring.'

She made a small, soft: 'Yes,' and then, more loudly: 'My God, yes. That's right. Always for ourselves . . .'

'You see how much the dead can teach, just by lying there, twiddling their thumb-bones?'

She laughed: he joined her in laughter. She had misjudged him on that initial meeting, thinking his face unused to smiles; it was not. But his features, when the laughter died, swiftly regained that eerie quiescence she had first noticed.

When, after a further half hour of his laconic remarks, he told her he had appointments to keep and had to be on his way, she thanked him for his company, and said:

'Nobody's made me laugh so much in weeks. I'm grateful.'

'You *should* laugh,' he told her. 'It suits you.' Then added: 'You have beautiful teeth.'

She thought of this odd remark when he'd gone, as she did of a dozen others he had made through the afternoon. He was undoubtedly one of the most off-beat individuals she'd ever encountered, but he had come into her life – with his eagerness to talk of crypts and the dead and the beauty of her teeth – at just the right moment. He was the perfect distraction from her buried sorrows, making her present aberrations seem minor stuff beside his own. When she started home she was in high spirits. If she had not known herself better she might have thought herself half in love with him.

On the journey back, and later that evening, she thought particularly of the joke he had made about the dead twiddling their thumb-bones, and that thought led inevitably to the mysteries that lay out of sight in the crypt. Her curiosity, once aroused, was not easily silenced; it grew on her steadily that she badly wanted to slip through that cordon of ribbon and see the burial chamber with her own eyes. It was a desire she would never previously have admitted to herself. (How many times had she walked from the site of an accident, telling herself to control the shameful inquisitiveness she felt?) But Kavanagh had legitimised her appetite with his flagrant enthusiasm for things funereal. Now, with the taboo shed, she wanted to go back to All Saints and look Death in its face, then next time she saw Kavanagh she would have some stories to tell of her own. The idea, no sooner budded, came to full flower, and in the middle of the evening she dressed for the street again and headed back towards the square.

She didn't reach All Saints until well after eleven-thirty, but there were still signs of activity at the site. Lights, mounted on stands and on the wall of the church itself, poured illumination on the scene. A trio of technicians, Kavanagh's so-called removal men, stood outside the tarpaulin shelter, their faces drawn with fatigue, their breath clouding the frosty air. She stayed out of sight and watched the scene. She was growing steadily colder, and her scars had begun to ache, but it was apparent that the night's work on the crypt was more or less over. After some brief exchange with the police, the technicians departed. They had extinguished all but one of the floodlights, leaving the site – church, tarpaulin and rimy mud – in grim chiaroscuro

The two officers who had been left on guard were not over-conscientious in their duties. What idiot, they apparently reasoned, would come grave-robbing at this hour, and in such temperatures? After a few minutes keeping a foot-stamping vigil they withdrew to the relative comfort of the workmen's hut. When they did not re- emerge, Elaine crept out of hiding and moved as cautiously as possible to the ribbon that divided one zone from the other. A radio had been turned on in the hut; its noise (music for lovers from dusk to dawn, the distant voice purred) covered her crackling advance across the frozen earth.

Once beyond the cordon, and into the forbidden territory beyond, she was not so hesitant. She swiftly crossed the hard ground, its wheel-ploughed furrows like concrete, into the lee of the church. The floodlight was dazzling; by it her breath appeared as solid as yesterday's smoke had seemed. Behind her, the music for lovers murmured on. No one emerged from the hut to summon her from her trespassing. No alarm-bells rang. She reached the edge of the tarpaulin curtain without incident, and peered at the scene concealed behind it.

The demolition men, under very specific instructions to judge by the care they had taken in their labours, had dug fully eight feet down the side of All Saints, exposing the foundations. In so doing they had uncovered an entrance to the burial-chamber which previous hands had been at pains to conceal. Not only had earth been piled up against the flank of the church to hide the entrance,

13

but the crypt door had also been removed, and stone masons sealed the entire aperture up. This had clearly been done at some speed; their handiwork was far from ordered. They had simply filled the entrance up with any stone or brick that had come to hand, and plastered coarse mortar over their endeavours. Into this mortar – though the design had been spoiled by the excavations – some artisan had scrawled a six-foot cross.

All their efforts in securing the crypt, and marking the mortar to keep the godless out, had gone for nothing however. The seal had been broken – the mortar hacked at, the stones torn away. There was now a small hole in the middle of the doorway, large enough for one person to gain access to the interior. Elaine had no hesitation in climbing down the slope to the breached wall, and then squirming through.

She had predicted the darkness she met on the other side, and had brought with her a cigarette lighter Mitch had given her three years ago. She flicked it on. The flame was small; she turned up the wick, and by the swelling light investigated the space ahead of her. It was not the crypt itself she had stepped into but a narrow vestibule of some kind: a yard or so in front of her was another wall, and another door. This one had not been replaced with bricks, though into its solid timbers a second cross had been gouged. She approached the door. The lock had been removed – by the investigators presumably – and the door then held shut again with a rope binding. This had been done quickly, by tired fingers. She did not find the rope difficult to untie, though it required both hands, and so had to be effected in the dark.

As she worked the knot free, she heard voices. The policemen – damn them – had left the seclusion of their hut and come out into the bitter night to do their rounds. She let the rope be, and pressed herself against the inside wall of the vestibule. The officers' voices were becoming louder: talking of their children, and the escalating cost of Christmas joy. Now they were within yards of the crypt entrance, standing, or so she guessed, in the shelter of the tarpaulin. They made no attempt to descend the slope however, but finished their cursory inspection on the lip of the earthworks, then turned back. Their voices faded.

Satisfied that they were out of sight and hearing of her, she re-ignited the flame and returned to the door. It was large and brutally heavy; her first attempt at hauling it open met with little success. She tried again, and this time it moved, grating across the grit on the vestibule floor. Once it was open the vital inches required for her to squeeze through she eased her straining. The lighter guttered as though a breath had blown from within; the flame briefly burned not yellow but electric blue. She didn't pause to admire it, but slid into the promised wonderland.

Now the flame fed – became livid – and for an instant its sudden brightness took her sight away. She pressed the corners of her eyes to clear them, and looked again.

So this was Death. There was none of the art or the glamour Kavanagh had talked of; no calm laying out of shrouded beauties on cool marble sheets; no elaborate reliquaries, nor aphorisms on the nature of human frailty: not even names and dates. In most cases, the corpses lacked even coffins.

The crypt was a charnel-house. Bodies had been thrown in heaps on every side; entire families pressed into niches that were designed to hold a single casket, dozens more left where hasty and careless hands had tossed them. The scene – though absolutely still – was rife with panic. It was there in the faces that stared from the piles of dead: mouths wide in silent protest, sockets in which eyes had withered gaping in shock at such treatment. It was there too in the way the system of burial had degenerated from the ordered arrangement of caskets at the far end of the crypt to the haphazard piling of crudely made coffins, their wood unplaned, their lids unmarked but for a scrawled cross, and thence – finally – to this hurried heaping of unhoused carcasses, all concern for dignity, perhaps even for the rites of passage, forgotten in the rising hysteria.

There had been a disaster, of that she could have no doubt; a sudden influx of bodies – men, women, children (there was a baby at her feet who could not have lived a day) – who had died in such escalating numbers that there was not even time to close their eyelids before they were shunted away into this pit. Perhaps the coffin-makers had also died, and were thrown here amongst their clients; the shroud-sewers too, and the priests. All gone in one apocalyptic month (or week), their surviving relatives too shocked or too frightened to consider the niceties, but only eager to have the dead thrust out of sight where they would never have to look on their flesh again.

There was much of that flesh still in evidence. The sealing of the crypt, closing it off from the decaying air, had kept the occupants intact. Now, with the violation of this secret chamber, the heat of decay had been rekindled, and the tissues were deteriorating afresh. Everywhere she saw rot at work, making sores and suppurations, blisters and pustules. She raised the flame to see

15

better, though the stench of spoilage was beginning to crowd upon her and make her dizzy. Everywhere her eyes travelled she seemed to alight upon some pitiful sight. Two children laid together as if sleeping in each other's arms; a woman whose last act, it appeared, had been to paint her sickened face so as to die more fit for the marriage-bed than the grave.

She could not help but stare, though her fascination cheated them of privacy. There was so much to see and remember. She could never be the same, could she, having viewed these scenes? One corpse – lying half-hidden beneath another – drew her particular attention: a woman whose long chestnut-coloured hair flowed from her scalp so copiously Elaine envied it. She moved closer to get a better look, and then, putting the last of her squeamishness to flight, took hold of the body thrown across the woman, and hauled it away. The flesh of the corpse was greasy to the touch, and left her fingers stained, but she was not distressed. The uncovered corpse lay with her legs wide, but the constant weight of her companion had bent them into an impossible configuration. The wound that had killed her had bloodied her thighs, and glued her skirt to her abdomen and groin. Had she miscarried, Elaine wondered, or had some disease devoured her there?

She stared and stared, bending close to study the faraway look on the woman's rotted face. Such a place to lie, she thought, with your blood still shaming you. She would tell Kavanagh when next she saw him, how wrong he had been with his sentimental tales of calm beneath the sod.

She had seen enough; more than enough. She wiped her hands upon her coat and made her way back to the door, closing it behind her and knotting up the rope again as she had found it. Then she climbed the slope into the clean air. The policemen were nowhere in sight, and she slipped away unseen, like a shadow's shadow.

There was nothing for her to feel, once she had mastered her initial disgust, and that twinge of pity she'd felt seeing the children and the woman with the chestnut hair; and even those responses – even the pity and the repugnance – were quite manageable. She had felt both more acutely seeing a dog run down by a car than she had standing in the crypt of All Saints, despite the horrid displays on every side. When she laid her head down to sleep that night, and realised that she was neither trembling nor nauseous, she felt strong. What was there to fear in all the world if the spectacle of mortality she had just witnessed could be borne so readily? She slept deeply, and woke refreshed.

16

She went back to work that morning, apologising to Chimes for her behaviour of the previous day, and reassuring him that she was now feeling happier than she'd felt in months. In order to prove her re-habilitation she was as gregarious as she could be, striking up conversations with neglected acquaintances, and giving her smile a ready airing. This met with some initial resistance; she could sense her colleagues doubting that this bout of sunshine actually meant a summer. But when the mood was sustained throughout the day and through the day following, they began to respond more readily. By Thursday it was as though the tears of earlier in the week had never been shed. People told her how well she was looking. It was true; her mirror confirmed the rumours. Her eyes shone, her skin shone. She was a picture of vitality.

On Thursday afternoon she was sitting at her desk, working through a backlog of inquiries, when one of the secretaries appeared from the corridor and began to babble. Somebody went to the woman's aid; through the sobs it was apparent she was talking about Bernice, a woman Elaine knew well enough to exchange smiles with on the stairs, but no better. There had been an accident, it seemed; the woman was talking about blood on the floor. Elaine got up and joined those who were making their way out to see what the fuss was about. The supervisor was already standing outside the women's lavatories, vainly instructing the curious to keep clear. Somebody else – another witness, it seemed – was offering her account of events:

'She was just standing there, and suddenly she started to shake. I thought she was having a fit. Blood started to come from her nose. Then from her mouth. Pouring out.'

'There's nothing to see,' Chimes insisted. 'Please keep back.' But he was substantially ignored. Blankets were being brought to wrap around the woman, and as soon as the toilet door was opened again the sight-seers pressed forward. Elaine caught sight of a form moving about on the toilet floor as if convulsed by cramps; she had no wish to see any more. Leaving the others to throng the corridor, talking loudly of Bernice as if she were already dead, Elaine returned to her desk. She had so much to do; so many wasted, grieving days to catch up on. An apt phrase flitted into her head. *Redeem the time*. She wrote the three words on her notebook as a reminder. Where did they come from? She couldn't recall. It didn't matter. Sometimes there was wisdom in forgetting.

* * *

17

Kavanagh rang her that evening, and invited her out to dinner the following night. She had to decline, however, eager as she was to discuss her recent exploits, because a small party was being thrown by several of her friends, to celebrate her return to health. Would he care to join them? she asked. He thanked her for the invitation, but replied that large numbers of people had always intimidated him. She told him not to be foolish: that her circle would be pleased to meet him, and she to show him off, but he replied he would only put in an appearance if his ego felt the equal of it, and that if he didn't show up he hoped she wouldn't be offended. She soothed such fears. Before the conversation came to an end she slyly mentioned that next time they met she had a tale to tell.

The following day brought unhappy news. Bernice had died in the early hours of Friday morning, without ever regaining consciousness. The cause of death was as yet unverified, but the office gossips concurred that she had never been a strong woman – always the first amongst the secretaries to catch a cold and the last to shake it off. There was also some talk, though traded less loudly, about her personal behaviour. She had been generous with her favours it appeared, and injudicious in her choice of partners. With venereal diseases reaching epidemic proportions was that not the likeliest explanation for the death?

The news, though it kept the rumourmongers in business, was not good for general morale. Two girls went sick that morning, and at lunch-time it seemed that Elaine was the only member of staff with an appetite. She compensated for the lack in her colleagues, however. She had a fierce hunger in her; her body almost seemed to ache for sustenance. It was a good feeling, after so many months of lassitude. When she looked around at the worn faces at the table she felt utterly apart from them: from their tittle-tattle and their trivial opinions, from the way their talk circled on the suddenness of Bernice's death as though they had not given the subject a moment's thought in years, and were amazed that their neglect had not rendered it extinct.

Elaine knew better. She had come close to death so often in the recent past: during the months leading up to her hysterectomy, when the tumours had suddenly doubled in size as though sensing that they were plotted against; on the operating table, when twice the surgeons thought they'd lost her; and most recently, in the crypt, face to face with those gawping carcasses. Death was everywhere. That they should be so startled by its entrance into their charmless circle struck her as almost comical. She ate lustily, and let them talk in whispers.

They gathered for her party at Reuben's house – Elaine, Hermione, Sam and Nellwyn, Josh and Sonja. It was a good night; a chance to pick up on how mutual friends were faring; how statuses and ambitions were on the change. Everyone got drunk very quickly; tongues already loosened by familiarity became progressively looser. Nellwyn led a tearful toast to Elaine; Josh and Sonja had a short but acrimonious exchange on the subject of evangelism; Reuben did his impersonations of fellow barristers. It was like old times, except that memory had yet to improve it. Kavanagh did not put in an appearance, and Elaine was glad of it. Despite her protestations when speaking to him she knew he would have felt out of place in such close-knit company.

About half past midnight, when the room had settled into a number of quiet exchanges, Hermione mentioned the yachtsman. Though she was almost across the room, Elaine heard the sailor's name mentioned quite distinctly. She broke off her conversation with Nellwyn and picked her way through the sprawling limbs to join Hermione and Sam.

'I heard you talking about Maybury,' she said.

'Yes,' said Hermione, 'Sam and I were just saying how strange it all was – '

'I saw him on the news,' Elaine said.

'Sad story, isn't it?' Sam commented. 'The way it happened.'

'Why sad?'

'Him saying that: about Death being on the boat with him – '

' – And then dying,' Hermione said.

'Dying?' said Elaine. 'When was this?'

'It was in all the papers.'

'I haven't been concentrating that much,' Elaine replied. 'What happened?'

'He was killed,' Sam said. 'They were taking him to the airport to fly him home, and there was an accident. He was killed just like that.' He snapped his middle finger and thumb. 'Out like a light.'

'So sad,' said Hermione.

She glanced at Elaine, and a frown crept across her face. The look baffled Elaine until – with that same shock of recognition she'd felt in Chimes' office, discovering her tears – she realized that she was smiling.

* * *

So the sailor was dead.

When the party broke up in the early hours of Saturday morning – when the embraces and the kisses were over and she was home again – she thought over the Maybury interview she'd heard, summoning a face scorched by the sun and eyes peeled by the wastes he'd almost been lost to, thinking of his mixture of detachment and faint embarrassment as he'd told the tale of his stowaway. And, of course, those final words of his, when pressed to identify the stranger:

'Death, I suppose,' he'd said.

He'd been right.

She woke up late on Saturday morning, without the anticipated hangover. There was a letter from Mitch. She didn't open it, but left it on the mantelpiece for an idle moment later in the day. The first snow of winter was in the wind, though it was too wet to make any serious impression on the streets. The chill was biting enough however, to judge by the scowls on the faces of passers-by. She felt oddly immune from it, however. Though she had no heating on in the flat she walked around in her bath-robe, and barefoot, as though she had a fire stoked in her belly.

After coffee she went through to wash. There was a spider clot of hair in the plug hole; she fished it out and dropped it down the lavatory, then returned to the sink. Since the removal of the dressings she had studiously avoided any close scrutiny of her body, but today her qualms and her vanity seemed to have disappeared. She stripped off her robe, and looked herself over critically.

She was pleased with what she saw. Her breasts were full and dark, her skin had a pleasing sheen to it, her pubic hair had regrown more lushly than ever. The scars themselves still looked and felt tender, but her eyes read their lividness as a sign of her cunt's ambition, as though any day now her sex would grow from anus to navel (and beyond perhaps) opening her up; making her terrible.

It was paradoxical, surely, that it was only now, when the surgeons had emptied her out, that she should feel so ripe, so resplendent. She stood for fully half an hour in front of the mirror admiring herself, her thoughts drifting off. Eventually she returned to the chore of washing. That done, she went back into the front room, still naked. She had no desire to conceal herself; quite the other way about. It was all she could do to prevent herself from stepping out into the snow and giving the whole street something to remember her by.

She crossed to the window, thinking a dozen such foolish thoughts. The snow had thickened. Through the flurries she caught a movement in the alley between the houses opposite. Somebody was there, watching her, though she couldn't see who. She didn't mind. She stood peeping at the peeper, wondering if he would have the courage to show himself, but he did not.

She watched for several minutes before she realised that her brazenness had frightened him away. Disappointed, she wandered back to the bedroom and got dressed. It was time she found herself something to eat; she had that familiar fierce hunger upon her. The fridge was practically empty. She would have to go out and stock up for the weekend.

Supermarkets were circuses, especially on a Saturday, but her mood was far too buoyant to be depressed by having to make her way through the crowds. Today she even found some pleasure in these scenes of conspicuous consumption; in the trolleys and the baskets heaped high with foodstuffs, and the children greedy-eyed as they approached the confectionery, and tearful if denied it, and the wives weighing up the merits of a leg of mutton while their husbands watched the girls on the staff with eyes no less calculating.

She purchased twice as much food for the weekend as she would normally have done in a full week, her appetite driven to distraction by the smells from the delicatessen and fresh meat counters. By the time she reached the house she was almost shaking with the anticipation of sustenance. As she put the bags down on the front step and fumbled for her keys she heard a car door slam behind her.

'Elaine?'

It was Hermione. The red wine she'd consumed the previous night had left her looking blotchy and stale.

'Are you feeling all right?' Elaine asked.

'The point is, are you?' Hermione wanted to know.

'Yes, I'm fine. Why shouldn't I be?'

Hermione returned a harried look. 'Sonja's gone down with some kind of food poisoning, and so's Reuben. I just came round to see that you were all right.'

'As I say, fine.'

'I don't understand it.'

'What about Nellwyn and Dick?'

21

'I couldn't get an answer at their place. But Reuben's in a bad way. They've taken him into hospital for tests.'

'Do you want to come in and have a cup of coffee?'

'No thanks, I've got to get back to see Sonja. I just didn't like to think of your being on your own if you'd gone down with it too.'

Elaine smiled. 'You're an angel,' she said, and kissed Hermione on the cheek. The gesture seemed to startle the other woman. For some reason she stepped back, the kiss exchanged, staring at Elaine with a vague puzzlement in her eyes.

'I must . . . I must go.' she said, fixing her face as though it would betray her.

'I'll call you later in the day,' Elaine said, 'and find out how they're doing.'

'Fine.'

Hermione turned away and crossed the pavement to her car. Though she made a cursory attempt to conceal the gesture, Elaine caught sight of her putting her fingers to the spot on her cheek where she had been kissed and scratching at it, as if to eradicate the contact.

It was not the season for flies, but those that had survived the recent cold buzzed around in the kitchen as Elaine selected some bread, smoked ham, and garlic sausage from her purchases, and sat down to eat. She was ravenous. In five minutes or less she had devoured the meats, and made substantial inroads into the loaf, and her hunger was scarcely tamed. Settling to a dessert of figs and cheese, she thought of the paltry omelette she'd been unable to finish that day after the visit to the hospital. One thought led to another; from omelette to smoke to the square to Kavanagh to her most recent visit to the church, and thinking of the place she was suddenly seized by an enthusiasm to see it one final time before it was entirely levelled. She was probably too late already. The bodies would have been parcelled up and removed, the crypt decontaminated and scoured; the walls would be rubble. But she knew she would not be satisfied until she had seen it for herself.

Even after a meal which would have sickened her with its excess a few days before, she felt light-headed as she set out for All Saints; almost as though she were drunk. Not the maudlin drunkenness she had been prone to when with Mitch, but a euphoria which made her feel well-nigh invulnerable, as if she had at last located some bright and incorruptible part of herself, and no harm would ever befall her again.

She had prepared herself for finding All Saints in ruins, but she did not. The building still stood, its walls untouched, its beams still dividing the sky. Perhaps it too could not be toppled, she mused; perhaps she and it were twin immortals. The suspicion was reinforced by the gaggle of fresh worshippers the church had attracted. The police guard had trebled since the day she'd been here, and the tarpaulin that had shielded the crypt entrance from sight was now a vast tent, supported by scaffolding, which entirely encompassed the flank of the building. The altar-servers, standing in close proximity to the tent, wore masks and gloves; the high priests – the chosen few who were actually allowed into the Holy of Holies – were entirely garbed in protective suits.

She watched from the cordon: the signs and genuflections between the devotees; the sluicing down of the suited men as they emerged from behind the veil; the fine spray of fumigants which filled the air like bitter incense.

Another onlooker was quizzing one of the officers.

'Why the suits?'

'In case it's contagious,' the reply came.

'After all these years?'

'They don't know what they've got in there.'

'Diseases don't last, do they?'

'It's a plague-pit.' the officer said. 'They're just being cautious.'

Elaine listened to the exchange, and her tongue itched to speak. She could save them their investigations with a few words. After all, she was living proof that whatever pestilence had destroyed the families in the crypt it was no longer virulent. She had breathed that air, she had touched that mouldy flesh, and she felt healthier now than she had in years. But they would not thank her for her revelations, would they? They were too engrossed in their rituals; perhaps even excited by the discovery of such horrors, their turmoil fuelled and fired by the possibility that this death was still living. She would not be so unsporting as to sour their enthusiasm with a confession of her own rare good health.

Instead she turned her back on the priests and their rites, on the drizzle of incense in the air, and began to walk away from the square. As she looked up from her thoughts she glimpsed a familiar figure watching her from the corner of the adjacent street. He turned away as she glanced up, but it was undoubtedly Kavanagh. She called to him, and went to the corner, but he was walking smartly away from her, head bowed. Again she called after him, and now he turned – a patently false look of surprise pasted onto his face – and retrod his escape-route to greet her.

'Have you heard what they've found?' she asked him.

'Oh yes,' he replied. Despite the familiarity they'd last enjoyed she was reminded now of her first impression of him: that he was not a man much conversant with feeling.

'Now you'll never get your stones,' she said.

'I suppose not,' he replied, not overtly concerned at the loss.

She wanted to tell him that she'd seen the plague-pit with her own eyes, hoping the news would bring a gleam to his face, but the corner of this sunlit street was an inappropriate spot for such talk. Besides, it was almost as if he knew. He looked at her so oddly, the warmth of their previous meeting entirely gone.

'Why did you come back?' he asked her.

'Just to see,' she replied.

'I'm flattered.'

'Flattered?'

'That my enthusiasm for mausoleums is infectious.'

Still he watched her, and she, returning his look, was conscious of how cold his eyes were, and how perfectly shiny. They might have been glass, she thought; and his skin suede-glued like a hood over the subtle architecture of his skull.

'I should go,' she said.

'Business or pleasure?'

'Neither,' she told him. 'One or two of my friends are ill.'

'Ah.'

She had the impression that he wanted to be away; that it was only fear of foolishness that kept him from running from her.

'Perhaps I'll see you again,' she said. 'Sometime.'

'I'm sure,' he replied, gratefully taking his cue and retreating along the street. 'And to your friends – my best regards.'

Even if she had wanted to pass Kavanagh's good wishes along to Reuben and Sonja, she could not have done so. Hermione did not answer the telephone, nor did any of the others. The closest she came was to leave a message with Reuben's answering service.

The light-headedness she'd felt earlier in the day developed into a strange dreaminess as the afternoon inched towards evening. She ate again, but the feast did nothing to keep the fugue-state from deepening. She felt quite well; that sense of inviolability that had come upon her was still intact. But time and again as the day wore on she found herself standing on the threshold of a room not knowing why she had come there; or watching the light dwindle in the street outside without being quite certain if she was the viewer or the thing viewed. She was happy with her company though, as the flies were happy. They kept buzzing attendance even though the dark fell.

About seven in the evening she heard a car draw up outside, and the bell rang. She went to the door of her flat, but couldn't muster the inquisitiveness to open it, step out into the hallway and admit callers. It would be Hermione again, most probably, and she didn't have any appetite for gloomy talk. Didn't want anybody's company in fact, but that of the flies.

The callers insisted on the bell; the more they insisted the more determined she became not to reply. She slid down the wall beside the flat door and listened to the muted debate that now began on the step. It wasn't Hermione; it was nobody she recognized. Now they systematically rang the bells of the flats above, until Mr Prudhoe came down from the top flat, talking to himself as he went, and opened the door to them. Of the conversation that followed she caught sufficient only to grasp the urgency of their mission, but her dishevelled mind hadn't the persistence to attend to the details. They persuaded Prudhoe to allow them into the hallway. They approached the door of her flat and rapped upon it, calling her name. She didn't reply. They rapped again, exchanging words of frustration. She wondered if they could hear her smiling in the darkness. At last – after a further exchange with Prudhoe – they left her to herself.

She didn't know how long she sat on her haunches beside the door, but when she stood up again her lower limbs were entirely numb, and she was hungry. She ate voraciously, more or less finishing off all the purchases of that morning. The flies seemed to have procreated in the intervening hours; they crawled on the table and picked at her slops. She let them eat. They too had their lives to live.

Finally she decided to take some air. No sooner had she stepped out of her flat, however, than the vigilant Prudhoe was at the top of the stairs, and calling down to her.

'Miss Rider. Wait a moment. I have a message for you.'

She contemplated closing the door on him, but she knew he would not rest until he had delivered his communiqué. He hurried down the stairs – a Cassandra in shabby slippers.

'There were policemen here,' he announced before he had even reached the bottom step, 'they were looking for you.'

'Oh,' she said. 'Did they say what they wanted?'

'To talk to you. *Urgently*. Two of your friends – '

'What about them?'

'They died,' he said. 'This afternoon. They have some kind of disease.'

He had a sheet of notepaper in his hand. This he now passed over to her, relinquishing his hold an instant before she took it.

'They left that number for you to call,' he said. 'You've to contact them as soon as possible.' His message delivered, he was already retiring up the stairs again.

Elaine looked down at the sheet of paper, with its scrawled figures. By the time she'd read the seven digits, Prudhoe had disappeared.

She went back into the flat. For some reason she wasn't thinking of Reuben or Sonja – who, it seemed, she would not see again – but of the sailor, Maybury, who'd seen Death and escaped it only to have it follow him like a loyal dog, waiting its moment to leap and lick his face. She sat beside the phone and stared at the numbers on the sheet, and then at the fingers that held the sheet and at the hands that held the fingers. Was the touch that hung so innocently at the end of her arms now lethal? Was that what the detectives had come to tell her?; that her friends were dead by *her* good offices? If so, how many others had she brushed against and breathed upon in the days since her pestilential education at the crypt? In the street, in the bus, in the supermarket: at work, at play. She thought of Bernice, lying on the toilet floor, and of Hermione, rubbing the spot where she had been kissed as if knowing some scourge had been passed along to her. And suddenly she *knew*, knew in her marrow, that her pursuers were right in their suspicions, and that all these dreamy days she had been nurturing a fatal child. Hence her hunger; hence the glow of fulfilment she felt.

She put down the note and sat in the semi-darkness, trying to work out precisely the plague's location. Was it her fingertips; in her belly; in her eyes? None, and yet all of these. Her first assumption had been wrong. It wasn't a child at all: she didn't carry it in some particular cell. It was *everywhere*. She and it were synonymous. That being so, there could be no slicing out of the offending part, as they had sliced out her tumours and all that had been devoured by them. Not that she would escape their attentions for that fact. They had come looking for her, hadn't they, to take

26

her back into the custody of sterile rooms, to deprive her of her opinions and dignity, to make her fit only for their loveless investigations. The thought revolted her; she would rather die as the chestnut-haired woman in the crypt had died, sprawled in agonies, than submit to them again. She tore up the sheet of paper and let the litter drop.

It was too late for solutions anyway. The removal men had opened the door and found Death waiting on the other side, eager for daylight. She was its agent, and it – in its wisdom – had granted her immunity; had given her strength and a dreamy rapture; had taken her fear away. She, in return, had spread its word, and there was no undoing those labours: not now. All the dozens, maybe hundreds, of people whom she'd contaminated in the last few days would have gone back to their families and friends, to their work places and their places of recreation, and spread the word yet further. They would have passed its fatal promise to their children as they tucked them into bed, and to their mates in the act of love. Priests had no doubt given it with Communion; shopkeepers with change of a five-pound note.

While she was thinking of this – of the disease spreading like fire in tinder – the doorbell rang again. They had come back for her. And, as before, they were ringing the other bells in the house. She could hear Prudhoe coming downstairs. This time he would know she was in. He would tell them so. They would hammer at the door, and when she refused to answer –

As Prudhoe opened the front door she unlocked the back. As she slipped into the yard she heard voices at the flat door, and then their rapping and their demands. She unbolted the yard gate and fled into the darkness of the alley-way. She was already out of hearing range by the time they had beaten down the door.

She wanted most of all to go back to All Saints, but she knew that such a tactic would only invite arrest. They would expect her to follow that route, counting upon her adherence to the first cause. But she wanted to see Death's face again, now more than ever. To speak with it. To debate its strategies. *Their* strategies. To ask why it had chosen her.

She emerged from the alley-way and watched the goings-on at the front of the house from the corner of the street. This time there were more than two men; she counted four at least, moving in and out of the house. What were they doing? Peeking through her underwear and her love-letters, most probably, examining the sheets on her bed for stray hairs, and the mirror for traces of her reflection. But even if they turned the flat upside-down, if they examined every print and pronoun, they wouldn't find the clues they sought. Let them search. The lover had escaped. Only her tear stains remained, and flies at the light bulb to sing her praises.

The night was starry, but as she walked down to the centre of the city the brightness of the Christmas illuminations festooning trees and buildings cancelled out their light. Most of the stores were well closed by this hour, but a good number of window-shoppers still idled along the pavements. She soon tired of the displays however, of the baubles and the dummies, and made her way off the main road and into the side streets. It was darker here, which suited her abstracted state of mind. The sound of music and laughter escaped through open bar doors; an argument erupted in an upstairs gaming-room: blows were exchanged; in one doorway two lovers defied discretion; in another, a man pissed with the gusto of a horse.

It was only now, in the relative hush of these backwaters, that she realised she was not alone. Footsteps followed her, keeping a cautious distance, but never straying far. Had the trackers followed her? Were they hemming her in even now, preparing to snatch her into their closed order? If so, flight would only delay the inevitable. Better to confront them now, and dare them to come within range of her pollution. She slid into hiding, and listened as the footsteps approached, then stepped into view.

It was not the law, but Kavanagh. Her initial shock was almost immediately superseded by a sudden comprehension of *why* he had pursued her. She studied him. His skin was pulled so tight over his skull she could see the bone gleam in the dismal light. How, her whirling thoughts demanded, had she not recognised him sooner?; not realised at that first meeting, when he'd talked of the dead and their glamour, that he spoke as their Maker?

'I followed you,' he said.

'All the way from the house?'

He nodded.

'What did they tell you?' he asked her. 'The policemen. What did they say?'

'Nothing I hadn't already guessed,' she replied.

'You knew?'

'In a manner of speaking. I must have done, in my heart of hearts. Remember our first conversation?'

28

He murmured that he did.

'All you said about Death. Such egotism.'

He grinned suddenly, showing more bone.

'Yes,' he said. 'What must you think of me?'

'It made a kind of sense to me, even then. I didn't know why at the time. Didn't know what the future would bring –'

'What does it bring?' he inquired of her softly.

She shrugged. 'Death's been waiting for me all this time, am I right?'

'Oh yes,' he said, pleased by her understanding of the situation between them. He took a step towards her, and reached to touch her face.

'You are remarkable,' he said.

'Not really.'

'But to be so unmoved by it all. So cold.'

'What's to be afraid of?' she said. He stroked her cheek. She almost expected his hood of skin to come unbuttoned then, and the marbles that played in his sockets to tumble out and smash. But he kept his disguise intact, for appearance's sake.

'I want you,' he told her.

'Yes,' she said. Of course he did. It had been in his every word from the beginning, but she hadn't had the wit to comprehend it. Every love story was – at the last – a story of death; this was what the poets insisted. Why should it be any less true the other way about?

They could not go back to his house; the officers would be there too, he told her, for they must know of the romance between them. Nor, of course, could they return to her flat. So they found a small hotel in the vicinity and took a room there. Even in the dingy lift he took the liberty of stroking her hair, and then, finding her compliant, put his hand upon her breast.

The room was sparsely furnished, but was lent some measure of charm by a splash of coloured lights from a Christmas tree in the street below. Her lover didn't take his eyes off her for a single moment, as if even now he expected her to turn tail and run at the merest flaw in his behaviour. He needn't have concerned himself; his treatment of her left little cause for complaint. His kisses were insistent but not over-powering; his undressing of her – except for the fumbling (a nice human touch, she thought) – was a model of finesse and sweet solemnity.

She was surprised that he had not known about her scar, only because she had become to believe this intimacy had begun on the

29

operating table, when twice she had gone into his arms, and twice been denied them by the surgeon's bullying. But perhaps, being no sentimentalist, he had forgotten that first meeting. Whatever the reason, he looked to be upset when he slipped off her dress, and there was a trembling interval when she thought he would reject her. But the moment passed, and now he reached down to her abdomen and ran his fingers along the scar.

'It's beautiful,' he said.

She was happy.

'I almost died under the anaesthetic,' she told him.

'That would have been a waste,' he said, reaching up her body and working at her breast. It seemed to arouse him, for his voice was more guttural when next he spoke. 'What did they tell you?' he asked her, moving his hands up to the soft channel behind her clavicle, and stroking her there. She had not been touched in months, except by disinfected hands; his delicacy woke shivers in her. She was so engrossed in pleasure that she failed to reply to his question. He asked again as he moved between her legs.

'What did they tell you?'

Through a haze of anticipation she said: 'They left a number for me to ring. So that I could be helped . . .'

'But you didn't want help?'

'No,' she breathed. 'Why should I?'

She half-saw his smile, though her eyes wanted to flicker closed entirely. His appearance failed to stir any passion in her; indeed there was much about his disguise (that absurd bow-tie, for one) which she thought ridiculous. With her eyes closed, however, she could forget such petty details; she could strip the hood off and imagine him pure. When she thought of him that way her mind pirouetted.

He took his hands from her; she opened her eyes. He was fumbling with his belt. As he did so somebody shouted in the street outside. His head jerked in the direction of the window; his body tensed. She was surprised at his sudden concern.

'It's all right,' she said.

He leaned forward and put his hand to her throat.

'Be quiet,' he instructed.

She looked up into his face. He had begun to sweat. The exchanges in the street went on for a few minutes longer; it was simply two late-night gamblers parting. He realized his error now.

'I thought I heard – '

'What?'

30

' – I thought I heard them calling my name.'

'Who would do that?' she inquired fondly. 'Nobody knows we're here.'

He looked away from the window. All purposefulness had abruptly drained from him; after the instant of fear his features had slackened. He looked almost stupid.

'They came close,' he said. 'But they never found me.'

'Close?'

'Coming to you.' He laid his head on her breasts. 'So *very* close,' he murmured. She could hear her pulse in her head. 'But I'm swift,' he said, 'and invisible.'

His hand strayed back down to her scar, and further.

'And always neat,' he added.

She sighed as he stroked her.

'They admire me for that, I'm sure. Don't you think they must admire me? For being so neat?'

She remembered the chaos of the crypt; its indignities, its disorders.

'Not always . . .' she said.

He stopped stroking her.

'*Oh yes,*' he said. 'Oh yes. I never spill blood. That's a rule of mine. *Never* spill blood.'

She smiled at his boasts. She would tell him now – though surely he already knew – about her visit to All Saints, and the handiwork of his that she'd séen there.

'Sometimes you can't help blood being spilt,' she said, 'I don't hold it against you.'

At these words, he began to tremble.

'What did they tell you about me? What *lies?*'

'Nothing,' she said, mystified by his response. 'What could they know?'

'I'm a professional,' he said to her, his hand moving back up to her face. She felt intentionality in him again. A seriousness in his weight as he pressed closer upon her.

'I won't have them lie about me,' he said. 'I won't have it.'

He lifted his head from her chest and looked at her.

'All I do is stop the drummer,' he said.

'The drummer?'

'I have to stop him cleanly. In his tracks.'

The wash of colours from the lights below painted his face one moment red, the next green, the next yellow; unadulterated hues, as in a child's paint-box.

'I won't have them tell lies about me,' he said again. 'To say I spill blood.'

'They told me nothing,' she assured him. He had given up his pillow entirely, and now moved to straddle her. His hands were done with tender touches.

'Shall I show you how clean I am?' he said: 'How easily I stop the drummer?'

Before she could reply, his hands closed around her neck. She had no time even to gasp, let alone shout. His thumbs were expert; they found her wind-pipe and pressed. She heard the drummer quicken its rhythm in her ears. 'It's quick; and clean,' he was telling her, the colours still coming in predictable sequence. Red, yellow, green; red, yellow, green.

There was an error here, she knew; a terrible misunderstanding which she couldn't quite fathom. She struggled to make some sense of it.

'I don't understand,' she tried to tell him, but her bruised larynx could produce no more than a gargling sound.

'Too late for excuses,' he said, shaking his head. 'You came to me, remember? You want the drummer stopped. Why else did you come?' His grip tightened yet further. She had the sensation of her face swelling; of the blood throbbing to jump from her eyes.

'Don't you see that they came to warn you about me?' frowning as he laboured. 'They came to seduce you away from me by telling you I spilt blood.'

'*No*,' she squeezed the syllable out on her last breath, but he only pressed harder to cancel her denial.

The drummer was deafeningly loud now; though Kavanagh's mouth still opened and closed she could no longer hear what he was telling her. It mattered little. She realised now that he was not Death; not the clean-boned guardian she'd waited for. In her eagerness, she had given herself into the hands of a common killer, a street-corner Cain. She wanted to spit contempt at him, but her consciousness was slipping, the room, the lights, the face all throbbing to the drummer's beat. And then it all stopped.

She looked down on the bed. Her body lay sprawled across it. One desperate hand had clutched at the sheet, and clutched still, though there was no life left in it. Her tongue protruded, there was spittle on her blue lips. But (as he had promised) there was no blood.

She hovered, her presence failing even to bring a breeze to the cobwebs in this corner of the ceiling, and watched while Kavanagh

32

observed the rituals of his crime. He was bending over the body, whispering in its ear as he rearranged it on the tangled sheets. Then he unbuttoned himself and unveiled that bone whose inflammation was the sincerest form of flattery. What followed was comical in its gracelessness; as her body was comical, with its scars and its places where age puckered and plucked at it. She watched his ungainly attempts at congress quite remotely. His buttocks were pale, and imprinted with the marks his underwear had left; their motion put her in mind of a mechanical toy.

He kissed her as he worked, and swallowed the pestilence with her spittle; his hands came off her body gritty with her contagious cells. He knew none of this, of course. He was perfectly innocent of what corruption he embraced, and took into himself with every uninspired thrust.

At last, he finished. There was no gasp, no cry. He simply stopped his clockwork motion and climbed off her, wiping himself with the edge of the sheet, and buttoning himself up again.

Guides were calling her. She had journeys to make, reunions to look forward to. But she did not want to go; at least not yet. She steered the vehicle of her spirit to a fresh vantage-point, where she could better see Kavanagh's face. Her sight, or whatever sense this condition granted her, saw clearly how his features were painted over a groundwork of muscle, and how, beneath that intricate scheme, the bones sheened. Ah, the bone. He was not Death of course; and yet he was. He had the face, hadn't he?; and one day, given decay's blessing, he'd show it. Such a pity that a scraping of flesh came between it and the naked eye.

Come away, the voices insisted. She knew they could not be fobbed off very much longer. Indeed there were some amongst them she thought she knew. *A moment*, she pleaded, *only a moment more*.

Kavanagh had finished his business at the murder-scene. He checked his appearance in the wardrobe mirror, then went to the door. She went with him, intrigued by the utter banality of his expression. He slipped out onto the silent landing and then down the stairs, waiting for a moment when the night-porter was otherwise engaged before stepping out into the street, and liberty.

Was it dawn that washed the sky, or the illuminations? Perhaps she had watched him from the corner of the room longer than she'd thought – hours passing as moments in the state she had so recently achieved.

Only at the last was she rewarded for her vigil, as a look she recognised crossed Kavanagh's face. Hunger! The man was hungry. He would not die of the plague, any more than she had. Its presence shone in him – gave a fresh lustre to his skin, and a new insistence to his belly.

He had come to her a minor murderer, and was going from her as Death writ large. She laughed, seeing the self-fulfilling prophecy she had unwittingly engineered. For an instant his pace slowed, as if he might have heard her. But no; it was the drummer he was listening for, beating louder than ever in his ear and demanding, as he went, a new and deadly vigour in his every step.

How Spoilers Bleed

Locke raised his eyes to the trees. The wind was moving in them, and the commotion of their laden branches sounded like the river in full spate. One impersonation of many. When he had first come to the jungle he had been awed by the sheer multiplicity of beast and blossom, the relentless parade of life here. But he had learned better. This burgeoning diversity was a sham; the jungle pretending itself an artless garden. It was not. Where the untutored trespasser saw only a brilliant show of natural splendours, Locke now recognised a subtle conspiracy at work, in which each thing mirrored some other thing. The trees, the river; a blossom, a bird. In a moth's wing, a monkey's eye; on a lizard's back, sunlight on stones. Round and round in a dizzying circle of impersonations, a hall of mirrors which confounded the senses and would, given time, rot reason altogether. See us now, he thought drunkenly as they stood around Cherrick's grave, look at how we play the game too. We're living; but we impersonate the dead better than the dead themselves.

The corpse had been one scab by the time they'd hoisted it into a sack and carried it outside to this miserable plot behind Tetelman's house to bury. There were half a dozen other graves here. All Europeans, to judge by the names crudely burned into the wooden crosses; killed by snakes, or heat, or longing.

Tetelman attempted to say a brief prayer in Spanish, but the roar of the trees, and the din of birds making their way home to their roosts before night came down, all but drowned him out. He gave up eventually, and they made their way back into the cooler interior of the house, where Stumpf was sitting, drinking brandy and staring inanely at the darkening stain on the floorboards.

Outside, two of Tetelman's tamed Indians were shovelling the rank jungle earth on top of Cherrick's sack, eager to be done with the work and away before nightfall. Locke watched from the window. The grave-diggers didn't talk as they laboured, but filled the shallow grave up, then flattened the earth as best they could with the leather-tough soles of their feet. As they did so the stamping of the ground took on a rhythm. It occurred to Locke that the men were probably the worse for bad whisky; he knew few Indians who didn't drink like fishes. Now, staggering a little, they began to dance on Cherrick's grave.

'Locke?'

Locke woke. In the darkness, a cigarette glowed. As the smoker drew on it, and the tip burned more intensely, Stumpf's wasted features swam up out of the night.

'Locke? Are you awake?'

'What do you want?'

'I can't sleep,' the mask replied, 'I've been thinking. The supply plane comes in from Santarem the day after tomorrow. We could be back there in a few hours. Out of all this.'

'Sure.'

'I mean permanently,' Stumpf said. 'Away.'

'Permanently?'

Stumpf lit another cigarette from the embers of his last before saying, 'I don't believe in curses. Don't think I do.'

'Who said anything about curses?'

'You saw Cherrick's body. What happened to him . . .'

'There's a disease,' said Locke, 'what's it called? – when the blood doesn't set properly?'

'Haemophilia,' Stumpf replied. 'He didn't have haemophilia and we both know it. I've seen him scratched and cut dozens of times. He mended like you or I.'

Locke snatched at a mosquito that had alighted on his chest and ground it out between thumb and forefinger.

'All right. Then what killed him?'

'You saw the wounds better than I did, but it seemed to me his skin just broke open as soon as he was touched.'

Locke nodded. 'That's the way it looked.'

'Maybe it's something he caught off the Indians.'

Locke took the point. '*I* didn't touch any of them,' he said.

'Neither did I. But he did, remember?'

Locke remembered; scenes like that weren't easy to forget, try as he might. 'Christ,' he said, his voice hushed. 'What a fucking situation.'

'I'm going back to Santarem. I don't want them coming looking for me.'

'They're not going to.'

'How do you know? We screwed up back there. We could have bribed them. Got them off the land some other way.'

'I doubt it. You heard what Tetelman said. Ancestral territories.'

'You can have my share of the land,' Stumpf said, 'I want no part of it.'

'You mean it then? You're getting out?'

'I feel dirty. We're spoilers, Locke.'

'It's your funeral.'

'I mean it. I'm not like you. Never really had the stomach for this kind of thing. Will you buy my third off me?'

'Depends on your price.'

'Whatever you want to give. It's yours.'

Confessional over, Stumpf returned to his bed, and lay down in the darkness to finish off his cigarette. It would soon be light. Another jungle dawn: a precious interval, all too short, before the world began to sweat. How he *hated* the place. At least he hadn't touched any of the Indians; hadn't even been within breathing distance of them. Whatever infection they'd passed on to Cherrick he could surely not be tainted. In less than forty-eight hours he would be away to Santarem, and then on to some city, *any* city, where the tribe could never follow. He'd already done his penance, hadn't he?; paid for his greed and his arrogance with the rot in his abdomen and the terrors he knew he would never quite shake off again. Let that be punishment enough, he prayed, and slipped, before the monkeys began to call up the day, into a spoiler's sleep.

A gem-backed beetle, trapped beneath Stumpf's mosquito net, hummed around in diminishing circles, looking for some way out. It could find none. Eventually, exhausted by the search, it hovered over the sleeping man, then landed on his forehead. There it wandered, drinking at the pores. Beneath its imperceptible tread, Stumpf's skin opened and broke into a trail of tiny wounds.

They had come into the Indian hamlet at noon; the sun a basilisk's eye. At first they had thought the place deserted. Locke and Cherrick had advanced into the compound, leaving the dysentery-ridden Stumpf in the jeep, out of the worst of the heat. It was Cherrick who first noticed the child. A pot-bellied boy of perhaps four or five, his face painted with thick bands of the scarlet vegetable dye *urucu*, had slipped out from his hiding place and come to peer at the trespassers, fearless in his curiosity. Cherrick stood still; Locke did the same. One by one, from the huts and from the shelter of the trees around the compound, the tribe

37

appeared and stared, like the boy, at the newcomers. If there was a flicker of feeling on their broad, flat-nosed faces, Locke could not read it. These people – he thought of every Indian as part of one wretched tribe – were impossible to decipher; deceit was their only skill.

'What are you doing here?' he said. The sun was baking the back of his neck. 'This is our land.'

The boy still looked up at him. His almond eyes refused to fear.

'They don't understand you,' Cherrick said.

'Get the Kraut out here. Let him explain it to them.'

'He can't move.'

'*Get him out here,*' Locke said. 'I don't care if he's shat his pants.'

Cherrick backed away down the track, leaving Locke standing in the ring of huts. He looked from doorway to doorway, from tree to tree, trying to estimate the numbers. There were at most three dozen Indians, two-thirds of them women and children; descendants of the great peoples that had once roamed the Amazon Basin in their tens of thousands. Now those tribes were all but decimated. The forest in which they had prospered for generations was being levelled and burned; eight-lane highways were speeding through their hunting grounds. All they held sacred – the wilderness and their place in its system – was being trampled and trespassed: they were exiles in their own land. But still they declined to pay homage to their new masters, despite the rifles they brought. Only death would convince them of defeat, Locke mused.

Cherrick found Stumpf slumped in the front seat of the jeep, his pasty features more wretched than ever.

'Locke wants you,' he said, shaking the German out of his doze. 'The village is still occupied. You'll have to speak to them.'

Stumpf groaned. 'I can't move,' he said, 'I'm dying – '

'Locke wants you dead or alive,' Cherrick said. Their fear of Locke, which went unspoken, was perhaps one of the two things they had in common; that and greed.

'I feel awful,' Stumpf said.

'If I don't bring you, he'll only come himself,' Cherrick pointed out. This was indisputable. Stumpf threw the other man a despairing glance, then nodded his jowly head. 'All right,' he said, 'help me.'

Cherrick had no wish to lay a hand on Stumpf. The man stank of his sickness; he seemed to be oozing the contents of his gut through his pores; his skin had the lustre of rank meat. He took the outstretched hand nevertheless. Without aid, Stumpf would never make the hundred yards from jeep to compound.

Ahead, Locke was shouting.

'Get moving,' said Cherrick, hauling Stumpf down from the front seat and towards the bawling voice. 'Let's get it over and done with.'

When the two men returned into the circle of huts the scene had scarcely changed. Locke glanced around at Stumpf.

'We got trespassers,' he said.

'So I see,' Stumpf returned wearily.

'Tell them to get the fuck off our land,' Locke said. 'Tell them this is our territory: we bought it. Without sitting tenants.'

Stumpf nodded, not meeting Locke's rabid eyes. Sometimes he hated the man almost as much as he hated himself.

'Go on . . .' Locke said, and gestured for Cherrick to relinquish his support of Stumpf. This he did. The German stumbled forward, head bowed. He took several seconds to work out his patter, then raised his head and spoke a few wilting words in bad Portuguese. The pronouncement was met with the same blank looks as Locke's performance. Stumpf tried again, re-arranging his inadequate vocabulary to try and awake a flicker of understanding amongst these savages.

The boy who had been so entertained by Locke's cavortings now stood staring up at this third demon, his face wiped of smiles. This one was nowhere near as comical as the first. He was sick and haggard; he smelt of death. The boy held his nose to keep from inhaling the badness off the man.

Stumpf peered through greasy eyes at his audience. If they *did* understand, and were faking their blank incomprehension, it was a flawless performance. His limited skills defeated, he turned giddily to Locke.

'They don't understand me,' he said.

'Tell them again.'

'I don't think they speak Portuguese.'

'Tell them anyway.'

Cherrick cocked his rifle. 'We don't have to talk with them,' he said under his breath. 'They're on our land. We're within our rights – '

'No,' said Locke. 'There's no need for shooting. Not if we can persuade them to go peacefully.'

'They don't understand plain common sense,' Cherrick said. 'Look at them. They're animals. Living in filth.'

Stumpf had begun to try and communicate again, this time accompanying his hesitant words with a pitiful mime.

'Tell them we've got work to do here,' Locke prompted him.

'I'm trying my best,' Stumpf replied testily.

'We've got papers.'

'I don't think they'd be much impressed,' Stumpf returned, with a cautious sarcasm that was lost on the other man.

'Just tell them to move on. Find some other piece of land to squat on.'

Watching Stumpf put these sentiments into word and sign-language, Locke was already running through the alternative options available. Either the Indians – the Txukahamei or the Achual or whatever damn family it was – accepted their demands and moved on, or else they would have to enforce the edict. As Cherrick had said, they were within their rights. They had papers from the development authorities; they had maps marking the division between one territory and the next; they had every sanction from signature to bullet. He had no active desire to shed blood. The world was still too full of bleeding heart liberals and doe-eyed sentimentalists to make genocide the most convenient solution. But the gun had been used before, and would be used again, until every unwashed Indian had put on a pair of trousers and given up eating monkeys.

Indeed, the din of liberals notwithstanding, the gun had its appeal. It was swift, and absolute. Once it had had its short, sharp say there was no danger of further debate; no chance that in ten years' time some mercenary Indian who'd found a copy of Marx in the gutter could come back claiming his tribal lands – oil, minerals and all. Once gone, they were gone forever.

At the thought of these scarlet-faced savages laid low, Locke felt his trigger-finger itch; physically *itch*. Stumpf had finished his encore; it had met with no response. Now he groaned, and turned to Locke.

'I'm going to be sick,' he said. His face was bright white; the glamour of his skin made his small teeth look dingy.

'Be my guest,' Locke replied.

'*Please*. I have to lie down. I don't want them watching me.'

Locke shook his head. 'You don't move 'til they listen. If we don't get any joy from them, you're going to see something to be sick about.' Locke toyed with the stock of his rifle as he spoke, running a broken thumb-nail along the nicks in it. There were perhaps a dozen; each one a human grave. The jungle concealed murder so easily; it almost seemed, in its cryptic fashion, to condone the crime.

Stumpf turned away from Locke and scanned the mute assembly. There were so many Indians here, he thought, and though he carried a pistol he was an inept marksman. Suppose they rushed Locke, Cherrick and himself?; he would not survive. And yet, looking at the Indians, he could see no sign of aggression amongst them. Once they had been warriors; now?; like beaten children, sullen and wilfully stupid. There was some trace of beauty in one or two of the younger women; their skins, though grimy, were fine, their eyes black. Had he felt more healthy he might have been aroused by their nakedness, tempted to press his hands upon their shiny bodies. As it was their feigned incomprehension merely irritated him. They seemed, in their silence, like another species, as mysterious and unfathomable as mules or birds. Hadn't somebody in Uxituba told him that many of these people didn't even give their children proper names?; that each was like a limb of the tribe, anonymous and therefore unfixable? He could believe that now, meeting the same dark stare in each pair of eyes; could believe that what they faced here was not three dozen individuals but a fluid system of hatred made flesh. It made him shudder to think of it.

Now, for the first time since their appearance, one of the assembly moved. He was an ancient; fully thirty years older than most of the tribe. He, like the rest, was all but naked. The sagging flesh of his limbs and breasts resembled tanned hide; his step, though the pale eyes suggested blindness, was perfectly confident. Once standing in front of the interlopers he opened his mouth – there were no teeth set in his rotted gums – and spoke. What emerged from his scraggy throat was not a language made of words, but only of sound; a pot-pourri of jungle noises. There was no discernible pattern to the outpouring, it was simply a display – awesome in its way – of impersonations. The man could murmur like a jaguar, screech like a parrot; he could find in his throat the splash of rain on orchids; the howl of monkeys.

The sounds made Stumpf's gorge rise. The jungle had diseased him, dehydrated him and left him wrung out. Now this rheumy-eyed stick-man was vomiting the whole odious place up at him. The raw heat in the circle of huts made Stumpf's head beat, and he was sure, as he stood listening to the sage's din, that the old man was measuring the rhythm of his nonsense to the thud at his temples and wrists.

41

'What's he saying?' Locke demanded.

'What does it sound like?' Stumpf replied, irritated by Locke's idiot questions. 'It's all noises.'

'The fucker's cursing us,' Cherrick said.

Stumpf looked round at the third man. Cherrick's eyes were starting from his head.

'It's a curse,' he said to Stumpf.

Locke laughed, unmoved by Cherrick's apprehension. He pushed Stumpf out of the way so as to face the old man, whose song-speech had now lowered in pitch; it was almost lilting. He was singing twilight, Stumpf thought: that brief ambiguity between the fierce day and the suffocating night. Yes, that was it. He could hear in the song the purr and the coo of a drowsy kingdom. It was so persuasive he wanted to lie down on the spot where he stood, and sleep.

Locke broke the spell. 'What are you saying?' he spat in the tribesman's mazy face. 'Talk sense!'

But the night-noises only whispered on, an unbroken stream.

'This is our village,' another voice now broke in; the man spoke as if translating the elder's words. Locke snapped round to locate the speaker. He was a thin youth, whose skin might once have been golden. '*Our* village. *Our* land.'

'You speak English,' Locke said.

'Some,' the youth replied.

'Why didn't you answer me earlier?' Locke demanded, his fury exacerbated by the disinterest on the Indian's face.

'Not my place to speak,' the man replied. 'He is the elder.'

'The Chief, you mean?'

'The Chief is dead. All his family is dead. This is the wisest of us – '

'Then you tell him – '

'No need to tell,' the young man broke in. 'He understands you.'

'He speaks English too?'

'No,' the other replied, 'but he understands you. You are . . . transparent.'

Locke half-grasped that the youth was implying an insult here, but wasn't quite certain. He gave Stumpf a puzzled look. The German shook his head. Locke returned his attention to the youth. 'Tell him anyway,' he said, 'tell all of them. This is our land. We bought it.'

'The tribe has always lived here,' the reply came.

42

'Not any longer,' Cherrick said.

'We've got papers – ' Stumpf said mildly, still hoping that the confrontation might end peacefully, ' – from the government.'

'We were here before the government,' the tribesman replied.

The old man had stopped talking the forest. Perhaps, Stumpf thought, he's coming to the beginning of another day, and stopped. He was turning away now, indifferent to the presence of these unwelcome guests.

'Call him back,' Locke demanded, stabbing his rifle towards the young tribesman. The gesture was unambiguous. 'Make him tell the rest of them they've got to go.'

The young man seemed unimpressed by the threat of Locke's rifle, however, and clearly unwilling to give orders to his elder, whatever the imperative. He simply watched the old man walk back towards the hut from which he had emerged. Around the compound, others were also turning away. The old man's withdrawal apparently signalled that the show was over.

'*No!*' said Cherrick, 'you're not *listening.*' The colour in his cheeks had risen a tone; his voice, an octave. He pushed forward, rifle raised. '*You fucking scum!*'

Despite his hysteria, he was rapidly losing his audience. The old man had reached the doorway of his hut, and now bent his back and disappeared into its recesses; the few members of the tribe who were still showing some interest in proceedings were viewing the Europeans with a hint of pity for their lunacy. It only enraged Cherrick further.

'Listen to me!' he shrieked, sweat flicking off his brow as he jerked his head at one retreating figure and then at another. '*Listen*, you bastards.'

'Easy . . .' said Stumpf.

The appeal triggered Cherrick. Without warning he raised his rifle to his shoulder, aimed at the open door of the hut into which the old man had vanished and fired. Birds rose from the crowns of adjacent trees; dogs took to their heels. From within the hut came a tiny shriek, not like the old man's voice at all. As it sounded, Stumpf fell to his knees, hugging his belly, his gut in spasm. Face to the ground, he did not see the diminutive figure emerge from the hut and totter into the sunlight. Even when he did look up, and saw how the child with the scarlet face clutched his belly, he hoped his eyes lied. But they did not. It was blood that came from between the child's tiny fingers, and death that had stricken his face. He fell forward on to the impacted earth of the hut's threshold, twitched, and died.

Somewhere amongst the huts a woman began to sob quietly. For a moment the world spun on a pin-head, balanced exquisitely between silence and the cry that must break it, between a truce held and the coming atrocity.

'You stupid bastard,' Locke murmured to Cherrick. Under his condemnation, his voice trembled. 'Back off,' he said. 'Get up, Stumpf. We're not waiting. Get up and come now, or don't come at all.'

Stumpf was still looking at the body of the child. Suppressing his moans, he got to his feet.

'Help me,' he said. Locke lent him an arm. 'Cover us,' he said to Cherrick.

The man nodded, deathly-pale. Some of the tribe had turned their gaze on the Europeans' retreat, their expressions, despite this tragedy, as inscrutable as ever. Only the sobbing woman, presumably the dead child's mother, wove between the silent figures, keening her grief.

Cherrick's rifle shook as he kept the bridgehead. He'd done the mathematics; if it came to a head-on collision they had little chance of survival. But even now, with the enemy making a getaway, there was no sign of movement amongst the Indians. Just the accusing facts: the dead boy; the warm rifle. Cherrick chanced a look over his shoulder. Locke and Stumpf were already within twenty yards of the jeep, and there was still no move from the savages.

Then, as he looked back towards the compound, it seemed as though the tribe breathed together one solid breath, and hearing that sound Cherrick felt death wedge itself like a fish-bone in his throat, too deep to be plucked out by his fingers, too big to be shat. It was just waiting there, lodged in his anatomy, beyond argument or appeal. He was distracted from its presence by a movement at the door of the hut. Quite ready to make the same mistake again, he took firmer hold of his rifle. The old man had re-appeared at the door. He stepped over the corpse of the boy, which was lying where it had toppled. Again, Cherrick glanced behind him. Surely they were at the jeep? But Stumpf had stumbled; Locke was even now dragging him to his feet. Cherrick, seeing the old man advancing towards him, took one cautious step backwards, followed by another. But the old man was fearless. He walked swiftly across the compound coming to stand so close to Cherrick, his body as vulnerable as ever, that the barrel of the rifle prodded his shrunken belly.

There was blood on both his hands, fresh enough to run down the man's arms when he displayed the palms for Cherrick's benefit. Had he touched the boy, Cherrick wondered, as he stepped out of the hut? If so, it had been an astonishing sleight-of-hand, for Cherrick had seen nothing. Trick or no trick, the significance of the display was perfectly apparent: he was being accused of murder. Cherrick wasn't about to be cowed, however. He stared back at the old man, matching defiance with defiance.

But the old bastard did nothing, except show his bloody palms, his eyes full of tears. Cherrick could feel his anger growing again. He poked the man's flesh with his finger.

'You don't frighten me,' he said, 'you understand? I'm not a fool.'

As he spoke he seemed to see a shifting in the old man's features. It was a trick of the sun, of course, or of bird-shadow, but there was, beneath the corruption of age, a hint of the child now dead at the hut door: the tiny mouth even seemed to smile. Then, as subtly as it had appeared, the illusion faded again.

Cherrick withdrew his hand from the old man's chest, narrowing his eyes against further mirages. He then renewed his retreat. He had taken three steps only when something broke cover to his left. He swung round, raised his rifle and fired. A piebald pig, one of several that had been grazing around the huts, was checked in its flight by the bullet, which struck it in the neck. It seemed to trip over itself, and collapsed headlong in the dust.

Cherrick swung his rifle back towards the old man. But he hadn't moved, except to open his mouth. His palate was making the sound of the dying pig. A choking squeal, pitiful and ridiculous, which followed Cherrick back up the path to the jeep. Locke had the engine running. 'Get in,' he said. Cherrick needed no encouragement, but flung himself into the front seat. The interior of the vehicle was filthy hot, and stank of Stumpf's bodily functions, but it was as near safety as they'd been in the last hour.

'It was a pig,' he said, 'I shot a pig.'

'I saw,' said Locke.

'That old bastard . . .'

He didn't finish. He was looking down at the two fingers with which he had prodded the elder. 'I touched him,' he muttered, perplexed by what he saw. The finger-tips were bloody, though the flesh he had laid his fingers upon had been clean.

Locke ignored Cherrick's confusion and backed the jeep up to turn it around, then drove away from the hamlet, down a track that seemed to have become choked with foliage in the hour since they'd come up it. There was no discernible pursuit.

The tiny trading post to the south of Averio was scant of civilisation, but it sufficed. There were white faces here, and clean water. Stumpf, whose condition had deteriorated on the return journey, was treated by Dancy, an Englishman who had the manner of a disenfranchised Earl and a face like hammered steak. He claimed to have been a doctor once upon a sober time, and though he had no evidence of his qualifications nobody contested his right to deal with Stumpf. The German was delirious, and on occasion violent, but Dancy, his small hands heavy with gold rings, seemed to take a positive delight in nursing his thrashing patient.

While Stumpf raved beneath his mosquito net, Locke and Cherrick sat in the lamp-lit gloom and drank, then told the story of their encounter with the tribe. It was Tetelman, the owner of the trading post's stores, who had most to say when the report was finished. He knew the Indians well.

'I've been here years,' he said, feeding nuts to the mangy monkey that scampered on his lap. 'I know the way these people think. They may act as though they're stupid; cowards even. Take it from me, they're neither.'

Cherrick grunted. The quicksilver monkey fixed him with vacant eyes. 'They didn't make a move on us,' Cherrick said, 'even though they outnumbered us ten to one. If that isn't cowardice, what is it?'

Tetelman settled back in his creaking chair, throwing the animal off his lap. His face was raddled and used. Only his lips, constantly rewetted from his glass, had any colour; he looked, thought Locke, like an old whore. 'Thirty years ago,' Tetelman said, 'this whole territory was their homeland. Nobody wanted it; they *went* where they liked, *did* what they liked. As far as we whites were concerned the jungle was filthy and disease-infected: we wanted no part of it. And, of course, in some ways we were right. It *is* filthy and disease-infected; but it's also got reserves we now want badly: minerals, oil maybe: power.'

'We paid for that land,' said Locke, his fingers jittery on the cracked rim of his glass. 'It's all we've got now.'

Tetelman sneered. 'Paid?' he said. The monkey chattered at his

46

feet, apparently as amused by this claim as its master. 'No. You just paid for a blind eye, so you could take it by force. You paid for the right to fuck up the Indians in any way you could. That's what your dollars bought, Mr Locke. The government of this country is counting off the months until every tribe on the sub-continent is wiped out by you or your like. It's no use to play the outraged innocents. I've been here too long . . .'

Cherrick spat on to the bare floor. Tetelman's speech had heated his blood.

'And so why'd *you* come here, if you're so fucking clever?' he asked the trader.

'Same reason as you,' Tetelman replied plainly, staring off into the trees beyond the plot of land behind the store. Their silhouettes shook against the sky; wind, or night-birds.

'What reason's that?' Cherrick said, barely keeping his hostility in check.

'Greed,' Tetelman replied mildly, still watching the trees. Something scampered across the low wooden roof. The monkey at Tetelman's feet listened, head cocked. 'I thought I could make my fortune out here, the same way you do. I gave myself two years. Three at the most. That was the best part of two decades ago.' He frowned; whatever thoughts passed behind his eyes, they were bitter. 'The jungle eats you up and spits you out, sooner or later.'

'Not me,' said Locke.

Tetelman turned his eyes on the man. They were wet. 'Oh yes,' he said politely. 'Extinction's in the air, Mr Locke. I can smell it.' Then he turned back to looking at the window.

Whatever was on the roof now had companions.

'They won't come here, will they?' said Cherrick. 'They won't follow us?'

The question, spoken almost in a whisper, begged for a reply in the negative. Try as he might Cherrick couldn't dislodge the sights of the previous day. It wasn't the boy's corpse that so haunted him; that he could soon learn to forget. But the elder – with his shifting, sunlit face – and the palms raised as if to display some stigmata, he was not so forgettable.

'Don't fret,' Tetelman said, with a trace of condescension. 'Sometimes one or two of them will drift in here with a parrot to sell, or a few pots, but I've never seen them come here in any numbers. They don't like it. This is civilisation as far as they're concerned, and it intimidates them. Besides, they wouldn't harm my guests. They need me.'

'Need you?' said Locke; who could need this wreck of a man?

'They use our medicines. Dancy supplies them. And blankets, once in a while. As I said, they're not so stupid.'

Next door, Stumpf had begun to howl. Dancy's consoling voice could be heard, attempting to talk down the panic. He was plainly failing.

'Your friend's gone bad,' said Tetelman.

'No friend,' Cherrick replied.

'It rots,' Tetelman murmured, half to himself.

'What does?'

'The soul.' The word was utterly out of place from Tetelman's whisky-glossed lips. 'It's like fruit, you see. It rots.'

Somehow Stumpf's cries gave force to the observation. It was not the voice of a wholesome creature; there was putrescence in it.

More to direct his attention away from the German's din than out of any real interest, Cherrick said: 'What do they give you for the medicine and the blankets? Women?'

The possibility clearly entertained Tetelman; he laughed, his gold teeth gleaming. 'I've no use for women,' he said. 'I've had the syph for too many years.' He clicked his fingers and the monkey clambered back up on to his lap. 'The soul,' he said, 'isn't the only thing that rots.'

'Well, what do you get from them then?' Locke said. 'For your supplies?'

'Artifacts,' Tetelman replied. 'Bowls, jugs, mats. The Americans buy them off me, and sell them again in Manhattan. Everybody wants something made by an extinct tribe these days. *Memento mori*.'

'Extinct?' said Locke. The word had a seductive ring; it sounded like life to him.

'Oh certainly,' said Tetelman. 'They're as good as gone. If you don't wipe them out, they'll do it themselves.'

'Suicide?' Locke said.

'In their fashion. They just lose heart. I've seen it happen half a dozen times. A tribe loses its land, and its appetite for life goes with it. They stop taking care of themselves. The women don't get pregnant any more; the young men take to drink, the old men just starve themselves to death. In a year or two it's like they never existed.'

Locke swallowed the rest of his drink, silently saluting the fatal wisdom of these people. They knew when to die, which was more than could be said for some he'd met. The thought of their death-

48

wish absolved him of any last vestiges of guilt. What was the gun in his hand, except an instrument of evolution?

On the fourth day after their arrival at the post, Stumpf's fever abated, much to Dancy's disappointment. 'The worst of it's over,' he announced. 'Give him two more days' rest and you can get back to your labours.'

'What are your plans?' Tetelman wanted to know.

Locke was watching the rain from the verandah. Sheets of water pouring from clouds so low they brushed the tree-tops. Then, just as suddenly as it had arrived, the downpour was gone, as though a tap had been turned off. Sun broke through; the jungle, new-washed, was steaming and sprouting and thriving again.

'I don't know what we'll do,' said Locke. 'Maybe get ourselves some help and go back in there.'

'There are ways,' Tetelman said.

Cherrick, sitting beside the door to get the benefit of what little breeze was available, picked up the glass that had scarcely been out of his hand in recent days, and filled it up again. 'No more guns,' he said. He hadn't touched his rifle since they'd arrived at the post; in fact he kept from contact with anything but a bottle and his bed. His skin seemed to crawl and creep perpetually.

'No need for guns,' Tetelman murmured. The statement hung on the air like an unfulfilled promise.

'Get rid of them without guns?' said Locke. 'If you mean waiting for them to die out naturally, I'm not that patient.'

'No,' said Tetelman, 'we can be swifter than that.'

'How?'

Tetelman gave the man a lazy look. 'They're my livelihood,' he said, 'or part of it. You're asking me to help you make myself bankrupt.'

He not only looks like an old whore, Locke thought, he thinks like one. 'What's it worth? Your wisdom?' he asked.

'A cut of whatever you find on your land,' Tetelman replied.

Locke nodded. 'What have we got to lose? Cherrick? You agree to cut him in?' Cherrick's consent was a shrug. 'All right,' Locke said, 'talk.'

'They need medicines,' Tetelman explained, 'because they're so susceptible to our diseases. A decent plague can wipe them out practically overnight.'

Locke thought about this, not looking at Tetelman. 'One fell swoop,' Tetelman continued. 'They've got practically no defences

49

against certain bacteria. Never had to build up any resistance. The clap. Smallpox. Even measles.'

'How?' said Locke.

Another silence. Down the steps of the verandah, where civilization finished, the jungle was swelling to meet the sun. In the liquid heat plants blossomed and rotted and blossomed again.

'I asked *how*,' Locke said.

'Blankets,' Tetelman replied, 'dead men's blankets.'

A little before the dawn of the night after Stumpf's recovery, Cherrick woke suddenly, startled from his rest by bad dreams. Outside it was pitch-dark; neither moon nor stars relieved the depth of the night. But his body-clock, which his life as a mercenary had trained to impressive accuracy, told him that first light was not far off, and he had no wish to lay his head down again and sleep. Not with the old man waiting to be dreamt. It wasn't just the raised palms, the blood glistening, that so distressed Cherrick. It was the words he'd dreamt coming from the old man's toothless mouth which had brought on the cold sweat that now encased his body.

What were the words? He couldn't recall them now, but wanted to; wanted the sentiments dragged into wakefulness, where they could be dissected and dismissed as ridiculous. They wouldn't come though. He lay on his wretched cot, the dark wrapping him up too tightly for him to move, and suddenly the bloody hands were there, in front of him, suspended in the pitch. There was no face, no sky, no tribe. Just the hands.

'Dreaming,' Cherrick told himself, but he knew better.

And now, the voice. He was getting his wish; here were the words he had dreamt spoken. Few of them made sense. Cherrick lay like a new-born baby, listening to its parents talk but unable to make any significance of their exchanges. He was ignorant wasn't he?; he tasted the sourness of his stupidity for the first time since childhood. The voice made him fearful of ambiguities he had ridden roughshod over, of whispers his shouting life had rendered inaudible. He fumbled for comprehension, and was not entirely frustrated. The man was speaking of the world, and of exile from the world; of being broken always by what one seeks to possess. Cherrick struggled, wishing he could stop the voice and ask for explanation. But it was already fading, ushered away by the wild address of parrots in the trees, raucous and gaudy voices erupting suddenly on every side. Through the mesh of Cherrick's mosquito net he could see the sky flaring through the branches.

He sat up. Hands and voice had gone; and with them all but an irritating murmur of what he had almost understood. He had thrown off in sleep his single sheet; now he looked down at his body with distaste. His back and buttocks, and the underside of his thighs, felt sore. Too much sweating on coarse sheets, he thought. Not for the first time in recent days he remembered a small house in Bristol which he had once known as home.

The noise of birds was filling his head. He hauled himself to the edge of the bed and pulled back the mosquito net. The crude weave of the net seemed to scour the palm of his hand as he gripped it. He disengaged his hold, and cursed to himself. There was again today an itch of tenderness in his skin that he'd suffered since coming to the post. Even the soles of his feet, pressed on to the floor by the weight of his body, seemed to suffer each knot and splinter. He wanted to be away from this place, and badly.

A warm trickle across his wrist caught his attention, and he was startled to see a rivulet of blood moving down his arm from his hand. There was a cut in the cushion of his thumb, where the mosquito net had apparently nicked his flesh. It was bleeding, though not copiously. He sucked at the cut, feeling again that peculiar sensitivity to touch that only drink, and that in abundance, dulled. Spitting out blood, he began to dress.

The clothes he put on were a scourge to his back. His sweat-stiffened shirt rubbed against his shoulders and neck; he seemed to feel every thread chafing his nerve-endings. The shirt might have been sack-cloth, the way it abraded him.

Next door, he heard Locke moving around. Gingerly finishing his dressing, Cherrick went through to join him. Locke was sitting at the table by the window. He was poring over a map of Tetelman's, and drinking a cup of the bitter coffee Dancy was so fond of brewing, which he drank with a dollop of condensed milk. The two men had little to say to each other. Since the incident in the village all pretence to respect or friendship had disappeared. Locke now showed undisguised contempt for his sometime companion. The only fact that kept them together was the contract they and Stumpf had signed. Rather than breakfast on whisky, which he knew Locke would take as a further sign of his decay, Cherrick poured himself a slug of Dancy's emetic and went out to look at the morning.

He felt strange. There was something about this dawning day which made him profoundly uneasy. He knew the dangers of courting unfounded fears, and he tried to forbid them, but they were incontestable.

Was it simply exhaustion that made him so painfully conscious of his many discomforts this morning? Why else did he feel the pressure of his stinking clothes so acutely? The rasp of his boot collar against the jutting bone of his ankle, the rhythmical chafing of his trousers against his inside leg as he walked, even the grazing air that eddied around his exposed face and arms. The world was pressing on him – at least that was the sensation – pressing as though it wanted him out.

A large dragonfly, whining towards him on iridescent wings, collided with his arm. The pain of the collision caused him to drop his mug. It didn't break, but rolled off the verandah and was lost in the undergrowth. Angered, Cherrick slapped the insect off, leaving a smear of blood on his tattooed forearm to mark the dragonfly's demise. He wiped it off. It welled up again on the same spot, full and dark.

It wasn't the blood of the insect, he realised, but his own. The dragonfly had cut him somehow, though he had felt nothing. Irritated, he peered more closely at his punctured skin. The wound was not significant, but it *was* painful.

From inside he could hear Locke talking. He was loudly describing the inadequacy of his fellow adventurers to Tetelman.

'Stumpf's not fit for this kind of work,' he was saying. 'And Cherrick – '

'What about me?'

Cherrick stepped into the shabby interior, wiping a new flow of blood from his arm.

Locke didn't even bother to look up at him. 'You're paranoid,' he said plainly. 'Paranoid and unreliable.'

Cherrick was in no mood for taking Locke's foul-mouthing. 'Just because I killed some Indian brat,' he said. The more he brushed blood from his bitten arm, the more the place stung. 'You just didn't have the balls to do it yourself.'

Locke still didn't bother to look up from his perusal of the map. Cherrick moved across to the table.

'Are you listening to me?' he demanded, and added force to his question by slamming his fist down on to the table. On impact his hand simply burst open. Blood spurted out in every direction, spattering the map.

Cherrick howled, and reeled backwards from the table with blood pouring from a yawning split in the side of his hand. The bone showed. Through the din of pain in his head he could hear a quiet voice. The words were inaudible, but he knew whose they were.

'I won't hear!' he said, shaking his head like a dog with a flea in its ear. He staggered back against the wall, but the briefest of contacts was another agony. *I won't hear, damn you!*

'What the hell's he talking about?' Dancy had appeared in the doorway, woken by the cries, still clutching the *Complete Works of Shelley* Tetelman had said he could not sleep without.

Locke re-addressed the question to Cherrick, who was standing, wild-eyed, in the corner of the room, blood spitting from between his fingers as he attempted to staunch his wounded hand. 'What are you saying?'

'He spoke to me,' Cherrick replied. 'The old man.'

'What old man?' Tetelman asked.

'He means at the village,' Locke said. Then, to Cherrick, 'Is that what you mean?'

'He wants us out. Exiles. Like them. *Like them!*' Cherrick's panic was rapidly rising out of anyone's control, least of all his own.

'The man's got heat-stroke,' Dancy said, ever the diagnostician. Locke knew better.

'Your hand needs bandaging . . .' he said, slowly approaching Cherrick.

'I heard him . . .' Cherrick muttered.

'I believe you. Just slow down. We can sort it out.'

'No,' the other man replied. 'It's pushing us out. Everything we touch. Everything we touch.'

He looked as though he was about to topple over, and Locke reached for him. As his hands made contact with Cherrick's shoulders the flesh beneath the shirt split, and Locke's hands were instantly soaked in scarlet. He withdrew them, appalled. Cherrick fell to his knees, which in their turn became new wounds. He stared down as his shirt and trousers darkened. 'What's happening to me?' he wept.

Dancy moved towards him. 'Let me help.'

'No! Don't touch me!' Cherrick pleaded, but Dancy wasn't to be denied his nursing.

'It's all right,' he said in his best bedside manner.

It wasn't. Dancy's grip, intended only to lift the man from his bleeding knees, opened new cuts wherever he took hold. Dancy felt the blood sprout beneath his hand, felt the flesh slip away from the bone. The sensation bested even his taste for agony. Like Locke, he forsook the lost man.

'He's rotting.' he murmured.

Cherrick's body had split now in a dozen or more places. He tried to stand, half staggering to his feet only to collapse again, his flesh breaking open whenever he touched wall or chair or floor. There was no help for him. All the others could do was stand around like spectators at an execution, awaiting the final throes. Even Stumpf had roused himself from his bed and come through to see what all the shouting was about. He stood leaning against the door-lintel, his disease-thinned face all disbelief.

Another minute, and blood-loss defeated Cherrick. He keeled over and sprawled, face down, across the floor. Dancy crossed back to him and crouched on his haunches beside his head.

'Is he dead?' Locke asked.

'Almost,' Dancy replied.

'Rotted,' said Tetelman, as though the word explained the atrocity they had just witnessed. He had a crucifix in his hand, large and crudely carved. It looked like Indian handiwork, Locke thought. The Messiah impaled on the tree was sloe-eyed and indecently naked. He smiled, despite nail and thorn.

Dancy touched Cherrick's body, letting the blood come with his touch, and turned the man over, then leaned in towards Cherrick's jittering face. The dying man's lips were moving, oh so slightly.

'What are you saying?' Dancy asked; he leaned closer still to catch the man's words. Cherrick's mouth trailed bloody spittle, but no sound came.

Locke stepped in, pushing Dancy aside. Flies were already flitting around Cherrick's face. Locke thrust his bull-necked head into Cherrick's view. 'You hear me?' he said.

The body grunted.

'You know me?'

Again, a grunt.

'You want to give me your share of the land?'

The grunt was lighter this time; almost a sigh.

'There's witnesses here,' Locke said. 'Just say yes. They'll hear you. Just say yes.'

The body was trying its best. It opened its mouth a little wider.

'Dancy – ' said Locke. 'You hear what he said?'

Dancy could not disguise his horror at Locke's insistence, but he nodded.

'You're a witness.'

'If you must,' said the Englishman.

Deep in his body Cherrick felt the fish-bone he'd first choked on in the village twist itself about one final time, and extinguish him.

54

'Did he say yes, Dancy?' Tetelman asked.

Dancy felt the physical proximity of the brute kneeling beside him. He didn't know what the dead man had said, but what did it matter? Locke would have the land anyway, wouldn't he?

'He said yes,'

Locke stood up, and went in search of a fresh cup of coffee.

Without thinking, Dancy put his fingers on Cherrick's lids to seal his empty gaze. Under that lightest of touches the lids broke open and blood tainted the tears that had swelled where Cherrick's sight had been.

They had buried him towards evening. The corpse, though it had lain through the noon-heat in the coolest part of the store, amongst the dried goods, had begun to putrify by the time it was sewn up in canvas for the burial. The night following, Stumpf had come to Locke and offered him the last third of the territory to add to Cherrick's share, and Locke, ever the realist, had accepted. The terms, which were punitive, had been worked out the next day. In the evening of that day, as Stumpf had hoped, the supply plane came in. Locke, bored with Tetelman's contemptuous looks, had also elected to fly back to Santarem, there to drink the jungle out of his system for a few days, and return refreshed. He intended to buy up fresh supplies, and, if possible, hire a reliable driver and gunman.

The flight was noisy, cramped and tedious; the two men exchanged no words for its full duration. Stumpf just kept his eyes on the tracts of unfelled wilderness they passed over, though from one hour to the next the scene scarcely changed. A panorama of sable green, broken on occasion by a glint of water; perhaps a column of blue smoke rising here and there, where land was being cleared; little else.

At Santarem they parted with a single handshake which left every nerve in Stumpf's hand scourged, and an open cut in the tender flesh between index finger and thumb.

Santarem wasn't Rio, Locke mused as he made his way down to a bar at the south end of the town, run by a veteran of Vietnam who had a taste for ad hoc animal shows. It was one of Locke's few certain pleasures, and one he never tired of, to watch a local woman, face dead as a cold manioc cake, submit to a dog or a donkey for a few grubby dollar bills. The women of Santarem were, on the whole, as unpalatable as the beer, but Locke had no eye for beauty in the opposite sex: it mattered only that their bodies be in reasonable working order, and not diseased. He found the bar, and settled down for an evening exchanging dirt with the American. When he tired of that – some time after midnight – he bought a bottle of whisky and went out looking for a face to press his heat upon.

The woman with the squint was about to accede to a particular peccadillo of Locke's – one which she had resolutely refused until drunkenness persuaded her to abandon what little hope of dignity she had – when there came a rap on the door.

'Fuck,' said Locke.

'*Si*,' said the woman. 'Fook. Fook.' It seemed to be the only word she knew in anything resembling English. Locke ignored her and crawled drunkenly to the edge of the stained mattress. Again, the rap on the door.

'Who is it?' he said.

'*Senhor* Locke?' the voice from the hallway was that of a young boy.

'Yes?' said Locke. His trousers had become lost in the tangle of sheets. 'Yes? What do you want?'

'*Mensagem*,' the boy said. '*Urgente. Urgente.*'

'For me?' He had found his trousers, and was pulling them on. The woman, not at all disgruntled by this desertion, watched him from the head of the bed, toying with an empty bottle. Buttoning up, Locke crossed from bed to door, a matter of three steps. He unlocked it. The boy in the darkened hallway was of Indian extraction to judge by the blackness of his eyes, and that peculiar lustre his skin owned. He was dressed in a T-shirt bearing the Coco-Cola motif.

'*Mensagem, Senhor* Locke,' he said again, '. . . *do hospital.*'

The boy was staring past Locke at the woman on the bed. He grinned from ear to ear at her cavortings.

'Hospital?' said Locke.

'*Sim. Hospital "Sacrado Coraçã de Maria".*'

It could only be Stumpf, Locke thought. Who else did he know in this corner of Hell who'd call upon him?; nobody. He looked down at the leering child.

'*Vem comigo*,' the boy said, '*vem comigo. Urgente.*'

'No,' said Locke. 'I'm not coming. Not now. You understand? Later. Later.'

The boy shrugged. '. . . *Tá morrendo*,' he said.

'Dying?' said Locke.

'*Sim. Tá morrendo.*'

'Well, let him. Understand me? You go back, and tell him, I won't come until I'm ready.'

Again, the boy shrugged. '*E meu dinheiro?*' he said, as Locke went to close the door.

'You go to Hell,' Locke replied, and slammed it in the child's face.

When, two hours and one ungainly act of passionless sex later, Locke unlocked the door, he discovered that the child, by way of revenge, had defecated on the threshold.

The hospital '*Sacrado Coraçã de Maria*' was no place to fall ill; better, thought Locke, as he made his way down the dingy corridors, to die in your own bed with your own sweat for company than come here. The stench of disinfectant could not entirely mask the odour of human pain. The walls were ingrained with it; it formed a grease on the lamps, it slickened the unwashed floors. What had happened to Stumpf to bring him here? a bar-room brawl, an argument with a pimp about the price of a woman? The German was just damn fool enough to get himself stuck in the gut over something so petty. '*Senhor* Stumpf?' he asked of a woman in white he accosted in the corridor. 'I'm looking for *Senhor* Stumpf.'

The woman shook her head, and pointed towards a harried-looking man further down the corridor, who was taking a moment to light a small cigar. He let go the nurse's arm and approached the fellow. He was enveloped in a stinking cloud of smoke.

'I'm looking for *Senhor* Stumpf,' he said.

The man peered at him quizzically.

'You are Locke?' he asked.

'Yes.'

'Ah.' He drew on the cigar. The pungency of the expelled smoke would surely have brought on a relapse in the hardiest patient. 'I'm Doctor Edson Costa,' the man said, offering his clammy hand to Locke. 'Your friend has been waiting for you to come all night.'

'What's wrong with him?'

'He's hurt his eye,' Edson Costa replied, clearly indifferent to Stumpf's condition. 'And he has some minor abrasions on his hands and face. But he won't have anyone go near him. He doctored himself.'

'Why?' Locke asked.

The doctor looked flummoxed. 'He pays to go in a clean room. Pays plenty. So I put him in. You want to see him? Maybe take him away?'

'Maybe,' said Locke, unenthusiastically.

'His head . . .' said the doctor. 'He has delusions.'

Without offering further explanation, the man led off at a considerable rate, trailing tobacco-smoke as he went. The route, that wound out of the main building and across a small internal courtyard, ended at a room with a glass partition in the door.

'Here,' said the doctor. 'Your friend. You tell him,' he said as a parting snipe, 'he pay more, or tomorrow he leaves.'

Locke peered through the glass partition. The grubby-white room was empty, but for a bed and a small table, lit by the same dingy light that cursed every wretched inch of this establishment. Stumpf was not on the bed, but squatting on the floor in the corner of the room. His left eye was covered with a bulbous padding, held in place by a bandage ineptly wrapped around his head.

Locke was looking at the man for a good time before Stumpf sensed that he was watched. He looked up slowly. His good eye, as if in compensation for the loss of its companion, seemed to have swelled to twice its natural size. It held enough fear for both it and its twin; indeed enough for a dozen eyes.

Cautiously, like a man whose bones are so brittle he fears an injudicious breath will shatter them, Stumpf edged up the wall, and crossed to the door. He did not open it, but addressed Locke through the glass.

'Why didn't you come?' he said.

'I'm here.'

'But *sooner*,' said Stumpf. His face was raw, as if he'd been beaten. 'Sooner.'

'I had business,' Locke returned. 'What happened to you?'

'It's true, Locke,' the German said, 'everything is true.'

'What are you talking about?'

'Tetelman told me. Cherrick's babblings. About being exiles. It's true. They mean to drive us out.'

'We're not in the jungle now,' Locke said. 'You've got nothing to be afraid of here.'

'Oh yes,' said Stumpf, that wide eye wider than ever. 'Oh yes! I saw him – '

'Who?'

'The elder. From the village. He was here.'

'Ridiculous.'

'*He was here*, damn you,' Stumpf replied. 'He was standing where you're standing. Looking at me through the glass.'

'You've been drinking too much.'

'It happened to Cherrick, and now it's happening to me. They're making it impossible to live – '

Locke snorted. 'I'm not having any problem,' he said.

'They won't let you escape,' Stumpf said. 'None of us'll escape. Not unless we make amends.'

'You've got to vacate the room,' Locke said, unwilling to countenance any more of this drivel. 'I've been told you've got to get out by morning.'

'No,' said Stumpf. 'I can't leave. I can't leave.'

'There's nothing to fear.'

'The dust,' said the German. 'The dust in the air. It'll cut me up. I got a speck in my eye – just a *speck* – and the next thing my eye's bleeding as though it'll never stop. I can't hardly lie down, the sheet's like a bed of nails. The soles of my feet feel as if they're going to split. You've got to help me.'

'How?' said Locke.

'Pay them for the room. Pay them so I can stay 'til you can get a specialist from Sao Luis. Then go back to the village, Locke. Go back and tell them. I don't want the land. Tell them I don't own it any longer.'

'I'll go back,' said Locke, 'but in my good time.'

'You must go *quickly*,' said Stumpf. 'Tell them to let me be.'

Suddenly, the expression on the partially-masked face changed, and Stumpf looked past Locke at some spectacle down the corridor. From his mouth, slack with fear, came the small word, 'Please.'

Locke, mystified by the man's expression, turned. The corridor was empty, except for the fat moths that were besetting the bulb. 'There's nothing there – ' he said, turning back to the door of Stumpf's room. The wire-mesh glass of the window bore the distinct imprint of two bloody palms.

'He's here,' the German was saying, staring fixedly at the miracle of the bleeding glass. Locke didn't need to ask who. He raised his hand to touch the marks. The handprints, still wet, were on *his* side of the glass, not on Stumpf's.

'My God,' he breathed. How could anyone have slipped between him and the door and laid the prints there, sliding away again in the brief moment it had taken him to glance behind him? It defied reason. Again he looked back down the corridor. It was still bereft of visitors. Just the bulb – swinging slightly, as if a breeze of passage had caught it – and the moth's wings, whispering. 'What's happening?' Locke breathed.

Stumpf, entranced by the handprints, touched his fingertips lightly to the glass. On contact, his fingers blossomed blood, trails of which idled down the glass. He didn't remove his fingers, but stared through at Locke with despair in his eye.

'See?' he said, very quietly.

'What are you playing at?' Locke said, his voice similarly hushed. 'This is some kind of trick.'

'No.'

'You haven't got Cherrick's disease. You can't have. You didn't touch them. We *agreed*, damn you,' he said, more heatedly. 'Cherrick touched them, *we didn't*.'

Stumpf looked back at Locke with something close to pity on his face.

'We were wrong,' he said gently. His fingers, which he had now removed from the glass, continued to bleed, dribbling across the backs of his hands and down his arms. 'This isn't something you can beat into submission, Locke. It's out of our hands.' He raised his bloody fingers, smiling at his own word-play: 'See?' he said.

The German's sudden, fatalistic calm frightened Locke. He reached for the handle of the door, and jiggled it. The room was locked. The key was on the inside, where Stumpf had paid for it to be.

'Keep out,' Stumpf said. 'Keep away from me.'

His smile had vanished. Locke put his shoulder to the door.

'Keep out, I said,' Stumpf shouted, his voice shrill. He backed away from the door as Locke took another lunge at it. Then, seeing that the lock must soon give, he raised a cry of alarm. Locke took no notice, but continued to throw himself at the door. There came the sound of wood beginning to splinter.

Somewhere nearby Locke heard a woman's voice, raised in response to Stumpf's calls. No matter; he'd have his hands on the German before help could come, and then, by Christ, he'd wipe every last vestige of a smile from the bastard's lips. He threw himself against the door with increased fervour; again, and again. The door gave.

In the antiseptic cocoon of his room Stumpf felt the first blast of unclean air from the outside world. It was no more than a light breeze that invaded his makeshift sanctuary, but it bore upon its back the debris of the world. Soot and seeds, flakes of skin itched off a thousand scalps, fluff and sand and twists of hair; the bright dust from a moth's wing. Motes so small the human eye only glimpsed them in a shaft of white sunlight; each a tiny, whirling speck quite harmless to most living organisms. But this cloud was lethal to Stumpf; in seconds his body became a field of tiny, seeping wounds.

He screeched, and ran towards the door to slam it closed again, flinging himself into a hail of minute razors, each lacerating him. Pressing against the door to prevent Locke from entering, his wounded hands erupted. He was too late to keep Locke out anyhow. The man had pushed the door wide, and was now stepping through, his every movement setting up further currents of air to cut Stumpf down. He snatched hold of the German's wrist. At his grip the skin opened as if beneath a knife.

Behind him, a woman loosed a cry of horror. Locke, realizing that Stumpf was past recanting his laughter, let the man go. Adorned with cuts on every exposed part of his body, and gaining more by the moment, Stumpf stumbled back, blind, and fell beside the bed. The killing air still sliced him as he sank down; with each agonised shudder he woke new eddies and whirlpools to open him up.

Ashen, Locke retreated from where the body lay, and staggered out into the corridor. A gaggle of onlookers blocked it; they parted, however, at his approach, too intimidated by his bulk and by the wild look on his face to challenge him. He retraced his steps through the sickness-perfumed maze, crossing the small courtyard and returning into the main building. He briefly caught sight of Edson Costa hurrying in pursuit, but did not linger for explanations.

In the vestibule, which, despite the late hour was busy with victims of one kind or another, his harried gaze alighted on a small boy, perched on his mother's lap. He had injured his belly apparently. His shirt, which was too large for him, was stained with blood; his face with tears. The mother did not look up as Locke moved through the throng. The child did however. He raised his head as if knowing that Locke was about to pass by, and smiled radiantly.

There was nobody Locke knew at Tetelman's store; and all the information he could bully from the hired hands, most of whom were drunk to the point of being unable to stand, was that their masters had gone off into the jungle the previous day. Locke chased the most sober of them and persuaded him with threats to accompany him back to the village as translator. He had no real

61

idea of how he would make his peace with the tribe. He was only certain that he had to argue his innocence. After all, he would plead, it hadn't been *he* who had fired the killing shot. There had been misunderstandings, to be certain, but he had not harmed the people in any way. How could they, in all conscience, conspire to hurt him? If they should require some penance of him he was not above acceding to their demands. Indeed, might there not be some satisfaction in the act? He had seen so much suffering of late. He wanted to be cleansed of it. Anything they asked, within reason, he would comply with; anything to avoid dying like the others. He'd even give back the land.

It was a rough ride, and his morose companion complained often and incoherently. Locke turned a deaf ear. There was no time for loitering. Their noisy progress, the jeep engine complaining at every new acrobatic required of it, brought the jungle alive on every side, a repertoire of wails, whoops and screeches. It was an urgent, hungry place, Locke thought: and for the first time since setting foot on this sub-continent he loathed it with all his heart. There was no room here to make sense of events; the best that could be hoped was that one be allowed a niche to breathe awhile between one squalid flowering and the next.

Half an hour before night-fall, exhausted by the journey, they came to the outskirts of the village. The place had altered not at all in the meagre days since he'd last been here, but the ring of huts was clearly deserted. The doors gaped; the communal fires, always alight, were ashes. There was neither child nor pig to turn an eye towards him as he moved across the compound. When he reached the centre of the ring he stood still, looking about him for some clue as to what had happened there. He found none, however. Fatigue made him foolhardy. Mustering his fractured strength, he shouted into the hush:

'*Where are you?*'

Two brilliant red macaws, finger-winged, rose screeching from the trees on the far side of the village. A few moments after, a figure emerged from the thicket of balsa and jacaranda. It was not one of the tribe, but Dancy. He paused before stepping fully into sight; then, recognising Locke, a broad smile broke his face, and he advanced into the compound. Behind him, the foliage shook as others made their way through it. Tetelman was there, as were several Norwegians, led by a man called Bjørnstrøm, whom Locke had encountered briefly at the trading post. His face, beneath a shock of sun-bleached hair, was like cooked lobster.

'My God,' said Tetelman, 'what are you doing here?'

'I might ask you the same question,' Locke replied testily.

Bjørnstrøm waved down the raised rifles of his three companions and strode forward, bearing a placatory smile.

'Mr Locke,' the Norwegian said, extending a leather-gloved hand. 'It is good we meet.'

Locke looked down at the stained glove with disgust, and Bjørnstrøm, flashing a self-admonishing look, pulled it off. The hand beneath was pristine.

'My apologies,' he said. 'We've been working.'

'At what?' Locke asked, the acid in his stomach edging its way up into the back of his throat.

Tetelman spat. 'Indians,' he said.

'Where's the tribe?' Locke said.

Again, Tetelman: 'Bjørnstrøm claims he's got rights to this territory . . .'

'The tribe,' Locke insisted. 'Where are they?'

The Norwegian toyed with his glove.

'Did you buy them out, or what?' Locke asked.

'Not exactly,' Bjørnstrøm replied. His English, like his profile, was impeccable.

'Bring him along,' Dancy suggested with some enthusiasm. 'Let him see for himself.'

Bjørnstrøm nodded. 'Why not?' he said. 'Don't touch anything, Mr Locke. And tell your carrier to stay where he is.'

Dancy had already about turned, and was heading into the thicket; now Bjørnstrøm did the same, escorting Locke across the compound towards a corridor hacked through the heavy foliage. Locke could scarcely keep pace; his limbs were more reluctant with every step he took. The ground had been heavily trodden along this track. A litter of leaves and orchid blossoms had been mashed into the sodden soil.

They had dug a pit in a small clearing no more than a hundred yards from the compound. It was not deep, this pit, nor was it very large. The mingled smells of lime and petrol cancelled out any other scent.

Tetelman, who had reached the clearing ahead of Locke, hung back from approaching the lip of the earthworks, but Dancy was not so fastidious. He strode around the far side of the pit and beckoned to Locke to view the contents.

The tribe were putrifying already. They lay where they had been thrown, in a jumble of breasts and buttocks and faces and limbs,

63

their bodies tinged here and there with purple and black. Flies built helter-skelters in the air above them.

'An education,' Dancy commented.

Locke just looked on as Bjørnstrøm moved around the other side of the pit to join Dancy.

'All of them?' Locke asked.

The Norwegian nodded. 'One fell swoop,' he said, pronouncing each word with unsettling precision.

'Blankets,' said Tetelman, naming the murder weapon.

'But so quickly . . .' Locke murmured.

'It's very efficient,' said Dancy. 'And difficult to prove. Even if anybody ever asks.'

'Disease is natural,' Bjørnstrøm observed. 'Yes? Like the trees.'

Locke slowly shook his head, his eyes pricking.

'I hear good things of you,' Bjørnstrøm said to him. 'Perhaps we can work together.'

Locke didn't even attempt to reply. Others of the Norwegian party had laid down their rifles and were now getting back to work, moving the few bodies still to be pitched amongst their fellows from the forlorn heap beside the pit. Locke could see a child amongst the tangle, and an old man, whom even now the burial party were picking up. The corpse looked jointless as they swung it over the edge of the hole. It tumbled down the shallow incline and came to rest face up, its arms flung up to either side of its head in a gesture of submission, or expulsion. It was the elder of course, whom Cherrick had faced. His palms were still red. There was a neat bullet-hole in his temple. Disease and hopelessness had not been entirely efficient, apparently.

Locke watched while the next of the bodies was thrown into the mass grave, and a third to follow that.

Bjørnstrøm, lingering on the far side of the pit, was lighting a cigarette. He caught Locke's eye.

'So it goes,' he said.

From behind Locke, Tetelman spoke.

'We thought you wouldn't come back,' he said, perhaps attempting to excuse his alliance with Bjørnstrøm.

'Stumpf is dead,' said Locke.

'Well, even less to divide up,' Tetelman said, approaching him and laying a hand on his shoulder. Locke didn't reply; he just stared down amongst the bodies, which were now being covered with lime, only slowly registering the warmth that was running

64

down his body from the spot where Tetelman had touched him. Disgusted, the man had removed his hand, and was staring at the growing bloodstain on Locke's shirt.

Twilight at the Towers

The photographs of Mironenko which Ballard had been shown in Munich had proved far from instructive. Only one or two pictured the KGB man full face; and of the others most were blurred and grainy, betraying their furtive origins. Ballard was not overmuch concerned. He knew from long and occasionally bitter experience that the eye was all too ready to be deceived; but there were other faculties – the remnants of senses modern life had rendered obsolete – which he had learned to call into play, enabling him to sniff out the least signs of betrayal. These were the talents he would use when he met with Mironenko. With them, he would root the truth from the man.

The truth? Therein lay the conundrum of course, for in this context wasn't sincerity a movable feast? Sergei Zakharovich Mironenko had been a Section Leader in Directorate S of the KGB for eleven years, with access to the most privileged information on the dispersal of Soviet Illegals in the West. In the recent weeks, however, he had made his disenchantment with his present masters, and his consequent desire to defect, known to the British Security Service. In return for the elaborate efforts which would have to be made on his behalf he had volunteered to act as an agent within the KGB for a period of three months, after which time he would be taken into the bosom of democracy and hidden where his vengeful overlords would never find him. It had fallen to Ballard to meet the Russian face to face, in the hope of establishing whether Mironenko's disaffection from his ideology was real or faked. The answer would not be found on Mironenko's lips, Ballard knew, but in some behavioural nuance which only instinct would comprehend.

Time was when Ballard would have found the puzzle fascinating; that his every waking thought would have circled on the unravelling ahead. But such commitment had belonged to a man convinced his actions had some significant effect upon the world. He was wiser now. The agents of East and West went about their secret works year in, year out. They plotted; they connived; occasionally (though rarely) they shed blood. There were débâcles and trade-offs and minor tactical victories. But in the end things were much the same as ever.

This city, for instance. Ballard had first come to Berlin in April of 1969. He'd been twenty-nine, fresh from years of intensive training, and ready to live a little. But he had not felt easy here. He found the city charmless; often bleak. It had taken Odell, his colleague for those first two years, to prove that Berlin was worthy of his affections, and once Ballard fell he was lost for life. Now he felt more at home in this divided city than he ever had in London. Its unease, its failed idealism, and – perhaps most acutely of all – its terrible isolation, matched his. He and it, maintaining a presence in a wasteland of dead ambition.

He found Mironenko at the Germälde Galerie, and yes, the photographs *had* lied. The Russian looked older than his forty-six years, and sicker than he'd appeared in those filched portraits. Neither man made any sign of acknowledgement. They idled through the collection for a full half-hour, with Mironenko showing acute, and apparently genuine, interest in the work on view. Only when both men were satisfied that they were not being watched did the Russian quit the building and lead Ballard into the polite suburbs of Dahlem to a mutually agreed safe house. There, in a small and unheated kitchen, they sat down and talked.

Mironenko's command of English was uncertain, or at least appeared so, though Ballard had the impression that his struggles for sense were as much tactical as grammatical. He might well have presented the same façade in the Russian's situation; it seldom hurt to appear less competent than one was. But despite the difficulties he had in expressing himself, Mironenko's avowals were unequivocal.

'I am no longer a Communist,' he stated plainly, 'I have not been a party-member – not *here* – ' he put his fist to his chest ' – for many years.'

He fetched an off-white handkerchief from his coat pocket, pulled off one of his gloves, and plucked a bottle of tablets from the folds of the handkerchief.

'Forgive me,' he said as he shook tablets from the bottle. 'I have pains. In my head; in my hands.'

Ballard waited until he had swallowed the medication before asking him, 'Why did you begin to doubt?'

The Russian pocketed the bottle and the handkerchief, his wide face devoid of expression.

67

'How does a man lose his . . . his faith?' he said. 'Is it that I saw too much; or too little, perhaps?'

He looked at Ballard's face to see if his hesitant words had made sense. Finding no comprehension there he tried again.

'I think the man who does not believe he is lost, is lost.'

The paradox was elegantly put; Ballard's suspicion as to Mironenko's true command of English was confirmed.

'Are you lost *now*?' Ballard inquired.

Mironenko didn't reply. He was pulling his other glove off and staring at his hands. The pills he had swallowed did not seem to be easing the ache he had complained of. He fisted and unfisted his hands like an arthritis sufferer testing the advance of his condition. Not looking up, he said:

'I was taught that the Party had solutions to everything. That made me free from fear.'

'And now?'

'Now?' he said. 'Now I have strange thoughts. They come to me from nowhere . . .'

'Go on,' said Ballard.

Mironenko made a tight smile. 'You must know me inside out, yes? Even what I dream?'

'Yes,' said Ballard.

Mironenko nodded. 'It would be the same with us,' he said. Then, after a pause: 'I've thought sometimes I would break open. Do you understand what I say? I would crack, because there is such rage inside me. And that makes me afraid, Ballard. I think they will see how much I hate them.' He looked up at his interrogator. 'You must be quick,' he said, 'or they will discover me. I try not to think of what they will do.' Again, he paused. All trace of the smile, however humourless, had gone. 'The Directorate has Sections even I don't have knowledge of. Special hospitals, where nobody can go. They have ways to break a man's soul in pieces.'

Ballard, ever the pragmatist, wondered if Mironenko's vocabulary wasn't rather high-flown. In the hands of the KGB he doubted if he would be thinking of his *soul*'s contentment. After all, it was the body that had the nerve-endings.

They talked for an hour or more, the conversation moving back and forth between politics and personal reminiscence, between trivia and confessional. At the end of the meeting Ballard was in no doubt as to Mironenko's antipathy to his masters. He was, as he had said, a man without faith.

The following day Ballard met with Cripps in the restaurant at the Schweizerhof Hotel, and made his verbal report on Mironenko.

'He's ready and waiting. But he insists we be quick about making up our minds.'

'I'm sure he does,' Cripps said. His glass eye was troubling him today; the chilly air, he explained, made it sluggish. It moved fractionally more slowly than his real eye, and on occasion Cripps had to nudge it with his fingertip to get it moving.

'We're not going to be rushed into any decision,' Cripps said.

'Where's the problem? I don't have any doubt about his commitment; or his desperation.'

'So you said,' Cripps replied. 'Would you like something for dessert?'

'Do you doubt my appraisal? Is that what it is?'

'Have something sweet to finish off, so that I don't feel an utter reprobate.'

'You think I'm wrong about him, don't you?' Ballard pressed. When Cripps didn't reply, Ballard leaned across the table. 'You do, don't you?'

'I'm just saying there's reason for caution,' Cripps said. 'If we finally choose to take him on board the Russians are going to be very distressed. We have to be sure the deal's worth the bad weather that comes with it. Things are so dicey at the moment.'

'When aren't they?' Ballard replied. 'Tell me a time when there wasn't some crisis in the offing?' He settled back in the chair and tried to read Cripps' face. His glass eye was, if anything, more candid than the real one.

'I'm sick of this damn game,' Ballard muttered.

The glass eye roved. 'Because of the Russian?'

'Maybe.'

'Believe me,' said Cripps, 'I've got good reason to be careful with this man.'

'Name one.'

'There's nothing verified.'

'What have you got on him?' Ballard insisted.

'As I say, rumour,' Cripps replied.

'Why wasn't I briefed about it?'

Cripps made a tiny shake of his head. 'It's academic now,' he said. 'You've provided a good report. I just want you to understand that if things don't go the way you think they should it's not because your appraisals aren't trusted.'

'I see.'

'No you don't,' said Cripps. 'You're feeling martyred; and I don't altogether blame you.'

'So what happens now? I'm supposed to forget I ever met the man?'

'Wouldn't do any harm,' said Cripps. 'Out of sight, out of mind.'

Clearly Cripps didn't trust Ballard to take his own advice. Though Ballard made several discreet enquiries about the Mironenko case in the following week it was plain that his usual circle of contacts had been warned to keep their lips sealed.

As it was, the next news about the case reached Ballard via the pages of the morning papers, in an article about a body found in a house near the station on Kaiser Damm. At the time of reading he had no way of knowing how the account tied up with Mironenko, but there was enough detail in the story to arouse his interest. For one, he had the suspicion that the house named in the article had been used by the Service on occasion; for another, the article described how two unidentified men had almost been caught in the act of removing the body, further suggesting that this was no crime of passion.

About noon, he went to see Cripps at his offices in the hope of coaxing him with some explanation, but Cripps was not available, nor would be, his secretary explained, until further notice; matters arising had taken him back to Munich. Ballard left a message that he wished to speak with him when he returned.

As he stepped into the cold air again, he realised that he'd gained an admirer; a thin-faced individual whose hair had retreated from his brow, leaving a ludicrous forelock at the high-water mark. Ballard knew him in passing from Cripps' entourage but couldn't put a name to the face. It was swiftly provided.

'Suckling,' the man said.

'Of course,' said Ballard. 'Hello.'

'I think maybe we should talk, if you have a moment,' the man said. His voice was as pinched as his features; Ballard wanted none of his gossip. He was about to refuse the offer when Suckling said: 'I suppose you heard what happened to Cripps.'

Ballard shook his head. Suckling, delighted to possess this nugget, said again: 'We should talk.'

They walked along the Kantstrasse towards the Zoo. The street was busy with lunchtime pedestrians, but Ballard scarcely noticed them. The story that Suckling unfolded as they walked demanded his full and absolute attention.

It was simply told. Cripps, it appeared, had made an arrangement to meet with Mironenko in order to make his own assessment of the Russian's integrity. The house in Schöneberg chosen for the meeting had been used on several previous occasions, and had long been considered one of the safest locations in the city. It had not proved so the previous evening however. KGB men had apparently followed Mironenko to the house, and then attempted to break the party up. There was nobody to testify to what had happened subsequently – both the men who had accompanied Cripps, one of them Ballard's old colleague Odell – were dead; Cripps himself was in a coma.

'And Mironenko?' Ballard inquired.

Suckling shrugged. 'They took him home to the Motherland, presumably,' he said.

Ballard caught a whiff of deceit off the man.

'I'm touched that you're keeping me up to date,' he said to Suckling. 'But *why*?'

'You and Odell were friends, weren't you?' came the reply. 'With Cripps out of the picture you don't have many of those left.'

'Is that so?'

'No offence intended,' Suckling said hurriedly. 'But you've got a reputation as a maverick.'

'Get to the point,' said Ballard.

'There is no point,' Suckling protested. 'I just thought you ought to know what had happened. I'm putting my neck on the line here.'

'Nice try,' said Ballard. He stopped walking. Suckling wandered on a pace or two before turning to find Ballard grinning at him.

'Who sent you?'

'Nobody sent me,' Suckling said.

'Clever to send the court gossip. I almost fell for it. You're very plausible.'

There wasn't enough fat on Suckling's face to hide the tic in his cheek.

'What do they suspect me of? Do they think I'm conniving with Mironenko, is that it? No, I don't think they're that stupid.'

Suckling shook his head, like a doctor in the presence of some incurable disease. 'You like making enemies?' he said.

'Occupational hazard. I wouldn't lose any sleep over it. I don't.'

'There's changes in the air,' Suckling said. 'I'd make sure you have your answers ready.'

'Fuck the answers,' Ballard said courteously. 'I think it's about time I worked out the right questions.'

Sending Suckling to sound him out smacked of desperation. They wanted inside information; but about what? Could they seriously believe he had some involvement with Mironenko; or worse, with the KGB itself? He let his resentment subside; it was stirring up too much mud, and he needed clear water if he was to find his way free of this confusion. In one regard, Suckling was perfectly correct: he *did* have enemies, and with Cripps indisposed he was vulnerable. In such circumstances there were two courses of action. He could return to London, and there lie low, or wait around in Berlin to see what manoeuvre they tried next. He decided on the latter. The charm of hide-and-seek was rapidly wearing thin.

As he turned North onto Leibnizstrasse he caught the reflection of a grey-coated man in a shop window. It was a glimpse, no more, but he had the feeling that he knew the fellow's face. Had they put a watch-dog onto him, he wondered? He turned, and caught the man's eye, holding it. The suspect seemed embarrassed, and looked away. A performance perhaps; and then again, perhaps not. It mattered little, Ballard thought. Let them watch him all they liked. He was guiltless. If indeed there was such a condition this side of insanity.

A strange happiness had found Sergei Mironenko; happiness that came without rhyme or reason, and filled his heart up to overflowing.

Only the previous day circumstances had seemed unendurable. The aching in his hands and head and spine had steadily worsened, and was now accompanied by an itch so demanding he'd had to snip his nails to the flesh to prevent himself doing serious damage. His body, he had concluded, was in revolt against him. It was that thought which he had tried to explain to Ballard: that he was divided from himself, and feared that he would soon be torn apart. But today the fear had gone.

Not so the pains. They were, if anything, worse than they'd been yesterday. His sinews and ligaments ached as if they'd been exercised beyond the limits of their design; there were bruises at all his joints, where blood had broken its banks beneath the skin. But that sense of imminent rebellion had disappeared, to be replaced with a dreamy peacefulness. And at its heart, such happiness.

When he tried to think back over recent events, to work out what had cued this transformation, his memory played tricks. He had been called to meet with Ballard's superior; *that* he remembered. Whether he had gone to the meeting, he did not. The night was a blank.

Ballard would know how things stood, he reasoned. He had liked and trusted the Englishman from the beginning, sensing that despite the many differences between them they were more alike than not. If he let his instinct lead, he would find Ballard, of that he was certain. No doubt the Englishman would be surprised to see him; even angered at first. But when he told Ballard of this new-found happiness surely his trespasses would be forgiven?

Ballard dined late, and drank until later still in The Ring, a small transvestite bar which he had been first taken to by Odell almost two decades ago. No doubt his guide's intention had been to prove his sophistication by showing his raw colleague the decadence of Berlin, but Ballard, though he never felt any sexual *frisson* in the company of The Ring's clientele, had immediately felt at home here. His neutrality was respected; no attempts were made to solicit him. He was simply left to drink and watch the passing parade of genders.

Coming here tonight raised the ghost of Odell, whose name would now be scrubbed from conversation because of his involvement with the Mironenko affair. Ballard had seen this process at work before. History did not forgive failure, unless it was so profound as to achieve a kind of grandeur. For the Odells of the world – ambitious men who had found themselves through little fault of their own in a cul-de-sac from which all retreat was barred – for such men there would be no fine words spoken nor medals struck. There would only be oblivion.

It made him melancholy to think of this, and he drank heavily to keep his thoughts mellow, but when – at two in the morning – he stepped out on to the street his depression was only marginally dulled. The good burghers of Berlin were well a-bed; tomorrow was another working day. Only the sound of traffic from the Kurfürstendamm offered sign of life somewhere near. He made his way towards it, his thoughts fleecy.

Behind him, laughter. A young man – glamorously dressed as a starlet – tottered along the pavement arm in arm with his unsmiling escort. Ballard recognised the transvestite as a regular at the bar; the client, to judge by his sober suit, was an out-of-towner slaking his thirst for boys dressed as girls behind his wife's back. Ballard picked up his pace. The young man's laughter, its musicality patently forced, set his teeth on edge.

He heard somebody running nearby; caught a shadow moving out of the corner of his eye. His watch-dog, most likely. Though alcohol had blurred his instincts, he felt some anxiety surface, the root of which he couldn't fix. He walked on. Featherlight tremors ran in his scalp.

A few yards on, he realised that the laughter from the street behind him had ceased. He glanced over his shoulder, half-expecting to see the boy and his customer embracing. But both had disappeared; slipped off down one of the alleyways, no doubt, to conclude their contract in darkness. Somewhere near, a dog had begun to bark wildly. Ballard turned round to look back the way he'd come, daring the deserted street to display its secrets to him. Whatever was arousing the buzz in his head and the itch on his palms, it was no commonplace anxiety. There was something wrong with the street, despite its show of innocence; it hid terrors.

The bright lights of the Kurfürstendamm were no more than three minutes' walk away, but he didn't want to turn his back on this mystery and take refuge there. Instead he proceeded to walk back the way he'd come, slowly. The dog had now ceased its alarm, and settled into silence; he had only his footsteps for company.

He reached the corner of the first alleyway and peered down it. No light burned at window or doorway. He could sense no living presence in the gloom. He crossed over the alley and walked on to the next. A luxurious stench had crept into the air, which became more lavish yet as he approached the corner. As he breathed it in the buzz in his head deepened to a threat of thunder.

A single light flickered in the throat of the alley, a meagre wash from an upper window. By it, he saw the body of the out-of-towner, lying sprawled on the ground. He had been so traumatically mutilated it seemed an attempt might have been made to turn him inside out. From the spilled innards, that ripe smell rose in all its complexity.

Ballard had seen violent death before, and thought himself indifferent to the spectacle. But something here in the alley threw his calm into disarray. He felt his limbs begin to shake. And then, from beyond the throw of light, the boy spoke.

74

'In God's name . . .' he said. His voice had lost all pretension to femininity; it was a murmur of undisguised terror.

Ballard took a step down the alley. Neither the boy, nor the reason for his whispered prayer, became visible until he had advanced ten yards. The boy was half-slumped against the wall amongst the refuse. His sequins and taffeta had been ripped from him; the body was pale and sexless. He seemed not to notice Ballard: his eyes were fixed on the deepest shadows.

The shaking in Ballard's limbs worsened as he followed the boy's gaze; it was all he could do to prevent his teeth from chattering. Nevertheless he continued his advance, not for the boy's sake (heroism had little merit, he'd always been taught) but because he was curious, more than curious, *eager*, to see what manner of man was capable of such casual violence. To look into the eyes of such ferocity seemed at that moment the most important thing in all the world.

Now the boy saw him, and muttered a pitiful appeal, but Ballard scarcely heard it. He felt other eyes upon him, and their touch was like a blow. The din in his head took on a sickening rhythm, like the sound of helicopter rotors. In mere seconds it mounted to a blinding roar.

Ballard pressed his hands to his eyes, and stumbled back against the wall, dimly aware that the killer was moving out of hiding (refuse was overturned) and making his escape. He felt something brush against him, and opened his eyes in time to glimpse the man slipping away down the passageway. He seemed somehow mis-shapen; his back crooked, his head too large. Ballard loosed a shout after him, but the berserker ran on, pausing only to look down at the body before racing towards the street.

Ballard heaved himself off the wall and stood upright. The noise in his head was diminishing somewhat; the attendant giddiness was passing.

Behind him, the boy had begun sobbing. 'Did you see?' he said. 'Did you *see*?'

'Who was it? Somebody you knew?'

The boy stared at Ballard like a frightened doe, his mascaraed eyes huge.

'Somebody . . .?' he said.

Ballard was about to repeat the question when there came a shriek of brakes, swiftly followed by the sound of the impact. Leaving the boy to pull his tattered *trousseau* about him, Ballard went back into the street. Voices were raised nearby; he hurried to their source. A large car was straddling the pavement, its headlights blazing. The driver was being helped from his seat, while his passengers – party-goers to judge by their dress and drink-flushed faces – stood and debated furiously as to how the accident had happened. One of the women was talking about an animal in the road, but another of the passengers corrected her. The body that lay in the gutter where it had been thrown was not that of an animal.

Ballard had seen little of the killer in the alleyway but he knew instinctively that this was he. There was no sign of the malformation he thought he'd glimpsed, however; just a man dressed in a suit that had seen better days, lying face down in a patch of blood. The police had already arrived, and an officer shouted to him to stand away from the body, but Ballard ignored the instruction and went to steal a look at the dead man's face. There was nothing there of the ferocity he had hoped so much to see. But there was much he recognised nevertheless.

The man was Odell.

He told the officers that he had seen nothing of the accident, which was essentially true, and made his escape from the scene before events in the adjacent alley were discovered.

It seemed every corner turned on his route back to his rooms brought a fresh question. Chief amongst them: why he had been lied to about Odell's death?; and what psychosis had seized the man that made him capable of the slaughter Ballard had witnessed? He would not get the answers to these questions from his sometime colleagues, that he knew. The only man whom he might have beguiled an answer from was Cripps. He remembered the debate they'd had about Mironenko, and Cripps' talk of 'reasons for caution' when dealing with the Russian. The Glass Eye had known then that there was something in the wind, though surely even he had not envisaged the scale of the present disaster. Two highly valued agents murdered; Mironenko missing, presumed dead; he himself – if Suckling was to be believed – at death's door. And all this begun with Sergei Zakharovich Mironenko, the lost man of Berlin. It seemed his tragedy was infectious.

Tomorrow, Ballard decided, he would find Suckling and squeeze some answers from him. In the meantime, his head and his hands ached, and he wanted sleep. Fatigue compromised sound judgement, and if ever he needed that faculty it was now. But despite his exhaustion sleep eluded him for an hour or more, and when it came it was no comfort. He dreamt whispers; and hard upon them, rising as if to drown them out, the roar of the helicopters. Twice he surfaced from sleep with his head pounding; twice a hunger to understand what the whispers were telling him drove him to the pillow again. When he woke for the third time, the noise between his temples had become crippling; a thought-cancelling assault which made him fear for his sanity. Barely able to see the room through the pain, he crawled from his bed.

'Please . . .' he murmured, as if there were somebody to help him from his misery.

A cool voice answered him out of the darkness:

'*What do you want?*'

He didn't question the questioner; merely said:

'Take the pain away.'

'*You can do that for yourself,*' the voice told him.

He leaned against the wall, nursing his splitting head, tears of agony coming and coming. 'I don't know *how*,' he said.

'*Your dreams give you pain,*' the voice replied, '*so you must forget them. Do you understand? Forget them, and the pain will go.*'

He understood the instruction, but not how to realise it. He had no powers of government in sleep. He was the object of these whispers; not they his. But the voice insisted.

'*The dream means you harm, Ballard. You must bury it. Bury it deep.*'

'Bury it?'

'*Make an image of it, Ballard. Picture it in detail.*'

He did as he was told. He imagined a burial party, and a box; and in the box, this dream. He made them dig deep, as the voice instructed him, so that he would never be able to disinter this hurtful thing again. But even as he imagined the box lowered into the pit he heard its boards creak. The dream would not lie down. It beat against confinement. The boards began to break.

'*Quickly!*' the voice said.

The din of the rotors had risen to a terrifying pitch. Blood had begun to pour from his nostrils; he tasted salt at the back of his throat.

'*Finish it!*' the voice yelled above the tumult. '*Cover it up!*'

Ballard looked into the grave. The box was thrashing from side to side.

'*Cover it, damn you!*'

He tried to make the burial party obey; tried to will them to pick up their shovels and bury the offending thing alive, but they would not. Instead they gazed into the grave as he did and watched as the contents of the box fought for light.

'*No!*' the voice demanded, its fury mounting. '*You must not look!*'

The box danced in the hole. The lid splintered. Briefly, Ballard glimpsed something shining up between the boards.

'*It will kill you!*' the voice said, and as if to prove its point the volume of the sound rose beyond the point of endurance, washing out burial party, box and all in a blaze of pain. Suddenly it seemed that what the voice said was true; that he was near to death. But it wasn't the dream that was conspiring to kill him, but the sentinel they had posted between him and it: this skull-splintering cacophony.

Only now did he realise that he'd fallen on the floor, prostrate beneath this assault. Reaching out blindly he found the wall, and hauled himself towards it, the machines still thundering behind his eyes, the blood hot on his face.

He stood up as best he could and began to move towards the bathroom. Behind him the voice, its tantrum controlled, began its exhortation afresh. It sounded so intimate that he looked round, fully expecting to see the speaker, and he was not disappointed. For a few flickering moments he seemed to be standing in a small, windowless room, its walls painted a uniform white. The light here was bright and dead, and in the centre of the room stood the face behind the voice, smiling.

'*Your dreams give you pain,*' he said. This was the first Commandment again. '*Bury them Ballard, and the pain will pass.*'

Ballard wept like a child; this scrutiny shamed him. He looked away from his tutor to bury his tears.

'*Trust us,*' another voice said, close by. '*We're your friends.*'

He didn't trust their fine words. The very pain they claimed to want to save him from was of their making; it was a stick to beat him with if the dreams came calling.

'*We want to help you.*' one or other of them said.

'No . . .' he murmured. 'No damn you . . . I don't . . . I don't believe . . .'

The room flickered out, and he was in the bedroom again, clinging to the wall like a climber to a cliff-face. Before they could come for him with more words, more pain, he edged his way to the bathroom door, and stumbled blindly towards the shower. There was a moment of panic while he located the taps; and then the water came on at a rush. It was bitterly cold, but he put his head beneath it, while the onslaught of rotor-blades tried to shake the plates of his skull apart. Icy water trekked down his back, but he let the rain come down on him in a torrent, and by degrees, the helicopters took their leave. He didn't move, though his body juddered with cold, until the last of them had gone; then he sat on the edge of the bath, mopping water from his neck and face and body, and eventually, when his legs felt courageous enough, made his way back into the bedroom.

He lay down on the same crumpled sheets in much the same position as he'd lain in before; yet nothing *was* the same. He didn't know what had changed in him, or how. But he lay there without sleep disturbing his serenity through the remaining hours of the night, trying to puzzle it out, and a little before dawn he remembered the words he had muttered in the face of the delusion. Simple words; but oh, their power.

'I don't believe . . .' he said; and the Commandments trembled.

It was half an hour before noon when he arrived at the small book exporting firm which served Suckling for cover. He felt quick-witted, despite the disturbance of the night, and rapidly charmed his way past the receptionist and entered Suckling's office unannounced. When Suckling's eyes settled on his visitor he started from his desk as if fired upon.

'Good morning,' said Ballard. 'I thought it was time we talked.'

Suckling's eyes fled to the office-door, which Ballard had left ajar.

'Sorry; is there a draught?' Ballard closed the door gently. 'I want to see Cripps,' he said.

Suckling waded through the sea of books and manuscripts that threatened to engulf his desk. 'Are you out of your mind, coming back here?'

'Tell them I'm a friend of the family,' Ballard offered.

'I can't believe you'd be so stupid.'

'Just point me to Cripps, and I'll be away.'

Suckling ignored him in favour of his tirade. 'It's taken two years to establish my credentials here.'

Ballard laughed.

'I'm going to report this, damn you!'

'I think you should,' said Ballard, turning up the volume. 'In the meanwhile: *where's Cripps?*'

Suckling, apparently convinced that he was faced with a lunatic, controlled his apoplexy. 'All right,' he said. 'I'll have somebody call on you; take you to him.'

'Not good enough,' Ballard replied. He crossed to Suckling in two short strides and took hold of him by his lapel. He'd spent at most three hours with Suckling in ten years, but he'd scarcely passed a moment in his presence without itching to do what he was doing now. Knocking the man's hands away, he pushed Suckling against the book-lined wall. A stack of volumes, caught by Suckling's heel, toppled.

'Once more,' Ballard said. 'The old man.'

'Take your fucking hands off me,' Suckling said, his fury redoubled at being touched.

'Again,' said Ballard. '*Cripps.*'

'I'll have you carpeted for this. I'll have you *out!*'

Ballard leaned towards the reddening face, and smiled.

'I'm out anyway. People have died, remember? London needs a sacrificial lamb, and I think I'm it.' Suckling's face dropped. 'So I've got nothing to lose, have I?' There was no reply. Ballard pressed closer to Suckling, tightening his grip on the man. '*Have I?*'

Suckling's courage failed him. 'Cripps is dead,' he said.

Ballard didn't release his hold. 'You said the same about Odell –' he remarked. At the name, Suckling's eyes widened. ' – And I saw him only last night.' Ballard said, 'out on the town.'

'You saw Odell?'

'Oh yes.'

Mention of the dead man brought the scene in the alleyway back to mind. The smell of the body; the boy's sobs. There were other faiths, thought Ballard, beyond the one he'd once shared with the creature beneath him. Faiths whose devotions were made in heat and blood, whose dogmas were dreams. Where better to baptise himself into that new faith than here, in the blood of the enemy?

Somewhere, at the very back of his head, he could hear the helicopters, but he wouldn't let them take to the air. He was strong today; his head, his hands, all *strong*. When he drew his nails towards Suckling's eyes the blood came easily. He had a sudden vision of the face beneath the flesh; of Suckling's features stripped to the essence.

'Sir?'

Ballard glanced over his shoulder. The receptionist was standing at the open door.

'Oh. I'm sorry,' she said, preparing to withdraw. To judge by her blushes she assumed this was a lover's tryst she'd walked in upon.

80

'*Stay*,' said Suckling. 'Mr Ballard . . . was just leaving.'

Ballard released his prey. There would be other opportunities to have Suckling's life.

'I'll see you again,' he said.

Suckling drew a handkerchief from his top pocket and pressed it to his face.

'Depend upon it,' he replied.

Now they would come for him, he could have no doubt of that. He was a rogue element, and they would strive to silence him as quickly as possible. The thought did not distress him. Whatever they had tried to make him forget with their brain-washing was more ambitious than they had anticipated; however deeply they had taught him to bury it, it was digging its way back to the surface. He couldn't see it yet, but he knew it was near. More than once on his way back to his rooms he imagined eyes at his back. Maybe he was still being tailed; but his instincts informed him otherwise. The presence he felt close-by – so near that it was sometimes at his shoulder – was perhaps simply another part of him. He felt protected by it, as by a local god.

He had half expected there to be a reception committee awaiting him at his rooms, but there was nobody. Either Suckling had been obliged to delay his alarm-call, or else the upper echelons were still debating their tactics. He pocketed those few keepsakes that he wanted to preserve from their calculating eyes, and left the building again without anyone making a move to stop him.

It felt good to be alive, despite the chill that rendered the grim streets grimmer still. He decided, for no particular reason, to go to the Zoo, which, though he had been visiting the city for two decades, he had never done. As he walked it occurred to him that he'd never been as free as he was now; that he had shed mastery like an old coat. No wonder they feared him. They had good reason.

Kantstrasse was busy, but he cut his way through the pedestrians easily, almost as if they sensed a rare certainty in him and gave him a wide berth. As he approached the entrance to the Zoo, however, somebody jostled him. He looked round to upbraid the fellow, but caught only the back of the man's head as he was submerged in the crowd heading onto Hardenbergstrasse. Suspecting an attempted theft, he checked his pockets, to find that a scrap of paper had been slipped into one. He knew better than to examine it on the spot, but casually glanced round again to see if he recognised the courier. The man had already slipped away.

He delayed his visit to the Zoo and went instead to the Tiergarten, and there – in the wilds of the great park – found a place to read the message. It was from Mironenko, and it requested a meeting to talk of a matter of considerable urgency, naming a house in Marienfelde as a venue. Ballard memorised the details, then shredded the note.

It was perfectly possible that the invitation was a trap of course, set either by his own faction or by the opposition. Perhaps a way to test his allegiance; or to manipulate him into a situation in which he could be easily despatched. Despite such doubts he had no choice but to go however, in the hope that this blind date was indeed with Mironenko. Whatever dangers this rendezvous brought, they were not so new. Indeed, given his long-held doubts of the efficacy of sight, hadn't every date he'd ever made been in some sense *blind*?

By early evening the damp air was thickening towards a fog, and by the time he stepped off the bus on Hildburghauserstrasse it had a good hold on the city, lending the chill new powers to discomfort.

Ballard went quickly through the quiet streets. He scarcely knew the district at all, but its proximity to the Wall bled it of what little charm it might once have possessed. Many of the houses were unoccupied; of those that were not most were sealed off against the night and the cold and the lights that glared from the watchtowers. It was only with the aid of a map that he located the tiny street Mironenko's note had named.

No lights burned in the house. Ballard knocked hard, but there was no answering footstep in the hall. He had anticipated several possible scenarios, but an absence of response at the house had not been amongst them. He knocked again; and again. It was only then that he heard sounds from within, and finally the door was opened to him. The hallway was painted grey and brown, and lit only by a bare bulb. The man silhouetted against this drab interior was not Mironenko.

'Yes?' he said. 'What do you want?' His German was spoken with a distinct Muscovite inflection.

'I'm looking for a friend of mine,' Ballard said.

The man, who was almost as broad as the doorway he stood in, shook his head.

'There's nobody here,' he said. 'Only me.'

'I was told – '

'You must have the wrong house.'

No sooner had the doorkeeper made the remark than noise erupted from down the dreary hallway. Furniture was being overturned; somebody had begun to shout.

The Russian looked over his shoulder and went to slam the door in Ballard's face, but Ballard's foot was there to stop him. Taking advantage of the man's divided attention, Ballard put his shoulder to the door, and pushed. He was in the hallway – indeed he was half-way down it – before the Russian took a step in pursuit. The sound of demolition had escalated, and was now drowned out by the sound of a man squealing. Ballard followed the sound past the sovereignty of the lone bulb and into gloom at the back of the house. He might well have lost his way at that point but that a door was flung open ahead of him.

The room beyond had scarlet floorboards; they glistened as if freshly painted. And now the decorator appeared in person. His torso had been ripped open from neck to navel. He pressed his hands to the breached dam, but they were useless to stem the flood; his blood came in spurts, and with it, his innards. He met Ballard's gaze, his eyes full to overflowing with death, but his body had not yet received the instruction to lie down and die; it juddered on in a pitiful attempt to escape the scene of execution behind him.

The spectacle had brought Ballard to a halt, and the Russian from the door now took hold of him, and pulled him back into the hallway, shouting into his face. The outburst, in panicked Russian, was beyond Ballard, but he needed no translation of the hands that encircled his throat. The Russian was half his weight again, and had the grip of an expert strangler, but Ballard felt effortlessly the man's superior. He wrenched the attacker's hands from his neck, and struck him across the face. It was a fortuitous blow. The Russian fell back against the staircase, his shouts silenced.

Ballard looked back towards the scarlet room. The dead man had gone, though scraps of flesh had been left on the threshold.

From within, laughter.

Ballard turned to the Russian.

'What in God's name's going on?' he demanded, but the other man simply stared through the open door.

Even as he spoke, the laughter stopped. A shadow moved across the blood-splattered wall of the interior, and a voice said:

'Ballard?'

83

There was a roughness there, as if the speaker had been shouting all day and night, but it was the voice of Mironenko.

'Don't stand out in the cold,' he said, 'come on in. And bring Solomonov.'

The other man made a bid for the front door, but Ballard had hold of him before he could take two steps.

'There's nothing to be afraid of, Comrade,' said Mironenko. 'The dog's gone.' Despite the reassurance, Solomonov began to sob as Ballard pressed him towards the open door.

Mironenko was right; it *was* warmer inside. And there no sign of a dog. There was blood in abundance, however. The man Ballard had last seen teetering in the doorway had been dragged back into this abattoir while he and Solomonov had struggled. The body had been treated with astonishing barbarity. The head had been smashed open; the innards were a grim litter underfoot.

Squatting in the shadowy corner of this terrible room, Mironenko. He had been mercilessly beaten to judge by the swelling about his head and upper torso, but his unshaven face bore a smile for his saviour.

'I knew you'd come,' he said. His gaze fell upon Solomonov. 'They followed me,' he said. 'They meant to kill me, I suppose. Is that what you intended, Comrade?'

Solomonov shook with fear – his eyes flitting from the bruised moon of Mironenko's face to the pieces of gut that lay everywhere about – finding nowhere a place of refuge.

'What stopped them?' Ballard asked.

Mironenko stood up. Even this slow movement caused Solomonov to flinch.

'Tell Mr Ballard,' Mironenko prompted. 'Tell him what happened.' Solomonov was too terrified to speak. 'He's KGB, of course,' Mironenko explained. 'Both trusted men. But not trusted enough to be warned, poor idiots. So they were sent to murder me with just a gun and a prayer.' He laughed at the thought. 'Neither of which were much use in the circumstances.'

'I beg you . . .' Solomonov murmured, '. . . let me go. I'll say nothing.'

'You'll say what they want you to say, Comrade, the way we all must,' Mironenko replied. 'Isn't that right, Ballard? All slaves of our faith?'

Ballard watched Mironenko's face closely; there was a fullness there that could not be entirely explained by the bruising. The skin almost seemed to crawl.

'They have made us forgetful,' Mironenko said.

'Of what?' Ballard enquired.

'Of ourselves,' came the reply, and with it Mironenko moved from his murky corner and into the light.

What had Solomonov and his dead companion done to him? His flesh was a mass of tiny contusions, and there were bloodied lumps at his neck and temples which Ballard might have taken for bruises but that they palpitated, as if something nested beneath the skin. Mironenko made no sign of discomfort however, as he reached out to Solomonov. At his touch the failed assassin lost control of his bladder, but Mironenko's intentions were not murderous. With eerie tenderness he stroked a tear from Solomonov's cheek. 'Go back to them,' he advised the trembling man. 'Tell them what you've seen.'

Solomonov seemed scarcely to believe his ears, or else suspected – as did Ballard – that this forgiveness was a sham, and that any attempt to leave would invite fatal consequences.

But Mironenko pressed his point. 'Go on,' he said. 'Leave us please. Or would you prefer to stay and eat?'

Solomonov took a single, faltering step towards the door. When no blow came he took a second step, and a third, and now he was out of the door and away.

'Tell them!' Mironenko shouted after him. The front door slammed.

'Tell them what?' said Ballard.

'That I've remembered,' Mironenko said. 'That I've found the skin they stole from me.'

For the first time since entering this house, Ballard began to feel queasy. It was not the blood nor the bones underfoot, but a look in Mironenko's eyes. He'd seen eyes as bright once before. But where?

'You – ' he said quietly, 'you did this.'

'Certainly,' Mironenko replied.

'How?' Ballard said. There was a familiar thunder climbing from the back of his head. He tried to ignore it, and press some explanation from the Russian. 'How, damn you?'

'We are the same,' Mironenko replied. 'I smell it in you.'

'No,' said Ballard. The clamour was rising.

'The doctrines are just words. It's not what we're taught but what we *know* that matters. In our marrow; in our souls.'

He had talked of souls once before; of places his masters had built in which a man could be broken apart. At the time Ballard

85

had thought such talk mere extravagance; now he wasn't so sure. What was the burial party all about, if not the subjugation of some secret part of him? The marrow-part; the soul-part.

Before Ballard could find the words to express himself, Mironenko froze, his eyes gleaming more brightly than ever.

'They're outside,' he said.

'Who are?'

The Russian shrugged. 'Does it matter?' he said. 'Your side or mine. Either one will silence us if they can.'

That much was true.

'We must be quick,' he said, and headed for the hallway. The front door stood ajar. Mironenko was there in moments. Ballard followed. Together they slipped out on to the street.

The fog had thickened. It idled around the street-lamps, muddying their light, making every doorway a hiding place. Ballard didn't wait to tempt the pursuers out into the open, but followed Mironenko, who was already well ahead, swift despite his bulk. Ballard had to pick up his pace to keep the man in sight. One moment he was visible, the next the fog closed around him.

The residential property they moved through now gave way to more anonymous buildings, warehouses perhaps, whose walls stretched up into the murky darkness unbroken by windows. Ballard called after him to slow his crippling pace. The Russian halted and turned back to Ballard, his outline wavering in the besieged light. Was it a trick of the fog, or had Mironenko's condition deteriorated in the minutes since they'd left the house? His face seemed to be seeping; the lumps on his neck had swelled further.

'We don't have to run,' Ballard said. 'They're not following.'

'They're always following,' Mironenko replied, and as if to give weight to the observation Ballard heard fog-deadened footsteps in a nearby street.

'No time to debate,' Mironenko murmured, and turning on his heel, he ran. In seconds, the fog had spirited him away again.

Ballard hesitated another moment. Incautious as it was, he wanted to catch a glimpse of his pursuers so as to know them for the future. But now, as the soft pad of Mironenko's step diminished into silence, he realised that the other footsteps had also ceased. Did they know he was waiting for them? He held his breath, but there was neither sound nor sign of them. The delinquent fog idled on. He seemed to be alone in it. Reluctantly, he gave up waiting and went after the Russian at a run.

A few yards on the road divided. There was no sign of Mironenko in either direction. Cursing his stupidity in lingering behind, Ballard followed the route which was most heavily shrouded in fog. The street was short, and ended at a wall lined with spikes, beyond which there was a park of some kind. The fog clung more tenaciously to this space of damp earth than it did to the street, and Ballard could see no more than four or five yards across the grass from where he stood. But he knew intuitively that he had chosen the right road; that Mironenko had scaled this wall and was waiting for him somewhere close by. Behind him, the fog kept its counsel. Either their pursuers had lost him, or their way, or both. He hoisted himself up on to the wall, avoiding the spikes by a whisper, and dropped down on the opposite side.

The street had seemed pin-drop quiet, but it clearly wasn't, for it was quieter still inside the park. The fog was chillier here, and pressed more insistently upon him as he advanced across the wet grass. The wall behind him – his only point of anchorage in this wasteland – became a ghost of itself, then faded entirely. Committed now, he walked on a few more steps, not certain that he was even taking a straight route. Suddenly the fog curtain was drawn aside and he saw a figure waiting for him a few yards ahead. The bruises now twisted his face so badly Ballard would not have known it to be Mironenko, but that his eyes still burned so brightly.

The man did not wait for Ballard, but turned again and loped off into insolidity, leaving the Englishman to follow, cursing both the chase and the quarry. As he did so, he felt a movement close by. His senses were useless in the clammy embrace of fog and night, but he saw with that other eye, heard with that other ear, and he knew he was not alone. Had Mironenko given up the race and come back to escort him? He spoke the man's name, knowing that in doing so he made his position apparent to any and all, but equally certain that whoever stalked him already knew precisely where he stood.

'Speak,' he said.

There was no reply out of the fog.

Then; movement. The fog curled upon itself and Ballard glimpsed a form dividing the veils. Mironenko! He called after the man again, taking several steps through the murk in pursuit and suddenly something was stepping out to meet him. He saw the phantom for a moment only; long enough to glimpse incandescent eyes and teeth grown so vast they wrenched the mouth into a permanent grimace. Of those facts – eyes and teeth – he was certain. Of the other bizarrities – the bristling flesh, the monstrous limbs – he was less sure. Maybe his mind, exhausted with so much noise and pain, was finally losing its grip on the real world; inventing terrors to frighten him back into ignorance.

'Damn you,' he said, defying both the thunder that was coming to blind him again and the phantoms he would be blinded to. Almost as if to test his defiance, the fog up ahead shimmered and parted and something that he might have taken for human, but that it had its belly to the ground, slunk into view and out. To his right, he heard growls; to his left, another indeterminate form came and went. He was surrounded, it seemed, by mad men and wild dogs.

And Mironenko; where was he? Part of this assembly, or prey to it? Hearing a half-word spoken behind him, he swung round to see a figure that was plausibly that of the Russian backing into the fog. This time he didn't walk in pursuit, he *ran*, and his speed was rewarded. The figure re-appeared ahead of him, and Ballard stretched to snatch at the man's jacket. His fingers found purchase, and all at once Mironenko was reeling round, a growl in his throat, and Ballard was staring into a face that almost made him cry out. His mouth was a raw wound, the teeth vast, the eyes slits of molten gold; the lumps at his neck had swelled and spread, so that the Russian's head was no longer raised above his body but part of one undivided energy, head becoming torso without an axis intervening.

'Ballard,' the beast smiled.

Its voice clung to coherence only with the greatest difficulty, but Ballard heard the remnants of Mironenko there. The more he scanned the simmering flesh, the more appalled he became.

'Don't be afraid,' Mironenko said.

'What disease is this?'

'The only disease I ever suffered was forgetfulness, and I'm cured of that – ' He grimaced as he spoke, as if each word was shaped in contradiction to the instincts of his throat.

Ballard touched his hand to his head. Despite his revolt against the pain, the noise was rising and rising.

'. . . You remember too, don't you? You're the same.'

'No,' Ballard muttered.

Mironenko reached a spine-haired palm to touch him. 'Don't be afraid,' he said. 'You're not alone. There are many of us. Brothers and sisters.'

'I'm not your brother,' Ballard said. The noise was bad, but the face of Mironenko was worse. Revolted, he turned his back on it, but the Russian only followed him.

'Don't you taste freedom, Ballard? And life. Just a breath away.' Ballard walked on, the blood beginning to creep from his nostrils. He let it come. 'It only hurts for a while,' Mironenko said. 'Then the pain goes . . .'

Ballard kept his head down, eyes to the earth. Mironenko, seeing that he was making little impression, dropped behind.

'They won't take you back!' he said. 'You've seen too much.'

The roar of helicopters did not entirely blot these words out. Ballard knew there was truth in them. His step faltered, and through the cacophony he heard Mironenko murmur:

'*Look* . . .'

Ahead, the fog had thinned somewhat, and the park wall was visible through rags of mist. Behind him, Mironenko's voice had descended to a snarl.

'*Look at what you are.*'

The rotors roared; Ballard's legs felt as though they would fold up beneath him. But he kept up his advance towards the wall. Within yards of it, Mironenko called after him again, but this time the words had fled altogether. There was only a low growl. Ballard could not resist looking; just once. He glanced over his shoulder.

Again the fog confounded him, but not entirely. For moments that were both an age and yet too brief, Ballard saw the thing that had been Mironenko in all its glory, and at the sight the rotors grew to screaming pitch. He clamped his hands to his face. As he did so a shot rang out; then another; then a volley of shots. He fell to the ground, as much in weakness as in self-defence, and uncovered his eyes to see several human figures moving in the fog. Though he had forgotten their pursuers, they had not forgotten him. They had traced him to the park, and stepped into the midst of this lunacy, and now men and half men and things not men were lost in the fog, and there was bloody confusion on every side. He saw a gunman firing at a shadow, only to have an ally appear from the fog with a bullet in his belly; saw a thing appear on four legs and flit from sight again on two; saw another run by carrying a human head by the hair, and laughing from its snouted face.

The turmoil spilled towards him. Fearing for his life, he stood up and staggered back towards the wall. The cries and shots and snarls went on; he expected either bullet or beast to find him with every step. But he reached the wall alive, and attempted to scale it.

His co-ordination had deserted him, however. He had no choice but to follow the wall along its length until he reached the gate.

Behind him the scenes of unmasking and transformation and mistaken identity went on. His enfeebled thoughts turned briefly to Mironenko. Would he, or any of his tribe, survive this massacre?

'Ballard,' said a voice in the fog. He couldn't see the speaker, although he recognised the voice. He'd heard it in his delusion, and it had told him lies.

He felt a pin-prick at his neck. The man had come from behind, and was pressing a needle into him.

'Sleep,' the voice said. And with the words came oblivion.

At first he couldn't remember the man's name. His mind wandered like a lost child, although his interrogator would time and again demand his attention, speaking to him as though they were old friends. And there was indeed something familiar about his errant eye, that went on its way so much more slowly than its companion. At last, the name came to him.

'You're Cripps,' he said.

'Of course I'm Cripps,' the man replied. 'Is your memory playing tricks? Don't concern yourself. I've given you some suppressants, to keep you from losing your balance. Not that I think that's very likely. You've fought the good fight, Ballard, in spite of considerable provocation. When I think of the way Odell snapped . . .' He sighed. 'Do you remember last night at all?'

At first his mind's eye was blind. But then the memories began to come. Vague forms moving in a fog.

'The park,' he said at last.

'I only just got you out. God knows how many are dead.'

'The other . . . the Russian . . .?'

'Mironenko?' Cripps prompted. 'I don't know. I'm not in charge any longer, you see; I just stepped in to salvage something if I could. London will need us again, sooner or later. Especially now they know the Russians have a special corps like us. We'd heard rumours of course; and then, after you'd met with him, began to wonder about Mironenko. That's why I set up the meeting. And of course when I saw him, face to face, I *knew*. There's something in the eyes. Something hungry.'

'I saw him change – '

'Yes, it's quite a sight, isn't it? The power it unleashes. That's why we developed the programme, you see, to harness that power, to have it work for us. But it's difficult to control. It took years of suppression therapy, slowly burying the desire for transformation, so that what we had left was a man with a beast's faculties. A wolf in sheep's clothing. We thought we had the problem beaten; that if the belief systems didn't keep you subdued the pain response would. But we were wrong.' He stood up and crossed to the window. 'Now we have to start again.'

'Suckling said you'd been wounded.'

'No. Merely demoted. Ordered back to London.'

'But you're not going.'

'I will now; now that I've found you.' He looked round at Ballard. 'You're my vindication, Ballard. You're living proof that my techniques are viable. You have full knowledge of your .condition, yet the therapy holds the leash.' He turned back to the window. Rain lashed the glass. Ballard could almost feel it upon his head, upon his back. Cool, sweet rain. For a blissful moment he seemed to be running in it, close to the ground, and the air was full of the scents the downpour had released from the pavements.

'Mironenko said –'

'Forget Mironenko,' Cripps told him. 'He's dead. You're the last of the old order, Ballard. And the first of the new.'

Downstairs, a bell rang. Cripps peered out of the window at the streets below.

'Well, well,' he said. 'A delegation, come to beg us to return. I hope you're flattered.' He went to the door. 'Stay here. We needn't show you off tonight. You're weary. Let them wait, eh? Let them sweat.' He left the stale room, closing the door behind him. Ballard heard his footsteps on the stairs. The bell was being rung a second time. He got up and crossed to the window. The weariness of the late afternoon light matched his weariness; he and his city were still of one accord, despite the curse that was upon him. Below a man emerged from the back of the car and crossed to the front door. Even at this acute angle Ballard recognised Suckling.

There were voices in the hallway; and with Suckling's appearance the debate seemed to become more heated. Ballard went to the door, and listened, but his drug-dulled mind could make little sense of the argument. He prayed that Cripps would keep to his word, and not allow them to peer at him. He didn't want to be a beast like Mironenko. It wasn't freedom, was it, to be so terrible?; it was merely a different kind of tyranny. But then he didn't want to be the first of Cripps' heroic new order either. He belonged to nobody, he realised; not even himself. He was hopelessly lost. And yet hadn't Mironenko said at that first meeting that the man who did not believe himself lost, *was* lost? Perhaps better that – better to exist in the twilight between one state and another, to prosper as best he could by doubt and ambiguity – than to suffer the certainties of the tower.

The debate below was gaining in momentum. Ballard opened the door so as to hear better. It was Suckling's voice that met him. The tone was waspish, but no less threatening for that.

'It's over . . .' he was telling Cripps '. . . don't you understand plain English?' Cripps made an attempt to protest, but Suckling cut him short. 'Either you come in a gentlemanly fashion or Gideon and Sheppard carry you out. Which is it to be?'

'What is this?' Cripps demanded, 'You're nobody, Suckling. You're comic relief.'

'That was yesterday,' the man replied. 'There've been some changes made. Every dog has his day, isn't that right? You should know that better than anybody. I'd get a coat if I were you. It's raining.'

There was a short silence, then Cripps said:

'All right. I'll come.'

'Good man,' said Suckling sweetly. 'Gideon, go check upstairs.'

'I'm alone,' said Cripps.

'I believe you,' said Suckling. Then to Gideon, 'Do it anyway.'

Ballard heard somebody move across the hallway, and then a sudden flurry of movement. Cripps was either making an escape-bid or attacking Suckling, one of the two. Suckling shouted out; there was a scuffle. Then, cutting through the confusion, a single shot.

Cripps cried out, then came the sound of him falling.

Now Suckling's voice, thick with fury. 'Stupid,' he said. 'Stupid.'

Cripps groaned something which Ballard didn't catch. Had he asked to be dispatched, perhaps, for Suckling told him: 'No. You're going back to London. Sheppard, stop him bleeding. Gideon; upstairs.'

Ballard backed away from the head of the stairs as Gideon began his ascent. He felt sluggish and inept. There was no way out of this trap. They would corner him and exterminate him. He was a beast; a mad dog in a maze. If he'd only killed Suckling when he'd had the strength to do so. But then what good would that have done? The world was full of men like Suckling, men biding their time until they could show their true colours; vile, soft, secret

92

men. And suddenly the beast seemed to move in Ballard, and he thought of the park and the fog and the smile on the face of Mironenko, and he felt a surge of grief for something he'd never had: the life of a monster.

Gideon was almost at the top of the stairs. Though it could only delay the inevitable by moments, Ballard slipped along the landing and opened the first door he found. It was the bathroom. There was a bolt on the door, which he slipped into place.

The sound of running water filled the room. A piece of guttering had broken, and was delivering a torrent of rain-water onto the window-sill. The sound, and the chill of the bathroom, brought the night of delusions back. He remembered the pain and blood; remembered the shower – water beating on his skull, cleansing him of the taming pain. At the thought, four words came to his lips unbidden.

'I do not believe.'

He had been heard.

'There's somebody up here,' Gideon called. The man approached the door, and beat on it. 'Open up!'

Ballard heard him quite clearly, but didn't reply. His throat was burning, and the roar of rotors was growing louder again. He put his back to the door and despaired.

Suckling was up the stairs and at the door in seconds. 'Who's in there?' he demanded to know. 'Answer me! Who's in *there*?' Getting no response, he ordered that Cripps be brought upstairs. There was more commotion as the order was obeyed.

'For the last time – ' Suckling said.

The pressure was building in Ballard's skull. This time it seemed the din had lethal intentions; his eyes ached, as if about to be blown from their sockets. He caught sight of something in the mirror above the sink; something with gleaming eyes, and again, the words came – 'I do not believe' – but this time his throat, hot with other business, could barely pronounce them.

'*Ballard*,' said Suckling. There was triumph in the word. 'My God, we've got Ballard as well. This is our lucky day.'

No, thought the man in the mirror. There was nobody of that name here. Nobody of any name at all, in fact, for weren't names the first act of faith, the first board in the box you buried freedom in? The thing he was becoming would not be named; nor boxed; nor buried. Never again.

For a moment he lost sight of the bathroom, and found himself hovering above the grave they had made him dig, and in the depths

93

the box danced as its contents fought its premature burial. He could hear the wood splintering – or was it the sound of the door being broken down?

The box-lid flew off. A rain of nails fell on the heads of the burial party. The noise in his head, as if knowing that its torments had proved fruitless, suddenly fled, and with it the delusion. He was back in the bathroom, facing the open door. The men who stared through at him had the faces of fools. Slack, and stupified with shock – seeing the way he was wrought. Seeing the snout of him, the hair of him, the golden eye and the yellow tooth of him. Their horror elated him.

'Kill it!' said Suckling, and pushed Gideon into the breach. The man already had his gun from his pocket and was levelling it, but his trigger-finger was too slow. The beast snatched his hand and pulped the flesh around the steel. Gideon screamed, and stumbled away down the stairs, ignoring Suckling's shouts.

As the beast raised his hand to sniff the blood on his palm there was a flash of fire, and he felt the blow to his shoulder. Sheppard had no chance to fire a second shot however before his prey was through the door and upon him. Forsaking his gun, he made a futile bid for the stairs, but the beast's hand unsealed the back of his head in one easy stroke. The gunman toppled forward, the narrow landing filling with the smell of him. Forgetting his other enemies, the beast fell upon the offal and ate.

Somebody said: 'Ballard.'

The beast swallowed down the dead man's eyes in one gulp, like prime oysters.

Again, those syllables. *'Ballard.'* He would have gone on with his meal, but that the sound of weeping pricked his ears. Dead to himself he was, but not to grief. He dropped the meat from his fingers and looked back along the landing.

The man who was crying only wept from one eye; the other gazed on, oddly untouched. But the pain in the living eye was profound indeed. It was *despair*, the beast knew; such suffering was too close to him for the sweetness of transformation to have erased it entirely. The weeping man was locked in the arms of another man, who had his gun placed against the side of his prisoner's head.

'If you make another move,' the captor said, 'I'll blow his head off. Do you understand me?'

The beast wiped his mouth.

'Tell him, Cripps! He's your baby. Make him understand.'

The one-eyed man tried to speak, but words defeated him. Blood from the wound in his abdomen seeped between his fingers.

'Neither of you need die,' the captor said. The beast didn't like the music of his voice; it was shrill and deceitful. 'London would much prefer to have you alive. So why don't you tell him, Cripps? Tell him I mean him no harm.'

The weeping man nodded.

'Ballard . . .' he murmured. His voice was softer than the other. The beast listened.

'Tell me, Ballard – ' he said, ' – how does it feel?'

The beast couldn't quite make sense of the question.

'Please tell me. For curiosity's sake – '

'Damn you – ' said Suckling, pressing the gun into Cripps' flesh. 'This isn't a debating society.'

'Is it good?' Cripps asked, ignoring both man and gun.

'Shut up!'

'Answer me, Ballard. *How does it feel?*'

As he stared into Cripps' despairing eyes the meaning of the sounds he'd uttered came clear, the words falling into place like the pieces of a mosaic. 'Is it good?' the man was asking.

Ballard heard laughter in his throat, and found the syllables there to reply.

'Yes,' he told the weeping man. 'Yes. It's good.'

He had not finished his reply before Cripps' hand sped to snatch at Suckling's. Whether he intended suicide or escape nobody would ever know. The trigger-finger twitched, and a bullet flew up through Cripps' head and spread his despair across the ceiling. Suckling threw the body off, and went to level the gun, but the beast was already upon him.

Had he been more of a man, Ballard might have thought to make Suckling suffer, but he had no such perverse ambition. His only thought was to render the enemy extinct as efficiently as possible. Two sharp and lethal blows did it. Once the man was dispatched, Ballard crossed over to where Cripps was lying. His glass eye had escaped destruction. It gazed on fixedly, untouched by the holocaust all around them. Unseating it from the maimed head, Ballard put it in his pocket; then he went out into the rain.

It was dusk. He did not know which district of Berlin he'd been brought to, but his impulses, freed of reason, led him via the back streets and shadows to a wasteland on the outskirts of the city, in the middle of which stood a solitary ruin. It was anybody's guess as to what the building might once have been (an abbatoir? an opera-house?) but by some freak of fate it had escaped demolition, though every other building had been levelled for several hundred yards in each direction. As he made his way across the weed-clogged rubble the wind changed direction by a few degrees and carried the scent of his tribe to him. There were many there, together in the shelter of the ruin. Some leaned their backs against the wall and shared a cigarette; some were perfect wolves, and haunted the darkness like ghosts with golden eyes; yet others might have passed for human entirely, but for their trails.

Though he feared that names would be forbidden amongst this clan, he asked two lovers who were rutting in the shelter of the wall if they knew of a man called Mironenko. The bitch had a smooth and hairless back, and a dozen full teats hanging from her belly.

'Listen,' she said.

Ballard listened, and heard somebody talking in a corner of the ruin. The voice ebbed and flowed. He followed the sound across the roofless interior to where a wolf was standing, surrounded by an attentive audience, an open book in its front paws. At Ballard's approach one or two of the audience turned their luminous eyes up to him. The reader halted.

'Ssh!' said one, 'the Comrade is reading to us.'

It was Mironenko who spoke. Ballard slipped into the ring of listeners beside him, as the reader took up the story afresh.

'*And God blessed them, and God said unto them, Be fruitful, and multiply, and replenish the earth . . .*'

Ballard had heard the words before, but tonight they were new.

'*. . . and subdue it: and have dominion over the fish of the sea, and over the fowl of the air . . .*'

He looked around the circle of listeners as the words described their familiar pattern.

'*. . , and over every living thing that moveth upon the earth.*'

Somewhere near, a beast was crying.

The Last Illusion

What happened then – when the magician, having mesmerised the caged tiger, pulled the tasselled cord that released a dozen swords upon its head – was the subject of heated argument both in the bar of the theatre and later, when Swann's performance was over, on the sidewalk of 51st Street. Some claimed to have glimpsed the bottom of the cage opening in the split second that all other eyes were on the descending blades, and seen the tiger swiftly spirited away as the woman in the red dress took its place behind the lacquered bars. Others were just as adamant that the animal had never been in the cage to begin with, its presence merely a projection which had been extinguished as a mechanism propelled the woman from beneath the stage; this, of course, at such a speed that it deceived the eye of all but those swift and suspicious enough to catch it. And the swords? The nature of the trick which had transformed them in the mere seconds of their gleaming descent from steel to rose-petals was yet further fuel for debate. The explanations ranged from the prosaic to the elaborate, but few of the throng that left the theatre lacked some theory. Nor did the arguments finish there, on the sidewalk. They raged on, no doubt, in the apartments and restaurants of New York.

The pleasure to be had from Swann's illusions was, it seemed, twofold. First: the spectacle of the trick itself – in the breathless moment when disbelief was, if not suspended, at least taken on tip-toe. And second, when the moment was over and logic restored, in the debate as to how the trick had been achieved.

'How do you do it, Mr Swann?' Barbara Bernstein was eager to know.

'It's magic,' Swann replied. He had invited her backstage to examine the tiger's cage for any sign of fakery in its construction; she had found none. She had examined the swords: they were lethal. And the petals, fragrant. Still she insisted:

'Yes, but *really* . . .' she leaned close to him. 'You can tell me,' she said, 'I promise I won't breathe a word to a soul.'

He returned her a slow smile in place of a reply.

97

'Oh, I know . . .' she said, 'you're going to tell me that you've signed some kind of oath.'

'That's right,' Swann said.

' – And you're forbidden to give away any trade secrets.'

'The intention is to give you pleasure,' he told her. 'Have I failed in that?'

'Oh no,' she replied, without a moment's hesitation. 'Everybody's talking about the show. You're the toast of New York.'

'No,' he protested.

'Truly,' she said, 'I know people who would give their eye-teeth to get into this theatre. And to have a guided tour backstage . . . well, I'll be the envy of everybody.'

'I'm pleased,' he said, and touched her face. She had clearly been anticipating such a move on his part. It would be something else for her to boast of: her seduction by the man critics had dubbed the Magus of Manhattan.

'I'd like to make love to you,' he whispered to her.

'Here?' she said.

'No,' he told her. 'Not within ear-shot of the tigers.'

She laughed. She preferred her lovers twenty years Swann's junior – he looked, someone had observed, like a man in mourning for his profile, but his touch promised wit no boy could offer. She liked the tang of dissolution she sensed beneath his gentlemanly façade. Swann was a dangerous man. If she turned him down she might never find another.

'We could go to a hotel,' she suggested.

'A hotel,' he said, 'is a good idea.'

A look of doubt had crossed her face.

'What about your wife . . . .?' she said. 'We might be seen.'

He took her hand. 'Shall we be invisible, then?'

'I'm serious.'

'So am I,' he insisted. 'Take it from me; seeing is not believing. I should know. It's the cornerstone of my profession.' She did not look much reassured. 'If anyone recognises us,' he told her, 'I'll simply tell them their eyes are playing tricks.'

She smiled at this, and he kissed her. She returned the kiss with unquestionable fervour.

'Miraculous,' he said, when their mouths parted. 'Shall we go before the tigers gossip?'

He led her across the stage. The cleaners had not yet got about their business, and there, lying on the boards, was a litter of rose-buds. Some had been trampled, a few had not. Swann took his hand from hers, and walked across to where the flowers lay.

She watched him stoop to pluck a rose from the ground, enchanted by the gesture, but before he could stand upright again something in the air above him caught her eye. She looked up and her gaze met a slice of silver that was even now plunging towards him. She made to warn him, but the sword was quicker than her tongue. At the last possible moment he seemed to sense the danger he was in and looked round, the bud in his hand, as the point met his back. The sword's momentum carried it through his body to the hilt. Blood fled from his chest, and splashed the floor. He made no sound, but fell forward, forcing two-thirds of the sword's length out of his body again as he hit the stage.

She would have screamed, but that her attention was claimed by a sound from the clutter of magical apparatus arrayed in the wings behind her, a muttered growl which was indisputably the voice of the tiger. She froze. There were probably instructions on how best to stare down rogue tigers, but as a Manhattanite born and bred they were techniques she wasn't acquainted with.

'Swann?' she said, hoping this yet might be some baroque illusion staged purely for her benefit. 'Swann. Please get up.'

But the magician only lay where he had fallen, the pool spreading from beneath him.

'If this is a joke –' she said testily, ' – I'm not amused.' When he didn't rise to her remark she tried a sweeter tactic. 'Swann, my sweet, I'd like to go now, if you don't mind.'

The growl came again. She didn't want to turn and seek out its source, but equally she didn't want to be sprung upon from behind.

Cautiously she looked round. The wings were in darkness. The clutter of properties kept her from working out the precise location of the beast. She could hear it still, however: its tread, its growl. Step by step, she retreated towards the apron of the stage. The closed curtains sealed her off from the auditorium, but she hoped she might scramble under them before the tiger reached her.

As she backed against the heavy fabric, one of the shadows in the wings forsook its ambiguity, and the animal appeared. It was not beautiful, as she had thought it when behind bars. It was vast and lethal and hungry. She went down on her haunches and reached for the hem of the curtain. The fabric was heavily weighted, and she had more difficulty lifting it than she'd expected, but she had managed to slide halfway under the drape when, head and hands pressed to the boards, she sensed the thump of the tiger's advance. An instant later she felt the splash of its breath on her bare back, and screamed as it hooked its talons into her body and hauled her from the sight of safety towards its steaming jaws.

Even then, she refused to give up her life. She kicked at it, and tore out its fur in handfuls, and delivered a hail of punches to its snout. But her resistance was negligible in the face of such authority; her assault, for all its ferocity, did not slow the beast a jot. It ripped open her body with one casual clout. Mercifully, with that first wound her senses gave up all claim to verisimilitude, and took instead to preposterous invention. It seemed to her that she heard applause from somewhere, and the roar of an approving audience, and that in place of the blood that was surely springing from her body there came fountains of sparkling light. The agony her nerve-endings were suffering didn't touch her at all. Even when the animal had divided her into three or four parts her head lay on its side at the edge of the stage and watched as her torso was mauled and her limbs devoured.

And all the while, when she wondered how all this could be possible – that her eyes could live to witness this last supper – the only reply she could think of was Swann's:

'*It's magic*,' he'd said.

Indeed, she was thinking that very thing, that this must *be* magic, when the tiger ambled across to her head, and swallowed it down in one bite.

Amongst a certain set Harry D'Amour liked to believe he had some small reputation – a coterie which did not, alas, include his ex-wife, his creditors or those anonymous critics who regularly posted dog's excrement through his office letterbox. But the woman who was on the phone now, her voice so full of grief she might have been crying for half a year, and was about to begin again, *she* knew him for the paragon he was.

' – I need your help, Mr D'Amour; very badly.'

'I'm busy on several cases at the moment,' he told her. 'Maybe you could come to the office?'

'I can't leave the house,' the woman informed him. 'I'll explain everything. Please come.'

He was sorely tempted. But there *were* several outstanding cases, one of which, if not solved soon, might end in fratricide. He suggested she try elsewhere.

'I can't go to just anybody,' the woman insisted.

'Why me?'

'I read about you. About what happened in Brooklyn.'

Making mention of his most conspicuous failure was not the surest method of securing his services, Harry thought, but it certainly got his attention. What had happened in Wyckoff Street had begun innocently enough, with a husband who'd employed him to spy on his adulterous wife, and had ended on the top storey of the Lomax house with the world he thought he'd known turning inside out. When the body-count was done, and the surviving priests dispatched, he was left with fear of stairs, and more questions than he'd ever answer this side of the family plot. He took no pleasure in being reminded of those terrors.

'I don't like to talk about Brooklyn,' he said.

'Forgive me,' the woman replied, 'but I need somebody who has experience with . . . with the occult.' She stopped speaking for a moment. He could still hear her breath down the line: soft, but erratic.

'I need you,' she said. He had already decided, in that pause when only her fear had been audible, what reply he would make.

'I'll come.'

'I'm grateful to you,' she said. 'The house is on East 61st Street – ' He scribbled down the details. Her last words were, 'Please hurry.' Then she put down the phone.

He made some calls, in the vain hope of placating two of his more excitable clients, then pulled on his jacket, locked the office, and started downstairs. The landing and the lobby smelt pungent. As he reached the front door he caught Chaplin, the janitor, emerging from the basement.

'This place stinks,' he told the man.

'It's disinfectant.'

'It's cat's piss,' Harry said. 'Get something done about it, will you? I've got a reputation to protect.'

He left the man laughing.

The brownstone on East 61st Street was in pristine condition. He stood on the scrubbed step, sweaty and sour-breathed, and felt like a slob. The expression on the face that met him when the door opened did nothing to dissuade him of that opinion.

'Yes?' it wanted to know.

'I'm Harry D'Amour,' he said. 'I got a call.'

The man nodded. 'You'd better come in,' he said, without enthusiasm.

It was cooler in than out; and sweeter. The place reeked of perfume. Harry followed the disapproving face down the hallway and into a large room, on the other side of which – across an oriental carpet that had everything woven into its pattern but the price – sat a widow. She didn't suit black; nor tears. She stood up and offered her hand.

'Mr D'Amour?'

'Yes.'

'Valentin will get you something to drink if you'd like.'

'Please. Milk, if you have it.' His belly had been jittering for the last hour; since her talk of Wyckoff Street, in fact.

Valentin retired from the room, not taking his beady eyes off Harry until the last possible moment.

'Somebody died,' said Harry, once the man had gone.

'That's right,' the widow said, sitting down again. At her invitation he sat opposite her, amongst enough cushions to furnish a harem. 'My husband.'

'I'm sorry.'

'There's no time to be sorry,' she said, her every look and gesture betraying her words. He was glad of her grief; the tear-stains and the fatigue blemished a beauty which, had he seen it unimpaired, might have rendered him dumb with admiration.

'They say that my husband's death was an accident,' she was saying. 'I know it wasn't.'

'May I ask . . . your name?'

'I'm sorry. My name is Swann, Mr D'Amour. Dorothea Swann. You may have heard of my husband?'

'The magician?'

'*Illusionist*,' she said.

'I read about it. Tragic.'

'Did you ever see his performance?'

Harry shook his head. 'I can't afford Broadway, Mrs Swann.'

'We were only over for three months, while his show ran. We were going back in September . . .'

'Back?'

'To Hamburg,' she said. 'I don't like this city. It's too hot. And too cruel.'

'Don't blame New York,' he said. 'It can't help itself.'

'Maybe,' she replied, nodding. 'Perhaps what happened to Swann would have happened anyway, wherever we'd been. People keep telling me: it was an accident. That's all. Just an accident.'

'But you don't believe it?'

Valentin had appeared with a glass of milk. He set it down on the table in front of Harry. As he made to leave, she said: 'Valentin. The letter?'

He looked at her strangely, almost as though she'd said something obscene.

'*The letter*,' she repeated.

He exited.

'You were saying – '

She frowned. 'What?'

'About it being an accident.'

'Oh yes. I lived with Swann seven and a half years, and I got to understand him as well as anybody ever could. I learned to sense when he wanted me around, and when he didn't. When he didn't, I'd take myself off somewhere and let him have his privacy. Genius needs privacy. And he *was* a genius, you know. The greatest illusionist since Houdini.'

'Is that so?'

'I'd think sometimes – it was a kind of miracle that he let me into his life . . .'

Harry wanted to say Swann would have been mad not to have done so, but the comment was inappropriate. She didn't want blandishments; didn't need them. Didn't need anything, perhaps, but her husband alive again.

'Now I think I didn't know him at all,' she went on, 'didn't *understand* him. I think maybe it was another trick. Another part of his magic.'

'I called him a magician a while back,' Harry said. 'You corrected me.'

'So I did,' she said, conceding his point with an apologetic look. 'Forgive me. That was Swann talking. He *hated* to be called a magician. He said that was a word that had to be kept for miracle-workers.'

'And he was no miracle-worker?'

'He used to call himself the Great Pretender,' she said. The thought made her smile.

Valentin had re-appeared, his lugubrious features rife with suspicion. He carried an envelope, which he clearly had no desire to give up. Dorothea had to cross the carpet and take it from his hands.

'Is this wise?' he said.

'Yes,' she told him.

He turned on his heel and made a smart withdrawal.

'He's grief stricken,' she said. 'Forgive him his behaviour. He was with Swann from the beginning of his career. I think he loved my husband as much as I did.'

She ran her finger down into the envelope and pulled the letter out. The paper was pale yellow, and gossamer-thin.

'A few hours after he died, this letter was delivered here by hand,' she said. 'It was addressed to him. I opened it. I think you ought to read it.'

She passed it to him. The hand it was written in was solid and unaffected.

Dorothea, he had written, *if you are reading this, then I am dead.*

You know how little store I set by dreams and premonitions and such; but for the last few days strange thoughts have just crept into my head, and I have the suspicion that death is very close to me. If so, so. There's no help for it. Don't waste time trying to puzzle out the whys and wherefores; they're old news now. Just know that I love you, and that I have always loved you in my way. I'm sorry for whatever unhappiness I've caused, or am causing now, but it was out of my hands.

I have some instructions regarding the disposal of my body. Please adhere to them to the letter. Don't let anybody try to persuade you out of doing as I ask.

I want you to have my body watched night and day *until I'm cremated. Don't try and take my remains back to Europe. Have me cremated here,* as soon as possible, *then throw the ashes in the East River.*

My sweet darling, I'm afraid. Not of bad dreams, or of what might happen to me in this life, but of what my enemies may try to do once I'm dead. You know how critics can be: they wait until you can't fight them back, then they start the character assassinations. It's too long a business to try and explain all of this, so I must simply trust you to do as I say.

Again, I love you, and I hope you never have to read this letter,
Your adoring,
Swann.'

'Some farewell note,' Harry commented when he'd read it through twice. He folded it up and passed it back to the widow.

'I'd like you to stay with him,' she said. 'Corpse-sit, if you will. Just until all the legal formalities are dealt with and I can make arrangements for his cremation. It shouldn't take them long. I've got a lawyer working on it now.'

'Again: why me?'

She avoided his gaze. 'As he says in the letter, he was never superstitious. But I am. I believe in omens. And there was an odd atmosphere about the place in the days before he died. As if we were watched.'

'You think he was murdered?'

She mused on this, then said: 'I don't believe it was an accident.'

'These enemies he talks about . . .'

'He was a great man. Much envied.'

'Professional jealousy? Is that a motive for murder?'

'Anything can be a motive, can't it?' she said. 'People get killed for the colour of their eyes, don't they?'

Harry was impressed. It had taken him twenty years to learn how arbitrary things were. She spoke it as conventional wisdom.

'Where is your husband?' he asked her.

'Upstairs,' she said. 'I had the body brought back here, where I could look after him. I can't pretend I understand what's going on, but I'm not going to risk ignoring his instructions.'

Harry nodded.

'Swann was my life,' she added softly, apropos of nothing; and everything.

She took him upstairs. The perfume that had met him at the door intensified. The master bedroom had been turned into a Chapel of Rest, knee-deep in sprays and wreaths of every shape and variety; their mingled scents verged on the hallucinogenic. In the midst of this abundance, the casket – an elaborate affair in black and silver – was mounted on trestles. The upper half of the lid stood open, the plush overlay folded back. At Dorothea's invitation he waded through the tributes to view the deceased. He liked Swann's face; it had humour, and a certain guile; it was even handsome in its weary way. More: it had inspired the love of Dorothea; a face could have few better recommendations. Harry stood waist high in flowers and, absurd as it was, felt a twinge of envy for the love this man must have enjoyed.

'Will you help me, Mr D'Amour?'

What could he say but: 'Yes, of course I'll help.' That, and: 'Call me Harry.'

He would be missed at Wing's Pavilion tonight. He had occupied the best table there every Friday night for the past six and a half years, eating at one sitting enough to compensate for what his diet lacked in excellence and variety the other six days of the week. This feast – the best Chinese cuisine to be had south of

105

Canal Street – came *gratis*, thanks to services he had once rendered the owner. Tonight the table would go empty.

Not that his stomach suffered. He had only been sitting with Swann an hour or so when Valentin came up and said:

'How do you like your steak?'

'Just shy of burned,' Harry replied.

Valentin was none too pleased by the response. 'I hate to overcook good steak,' he said.

'And I hate the sight of blood,' Harry said, 'even if it isn't my own.'

The chef clearly despaired of his guest's palate, and turned to go.

'Valentin?'

The man looked round.

'Is that your Christian name?' Harry asked.

'Christian names are for Christians,' came the reply.

Harry nodded. 'You don't like my being here, am I right?'

Valentin made no reply. His eyes had drifted past Harry to the open coffin.

'I'm not going to be here for long,' Harry said, 'but while I am, can't we be friends?'

Valentin's gaze found him once more.

'I don't have any friends,' he said without enmity or self-pity. 'Not now.'

'OK. I'm sorry.'

'What's to be sorry for?' Valentin wanted to know. 'Swann's dead. It's all over, bar the shouting.'

The doleful face stoically refused tears. A stone would weep sooner, Harry guessed. But there was grief there, and all the more acute for being dumb.

'One question.'

'Only one?'

'Why didn't you want me to read his letter?'

Valentin raised his eyebrows slightly; they were fine enough to have been pencilled on. 'He wasn't insane,' he said. 'I didn't want you thinking he was a crazy man, because of what he wrote. What you read you keep to yourself. Swann was a legend. I don't want his memory besmirched.'

'You should write a book,' Harry said. 'Tell the whole story once and for all. You were with him a long time, I hear.'

'Oh yes,' said Valentin. 'Long enough to know better than to tell the truth.'

So saying he made an exit, leaving the flowers to wilt, and Harry with more puzzles on his hands than he'd begun with.

Twenty minutes later, Valentin brought up a tray of food: a large salad, bread, wine, and the steak. It was one degree short of charcoal.

'Just the way I like it,' Harry said, and set to guzzling.

He didn't see Dorothea Swann, though God knows he thought about her often enough. Every time he heard a whisper on the stairs, or footsteps along the carpeted landing, he hoped her face would appear at the door, an invitation on her lips. Not perhaps the most appropriate of thoughts, given the proximity of her husband's corpse, but what would the illusionist care now? He was dead and gone. If he had any generosity of spirit he wouldn't want to see his widow drown in her grief.

Harry drank the half-carafe of wine Valentin had brought, and when – three-quarters of an hour later – the man re-appeared with coffee and Calvados, he told him to leave the bottle.

Nightfall was near. The traffic was noisy on Lexington and Third. Out of boredom he took to watching the street from the window. Two lovers feuded loudly on the sidewalk, and only stopped when a brunette with a hare-lip and a pekinese stood watching them shamelessly. There were preparations for a party in the brownstone opposite: he watched a table lovingly laid, and candles lit. After a time the spying began to depress him, so he called Valentin and asked if there was a portable television he could have access to. No sooner said than provided, and for the next two hours he sat with the small black and white monitor on the floor amongst the orchids and the lilies, watching whatever mindless entertainment it offered, the silver luminescence flickering on the blooms like excitable moonlight.

A quarter after midnight, with the party across the street in full swing, Valentin came up. 'You want a night-cap?' he asked.

'Sure.'

'Milk; or something stronger?'

'Something stronger.'

He produced a bottle of fine cognac, and two glasses. Together they toasted the dead man.

'Mr Swann.'

'Mr Swann.'

'If you need anything more tonight,' Valentin said, 'I'm in the room directly above. Mrs Swann is downstairs, so if you hear

107

somebody moving about, don't worry. She doesn't sleep well these nights.'

'Who does?' Harry replied.

Valentin left him to his vigil. Harry heard the man's tread on the stairs, and then the creaking of floorboards on the level above. He returned his attention to the television, but he'd lost the thread of the movie he'd been watching. It was a long stretch 'til dawn; meanwhile New York would be having itself a fine Friday night: dancing, fighting, fooling around.

The picture on the television set began to flicker. He stood up, and started to walk across to the set, but he never got there. Two steps from the chair where he'd been sitting the picture folded up and went out altogether, plunging the room into total darkness. Harry briefly had time to register that no light was finding its way through the windows from the street. Then the insanity began.

Something moved in the blackness: vague forms rose and fell. It took him a moment to recognise them. The flowers! Invisible hands were tearing the wreaths and tributes apart, and tossing the blossoms up into the air. He followed their descent, but they didn't hit the ground. It seemed the floorboards had lost all faith in themselves, and disappeared, so the blossoms just kept falling – *down, down* – through the floor of the room below, and through the basement floor, away to God alone knew what destination. Fear gripped Harry, like some old dope-pusher promising a terrible high. Even those few boards that remained beneath his feet were becoming insubstantial. In seconds he would go the way of the blossoms.

He reeled around to locate the chair he'd got up from – some fixed point in this vertiginous nightmare. The chair was still there; he could just discern its form in the gloom. With torn blossoms raining down upon him he reached for it, but even as his hand took hold of the arm, the floor beneath the chair gave up the ghost, and now, by a ghastly light that was thrown up from the pit that yawned beneath his feet, Harry saw it tumble away into Hell, turning over and over 'til it was pin-prick small.

Then it was gone; and the flowers were gone, and the walls and the windows and every damn thing was gone but *him*.

Not quite everything. Swann's casket remained, its lid still standing open, its overlay neatly turned back like the sheet on a child's bed. The trestle had gone, as had the floor beneath the trestle. But the casket floated in the dark air for all the world like some morbid illusion, while from the depths a rumbling sound accompanied the trick like the roll of a snare-drum.

Harry felt the last solidity failing beneath him; felt the pit call. Even as his feet left the ground, that ground faded to nothing, and for a terrifying moment he hung over the Gulfs, his hands seeking the lip of the casket. His right hand caught hold of one of the handles, and closed thankfully around it. His arm was almost jerked from its socket as it took his body-weight, but he flung his other arm up and found the casket-edge. Using it as purchase, he hauled himself up like a half-drowned sailor. It was a strange life-boat, but then this was a strange sea. Infinitely deep, infinitely terrible.

Even as he laboured to secure himself a better hand-hold, the casket shook, and Harry looked up to discover that the dead man was sitting upright. Swann's eyes opened wide. He turned them on Harry; they were far from benign. The next moment the dead illusionist was scrambling to his feet – the floating casket rocking ever more violently with each movement. Once vertical, Swann proceeded to dislodge his guest by grinding his heel in Harry's knuckles. Harry looked up at Swann, begging for him to stop.

The Great Pretender was a sight to see. His eyes were starting from his sockets; his shirt was torn open to display the exit-wound in his chest. It was bleeding afresh. A rain of cold blood fell upon Harry's upturned face. And still the heel ground at his hands. Harry felt his grip slipping. Swann, sensing his approaching triumph, began to smile.

'Fall, boy!' he said. 'Fall!'

Harry could take no more. In a frenzied effort to save himself he let go of the handle in his right hand, and reached up to snatch at Swann's trouser-leg. His fingers found the hem, and he pulled. The smile vanished from the illusionist's face as he felt his balance go. He reached behind him to take hold of the casket lid for support, but the gesture only tipped the casket further over. The plush cushion tumbled past Harry's head; blossoms followed.

Swann howled in his fury and delivered a vicious kick to Harry's hand. It was an error. The casket tipped over entirely and pitched the man out. Harry had time to glimpse Swann's appalled face as the illusionist fell past him. Then he too lost his grip and tumbled after him.

The dark air whined past his ears. Beneath him, the Gulfs spread their empty arms. And then, behind the rushing in his head, another sound: a human voice.

'Is he dead?' it inquired.

'No,' another voice replied, 'no, I don't think so. What's his name, Dorothea?'

'D'Amour.'

'Mr D'Amour? Mr D'Amour?'

Harry's descent slowed somewhat. Beneath him, the Gulfs roared their rage.

The voice came again, cultivated but unmelodious. 'Mr D'Amour.'

'Harry,' said Dorothea.

At that word, from that voice, he stopped falling; felt himself borne up. He opened his eyes. He was lying on a solid floor, his head inches from the blank television screen. The flowers were all in place around the room, Swann in his casket, and God – if the rumours were to be believed – in his Heaven.

'I'm alive,' he said.

He had quite an audience for his resurrection. Dorothea of course, and two strangers. One, the owner of the voice he'd first heard, stood close to the door. His features were unremarkable, except for his brows and lashes, which were pale to the point of invisibility. His female companion stood nearby. She shared with him this distressing banality, stripped bare of any feature that offered a clue to their natures.

'Help him up, angel,' the man said, and the woman bent to comply. She was stronger than she looked, readily hauling Harry to his feet. He had vomited in his strange sleep. He felt dirty and ridiculous.

'What the hell happened?' he asked, as the woman escorted him to the chair. He sat down.

'He tried to poison you,' the man said.

'Who did?'

'Valentin, of course.'

'Valentin?'

'He's gone,' Dorothea said. 'Just disappeared.' She was shaking. 'I heard you call out, and came in here to find you on the floor. I thought you were going to choke.'

'It's all right,' said the man, 'everything is in order now.'

'Yes,' said Dorothea, clearly reassured by his bland smile. 'This is the lawyer I was telling you about, Harry. Mr Butterfield.'

Harry wiped his mouth. 'Pleased to meet you,' he said.

'Why don't we all go downstairs?' Butterfield said. 'And I can pay Mr D'Amour what he's due.'

110

'It's all right,' Harry said, 'I never take my fee until the job's done.'

'But it is done,' Butterfield said. 'Your services are no longer required here.'

Harry threw a glance at Dorothea. She was plucking a withered anthurium from an otherwise healthy spray.

'I was contracted to stay with the body – '

'The arrangements for the disposal of Swann's body have been made,' Butterfield returned. His courtesy was only just intact. 'Isn't that right, Dorothea?'

'It's the middle of the night,' Harry protested. 'You won't get a cremation until tomorrow morning at the earliest.'

'Thank you for your help,' Dorothea said. 'But I'm sure everything will be fine now that Mr Butterfield has arrived. Just fine.'

Butterfield turned to his companion.

'Why don't you go out and find a cab for Mr D'Amour?' he said. Then, looking at Harry: 'We don't want you walking the streets, do we?'

All the way downstairs, and in the hallway as Butterfield paid him off, Harry was willing Dorothea to contradict the lawyer and tell him she wanted Harry to stay. But she didn't even offer him a word of farewell as he was ushered out of the house. The two hundred dollars he'd been given were, of course, more than adequate recompense for the few hours of idleness he'd spent there, but he would happily have burned all the bills for one sign that Dorothea gave a damn that they were parting. Quite clearly she did not. On past experience it would take his bruised ego a full twenty-four hours to recover from such indifference.

He got out of the cab on 3rd around 83rd Street, and walked through to a bar on Lexington where he knew he could put half a bottle of bourbon between himself and the dreams he'd had.

It was well after one. The street was deserted, except for him, and for the echo his footsteps had recently acquired. He turned the corner into Lexington, and waited. A few beats later, Valentin rounded the same corner. Harry took hold of him by his tie.

'Not a bad noose,' he said, hauling the man off his heels.

Valentin made no attempt to free himself. 'Thank God you're alive,' he said.

'No thanks to you,' Harry said. 'What did you put in the drink?'

'Nothing,' Valentin insisted. 'Why should I?'

'So how come I found myself on the floor? How come the bad dreams?'

'Butterfield,' Valentin said. 'Whatever you dreamt, he brought with him, believe me. I panicked as soon as I heard him in the house, I admit it. I know I should have warned you, but I knew if I didn't get out quickly I wouldn't get out at all.'

'Are you telling me he would have killed you?'

'Not personally; but yes.' Harry looked incredulous. 'We go way back, him and me.'

'He's welcome to you,' Harry said, letting go of the tie. 'I'm too damn tired to take any more of this shit.' He turned from Valentin and began to walk away.

'Wait – ' said the other man, ' – I know I wasn't too sweet with you back at the house, but you've got to understand, things are going to get bad. For both of us.'

'I thought you said it was all over bar the shouting?'

'I thought it was. I thought we had it all sewn up. Then Butterfield arrived and I realised how naïve I was being. They're not going to let Swann rest in peace. Not now, not ever. We have to save him, D'Amour.'

Harry stopped walking and studied the man's face. To pass him in the street, he mused, you wouldn't have taken him for a lunatic.

'Did Butterfield go upstairs?' Valentin enquired.

'Yes he did. Why?'

'Do you remember if he approached the casket?'

Harry shook his head.

'Good,' said Valentin. 'Then the defences are holding, which gives us a little time. Swann was a fine tactician, you know. But he could be careless. That was how they caught him. Sheer carelessness. He knew they were coming for him. I told him outright, I said we should cancel the remaining performances and go home. At least he had some sanctuary there.'

'You think he was murdered?'

'Jesus Christ,' said Valentin, almost despairing of Harry, 'of course he was murdered.'

'So he's past saving, right? The man's dead.'

'Dead; yes. Past saving? no.'

'Do you talk gibberish to everyone?'

Valentin put his hand on Harry's shoulder, 'Oh no,' he said, with unfeigned sincerity. 'I don't trust anyone the way I trust you.'

'This is very sudden,' said Harry. 'May I ask why?'

'Because you're in this up to your neck, the way I am,' Valentin replied.

'No I'm not,' said Harry, but Valentin ignored the denial, and went on with his talk. 'At the moment we don't know how many of them there are, of course. They might simply have sent Butterfield, but I think that's unlikely.'

'Who's Butterfield with? The Mafia?'

'We should be so lucky,' said Valentin. He reached in his pocket and pulled out a piece of paper. 'This is the woman Swann was with,' he said, 'the night at the theatre. It's possible she knows something of their strength.'

'There was a witness?'

'She didn't come forward, but yes, there was. I was his procurer you see. I helped arrange his several adulteries, so that none ever embarrassed him. See if you can get to her – ' He stopped abruptly. Somewhere close by, music was being played. It sounded like a drunken jazz band extemporising on bagpipes; a wheezing, rambling cacophony. Valentin's face instantly became a portrait of distress. 'God help us . . .' he said softly, and began to back away from Harry.

'What's the problem?'

'Do you know how to pray?' Valentin asked him as he retreated down 83rd Street. The volume of the music was rising with every interval.

'I haven't prayed in twenty years,' Harry replied.

'Then *learn*,' came the response, and Valentin turned to run.

As he did so a ripple of darkness moved down the street from the north, dimming the lustre of bar-signs and street-lamps as it came. Neon announcements suddenly guttered and died; there were protests out of upstairs windows as the lights failed and, as if encouraged by the curses, the music took on a fresh and yet more hectic rhythm. Above his head Harry heard a wailing sound, and looked up to see a ragged silhouette against the clouds which trailed tendrils like a man o' war as it descended upon the street, leaving the stench of rotting fish in its wake. Its target was clearly Valentin. He shouted above the wail and the music and the panic from the black-out, but no sooner had he yelled than he heard Valentin shout out from the darkness; a pleading cry that was rudely cut short.

He stood in the murk, his feet unwilling to carry him a step nearer the place from which the plea had come. The smell still stung his nostrils; nosing it, his nausea returned. And then, so did the lights; a wave of power igniting the lamps and the bar-signs as it washed back down the street. It reached Harry, and moved on to the spot where he had last seen Valentin. It was deserted; indeed the sidewalk was empty all the way down to the next intersection.

The drivelling jazz had stopped.

Eyes peeled for man, beast, or the remnants of either, Harry wandered down the sidewalk. Twenty yards from where he had been standing the concrete was wet. Not with blood, he was pleased to see; the fluid was the colour of bile, and stank to high Heaven. Amongst the splashes were several slivers of what might have been human tissue. Evidently Valentin had fought, and succeeded in opening a wound in his attacker. There were more traces of the blood further down the sidewalk, as if the injured thing had crawled some way before taking flight again. With Valentin, presumably. In the face of such strength Harry knew his meagre powers would have availed him not at all, but he felt guilty nevertheless. He'd heard the cry – seen the assailant swoop – and yet fear had sealed his soles to the ground.

He'd last felt fear the equal of this in Wyckoff Street, when Mimi Lomax's demon-lover had finally thrown off any pretence to humanity. The room had filled with the stink of ether and human dirt, and the demon had stood there in its appalling nakedness and shown him scenes that had turned his bowels to water. They were with him now, those scenes. They would be with him forever.

He looked down at the scrap of paper Valentin had given him: the name and address had been rapidly scrawled, but they were just decipherable.

A wise man, Harry reminded himself, would screw this note up and throw it down into the gutter. But if the events in Wyckoff Street had taught him anything, it was that once touched by such malignancy as he had seen and dreamt in the last few hours, there could be no casual disposal of it. He had to follow it to its source, however repugnant that thought was, and make with it whatever bargains the strength of his hand allowed.

There was no good time to do business like this: the present would have to suffice. He walked back to Lexington and caught a cab to the address on the paper. He got no response from the bell marked Bernstein, but roused the doorman, and engaged in a frustrating debate with him through the glass door. The man was angry to have been raised at such an hour; Miss Bernstein was not in her apartment, he insisted, and remained untouched even when

114

Harry intimated that there might be some life-or-death urgency in the matter. It was only when he produced his wallet that the fellow displayed the least flicker of concern. Finally, he let Harry in.

'She's not up there,' he said, pocketing the bills. 'She's not been in for days.'

Harry took the elevator: his shins were aching, and his back too. He wanted sleep; bourbon, then sleep. There was no reply at the apartment as the doorman had predicted, but he kept knocking, and calling her.

'Miss Bernstein? Are you there?'

There was no sign of life from within; not at least, until he said: 'I want to talk about Swann.'

He heard an intake of breath, close to the door.

'Is somebody there?' he asked. 'Please answer. There's nothing to be afraid of.'

After several seconds a slurred and melancholy voice murmured: 'Swann's dead.'

At least *she* wasn't, Harry thought. Whatever forces had snatched Valentin away, they had not yet reached this corner of Manhattan. 'May I talk to you?' he requested.

'No,' she replied. Her voice was a candle flame on the verge of extinction.

'Just a few questions, Barbara.'

'I'm in the tiger's belly,' the slow reply came, 'and it doesn't want me to let you in.'

Perhaps they *had* got here before him.

'Can't you reach the door?' he coaxed her. 'It's not so far . . .'

'But it's eaten me,' she said.

'*Try*, Barbara. The tiger won't mind. *Reach*.'

There was silence from the other side of the door, then a shuffling sound. Was she doing as he had requested? It seemed so. He heard her fingers fumbling with the catch.

'That's it,' he encouraged her. 'Can you turn it? Try to turn it.'

At the last instant he thought: suppose she's telling the truth, and there *is* a tiger in there with her? It was too late for retreat, the door was opening. There was no animal in the hallway. Just a woman, and the smell of dirt. She had clearly neither washed nor changed her clothes since fleeing from the theatre. The evening gown she wore was soiled and torn, her skin was grey with grime. He stepped into the apartment. She moved down the hallway away from him, desperate to avoid his touch.

'It's all right,' he said, 'there's no tiger here.'

115

Her wide eyes were almost empty; what presence roved there was lost to sanity.

'Oh there is,' she said, 'I'm in the tiger. I'm in it forever.'

As he had neither the time nor the skill required to dissuade her from this madness, he decided it was wiser to go with it.

'How did you get there?' he asked her. 'Into the tiger? Was it when you were with Swann?'

She nodded.

'You remember that, do you?'

'Oh yes.'

'What do you remember?'

'There was a sword; it fell. He was picking up – ' She stopped and frowned.

'Picking up what?'

She seemed suddenly more distracted than ever. 'How can you hear me,' she wondered, 'when I'm in the tiger? Are you in the tiger too?

'Maybe I am,' he said, not wanting to analyse the metaphor too closely.

'We're here forever, you know,' she informed him. 'We'll never be let out.'

'Who told you that?'

She didn't reply, but cocked her head a little.

'Can you hear?' she said.

'Hear?'

She took another step back down the hallway. Harry listened, but he could hear nothing. The growing agitation on Barbara's face was sufficient to send him back to the front door and open it, however. The elevator was in operation. He could hear its soft hum across the landing. Worse: the lights in the hallway and on the stairs were deteriorating; the bulbs losing power with every foot the elevator ascended.

He turned back into the apartment and went to take hold of Barbara's wrist. She made no protest. Her eyes were fixed on the doorway through which she seemed to know her judgement would come.

'We'll take the stairs,' he told her, and led her out on to the landing. The lights were within an ace of failing. He glanced up at the floor numbers being ticked off above the elevator doors. Was this the top floor they were on, or one shy of it? He couldn't remember, and there was no time to think before the lights went out entirely.

116

He stumbled across the unfamiliar territory of the landing with the girl in tow, hoping to God he'd find the stairs before the elevator reached this floor. Barbara wanted to loiter, but he bullied her to pick up her pace. As his foot found the top stair the elevator finished its ascent.

The doors hissed open, and a cold fluorescence washed the landing. He couldn't see its source, nor did he wish to, but its effect was to reveal to the naked eye every stain and blemish, every sign of decay and creeping rot that the paintwork sought to camouflage. The show stole Harry's attention for a moment only, then he took a firmer hold of the woman's hand and they began their descent. Barbara was not interested in escape however, but in events on the landing. Thus occupied she tripped and fell heavily against Harry. The two would have toppled but that he caught hold of the banister. Angered, he turned to her. They were out of sight of the landing, but the light crept down the stairs and washed over Barbara's face. Beneath its uncharitable scrutiny Harry saw decay busy in her. Saw rot in her teeth, and the death in her skin and hair and nails. No doubt he would have appeared much the same to her, were she to have looked, but she was still staring back over her shoulder and up the stairs. The light-source was on the move. Voices accompanied it.

'The door's open,' a woman said.

'What are you waiting for?' a voice replied. It was Butterfield.

Harry held both breath and wrist as the light-source moved again, towards the door presumably, and then was partially eclipsed as it disappeared into the apartment.

'We have to be quick,' he told Barbara. She went with him down three or four steps and then, without warning, her hand leapt for his face, nails opening his cheek. He let go of her hand to protect himself, and in that instant she was away – back up the stairs.

He cursed and stumbled in pursuit of her, but her former sluggishness had lifted; she was startlingly nimble. By the dregs of light from the landing he watched her reach the top of the stairs and disappear from sight.

'Here I am,' she called out as she went.

He stood immobile on the stairway, unable to decide whether to go or stay, and so unable to move at all. Ever since Wyckoff Street he'd hated stairs. Momentarily the light from above flared up, throwing the shadows of the banisters across him; then it died again. He put his hand to his face. She had raised weals, but

117

there was little blood. What could he hope from her if he went to her aid? Only more of the same. She was a lost cause.

Even as he despaired of her he heard a sound from round the corner at the head of the stairs; a soft sound that might have been either a footstep or a sigh. Had she escaped their influence after all? Or perhaps not even reached the apartment door, but thought better of it and about-turned? Even as he was weighing up the odds he heard her say:

'Help me . . .' The voice was a ghost of a ghost; but it was indisputably her, and she was in terror.

He reached for his .38, and started up the stairs again. Even before he had turned the corner he felt the nape of his neck itch as his hackles rose.

She was there. But so was the tiger. It stood on the landing, mere feet from Harry, its body humming with latent power. Its eyes were molten; its open maw impossibly large. And there, already in its vast throat, was Barbara. He met her eyes out of the tiger's mouth, and saw a flicker of comprehension in them that was worse than any madness. Then the beast threw its head back and forth to settle its prey in its gut. She had been swallowed whole, apparently. There was no blood on the landing, nor about the tiger's muzzle; only the appalling sight of the girl's face disappearing down the tunnel of the animal's throat.

She loosed a final cry from the belly of the thing, and as it rose it seemed to Harry that the beast attempted a grin. Its face crinkled up grotesquely, the eyes narrowing like those of a laughing Buddha, the lips peeling back to expose a sickle of brilliant teeth. Behind this display the cry was finally hushed. In that instant the tiger leapt.

Harry fired into its devouring bulk and as the shot met its flesh the leer and the maw and the whole striped mass of it unwove in a single beat. Suddenly it was gone, and there was only a drizzle of pastel confetti spiralling down around him. The shot had aroused interest. There were raised voices in one or two of the apartments, and the light that had accompanied Butterfield from the elevator was brightening through the open door of the Bernstein residence. He was almost tempted to stay and see the light-bringer, but discretion bettered his curiosity, and he turned and made his descent, taking the stairs two and three at a time. The confetti tumbled after him, as if it had a life of its own. Barbara's life, perhaps; transformed into paper pieces and tossed away.

He reached the lobby breathless. The doorman was standing there, staring up the stairs vacantly.

'Somebody get shot?' he enquired.

'No,' said Harry, 'eaten.'

As he headed for the door he heard the elevator start to hum as it descended. Perhaps merely a tenant, coming down for a pre-dawn stroll. Perhaps not.

He left the doorman as he had found him, sullen and confused, and made his escape into the street, putting two block lengths between him and the apartment building before he stopped running. They did not bother to come after him. He was beneath their concern, most likely.

So what was he to do now? Valentin was dead, Barbara Bernstein too. He was none the wiser now than he'd been at the outset, except that he'd learned again the lesson he'd been taught in Wyckoff Street: that when dealing with the Gulfs it was wiser never to believe your eyes. The moment you trusted your senses, the moment you believed a tiger to *be* a tiger, you were half theirs.

Not a complicated lesson, but it seemed he had forgotten it, like a fool, and it had taken two deaths to teach it him afresh. Maybe it would be simpler to have the rule tattooed on the back of his hand, so that he couldn't check the time without being reminded: *Never believe your eyes.*

The principle was still fresh in his mind as he walked back towards his apartment and a man stepped out of the doorway and said:

'Harry.'

It *looked* like Valentin; a wounded Valentin, a Valentin who'd been dismembered and sewn together again by a committee of blind surgeons, but the same man in essence. But then the tiger had looked like a tiger, hadn't it?

'It's me,' he said.

'Oh no,' Harry said. 'Not this time.'

'What are you talking about? *It's Valentin.*'

'So prove it.'

The other man looked puzzled. 'This is no time for games,' he said, 'we're in desperate straits.'

Harry took his .38 from his pocket and pointed at Valentin's chest. 'Prove it or I shoot you,' he said.

'Are you out of your mind?'

'I saw you torn apart.'

'Not quite,' said Valentin. His left arm was swathed in makeshift bandaging from fingertip to mid-bicep. 'It was touch

119

and go . . .' he said, '. . . but everything has its Achilles' heel. It's just a question of finding the right spot.'

Harry peered at the man. He wanted to believe that this was indeed Valentin, but it was too incredible to believe that the frail form in front of him could have survived the monstrosity he'd seen on 83rd Street. No; this was another illusion. Like the tiger: paper and malice.

The man broke Harry's train of thought. 'Your steak . . .' he said.

'My steak?'

'You like it almost burned,' Valentin said. 'I protested, remember?'

Harry remembered. 'Go on,' he said.

'And you said you hated the sight of blood. Even if it wasn't your own.'

'Yes,' said Harry. His doubts were lifting. 'That's right.'

'You asked me to prove I'm Valentin. That's the best I can do.' Harry was almost persuaded. 'In God's name,' Valentin said, 'do we have to debate this standing on the street?'

'You'd better come in.'

The apartment was small, but tonight it felt more stifling than ever. Valentin sat himself down with a good view of the door. He refused spirits or first-aid. Harry helped himself to bourbon. He was on his third shot when Valentin finally said:

'We have to go back to the house, Harry.'

'*What?*'

'We have to claim Swann's body before Butterfield.'

'I did my best already. It's not my business any more.'

'So you leave Swann to the Pit?' Valentin said.

'*She* doesn't care, why should I?'

"You mean Dorothea? She doesn't know what Swann was involved with. That's why she's so trusting. She has suspicions maybe, but, insofar as it is possible to be guiltless in all of this, she is.' He paused to adjust the position of his injured arm. 'She was a prostitute, you know. I don't suppose she told you that. Swann once said to me he married her because only prostitutes know the value of love.'

Harry let this apparent paradox go.

'Why did she stay with him?' he asked. 'He wasn't exactly faithful, was he?'

'She loved him,' Valentin replied. 'It's not unheard of.'

'And you?'

'Oh I loved him too, in spite of his stupidities. That's why we have to help him. If Butterfield and his associates get their hands on Swann's mortal remains, there'll be all Hell to pay.'

'I know. I got a glimpse at the Bernstein place.'

'What did you see?'

'Something and nothing,' said Harry. 'A tiger, I thought; only it wasn't.'

'The old paraphernalia,' Valentin commented.

'And there was something else with Butterfield. Something that shed light: I didn't see what.'

'The Castrato,' Valentin muttered to himself, clearly discomfited. 'We'll have to be careful.'

He stood up, the movement causing him to wince. 'I think we should be on our way, Harry.'

'Are you paying me for this?' Harry inquired, 'or am I doing it all for love?'

'You're doing it because of what happened at Wyckoff Street,' came the softly-spoken reply. 'Because you lost poor Mimi Lomax to the Gulfs, and you don't want to lose Swann. That is, if you've not already done so.'

They caught a cab on Madison Avenue and headed back uptown to 61st Street, keeping their silence as they rode. Harry had half a hundred questions to ask of Valentin. Who was Butterfield? for one, and what was Swann's crime was that he be pursued to death and beyond? So many puzzles. But Valentin looked sick and unfit for plying with questions. Besides, Harry sensed that the more he knew the less enthusiastic he would be about the journey they were now taking.

'We have perhaps one advantage – ' Valentin said as they approached 61st Street. 'They can't be expecting this frontal attack. Butterfield presumes I'm dead, and probably thinks you're hiding your head in mortal terror.'

'I'm working on it.'

'You're not in danger,' Valentin replied, 'at least not the way Swann is. If they were to take you apart limb by limb it would be nothing beside the torments they have waiting for the magician.'

'Illusionist,' Harry corrected him, but Valentin shook his head.

'Magician he was; magician he will always be.'

The driver interrupted before Harry could quote Dorothea on the subject.

'What number you people want?' he said.

'Just drop us here on the right,' Valentin instructed him. 'And wait for us, understand?'

'Sure.'

Valentin turned to Harry. 'Give the man fifty dollars.'

'*Fifty?*'

'Do you want him to wait or not?'

Harry counted four tens and ten singles into the driver's hand. 'You'd better keep the engine running,' he said.

'Anything to oblige,' the driver grinned.

Harry joined Valentin on the sidewalk and they walked the twenty-five yards to the house. The street was still noisy, despite the hour: the party that Harry had seen in preparation half a night ago was at its height. There was no sign of life at the Swann residence however.

Perhaps they *don't* expect us, Harry thought. Certainly this head-on assault was about the most foolhardy tactic imaginable, and as such might catch the enemy off-guard. But were such forces ever off-guard? Was there ever a minute in their maggoty lives when their eyelids drooped and sleep tamed them for a space? No. In Harry's experience it was only the good who needed sleep; iniquity and its practitioners were awake every eager moment, planning fresh felonies.

'How do we get in?' he asked as they stood outside the house.

'I have the key,' Valentin replied, and went to the door.

There was no retreat now. The key was turned, the door was open, and they were stepping out of the comparative safety of the street. The house was as dark within as it had appeared from without. There was no sound of human presence on any of the floors. Was it possible that the defences Swann had laid around his corpse had indeed rebuffed Butterfield, and that he and his cohorts had retreated? Valentin quashed such misplaced optimism almost immediately, taking hold of Harry's arm and leaning close to whisper:

'*They're here.*'

This was not the time to ask Valentin how he knew, but Harry made a mental note to enquire when, or rather *if*, they got out of the house with their tongues still in their heads.

Valentin was already on the stairs. Harry, his eyes still accustoming themselves to the vestigial light that crept in from the street, crossed the hallway after him. The other man moved confidently in the gloom, and Harry was glad of it. Without

Valentin plucking at his sleeve, and guiding him around the half-landing he might well have crippled himself.

Despite what Valentin had said, there was no more sound or sight of occupancy up here than there had been below, but as they advanced towards the master bedroom where Swann lay a rotten tooth in Harry's lower jaw that had lately been quiescent began to throb afresh, and his bowels ached to break wind. The anticipation was crucifying. He felt a barely suppressible urge to yell out, and to oblige the enemy to show its hand, if indeed it had hands to show.

Valentin had reached the door. He turned his head in Harry's direction, and even in the murk it was apparent that fear was taking its toll on him too. His skin glistened; he stank of fresh sweat.

He pointed towards the door. Harry nodded. He was as ready as he was ever going to be. Valentin reached for the door handle. The sound of the lock-mechanism seemed deafeningly loud, but it brought no response from anywhere in the house. The door swung open, and the heady scent of flowers met them. They had begun to decay in the forced heat of the house; there was a rankness beneath the perfume. More welcome than the scent was the light. The curtains in the room had not been entirely drawn, and the street-lamps described the interior: the flowers massed like clouds around the casket; the chair where Harry had sat, the Calvados bottle beside it; the mirror above the fireplace showing the room its secret self.

Valentin was already moving across to the casket, and Harry heard him sigh as he set eyes on his old master. He wasted little time, but immediately set to lifting the lower half of the casket lid. It defeated his single arm however and Harry went to his assistance, eager to get the job done and be away. Touching the solid wood of the casket brought his nightmare back with breath-snatching force: the Pit opening beneath him, the illusionist rising from his bed like a sleeper unwillingly woken. There was no such spectacle now, however. Indeed a little life in the corpse might have made the job easier. Swann was a big man, and his limp body was uncooperative to a fault. The simple act of lifting him from his casket took all their breath and attention. He came at last, though reluctantly, his long limbs flopping about.

'Now . . .' said Valentin '. . . downstairs.'

As they moved to the door something in the street ignited, or so it seemed, for the interior suddenly brightened. The light was not kind to their burden. It revealed the crudity of the cosmetics applied to Swann's face, and the burgeoning putresence beneath. Harry had an instant only to appreciate these felicities, and then the light brightened again, and he realised that it wasn't *out*side, but *in*.

He looked up at Valentin, and almost despaired. The luminescence was even less charitable to servant than to master; it seemed to strip the flesh from Valentin's face. Harry caught only a glimpse of what it revealed beneath – events stole his attention an instant later – but he saw enough to know that had Valentin not been his accomplice in this venture he might well have run from him.

'*Get him out of here!*' Valentin yelled.

He let go of Swann's legs, leaving Harry to steer Swann single-handed. The corpse proved recalcitrant however. Harry had only made two cursing steps towards the exit when things took a turn for the cataclysmic.

He heard Valentin unloose an oath, and looked up to see that the mirror had given up all pretence to reflection, and that something was moving up from its liquid depths, bringing the light with it.

'What is it?' Harry breathed.

'The Castrato,' came the reply. 'Will you *go*?'

There was no time to obey Valentin's panicked instruction however, before the hidden thing broke the plane of the mirror and invaded the room. Harry had been wrong. It did not carry the light with it as it came: it *was* the light. Or rather, some holocaust blazed in its bowels, the glare of which escaped through the creature's body by whatever route it could. It had once been human; a mountain of a man with the belly and the breasts of a neolithic Venus. But the fire in its body had twisted it out of true, breaking out through its palms and its navel, burning its mouth and nostrils into one ragged hole. It had, as its name implied, been unsexed; from that hole too, light spilled. By it, the decay of the flowers speeded into seconds. The blossoms withered and died. The room was filled in moments with the stench of rotting vegetable matter.

Harry heard Valentin call his name, once, and again. Only then did he remember the body in his arms. He dragged his eyes from the hovering Castrato, and carried Swann another yard. The door was at his back, and open. He dragged his burden out into the landing as the Castrato kicked over the casket. He heard the din, and then shouts from Valentin. There followed another terrible commotion, and the high-pitched voice of the Castrato, talking through that hole in its face.

'Die and be happy,' it said, and a hail of furniture was flung against the wall with such force chairs embedded themselves in the plaster. Valentin had escaped the assault however, or so it seemed, for an instant later Harry heard the Castrato shriek. It was an appalling sound: pitiful and revolting. He would have stopped his ears, but that he had his hands full.

He had almost reached the top of the stairs. Dragging Swann a few steps further he laid the body down. The Castrato's light was not dimmed, despite its complaints; it still flickered on the bedroom wall like a midsummer thunderstorm. For the third time tonight – once on 83rd Street, and again on the stairs of the Bernstein place – Harry hesitated. If he went back to help Valentin perhaps there would be worse sights to see than ever Wyckoff Street had offered. But there could be no retreat this time. Without Valentin he was lost. He raced back down the landing and flung open the door. The air was thick; the lamps rocking. In the middle of the room hung the Castrato, still defying gravity. It had hold of Valentin by his hair. Its other hand was poised, first and middle fingers spread like twin horns, about to stab out its captive's eyes.

Harry pulled his .38 from his pocket, aimed, and fired. He had always been a bad shot when given more than a moment to take aim, but *in extremis*, when instinct governed rational thought, he was not half bad. This was such an occasion. The bullet found the Castrato's neck, and opened another wound. More in surprise than pain perhaps it let Valentin go. There was a leakage of light from the hole in its neck, and it put its hand to the place.

Valentin was quickly on his feet.

'Again,' he called to Harry. '*Fire again!*'

Harry obeyed the instruction. His second bullet pierced the creature's chest, his third its belly. This last wound seemed particularly traumatic; the distended flesh, ripe for bursting, broke – and the trickle of light that spilled from the wound rapidly became a flood as the abdomen split.

Again the Castrato howled, this time in panic, and lost all control of its flight. It reeled like a pricked balloon towards the ceiling, its fat hands desperately attempting to stem the mutiny in its substance. But it had reached critical mass; there was no making good the damage done. Lumps of its flesh began to break from it. Valentin, either too stunned or too fascinated, stood staring up at the disintegration while rains of cooked meat fell around him. Harry took hold of him and hauled him back towards the door.

The Castrato was finally earning its name, unloosing a desolate

125

ear-piercing note. Harry didn't wait to watch its demise, but slammed the bedroom door as the voice reached an awesome pitch, and the windows smashed.

Valentin was grinning.

'Do you know what we did?' he said.

'Never mind. Let's just get the fuck out of here.'

The sight of Swann's corpse at the top of the stairs seemed to chasten Valentin. Harry instructed him to assist, and he did so as efficiently as his dazed condition allowed. Together they began to escort the illusionist down the stairs. As they reached the front door there was a final shriek from above, as the Castrato came apart at the seams. Then silence.

The commotion had not gone unnoticed. Revellers had appeared from the house opposite, a crowd of late-night pedestrians had assembled on the sidewalk. 'Some party,' one of them said as the trio emerged.

Harry had half expected the cab to have deserted them, but he had reckoned without the driver's curiosity. The man was out of his vehicle and staring up at the first floor window.

'Does he need a hospital?' he asked as they bundled Swann into the back of the cab.

'No,' Harry returned. 'He's about as good as he's going to get.'

'Will you *drive*?' said Valentin.

'Sure. Just tell me where to.'

'Anywhere,' came the weary reply. 'Just get out of here.'

'Hold it a minute,' the driver said, 'I don't want any trouble.'

'Then you'd better *move*,' said Valentin. The driver met his passenger's gaze. Whatever he saw there, his next words were:

'I'm driving,' and they took off along East 61st like the proverbial bat out of Hell.

'We did it, Harry,' Valentin said when they'd been travelling for a few minutes. 'We got him back.'

'And that *thing*? Tell me about it.'

'The Castrato? What's to tell? Butterfield must have left it as a watch-dog, until he could bring in a technician to de-code Swann's defence mechanisms. We were lucky. It was in need of milking. That makes them unstable.'

'How do you know so much about all of this?'

'It's a long story,' said Valentin. 'And not for a cab ride.'

'So what now? We can't drive round in circles all night.'

Valentin looked across at the body that sat between them, prey to every whim of the cab's suspension and road-menders' craft. Gently, he put Swann's hands on his lap.

'You're right of course,' he said. 'We have to make arrangements for the cremation, as swiftly as possible.'

The cab bounced across a pot-hole. Valentin's face tightened.

'Are you in pain?' Harry asked him.

'I've been in worse.'

'We could go back to my apartment, and rest there.'

Valentin shook his head. 'Not very clever,' he said, 'it's the first place they'll look.'

'My offices, then – '

'The second place.'

'Well, Jesus, this cab's going to run out of gas eventually.'

At this point the driver intervened.

'Say, did you people mention cremation?'

'Maybe,' Valentin replied.

'Only my brother-in-law's got a funeral business out in Queens.'

'Is that so?' said Harry.

'Very reasonable rates. I can recommend him. No shit.'

'Could you contact him *now*?' Valentin said.

'It's two in the morning.'

'We're in a hurry.'

The driver reached up and adjusted his mirror; he was looking at Swann.

'You don't mind me asking, do you?' he said. 'But is that a body you got back there?'

'It is,' said Harry. 'And he's getting impatient.'

The driver made a whooping sound. 'Shit!' he said. 'I've had a woman drop twins in that seat; I've had whores do business; I even had an alligator back there one time. But this beats them all!' He pondered for a moment, then said: 'You kill him, did you?'

'No,' said Harry.

'Guess we'd be heading for the East River if you had, eh?'

'That's right. We just want a decent cremation. And *quickly*.'

'That's understandable.'

'What's your name?' Harry asked him.

'Winston Jowitt. But everybody calls me Byron. I'm a poet, see? Leastways, I am at weekends.'

'Byron.'

'See, any other driver would be freaked out, right? Finding two guys with a body in the back seat. But the way I see it, it's all material.'

'For the poems.'

'Right,' said Byron. 'The Muse is a fickle mistress. You have to take it where you find it, you know? Speaking of which, you gentlemen got any idea where you want to go?'

'Make it your offices,' Valentin told Harry. 'And he can call his brother-in-law.'

'Good,' said Harry. Then, to Byron:

'Head west along 45th Street to 8th.'

'You got it,' said Byron, and the cab's speed doubled in the space of twenty yards. 'Say,' he said, 'you fellows fancy a poem?'

'Now?' said Harry.

'I like to improvise,' Byron replied. 'Pick a subject. Any subject.'

Valentin hugged his wounded arm close. Quietly, he said: 'How about the end of the world?'

'Good subject,' the poet replied, 'just give me a minute or two.'

'So soon?' said Valentin.

They took a circuitous route to the offices, while Byron Jowitt tried a selection of rhymes for Apocalypse. The sleep-walkers were out on 45th Street, in search of one high or another; some sat in the doorways, one lay sprawled across the sidewalk. None of them gave the cab or its occupants more than the briefest perusal. Harry unlocked the front door and he and Byron carried Swann up to the third floor.

The office was home from home: cramped and chaotic. They put Swann in the swivel chair behind the furred coffee cups and the alimony demands heaped on the desk. He looked easily the healthiest of the quartet. Byron was sweating like a bull after the climb; Harry felt – and surely looked – as though he hadn't slept in sixty days; Valentin sat slumped in the clients' chair, so drained of vitality he might have been at death's door.

'You look terrible,' Harry told him.

'No matter,' he said. 'It'll all be done soon.'

Harry turned to Byron. 'How about calling this brother-in-law of yours?'

While Byron set to doing so, Harry returned his attention to Valentin.

'I've got a first-aid box somewhere about,' he said. 'Shall I bandage up that arm?'

'Thank you, but no. Like you, I hate the sight of blood. Especially my own.'

Byron was on the phone, chastising his brother-in-law for his ingratitude. 'What's your beef? I got you a client! I *know* the time, for Christ's sake, but business is business . . .'

'Tell him we'll pay double his normal rate,' Valentin said.

'You hear that, Mel? *Twice* your usual fee. So get over here, will you?' He gave the address to his brother-in-law, and put down the receiver. 'He's coming over,' he announced.

'Now?' said Harry.

'Now,' Byron glanced at his watch. 'My belly thinks my throat's cut. How about we eat? You got an all night place near here?'

'There's one a block down from here.'

'You want food?' Byron asked Valentin.

'I don't think so,' he said. He was looking worse by the moment.

'OK,' Byron said to Harry, 'just you and me then. You got ten I could borrow?'

Harry gave him a bill, the keys to the street door and an order for doughnuts and coffee, and Byron went on his way. Only when he'd gone did Harry wish he'd convinced the poet to stave off his hunger pangs a while. The office was distressingly quiet without him: Swann in residence behind the desk, Valentin succumbing to sleep in the other chair. The hush brought to mind another such silence, during that last, awesome night at the Lomax house when Mimi's demon-lover, wounded by Father Hesse, had slipped away into the walls for a while, and left them waiting and waiting, knowing it would come back but not certain of when or how. Six hours they'd sat – Mimi occasionally breaking the silence with laughter or gibberish – and the first Harry had known of its return was the smell of cooking excrement, and Mimi's cry of 'Sodomite!' as Hesse surrendered to an act his faith had too long forbidden him. There had been no more silence then, not for a long space: only Hesse's cries, and Harry's pleas for forgetfulness. They had all gone unanswered.

It seemed he could hear the demon's voice now; its demands, its invitations. But no; it was only Valentin. The man was tossing his head back and forth in sleep, his face knotted up. Suddenly he started from his chair, one word on his lips:

'*Swann!*'

His eyes opened, and as they alighted on the illusionist's body, which was propped in the chair opposite, tears came uncontrollably, wracking him.

129

'He's dead,' he said, as though in his dream he had forgotten that bitter fact. 'I failed him, D'Amour. That's why he's dead. Because of my negligence.'

'You're doing your best for him now,' Harry said, though he knew the words were poor compensation. 'Nobody could ask for a better friend.'

'I was never his friend,' Valentin said, staring at the corpse with brimming eyes. 'I always hoped he'd one day trust me entirely. But he never did.'

'Why not?'

'He couldn't afford to trust anybody. Not in his situation.' He wiped his cheeks with the back of his hand.

'Maybe,' Harry said, 'it's about time you told me what all this is about.'

'If you want to hear.'

'I want to hear.'

'Very well,' said Valentin. 'Thirty-two years ago, Swann made a bargain with the Gulfs. He agreed to be an ambassador for them if they, in return, gave him magic.'

'*Magic?*'

'The ability to perform miracles. To transform matter. To bewitch souls. Even to drive out God.'

'That's a miracle?'

'It's more difficult than you think,' Valentin replied.

'So Swann *was* a genuine magician?'

'Indeed he was.'

'Then why didn't he use his powers?'

'He did,' Valentin replied. 'He used them every night, at every performance.'

Harry was baffled. 'I don't follow.'

'Nothing the Prince of Lies offers to humankind is of the least value,' Valentin said, 'or it wouldn't be offered. Swann didn't know that when he first made his Covenant. But he soon learned. Miracles are useless. Magic is a distraction from the real concerns. It's rhetoric. Melodrama.'

'So what exactly are the real concerns?'

'You should know better than I,' Valentin replied. 'Fellowship, maybe? Curiosity? Certainly it matters not in the least if water can be made into wine, or Lazarus to live another year.'

Harry saw the wisdom of this, but not how it had brought the magician to Broadway. As it was, he didn't need to ask. Valentin had taken up the story afresh. His tears had cleared with the telling; some trace of animation had crept back into his features.

'It didn't take Swann long to realise he'd sold his soul for a mess of pottage,' he explained. 'And when he did he was inconsolable. At least he was for a while. Then he began to contrive a revenge.'

'How?'

'By taking Hell's name in vain. By using the magic which it boasted of as a trivial entertainment, degrading the power of the Gulfs by passing off their wonder-working as mere illusion. It was, you see, an act of heroic perversity. Every time a trick of Swann's was explained away as sleight-of-hand, the Gulfs squirmed.'

'Why didn't they kill him?' Harry said.

'Oh they tried. Many times. But he had allies. Agents in their camp who warned him of their plots against him. He escaped their retribution for years that way.'

'Until now?'

'Until now,' Valentin sighed. 'He was careless, and so was I. Now he's dead, and the Gulfs are itching for him.'

'I see.'

'But we were not entirely unprepared for this eventuality. He had made his apologies to Heaven; and I dare to hope he's been forgiven his trespasses. Pray that he has. There's more than *his* salvation at stake tonight.'

'Yours too?'

'All of us who loved him are tainted,' Valentin replied, 'but if we can destroy his physical remains before the Gulfs claim them we may yet avoid the consequences of his Covenant.'

'Why did you wait so long? Why didn't you just cremate him the day he died?'

'Their lawyers are not fools. The Covenant specifically proscribes a period of lying-in-state. If we had attempted to ignore that clause his soul would have been forfeited automatically.'

'So when is this period up?'

'Three hours ago, at midnight,' Valentin replied. 'That's why they're so desperate, you see. And so dangerous.'

Another poem came to Byron Jowitt as he ambled back up 8th Avenue, working his way through a tuna salad sandwich. His Muse was not to be rushed. Poems could take as long as five minutes to be finalised; longer if they involved a double rhyme. He didn't hurry on his journey back to the offices therefore, but wandered in a dreamy sort of mood, turning the lines every which way to make them fit. That way he hoped to arrive back with another finished poem. Two in one night was damn good going.

He had not perfected the final couplet however, by the time he reached the door. Operating on automatic pilot he fumbled in his pocket for the keys D'Amour had loaned him, and let himself in. He was about to close the door again when a woman stepped through the gap, smiling at him. She was a beauty, and Byron, being a poet, was a fool for beauty.

'Please,' she said to him, 'I need your help.'

'What can I do for you?' said Byron through a mouthful of food.

'Do you know a man by the name of D'Amour? Harry D'Amour?'

'Indeed I do. I'm going up to his place right now.'

'Perhaps you could show me the way?' the woman asked him, as Byron closed the door.

'Be my pleasure,' he replied, and led her across the lobby to the bottom of the stairs.

'You know, you're very sweet,' she told him; and Byron melted.

Valentin stood at the window.

'Something wrong?' Harry asked.

'Just a feeling,' Valentin commented.' I have a suspicion maybe the Devil's in Manhattan.'

'So what's new?'

'That maybe he's coming for us.' As if on cue there was a knock at the door. Harry jumped. 'It's all right,' Valentin said, 'he never knocks.'

Harry went to the door, feeling like a fool.

'Is that you, Byron?' he asked before unlocking it.

'Please,' said a voice he thought he'd never hear again. 'Help me . . .'

He opened the door. It was Dorothea, of course. She was colourless as water, and as unpredictable. Even before Harry had invited her across the office threshold a dozen expressions, or hints of such, had crossed her face: anguish, suspicion, terror. And now, as her eyes alighted upon the body of her beloved Swann, relief and gratitude.

'You *do* have him,' she said, stepping into the office.

Harry closed the door. There was a chill from up the stairs.

'Thank God. Thank God.' She took Harry's face in her hands

132

and kissed him lightly on the lips. Only then did she notice Valentin.

She dropped her hands.

'What's *he* doing here?' she asked.

'He's with me. With us.'

She looked doubtful.' No,' she said.

'We can trust him.'

'I said *no*! Get him out, Harry.' There was a cold fury in her; she shook with it. '*Get him out!*'

Valentin stared at her, glassy-eyed. 'The lady doth protest too much,' he murmured.

Dorothea put her fingers to her lips as if to stifle any further outburst. 'I'm sorry,' she said, turning back to Harry, 'but you must be told what this man is capable of – '

'Without him your husband would still be at the house, Mrs Swann,' Harry pointed out. '*He's* the one you should be grateful to, not me.'

At this, Dorothea's expression softened, through bafflement to a new gentility.

'Oh?' she said. Now she looked back at Valentin. 'I'm sorry. When you ran from the house I assumed some complicity . . .'

'With whom?' Valentin inquired.

She made a tiny shake of her head; then said, 'Your arm. Are you hurt?'

'A minor injury,' he returned.

'I've already tried to get it rebandaged,' Harry said. 'But the bastard's too stubborn.'

'Stubborn I am,' Valentin replied, without inflection.

'But we'll be finished here soon – ' said Harry.

Valentin broke in. 'Don't tell her anything,' he snapped.

'I'm just going to explain about the brother-in-law – ' Harry said.

'The brother-in-law?' Dorothea said, sitting down. The sigh of her legs crossing was the most enchanting sound Harry had heard in twenty-four hours. 'Oh please tell me about the brother-in-law . . .'

Before Harry could open his mouth to speak, Valentin said: 'It's not her, Harry.'

The words, spoken without a trace of drama, took a few seconds to make sense. Even when they did, their lunacy was self-evident. Here she was in the flesh, perfect in every detail.

'What are you talking about?' Harry said.

133

'How much more plainly can I say it?' Valentin replied. *'It's not her.* It's a trick. An illusion. They know where we are, and they sent *this* up to spy out our defences.'

Harry would have laughed, but that these accusations were bringing tears to Dorothea's eyes.

'Stop it,' he told Valentin.

'No, Harry. You *think* for a moment. All the traps they've laid, all the beasts they've mustered. You suppose she could have escaped that?' He moved away from the window towards Dorothea. 'Where's Butterfield?' he spat. 'Down the hall, waiting for your signal?'

'Shut up,' said Harry.

'He's scared to come up here himself, isn't he?' Valentin went on. 'Scared of Swann, scared of us, probably, after what we did to his gelding.'

Dorothea looked at Harry. 'Make him stop,' she said.

Harry halted Valentin's advance with a hand on his bony chest. 'You heard the lady,' he said.

'That's no lady,' Valentin replied, his eyes blazing. 'I don't know what it is, but it's no lady.'

Dorothea stood up. 'I came here because I hoped I'd be safe,' she said.

'You *are* safe,' Harry said.

'Not with him around, I'm not,' she replied, looking back at Valentin. 'I think I'd be wiser going.'

Harry touched her arm.

'No,' he told her.

'Mr D'Amour,' she said sweetly, 'you've already earned your fee ten times over. Now I think it's time *I* took responsibility for my husband.'

Harry scanned that mercurial face. There wasn't a trace of deception in it.

'I have a car downstairs,' she said. 'I wonder . . . could you carry him downstairs for me?'

Harry heard a noise like a cornered dog behind him and turned to see Valentin standing beside Swann's corpse. He had picked up the heavy-duty cigarette lighter from the desk, and was flicking it. Sparks came, but no flame.

'What the hell are you doing?' Harry demanded.

Valentin didn't look at the speaker, but at Dorothea.

'She knows,' he said.

He had got the knack of the lighter; the flame flared up.

134

Dorothea made a small, desperate sound.

'Please don't,' she said.

'We'll all burn with him if necessary,' Valentin said.

'He's insane,' Dorothea's tears had suddenly gone.

'She's right,' Harry told Valentin, 'you're acting like a madman.'

'And you're a fool to fall for a few tears!' came the reply. 'Can't you see that if she takes him we've lost everything we've fought for?'

'Don't listen,' she murmured. 'You know me, Harry. You trust me.'

'What's under that face of yours?' Valentin said. 'What are you? A Coprolite? Homunculus?'

The names meant nothing to Harry. All he knew was the proximity of the woman at his side; her hand laid upon his arm.

'And what about you?' she said to Valentin. Then, more softly, 'why don't you show us your wound?'

She forsook the shelter of Harry's side, and crossed to the desk. The lighter flame guttered at her approach.

'Go on . . .' she said, her voice no louder than a breath. '. . . I *dare* you.'

She glanced round at Harry. 'Ask him, D'Amour,' she said. 'Ask him to show you what he's got hidden under the bandages.'

'What's she talking about?' Harry asked. The glimmer of trepidation in Valentin's eyes was enough to convince Harry there was merit in Dorothea's request. 'Explain,' he said.

Valentin didn't get the chance however. Distracted by Harry's demand he was easy prey when Dorothea reached across the desk and knocked the lighter from his hand. He bent to retrieve it, but she seized on the *ad hoc* bundle of bandaging and pulled. It tore, and fell away.

She stepped back. 'See?' she said.

Valentin stood revealed. The creature on 83rd Street had torn the sham of humanity from his arm; the limb beneath was a mass of blue-black scales. Each digit of the blistered hand ended in a nail that opened and closed like a parrot's beak. He made no attempt to conceal the truth. Shame eclipsed every other response.

'I warned you,' she said, 'I warned you he wasn't to be trusted.'

Valentin stared at Harry. 'I have no excuses,' he said. 'I only ask you to believe that I want what's best for Swann.'

'How can you?' Dorothea said. 'You're a demon.'

'More than that,' Valentin replied, 'I'm Swann's Tempter. His

135

familiar; his creature. But I belong to him more than I ever belonged to the Gulfs. And I will defy them – ' he looked at Dorothea, ' – and their agents.'

She turned to Harry. 'You have a gun,' she said. 'Shoot the filth. You mustn't suffer a thing like that to live.'

Harry looked at the pustulent arm; at the clacking fingernails: what further repugnance was there in wait behind the flesh façade?

'Shoot it,' the woman said.

He took his gun from his pocket. Valentin seemed to have shrunk in the moments since the revelation of his true nature. Now he leaned against the wall, his face slimy with despair.

'Kill me then,' he said to Harry, 'kill me if I revolt you so much. But Harry, I *beg* you, don't give Swann to her. Promise me that. Wait for the driver to come back, and dispose of the body by whatever means you can. Just don't give it to her!'

'Don't listen,' Dorothea said. 'He doesn't care about Swann the way I do.'

Harry raised the gun. Even looking straight at death, Valentin did not flinch.

'You've failed, Judas,' she said to Valentin. 'The magician's mine.'

'What magician?' said Harry.

'Why Swann, of course!' she replied lightly. 'How many magicians have you got up here?'

Harry dropped his bead on Valentin.

'He's an illusionist,' he said, 'you told me that at the very beginning. Never call him a magician, you said.'

'Don't be pedantic,' she replied, trying to laugh her off *faux pas*.

He levelled the gun at her. She threw back her head suddenly, her face contracting, and unloosed a sound of which, had Harry not heard it from a human throat, he would not have believed the larynx capable. It rang down the corridor and the stairs, in search of some waiting ear.

'Butterfield is here,' said Valentin flatly.

Harry nodded. In the same moment she came towards him, her features grotesquely contorted. She was strong and quick; a blur of venom that took him off-guard. He heard Valentin tell him to kill her, before she transformed. It took him a moment to grasp the significance of this, by which time she had her teeth at his throat. One of her hands was a cold vice around his wrist; he sensed strength in her sufficient to powder his bones. His fingers were already numbed by her grip; he had no time to do more than depress the trigger. The gun went off. Her breath on his throat seemed to gush from her. Then she loosed her hold on him, and staggered back. The shot had blown open her abdomen.

He shook to see what he had done. The creature, for all its shriek, still resembled a woman he might have loved.

'Good,' said Valentin, as the blood hit the office floor in gouts. 'Now it must show itself.'

Hearing him, she shook her head. 'This is all there is to show,' she said.

Harry threw the gun down. 'My God,' he said softly, 'it's her . . .'

Dorothea grimaced. The blood continued to come. 'Some *part* of her,' she replied.

'Have you always been with them then?' Valentin asked.

'Of course not.'

'Why then?'

'Nowhere to go . . .' she said, her voice fading by the syllable. 'Nothing to believe in. All lies. Everything: *lies.*'

'So you sided with Butterfield?'

'Better Hell,' she said, 'than a false Heaven.'

'Who taught you that?' Harry murmured.

'Who do you think?' she replied, turning her gaze on him. Though her strength was going out of her with the blood, her eyes still blazed. 'You're finished, D'Amour,' she said. 'You, and the demon, and Swann. There's nobody left to help you now.'

Despite the contempt in her words he couldn't stand and watch her bleed to death. Ignoring Valentin's imperative that he keep clear, he went across to her. As he stepped within range she lashed out at him with astonishing force. The blow blinded him a moment; he fell against the tall filing cabinet, which toppled sideways. He and it hit the ground together. *It* spilled papers; he, curses. He was vaguely aware that the woman was moving past him to escape, but he was too busy keeping his head from spinning to prevent her. When equilibrium returned she had gone, leaving her bloody handprints on wall and door.

Chaplin, the janitor, was protective of his territory. The basement of the building was a private domain in which he sorted through office trash, and fed his beloved furnace, and read aloud his favourite passages from the Good Book; all without fear of interruption. His bowels – which were far from healthy – allowed him little slumber. A couple of hours a night, no more, which he supplemented with dozing through the day. It was not so bad. He had the seclusion of the basement to retire to whenever life upstairs became too demanding; and the forced heat would sometimes bring strange waking dreams.

Was this such a dream: this insipid fellow in his fine suit? If not, how had he gained access to the basement, when the door was locked and bolted? He asked no questions of the intruder. Something about the way the man stared at him baffled his tongue. 'Chaplin,' the fellow said, his thin lips barely moving, 'I'd like you to open the furnace.'

In other circumstances he might well have picked up his shovel and clouted the stranger across the head. The furnace was his baby. He knew, as no-one else knew, its quirks and occasional petulance; he loved, as no-one else loved, the roar it gave when it was content; he did not take kindly to the proprietorial tone the man used. But he'd lost the will to resist. He picked up a rag and opened the peeling door, offering its hot heart to this man as Lot had offered his daughters to the stranger in Sodom.

Butterfield smiled at the smell of heat from the furnace. From three floors above he heard the woman crying out for help; and then, a few moments later, a shot. She had failed. He had thought she would. But her life was forfeit anyway. There was no loss in sending her into the breach, in the slim chance that she might have coaxed the body from its keepers,. It would have saved the inconvenience of a full-scale attack, but no matter. To have Swann's soul was worth any effort. He had defiled the good name of the Prince of Lies. For that he would suffer as no other miscreant magician ever had. Beside Swann's punishment, Faust's would be an inconvenience, and Napoleon's a pleasure-cruise.

As the echoes of the shot died above, he took the black lacquer box from his jacket pocket. The janitor's eyes were turned heavenward. He too had heard the shot.

'It was nothing,' Butterfield told him. 'Stoke the fire.'

Chaplin obeyed. The heat in the cramped basement rapidly grew. The janitor began to sweat; his visitor did not. He stood mere feet from the open furnace door and gazed into the brightness with impassive features. At last, he seemed satisfied.

'Enough,' he said, and opened the lacquer box. Chaplin thought he glimpsed movement in the box, as though it were full to the lid with maggots, but before he had a chance to look more closely both the box and contents were pitched into the flames.

'Close the door,' Butterfield said. Chaplin obeyed. 'You may

138

watch over them awhile, if it pleases you. They need the heat. It makes them mighty.'

He left the janitor to keep his vigil beside the furnace, and went back up to the hallway. He had left the street door open, and a pusher had come in out of the cold to do business with a client. They bartered in the shadows, until the pusher caught sight of the lawyer.

'Don't mind me,' Butterfield said, and started up the stairs. He found the widow Swann on the first landing. She was not quite dead, but he quickly finished the job D'Amour had started.

'We're in trouble,' said Valentin. 'I hear noises downstairs. Is there any other way out of here?'

Harry sat on the floor, leaning against the toppled cabinet, and tried not to think of Dorothea's face as the bullet found her, or of the creature he was now reduced to needing.

'There's a fire escape,' he said, 'it runs down to the back of the building.'

'Show me,' said Valentin, attempting to haul him to his feet.

'Keep your hands off me!'

Valentin withdrew, bruised by the rebuffal. 'I'm sorry,' he said. 'Maybe I shouldn't hope for your acceptance. But I do.'

Harry said nothing, just got to his feet amongst the litter of reports and photographs. He'd had a dirty life: spying on adulteries for vengeful spouses; dredging gutters for lost children; keeping company with scum because it rose to the top, and the rest just drowned. Could Valentin's soul be much grimier?

'The fire escape's down the hall,' he said.

'We can still get Swann out,' Valentin said. 'Still give him a decent cremation – ' The demon's obsession with his master's dignity was chastening, in its way. 'But you have to help me, Harry.'

'I'll help you,' he said, avoiding sight of the creature. 'Just don't expect love and affection.'

If it were possible to hear a smile, that's what he heard.

'They want this over and done with before dawn,' the demon said.

'It can't be far from that now.'

'An hour, maybe,' Valentin replied. 'But it's enough. Either way, it's enough.'

The sound of the furnace soothed Chaplin; its rumbles and rattlings were as familiar as the complaint of his own intestines. But there was another sound growing behind the door, the like of which he'd never heard before. His mind made foolish pictures to go with it. Of pigs laughing; of glass and barbed wire being ground between the teeth; of hoofed feet dancing on the door. As the noises grew so did his trepidation, but when he went to the basement door to summon help it was locked; the key had gone. And now, as if matters weren't bad enough, the light went out.

He began to fumble for a prayer –

'Holy Mary, Mother of God, pray for us sinners now and at the hour – '

But he stopped when a voice addressed him, quite clearly.

'Michelmas,' it said.

It was unmistakably his mother. And there could be no doubt of its source, either. It came from the furnace.

'*Michelmas*,' she demanded, 'are you going to let me cook in here?'

It wasn't possible, of course, that she was there in the flesh: she'd been dead thirteen long years. But some phantom, perhaps? He believed in phantoms. Indeed he'd seen them on occasion, coming and going from the cinemas on 42nd Street, arm in arm.

'Open up, Michelmas,' his mother told him, in that special voice she used when she had some treat for him. Like a good child, he approached the door. He had never felt such heat off the furnace as he felt now; he could smell the hairs on his arms wither.

'*Open the door*,' Mother said again. There was no denying her. Despite the searing air, he reached to comply.

'That fucking janitor,' said Harry, giving the sealed fire escape door a vengeful kick. 'This door's supposed to be left unlocked at all times.' He pulled at the chains that were wrapped around the handles. 'We'll have to take the stairs.'

There was a noise from back down the corridor; a roar in the heating system which made the antiquated radiators rattle. At that moment, down in the basement, Michelmas Chaplin was obeying his mother, and opening the furnace door. A scream climbed from below as his face was blasted off. Then, the sound of the basement door being smashed open.

Harry looked at Valentin, his repugnance momentarily forgotten.

'We shan't be taking the stairs,' the demon said.

Bellowings and chatterings and screechings were already on the rise. Whatever had found birth in the basement, it was precocious.

'We have to find something to break down the door,' Valentin said, '*anything.*'

Harry tried to think his way through the adjacent offices, his mind's eye peeled for some tool that would make an impression on either the fire door or the substantial chains which kept it closed. But there was nothing useful: only typewriters and filing cabinets.

'*Think*, man,' said Valentin.

He ransacked his memory. Some heavy-duty instrument was required. A crowbar; a hammer. An axe! There was an agent called Shapiro on the floor below, who exclusively represented porno performers, one of whom had attempted to blow his balls off the month before. She'd failed, but he'd boasted one day on the stairs that he had now purchased the biggest axe he could find, and would happily take the head of any client who attempted an attack upon his person.

The commotion from below was simmering down. The hush was, in its way, more distressing than the din that had preceded it.

'We haven't got much time,' the demon said.

Harry left him at the chained door. 'Can you get Swann?' he said, as he ran.

'I'll do my best.'

By the time Harry reached the top of the stairs the last chatterings were dying away; as he began down the flight they ceased altogether. There was no way now to judge how close the enemy were. On the next floor? Round the next corner? He tried not to think of them, but his feverish imagination populated every dirty shadow.

He reached the bottom of the flight without incident, however, and slunk along the darkened second-floor corridor to Shapiro's office. Half way to his destination, he heard a low hiss behind him. He looked over his shoulder, his body itching to run. One of the radiators, heated beyond its limits, had sprung a leak. Steam was escaping from its pipes, and hissing as it went. He let his heart climb down out of his mouth, and then hurried on to the door of Shapiro's office, praying that the man hadn't simply been shooting the breeze with his talk of axes. If so, they were done for. The office was locked, of course, but he elbowed the frosted glass out, and reached through to let himself in, fumbling for the light switch. The walls were plastered with photographs of sex-goddesses. They scarcely claimed Harry's atention; his panic fed upon itself with every heartbeat he spent here. Clumsily he scoured the office, turning furniture over in his impatience. But there was no sign of Shapiro's axe.

Now, another noise from below. It crept up the staircase and along the corridor in search of him – an unearthly cacophony like the one he'd heard on 83rd Street. It set his teeth on edge; the nerve of his rotting molar began to throb afresh. What did the music signal? Their advance?

In desperation he crossed to Shapiro's desk to see if the man had any other item that might be pressed into service, and there tucked out of sight between desk and wall, he found the axe. He pulled it from hiding. As Shapiro had boasted, it was hefty, its weight the first reassurance Harry had felt in too long. He returned to the corridor. The steam from the fractured pipe had thickened. Through its veils it was apparent that the concert had taken on new fervour. The doleful wailing rose and fell, punctuated by some flaccid percussion.

He braved the cloud of steam and hurried to the stairs. As he put his foot on the bottom step the music seemed to catch him by the back of the neck, and whisper: *'Listen'* in his ear. He had no desire to listen; the music was vile. But somehow – while he was distracted by finding the axe – it had wormed its way into his skull. It drained his limbs of strength. In moments the axe began to seem an impossible burden.

'Come on down,' the music coaxed him, *'come on down and join the band.'*

Though he tried to form the simple word 'No', the music was gaining influence upon him with every note played. He began to hear melodies in the caterwauling; long circuitous themes that made his blood sluggish and his thoughts idiot. He knew there was no pleasure to be had at the music's source – that it tempted him only to pain and desolation – yet he could not shake its delirium off. His feet began to move to the call of the pipers. He forgot Valentin, Swann and all ambition for escape, and instead began to descend the stairs. The melody became more intricate. He could hear voices now, singing some charmless accompaniment in a language he didn't comprehend. From somewhere above, he heard his name called, but he ignored the summons. The music clutched him close, and now – as he descended the next flight of stairs – the musicians came into view.

They were brighter than he had anticipated, and more various. More baroque in their configurations (the manes, the multiple heads); more particular in their decoration (the suit of flayed faces; the rouged anus); and, his drugged eyes now stung to see, more atrocious in their choice of instruments. Such instruments! Byron was there, his bones sucked clean and drilled with stops, his bladder and lungs teased through slashes in his body as reservoirs for the piper's breath. He was draped, inverted, across the musician's lap, and even now was played upon – the sacs ballooning, the tongueless head giving out a wheezing note. Dorothea was slumped beside him, no less transformed, the strings of her gut made taut between her splinted legs like an obscene lyre; her breasts drummed upon. There were other instruments too, men who had come off the street and fallen prey to the band. Even Chaplin was there, much of his flesh burned away, his rib-cage played upon indifferently well.

'I didn't take you for a music lover,' Butterfield said, drawing upon a cigarette, and smiling in welcome. 'Put down your axe and join us.'

The word *axe* reminded Harry of the weight in his hands, though he couldn't find his way through the bars of music to remember what it signified.

'Don't be afraid,' Butterfield said, 'you're an innocent in this. We hold no grudge against you.'

'Dorothea . . .' he said.

'She was an innocent too,' said the lawyer, 'until we showed her some sights.'

Harry looked at the woman's body; at the terrible changes that they had wrought upon her. Seeing them, a tremor began in him, and something came between him and the music; the imminence of tears blotted it out.

'Put down the axe,' Butterfield told him.

But the sound of the concert could not compete with the grief that was mounting in him. Butterfield seemed to see the change in his eyes; the disgust and anger growing there. He dropped his half-smoked cigarette and signalled for the music-making to stop.

'Must it be death, then?' Butterfield said, but the enquiry was scarcely voiced before Harry started down the last few stairs towards him. He raised the axe and swung it at the lawyer but the blow was misplaced. The blade ploughed the plaster of the wall, missing its target by a foot.

At this eruption of violence the musicians threw down their instruments and began across the lobby, trailing their coats and tails in blood and grease. Harry caught their advance from the

143

corner of his eye. Behind the horde, still rooted in the shadows, was another form, larger than the largest of the mustered demons, from which there now came a thump that might have been that of a vast jack-hammer. He tried to make sense of sound or sight, but could do neither. There was no time for curiosity; the demons were almost upon him.

Butterfield glanced round to encourage their advance, and Harry – catching the moment – swung the axe a second time. The blow caught Butterfield's shoulder; the arm was instantly severed. The lawyer shrieked; blood sprayed the wall. There was no time for a third blow, however. The demons were reaching for him, smiles lethal.

He turned on the stairs, and began up them, taking the steps two, three and four at a time. Butterfield was still shrieking below; from the flight above he heard Valentin calling his name. He had neither time nor breath to answer.

They were on his heels, their ascent a din of grunts and shouts and beating wings. And behind it all, the jack-hammer thumped its way to the bottom of the flight, its noise more intimidating by far than the chatterings of the berserkers at his back. It was in his belly, that thump; in his bowels. Like death's heartbeat, steady and irrevocable.

On the second landing he heard a whirring sound behind him, and half turned to see a human-headed moth the size of a vulture climbing the air towards him. He met it with the axe blade, and hacked it down. There was a cry of excitement from below as the body flapped down the stairs, its wings working like paddles. Harry sped up the remaining flight to where Valentin was standing, listening. It wasn't the chatter he was attending to, nor the cries of the lawyer; it was the jack-hammer.

'They brought the Raparee,' he said.

'I wounded Butterfield – '

'I heard. But that won't stop them.'

'We can still try the door.'

'I think we're too late, my friend.'

'*No!*' said Harry, pushing past Valentin. The demon had given up trying to drag Swann's body to the door, and had laid the magician out in the middle of the corridor, his hands crossed on his chest. In some last mysterious act of reverence he had set folded paper bowls at Swann's head and feet, and laid a tiny origami flower at his lips. Harry lingered only long enough to re-acquaint himself with the sweetness of Swann's expression, and then ran to

144

the door and proceeded to hack at the chains. It would be a long job. The assault did more damage to the axe than to the steel links. He didn't dare give up, however. This was their only escape route now, other than flinging themselves to their deaths from one of the windows. That he would do, he decided, if the worst came to the worst. Jump and die, rather than be their plaything.

His arms soon became numb with the repeated blows. It was a lost cause; the chain was unimpaired. His despair was further fuelled by a cry from Valentin – a high, weeping call that he could not leave unanswered. He left the fire door and returned past the body of Swann to the head of the stairs.

The demons had Valentin. They swarmed on him like wasps on a sugar stick, tearing him apart. For the briefest of moments he struggled free of their rage, and Harry saw the mask of humanity in rags and the truth glistening bloodily beneath. He was as vile as those besetting him, but Harry went to his aid anyway, as much to wound the demons as to save their prey.

The wielded axe did damage this way and that, sending Valentin's tormentors reeling back down the stairs, limbs lopped, faces opened. They did not all bleed. One sliced belly spilled eggs in thousands, one wounded head gave birth to tiny eels, which fled to the ceiling and hung there by their lips. In the mêlée he lost sight of Valentin. Forgot about him, indeed, until he heard the jack-hammer again, and remembered the broken look on Valentin's face when he'd named the thing. He'd called it the *Raparee*, or something like.

And now, as his memory shaped the word, it came into sight. It shared no trait with its fellows; it had neither wings nor mane nor vanity. It seemed scarcely even to be flesh, but *forged*, an engine that needed only malice to keep its wheels turning.

At its appearance, the rest retreated, leaving Harry at the top of the stairs in a litter of spawn. Its progress was slow, its half dozen limbs moving in oiled and elaborate configurations to pierce the walls of the staircase and so haul itself up. It brought to mind a man on crutches, throwing the sticks ahead of him and levering his weight after, but there was nothing invalid in the thunder of its body; no pain in the white eye that burned in his sickle-head.

Harry thought he had known despair, but he had not. Only now did he taste its ash in his throat. There was only the window left for him. That, and the welcoming ground. He backed away from the top of the stairs, forsaking the axe.

Valentin was in the corridor. He was not dead, as Harry had

presumed, but kneeling beside the corpse of Swann, his own body drooling from a hundred wounds. Now he bent close to the magician. Offering his apologies to his dead master, no doubt. But no. There was more to it than that. He had the cigarette lighter in his hand, and was lighting a taper. Then, murmuring some prayer to himself as he went, he lowered the taper to the mouth of the magician. The origami flower caught and flared up. Its flame was oddly bright, and spread with supernatural efficiency across Swann's face and down his body. Valentin hauled himself to his feet, the firelight burnishing his scales. He found enough strength to incline his head to the body as its cremation began, and then his wounds overcame him. He fell backwards, and lay still. Harry watched as the flames mounted. Clearly the body had been sprinkled with gasoline or something similar, for the fire raged up in moments, gold and green.

Suddenly, something took hold of his leg. He looked down to see that a demon, with flesh like ripe raspberries, still had an appetite for him. Its tongue was coiled around Harry's shin; its claws reached for his groin. The assault made him forget the cremation or the Raparee. He bent to tear at the tongue with his bare hands, but its slickness confounded his attempts. He staggered back as the demon climbed his body, its limbs embracing him.

The struggle took them to the ground, and they rolled away from the stairs, along the other arm of the corridor. The struggle was far from uneven; Harry's repugnance was at least the match of the demon's ardour. His torso pressed to the ground, he suddenly remembered the Raparee. Its advance reverberated in every board and wall.

Now it came into sight at the top of the stairs, and turned its slow head towards Swann's funeral pyre. Even from this distance Harry could see that Valentin's last-ditch attempts to destroy his master's body had failed. The fire had scarcely begun to devour the magician. They would have him still.

Eyes on the Raparee, Harry neglected his more intimate enemy, and it thrust a piece of flesh into his mouth. His throat filled up with pungent fluid; he felt himself choking. Opening his mouth he bit down hard upon the organ, severing it. The demon did not cry out, but released sprays of scalding excrement from pores along its back, and disengaged itself. Harry spat its muscle out as the demon crawled away. Then he looked back towards the fire.

All other concerns were forgotten in the face of what he saw.
Swann had stood up.

146

He was burning from head to foot. His hair, his clothes, his skin. There was no part of him that was not alight. But he was standing, nevertheless, and raising his hands to his audience in welcome.

The Raparee had ceased its advance. It stood a yard or two from Swann, its limbs absolutely still, as if it were mesmerised by this astonishing trick.

Harry saw another figure emerge from the head of the stairs. It was Butterfield. His stump was roughly tied off; a demon supported his lop-sided body.

'Put out the fire,' demanded the lawyer of the Raparee. 'It's not so difficult.'

The creature did not move.

'*Go on*,' said Butterfield. 'It's just a trick of his. He's dead, damn you. It's just conjuring.'

'No,' said Harry.

Butterfield looked his way. The lawyer had always been insipid. Now he was so pale his existence was surely in question.

'What do you know?' he said.

'It's not conjuring,' said Harry. 'It's *magic*.'

Swann seemed to hear the word. His eyelids fluttered open, and he slowly reached into his jacket and with a flourish produced a handkerchief. It too was on fire. It too was unconsumed. As he shook it out tiny bright birds leapt from its folds on humming wings. The Raparee was entranced by this sleight-of-hand. Its gaze followed the illusory birds as they rose and were dispersed, and in that moment the magician stepped forward and embraced the engine.

It caught Swann's fire immediately, the flames spreading over its flailing limbs. Though it fought to work itself free of the magician's hold, Swann was not to be denied. He clasped it closer than a long-lost brother, and would not leave it be until the creature began to wither in the heat. Once the decay began it seemed the Raparee was devoured in seconds, but it was difficult to be certain. The moment – as in the best performances – was held suspended. Did it last a minute? Two minutes? Five? Harry would never know. Nor did he care to analyse. Disbelief was for cowards; and doubt a fashion that crippled the spine. He was content to watch – not knowing if Swann lived or died, if birds, fire, corridor or if he himself – Harry D'Amour – were real or illusory.

Finally, the Raparee was gone. Harry got to his feet. Swann was also standing, but his farewell performance was clearly over.

The defeat of the Raparee had bested the courage of the horde. They had fled, leaving Butterfield alone at the top of the stairs.

'This won't be forgotten, or forgiven,' he said to Harry. 'There's no rest for you. Ever. I am your enemy.'

'I hope so,' said Harry.

He looked back towards Swann, leaving Butterfield to his retreat. The magician had laid himself down again. His eyes were closed, his hands replaced on his chest. It was as if he had never moved. But now the fire was showing its true teeth. Swann's flesh began to bubble, his clothes to peel off in smuts and smoke. It took a long while to do the job, but eventually the fire reduced the man to ash.

By that time it was after dawn, but today was Sunday, and Harry knew there would be no visitors to interrupt his labours. He would have time to gather up the remains; to pound the bone-shards and put them with the ashes in a carrier bag. Then he would go out and find himself a bridge or a dock, and put Swann into the river.

There was precious little of the magician left once the fire had done its work; and nothing that vaguely resembled a man.

Things came and went away; that was a kind of magic. And in between?; pursuits and conjurings; horrors, guises. The occasional joy.

That there was room for joy; ah! that was magic too.

The Book of Blood
(a postscript):
On Jerusalem Street

Wyburd looked at the book, and the book looked back. Everything he'd ever been told about the boy was true.

'How did you get in?' McNeal wanted to know. There was neither anger nor trepidation in his voice; only casual curiosity.

'Over the wall,' Wyburd told him.

The book nodded. 'Come to see if the rumours were true?'

'Something like that.'

Amongst connoisseurs of the bizarre, McNeal's story was told in reverential whispers. How the boy had passed himself off as a medium, inventing stories on behalf of the departed for his own profit; and how the dead had finally tired of his mockery, and broken into the living world to exact an immaculate revenge. They had *written* upon him; tattooed their true testaments upon his skin so that he would never again take their grief in vain. They had turned his body into a living book, a book of blood, every inch of which was minutely engraved with their histories.

Wyburd was not a credulous man. He had never quite believed the story – until now. But here was living proof of its veracity, standing before him. There was no part of McNeal's exposed skin which was not itching with tiny words. Though it was four years and more since the ghosts had come for him, the flesh still looked tender, as though the wounds would never entirely heal.

'Have you seen enough?' the boy asked. 'There's more. He's covered from head to foot. Sometimes he wonders if they didn't write on the inside as well.' He sighed. 'Do you want a drink?'

Wyburd nodded. Maybe a throatful of spirits would stop his hands from trembling.

McNeal poured himself a glass of vodka, took a slug from it, then poured a second glass for his guest. As he did so, Wyburd saw that the boy's nape was as densely inscribed as his face and hands, the writing creeping up into his hair. Not even his scalp had escaped the authors' attentions, it seemed.

'Why do you talk about yourself in the third person?' he asked

McNeal, as the boy returned with the glass. 'Like you weren't here . . .?'

'The boy?' McNeal said. 'He isn't here. He hasn't been here in a long time.'

He sat down; drank. Wyburd began to feel more than a little uneasy. Was the boy simply mad, or playing some damn-fool game?

The boy swallowed another mouthful of vodka, then asked, matter of factly: 'What's it worth to you?'

Wyburd frowned. 'What's what worth?'

'His skin,' the boy prompted. 'That's what you came for, isn't it?' Wyburd emptied his glass with two swallows, making no reply. McNeal shrugged. 'Everyone has the right to silence,' he said. 'Except for the boy of course. No silence for him.' He looked down at his hand, turning it over to appraise the writing on his palm. 'The stories go on, night and day. Never stop. They tell themselves, you see. They bleed and bleed. You can never hush them; never heal them.'

He *is* mad, Wyburd thought, and somehow the realisation made what he was about to do easier. Better to kill a sick animal than a healthy one.

'There's a road, you know . . .' the boy was saying. He wasn't even looking at his executioner. 'A road the dead go down. He saw it. Dark, strange road, full of people. Not a day gone by when he hasn't . . . hasn't wanted to go back there.'

'Back?' said Wyburd, happy to keep the boy talking. His hand went to his jacket pocket; to the knife. It comforted him in the presence of this lunacy.

'Nothing's enough,' McNeal said. 'Not love. Not music. Nothing.'

Clasping the knife, Wyburd drew it from his pocket. The boy's eyes found the blade, and warmed to the sight.

'You never told him how much it was worth,' he said.

'Two hundred thousand,' Wyburd replied.

'Anyone he knows?'

The assassin shook his head. 'An exile,' he replied. 'In Rio. A collector.'

'Of skins?'

'Of skins.'

The boy put down his glass. He murmured something Wyburd didn't catch. Then, very quietly, he said:

'Be quick, and do it.'

150

He juddered a little as the knife found his heart, but Wyburd was efficient. The moment had come and gone before the boy even knew it was happening, much less felt it. Then it was all over, for him at least. For Wyburd the real labour was only just beginning. It took him two hours to complete the flaying. When he was finished – the skin folded in fresh linen, and locked in the suitcase he'd brought for that very purpose – he was weary.

Tomorrow he would fly to Rio, he thought as he left the house, and claim the rest of his payment. Then, Florida.

He spent the evening in the small apartment he'd rented for the tedious weeks of surveillance and planning which had preceded this afternoon's work. He was glad to be leaving. He had been lonely here, and anxious with anticipation. Now the job was done, and he could put the time behind him.

He slept well, lulled to sleep by the imagined scent of orange groves.

It was not fruit he smelt when he woke, however, but something savoury. The room was in darkness. He reached to his right, and fumbled for the lamp-switch, but it failed to come on.

Now he heard a heavy slopping sound from across the room. He sat up in bed, narrowing his eyes against the dark, but could see nothing. Swinging his legs over the edge of the bed, he went to stand up.

His first thought was that he'd left the bathroom taps on, and had flooded the apartment. He was knee-deep in warm water. Confounded, he waded towards the door and reached for the main light-switch, flipping it on. It was not water he was standing in. Too cloying, too precious; too red.

He made a cry of disgust, and turned to haul open the door, but it was locked, and there was no key. He beat a panicked fusillade upon the solid wood, and yelled for help. His appeals went unanswered.

Now he turned back into the room, the hot tide eddying about his thighs, and sought out the fountainhead.

The suitcase. It sat where he had left it on the bureau, and bled copiously from every seam; and from the locks; and from around the hinges – as if a hundred atrocities were being committed within its confines, and it could not contain the flood these acts had unleashed.

He watched the blood pouring out in steaming abundance. In the scant seconds since he'd stepped from the bed the pool had deepened by several inches, and still the deluge came.

151

He tried the bathroom door, but that too was locked and keyless. He tried the windows, but the shutters were immovable. The blood had reached his waist. Much of the furniture was floating. Knowing he was lost unless he attempted some direct action, he pressed through the flood towards the case, and put his hands upon the lid in the hope that he might yet stem the flow. It was a lost cause. At his touch the blood seemed to come with fresh eagerness, threatening to burst the seams.

The stories go on, the boy had said. *They bleed and bleed*. And now he seemed to hear them in his head, those stories. Dozens of voices, each telling some tragic tale. The flood bore him up towards the ceiling. He paddled to keep his chin above the frothy tide, but in minutes there was barely an inch of air left at the top of the room. As even that margin narrowed, he added his own voice to the cacophony, begging for the nightmare to stop. But the other voices drowned him out with their stories, and as he kissed the ceiling his breath ran out.

The dead have highways. They run, unerring lines of ghost-trains, of dream-carriages, across the wasteland behind our lives, bearing an endless traffic of departed souls. They have sign-posts, these highways, and bridges and lay-bys. They have turnpikes and intersections.

It was at one of these intersections that Leon Wyburd caught sight of the man in the red suit. The throng pressed him forward, and it was only when he came closer that he realised his error. The man was not wearing a suit. He was not even wearing his skin. It was not the McNeal boy however; he had gone on from this point long since. It was another flayed man entirely. Leon fell in beside the man as he walked, and they talked together. The flayed man told him how he had come to this condition; of his brother-in-law's conspiracies, and the ingratitude of his daughter. Leon in turn told of his last moments.

It was a great relief to tell the story. Not because he wanted to be remembered, but because the telling relieved him of the tale. It no longer belonged to him, that life, that death. He had better business, as did they all. Roads to travel; splendours to drink down. He felt the landscape widen. Felt the air brightening.

What the boy had said was true. The dead have highways.

Only the living are lost.

THE DAMNATION GAME

Clive Barker

'It was an odd disease. Its symptoms were like infatuation – palpitations, sleeplessness. Its only certain cure, Death . . .'

Chance had ruled Marty Strauss' life for as long as he could remember. Now at last luck was turning his way.

Parolled from prison, he becomes bodyguard to Joseph Whitehead, one of the richest men in Europe.

But Whitehead has also played with chance – an ancient game which gave him vast power and wealth, in exchange for his immortal soul.

Now the forces he played against are back to claim what's theirs. Terrifying forces, with the power to raise the dead; and Marty is trapped between his human masters and Hell itself, with just one last, desperate game left to play . . .

'I think Clive Barker is so good that I am almost literally tongue-tied' Stephen King

'Clive Barker writes about horrors most of us would scarcely dare imagine' Ramsey Campbell

'The most impressive first novel I've read for a long, long time. Touches of sheer brilliance throughout.' James Herbert

Also by Clive Barker:
BOOKS OF BLOOD volumes 1–6

Other bestselling Warner titles available by mail:

☐	Books of Blood 1st Omnibus	Clive Barker	£7.99
☐	The Damnation Game	Clive Barker	£5.99
☐	The Vampyre	Tom Holland	£5.99
☐	Supping With Panthers	Tom Holland	£5.99
☐	Spanky	Christopher Fowler	£5.99
☐	Psychoville	Christopher Fowler	£5.99

The prices shown above are correct at time of going to press, however the publishers reserve the right to increase prices on covers from those previously advertised, without further notice.

WARNER BOOKS   WARNER BOOKS
Cash Sales Department, P.O. Box 11, Falmouth, Cornwall, TR10 9EN
Tel: +44 (0) 1326 372400, Fax: +44 (0) 1326 374888
Email: books@barni.avel.co.uk.

POST AND PACKING:
Payments can be made as follows: cheque, postal order (payable to Warner Books) or by credit cards. Do not send cash or currency.
All U.K. Orders   **FREE OF CHARGE**
E.E.C. & Overseas   25% of order value

Name (Block Letters) _____

Address_____

_____

Post/zip code:_____

☐ Please keep me in touch with future Warner publications

☐ I enclose my remittance £_____

☐ I wish to pay by Visa/Access/Mastercard/Eurocard

Card Expiry Date

_____